Juliet E. McKenna has been interested in fantasy stories since childhood, from *Winnie the Pooh* to the *Iliad*. An abiding fascination with other worlds and their peoples played its part in her subsequently reading Classics at St Hilda's College, Oxford. While working in recruitment and personnel, she continued to read across all genres, and started to write herself. After combining book-selling and motherhood for a couple of years, she now fits in her writing around her family and vice versa. She lives with her husband and children in West Oxfordshire.

Find out more about Juliet E. McKenna and other Orbit authors by registering for the free monthly newsletter at www.orbitbooks.co.uk

By Juliet E. McKenna

The Tales of Einarinn
THE THIEF'S GAMBLE
THE SWORDSMAN'S OATH
THE GAMBLER'S FORTUNE
THE WARRIOR'S BOND
THE ASSASSIN'S EDGE

The Aldabreshin Compass
SOUTHERN FIRE
NORTHERN STORM

NORTHERN STORM

Juliet E. McKenna

www.orbitbooks.co.uk

An *Orbit* Book

First published in Great Britain by Orbit, 2004

A CIP catalogue record for this book is available from the British Library.

ISBN 1 84149 167 5

Typeset in Ehrhardt by
Palimpsest Book Production Limited,
Polmont, Stirlingshire
Printed and bound in Great Britain by
Mackays of Chatham plc, Chatham, Kent

Orbit
An imprint of
Time Warner Book Group UK
Brettenham House
Lancaster Place
London WC2E 7EN

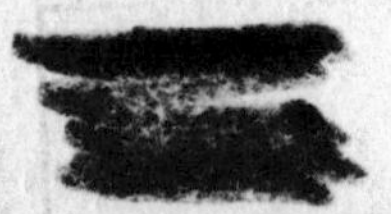

For Ernie and Betty,
for all they do to ease my working life
and all they do to enrich our sons' lives.

ACKNOWLEDGEMENTS

After waiting with bated breath for reaction to *Southern Fire*, my thanks to everyone who's been so enthusiastic about this new direction.

My faithful test readers, Steve, Sue and Mike, have done sterling service once again; my thanks to them. I'm also indebted to Rachel for tropical atmosphere and sub-aqua notes and to Alex for the ophthalmology. For their ongoing enthusiasm, friendship and plausible names for things and places, I'm sincerely grateful to Matt, Michele and Toby.

The pals' network continues to make this writing life possible, with much practical help and moral support. My thanks to Gill and Mike, Penny, Helen, Corinne and Liz, and to all the friends who brighten up my days with their emails or a quick chat at the school gate.

Family support often goes without saying but it's invaluable, so I think it deserves acknowledgement. My mum deserves a special mention in this last year and a half that's seen the loss of my grandparents, her parents, in their mid-90s.

On the business side, sincerest thanks to Tim, Gabby, Jess, and the wonderful team at Orbit, as well as to Lisa and to Moshe. Also to my agent Maggie, and to Jill and Camilla.

On the professional side, I would like to thank all those generous writers, across so many genres, who continue to share their cautionary tales and useful tips, and to inspire me with their friendship.

CHAPTER ONE

What does this sunrise bring, beyond another day of trying to read all the faces turned to me? What omens might there be as to whether or not I'll meet whatever challenges are set before me before sunset? Will I fail? Who will I fail – myself or these people who never foresaw that I would become their ruler?

Idly rubbing a hand over his close-trimmed beard, he glanced from side to side to see if any portent offered itself in any arc of the compass, firstly in the pale skies of the early morning, the clouds iridescent as mother-of-pearl. Dropping his gaze, he studied the indigo waters broken by ruffles of foam and mysterious swirls of lighter blue. The waters rose and fell as gently as a sleeping child's chest.

No sign of any sea serpent lurking in the channels between coral and sand. No whale rising unexpectedly from the distant deeps further out. No detritus floating in our path as portent of good or ill. There are no omens that I can see. The future is as bare of signs to guide me as the empty ocean.

A dutiful voice interrupted his fruitless survey.

'We're nearly there, my lord Chazen Kheda,' the helmsman announced, sitting alert on his stool on the raised platform at the stern of the little galley. One brown hand rested on the steering oar, his dark eyes fixed on the man standing in the prow. The ship's master kept an alert watch for reefs and skerries beneath the waves, his dun cotton tunic and trousers flattened against his muscular body by the breeze. In the belly of the ship, the rowers bent and hauled and sent the *Yellow Serpent* speeding through the water, three men to a bench, each with his own long oar lashed to its thole-pin. With the crew of the warlord's vessel drawn from the most practised oarsmen, they barely needed the regular drone of the piper's flute amidships to keep their strokes even, making light of pulling the long, lithe vessel against the wind.

'We're in good time, as always.' Kheda eased his shoulders beneath the weight of his chain-mail hauberk and adjusted the silk scarf around his neck before raising his voice so that the rowers on the open deck below could hear him. 'The *Yellow Serpent* has served me well throughout this voyage.'

As I have served this domain, I hope. But this voyage is all but over and I will have a whole new set of challenges to meet when I return to what I suppose I must call my home now.

'Seen any omens for our day?' A man whose bald head barely topped Kheda's shoulder held out a round brass and steel helmet with a chain-mail veil hanging down to protect the wearer's neck and shoulders. Diamonds around the gold brow band spat defiant fire back at the strengthening sun.

'I won't want that till we land.' Kheda relished the breeze brushing his short-cropped, tightly curled hair as he kept his eyes on the rapidly approaching drifts of foam that ringed the few scraps of sandy land in the midst of the reefs and sandbanks. Sparkling beaches circled dense clumps of midar shrub pierced here and there with stands of nut palms. The trees waved exuberant fronds of lush new growth, still drawing on the water hoarded by the earth since the drenching of last year's rains.

'The final outposts of your domain, my lord Chazen Kheda, before the countless islands of the Aldabreshin Archipelago yield to the boundless southern ocean.' The shorter man's tone was faintly mocking.

'Not so boundless, Dev.' Kheda shot a glare at him. 'We know all too well there must be land beyond the horizon to spawn our enemies.'

Dev affected not to see Kheda's irritation as he adjusted the broad brass-studded belt around his sturdy waist, armour jingling softly as he shifted his bare feet on the smooth planking. His hauberk was plain, wholly made from polished steel rings, in contrast to Kheda's which boasted a diamond pattern of brazen links and engraved metal plates inset to protect his vitals from piercing arrows or murderous sword-thrusts. The fine leather of the warlord's belt was invisible beneath golden plaques embossed with intricate sprays of canthira leaves.

'Have there been omens of battle ahead, my lord?' the helmsman asked with alarm. 'Do you think some new wave of invaders will come to support those still trapped in the western isles?'

'No.' Kheda smiled easily to calm the mariner's fears. 'There's been no such sign.'

Fool. Watch what you say. These men of Chazen haven't known and trusted you since your birth or theirs. You cannot rely on them to read your words aright, or keep them to themselves as those of Daish would have done.

'We will throw the last sorry remnants of those savages into the sea soon enough. Let the currents carry their bloated corpses back to wash up and warn their kin against quitting their own shores again.' As he continued in the same confident tone, Kheda waved one hand airily and the uncut emerald on the heavy silver ring he wore glowed vividly in the brilliant light.

'We'll be getting back to clearing out the last of the invaders, will we, as soon as we've completed this interminable tour of every last rock and reef?' Dev demanded abruptly.

Kheda glanced at him, face stern. 'Dev, as a barbarian,

I'll allow you more leeway than I would any true-born Archipelagan, but use that tone to me again and I will have you flogged. Better yet, I will do it myself.'

Do you remember what I told you? That one of my father Daish Reik's precepts of leadership was never make a threat you're not prepared to carry out? You can be sure that's no idle warning, barbarian.

He looked into Dev's dark eyes but couldn't read anything there. No matter. The barbarian looked away first.

'My lord, if you please, where's the *Mist Dove*?' The helmsman was still gazing resolutely over the heads of the rowers on their serried benches towards the *Yellow Serpent*'s burly shipmaster on the prow platform. A flurry of foam blew up over the prow as the knife edge of the brass-sheathed ram sliced through the waves.

'Staying well clear.' Kheda looked back astern to see the heavy trireme that had accompanied them slowing in the more open waters, oars idling. The weapons and armour of the fighting men aboard glinted in the sun.

And if by some mischance I have failed to note any portent of some new assault by the savages, we have steel and hatred to use against them. But let's not tempt the future with such thoughts. There's been no sign of any new invasion. You had better turn your attention to what awaits you here, and whatever portents for your rule of this domain that'll be set out for all to see.

Shallow enough to negotiate the encircling corals, the light galley headed towards the largest of the scatter of low islands. The ragged fronds of the tallest trees were stirring in the rising breeze and the channels between the islands were thronged with little boats.

'So where exactly are the pearl beds?' Dev studied the shipmasters raising their sails, the divers busy on deck checking the weighted ropes that would take them down to the sea bed and the lifelines that should ensure they would survive to enjoy the fruits of their labours. Lookouts on each boat sharpened broad-bladed shark spears and viciously barbed gaff hooks.

'They shift from year to year.' Kheda watched the youths and young girls trading their sweat and muscle for the right to learn the skills of diver and sailor. Some were wading out to the skiffs carrying food and water on their heads; others were stowing the stacks of baskets waiting to bring the year's greatest bounty up from the deep.

And sometimes the pearl oysters vanish altogether. What manner of omen would that be?

The tremor that ran through Kheda had nothing to do with the surge beneath his feet as the *Yellow Serpent*'s rowers bent over their oars. Pearl skiffs scattered as the galley headed towards a wide beach where a veritable village had been thrown up. Huts built from woven panels of palm fronds were roughly thatched with bundles of coarse grass tied with tangling vines. The greenery was barely faded but Kheda knew it wouldn't be long before the punishing sun parched roofs and walls to a yellowy brown.

Then the pearl harvest will be over and the huts will be left to the sand lizards and the sooty shrews hunting sickle snakes and scorpions. The pearl gulls and coral fishers will plunder the roofs for their own nests and prey on unwary shrews to feed their young. The dry season will bleach these huts to frail straw and the rainy season's storms will rip them apart. There'll be barely a sign that there was anything here when the last full moons of the year ahead of us will summon the divers to search the reefs for the shifting pearl beds.

I wonder if I will be here to see next year's harvest.

The wind shifted, bringing a startling stench. 'Saedrin save me!' Dev barely reached the stern before he lost his breakfast noisily over the rail.

Kheda exchanged a rueful grin with the helmsman,

trying to breathe as shallowly as possible. 'You always tell yourself it can't be as bad as you remember.'

And perhaps that's a sign: to concentrate on the here and now rather than indulging in idle speculations about future paths.

'Then you realise it's worse.' The helmsman's weather-beaten brown face grimaced as he hauled on the steering oar in response to a signal from the shipmaster.

The rowers pulled on their oars with a will, even those gagging on their own nausea. The *Yellow Serpent* accelerated past the bare sandy reef that was the source of the stink. Masked with swathes of cotton cloth, one of the few men ashore waved. Another was more concerned with throwing an old dry shell at a gull darting down from the cloud of birds wheeling above, squawking their outrage as mats of woven palm fronds frustrated their efforts to plunder the vast tubs the men were guarding. Emerald finches and dusky gnatcatchers swooped unopposed, gorging on the red-eyed flies that hung around the tubs in smoky swarms.

As the *Yellow Serpent* passed the reeking islet and the breeze brought clean, salt-scented air, Kheda dipped a cup of water from a lidded barrel lashed to the light galley's rearmost signal mast. He passed it to Dev, who was still leaning over the stern, pale beneath his coppery tan.

'You people can't just open your oysters with a sharp knife and dig out the pearls?' Dev swilled water around his mouth and spat sourly over the rail.

'Not when we want every pearl, right down to the seed and dust pearls.' Kheda watched the water turning from mysterious green to crystal clarity over the brilliant sands as the shipmaster skilfully guided the vessel into the shallows. 'The only way to get those is to let maggots strip the oysters clean.'

'We're sailing west again after this?' the barbarian growled beneath his breath.

'No, back to the residence. I told you.' Kheda shot the scowling Dev a warning look, his voice low and rapid. 'After all they've suffered in the last year, these people need the reassurance of correct observance of every ritual. As warlord, I have to be there when the new-year stars come into alignment. It's my duty to read the skies for the domain and give judgement on any other portent.'

'What portents do you think they will bring you? Lizards caught in bizarre places?' Dev mocked. 'Or patterns imagined in a pot of beans?'

'Just keep your mouth shut on your ignorance.' Kheda didn't hide his contempt.

'Some new year it'll be, without so much as a sniff of liquor,' Dev muttered, sipping at his water with distaste. 'What then?'

'We'll see.' Kheda smiled thinly. 'In the omens of the heavenly and the earthly compasses.'

He left Dev and went to stand beside the helmsman's chair. The rowers had slowed, listening for the ship-master's shouts of command and the piper's signals. Some glanced up at the stern platform with discreet curiosity. Kheda kept his face impassive as he made a covert survey of the crew's bearded faces.

They're as curious as everyone else to see what kind of pearl harvest will mark the turn of my first year as unexpected lord of this Chazen domain. And I can see a measure of private anticipation, naturally, in their hopes that serving the warlord in person will win them some share in the bounty.

What can they see in you? Very little, hopefully. 'Show no more emotion than a statue of the finest marble,' that's what your father used to say. Because people looking at a statue see in it what they want to see more often than not.

But I'm not seeing that trust I was so used to as ruler of the Daish domain that I took it for granted.

What did your father Daish Reik have to say about respect? That a wise warlord would earn it before he demanded it.

Let's see if I can do that in this domain.

'Excuse me, my lord.' The helmsman interrupted his reverie as a couple of men tossed anchors over the prow at the shipmaster's nod and two more came up to secure the galley's stern with a rattle of ropes and a clatter of iron.

'Time to go ashore, Dev.' Kheda halted by the steps leading down to the main deck, lowering his voice. 'Try to look as if you have some idea of what to do with those swords.'

'I could kill any man on this beach in a knife fight.' Dev thrust Kheda's helm into his hands with scant ceremony.

'Which would prove you're no true body slave.' Kheda looked hard at the shorter man, unsmiling eyes shaded by the face plate of the helm, which was held up over his forehead by a sliding nasal bar. 'And set everyone wondering just what you might be, barbarian born and so far from home.'

Fleeting uncertainty momentarily replaced the veiled antagonism in Dev's dark eyes. 'Then you'd best make sure there's no need for me to fight for your honour, hadn't you?' He thrust his own helm on his head and pulled the strap tight beneath his belligerent, clean-shaven chin.

Seeing that their pause was prompting unwelcome curiosity, Kheda went down the steps and strode along the central gangway between the rows of benches. He took the double step to the shallow bow platform in a single lithe stride and nodded his approval to the shipmaster. 'A swift voyage and a smooth one, Hesi. Thank you.'

'It is my honour to serve you, my lord.' The burly shipmaster bowed low.

Kheda looked over the *Yellow Serpent*'s prow to see a waiting rowing boat and climbed carefully down the rope ladder slung ready.

Falling into the water would hardly suit a warlord's dignity. Besides, every man, woman and child here would see some truly awful omen in such a mishap.

The islander at the oars of the little boat smiled ingratiatingly at Kheda, then his eyes widened as Dev cautiously descended the flexing rope rungs. Even tanned by his years beneath the strong Aldabreshin sun, the northerner's skin was paler than either Kheda's or the boatman's, an oddity made all the more obvious given his lack of a beard.

'Any time you're ready.' Dev settled himself on the stern thwart of the boat.

The boatman's confusion visibly deepened. Dev's accent wasn't from any of the southerly Aldabreshin domains but his speech was as fluently Archipelagan as if he'd learned the tongue at his mother's knee.

Kheda demanded the islander's attention with a wry smile. 'We smelled the first hauls of oysters putrefying nicely.'

'The first fruits are already gathered, my lord.' The boatman recalled his purpose and bent to his oars. 'The reefs are as thick with oysters as we've ever seen them.'

As relief flooded through Kheda, the pearl skiffs clustered close, divers shouting out to support the rower's verdict with eager claims of their own.

'Excellent news,' Kheda called back with warm approval.

'Indeed, my lord,' echoed Dev with unashamed calculation.

I suppose that will pass unremarked. He's obviously a barbarian and we all know that rampant greed rules the unbroken lands of the north. Besides, a loyal body slave would know that the quantity and quality of this year's harvest are crucial to all our hopes. And surely every islander will want to see my rule sanctioned by the best possible omens?

'I've brought swords and archers to keep your harvest safe,' Kheda called out to the pearl skiffs. 'Carry water to my ships to refill their barrels, if you please.'

Leaving behind a robust chorus of earnest assurances, the rowing boat soon reached the shallows. The boatman shipped his oars and jumped lithely over the side, grabbing for the bow rope to begin hauling the boat up on to the drier sand.

'This will do.' Kheda raised a hand, inclining his head courteously to the boatman as he got out. 'Make yourself known to my slave before we leave.' The cool ruffles of surf around his shins were refreshing after the sun-baked wood of the galley's deck beneath his bare feet. 'Remember that boatman and give him a few pearls,' he said quietly to Dev as they walked up the beach.

'Naturally, my lord,' murmured Dev with a touch of sarcasm. 'A memory for faces is essential in my proper trade.'

Kheda's spine stiffened despite himself. Before he could find a reprimand for the barbarian, a handful of men advanced down the beach towards them, leaving more waiting in a respectful half-circle where the white coral sands gave way to dusty soil and sparse coils of parched, grey midar stems. Dev had been walking a pace behind Kheda on his open side, one hand resting lightly on the twin hilts thrust through his double-looped sword belt. As the islanders approached, the barbarian moved swiftly to stand between the warlord and these newcomers, stony faced, until Kheda gave him the nod to stand aside, his smile one of nicely calculated superiority.

You can feign this much of a true body slave's duties at least.

The leader of the delegation bowed low. The bold yellow cloth of his simply cut cotton tunic and trousers was rich with embroidery mimicking turtleshell. He had a darker complexion than his companions and the more tightly curled hair of a hill-dweller, showing that blood from some larger domain had mingled with his more local ancestry. 'My lord Chazen Kheda.'

'Borha.' Kheda smiled widely to conceal how much that new title still grated on his ears.

Get used to it, fool. You're not Daish Kheda, nor ever will be again.

'I see you've brought plenty of strong arms to reap the pearl harvest,' Kheda continued smoothly.

'We left plenty of men to continue our rebuilding.' The man beamed with pleasure at being recognised but fingered a white crab-shell talisman on a cord around his neck, betraying an unconscious anxiety.

'I know – we've just come from Salgaru. Your village is certainly prospering, and all the others besides.' Kheda widened his smile and looked beyond Borha to include all the waiting men in his approval.

One of the others spoke up. 'Will you take some refreshment while we wait for our fishermen to return, my lord?'

'Thank you.' Kheda walked on up the beach and the islanders moved to either side, giving Dev a respectful distance. A few had darker skin and curly hair like Borha. More had the rich brown complexion and straighter hair prevalent in these southerly reaches. All wore crisp new cottons in reds, blues and yellows decorated with skilful embroidery. Some bore vivid butterflies across their shoulders or patterns echoing any one of the myriad bright birds that graced the bigger islands. Other decorations recalled the intricate traceries of thorn coral or the spirals of seashells. A couple wore bracelets of twisted silver wire and one boasted a chain of gold lozenge links around his neck. Most wore more simple talismans – a plaited wristband of the silky fibres from a tandra seed pod or a string of polished ironwood beads. All the men wore daggers at their hips, but Kheda and Dev were the only ones with swords.

They're all so careful to match my pace exactly, with the same diffidence I've seen throughout this voyage around the domain. They bow and simper and answer all my questions, barely asking any of their own. This is obviously how they treated Chazen Saril. But Saril's dead and gone. These people must learn how different a ruler I am.

Kheda headed for a temporary pavilion set up among the palm huts. Polished berale wood supported azure cotton embroidered with fan-shaped midar leaves shading a bank of plump indigo cushions. Hopeful maidens in simple silk dresses of yellow and white that flattered the warm bronze of their bare arms and faces stood holding beaten brass plates laden with dainties. Idling unconvincingly among the crude huts, men and women clad in sober unbleached cotton eyed the spectacle.

'Please, join me.' Kheda swept a hand around to include all the spokesmen in his invitation.

Dev was already moving to take a tray of goblets from a girl who had found time to weave crimson striol-vine flowers into her glossy black curls. He surprised her into a giggle with a mischievous wink before offering the salver deftly to Kheda, eyes dutifully downcast.

'Admire if you want but lay a finger on any of them –' Kheda raised the goblet to hide his lips '– and I'll cut it off.'

'Naturally, my lord.' Dev's answering murmur dripped with sarcasm.

Kheda sipped velvety sard-berry juice, its richness quenching his thirst as the heady scent cleansed the lurking memory of the rotting oysters.

'My lord Chazen Kheda.' Another of the islanders' spokesmen addressed him, stumbling over his words.

Kheda searched his memory for the stained yellow talisman the man wore on a leather thong: a tooth from some piebald whale either taken by a valiant ancestor or washed up on these shores as a sign to bemuse anyone other than a seer or a warlord. 'Isei, isn't it?'

Tell me, why is your fist so tight around the stem of that goblet that your knuckles are white?

'You come dressed for war, my lord.' Isei cleared his throat. 'I was wondering how the western isles fare. Are the invaders finally defeated?'

Some of the other spokesmen edged away to dissociate themselves from such boldness and a few closed their eyes, helplessly struggling to hide their expressions of pain.

Do you think I would disapprove of such a question? That I don't have my own unwelcome memories of the destruction that swept across your islands not even a year ago?

'I was taught to always travel armoured.' Kheda shrugged.

Taught by my father, Daish Reik, warlord of the stronger, richer Daish domain to your north, a man to be treated with all due respect lest he make your lives intolerable by closing the seaways to you. Who would ever have foreseen that his son would become your warlord? Not Daish Reik. Not me, that's for sure, when I was Daish Kheda. Not Chazen Saril. But then none of us foresaw the invasion of Chazen by brutal savages from some unknown land beyond the southern horizon.

He looked slowly around the circle of intent faces. 'As for the invaders, we wrought your vengeance with the death of nearly all of them in that first sustained assault, with Daish lending their swordsmen and ships and warriors from Ritsem and Redigal domains coming to our aid as well. The last sorry remnant disappeared into the thickets of our most remote southern and western islets. We continue to hunt them down, making sure we have cleared each island entirely before we move on to the next.

But we are being cautious, yes. I don't intend to spend a single Chazen life for the sake of a hundred savages, not if I can help it.'

Kheda paused and drank from his goblet, noting one of the spokesmen pressing the back of a burn-scarred hand to his tight-shut eyes.

He hardened his voice. 'Their savage wizards are all dead, so they cannot visit the foul evils of their magic on us ever again. They have no ships, so they cannot escape. Our triremes keep vigil along the seaways and crush any of their log boats trying to put to sea. Few of the islands they hold have water year round. They'll be as thirsty as these reefs before much longer into the dry season.'

He gestured at the temporarily flourishing greenery beyond the pavilion before startling the assembled spokesmen with sudden entreaty. 'Leave me and the warriors of Chazen to serve the domain in fighting these vermin. Let us take your vengeance on a people so debased they brought magic to fight their battles for them. Your strong arms and backs are better used in rebuilding your homes and your boats, in restoring your vegetable gardens and grain plots, in recapturing your house fowls. Then, when we have put the last invader to his richly deserved death, you will be ready to help restore those islands in their turn.'

'You don't fear that the presence of such vile savages will have corrupted those islands beyond cleansing?' Isei's free hand strayed to the hilt of the dagger at his plaited-leather belt.

Crescent-moon Chazen dagger like the one I wear now, not the smoother curve of a Daish blade like the one my father gave me.

Kheda looked him straight in the eye. 'Not after every trace of their foul presence has been burned to ash and scattered to the seas and the winds.'

For retribution as well as purification, for the sake of all those innocents they slaughtered and all the villages they burned in their accursed rampage.

'My lord, something to eat?' Borha broke the tense silence with a snap of his fingers at the waiting maidens. One immediately proffered candied lilla fruit slices set on cakes of steamed saller grain glistening with honey.

'Thank you, no.' Kheda smiled to mitigate the rebuff. 'Passing by the oyster vats has left me without an appetite. Tell me, are the divers correct? Are we going to see a good harvest of pearls for the Chazen domain?'

'It's early days yet, my lord, but yes, I think it will be a truly splendid year.' Borha's smile was wide and ingratiating.

'Let's go and see for ourselves.' Kheda abandoned the pavilion and strode towards the crude awnings sheltering those sifting through the pearls already won from the close-mouthed oysters. The assembled spokesmen hurried after him, other islanders trailing after.

Let's keep you all looking to the future and let's hope it's a favourable one. Let's not remember the invaders who brought chaos and death last year. Let's not recall the calamity or your erstwhile lord Chazen Saril dead in exile from his birthright. Let's not wonder how rumours of my own death turned out to be falsehood or contemplate those events that set me over you as your new ruler. Let's not ponder just why it proved impossible for me to return to my home and my family and the Daish domain I was born to rule.

Borha drew level with Kheda's elbow. 'We filled the vats within a few days of starting to dive. They were already rotted down enough to be emptied yesterday. We've had a fine haul of pearls and there are plenty of shells warranting a closer look.' He gestured to the baskets of dark mottled ovals in the midst of a gang of old men sitting cross-legged on a stretch of faded, sandy carpet.

'My lord.' One acknowledged Kheda with easy self-assurance. His hair and beard were white in stark contrast to skin as wrinkled and dark as a sun-dried berry. Unhurried, he studied the empty oyster shell, fine-bladed knife hovering around a sizeable blister marring the iridescent nacre that so closely mimicked the pearls it bore.

Kheda found he was holding his breath as the old man scored a fine line around the bulbous swelling.

A trivial omen, but an omen nevertheless. Will he find a pearl? Or will this be one of those pockets of stinking black slime?

The old man eased the sharp steel into the nacre and the swelling burst to leave a perfect milky sphere rolling in the hollow of the shell. 'Should clean up well enough.' Putting the pearl carefully in a cotton-lined box, he took another shell from the basket and contemplated a cyst of three half-moon pearls clinging stubbornly to one edge.

'You're polishing them here?' Kheda moved on towards an awning shading men and women gently scouring impurities from gleaming pearls held in scraps of soft deer hide, their forearms shimmering with pearl dust.

'And drilling them, my lord.' Borha bowed obsequiously, simultaneously indicating a tent some way beyond where the most skilled craftsmen were studying pearls through handheld lenses or marking them precisely with callipers tipped with lampblack.

As Kheda approached, he observed that one man had already drilled a large silvery pearl from one side and was plucking it from the moist scrap of leather holding it in a notch in the wooden block gripped between his knees. Deftly reversing it, he set the needle-fine tip of his drill on the sooty pinpoint he had made earlier and cupped the upper end of his drill rod in a discarded oyster shell. As he worked the bow back and forth, slowly at first and then more swiftly, the string whirled the steel-tipped drill around.

'Ever seen this done, Dev?' Kheda asked.

'No.' The barbarian grinned with open appreciation. 'It's quite some trick.'

Using his little finger on every other stroke, the craftsman was deftly flicking water from a larger hollow in the block on to the pearl. His apprentice watched attentively, pausing in his own duty of sharpening drill points on a broad whetstone. As the driller pulled rod and bow away, the lad instantly picked the pearl out of the hollow and washed it carefully in a little pot of fresh seawater.

'Are you having many pearls break?' Kheda asked casually.

'Very few, my lord,' the craftsman assured him with a half-smile.

'They're still getting their eye in on the biggest pearls.' Unbidden, Isei spoke up. 'There'll be more losses with the smaller ones.'

'True enough,' said Kheda mildly.

But the fewer losses the better, both as portent for my rule and for the sake of the domain's trade, when we need every resource to make good all the losses of this last year.

'Please take these to our lady Itrac Chazen, my lord.' Borha had stepped away for a moment, returning with a box of berale-tree wood still pale and fresh from the joiner's hands. Dev stepped up smartly to claim it.

'We'll be hard pressed to have all the pearls polished and drilled by the time our lady Itrac wishes to sail north.' Isei's beard jutted defiantly. 'So many of our craftsmen were murdered by the invaders. And there are those who would say those of us that remain would be better spending our energies elsewhere.'

I'd wager that whale-tooth talisman wasn't won by some ancestor who found the beast dead on the shore. He was probably master of the ship risking life and limb to drive it into the shallows and the waiting spears.

'I take it you're one of them?' Kheda looked straight at Isei once again. 'Then make your case. What concerns do you have? Speak freely,' he commanded.

I'm not some lord like Ulla Safar who can kill a messenger for bringing undesirable news. Nor, to his credit, was Chazen Saril.

Isei hesitated before drawing a deep breath and plunging on. 'We'll run short of food before the end of the dry season, my lord. The rains were more than half-gone before we could get our saller seedlings in the ground. We have fewer men to work the land, with so many dead or fled, and fewer still to tend what we could salvage from the fruit and vegetable plantations. Even with all the women and children lending their strength to bring in the harvest, we nowhere near filled the granaries.'

Kheda raised a hand to quell the voices of the other spokesmen suddenly emboldened by Isei's words. 'I'm hardly ignorant of such vital matters but you're right to make certain that I appreciate your situation.'

'What do you propose to do about it?' Isei looked straight back at him, unabashed.

'I propose to discuss all the domain's necessities with my lady Itrac Chazen,' replied Kheda with a hint of reproof, 'so that she may trade these pearls with the ladies of Redigal and Daish and the domains beyond, to Chazen's best advantage.'

'We have concerns there as well, my lord,' asserted Isei boldly.

'Explain yourself,' Kheda prompted tersely, noting Borha wincing out of the corner of his eye.

'My lady Itrac will doubtless feel that Chazen is under obligation to Daish, Redigal and other domains for their help in driving out the invaders.' Isei folded his arms across his chest. 'Which is certainly true. But I believe Daish owes Chazen some debt that should be weighed in the scales before any price in pearls is agreed for saller grain or dried meats. Many Chazen who had no choice but to flee before the invaders were given sanctuary among the Daish islands. The Chazen repaid this generosity with their labour in the Daish saller fields and vegetable plots.' Isei hastily qualified his words. 'And such labour was gladly given, don't mistake me. Daish harvests have been plentiful and we're glad of it, and to see Daish Sirket's rule begun under such good auspices. But it's a fact that Daish Sirket's decree that all those of Chazen quit his domain before the stars of the new year has left his islands with fewer mouths to feed while we have more come home with every tide and little enough to share as it is.'

'You think Chazen might rightfully claim some share from the Daish granaries and storehouses?' Kheda hazarded.

Is this some test, honest Isei? Do you think I should prove my fitness to wear a Chazen dagger by challenging my own son, who was forced to declare himself Daish warlord because I was believed dead? Don't think I haven't heard the murmuring, honest Isei, the whispers of those who say I should have raised my sword against Sirket instead of turning to claim this leaderless domain. Do you think I should have brought internal warfare on the people of Daish, with untamed savages massing on their southern border? Who would have driven the invaders out of your islands then, after Chazen Saril had fled in abject terror?

Isei made no reply, staring at the ground in front of him. The uncomfortable silence lengthened.

'I will discuss all the domain's concerns with my lady Itrac Chazen.' Kheda turned from Isei to address Borha with a friendly smile. 'I know it's early days but are there many pearls of unusual colour or shape?'

'This way, my lord.' Borha eagerly ushered Kheda towards an open-sided tent surrounded by shallow baskets redolent of decayed shellfish. Women sat at trestle tables, sorting through layers of salt-stained cotton to retrieve smooth orbs, tear drops, angular hound's teeth, flattened petals and half-moons.

Kheda paused by a plump matron comfortable in a shapeless gown of orange patterned with yellow vizail blossoms, a turtleshell comb in her grizzled curly hair. Her deft brown fingers were quick as a silver crane plucking shrimp from the shallows as she dropped each style of pearl into separate silk-lined boxes.

'How are the pickings?' Kheda enquired genially.

She didn't look up, intent on her task. 'Far better than last year.'

'Here, my lord.' The woman on his other side surprised Kheda by taking his hand and dropping two coloured pearls into his palm. One was a deep vibrant gold, the other a mysterious cloudy blue. Both were as big as the nail on Kheda's smallest finger.

'Isei.' He held them up. 'Your village chose you to speak for them so you must read the day-to-day omens. What do these signify to you?'

'Yellow for wealth, my lord.' Isei's eyes brightened with faint hope. 'Blue for good fortune.'

'A fine portent to greet your visit, my lord,' said Borha obsequiously.

A fine portent and, better yet, one that I had no hand in seeking out. An interpretation that we've all known since childhood, plain enough for even the disaffected to read. A sign I can trust? That the fortunes of this hapless domain are finally turning to good after the ills that have plagued it? Reassurance that my actions haven't irrevocably blighted my future or theirs?

'I'm interrupting you, forgive me.' Kheda smiled at the

women whose fingers hadn't stopped working. He walked on, beyond the shade of the tents where bolts of closely woven black material were stretched along the dry sand. Buckets were being emptied out on to the cloth and the scent of decay was inescapable.

'What's going on here?' Dev wrinkled his nose.

'After fifteen days the vats are filled with seawater, to float out the maggots and slime and leave the pearls and the shells.' Kheda nodded towards the detritus on the cloth: tiny scraps of shell, a few dead and broken maggots, nameless sparkling fragments and sand of every colour the reefs offered. 'The slurry from the bottom is sieved for seed pearls. Then it's dried and picked over for dust pearls.'

'I didn't think Daish went to so much bother,' commented a man searching the debris in front of them. He only had one hand, and was propping himself on the stump of his other wrist. His leg on that same side ended abruptly at mid-thigh.

'Daish doesn't. This is Chazen.' Kheda looked out towards the reefs where the pearl skiffs were now anchored for their day's work, distant bobbing specks. 'Tell me, has there been much sight of sharks? Any word of sea serpents?'

'Not so far.' The man looked up with frank thankfulness.

'You've got funny eyes.' A little boy squatting beside the crippled diver to search the dark cloth for minuscule treasures stood up. His curly black head barely reached Kheda's sword belt as he peered up with open curiosity. 'They're green.'

'Su, that's your lord Chazen Kheda,' a slim girl said in strangled embarrassment, scrambling to her feet and dusting her hands against well-worn cotton trousers.

'He's still got green eyes,' said the lad forcefully.

'You're plainly your father's son.' Kheda hunkered down to meet the child on his own level. 'My forefathers and foremothers made alliances that brought barbarian blood into my line. See, my hair's more brown than black, isn't it?' He took off his helmet and relished the breeze on his sweating forehead.

'*He's* a barbarian.' Su's glance flickered dubiously to Dev. 'But he's got *brown* eyes.'

'So he's not that different from you.' Kheda ruffled the lad's tousled black hair. 'And now he lives among civilized folk, so that makes him an Archipelagan.'

Su looked wide-eyed at Kheda. 'Is is true the northern lands run unbroken all the way across the horizon?'

'I've never seen that myself,' Kheda answered apologetically. 'Dev?'

'It's true enough,' the barbarian confirmed with a grin.

'I'm going to take ship to the north and see for myself when I'm grown,' the little boy said robustly. 'I'll take an oar on a galley and work my way up to helmsman and then shipmaster.'

'When will the merchant galleys be coming, my lord, from the other domains?' The girl bit her lip at her own daring. 'It's just that we'll need silk, for stringing the pearls.' Someone behind Kheda caught her eye and she fell silent, dropping her gaze to the ground.

'I shall remind my lady Itrac Chazen,' Kheda assured her, 'just as soon as may be.' He stood and thrust his helmet back on his head to hide a furtive sting of tears in his eyes.

Sirket was like that as a child, always ready to speak his mind and full of questions. Mesil was more of a thinker, doubtless still is, certainly not one to play a wager against unless you've all your wits about you. Which will my third son grow [illegible] – eager seeker or careful observer? How will I ever know, separated from him and all my other children, my beautiful, beloved daughters?

He cleared his throat and nodded to the crippled diver. 'You are certainly blessed in your children, my friend.'

The importunate Isei was at Kheda's shoulder as he turned to walk away. 'Children are indeed a man's greatest good fortune. And the domain's.'

That's another of your concerns, is it? You and everyone else speculating around the evening cookfires. What would you have me say to my lady Itrac Chazen on that score?

Kheda found his patience abruptly exhausted. 'Thank you, Borha, this has all been most interesting. I shall take some refreshment now, until you have need of me to read the omens.'

With his sudden about-face leaving them wrong-footed, he strode past the startled spokesmen. The islanders who had trailed around after their progress hurriedly got out of his way. With Dev at his shoulder, Kheda headed for the little blue pavilion and dropped on to the down-filled cushions, ignoring the girls.

'Some privacy for my lord. No, leave that.' Dev nodded at a girl carrying a ewer of juice. She put it on a small table wedged firmly into the sandy ground where Dev set the berale-wood box of pearls before shooing the patiently waiting maidens away, taking a tray of little cakes from one and a goblet of sard-berry juice from another.

Kheda reached up to take the drink the barbarian offered him. 'That should be "our lord".'

'Who expects an ignorant barbarian to get it right every time?' Dev said, sardonic.

'Too many lapses and they'll expect me to beat it into you if necessary,' warned Kheda, 'and they may start wondering why I don't. We can't either of us afford that.'

'You've got them wondering about more than your unusual body slave.' Dev glanced idly around at the village spokesmen who were engaging in desultory conversations with various islanders. 'I think they're trying to guess if you'll turn out to be some vicious tyrant like Ulla Safar or the enlightened ruler they were so used to hearing Daish traders boast of.'

'They should be used to uncertainty. Chazen Saril's moods were apt to change as quick as a weather vane in the rainy season.' Kheda took one of the little sweetmeats Dev was offering and bit into it. Taken unawares by the glutinous sweetness of the filling, he grimaced before forcing himself to swallow it. 'And as my dutiful body slave, can you please spread the word as tactfully as you can that I have nothing like Saril's sweet tooth.'

'Anything else?' asked Dev, amused.

'Yes.' Kheda looked up, tone forthright. 'You can find out just what history there might be between Borha and Isei. If there are any tensions between the two of them or their villages, I want to know every detail. Everyone's all co-operation now, with the first excitement of a rich pearl harvest in view. That might last or it might not, once all the late nights and early mornings take their toll. And this cheerfulness will float away on the tide if sharks or sea serpents start taking divers on the reefs, or if too many of them find their eyesight fails this season.'

Healer I may be, but there's nothing I can do for eyes grown clouded, silvered as the pearls they've sought for so many years. Nor for those who find blurring in their vision means they can only see what they're not actually looking at. I may be their augur but I've no explanation for that paradox.

But the divers are always remarkably sanguine; they know some will pay that price for the ocean's bounty. Everything has its price.

'Leave it to me,' Dev said confidently. 'I can be your eyes and ears, just like a proper body slave.'

'I don't have a lot of choice, do I?' retorted Kheda,

waving away the sweetmeats and taking another drink to try to rid his mouth of the cloying taste.

But you're right. You are an accomplished spy and one who spent enough years sailing the length and breadth of the Archipelago's domains to know all the ins and outs of masquerading as a body slave. Everything except the sword skills.

But are you still spying for those mysterious barbarian powers that first sent you into Aldabreshin waters? And how will you seek to profit on your own account with whatever you learn, with your northern greed and utter lack of scruple? What will these people of Chazen think of me, if you're caught out in some despicable connivance?

What wouldn't I give to have Telouet back as my body slave, strong sword arm and faithful friend besides? The only consolation for his loss is that he serves Sirket now. There's no one I would rather have trusted my son to.

Dev grinned as Kheda handed him the empty goblet. 'I can tell you one thing none of you Archipelagans seem to know: you can do better than silk for stringing pearls. Horsehair, that's what you want, white horsehair. That's what all the gem traders on the mainland use. It's the first thing they do when they get their hands on Aldabreshin pearls – restring them.'

Taken aback despite himself, Kheda rallied. 'Just how am I supposed to get such stuff when we're as far from the unbroken lands as it's possible to get? And every northern domain that's been tempted to trade for horses from you barbarians has seen their investment sicken and die before the year's out. No, I'll settle for safer trades and more immediately useful ones, food most of all. Isei may be overbold but he's not wrong to worry about a hungry end to the dry season.'

'Well, you'd better not go hungry here or you'll be insulting all these fine people.' Dev searched through the sweetmeats with careful fingers. 'I think that's a plainer one. If you're worried about them running short of food hereabouts, can't they just eat the pearl oysters instead of fattening up maggots for the fish and the seabirds and raising a stink to curdle the clouds?'

'Have you ever tried eating a pearl oyster, you ignorant barbarian?' Kheda was surprised into laughing and nearly choked on the little cake. 'I'd eat the coral gulls first and they taste disgusting.' He paused to catch his breath before continuing, face serious. 'No, I don't want anyone in the domain reduced to such straits; they'd give up on my rule for good if they were. Besides, it's an ill omen to cook any kind of shellfish and find you've ruined a pearl with the heat of a fire. Haven't you seen how thoroughly the divers cut up purple conch flesh, to make sure there's nothing hidden in the folds?'

'If you're not hungry, can I eat something?' Dev asked as he handed Kheda the refilled goblet. 'I lost my breakfast, if you recall.' He barely waited for Kheda's nod of permission before cramming a couple of sticky morsels into his mouth, speaking through the food. 'It doesn't look as if you've much to worry about. If this year's harvest is as good as everyone's saying it will be, you'll have enough pearls to buy each islander their own sack of saller grain.'

Kheda shook his head as he sipped sard-berry juice. 'It's a good start but it's only pearls. You might only get a handful out of every thousand oysters. The shells in these reaches are too small and too thin to provide much nacre. That's the foundation of Daish prosperity, the inner face of the oyster shells. That's why they don't have to trouble themselves salvaging every last dust pearl from the slurry in the vats.'

'You should let me take a boat back to the northern lands and do some trading for you there.' Dev looked out towards the ocean, face unreadable. 'That little box they gave you just now would fetch a king's ransom on its own.'

'All the trading and bargaining done in Chazen's name is my lady Itrac's responsibility,' Kheda said repressively. 'I won't encroach on her prerogatives nor yet insult her with such a proposal.'

And I wouldn't wager an empty oyster shell on my chances of ever seeing you again. You may be as much of a liability as you are an asset as a body slave but I want you where I can see you.

'Your loss.' Dev shrugged and sighed as he looked over towards the reefs. 'Remind me, what are we doing now?'

'We're waiting until one of the fishermen Borha sent out comes back with something by which I can read the omens for the rest of the pearl harvest.'

'How long's that going to be?' Dev looked askance at the warlord.

'Who knows?' Kheda shrugged. 'Which is all part of the omen in itself.'

And who else will be here to read the omens and cast their own interpretations around once the Yellow Serpent *has carried me away?*

As he drank his juice, the warlord glanced idly around the crude huts, eyes alert for any man with the long, untrimmed hair and beard of a soothsayer. There was none to be seen, wherever he looked.

Does that mean there are no seers here? Or are they just staying out of sight till I'm gone?

Kheda tried to put such thoughts out of his mind and enjoy the shade beneath the pavilion. They had waited there long enough for Dev to discreetly eat most of the sweet cakes before a cry of anticipation went up along the waterline. A sturdy skiff was approaching the beach, the two men crewing it shouting and waving urgent hands. Chazen islanders abandoned their toils over baskets and tubs to splash into the shallows and help drag the craft on to drier, firmer ground. Pearl drillers and pickers alike stood up, their tasks forgotten as they strained to see what was being brought ashore. The spokesmen forgot their dignity as they hurried down to the shore with everyone else, Borha and Isei shoving their way to the fore.

'There's a favourable portent in itself, that they've found something so soon.' Kheda got to his feet, feeling a welcome lightening of his mood.

'Here you go again,' Dev said under his breath, 'getting up to your elbows in something's innards. Have you any idea how the laundry maids complain when I take them a tunic with blood up to the armpits?'

Kheda laid a hand in the middle of the sarcastic barbarian's mailed chest. 'I've told you before: curb your tongue. For a man so keen to boast of his cleverness, you can be remarkably stupid.' Not waiting for the barbarian to find a reply, he strode out from the shade of the little pavilion, the sunlight striking down hard on his unprotected head.

Which is pretty stupid of you, oh wise and powerful warlord, and you can hardly ruin the moment for all these onlookers by going back for your helmet, you fool. You need to curb your temper or you'll both end up dead, your blood spilled along with Dev's. There are some things no domain's people will forgive.

'It's a flail-tailed shark, my lord!' The press of people around the pearl skiff parted to reveal Borha.

'Have you seen many of them this harvest?' Kheda looked around for some diver or boatmaster among the anxious, anticipatory faces clustering close.

'This is the first sign of any shark, my lord.' A thickset man spoke up, bare-chested in coarse cotton trousers faded to colourlessness. 'And we've manned a ring of watch boats at first light every day, well before the divers take to the water.'

'Then it's a good omen when the very first shark to come sniffing around ends up on a spear.' Kheda nodded his approval. 'What else can we read into this? A flail-tail is a dangerous shark but nowhere near as deadly as a ragged-tooth. A ragged-tooth will eat a flail-tail, so the very fact that a flail-tail is in these waters should mean the bigger sharks are elsewhere.'

'Very true, my lord,' agreed the confident diver and the crowd's smiles broadened perceptibly at this happy thought.

Though it's no meagre specimen, at least as long as I am tall and doubtless as heavy as any three men here.

'Let's see what else we can learn from this fish.' Kheda stepped back to let the crowd press forward, eager hands grabbing at the harsh-skinned bluish-grey fins and tail. There didn't seem to be any life left in the creature but he kept a prudent distance from the vicious maw all the same. The skiff's master and his helmsman lifted the shark's head between them, using the broad-bladed spears that had slain it and which were still embedded deep in its gills and through its snout. The islanders wrestled the inert mass over the side of the boat and dumped it on the ground. Dark blood oozed from its mouth, staining the sand.

'Show me its belly.' Kheda held out a hand and Dev provided him with a heavy barbed spear acquired from someone. The skiff's crew rolled the unwieldy creature over to lie half on its back, half on its side, glaucous underside pallid in the sun, the long pennant of its tail trailing lifeless across the sand. Kheda lifted the spear high above his head with both hands and with a grunt of effort thrust it clean through the shark just below the vicious curve of its jaw, pinning the creature to the ground. There was a murmur of uncertainty from a few directions.

Not what Chazen Saril used to do, then? Perhaps his father never told him of warlords who'd been surprised by a moribund shark and bitten even after they'd cut the beast's head off. That's not the kind of omen we want today.

'A knife.' Kheda reached behind him.

'Here.' Dev slapped a long, brutally serrated blade into his palm.

'My lord?' Isei was looking expectantly at him.

Kheda took a deep breath and pinioned the fish's tail firmly with one foot. He dug the point of the blade into the fish's cloaca and ripped a jagged slit up its length, fighting against the tough, clinging skin, harsh as a carpenter's rasp against his knuckles.

Not too deep. Don't pierce the intestines or mar the liver, blighting the interpretation before it's even begun. Stars above, this is easier with a deer or a hog.

Wiping sweat from his forehead, he persisted until he had laid the shark's entrails bare for all to see. A powerful smell rose from the dead fish, not yet edged with the sickly stench of decay, though that wouldn't take long in this strong sun.

'The beast is certainly healthy, nothing ill-omened among its entrails, no marks, no deformities.' Kheda waited to be quite sure that the shark was motionless, then stuck the knife into the sand by his foot. He reached both hands into the cavity to lift out the dark liver, searching for stains or blemishes.

What's the first thing I will see mirrored in its sheen? That's always the crucial portent.

As he sought to get a grip on the solid, slippery mass, something squirmed among the coiled lengths of the shark's guts. Kheda abandoned all thoughts of securing the liver and snatched up the knife instead.

'Has it eaten something alive?' Dev peered into the beast with lively curiosity.

'Or someone?' quavered Borha.

'It's a flail-tail, not a ragged-tooth.' Kheda took a firm grip on the salt-roughened handle of the knife.

Which is fortunate because we've all heard the tales of ragged-toothed sharks cut open to reveal whole skeletons inside them or at very least fateful collections of skulls and bones. Flail-tails can only take an arm or a leg at worst and one of those could hardly be still fighting or kicking. Besides, the divers said there'd been no mishaps on the reefs.

Dismissing his incoherent thoughts, Kheda used the point of the blade to push aside the pallid loops of the shark's gut, less concerned with piercing them now than with revealing this mystery. He exposed a swollen sac, feebly contorted by whatever lay within in. 'Whatever this is, it isn't in the creature's belly,' he said, bemused. Setting his jaw, he seized one end of the sac where it was anchored within the fish and sliced it open with a deft stroke of the knife.

A miniature shark twisted out of the wound, as long as a man's arm and about as thick, perfect in every detail. Black eyes bright, its snapping white teeth missed Kheda's hand by a hair's breadth. A *frisson* ran through the mesmerised islanders.

Teeth more than big enough to do damage. How would that have been for an omen?

He skewered the wriggling infant through its flapping gills and hoisted it out of the dead shark's belly on the knife blade. It was surprisingly heavy.

'Has anyone ever seen such a thing?' he enquired, letting a hint of amusement colour his query.

Heads shook all around, some faces awestruck, others apprehensive.

'Then we certainly have a mighty portent to read.' Kheda smiled and threw the baby shark down on the sand, sending the nearest islanders stumbling backwards into those pressing close behind them. 'But let's not get ahead of ourselves. What has the liver to tell us?' As he bent to tug at the uncooperative mass, using the knife to cut it free, he thought furiously.

What might be read into such a thing? A shark with a live baby in its belly? What is that an omen for? Who is such a portent meant for?

The dark, unwieldy mass of the adult shark's liver came free with a suddenness that surprised him and Kheda felt Dev's steadying hand in the small of his back. The ground was treacherous now, slick with the shark's blood, and the stench was growing heady, red-eyed flies gathering to defy the islanders' swatting hands.

'My lord?' It was the bare-chested diver, the confident one.

Kheda saw the man's face reflected in the last gloss on the rapidly drying surface of the shark's liver and let the weighty organ fall back into the gutted hollow of the great fish with a soggy thud. He smiled at Borha, hovering anxiously on the other side of the shark. 'We've seen all we need to, so I'll wash now, if I may.'

'Here, girl!' The spokesman beckoned to the maidens who had been serving by the pavilion. One hurried forward cradling a broad silver bowl of scented water and, tense beside her, a younger girl clutched a sizeable sponge.

'In the water with it,' Dev prompted briskly, taking the bowl. 'The sponge, girl, the sponge!'

'I see most favourable omens in this shark's death,' Kheda announced as he squeezed water over his arms to wash the worst of the blood and slime off on to the sand. To his relief, besa oil's astringency cut through the fishy stench hanging all around. 'To add to all the other positive portents favouring this pearl harvest and this domain at present.' He submerged one forearm in the bowl and scrubbed with the sponge.

'This shark came to feed at dawn, as is their habit. But it came alone, so we need not fear a season of losses among the divers, not to the sea's predators. That's how I read the matter, anyway. Mind you, I believe it came to lay claim to the reefs and whatever prey it might find there. To give birth in a place is to tie your future to it.' He looked around to see rapt agreement on every face. 'It didn't succeed, did it? Your watch boats spotted the creature and your fishermen speared it before it had a chance to flee or to hide. It had no chance to make its bid for a stake in these waters.' He gestured to the dead infant shark before beginning to wash his other arm.

'The mother was a healthy beast which indicates that the omens overall are to be read in a positive light and everything that I saw in the mirror of its liver was a favourable indicator for the success of our pearl harvest. The spawn did its best to bite me. It failed and, more significantly, it died at the hands of your warlord, which suggests that Chazen interests will be safe for some while, wouldn't you say? Dev, we'll take that with us.' He nodded at the infant shark. 'Borha, have the jaw cut out of the adult's head and share out the teeth among the divers for talismans. Take the carcass well out to sea before you dump it, where the currents will take it away from the reefs. We don't want its kin coming to see where it got to.'

The burly diver was the first to raise a cheer. Loud approbation spread among the islanders, even those faces that had been uneasy before soon clearing. Kheda waited, smiling, as he dried his arms on a white cotton cloth offered by yet another maiden, this one all coquettish smiles that faded a little as he waved her away. At the first hint of an ebb in the surge of fervour, he turned to walk unhurriedly back up the slope towards the pavilion and the crowd drifted apart.

Dev walked at his shoulder, studying the infant shark as he carried it skewered on a spear he had pulled from the larger fish. 'So all the omens are good.' His face was studiedly neutral. 'Does that mean we can get back to hunting down those invaders? There's no telling what might have happened out to the west while we've been trailing around the rest of the domain,' he concluded with ill-concealed frustration.

'For the pearl harvest, the portents are certainly most favourable. As for that shark spawn, I'm not sure what such a thing might mean,' Kheda admitted in a low voice as they returned to the shade of the pavilion and its illusion of privacy.

'Does it really matter?' Dev was unexpectedly curious.

'It almost got its teeth into me,' Kheda said soberly. 'That has to mean it's a personal portent. I'll have to consult Chazen Saril's library when we rejoin Itrac at the residence. I'm really not clear on the lore of sharks.'

And I had better be before I have to counter whatever verdict any other soothsayer sets running around as rumour, out of honest belief or treacherous intent.

He tossed Dev the cloth he'd been wiping his arms with. 'Wrap it in that. I don't want to be mobbed by gulls all the way back.'

'What now?' Dev took the cloth and swaddled the infant shark securely.

'Favourable portents are all well and good but once word spreads, that'll encourage any hovering sea hawks to prey on such a plentiful pearl harvest.' Kheda shaded his eyes with a hand as he stared out to the strait where the *Yellow Serpent* waited; light skiffs were busy ferrying food and water to the rowers. 'There are still too many opportunists sneaking about Chazen waters for my peace of mind. Itrac won't do much trade for saller grain or horsehair or anything else if some enterprising pirate plunders the galleys she sends to collect the pearl chests.'

'Which would be an unfortunate omen,' Dev commented sarcastically.

'Quite,' said Kheda shortly. 'So when you've dropped a pearl or two into every hand that's done us a service here, we need to get back to the *Yellow Serpent* and tell Hesi to set a course to check up on that motley flotilla of boats we left to guard the seaways. Share out the rest of that box between Hesi and the trireme's shipmaster.'

'Which means yet more delay before we sail back to the western isles,' muttered Dev with stifled anger.

'We will still be back at the residence for the night of the new year.' Kheda looked at the barbarian, his green eyes cold as jade. 'Though if I deem it necessary after that, we'll repeat this entire voyage around the domain, just to be sure all is well.'

'Why?' demanded Dev. 'When I can tell you precisely where every boat might be – every islander if you give me time – be they friendly or unfriendly, without you having to move a muscle.'

'And how do we explain how we came by such knowledge? What will you do when we're discovered?' Kheda looked at him with ill-concealed anger. 'You using magic and me condoning it? You think I'd escape having my throat cut so that my blood might dilute the stain of wizardry in yours, as it soaks into the ground while you're skinned alive and your hide turned inside out to expiate your every touch on Aldabreshin soil?' His voice thickened. 'Do you think Itrac would lift a finger to save either of us? Do you think she could? These people of Chazen don't just detest wizardry like the other domains of the Archipelago, for all its foul assault on the natural order of things. They truly fear and loathe it after all the misery and death those invaders and their brutal enchanters brought with them. The day your secret is out is the day you die.'

'Fools, the lot of them.' Dev gritted his teeth. 'When it was my magic saved them from those savage mages. Just so long as we head west as soon as we can after you've played your new-year games.' The barbarian wizard bent to retrieve Kheda's helmet. As Kheda reached out to take it, Dev's fingers closed over the warlord's, pressing them painfully against the hard metal and unyielding facets of the diamonds on the brow band.

'You promised me I'd be there to see the last nests of those savages rooted out. I killed their wizards for you but the survivors may be hoarding something that could give me a hint of how they worked their magic. You really don't want to break your word to me, Kheda. You shouldn't need any portents to warn you just what a bad idea that would be.'

CHAPTER TWO

'Just where have our supposed guardians of these seaways got to?' Kheda scowled past the upswept stern posts of the *Mist Dove* as the trireme pulled away from yet another landing empty of Chazen ships.

'At least no one's offered tales of trouble washing up on their beaches.' Dev waved as the trireme eased along the shore watched by a party of huntsmen clutching the heavy square-ended blades they used for hacking paths through the dense forest.

'And at least they look ready to drive it off, if trouble turns up.' Kheda raised a hand to acknowledge two fishermen pausing to raise their long spears in salute on their hunt for the ugly bristle-mouthed fish that lurked among the roots of the coppery reed beds.

'There should be more boats on the waters, shouldn't there?' Dev queried idly. 'Trade's in the Aldabreshin blood around here as much as in the central domains.'

Where you hid so effectively under the mask of a thoroughly amoral merchant for so many years.

'Village spokesmen should be keeping in touch with one another, at the very least.' Kheda's irritation was unabated. 'I want to know where Nyral is.'

The trireme continued to pick a cautious path between low, muddy islets, slowing almost to walking pace to navigate the turbid channel between the encroaching groves of knot trees. The breezes off the open seas were baffled by the smothering vegetation and the sun beat down ever hotter from above. The still air smelled more of silt than of salt and the raucous cries of crookbeaks crashed through the taller lilla trees set back from the shore.

Kheda wiped sweat from his face and accepted a cup of water from Dev. 'Shaiam? Any suggestions where we might look for Nyral next?'

A tall, wiry man with plaited black hair and beard climbed up the ladderlike stair from the rowing deck. 'Nothing we haven't already thought of, my lord.' The trireme's shipmaster clutched a battered and salt-stained black book in a hand almost the same hue as the leather cover. His naturally dark complexion had been deepened by years in the strong southern sun, striking against the vivid red of the long sleeveless mantle he wore over his bare chest. His russet trousers were cut short just below the knee, revealing sturdy calves and long splayed toes that gripped the smooth wood of the deck.

'So we're still heading for Kalan?' Alert in his seat just in front of the shipmaster's lofty chair, the helmsman Yere gripped the twin stern oars that governed the mighty trireme's movements. He spared a glance for the book open on his knees, bound in unfaded indigo leather.

Kheda noted that the helmsman's painstakingly compiled record of Chazen's sea lanes was nowhere near as thick as Shaiam's mute testament to the older man's years of experience.

A book holding so many of the secrets that the shipmasters barter between themselves. How many of Chazen's hapless mariners were forced to trade away such precious knowledge as they fled the invaders? What else could they offer in return for water or food or a secure anchorage? Who has such knowledge now?

He stared out over the clouded waters as the narrow channel opened up and the rowing master down below signalled for the piper to pick up the pace.

'We'd best not make a long stop at Kalan, my lord, not if we want to be back at the dry-season residence for the new-year rites.' Yere's serious expression sat oddly on his cheerful brown face, exuberant black hair curling untamed to his shoulders.

'Let's hope we find Shipmaster Nyral quickly, then,' Kheda said curtly. 'I'll be interested to hear just how he and his crew plan on keeping bilge rats out of our waters when he's nowhere to be found in the reach he was set to guard.'

'We can make up some time here, my lord.' Shaiam lifted callused fingers to his mouth to whistle down to the rowing master, who looked up from the sunlit aisle between the rowers on their staggered seats. Nodding, he clapped his hands briskly to encourage the oarsmen, indistinct on each side in the shade cast by the split upper deck of the trireme. The shrill note of the flute gathered speed, the piper sitting on the wooden block half-way down the aisle where the mast would be stepped, should Shaiam decide that the wind was favourable enough to call for the sail.

Kheda looked down at the shadowy oarsmen as the trireme shivered beneath his feet.

What would you rowers think if you knew I'd taken an oar in a merchant galley, pulling my weight all the way to the northernmost domains in search of lore to drive the invaders and their magic out of these southern waters? Would it strengthen your loyalty to know that I understand how the world shrinks to the oar in your hands and the pipe note in your ears after a long day's haul? Would you be impressed that I know all the tricks of tying a rope grommet to secure an oar and how best to repair an oar port's leather sleeve?

Or would you just want to know exactly what it was that I found in the far north? Would you guess it was Dev? Would you start speculating on just how it was that he could help me kill the savages' wizards?

The oarsmen murmured a count among themselves to measure their increasing pace. The ship gathered speed, driven on by the rushing oars. The rowers fell silent as they settled into a regular rhythm, the only sounds from the lower deck the pipe, the creak of rope, leather and wood and, lower still, the susurration of water beneath the trireme's long, lithe hull.

'Of course, Nyral could have found someone making free with Chazen resources,' remarked Dev thoughtfully, 'and come to grief himself.'

Kheda shot a glance at the barbarian before nodding slowly. 'It's possible. Let's be certain we're ready for a fight.'

He walked swiftly forward along one half of the uppermost deck as the *Mist Dove* ploughed through a broad, shallow channel thick with mats of floating lily leaves. The small detachment of armoured men on the trireme's bow platform rose dutifully to their feet at his approach and bowed low.

Ten swordsmen and four archers is the complement for a fast trireme sailing as advance scout or messenger. A heavy trireme like this should have fifty men ready to put paid to any mischief. And loyal as they are, these hopeful warriors are the remnants of those too old and too young to fight the savages last year. All Chazen's best swordsmen died in defence of their women and children as they fled the murderous magic.

'My lord.' The senior warrior stepped forward and bowed low. In a plain chain-mail hauberk like the rest, helm of dull steel unadorned, he was sweating profusely in the breathless heat.

'Aysi.' Kheda inclined his head by way of acknowledgement. 'I was wondering if Shipmaster Nyral might have run into trouble. Will you be ready to meet any challenge that comes our way?'

'Ready and willing to serve, my lord.' The grizzled swordsman stroked his close-cropped beard thoughtfully. 'Ridu will probably be safest in a fight. His strokes are still so wild no one will dare come near him, for fear of losing their head by accident.' He spared a glance for the youngest of his ill-assorted detachment, a lad with a beard barely a hopeful shadow on his round jaw. The lad ducked his head in discomfiture as the others studiously avoided catching each other's gaze.

Atoun would never have embarrassed a lad like that. He had the knack of welding the most ill-matched men into a fighting force that won respect for Daish from all our neighbours. There's no one in Chazen to equal him, to take his place as commander of the warlord's warriors. Any man who could is probably dead like Atoun, at the claws of the monsters the invaders wrought with their magic.

Kheda turned to the archers. 'Will we have fresh meat to feed these brave warriors this evening, Tawai?'

'Give us half a day and we could feed a fleet, my lord.' The oldest of the archers grinned, then his lined, leathery face turned serious as he patted the quiver at his hip, bristling with red and brown goose feathers. 'But we can't bring down armoured men with blunt fowling arrows. We need chisel-heads to get through armour and broad-heads with barbs to be sure of a crippling wound, and we've few enough of those.'

'I'll be happy to let Tawai and his lads drop any scoundrels from a distance. It's too hot for close-quarters fighting.' Aysi didn't quite succeed in making a joke of his interjection.

'I'm sure you'll make every shot count, if we do run into trouble,' Kheda assured the archers with an encouraging smile.

Because I can hardly give Dev your fowling blunts and watch while he melts the very metal of the arrowheads in the palm of his hand, then reshapes it with his sorcery to suit your needs.

Out of the corner of his eye, Kheda saw the wizard intent on something ahead of the *Mist Dove*, the creases around his eyes deepening as he squinted against the brilliance of sea and sky. His already thin lips narrowed further. 'There's the *Yellow Serpent*!'

As Dev pointed, Kheda saw the light galley emerge from a distant channel. A brassy flourish from the *Mist Dove*'s signal horn rang out and the *Yellow Serpent* altered her course with a crash of oars stirring dirty foam from the sluggish waters.

'Still on her own, I see.' Forcing his face into a polished mask of serenity, Kheda left the *Mist Dove*'s bow to her paltry fighting force and returned to the stern platform.

'No sign of Nyral, it seems.' Shaiam sat in the shipmaster's chair, signal horn loose in his lap as he looked over Yere's head to gauge the distant galley's speed.

'My lord, let's have both of our ships draw into that bay.' Dev pointed abruptly to one of the few lumps of land where tandra trees reinforced by the lofty grey trunks of ironwoods defied the all-pervasive knot trees.

'Why?' Kheda looked at the wizard, bemused.

'You could go ashore and see if there's any bird pepper growing thereabouts,' said Dev with heavy emphasis. 'You were saying you would be needing some if the turn of the year brought any cases of worm fever. It'll only take the two of us and we'll barely be delayed.'

'What?' Kheda stared for a moment before realisation dawned. 'Yes, that's very true. Good thinking, Dev.' He glanced at the shipmaster with an apologetic smile. 'If you would, Shaiam. I imagine there will be a shortage of healers this year.'

'My lord.' At Shaiam's nod, Yere leaned against his steering oar to turn the ship towards the shore.

Kheda jerked his head at Dev and the two men passed behind the shipmaster's chair to lean against the solid baulk of timber made by the curved stern planking rising up above their heads.

Good thinking, Dev, if you're thinking what I think you're thinking, but you could have been more tactful. Telouet would have made some joke about making landfall to look for plants at every opportunity, to disguise any true intention.

He studied the uncommunicative back of Shaiam's head.

And Jatta would have had something to say about it, as shipmaster of my personal trireme for six years and more. Smooth as the seas he sailed, he'd still have reminded me of all the reasons why I was needed back at the residence sooner rather than later and that any delay should be avoided. Let's hope he still serves Daish as loyally.

Kheda glanced at Dev but the wizard was intent on the *Yellow Serpent*, which had noted the *Mist Dove*'s change of course and was following suit. The gap between the two ships was narrowing rapidly and every eye on the trireme was on the light galley.

You people are always so hesitant about speaking your mind, on this ship, at the residence, in any village I visit. Why so diffident? Chazen Saril was no brute. Though his father had a harsh reputation and his grandfather was a byword for ruthlessness according to Daish Reik. I don't suppose anyone taught Saril that encouraging friendship and even honest disagreement would strengthen his people's loyalty, not weaken his authority.

But how do I encourage openness and honesty when I have so much to hide, such deceits burdening me?

The *Mist Dove* slowed and the rowers deftly turned the vessel before backing the trireme into a shelving landing. Gritty mud grated beneath the shallow hull and anchors splashed into the water at Shaiam's command, an answering shout coming from the sailmaster up on the prow platform.

Dev threw a rope ladder down beside the stern posts, the perfect attentive slave. 'Let's be quick, my lord, then we can be back aboard before the *Yellow Serpent* reaches us with her news.'

'Indeed.' Kheda climbed down the ladder to discover that the water at the trireme's stern was waist deep. Pausing to thread one arm through the rope rungs, he unbuckled his sword belt and held his blades shoulder high as he waded ashore, bare toes feeling more mud than sand underfoot. At least the cool seawater was refreshing in the heat of the day. Reaching the water's edge, he paused to don his twin-looped sword belt and secure his weapons again, watching Dev stride through the sea towards him.

'Finally, some privacy.' The wizard grinned with satisfaction as he paused on the water's edge. 'Though there's not much point having a password for our excursions if you can't remember it. I thought it'd take you till sunset to catch my meaning.'

'You'll be spending the rest of the day polishing our chain mail after this wetting,' Kheda pointed out with faint malice.

'What are you going to wear in the meantime, my lord?' Sarcasm sharpened Dev's voice. 'The threadbare blue silk or the yellow with the mould stain on the back?'

Kheda grimaced. 'Let's hope Itrac has managed to replenish my wardrobe with the necessary elegance by the time we get back. Now, what have you got to say that you don't want Shaiam hearing?'

'Let's find some still water.' Dev walked into the green gloom beneath the tandra trees. The air was still, perfumed by the yellow flowers of cat's-claw creepers.

'We can find Nyral without resorting to magic,' Kheda said curtly, not moving.

'Not and be sure of getting back to the residence for your new year. Isn't that your overriding priority?' Dev looked back over his shoulder. 'Come on. And keep your eyes open for bird pepper,' he added as an amused afterthought.

Kheda followed the barbarian reluctantly away from the shore and in among the taller trees where green pods were swelling in the forks of the tandra tree branches. Emerald and sapphire glory-birds were picking their way carefully around a striol vine's vicious spines to reach a sard-berry bush's bounty. Avid ruby butterflies flitted between the scarlet blooms while glittering beetles feasted on the fallen fruit. Beyond the dense shade cast by the mighty ironwoods, the orange-gold trefoils of fire-daggers carpeted the ground.

'This'll do.' Dev halted by a hollow where some storm had scoured the soil away from the buttress roots of an ironwood tree to leave a little pool as nursery for some blithely paddling froglets, their brown and yellow mottling a perfect match for the forest floor. 'Would this be a sign for you?' the wizard asked with mild derision. 'Or shall I just get on and find some certainty for us?'

'You may be a man without convictions, Dev, but don't scoff at those of us who see more than the here and now.' Kheda studied the leaf-stained water. 'As it happens, frogs can be a sign of many things. It's certainly a good omen to find them thriving in a pond this long after the rains, especially since the last rains were so short.' He grimaced. 'Though a frog's croaking can signify someone talking nonsense. They can be a symbol of foolish aspiration or a reminder to stay close to one's home and birthplace.'

Do you talk nonsense, wizard, when you try to convince me to meet your demands? Am I deluding myself if I think

I can make a success of ruling a domain I wasn't born to? Would our lives have been better if we had both stayed close to home and never become entangled like this?

Dev chuckled as emerald light dripped from his fingers into the water and the frogs hopped frantically in all directions. 'They don't want to hang around. Make of that what you will, Kheda, while I do something useful.' The wizard crouched by the pool, which was now suffused with a mossy light.

'Just be quick about it.' Kheda turned his back, trying to ascertain if anyone else had come ashore from the *Mist Dove*. 'If you can see Nyral, try to find some excuse for whatever detour we'll need to take to happen to encounter him. I want to see what he's got to say for himself before I quit these waters.' There was no sign of any movement by the shoreline, so Kheda searched the undergrowth for bird pepper or any other medicinal plant.

Better find something to justify this trip ashore. And curse him, Dev's right. How else am I going to find out what's afoot in these islands? But we're not going to be doing this for much longer. Not once I've woven a proper net of eyes and ears to sustain my rule. Not once I've reinstated the beacon chains and we've bred enough courier doves to send the length and breadth of the domain.

Chazen will recover, surely? These people are strong and they are bound together in so many ways. They've known each other, traded with each other's villages, since they were old enough to sail the waters in between. More than that, they've been through the sorest of trials this last year and survived, not least because every one of them lent a helping hand to anyone who needed it, in the face of the invaders' malevolence.

Let's hope such ties are strong enough to hold the domain together until they accept me as reader of portents, giver of their laws and healer of their sick. Let's hope they are strong enough to defy any menace I've inadvertently brought into these waters through my compromises with magic.

'I can't find Nyral,' Dev said slowly, 'but you should have a look at this. You've got vermin in your waters.'

'What?' Kheda threw aside a handful of feathery raposa stems.

'See for yourself,' Dev invited, hands spread palms down over the water.

Reluctantly, Kheda looked into the ensorcelled pool. An image floated on the iridescent magic. Several sailing boats scarcely bigger than pearl skiffs were drawn up on a muddy landing.

'Not such unusual boats for fishermen.' Kheda scowled dubiously all the same.

'With enough men to crew them five times over and no sign of nets?' scoffed Dev. 'Granted, they've got women with them, but no children, no elders. And if they are honest islanders come back to Chazen, why are they hiding their boats?'

Kheda watched the minuscule figures hastily concealing the vessels under green branches hacked and ripped from the knot trees. 'Show me those huts.'

Dev swept his hands over the pool and the image shivered, clearing to reveal the battered remnants of a village set just out of reach of tide and storm where ironwood trees offered shade.

'There's not a saller seedling planted and no one's tended those vegetable plots this side of the rains,' Kheda said more to himself than to Dev. 'What do you suppose they're here for?'

'It's half a year since you drove out the invaders.' Dev shrugged, unconcerned. 'It's a fair bet some island or other will have something worth stealing by now.'

'Not in that village.' Kheda studied the crude repairs made to those few houses still standing after the torrential rains of the wet season had added to the depredations of the invaders. Holes and burned patches in thatch and walls had simply been roughly patched with woven panels torn from the remnants of wrecked huts. 'Where exactly are they? They're not staying anywhere in Chazen without explaining themselves to me.'

'Which will just mean more delay,' said Dev with distaste. 'You can see as well as I can that they're no loyal Chazen folk come home to rebuild their lives.' He grinned wickedly. 'I can chase them off for you from here. They won't stop rowing till they run aground on the northern mainland.'

'You use no magic without my sanction,' snapped Kheda. 'And remember what I said. If anyone sees you using any enchantment, I'll behead you myself.'

The mage gazed at him, untroubled. 'Do you think they'll believe you when you swear you'd no idea that I could be such a foul thing as a wizard? Who knows, they might. Stranger things have happened,' he taunted, 'like wild men coming out of the empty ocean, following wizards who clear their path with torrents of murderous fire. And stranger still, those same wizards suddenly all starting a fight to the death among themselves, presumably to be cock of the dunghill they've made of the Chazen domain. And strangest of all, Daish Kheda, who everyone would swear was dead, just happens to be there to see it and to spearhead an Archipelagan riposte. Which does at least entitle him to lay claim to the domain when Chazen Saril, coward though he was, happens to die in most peculiar circumstances.'

Kheda gritted his teeth. 'We can deal with this without your enchantments. Just show me where they are.'

Dev concentrated on the shimmering pool. 'We can accidentally run across these people if you can talk Shaiam into cutting across to the more northerly sea lane that runs back to the residence.' He looked up at Kheda, dark eyes unfathomable. 'Then we set sail for the western isles as soon as you've seen your new year in. I don't want to lose my chance of finding some clue as to where those invaders came from before your swordsmen slaughter the last of them. And I'll be going looking in my own way and be cursed to your Aldabreshin ignorance and fear of magic. You owe me, Kheda, and don't think you can settle our account with a knife in my ribs.'

'First things first. Let's see who these beggars washed up on Chazen shores might be.' Kheda looked down to find he was gripping one of his sword hilts and thrust it back into its scabbard with a muted click. 'And let's get back to the ships before someone comes looking for us.'

Clearing out such parasites is something honest I can do for Chazen's good at least. Will they prove to be thieves, though, or truly paupers in need of our care?

Do you want to make any wager against the future here? If Dev is proved right, does that mean your best course will be to take him to the western isles in the hope of unravelling the mysteries of those savages?

The warlord turned his back on the wizard, heading for the shore with rapid strides. He barely slowed as he entered the water, wading out to the ladders hanging from the *Mist Dove*.

'Hesi hasn't seen any sign of Nyral,' Shaiam announced without preamble.

'Why doesn't that surprise me?' Kheda glanced over at the *Yellow Serpent* waiting patiently out in deeper water. 'But he had better keep looking. As for ourselves, we had best set a course to the residence if we're to be sure of arriving for the turn of the year. Won't we make a quicker passage if we cut across towards the main sea lane coming down from the north?' He looked at Shaiam, brows raised in query.

I hope that makes sense. I could almost wish for one of Dev's treacherous barbarian maps of these waters. I don't think I will ever understand Chazen's isles and backwaters the way I did those of Daish. You have to be born to a domain to truly know it.

Shaiam nodded slowly, a little perplexed. 'I don't see it making much difference but we might pick up some wind to win us a few ship lengths.'

Kheda hid his relief as he feigned a new thought. 'It's always possible Nyral has sailed that way. Signal Hesi to follow us and the *Yellow Serpent* can search those reaches.'

As Dev climbed over the rail on to the stern platform, Shaiam moved to shout this new plan across to Hesi. Yere glanced curiously at Dev, to be met with a blank look that the barbarian edged with just a hint of challenge. The youthful helmsman turned his attention to calling down to the rowing master and settling himself at his steering oars.

As Shaiam set his crew hauling on their oars with a shout of encouragement, Kheda moved to sit cross-legged at the rear of the stern platform. He took off his helm and stared ahead, unseeing. Muddy seawater from his trousers spread across the deck, glistening briefly before the breeze brushed it away. Dev sat silently beside him, the barbarian fingering the links of his chain-mail hauberk as he dried in the sun.

Have there truly been such positive omens and so many favourable portents on this voyage? Can I be sure I'm not misreading them? Could the corruption of the savages' enchantments still be perverting the natural order in Chazen? Could my ties to past and present have been severed by the touch of Dev's magic?

I'm sick of such uncertainty. My commitment to this domain must surely link me to its future. I must start looking to the heavens again. The stars ride far above any earthly taint. And I must be sure I am committed to Chazen. I must turn my back on Daish once and for all if I'm to be any kind of warlord to these people, or any kind of husband to Itrac Chazen.

As Kheda looked up, resolutely banishing recollections of clearer seas, the trireme broke free of the clinging islands to reach a broad channel opening still wider to the south. Kheda took an appreciative breath of the fresher air but noted the empty vista with displeasure.

Dev's right to wonder at the lack of trade. There should be merchant galleys sailing north and south at this season – Chazen's own and visitors from all the local domains proud to fly the pennants that give them the right of passage in our waters.

'My lord!' A shout from the prow was half-surprised, half-alarmed, and one of the youthful swordsmen came running back along the side deck. 'There's a boat in the water, my lord, overturned.' His voice turned to outrage. 'It's been holed, my lord, deliberately. Looks like an axe did it.'

Is this a sign that we need not resort to any more lies to find these people?

Kheda forced himself not to look at Dev. 'Where has it come from? Shaiam, can you tell? Yere?'

'On that side of the channel?' The helmsman searched the murky water for the wreckage before leafing through his route record to confirm exactly where the navigable backwaters ran hereabouts. 'It'll have washed out of that inlet, I think?' He pointed, looking to Shaiam for support.

The shipmaster nodded, tugging at his braided beard. 'Or the one to the north.'

Kheda got to his feet. 'Raise signal flags for the *Yellow Serpent*. We'll take the northern channel, they can take the southern. Let's see who thinks Chazen can afford to lose a serviceable boat for firewood.'

He stifled a qualm of apprehension as the vessel shot towards a gap in the chain of islands on the far side of the channel. At first glance, the narrow entrance offered no more than a stagnant dead end for the unwary, or worse, a deathtrap for the uninvited. The shore was thick with grey-brown knot-tree roots clawing at tangles of lily leaves. As the *Yellow Serpent* vanished down a similarly uninviting watercourse, the air grew thick and stifling once again. Kheda felt sweat trickle down his spine.

In contrast to his apprehension, this unexpected turn of events prompted a surge of enthusiasm from the rowing deck. The *Mist Dove* forced a path through the dense vegetation, branches yielding in a flurry of snapping noises.

'My lord!' Another of Aysi's hopeful swordsmen was perched precariously out on the timbers that projected from the trireme's bow to protect the foremost oars when ramming an enemy. He clung to the upswept prow with one hand. 'A trading boat but flying no pennant!'

'Follow it!' Kheda shouted back.

Shaiam caught up his coiled brass horn and blew a terse demand that the smaller vessel stop to identify itself. Its master plainly had no such intention, hastily canting his sail to catch the wind and speed away.

'Sound a signal for the *Yellow Serpent*,' Kheda ordered Shaiam, keeping his eyes on the fugitive.

As the horn's cry echoed back from the green-cloaked isles all around, the *Mist Dove*'s piper picked up his pace and the trireme's rowers followed suit. They were nearly on top of the trading boat as it rounded a shallow headland foul with muck and flotsam and fled headlong for a muddy cove. With a shock of relief, Kheda recognised the landing that Dev's spell had shown him. Small figures on the shore froze in startled confusion as they saw the trireme bearing down on them.

'We're going ashore,' said Kheda tersely.

'My lord?' Shaiam looked at him with surprise.

Kheda could see the unspoken words in the shipmaster's dark eyes.

It's not the place of warlords to get themselves killed in skirmishes like common swordsmen.

That's all very well, as long as a warlord has plenty of common swordsmen to do his bidding.

'I'm going ashore,' he reiterated, 'and I want every oarsman trained with a sword to follow.'

At least they have proper swords, even if each lesson Dev gives them is the one I've just finished drilling into him.

'Hold on to something,' Shaiam advised before shouting down to the rowing master, 'Turn and beach us!'

The piper sounded a shrill note and every blade rose clear of the water. Kheda held tightly on to the back of the shipmaster's chair as Yere hauled on his steering oars to twist the *Mist Dove*'s stern to the land. Below, the rowers lifted their feet and spun around on their seats, each man now facing the prow. Turning almost inside its own length, the *Mist Dove* wallowed for a moment before the rowers dug their first stroke deep with a guttural shout. The oars crashed into the water and the galley surged stern-first for the shore.

Dev threw the ladders down over the stern while the timbers were still reverberating with the impact. Aysi and his men came running along the side decks, the archers scanning the shore, arrows nocked and ready. Below, the innermost ranks of rowers abandoned their sweeps to their neighbours as the sail crew handed out the weapons the ship carried in lieu of a full contingent of warriors. Kheda pulled on mail-backed gloves and steadied his swords as he made ready to drop over the stern.

'Running like rats.' Dev observed the commotion ashore with contempt.

'A cornered rat can still take your finger off.' Kheda watched the men and women on the beach scattering. A few were running to the huts just visible in the trees. More were retreating towards the three ships they had beached, drawing swords of their own. Some had clambered aboard the vessels, throwing aside the concealing knot-tree branches with frantic haste.

'They won't get them afloat, not with the tide as it is,' Dev said with cruel amusement before sliding lithely down a rope ladder.

'If they do, Hesi will catch them.' Kheda glanced over his shoulder to see the distinctive silhouette of the *Yellow Serpent* approaching. He settled his helm firmly on his head and drew the chain-mail veil around his neck and throat, snapping the clasp below his chin. Sliding the ornate face plate down the nasal bar, he locked it in place. But as he climbed down the ladder, he realised he was lacking the metal-plated leggings that should complete his armour.

You still have a lot to learn about being a decent body slave, Dev. Telouet would never have let me on to a hostile shore with bare knees.

He had no chance to do anything about it. The trireme's swordsmen were pressing close behind him, drawing their blades in a flurry of flashing sunlight as they splashed through the shallows.

'If they yield, take them prisoner.' Kheda's words rang out across the beach for the benefit of these unknown newcomers as well as Aysi's warriors. 'If they fight, kill them. This is Chazen land and my writ runs here.' His voice was harsh behind the steely lattice of his visor.

At the centre of the ragged line of armoured men, Kheda led a slow advance across the damp, muddy ground. The youth Ridu raised a cry of 'Chazen!' and the oarsmen backing the swordsmen picked it up, every repetition gathering menace.

The unknown men and women drew back till they had their boats at their backs, swords thrust forward. All Kheda could see was ugly defiance. Men and women alike, all were young, their feet planted firmly on this ground they had claimed and brandishing swords with more ferocity than skill. A couple wore chain mail and a handful more had somehow scrounged the coats of nail-studded leather that were customarily a village spokesman's privilege. The rest were relying on hastily sewn jerkins of turtle hide or sharkskin.

The Chazen line advanced to within twenty paces of the beached boats. With an inarticulate roar the enemy rushed forward, wild strokes cleaving the air until Chazen blades met them with a grating clash of steel.

Kheda's vision shrank to the foe before him, anything to either side a blur. His opponent thrust desperately, a last instant of hesitation robbing his sword of any real strength. Kheda parried easily before turning his stroke into a backhanded slash to bite deep into the man's upper arm. With skills honed since his earliest youth, he swept up his off-hand sword to run the man clean through just below his ribcage.

Not so low as to strike a hip. Not so deep into the body as to risk binding on the backbone.

Kheda ripped his sword free of the dying man and took an instant to assess the combat on either side. Dev was more than holding his own, even if his strokes owed more to natural viciousness than real skill. A rower to Kheda's open side was not doing so well, already bleeding from a ragged slash to his thigh. Kheda moved to shield the man with his armoured body and a killing stroke came down to rasp impotently along the warlord's mail-clad arm as Kheda forced the rusty sword aside.

Kheda brought his second blade round at waist height to disembowel this new adversary but the man leapt backwards in the nick of time. Even as he shied away, the man twisted his own sword into a brutal thrust at Kheda's face. The warlord couldn't help but flinch, knocking the blade away with an instinctive blow. The nameless adversary followed up his advantage, sword spiralling down to hack at Kheda's unprotected legs. Kheda dropped instantly to one knee, arms rising as he did so. The solid steel side plate of his hauberk met the enemy's notched blade as Kheda's leading sword swept up and across to cut the man's hand off at the wrist. The spray of blood had barely reached the warlord before his second blade bit deep into the man's thigh. Springing to his feet, Kheda ripped the blade backwards and bright heart's blood soaked the man's grubby cotton trews. As he cried out, he locked gazes with Kheda for a timeless instant.

You've been in battle before. You've a deftness in your swordplay that speaks of decent training. And you've seen enough blood to know that you're dying.

As the man let his sword arm fall, unprotesting, Kheda put all his strength into a backhanded scything stroke. The man's severed head flew a few paces sideways to startle another foe rushing in to attack Dev. The man stumbled and Dev was on him, running him through the breast. The wizard's enthusiasm betrayed him and he found himself struggling to extricate his sword from the clinging embrace of the dead man's ribs.

Kheda saw a youth lift his sword in a shaking hand to thrust at Dev's face. The warlord shoved Dev aside and stepped forward to sweep the stained and notched blade away before bringing the youth down with a sharp slice to the side of his leg. The lad fell to the trampled and bloodied ground, clutching the crippling wound to his knee, his shrieks lost in the all-encircling clamour.

As Dev finally ripped his sword free, Kheda heard a new sound shoot across the tumult. Getting Dev's attention with an emphatic elbow, he jerked his head backwards and the two of them retreated from the thick of the fight, the *Mist Dove*'s eager rowers closing up the gap they had left.

A second hiss of arrows flew across the beach and Kheda looked to see Tawai and his archers up on the *Mist Dove*'s side decks sending a rain of arrows soaring towards the village. Aysi and a handful of his swordsmen were advancing towards the huts. As the cascade of shafts ceased, Aysi broke into a run, the others hard on his heels.

'After them!' Kheda ran inland, Dev at his side, his breath rasping within the confines of his helmet. Sweat soaked the padded cotton beneath his armour, hot between his shoulder blades and trickling down the hollow of his spine to disappear into the cleft of his buttocks. His shoulders protested at the unrelenting weight of his armour and his thighs burned with the effort of running up the incline towards the sorry huts.

When they arrived, no enemy was still standing. Several were dead with arrows ripped through their bodies or dying of mortal sword wounds. Two were face down in the dirt with a Chazen foot on their necks to make sure they stayed that way.

'My lord!' Ridu appeared from behind one of the tumbledown huts, gore clotting on both of his swords. 'Here, quickly!'

Kheda sheathed one sword and raised the face plate of his helmet. 'What is it?'

'Aysi,' Ridu gasped, face ashen.

Kheda rounded the hut to find the old warrior flat on his back, his helmet cast aside. One side of his face had been laid open by an axe blow, the weapon lying beside him. Its owner was sprawled some distance away with enough gaping wounds to kill him three times over.

Aysi's nose and cheekbone were smashed, white

splinters sinking beneath the welling blood that had already drowned his ruined eye. It pooled in his ear, soaking through his grizzled hair to puddle on the ground beneath his head. The warrior's jaw worked desperately as he choked on blood and spittle.

'Don't try to talk.' Kheda knelt and gripped Aysi's hands as the old man feebly sought to clutch at his pain. As the blood trickled away from the hideous wound, Kheda saw just how deep it had gone.

'Get the warlord's physic chest!' Dev bellowed and other voices carried the order down to the beached trireme.

There's no staunching this, no salve that can do anything, not even dull the pain before he dies.

Kheda held both of Aysi's hands firmly in his mail gauntlets. 'You proved yourself a mighty warrior today. You have won a warlord's consideration for your family and your whole village.'

Aysi's unwounded eye looked up past Kheda, uncomprehending, as his lips moved soundlessly. He coughed up more blood and froze in a rigid spasm of agony before going limp.

Kheda heaved a sigh and laid the old man's lifeless hands gently on his breast. 'Is anyone else hurt? Ridu!' He raised his voice to get the youth's attention.

'No more than scratches.' The youth looked down at his dead mentor, distraught. 'Apart from Aysi.'

'Let's make sure his death hasn't been in vain.' Kheda rose to his feet and gripped the lad's shoulder hard with one mailed hand. 'Did you catch them all?'

Dev glowered at his side. 'Are you sure none of them fled into the trees?'

'No, that is, we got them all.' Ridu scrubbed tears from his cheeks, his hazel eyes still white-rimmed with shock.

'Bring your captives down to join their friends.'

Kheda waited a moment to be sure the youthful warriors had themselves in hand before striding back down to the shore. 'Let's see what these scum have to say for themselves.'

'Now what?' Dev's brown eyes were avid.

'Now you'll see what it means to have me as your warlord,' said Kheda shortly. 'You and everyone else.'

I didn't look for an opportunity to send this kind of message, but I can't afford to pass it up.

Down by the sea, the dead had already been dragged aside into a loose-limbed heap, the dying left to whimper out their last moments. Those who had thrown down their weapons were circled by oarsmen holding ready blades. The prisoners knelt with their foreheads pressed to the damp earth.

Kheda saw that the trireme's archers had come ashore and were gathering up the abandoned blades. He summoned Tawai with a snap of his fingers. 'Did they carry daggers?'

'None, my lord, just rough knives.' The archer came over with an armful of swords, some scabbarded, most not.

'They had some warrior's weapons.' Kheda carefully extricated one naked blade from the pile. The steel was stained with rust as well as blood and the filthy silken cord braiding the handle was inexpertly wound. 'But scarcely cared for and clumsily sharpened.'

'Salvaged from some isle where the invaders slaughtered Chazen warriors?' Tawai hazarded. 'The savages never bothered picking up fallen blades.'

'Didn't know how to use them,' remarked Dev derisively.

'They killed enough of our people with their stone clubs and wooden spears.' Tawai looked at the barbarian with as much distaste as he dared.

'We are hardly likely to forget that,' said Kheda with

mild reproof. 'No, nothing about this sword tells me where it came from, or whose armoury it was made for.'

Telouet might have seen similar somewhere, might have known enough to hazard a guess. No one here is going to be able to.

He tossed the ruined blade aside. 'Let's see if one of these vermin can tell us where they got their blades.'

The circle of rowers parted obediently to give him access to the cowering captives, who raised hopeless eyes to the armoured warlord.

'Who led you here?' barked Kheda.

Most immediately dropped their gaze to the patch of ground in front of their knees. A few were startled into betraying the same man with an unguarded glance.

'Bring him here.' Kheda pointed a merciless finger.

Dev promptly stepped forward and wound one hand in the loose cloth of the man's tunic, throwing him down in front of Kheda, who studied him dispassionately.

'One of our warriors died today, reclaiming this land for Chazen. You owe the domain a death.' Kheda nodded at Dev, who looked back at him with faint confusion.

Much as I like to see you disconcerted, wizard, this is hardly the time.

Kheda held his breath as understanding dawned in Dev's eyes and the barbarian drew his sword with slow deliberation.

'My lord, please . . .' The prisoner shrank into himself, shoulders hunched.

His plea was silenced as Dev's blade flashed in the sunlight. The captive's head leapt from his shoulders, the cut clean and barely bleeding.

Hopefully no one else will have seen enough beheadings to know what an impossible stroke that was. Hopefully I was the only one who saw that shimmer of fire edging Dev's blade.

His face a mask of implacable severity, Kheda looked

around the cove to see the *Mist Dove*'s oarsmen wide-eyed with awe at their warlord's decisive action. The swordsmen and archers were more open in their vengeful appreciation of such immediate retribution. Kheda addressed himself to the rest of the quaking prisoners with cold condemnation.

'You came unbidden into Chazen waters. Far from seeking my permission to stay and promising your duty to me, to this domain and its blood, you have plundered this island and who knows what else besides. Shall we see what we find in your ships and your huts to answer that question?' he wondered ominously. He paused for a moment and was relieved to see guilty glances passing between some of the captives, condemning them as thieves as well as interlopers.

'None of you carries any dagger to acknowledge the domain that bore you, so you've plainly abandoned such allegiances,' he continued with scorn. 'At least that spares me the tiresome chore of seeking recompense for your malfeasance from any other warlord. You can all pay for your offences with your bodies, as slaves. My lady Itrac Chazen will be opening her dealings with the domains to the north shortly. I'm sure she can find some value in your worthless carcasses.'

Kheda turned his back on a despairing wail of protest stifled by a heavy blow behind him. He summoned Tawai with a curt gesture. 'Call the *Mist Dove*'s sail crew ashore. They can flog these wretches into submission and stow them aboard the *Yellow Serpent*. I'm not carrying that amount of dead weight on the voyage back to the residence. Light a fire and burn those bodies, they deserve no better. Set Ridu and his boys to burying Aysi fittingly. His body in the soil of this place will assuredly confer strength and courage on those who may dwell here in the future.'

'As you wish, my lord.' Tawai bowed low.

'And tell your men I am most impressed with their skills. You are obviously an excellent teacher. I'd be grateful if you'd share your talents with the residence garrison.' Surprising the archer with a smile of warm approbation, Kheda walked away along the shore towards the beached trireme.

Dev drew level with him. 'You don't want to spring surprises like that on me,' the mage said frankly.

Kheda glanced around to make sure there was no one close enough to overhear them. 'At least you rose to the occasion.'

'I always do that.' Dev chuckled.

'I think I saw how,' said Kheda, unsmiling. 'Just be thankful no one else did.'

'So what do we do now? My lord,' Dev added for the benefit of Shaiam, who was climbing down from the trireme's stern.

Kheda addressed himself to the shipmaster. 'The *Yellow Serpent* can stay to patrol these waters as we decided earlier, even with captives in her hold. We don't need them weighing us down—'

'My lord.' Excessively apologetic, Shaiam interrupted and gestured out to sea. 'The *Thorn Circle* has appeared.'

'Nyral's ship?' Kheda moved to get a clear view and found that he recognised the fast trireme. 'Well, well. I wonder what he will have to say for himself.'

'Was it just his laziness that let these scavengers get a foothold here?' Shaiam looked dubiously at the slowly approaching vessel. 'Or could he be in league with them?'

'Either way I'll be stripping him of his command for failing the domain so grievously,' Kheda said severely. 'The only question is should he just be flogged bloody or until we see the bones of his ribs.'

'Care for a wager on that?' Dev cocked a sardonic brow at the shipmaster.

Kheda continued as if the barbarian hadn't spoken. 'The *Thorn Circle* can follow the *Yellow Serpent* under a new master. You and Hesi decide between you if it's Yere or the *Yellow Serpent*'s helmsman who's earned the promotion.'

'The *Thorn Circle*'s crew have sailed with Nyral a long time, my lord,' said Shaiam doubtfully. 'I don't know how they'll take to a new shipmaster.'

'Then tell Hesi to remove any who look as if they might be trouble and to mix plenty of the *Yellow Serpent*'s oarsmen in with the rest.' Kheda looked steadily at the tall mariner. 'And let the *Thorn Circle*'s men know that Hesi has order to ram them at the first sign of mutiny. A light galley won't sink a fast trireme but the *Yellow Serpent* could certainly spring enough planks to cripple it. Tell Hesi to drive it into shallow water first, though, if it comes to it,' he added wryly. 'Truth be told, we can't afford to lose any vessels and I don't want to lose any men if we can help it. I just want Nyral and the rest of his crew to know that I am master here.'

'There'll be fewer doubters when word of this day's work spreads.' A broad grin cracked Shaiam's dark face.

'I certainly hope so.' Kheda smiled conspiratorially before nodding towards the captured boats now stripped of their ineffectual cloak of knot-tree branches. 'Pick the best men you can spare to crew those and to spread that word a little wider. Have them tell Hesi if there are any honest folk living in these backwaters. I'd like to have someone ready to send word if they see any unknown ships that might be considering a sniff down towards the pearl reefs. Tell Hesi I'll send him out a cage of courier doves when I get back to the residence so that he can report to me directly.'

'Yes, my lord,' said Shaiam with satisfaction.

'And now let's deal with Nyral,' concluded Kheda softly.

The *Thorn Circle* was drawing cautiously alongside the *Mist Dove*. The three men stood silently as the fast trireme grounded softly and her stern ladders promptly lowered. Dev turned and whistled and the *Mist Dove*'s swordsmen quickly drew up behind Kheda in a guard that made up in grimness for what it lacked in polish. Tawai and the archers moved casually to one side, making sure they all had a clear shot at whoever disembarked from the newly arrived ship.

There's nothing like the unity that comes from having been in a battle together. I'll settle for that, even if it isn't inborn loyalty to me as their warlord.

Kheda nodded to acknowledge the fast trireme's shipmaster as the man splashed through the shallows to bow before him. 'Nyral.'

'My lord.' There was no hint of obsequiousness in the heavy-set mariner's voice or in his brown face, with his long black beard plaited to a sharp point. He wore a Redigal dagger on his scarlet leather belt, just like the helmsman standing at his shoulder, one massive hand dwarfing the thin and tattered route record that he clutched. There was a strong resemblance between the two men: both had deep-set, circumspect eyes and tip-tilted noses, though something forceful had sent the helmsman's all lopsided a few years ago.

'What traffic have you seen since we left you to watch these sea lanes?' Kheda demanded.

'A Daish flotilla, my lord.' The man's confident answer was entirely unexpected. 'A great galley escorted by two fast triremes and two heavy.' Nyral shrugged, curly head canted arrogantly. 'They flew the old pennants from Chazen Saril's day but we didn't feel inclined to try stopping them, did we, Banse?'

The helmsman cleared his throat. 'I recognised the steersman of the galley and the shipmaster of one of the light triremes.'

'I knew several of the swordsmen on the heavy triremes' upper decks.' Unbidden, the *Thorn Circle*'s rowing master joined them. Like the other men, he wore a sleeveless tunic and loose trousers of dirty white cotton. He wore the narrow double-edged dagger of the Aedis domain on his belt of plaited rainbow cords.

Aedis and Redigal rowers make up more than half the Thorn Circle*'s crew. Even their carpenter's from Ritsem Caid's domain. What choice did I have? Chazen has few enough triremes left after all the invaders' destruction and less than half the mariners needed to man them. And why shouldn't I believe men seeking to better themselves by helping to rebuild Chazen when opportunities prove limited in the domains that bore them?*

Kheda gestured towards Nyral's dagger. 'When you come back to the residence anchorage we should have Chazen knives for you all.'

'Thank you, my lord.' There was a marked lack of enthusiasm in the mariner's voice.

'It has always been my practice to reward loyalty.' Kheda kept his face impassive despite noting a scowl fleet across the helmsman's face. 'As well as punishing laxity, naturally.'

'My lord?' Nyral looked puzzled but his henchmen's expressions verged on insolent.

'You have been lax, haven't you, to allow these vermin to dig in like sand lice on a lizard too sluggish to move?' Kheda gestured at the wretched captives now firmly bound hand and foot. 'I don't want to contemplate any alternative explanation.'

'I'm not quite sure what you mean, my lord.' Nyral's words were polite but uncertainty hooded his eyes as he tried to work out his safest course here.

'You've either been lax in your watch on these reaches or you've allowed these people to make landfall.' Kheda shrugged. 'What next? Will we find pirates preying on this pitiful domain, once you've let them spy out Chazen's seaways?'

'We've been patrolling the lesser channels, my lord,' Nyral insisted with a hint of defiance.

'Not very effectively, if this is any example of your diligence,' countered Kheda calmly. 'Have you built a full chain of beacons yet?'

'We've done all we can but we need metal fire baskets, my lord,' Nyral protested with every appearance of sincerity. 'We daren't set a blaze without one and the season grows drier every day.'

Which is one honest answer, at least. Itrac Chazen had better add iron to the list of things she needs to trade for. The pearl harvest is going to have to be truly spectacular if she's to secure half the things we need.

'So if you haven't been busy setting beacons, how do you explain your laxity in letting these vermin sneak past and make themselves at home?' Kheda gestured towards the captives once again.

The *Thorn Circle*'s rowing master and helmsman slid each other dubious looks behind their shipmaster's back.

'We can't be everywhere at once, my lord.' Nyral shrugged broad shoulders with scant contrition.

Kheda took a moment to pretend to consider this defence, looking past Nyral and his henchmen to the *Thorn Circle*'s side decks. The fast trireme's rowers were surveying the carnage on shore, heads close together in discreet deliberation.

Counting heads and realising that they're outnumbered, as well as seeing that these men have had a taste of blood today. Besides, I am the warlord here. I've proved it in this fight.

Does anyone really want to raise his sword against me and find no one follows his lead?

'So you simply didn't know these vermin were here?' Kheda shook his head.

'No, my lord,' said Nyral with belated regret.

'Yet you were close enough to hear our horns and come to see what was amiss?' Kheda wondered, apparently puzzled.

'A stroke of fortune, my lord.' The boldness in Nyral's voice ebbed away. 'We came as fast as we could, to lend our strength to yours.'

The *Thorn Circle*'s rowing master and helmsman were looking past Kheda to the belligerent half-circle of the *Mist Dove*'s swordsmen with growing apprehension.

'I'm glad of it.' Kheda nodded. 'And since you admit your dereliction, I am inclined to be merciful. You will merely be flogged and chained to an oar in the lowest bank of the *Mist Dove* until Shipmaster Shaiam is inclined to release you.'

Nyral's face turned ugly and he took a pace forward before abruptly freezing.

Kheda took a step forward to match the shipmaster's, gripping the man's forearm so he couldn't go for his knife and leaning close. 'Do you want me to ask those new slaves if anyone recognises you and your ship? If they've paid for your blindness with loot or their women's favours? I'll get whatever answer I want and you can settle your account with your head. No one will lift a finger to save you.'

As he spoke, Kheda felt an unnatural tension in Nyral, the muscles cording his arm shuddering as if the man strained against invisible bonds. He looked the shipmaster in the eye and saw panic there instead of rebellion. Nyral's jaw worked beneath his beard, the man struggling to speak even as his own mouth refused to obey him.

Dev, you disobedient, bloody-minded, lizard-eating barbarian.

As quick as that thought came to him, Kheda drew his own dagger and sunk it to the hilt into Nyral's unprotected midriff. Pulling the mariner towards him, he drove the blade deeper and twisted it up behind the man's ribs. Dev already had a drawn sword at the throat of the *Thorn Circle*'s helmsman and Shaiam had his own dagger levelled at the fast trireme's rowing master. As Kheda stepped back, heartsick and withdrawing his dagger with remarkably little blood, Nyral collapsed dead to the damp ground. The other two men from the *Thorn Circle* dropped to their knees, arms outstretched, hands nowhere near their belt weapons.

'You two can pay his penalty, for standing with him,' snarled Shaiam. The *Mist Dove*'s swordsmen seized them, four or five to each unresisting man, and dragged them away. 'Bring me a lash!' Shaiam bellowed as he stalked after them.

Everyone else retreated to leave Kheda and Dev isolated on the water's edge.

'I thought flogging was the sailmaster's job, what with all that hauling on ropes to build the shoulders,' Dev commented lightly. 'Though I suppose Shaiam's got the muscles to make a decent enough job of it.'

'Why did you do that?' Kheda glared at the wizard with discreet fury. 'How could I let Nyral let live after you had wrapped him in the toils of some cursed enchantment?'

'What was I supposed to do? Let that bastard cut your throat for you while the rest of us stood there with our hands down our trousers?' Dev was unmoved. 'Maybe you could have taken him in a fight. I'm no augur but I could see that turning into a battle that would leave this beach knee-deep in blood if the *Thorn Circle*'s men decided to make a fight of it. As long as I'm playing your body slave it's my duty to keep you alive, and you know I'm no swordsman.' Dev looked down at Nyral's lifeless body and poked it with one foot. 'Anyway, what have you lost besides one half-competent and likely corrupt shipmaster? All these men have just seen you act with the resolution of an awesome warlord. That's no bad trade for one life.' The wizard turned from the corpse at his feet to speak softly into Kheda's ear. 'Besides, what are you going to do about it?'

'I do not wish to rule these people through fear,' said Kheda through gritted teeth.

'And you can be as generous and kindly as you like when your rule is truly secure,' Dev retorted. 'In the meantime, settle for knowing that everyone hereabouts is cowed by your ruthlessness. Now we can sail back to the residence without worrying what's going on behind our backs. After you've done whatever you people do to celebrate your new year, we can sail west.'

'We'll certainly sail west as soon as possible,' Kheda assured him grimly. 'I've decided I want every last mud-painted, feather-wearing savage dead. If you can learn anything that serves your purpose while we do it, that's your affair.'

'You're finally talking about a proper campaign to hunt them out?' Dev was openly surprised. 'No more of this slowly drawing a noose around them to see if thirst and heat can do the job for you?'

'I can't afford to keep those triremes in the west if we need our trade routes hereabouts guarded. We plainly can't trust Nyral and his like and word of the pearl harvest will soon spread, especially if Daish galleys are finally risking these waters again. Come to that, I want to show Daish all the triremes we can muster until I know how the wind blows in that quarter.'

Kheda looked at the wizard, unsmiling. 'So yes, it's

time to put an end to those last skulking invaders, even if it does cost us Chazen blood. I'll find another body slave from somewhere and you can go looking for whatever it is you think you'll find among them. That should settle all accounts between us. As soon as they are all dead, you can sail north and lose yourself wherever you see fit. Then I can concentrate on looking to this domain's future without the dubious benefit of your particular services.'

CHAPTER THREE

I don't think I'll ever get used to the notion of a warlord's residence without walls. It was strange enough visiting this place when it was Chazen Saril's. Now that it's mine, this openness feels more wrong than ever.

'Well done, Shaiam, we're here in good time to celebrate the new-year stars.' Kheda made sure warm approval rang through his words as he called out to the shipmaster. 'You've all earned a consideration when the pearl harvest is gathered in.'

That declaration garnered Kheda loud cheers from rowers bone weary from nine days' hard labour. He was more concerned with searching the seas ahead for any sign of visiting ships.

What interest does Daish have in the Chazen pearl harvest? What prompted a trading flotilla to sail south when no other domain feels inclined to risk these waters just yet? How long have they been here and what have they done? Who is leading their delegation?

The sun was low in the west and Kheda shaded his eyes with one hand to try to see what vessels might be at anchor within the lagoon surrounding the chain of islets long favoured by Chazen's warlords as their dry-season home. The ships remained stubbornly anonymous, mere black silhouettes against the vivid orange of the evening sky.

The *Mist Dove* slowed. Shaiam showed no sign of having heard Kheda's words of praise, intent as he was on negotiating the maze of reefs that served as the first line of defence for the residence. Yere gripped his steering oars, sitting with back straight and alert for any word from the shipmaster or any signal from the lookouts perched on the projecting bow timbers.

Kheda moved to look down over the trireme's side. Reddish coral crags appeared impossibly close as the galley's hull slid through the crystal-clear water. Brilliant fish darted in and out of the crevices with a twitch of their tails. Jaunty painted fools with wide white masks stayed close to the deceptive tentacles of sea flowers vivid as living ruby or golden quartz. Steel and sapphire shoals of blade fish cut circles around the duller humpbacked drift fish idling along. Down in the deeps, cobalt sea stars and giant green-lipped clams sat placidly in patches of rippled whiteness among mossy green fernlike fronds.

Dev came to stand beside Kheda. 'What by all that's holy is he doing?' the barbarian demanded, gazing down incredulously at a figure beneath the water.

'Fishing.' Kheda smiled despite himself. 'He's a pearl diver in from the outer reefs.'

An islander sat quite motionless on the sandy sea floor near a round bulge of mottled brown coral. A shoal of sunset fish nosed along the contorted grooves incised in the outcrop, turning from orange to yellow as the light struck them. Then everything vanished in a flurry of sand and shimmering scales.

'See.' Kheda pointed as the islander emerged from the cloud of sand, kicking urgently for the surface. He had a fish in each hand, his thumbs hooked through their gills. The man surfaced with an explosive gasp for air, treading water for a moment before swimming towards a basket he had left floating between two empty wax-sealed gourds. A rope with a stone on the end was anchoring it against the ebb and flow of the curious tide.

'You don't think he'd find it easier to use a net?' Dev wondered sarcastically.

'Easier but less impressive where the residence girls are concerned.' Kheda smiled.

'I should try that.' There was a lascivious edge to Dev's chuckle. 'If that's what it takes to get a girl to spread her legs.'

'You don't think you might get invited into some maid's quilts if you just let your hair and beard grow in?' Kheda queried. 'Half the girls think you must be a man's man and the rest keep trying to find a discreet way of confirming you're *zamorin*.'

'Ah, but looking so different – that's all part of my intriguing barbarian mystery, isn't it?' Dev ran a hand over his bald head and clean-shaven chin. 'But maybe I should let some lass into my secret. That would get me half-way to a decent new-year celebration at the very least.' He glanced over his shoulder to be sure Yere and Shaiam were still intent on their tasks and lowered his voice still further. 'How long do you think I could get away with staying down for? A count of a hundred? You could win all the wagers you wanted on me – if you shared the take.'

Kheda quelled the barbarian with a warning glare and the heavy trireme went on to pass through the main channel between the outer reefs without incident. Warlord and wizard gazed at the islands lying within the thorny palisade of corals. Men and women were busy around fire pits dug into the white beaches, others hurrying in and out of the long huts set among the nut palms and neat gardens that patterned each scrap of land. Savoury smoke floating across the evening stillness promised feasting and the rowers below stirred and murmured among themselves.

At the centre of the broad lagoon a string of islets lay like gems in a necklace separated by golden links. With no more than a few buildings on each one, these islands were linked by chains of bridges.

Which can be cut if needs must, to defend one avenue of attack while Chazen swordsmen take other paths over bridges, ropes and boats to strike back at an enemy from side and rear. Defence doesn't always mean ramparts. With few enough walls to hide behind, any attackers would always be open to arrows from some direction. And if they did take the buildings, what then? The rulers of Chazen would be long gone. No enemy could hope to maintain a blockade around such an expanse of reef. And what enemy could arrive unexpected, with the bulwark of the entire domain between this warlord's residence and any peril sailing south from the wider Archipelago?

Kheda looked at the well-tended gardens set here and there along the innermost islands. Trees and underbrush had been long since cleared to leave only the most carefully selected specimens. The beds around them weren't planted with saller grain or kitchen vegetables like the outer islands devoted to the prosaic business of growing food and necessities to keep the warlord's residence supplied. A wide variety of shrubs and plants was carefully tended, some vivid with flowers or brightly coloured leaves, others mere creeping mats of dullness but cherished all the same.

'I imagine there'll be a fair few healers come to ask my advice and beg for seedlings,' Kheda said to Dev. 'Let them know I'll make myself available tomorrow afternoon.'

I'll have more than enough to occupy me till then, even if that will give you all the more time to line your pockets with whatever the most desperate will offer you for a chance to reach my presence ahead of the others.

'You'll be letting them take away some of your distilled liquor, I take it?' Dev shot a sideways glance at Kheda.

'Because they will use it in tinctures and lotions for healing the sick, not for addling their wits,' retorted the warlord. 'And you'll have no credibility as my slave if anyone sees you drunk, even if you are a barbarian.'

'So much for the comforts of home.' Dev glowered. 'We'll be toasting the new year with your piss-poor excuse for wine, then, will we?'

Kheda was unmoved. 'And no one will start a fight like some drunken barbarian or fall down dead tomorrow morning with the blood too thick to flow in their veins.'

'That's just a myth to keep your swordsmen clear-headed and you know it.' Dev stared moodily out over the anchorage. 'I'd have found plenty of people here willing to trade something shiny for northern liquor or leaf if I still had my own boat.'

'Then I'd definitely have had you flogged.' Kheda gave a noncommittal shrug. 'And I've seen more than one man who dropped dead for no more reason than an uncommonly hot day following a drunken night.'

The trireme picked its way carefully towards the innermost islands. The buildings were markedly different from the huts of polished wood and tidy palm thatch elsewhere – here they were stone-built pavilions, some long and low, some hollow squares, all roofed with gleaming turquoise tiles. Broad eaves shaded wide steps on all sides where benches were set for those summoned to their lord or lady's presence but not yet admitted to the inner courts. Generous windows stood open to the breezes; pale yellow muslin drapes within teased out over the sills here and there. Sturdy hakali-wood shutters were pinned back against the white walls, ready to be closed with the fall of rapidly approaching dusk.

'It'll be some job packing all this up when the rains come.' Dev shook his head at the flurry of activity along the shore as servants and slaves hurried to make ready for the trireme's arrival.

'It's that or spend the wet season up to our ankles in

water,' Kheda pointed out. 'And we'd get blown clear across the domain by the storms in any case.'

Then these luxurious dwellings will be stripped bare of everything up to and including those shutters. House lizards and palm finches can come and go as they wish and the fiercest winds can rush through the buildings unhindered. We will all have sailed north to bigger islands less vulnerable to the whirlwinds, trading the safety of this openness for a very different fortress and relying on the rains to close the waterways to all but Chazen vessels. If I feel an interloper here, how much more will I seem a trespasser there?

The *Mist Dove* approached her customary berth, careful not to hinder the six-oared supply boats toiling across the lapis lazuli water, weighed down with baskets and bundles for the warlord's household.

Kheda noted the bare patches still scarring the physic gardens and black charring on the trunks of the larger trees.

Should we be risking ourselves by staying? Building here with the rest of the domain between them and the wider Archipelago had been a sound enough strategy for the rulers of Chazen until invaders appeared out of the southern ocean that everyone believed was an empty waste of water. What use were all these carefully planned networks of bridges and channels when the savages' wizards could send fire leaping across the empty air and throw paths of solid cloud across the seas?

Visceral loathing of magic curdled Kheda's belly.

But you were the one who brought Dev here, as the only hope you could find to battle the savages' wizards. And you still owe him a mighty debt, after he nearly lost his life in doing so.

Oblivious, the barbarian mage was gazing at the beautiful pavilions. 'Itrac Chazen has worked wonders, hasn't she?'

'Indeed,' Kheda agreed, his face a neutral mask.

Because what little wealth this devastated domain could salvage has been traded for pretty tiles, costly marbles and whitewash to cover the smoke stains. And men and women have been taken from trying to rebuild their pitiful homes to bring shiploads of clean sand to cover the blood on the beaches.

But how could they believe themselves secure or have any confidence in their future if they did not have their warlord and his lady displaying the pride and honour of the domain in their luxurious home and their lavish household? What other domains would deign to trade with Chazen if all we had to offer was a pauper's hovel?

He glanced across to one of the anchorages cut into the reef to accommodate any deep-keeled ship visiting this restored seat of Chazen power. A great galley wallowed between sturdy hawsers secured to wooden piles driven deep into the coral. Oars were shipped in their ports on the middle of the three roomy decks, rowers doubtless now resting in the vast cargo holds beneath. Varka gulls wheeled around the tops of the three permanent masts that were always ready to take advantage of any wind that might aid the toiling oarsmen in their voyages between the domains.

My shoulders ache just at the recollection of taking an oar on such a vessel.

'One of yours?' Dev asked Kheda as he studied the galley with interest. 'Daish's, I mean.'

Kheda chewed his lip. 'It's the *Sun Bird*. Rekha Daish's favourite ship.'

Her favourite sun birds are the roseate kind barely bigger than the thumb-sized myrtali flowers they feed from. That's the only gardening Rekha does, cultivating the bushes to attract them. Tiny birds, so dainty and quick, and she names a lumbering hulk for them. Why did she do that?

'So every man aboard will be loyal to her, with all their hopes of profit tight in her manicured hand.' Dev regarded the deserted deck of the galley with something perilously close to a scowl.

'No Daish islander ever lost out following Rekha's lead on what to trade and where,' commented Kheda. 'And plenty of warlords' wives reckon they've done well if their ledgers come out even when they've concluded a deal with her. You can count the number of those coming out ahead of her over the course of a year on the fingers of one hand.'

'I don't see Itrac being one of them,' Dev murmured under his breath.

No, nor do I, but I don't see Rekha coming here just for trade, not at the very start of the year when everyone should be close to home and family, to share in the celebrations and debate the auguries of such an auspicious day.

Sirket will be taking the auguries alone this year. I hope they are favourable for you, my son.

'She's brought her own triremes, I see.' Dev squinted at the lithe vessels with their upcurved sterns and prows anchored in the open water of the lagoon.

'We can hardly take offence at that,' said Kheda reluctantly. 'Chazen waters haven't been overly safe of late.'

Is that why Rekha's here, rather than Janne Daish? Second wife rather than first wouldn't be quite such an ominous loss. Though the loss of Rekha's acumen would be a grievous blow to Daish. What is she seeking that she reckons worth the risk of this voyage? What has she brought here in those capacious holds and what might she be looking to take away in them?

The *Mist Dove* lurched gently as the trireme eased into her berth and those rowers taking a rest from their oars to act as the sail crew hurried to secure the mooring ropes.

'So what's the plan when we're ashore?' Dev watched islanders ashore throw ropes to enable the trireme's crew to haul a floating walkway alongside.

'I'll go and read the immediate auguries from the observatory while you see what Itrac's come up with by way of suitable finery for me.' Kheda nodded at the modest tower rising three storeys high beyond a low pavilion set alone on the most easterly islet. He grimaced. 'Then I will greet my present lady wife and we'll discuss how best to deal with my former spouse.'

'Do you think there'll be a cat-fight for your favours?' Dev chuckled unsympathetically. 'Are you sure you wouldn't rather sail straight for the western isles and some open, honest warfare?'

'Just keep your mouth shut and your eyes open,' said Kheda brusquely.

I'd gag you if I thought I could get away with it. You may make a convincing enough show as a body slave when it comes to fetching and carrying and exploiting all the feuds and alliances of a household but you're not going to be much use in these skirmishes, barbarian. I can't send you to practise your sword skills with Rekha's slave; Andit would know you for a fraud before you'd even drawn your blades. So there's no chance of discreet backhand communications to temper what might be said in public for reasons of dignity or deception.

Will Itrac be inclined to share whatever she might learn through her Jevin's not-so-casual conversations? Though he's as green as she is, both of them out of their depth when it comes to dealing with a seasoned traveller like Rekha. What wouldn't I give for just one slave as astute and experienced as Telouet?

'My thanks once again, Shipmaster Shaiam, to you and all your crew. Now, my final order is that you celebrate your new year with all the feasting and merriment that this place can offer you!' Kheda waved towards a long sand bar in the midst of the anchorage where bonfires and torches were being lit. The pipers from a handful of ships were already playing for a circle of girls dancing between trestle tables being stacked high with platters of meat and steaming cook pots. As the *Mist Dove*'s crew turned to the prospect with an approving cheer, the warlord vaulted over the trireme's stern rail without further ceremony.

Dev hit the planks behind him with a solid thump and a jingle of chain mail. 'I don't know about you, my lord,' he said fervently, 'but I will be truly glad to get out of this armour.'

'Indeed.' Kheda strode on ahead to solid ground, taking a fork in the path of raked sand that led towards the observatory tower. Maidservants were coming the other way, all clothed in simple white dresses with embroidery echoing the patterns of the reef fish or the brilliant birds twittering in the trees and shrubs. One carried a basket laden with green leaves wrapped around tiny blue flower spikes, the next a bushel of yellow zera shoots, black earth still clinging to their red roots.

As the girls bowed and withdrew to the sides of the path, Kheda smiled at them. 'We'll be greeting the year's new stars with a fine feast, I see.'

'Absolutely, my lord,' one replied, the girls dipping in demure obeisance.

Two men behind hesitated. They carried a turtle between them in a plaited rope sling, its scaled flippers tied tight to the brown and grey shell as long as a man's leg.

'We'll go around you.' Kheda raised a hand and suited his actions to his words before the turtle hunters could demur. Off the path the ground was sandy, sparse grass soft beneath his feet.

'Turtle meat's such a rare luxury in the north,' Dev observed wryly. 'I never thought to tire of it, but if you could find a sack of pearls for a side of beef, I'd be truly grateful.'

Kheda spared him a glance as they crossed the swaying

walkway to the next small island. 'I wouldn't mind a decent-sized deer to roast.'

But I'll look ver carefully for the snare that comes with it if Rekha offers me one.

Clusters of palm saplings surrounded the pavilion on the furthest island, each one sheltering carefully tended seedlings of red cane and vizail. Servants and slaves hovered on the steps, smiles ingratiating, all dressed alike in cerulean blue, trousers and tunics spotless. Gold and silver clasps shone brightly at wrists and ankles and the men all had hair and beards neatly trimmed and dressed with oil. The women wore fresh flowers woven into their braids or tucked behind turtleshell combs holding flowing black locks away from their round, smiling faces.

Itrac's doing her best to show Rekha Daish that we of Chazen are no paupers.

Kheda smiled in return and paused to hand Dev his helmet, then unbuckled his swords. 'Take this inside, all of it.' He unlaced the neck of his hauberk and, ducking his head with practised suddenness, shook the chain mail down over his body and outstretched arms. As the weight of the metal pulled the armour to the ground with a rattling thump, Kheda stood upright with a heartfelt sigh of relief and ripped off the sweat-stained padded tunic that had protected him from the bruising rings. He relished the touch of the evening breeze on his sweaty skin, then wrinkled his nose at his own odour.

'Get a bath ready, Dev, while I look for any immediate auguries relating to our return. Send a message to my lady Itrac to say I'll call on her shortly. Find out if we're dining with Rekha Daish. Oh, and put the talismans we collected on the voyage in the observatory.'

Ignoring the uncertain glances the resident slaves were exchanging among themselves, he headed for the observatory clad only in his worn and crumpled trousers.

Of course I could just strip off and swim in the sea. No, better not set everyone fretting about how I fail to conduct myself with all the decorum of a warlord. There are always so many eyes on me here. And Daish eyes, too, today. What do they see, now I'm no longer their lord?

Because I am Chazen's warlord. I chose to seize this domain rather than fight Sirket for the one I was born to. Let's start this new year remembering that, as I read the skies when the stars align to mark the return of the heavenly compass. But what are the immediate portents for our return?

The lowest level of the observatory was a broad circular building roofed with the same turquoise tiles as the pavilion. The tower rose in the centre, a white pillar with its uppermost level open to the sky. Kheda pushed open the door and, ignoring the arches opening to wide half-circular halls on either side, he took the spiral stairs up the core of the tower. The upper floor of glazed black tiles was marked with curling ochre patterns within each quarter of the compass. The carvings on the waist-high balustrade divided each quarter into three.

Kheda had no need to read the lyrical script scrolling along the wooden rail, detailing the wisdom of generations in divining the omens that would arise in each arc of the heavenly and earthly compasses. He turned to the east, his expression hard.

Is it significant that it's customary to look first to the arc of marriage, when I'm about to dine with one former, doubtless angry wife and one quite likely still resentful at being forced into wedding me?

The eastern sky was unhelpfully blank. Kheda dropped his gaze to the lavender-tinted sea below. There was nothing to see; no birds in flight, no ripple running against the flow of the waters. There was nothing cast up on the white sand of a distant barren reef or on the narrow shore below him.

But there is always a portent. Daish Reik told you that. You just need the wit to see it and the skill to read it. Are you still stained by magic, unable to read the signs that tie you to past and future?

He swung around in an impatient arc, scanning the horizon. The setting sun dazzled him. Kheda raised an involuntary hand to shield his eyes.

This is where I should be reading the sky, where the new-year stars, brightest in the sky, rise in direct opposition to the coming dawn. This is where our futures will be seen, my own and the domain's together. For our futures are as one from now on, aren't they?

Well, you can't do that till the sun has set, so what else can you learn from the skies?

Slowly, he turned back to look at the darkening east. Even with the augural constellations barely visible, Kheda knew exactly where they lay. It took him but a moment to calculate where the vibrant jewels that traversed the heavens would appear as the night deepened.

There's nothing to see in the arc that governs marriage beyond the stars of the Yora Hawk that signify adversaries to hand. I hardly need the skies to tell me that. What I don't see is any clue as to what lies ahead for me in my dealings with Itrac and Rekha both.

No such confusion clouds the arc of death, next around the compass. The Lesser Moon, the Pearl of the heavens, is a mere nail-paring. With the Pearl the most potent talisman for the Daish domain, is that the final sign for me at the close of the year, that I am truly dead to Daish? The Amethyst shines there, too, gem to counsel reflection and humility in accepting one's fate.

But even in the arc of death omens, the Sailfish swims through the deep distances of the sky. That's a symbol of good fortune when it coincides with either moon, and of life, like the sailfish in the sea rising to spawn in the moonlight.

Kheda turned abruptly to look to the arc of the compass

opposite the faint sickle of the Lesser Moon and the dimly seen Amethyst.

I should have sought guidance from the heavens before now. There are potent conjunctions in this sky for all who rule. The Diamond will shine there before much longer, gem of clarity of mind, of warding against corruption, talisman for all warlords. It rises in the arc of wealth, both material possessions and those intangible things that a wise man values: peace, health and goodwill. That's where the Sapphire rides, too, slowest of the heavenly gems tracing through the sky, patient counsellor reminding us to trust our intuition.

What do those jewels signify in collaboration with the Sea Serpent's writhing stars? That's a sign of mysteries, of hidden forces and conundrums that will be resolved in time. Is that what I must do, bide my time and value what I have, trusting that all will be well?

The hairs on Kheda's neck bristled as a cool breeze brushed across his back.

But there are calls to action elsewhere in the sky. The Greater Moon, Opal talisman for harmony and truth, shines beside the Hoe that reminds us how a man must toil in nurturing the land that supports us all. Constellation and gem are both in the arc of travel. Is this where my journey has brought me, to a future working for Chazen?

What of the arc of duty? The Ruby calls for courage and shines among the stars of the Spear that reminds all men, rulers most of all, of the need for determination in meeting any challenge. And the Ruby is talisman against fire. With the Emerald there as talisman of valour for all those taking up arms to secure peace. The Topaz that takes a full year to traverse each separate arc of the sky will move into the arc of foes directly opposite, tomorrow when the stars are aligned. Topaz, talisman gem for all who seek wisdom. My path is clear, surely? Let's start the new year sailing west to put an end to these invaders once and for all.

Kheda looked across the observatory. A line drawn between the Emerald and Ruby and the Diamond and Sapphire cut across one-third of the circle.

The last corner of that triangle should offer a potent sign in the arc of the compass governing honour and ambition. What stars are there? The Canthira Tree, symbol of death and rebirth, whose seeds need the fire that consumes the parent before they can sprout anew.

Can you doubt it any longer, that Chazen is where your future lies, where you must make your mark as man and warlord alike?

Why does such incontrovertible testimony bring no relief but rather an ever heavier sense of burden?

Footsteps in the halls below caught Kheda's ear. He turned his back on the sky and hurried down the stairs. 'Dev? Is my bath ready? Oh, Rekha—'

His erstwhile wife was standing in the archway that led to the west-facing hall on the ground floor of the observatory. Leaning casually against the plastered stone painted with flowering vines, Rekha Daish was long-limbed and effortlessly elegant. The merest sheen of silver highlighted her dark eyes and a gloss of red softened her tempting lips. Her sleeveless travelling gown was a simple affair of fine rose silk, the lustrous colour flattering the warm brown of her flawless skin. The dress was fastened on each shoulder with a pair of simple silver brooches, her long earrings fashioned to match. A necklace in the same design nestled at the base of her throat and Kheda noted how the low-cut neck of the gown exposed the firm swell of her breasts. A belt of broad silver links emphasised her slender waist and as she took a step forward, he glimpsed the smoothness of her thigh through the side-slit skirt.

'Kheda.' Half-smiling, she brushed back a lock of her lustrous black hair that had escaped the confines of an array of silver combs. Silver bangles whispered musically down her arm.

'Rekha Daish.' Kheda made a formal bow and laid just the faintest emphasis on her domain name. 'I didn't expect to see you at this residence at such a time, never mind in my personal halls. Where's Andit?' he asked with scant courtesy.

'Seeing to my unpacking in the guest pavilion on the central isle. I never knew that Chazen Saril collected star circles,' Rekha mused, with an inconsequential wave towards the westerly hall where lamplight shone on an array of bronze and copper discs hanging on the walls. Then she took a pace forward and laid one slender hand on his bare chest. 'You look well, Kheda, for a man we all thought dead and lost to us. Forgive my lack of etiquette, but I had to see you for myself, just the two of us.'

His skin tensed at her touch. Her perfume was attar of roses, subtle and intoxicating and powerfully reminiscent of the pale golden blooms, ruby-hearted, that grew only in the compound of the Daish rainy season residence, nowhere else in the entire domain. Kheda looked down at Rekha's hand, her long fingers tipped with silver-varnished almond-shaped nails.

Beautifully manicured. Just as Dev predicted.

'It can never just be the two of us.' Kheda took Rekha's hand off his chest and stepped away. 'It never was.'

'No,' she agreed warmly, moving closer once more. 'We shared our children—'

'You misunderstand me, my lady of Daish,' Kheda said sharply. 'Far more things divide us now, you and me, than ever tied us together. That was your choice, yours and my lady Janne's.'

'What of your choice, Kheda, to leave us all mourning you as dead?' Rekha's fine features hardened slightly, the tip of her aquiline nose thinning. 'To set Sirket the challenge of establishing himself as warlord, with him barely grown and in a time of unprecedented upheaval?'

'Unprecedented upheaval and attack from beyond the Archipelago, with magic no less, something not seen in these southerly reaches for time out of mind.' Kheda spoke with biting precision. 'When far from uniting against this appalling threat, our neighbouring domains could only bicker among themselves. Ulla Safar even tried to kill me for his own selfish purposes, you know that.' He paused to swallow his rising ire.

'I read the omens and saw the signs telling me I had to go in search of some means to counter these savage sorceries. I couldn't do that with every eye following me, with the pomp of a warlord weighing me down and hindering my progress through every domain. And I didn't feign my own death; I merely let people believe that Ulla Safar had finally succeeded in murdering me. Desperate times call for desperate courses, Rekha. I wish I hadn't had to do it, but isn't our victory over the savages proof that I was following the right path?'

Though I still have to extricate myself from the mire I've landed myself in as a consequence. Where are the signs to show me a way out of this?

'But what of us – your wives, your heartbroken, grieving sons and daughters?' Rekha's dark eyes searched Kheda's face.

'I would have come back to you and made all amends I could,' Kheda said with low fury. 'It was Janne Daish who made that impossible for me. Go and seek answers from her.'

Neither of them spoke for a long, still moment, then Rekha shifted her gaze to the archway behind Kheda with a shake of her head that sent her long black hair rippling to her waist. The familiar gesture teased Kheda's memory.

She shakes her head like that when she's unsure of herself, not that that happens much more often than a moonless night. Or unsure of me – she did that a lot when we were first married.

'You assuredly saved the Chazen domain from calamity.' Rekha's tone was more conciliatory. 'And it was only right that you should claim these isles with Chazen Saril dead. You certainly earned such a reward with your sacrifices. And don't blame Janne for doing all she could be sure Daish Sirket was able to continue his rule unchallenged as his reward for securing the domain in such a time of fear and peril. You could only have returned by taking up arms against your own son and none of us would have wanted that.'

'I'm sure Sirket and I could have settled matters between us, if Janne Daish hadn't set herself so implacably against my return,' Kheda said coldly.

And fed Chazen Saril a meal of poisoned shellfish to leave him dead at my feet, to force me into a choice between fighting with my own son to reclaim my birthright or turning to secure this masterless domain before some other of my rivals or enemies did so. Where would Daish have been then?

'You would never guess what devastation had been done here.' Rekha was looking all around the hallway, her face admiring. She smiled, this time conspiratorial. 'I would dearly love to know just how you defeated those wild mages, my husband.'

'That is a Chazen secret, my lady of Daish,' Kheda replied, unmoved. 'And I am most assuredly no longer your husband, nor you my wife.'

'From all I hear, Itrac Chazen is a wife in name only and you've taken no concubines or slaves to your bed.' As she spoke, Rekha's swift steps closed the gap between them. She laid her elegant hand on Kheda's chest again, fingertips caressing. 'You must be having a long, dry season.' She raised her eyes to his, running the tip of her tongue along her luscious lips. 'As, of course, am I. We can none of us marry again, me or Janne or Sain, without being forced to choose between abandoning the children we've borne to Daish or running the risk of bringing a man to the domain who might rise to challenge Sirket.'

Kheda laughed out loud in sheer surprise. 'You're inviting me to your bed, Rekha? Or what, to lay you down on these bare tiles and quench my thirst between your thighs?' He shook his head, pretending more amusement than he felt. 'Forgive me, but of all we shared when we were married, lusts of the flesh came a long way down the list. Be honest, Rekha, you only invited me to your bed under the stars you favoured for getting pregnant and you were always swift to call a halt to such pleasures once you had quickened.'

'You don't think I might regret such hardhearted practicality?' She raised one perfectly shaped brow. 'Or desire what I have lost?'

She pressed against him, so close that he could feel her warmth through the fine silk of her dress, her soft breasts against his bare chest. Perfidious memory reminded him of her nakedness, clad only in the unbound midnight of her hair scented with roses.

Her voice trembled. 'I wept for you, Kheda, until I had no more tears to shed.'

'I never thought you hardhearted, Rekha.' Kheda fought a rising desire to take her in his arms and kiss her. That wasn't the only thing rising and he backed away, hoping she had not felt his body's treacherous urgency. 'I thought you the most clear-headed woman born to any domain I knew and that's what I prized in you above all else. No warlord's lady ever served her domain better in her trading. I take it that's what's brought you here? But surely you could have waited to see in the new year back in Daish before bringing your proposals for Itrac's consideration?'

Rekha was making a considerable business of taking out and replacing one of her silver combs. When she looked at Kheda again, her face was calm, her voice composed. 'Itrac is a dear girl and we are very fond of her, Janne and me, having sheltered her through the crisis that overwhelmed her domain last year. We wouldn't dream of seeking to take advantage of her in trade, any more than we would one of our own daughters. Ask her yourself.' Rekha gestured vaguely at the ceiling of the entrance hall with its ornate paintwork. 'Mirrel Ulla would never have let the tiles to reroof these buildings leave her craftsmen if she had known where they would end up. It was Janne and me who persuaded Taisia Ritsem to act as go-between. Now Itrac has her home restored, as was her heart's desire.' She sounded genuinely pleased.

'I'm sure she will be properly grateful for a long time to come,' agreed Kheda. 'But I'm still curious to know what brings you here at the turn of the year.'

Rekha folded her arms and looked frankly at him. 'Every warlord will be reading the omens for trade in the new-year stars and the wives of every domain will be sending the order to ready their fleets. No one will sail with the Greater Moon waning but by the time it's back to the full, the sea lanes will be thronged with galleys.'

'So you're looking to get ahead of the tide?' Kheda queried sceptically.

'Precious few will be coming here,' said Rekha bluntly. 'Not to islands stormed by savage magic, where the seas ran red with the blood of slaughtered islanders.'

'A stain cleansed by the blood of those invaders as soon as I made it safe for Daish and Ritsem to attack without fear,' Kheda retorted.

Rekha nodded with a regretful *moue*. 'Most domains

honour you for that, but they still won't risk their ships and goods in these waters. Not when we are all still unsure how deep the taint of magic runs in Chazen. Not when there are still the remnants of those unspeakable savages lurking in your westernmost isles.'

'Then I'll offer you valuable news to take north with you,' Kheda said curtly. 'I will be sailing to put the last of them to sword and cleansing fire just as soon as the new-year festivities are done.'

'How long will that take, Kheda? Even one fugitive can lead a hunting party a merry chase and you dare not leave the smallest of islands until you are sure beyond doubt that not a single savage remains.' Rekha shook her head. 'Merchants won't be sailing this far south, not till word spreads that it's truly safe and that won't be soon enough to save your trade this year. And you need trade to restore this domain. You need tools and seasoned wood to rebuild, pots and cloth and so much else to refurnish your people's homes. But merchants need not risk your waters. They have plenty of other places to trade their wares. And none of the neighbouring domains' ladies will risk their standing with their people by ordering reluctant vessels south.'

Her tone became ominous. 'You need ships and swords in case these invaders return. You need food to see you all through the end of the dry season, until the rains bring your next round of crops to harvest. You need full storehouses so your young men can be spared to train with those swords, rather than spending all their time with their hoes and their hunting dogs just to keep everyone fed.'

'Itrac Chazen is fully mindful of her responsibilities and I of mine,' interrupted Kheda.

'We don't want to see Itrac fail, Janne and I.' Rekha moved to stand silhouetted against the evening light falling through the doorway. The silk of her dress was sheer enough that her slender nakedness beneath was clearly outlined. 'We don't want to see her rebuffed and humiliated if she tries dealing with the other domains herself. We want to help. We can make the trades for her. We can pass off Chazen pearls as our own.'

Did you think I would miss that calculating glint in your eye, Rekha, if I was satiated with the pleasures of your flesh? Do you think I have forgotten that your body has always been a commodity you trade when it suits you? No harm in that and you've often done well by Daish as a consequence. Not this time, though, and I am no longer Daish to admire you for trying.

'All such matters are Itrac Chazen's concern.' Kheda skirted around Rekha to reach the door. 'She is this domain's first wife.'

'First wife?' Rekha called after him. 'When she had been third wife and barely wed a year to Chazen Saril, who chose her for her charms far more than her brains. Why shouldn't he, when there was no reason to expect she'd have such burdens thrust upon her?'

She shook her head so vehemently that her earrings jingled. 'Which was all very well, Kheda, but now she has burdens beyond her strength to shoulder. How is she to fulfil all the duties of a warlord's wives on her own? Shouldn't you be looking to your posterity by now? There's no sign of her being with child and there's no chance she will quicken any time soon with you spending all your time apart, each busy about your own duties round the domain and seldom in the same residence inside the same phase of either moon.'

'Is this why you're here?' Kheda rounded angrily on Rekha. 'What are you hoping for? That I'd plough your furrow for old times' sake and if you should prove fertile ground, I'd invite you to quit Daish for Chazen? Of course, as mother of this domain's only child, you would naturally become first wife. Is that it? Are you finally tired of standing in Janne's shadow?'

Or is Janne's shadow falling between us here? This smells far more of her perfume than yours, Rekha. And Janne would know what I have been missing through this long, solitary season. She was the one who first taught me the delights of the marriage bed, when I was just a callow youth and she the sophisticated beauty in her glorious prime.

Rekha's stinging slap rocked Kheda's head sideways and scattered his wrathful thoughts. 'How dare you think I am anything but loyal to Daish,' she hissed furiously.

'Excuse me, Rekha Daish.' He managed to turn his heated thoughts into icy formality. 'As I'll forgive you for presuming on our previous acquaintance to risk such a remarkable breach of etiquette in speaking to me like this. I will see you at dinner. I certainly don't want to see you again before.'

Without a backward glance, he turned and walked swiftly out of the building. Two men pushed themselves away from the outer wall where they had been leaning. Both wore the same vivid blue silk that now clad all the household.

'Dev.' Kheda gave a curt nod to either side as they flanked him. 'Jevin. How long were you there?'

'Long enough,' Dev replied smugly. 'Do you want a poultice for that cheek?' he asked with unctuous solicitude.

Kheda ignored the barbarian, fixing his attention on the Archipelago-born slave. 'My lady Itrac will be most interested to learn what Rekha Daish had to say to me.'

'Yes, my lord.' There was a certain wariness in the youthful Jevin's words.

'Go and tell her everything, you understand me?' Kheda paused on the steps of his personal pavilion. 'I'll bathe and come to her as quickly as I can. I want to know her thoughts on this before we dine with my lady of Daish.'

'Very good, my lord.' Jevin loped off with alacrity.

'Everything's ready.' Dev jerked his head towards the warlord's personal pavilion. The slaves on the broad steps bowed low. With a grunt of acknowledgement for the hovering steward, Kheda went inside and crossed the cool cream-tiled hall to the bathroom door.

'Out, all of you.' His scowl cleared the room of a trio of anxious servants in an instant. 'Not, not you, Dev. Keep an eye on the path.'

'There she goes,' Dev observed, peering through the slatted shutters. 'At quite a pace for such an elegant piece.'

The drawstring of his trousers was knotted stubbornly tight. Too irritated to try unpicking it, Kheda snapped the cord and kicked the garment aside. Stepping into the deep bath set in the floor, he emptied a ewer of standing water over his head. It was colder than he had expected on his sun-warmed skin and he gasped. 'Where's she heading?'

'That must be her slave waiting for her at the next bridge.' Dev moved a little for a better view. 'Yes, he's tagging after her like a well-trained hound. She's going back to the guest pavilion.'

'To gather her wits in privacy.' Kheda dipped a handful of aromatic liquid soap from a bowl and lathered his hair and beard briskly.

'I reckon she might try for some privacy with you again before she goes back home,' said Dev with lewd emphasis.

'Then you will play the proper slave for a change and sleep across my threshold to keep her out.' Kheda washed himself vigorously with a soapy cloth.

'I don't think so,' said Dev with distaste. 'I'll find some little maid girl to keep watch on the footbridge and come and warn me if her ladyship goes for a midnight stroll.'

'Find someone to keep an eye on that galley of hers.' Kheda began rinsing away the suds that covered him. 'I want to know exactly when she lets a message bird fly.'

'Do you want it brought down?' Dev suggested. 'I could do that without anyone noticing and you can always blame one of the gull hawks.'

'No.' Kheda ran firm hands over his head and face to force water out of his hair and beard.

'There have been plenty of Chazen courier doves winging their way home over the last ten days or so, from what Jevin tells me. I'll go and check if any of them are bringing news from the west. You'll want to know exactly where the remaining wild men are to be found, so you can plan your new campaign against them properly.' Dev threw Kheda a towel as he climbed out of the bath. 'And whatever her haughtiness Rekha Daish might say, Itrac is managing to trade with other domains. At least, she's found someone to give her enough silk to cover your arse in suitable style. Come and see.'

Drying himself, Kheda followed the barbarian through the door that led straight from the bathroom into his spacious bedchamber. Dev lifted two full-sleeved tunics from the broad, low bed. 'The grey or the tan, my lord?' he asked with mock obsequiousness.

'I don't suppose you thought to ask what Itrac will be wearing?' Kheda considered the skilfully cut and sewn garments. The grey was a dark hue shot through with blue like a rainy-season cloud. The tan was a warmer colour with a vibrant golden gloss. There hadn't been time for any embroidery on either, however.

'As it happens, I did,' retorted Dev. 'Yellow, so the lad said.'

'The tan then.' Kheda reached for the trousers. 'What gems do we have to dress it up?'

'Precious few.' Dev tossed the tunic across and Kheda pulled it over his head.

'I suppose it's too much to hope that any more of the domain's heirlooms have come to light while we've been away?' The cloth muffled his words.

'No such luck,' the barbarian confirmed as he unlocked a coffer set on a stand beside the bed. 'I'll bet Daish and Ritsem skippers are trading them even as we speak.'

'Keep that opinion to yourself, barbarian,' Kheda warned, 'unless you want me to read your fate in your entrails when some mariner guts you. Archipelagans aren't thieves like you northerners. We'll find most of the loot with those last savages penned up in the west.'

'Which is another good reason to finally see them all dead,' said Dev with happy anticipation.

'So you can try your hand at plundering the wealth they stole?' Kheda challenged. 'Not when Itrac needs those talismans and heirlooms to trade for everything this domain so desperately lacks.'

'You don't think she'll have enough pearls?' Dev stirred the paltry selection of ornaments in the upper tray of the chest with a disdainful finger. 'What do you want out of here?'

'Not pearls, with this colour silk,' Kheda commented as he came to pull a fine gold chain out of a tangle of links. He took off his silver ring with its uncut talisman emerald and threaded the chain through it.

'If you say so.' Dev shrugged. 'I never had to play the lady's maid back home.'

'Just be thankful I didn't end up saving your skin by making you a slave to my lady wife,' Kheda taunted as he slipped the chain over his neck and tucked the ring beneath the neck of his tunic. 'Do you think you would have liked learning how to paint Itrac's face and nails? What else have we got?'

'Turtleshell and that's about it.' Dev lifted out the padded silk tray to reveal variegated bracelets polished to a mirror finish.

'Those will do.' Kheda pushed a matched pair over his knuckles and thrust heavy gold rings on all his fingers. 'And that belt.'

'This one?' Dev picked out the piece Kheda had indicated with his nod. It was made of plaques of turtleshell joined by chased gold links.

And carefully adjusted to fit me, not Chazen Saril's greater girth.

'And anklets to finish the set?' Dev held out two more pieces with faint derision.

Kheda settled the belt on his hips and secured the clasp before taking the anklets and snapping them around the hems of his trousers, drawing in the loose cloth. 'You don't reckon much to turtleshell, do you? Nor pearls, if you're honest, not for more than they can buy you. Why is that?'

'Probably because I'm an ignorant barbarian with no understanding of their talismanic value,' said Dev smoothly.

Or is it because you are a wizard? The savage mages that came with the invaders, they spurned pearls and turtleshell alike, seeking only to loot our gemstones. You claim to have no idea why. Is that the truth?

Kheda let that question pass unspoken and unanswered. 'Whatever Rekha's plotting, I don't think we'll need armoured guards at dinner but you should wear your swords if not your hauberk. Go and get them.'

'Yes, my lord.' Sarcasm and relief weighted Dev's words in equal measure.

'And now I had best go to see Itrac.' Kheda smoothed his hair and beard, already as good as dry with the heat of the day slow to fade till the sun was utterly set. 'So we can decide our strategy before we go to dine with Rekha.'

CHAPTER FOUR

Kheda headed for the door leading from the bedchamber into the hall. Dev followed and slid away towards the rear of the building.

The stocky steward who had been waiting outside the pavilion stepped up smartly and bowed low. 'It's good to see you back, my lord.'

'I'm happy to be back, Beyau,' Kheda replied courteously. 'Is everything in good order here? Please, walk with me to my lady Itrac's pavilion.'

Would you tell me if things weren't going smoothly or try to fix any problem before I discovered it, rather than come and seek my counsel? How am I ever going to be wholly at ease with this household or they with me? Daish slaves knew they were free to speak their minds at all times, but we'd known each other since I was a child, for the most part. I don't feel I know anyone here. But never take your servants for granted, that's what Daish Reik always said, or one day you'll stretch out your hand for something and it'll stay empty.

'We're managing well enough now we've a full complement of servants,' the steward said slowly as they walked across the island into the fast-fading evening light. 'Hopefuls wash up with every tide but I'm not letting them stay unless they were part of the household before – or unless they look as if they'd be handy with a sword.' He hesitated, muscular hands clasped behind his stiff back as he walked. 'I've nearly doubled the warriors in your retinue.'

'Those you're sending away, are they returning to their

homes?' Kheda glanced at the man as they reached the first bridge over the shimmering water. Beyau's burly build was ill-suited to the elegantly cut silk of a household slave's formal tunic and Kheda noted that he still affected the close-cropped hair and beard of a fighting man. 'Are you giving them all you can to help them rebuild what they have lost?'

'All we can spare, my lord,' Beyau assured him fervently before hesitating again. 'Touai, who is first among my lady Itrac's attendants, she thinks we could spare more if we weren't maintaining so many warriors in the residence.'

'Do we have the same numbers of swords as in Chazen Saril's day yet?' Kheda nodded as Beyau shook his head. 'Then you can take on every likely swordsman until we do. The domain must present a decent show of force to our neighbours.'

Not that all the swords of the Archipelago could turn aside the magic of the savages, if they invade again.

'And you're right to encourage those who are coming back to return to their homes, to rebuild their villages,' the warlord continued. 'We need all hands working the land, not outstretched for unearned food.' Then Kheda hesitated in his turn. 'All able hands, that is. Are there many coming back unable to make shift for themselves, out of injury to mind or body?'

Is that one of the mysteries we might solve in hunting down the last of the savages? Why did they imprison so many of our people and treat them so abominably?

'No.' Beyau looked grim, dark scowl gilded by the sun on the far horizon. 'Those who were held captive by the savages mostly just come back to die, my lord, if they come back at all.'

Dying of despair as much as the injuries they suffered being starved and beaten and worked till they dropped.

'Whereas you came back to take up your father's role.'

Kheda paused to look the thickset man in the eye. 'Don't think I don't appreciate that.'

'We'll be ready for them if they ever come again.' Beyau looked away, out over the southern waters, sword hand straying to the crescent dagger at his belt.

'We will,' Kheda assured him.

As long as you keep Dev happy, and keep his true nature a secret, so you can meet sorcerous fire with sorcerous fire. Can you really afford to send him away once he's satisfied his curiosity about the savages?

But what will these people think if they ever uncover such a deception?

Kheda gestured towards one of the islands on the outer edge of the reef where long huts surrounded a pounded expanse of sandy soil. 'I take it you're drilling the swordsmen yourself?'

Beyau looked uncertain. 'I know it's not my place—'

'We're none of us in the places we held before the invaders came,' Kheda said unguardedly. 'Your father may have been the residence steward but you were rising fast in the ranks of the guard – Itrac told me as much. There's no one better to train them, is there? Tell me honestly,' he commanded, seeing the man's reluctance.

The steward squared his impressively muscled shoulders. 'Jevin just isn't used to assuming command, my lord, and some of the older ones aren't inclined to take orders from a lad as young as him. I thought it best to step in till you returned.'

'Good. Then you can continue taking charge until you find someone fit to be raised to captain. Dev's less experience of command than Jevin,' Kheda said bluntly, 'and there's nothing a barbarian can teach an Archipelagan about swordplay.'

'No, my lord.' Beyau's voice was neutral but a grin plucked at the corners of his generous mouth.

'Mind you,' Kheda said thoughtfully, 'Rekha Daish's body slave, Andit, he's both experienced and old enough to command respect among your would-be warriors. Your younger boys could learn some useful tricks from him, if you invite him to share in the daily training sessions while he's here. I take it Jevin has extended the usual courtesies to him?'

'I wouldn't know, my lord,' said Beyau stolidly, 'but I was thinking I might breakfast with him and Andit tomorrow.'

So Jevin still needs a hint or two. Let's hope Andit will know how to give a few tactful suggestions to a lad thrust into precedence over a residence guard with no elder body slave's example to follow. That wouldn't compromise his loyalty to Rekha Daish.

They walked across the islet to the next bridge in thoughtful silence.

'Where are we dining tonight?' Kheda asked as they crossed the gently flexing planks. 'And who is dining with us, besides Rekha Daish?'

'A banquet is to be served in my lady Itrac Chazen's great hall.' Beyau didn't hide his unease. 'With all the shipmasters invited.' He waved a hand at the various galleys and triremes safely anchored around the reefs.

'Whose idea was that?' Kheda frowned as they reached a sandy nub of reef where walkways branched off in several directions across the corals.

'I believe it was Rekha Daish's suggestion,' Beyau answered neutrally. 'My lady Itrac agreed it would be a splendid way to celebrate the turn of the year.'

'Then you must have a great deal to organise. Don't let me keep you. Unless there's anything else?'

'No, my lord.' Beyau bowed low.

Kheda dismissed him with a nod and walked on alone.

So Rekha has some plan to show all the shipmasters –

what? That she and I still share the familiarity of husband and wife? That I still find her desirable? That Itrac has none of Rekha's poise or her daunting experience in the complexities of trade?

Itrac must want to make a fight of it, though, otherwise she'd have come up with some reason for the three of us to dine alone. Or would she have thought of that in time? I don't think I need any omens to tell me this isn't going to be a relaxing meal.

Seeing Chazen islanders on all sides as well as servants and slaves, Kheda went on his way with a calculatedly carefree expression, acknowledging dutiful obeisance with a smile. By the time he reached the wide island where the first wife of Chazen always dwelt, his face felt tense and his shoulders stiff under the heavy weight of the unspoken expectation he saw on every face.

The central pavilion was huge, a hollow square offering luxurious accommodation for the extended household customary for every noblewoman of an Archipelagan domain. Wings on either side would house her faithful retainers and those craftsmen she summoned from time to time to consult on the domain's wealth and prospects. Lesser quarters for her countless servants and slaves were tucked discreetly away at the rear.

Kheda went up the broad, shallow steps and pushed open the wide double doors to enter the spacious hall that occupied one whole side of the building. The floor was tiled in soft green and the lofty walls were decorated with hangings of translucent silk painted with seascapes in countless shades of blue. There was room for Itrac to meet with every diver and polisher whose pearls and turtleshell she would trade for the good of the domain.

Two servants were unrolling a thick carpet of mottled-blue silk with white and silver fish darting through a pattern of green seaweed and a border of multicoloured squid. They froze at Kheda's entrance, along with a waiting crowd of household slaves, their arms full of sapphire cushions. Outdoor servants in undyed cotton appeared at a side door carrying long, low tables and an indignant exclamation died away to nothing as whoever had uttered it realised that the warlord was among them.

'Don't let me interrupt you.' Waving away dutiful bows, Kheda walked across the hall and out through the tall doors on the far side into the enclosed garden beyond. It was hot and still, the mingled perfumes of vizail, jessamine and white basket flowers heavy in the air. Grey and scarlet shadow-finches were clustered in a corner of their aviary at the heart of the garden and barely chirruped as Kheda passed. Three different gaudy glory-birds in a spinefruit tree watched him without stirring a feather.

Kheda walked slowly towards the steps leading to the central entrance to the fourth side of the pavilion's hollow heart. Doors on either side stood closed and barred. The apartments for those children of the domain grown to an age of discretion and ready to learn all their complex duties from their first mother stood in echoing emptiness.

Even if Itrac invited me to her bed tonight and my seed took root, it would be many years before I had a son grown into his strength or a daughter grown to the wisdom needed to rule in her own right. I had sons and daughters in Daish and I loved them more than I thought possible. Could I ever love children born here in the same way?

Would Rekha come here as a Chazen wife? Janne would have no right to stop her bringing her younger children, the ones below the age of reason – Vida, little Mie and Noi.

You could see your daughters taught all they would need to know to rule Chazen. Vida could be promised to some lesser son of Ritsem or Redigal and the other two married to the heirs of those domains. Ritsem Caid and Redigal Coron were always your friends. Chazen would be more secure in its alliances than it has been for generations.

Wouldn't that be doing your duty by these people?

'My lord Chazen Kheda.' Jevin's precipitate arrival beside him interrupted the perfidious notions that Kheda found so hard to shake off. The youthful slave opened the door with a smile of relief. 'Your lady wife is pleased to see you.'

'And I to see her.' Kheda recovered himself and went inside.

Itrac Chazen's personal audience chamber was an airy room floored with the Ulla domain's most prized lustre tiles. The sunrise-pink walls were hung with draperies of white silk painted with a riot of colourful birds flitting among nut palms and lilla trees. A low table of creamy marbled halda wood in the middle of the floor was surrounded by plum-coloured cushions. Kheda noted a litter of the thin silver cylinders that courier doves carried clasped to their scaly legs and slips of coiled paper fine as onion skin. Reed pens lay across an open inkwell in the midst of them.

'I was glad to hear you'd returned safely. How fares our domain, my husband?' Standing by the table, Itrac Chazen wore a gown of sunshine silk shot with a blush of pink, the whispering pleats of the full skirt belted close to her slim waist with a heavy golden chain. The modest bodice rose to a high neck, leaving her slender arms and shoulders bare. She wore a triple-stranded collar of lustrous pink conch pearls and bracelets of the same sea gems. More gleamed in the net of fine braids woven from her own long hair, holding the wealth of midnight locks off her face to cascade down her back to her waist. Subtle paints of gold and shell-pink made an exquisite mask of her eyes and mouth.

'Well enough, my lady wife. I visited every major island

and every group of lesser ones and the spokesmen brought me word of each village. There were few enough healers bringing illnesses or injuries for my advice and I didn't need to sit in judgement on any disputes. Our people are busy rebuilding their homes and their lives and looking forward to a better future.'

Whereas you're looking thinner than is good for you and even Jevin's skilled hand with a cosmetic brush can't hide your weariness and apprehension. Though I see determination in your eyes. That's better than the grief and confusion when we first came here.

Kheda took her hands in his and kissed her chastely on one cheek. His skin was lighter than most in these southern reaches but Itrac's was paler still, the colour of honey. With the much-mingled blood of the central domains, she was taller than most women hereabouts, with a sparer build. 'I gather we're to enjoy a dinner that will be a credit to the domain.'

'As long as there are fish in the sea and fruit on the trees we won't go hungry.' Itrac's taut smile faded a little. 'Though I see us tightening our belts before the rains, even with us drying and pickling all the excess.'

'Daish must have some surplus, after Chazen labour helped to plant their saller and reap their harvest last year,' Kheda remarked with studied casualness. 'You might like to propose some mutually beneficial exchange with Rekha.'

'I gather she had hopes of some more personal exchange with you.' Itrac's hazel eyes searched Kheda's green ones.

'Now dashed, sadly for her.' Kheda surprised Itrac with a grin and a nod at Jevin who was filling two crystal goblets with the pale wine of the Archipelago from a long-spouted ewer of gold embossed with silver sea birds. 'As I hope Jevin told you. She seems very eager for me to interfere with your trading of the pearl harvest,' he added sceptically.

'I'll bet she is.' A smile lightened Itrac's face, her teeth white and even.

Kheda narrowed his eyes as he accepted a goblet from Jevin. 'That doesn't sound like a wager I want to take.' He sipped at the wine: refreshing without being intoxicating.

Because we want all our wits about us for dealings with Rekha. How can barbarians conduct their commerce or their warfare when they are so fuddled with alcohol?

'I've been picking up the threads of the network that brought news to Olkai.' Itrac's voice wavered a little at the mention of the domain's former first wife. 'Some of her favoured craftsmen have only recently returned from Daish waters and they bring interesting news.'

'Do they?' Kheda couldn't restrain a qualm at the notion of Daish concerns so blithely carried south.

Itrac's eyes shone with glee. 'The pearl oysters have deserted the Daish reefs.'

'A barren year?' The shock left Kheda hollow.

What an appalling omen for Sirket's first full year as warlord.

'Which is why Rekha's come looking for Chazen pearls to help them weather this calamity.' Itrac's tone didn't bode well for the Daish woman.

'Janne and Rekha are always prepared for a lean year,' Kheda said slowly. 'They will have pearls and nacre stockpiled, doubtless enough to settle trades already agreed with the Ritsem and Aedis domains.'

'Then why is Rekha so desperate to get her hands on our harvest?' Itrac challenged him. 'And she is desperate, believe me.'

'I know,' Kheda assured her. He closed his eyes, the better to scour his memory as recollection teased him. 'I think I have it. Rekha made a deal with Moni Redigal towards the end of the last dry season for a shipload of brassware. Redigal is owed a full eighth share in this oyster harvest as it leaves the sea.'

Itrac clicked her tongue. 'Moni Redigal is always too ready to gamble. So Daish has its brassware in return for a cupful of pearls, if Moni's lucky.'

'Daish won't relish such a bargain.' Kheda drained his goblet. 'How can they conceal this disaster, if Redigal boats are out on their reefs waiting for their share of the unopened oysters?'

'Moni would want pearls equal to an eighth share of a fair harvest, at the very least, as the price of her silence.' Itrac pursed her lips.

'Which would seriously deplete Daish reserves.' Kheda did his best to hide his concern. 'And they would hardly want to trade the rest in case the reefs prove barren again next year.'

It happened in my grandsire's time: a full seven years when the best reefs were bare and the lesser oyster beds offered only the poorest nacre.

What does this portend, when Chazen has the richest pearl harvest within living memory?

'So Daish has a grave problem.' Itrac looked closely at him. 'And we have an interesting opportunity.'

And I am now of Chazen, not of Daish.

Kheda hid his misgivings in his empty goblet, pretending to drink. 'How do you propose to make the best of it?'

'What do you make of the omen in this?' Itrac's gaze still held his. 'That Daish suffers such an ill-fated start to their year? Do we want dealings with a domain facing such misfortune? We have reason enough to shun their waters, after Chazen Saril died while enjoying their hospitality.'

Kheda's mind's eye showed him Chazen Saril's agonised death once again.

Am I truly innocent because I had no notion that Janne was feeding all three of us mussels gathered after a red tide, potentially lethal? The wife of my youth and I had no idea she could be so ruthless, wagering all our lives against her judgement that Chazen Saril's cowardice forfeited his right to rule and to life, and that my choice to cloak myself in a deceit of death and search out lore to counter the invaders' magic forfeited any right of return to my own domain.

'Chazen Kheda?' Itrac's pointed prompting struck him harder than Rekha's slap to his face.

He blinked and chose his words carefully. 'Whatever this portent means for Daish, we must consider Chazen's situation. The safest seaways to the rest of the Archipelago run through Daish waters. Crossing open water to Redigal is far more dangerous for our galleys. If we don't give Rekha something of what she wants, we risk her closing Daish waters to anyone wanting to trade with us. That's if they have overcome their doubts about our domain's recovery from the magic that swept over us last year.'

'Word will have spread fast enough that the wild wizards spurned any wealth born of the seas and only sought gemstones.' Itrac was scornful. 'And I want the entire Archipelago to know that our new year is blessed with such a potent omen. I am not about to let Rekha pass off our pearls or our good fortune as her own.'

'And Chazen needs so many things that you can buy with those pearls.' Kheda inclined his head slowly. 'Of course, drilled pearls are more valuable, as are finished ornaments made from the petals and dog's teeth. But I do have some unwelcome news from my voyage around the domain, Itrac. Many of our best craftsmen fled the invaders to Daish waters and they're slow to return, whatever Daish Sirket might decree. You might allow Rekha some limited share in our pearl harvest on the strict understanding that such valuable men and women of Chazen be sent home.'

'Possibly.' Itrac looked a little mutinous before smiling with new boldness. 'You're right to say it would be better to keep our access to their sea lanes. Trade with Ritsem is certainly easier with passage through Daish waters and I've a proposal for Taisia. Ulla Safar's wives are doing all they can to deny Ritsem the limestone they need to smelt the iron ore they discovered last year. Given how little nacre our harvest yields, I propose to burn thc oyster shells for lime. We can trade that with Taisia Ritsem for swords and armour.'

'An excellent opportunity for Chazen to help Ritsem and to snub Ulla,' observed Kheda. 'And no one will weep to see Ulla Safar's power as the only purveyor of iron in these reaches undermined.'

I owe Ulla Safar and his pack of bitches every ill turn I can contrive. He would have killed me for pure malice before lifting a finger to help Daish against the invaders. But would all the warriors from the Ulla domain have been any use against magic?

Though without his attempts on your life, you'd never have been able to play dead and go in search of lore to combat the invaders' sorceries.

But the price of that was being landed with Chazen and with Dev. And where is he?

'Taisia Ritsem sends me plenty of news.' Itrac didn't notice his preoccupation, looking down at the message slips brought by the courier doves. Her voice shook a little. 'For the sake of Olkai Chazen, who was her sister before she was mine.'

'You could make it a condition of trading pearls with Rekha,' Kheda said without thinking, 'that Olkai's bones are returned from the Daish tower of silence where we laid her.'

He looked through the far window over towards the only other tower on these islands. Out on the most distant islet at the far end of the reef, a tall wall with a single gate ringed a solid pillar. Unrailed stairs spiralled up the outside to the open platform where the most honoured dead of the domain were laid. There were no carrion birds wheeling around in the fading sky. There was nothing to bring them to play their part in returning all that the dead had been to the islands they had lived in, to bind them to the future of the whole domain.

Forgive me, Sekni Chazen, on your own behalf and for the three little children of the domain who died with you. There was simply no way of telling your charred bones from all those others killed here. At least you are buried with your people and your virtues will bless this residence at least.

'I miss her so much.' Itrac choked on an abrupt sob and tears spilled from her long painted lashes. 'Olkai and Sekni.'

'You did all you could.' Kheda laid gentle hands on her bare shoulders and felt her trembling with the effort of holding back hysterical weeping. 'You brought Olkai out of the fires of the wild men's attack. I used all the healing lore I had. There was just no saving her from such burns.'

Not with more than half her body blistered and blackened by magical fires. One of the kindest and most amiable women I have ever known, from her earliest girlhood as Olkai Ritsem. She was far more wife than Chazen Saril deserved, the best first wife this domain had had in a long while.

'Perhaps –' Itrac took a deep breath and wiped the tears from her decorated eyes with careful fingers '– it might have been better for the domain if I had died and she had lived.'

'Never think that.' Kheda tightened his grip on her shoulders. 'When someone dies despite all we can do, we must accept that fate. All we can do is seek to understand the omens in that death.'

'I'll never understand why Olkai had to die like that. Omens are your business and trade is mine.' Itrac twisted free of Kheda's hands, her chin trembling. 'But perhaps I'll make a deal with Rekha for Olkai's bones. Then I might at least feel her presence in my dreams here.'

'You will prove as fine a first wife for this domain as she was,' Kheda said warmly.

'You've seen that in the portents, have you?' Itrac demanded with sudden brittle anger. 'When I'm so terrified of dying like Olkai that I spend half my days staring out over the southern ocean, wondering when those savages will return? When every day I spend here reminds me of Sekni and the children she and Olkai bore to Saril, all dead at the invaders' hands? I wake expecting their laughter and hear only the endless silence in their empty rooms.'

She pressed her hands to her flat stomach. 'Don't say it, Kheda. I hear it whispered in corners day after day. I see the way everyone looks at my belly before they look me in the eye, as if all I need is to get with child to make me forget the babies I took in my arms when they were still wet with their birth blood.'

Her voice rose in wild accusation. 'And don't tell me all the village spokesmen and half the shipmasters weren't making tactful enquires after my health on your voyage. Or were they offering up travelling seers to predict an auspicious future for our children, as soon as I care to supply them? Well, I don't care to, Kheda, not until you can show me a future beyond doubt where I'll never see those I love murdered by wild men and their vicious magics. And I don't care if that does send you to Rekha's bed!'

Is this why Rekha came instead of Janne? Itrac would

always have the advantage of youth over Janne's grey hair and thickened waist. But she's a bud blighted by drought and uncertainty compared to Rekha in the full bloom of her womanhood. And I see some things remain consistent in my marriages. Such as impossible conversations where I'll be in the wrong whatever I say. But if I don't at least try, I'm definitely condemned.

'Itrac, listen to me.' Kheda seized her shoulders again and this time he shook her, sending Jevin backwards with a fierce glare when the slave would have intervened. 'Yes, I've had all the veiled hints you can imagine, and some not so veiled. True, the islanders would be greatly reassured if you bore a baby to the domain as token of your confidence in Chazen's future. If you chose me to father your child, many would feel more certain of my commitment to them and their domain, given that I was not born here.'

He waved a hand at the darkening skies beyond the window where stars were now visible. 'The Winged Serpent rides in the arc of the heavens where we could seek signs concerning children and serpents of any kind are a reminder of male and female intertwined. None of this gives me any rights over your choices. It is ever a wife's prerogative to decide when and if to give her husband a child, from the least to the highest born in any domain.'

Itrac stood frozen between his hands. Kheda leaned forward to kiss her cheek once again before speaking more softly. 'If you invite me to your bed, when you judge that the time is right, I will be honoured. You're a beautiful and desirable woman. Forgive me if I haven't made myself clear on that; I wanted to leave you to grieve for Chazen Saril in peace. I know you married him for love more than any alliance. I can wait, and if I find myself in need of companionship in the meantime, I'll find some bedmate who won't exact the kind of price Rekha Daish would be seeking for her favours,' he concluded frankly.

'I'm sorry . . .' Itrac stammered. 'I shouldn't have said—'

Kheda shook his head. 'Don't apologise. We should have had this conversation long since but that's as much my fault as yours. And since the subject of children has come up, you should think very carefully whether or not you want to me to father any child of yours. For every learned sage who declares an innocent touched by magic is not stained with it, there's another who says merely being in the presence of magic taints us. I was in the presence of magic time and again, Itrac, however honest my motives. If you don't want to risk blighting your baby's future with such a father, I couldn't blame you. There's always Jevin.' He was careful not to look at the youthful slave. 'He was a gift from Taisia Ritsem and that domain's certainly untouched by magic.'

Are you untouched by him or have you already turned to him for consolation? Does it matter? I've no right to dictate who you may or may not take to your bed and Dev's presence in my life doesn't exactly leave me feeling very wholesome.

Itrac surprised the warlord with a tremulous smile. 'I never thought of that – not Jevin, I mean, but the whole business of the taint of magic.' She shrugged. 'If just encountering magic contaminates us with its evil, I've been touched along with everyone else who survived the savages.' She shivered despite the warmth. 'Have you had any news from the triremes to the west? I dream about those wild men out there over the horizon, and all they did to us.'

If a warlord's prerogative is the reading of omens written in the world around us, it's women whose dreams link their inner lives to past and future through the unbroken thread of blood.

'The time has come to make an end of them,' Kheda said firmly. 'The portents are clear about that. As soon as we've celebrated the alignment of the new year, I'll summon every swordsman and ship we can call on and cleanse every last isle of the domain. I'll burn their bolt-holes to black ash and throw their splintered bones into the sea.'

Itrac's eyes widened at his vehemence. 'Be careful.'

'I will be,' Kheda assured her.

A peremptory knock on the door leading to the garden startled them both and Jevin hastily gathered his wits to hurry over to open it.

Dev stood there, scanning the room with amused curiosity. 'Are we ready to dine with Rekha Daish in sufficient state to convince her that Chazen is set fair for a successful year?' The barbarian mage was wearing a plain tunic and trousers of rich brown silk, his paired swords thrust through a wide sash. His coppery skin gleamed with oil and he wore a single earring, a ruby faceted in the fashion of the unbroken lands of his birth.

'Not till I've seen to your cosmetics, my lady.' Jevin spoke up apologetically. 'You're a bit smudged.'

'Then there's a messenger you might like to see, my lord,' said Dev briskly. 'If we've a bit of time in hand.'

'I think we can feel free to keep Rekha waiting.' Kheda kissed Itrac's mouth firmly now that he didn't need to be so careful not to mar her face paint. 'Any lesser wife must expect to serve a first wife's convenience.'

He followed Dev across the dusky garden and out through the reception hall where everything was nearly ready for the celebratory feast. They skirted servants carefully bringing in tall lamp stands and a slave boy waiting with a pitcher of oil.

'Green oil, my lord,' Dev observed with a grin, 'just to show anyone who might be wondering that Chazen trade-links still reach all the way to the unbroken lands of the barbarous north.'

Kheda glanced around the room. 'We're not exactly dressed to match the furnishings, though. That will give Rekha something to gloat over.'

'Which will doubtless spur Itrac on to make the most profitable trades she can,' said Dev comfortably, 'so that she can invite all the neighbouring domain's women here along with the Daish wives next year, to see hangings, carpets, cushions and everyone's clothes matched to a shade. Care to make a wager on it?'

'Was that the first Archipelagan habit you acquired?' Kheda wondered. 'Laying bets whenever you get the chance?'

Not that you have any true understanding of testing your perception of the present against the chances of the future. You just seize any opportunity to enrich yourself like the barbarian you were born.

Kheda paused on the outer steps and surveyed the wide expanse of the reef and lagoon. Triremes and galleys had their stern lanterns lit, rocking peaceably at anchor. A woman's song swelled above the shimmering music of a round harp and laughter rang across the water as the resident islanders welcomed Chazen mariners and Daish newcomers alike to their celebrations. The pungent scents of finger-fish fried in peppery oil and spit-roasted ducks stuffed with herbs made Kheda's stomach rumble.

'There's your messenger, my lord.' Dev pointed to a drifting lantern and Kheda peered through the half-light to see a small boat picking its cautious way towards the far isle where his pavilion and the observatory stood.

It was a sturdy little vessel of the kind that travelled unremarked between the islands of a domain, with a capacious hold full of useful items. A boat easily handled by two crew and manageable enough for a solitary mariner who knew the ropes of its triangular rigged sail. A boat big enough for someone bold enough to sail across the more open seas to another warlord's waters and negotiate for the pennants granting safe passage to go and see what was on offer at the beaches where islanders and traders swapped their wares. Kheda felt the first uncalculated smile of the day widen on his face.

Better not run, however much you want to. That would attract attention and someone would jump to a wrong conclusion or start some panic.

He began walking more briskly and, schooling his face into placid affability for the servants and islanders he passed, always kept the little boat in view as it nosed into a modest berth close by the observatory. Leaving the busier pavilions behind, Kheda made his way across the walkways to the far island as rapidly as possible.

Just as eager at his shoulder, Dev was concentrating on watching the little ship easing up to the unforgiving coral. 'You watch what you're doing, girlie. That's still my ship.'

'Nice to see you, too, Dev,' called the female mariner wielding a single weighty oar at the stern. Shipping her sweep, she threw out a heavy anchor that landed on the reef with a crunch. 'You could come and lend a hand, you idle barbarian.' She hauled on the rope to make sure all was secure.

Dev spread mock-apologetic hands. 'My lord would hardly approve of me getting all dirty before such an important evening.'

'The first thing I want is a decent bath.' The girl wiped her forehead with the back of one hand before deftly throwing a loop of rope over a mooring post. 'I'm sick of being all sticky with salt.'

'Have you brought my *Amigal* back in one piece?' Dev laid a proprietorial hand on the rail.

'You can go aboard and satisfy yourself while Risala

tells me her news.' Kheda held out a hand to the girl. 'Or at least the most important details. We don't have long before we have to go and play our parts at Itrac's dinner table.'

The girl jumped deftly over the little ship's stern, ragged grey trousers hanging loose on her skinny frame, her overlarge red tunic patterned with faded black canthira leaves. She brushed tousled black hair out of her vivid blue eyes. 'Where can we talk without some maid bobbing up?' She cocked her head at Kheda, thin face alert.

'In there.' Kheda nodded towards the observatory tower. 'Dev, stay on deck and keep an eye out. Don't let anyone interrupt us.'

'Naturally, my lord.' Dev's face was intent as he climbed aboard the *Amigal*, keen eyes searching the mast, sail and boom.

'No chance of you getting your dinner till he's satisfied I've kept his precious ship safe.' Risala chuckled as she followed Kheda to the round building at the base of the tower. With only the sun's afterglow fading fast on the horizon it was dark inside.

'Wait a moment.' Kheda felt for the lamp set in a niche in the wall and found the spark-maker beside it. A few snaps and the toothed steel stuck a spark from the glaucous firestone to catch in the tandra-tree fluff. Kheda lit the lamp's wick and crushed the flame from the tinder with licked fingers.

'You haven't forgotten how to do things for yourself, then?' Risala was amused. 'With all these slaves and lackeys running around after you again? I take it they're all still as desperate to serve your every whim?'

'Desperate to prove to themselves that things are back to normal. I do wonder if Chazen Saril ever lifted a finger for himself,' said Kheda wryly as he led the way through the open archway to the half-moon hall beyond. 'We of

Daish used to do the little things for ourselves when it was just us, when there was no one else to be impressed by the devotion of our servants keeping us in indolence. My father wouldn't have it any other way.'

He set the shell-shaped lamp on one of the several tables lining the long room. The warm golden glow reflected back from brass discs of all sizes hung on the walls, each engraved with curving lines like the patterns of tiles on the observatory floor and overlaid with a second disc pierced to the likeness of a net of burnished metal.

'The ordinary islanders of Chazen were impressed to see you making shift for yourself when need be on your voyage,' Risala said without preamble. 'They like that idea much better than having you take them away from rebuilding their homes and re-establishing their vegetable gardens and saller plots just to dance attendance on you when you visit their villages.'

Kheda was relieved. 'How many days behind us were you?'

Risala swatted with a bony hand at an importunate insect humming around her head. 'Five or six, depending on the winds and tides.'

'Your arrival didn't cause comment?' Kheda moved to the unshuttered window and looked out towards the north, now hidden in the night. He pulled the fine cotton curtains closed to baffle the winged night-biters. 'I didn't see many boats on the waters as we travelled.'

'There still aren't that many people moving around the domain.' Risala shrugged. 'But most villages were happy enough to see a poet as they turned their thoughts to the new-year stars.' She twisted a heavy silver ring set with an uncut emerald around on one finger. 'And everyone knows poets are mad, so no one really asked why I was sailing alone.'

'What did you say to those who did?' Kheda asked.

'That my brother who had shared the boat with me had drowned when we fled the wild men through a rainy season storm,' Risala explained, 'which generally set people off on their own tales of last year's deaths and disasters.'

'Are they still burdened by the past?' Kheda lifted a hand to one of the larger star circles hanging on the wall by the window. The paths of every constellation were incised on the brass plate, heavenly jewels inlaid on the net, measuring bar precisely aligned across it. 'I read the local omens for the new year wherever we stopped. The portents were positive as far as they went. Were the islanders inclined to take my word on that?'

'I came across quite a few who'd won wagers with their neighbours over signs that said you were right. There were a few muttering about you not being born to the domain.' Risala perched on the table by the lamp, bare feet swinging idly. 'They wondered how you could hope to draw together the threads of the past hereabouts and see how the future would be woven. Don't let that keep you awake at night. They were generally the ones complaining that you weren't travelling in the style befitting a warlord and they mostly got short shrift from everyone else.'

She rubbed a hand through her tousled hair and yawned. 'You wouldn't have made any friends parading around in silks and jewels. Seeing the domain's prosperity reflected in their warlord's finery is all very well in times of peace and plenty, but not when half the islanders have to go naked if they want to launder their one pair of trousers. Most are quite content that you showed your commitment to the domain by driving out the invaders and then by claiming the lordship and marrying Itrac when Chazen Saril died. They know full well they'd have been meat for the bone hawks if the domain had ended up without a warlord and Ritsem, Redigal and Ulla had joined battle over it.'

'If they hadn't been too afraid of the magic loose down here.' Kheda moved closer. 'They're content not knowing exactly how I drove out the invaders?' he asked with low intensity. 'There aren't too many wondering just how I managed to defeat the wild magic?'

'There are enough survivors who were held captive in that final encampment and saw the savage mages fighting among themselves.' Risala glanced involuntarily towards the archway and the darkness outside the hall. 'Everyone I spoke to is happy enough to believe that a battle for overall power broke out among the strongest invaders and their wizards. No one but the three of us need ever know that it was Dev who started the slaughter with his enchanter's illusions.' She managed a crooked smile. 'I found Bukai's song cycle very popular, especially when I gave them the poet's vision of the Winged Snake and the Sea Serpent eating each other's tails. Everyone agreed the moral of that was more than proven: magic twists men's natures and sweeps them to disaster like serpents mad with heat frenzy.'

'Just as long as it doesn't sweep Dev to disaster while he's still masquerading as my body slave.' Kheda pulled a stool out from beneath the table and sat down with a sigh.

'Indeed,' Risala agreed dryly, looking down at him. 'I take it he's still itching to go and see if there are any wizardly secrets to be learned from the last remnants hiding out in the western isles? The anchorage is full of the news that you're going to lead a campaign against them instead of waiting for thirst and disease to make an end of them.'

'It's time to do it, now that I've acquitted my responsibilities in surveying the domain before the new year.

There are portents saying as much wherever I look.' Kheda nodded, fingering a crystal inkwell with a silver lid. 'What were the augurs around the islands saying? Do I need to fear travelling soothsayers muttering dire predictions of disaster under my rule?'

'No,' said Risala slowly. 'Not that they're seeing a bright new future of peace and plenty, either. Most are talking about uncertainty, in the future and in the omens, and are sticking to strictly limited and local forecasts.'

'Which is as good as I can hope for.' Kheda nodded. 'What else did you manage to do for me? We really need some means of getting reliable news from the domain, and fast, without having to rely on Dev snooping with his bowls of scrying spells.'

'I've found us eyes and ears on all the big islands and in nearly all the coastal villages, and most are well placed to hear news from inland and from the lesser isles.' Risala swung her legs, leaning forward with her hands on the edge of the table. 'We've agreed a few basic ciphers and there should be enough boats doing the rounds to carry routine reports soon enough. Though the key men and women need courier doves, for the news we need fast.' She looked at Kheda, black brows rising to be lost in her ragged hair.

'I'll ask Itrac for all she can spare.' Kheda pushed the inkwell away. 'I'm grateful for your help, as always. Now you've done this . . .' He hesitated. 'Don't forget you're free to sail north, to go back home, whenever you like. You were Shek Kul's poet and emissary before you were mine. If you want to return to your own domain to make a new start with the new year, to tell Shek Kul how he helped me find the means to save Chazen—'

'I think the last thing he'll want to hear is that his suspicions were right and Dev did prove to be a spying barbarian mage,' said Risala with a shudder. 'No, I'll wait.

When Shek Kul sent me his token, he ordered me to do all I could to make these southern islands safe from the evils of magic. I don't think we've achieved that yet.' She twisted her heavy silver ring with its uncut emerald.

'Do you think your lord would understand that we had no choice but to use Dev's powers as the lesser evil?' Kheda rubbed a hand over his beard, staring unseeing at the far wall with its array of star circles.

'He gave us the blend of herbs to dull a mage's powers.' Risala laid a hand over Kheda's where it rested on the table.

'Don't you think he intended we should use it to cripple the savage wizards so that we could kill them by less dubious means?' Kheda looked up at the girl.

'Which is what we did,' she pointed out firmly, 'as far as your friends among the neighbouring warlords and their wives are concerned. You needn't favour the rest with any explanation.'

'I don't think Rekha believes that fireside tale of me as the bold hero, risking my own life to sneak in among the invaders to poison their mages' cook pots, however far and wide you've got village versifiers proclaiming it.' There was little humour in Kheda's words. 'I can't see her and Janne letting their curiosity lie any time soon.'

'You still have some of Shek Kul's powder, don't you? Couldn't you show it to Rekha?' wondered Risala.

'And feed some to Dev to show her how it works?' Kheda smiled to take the sting out of his words. 'Then tell how we half-poisoned, half-blackmailed this mage from the north into using his own enchantments to defeat the sorcerous southerners? Then explain how we didn't let him die of the wounds he suffered from their spells but patched him up and gave him the protection of being my body slave?'

'When you put it like that, no, let's not.' Risala grinned

back but Kheda could see the shadow in her eyes.

The same shadow that lies over me.

'I don't imagine Itrac would be any too pleased to learn just what her new lord and master is capable of,' he said wearily. 'And you could be certain Rekha would tell her. I don't think the ladies of Daish want to see me making a success of this marriage they wished on us.'

'You couldn't very well do anything but marry Itrac.' Risala sounded indignant, folding her arms across her meagre chest. 'When Janne Daish refused her further shelter and the domain she was born to spurned her as irrevocably tainted with magic. What were you supposed to do? Let some brute like Ulla Safar catch her, call her rape a marriage and try claiming the Chazen domain for himself on the strength of wedding the last living survivor of the true warlord's family?'

'Since you put it like that, no, not really.' Kheda shared another brief smile with Risala.

'Speaking of Itrac, she's making a fair job of patching up Olkai Chazen's web of informers,' Risala said briskly. 'I found myself nearly tripping over their snares more than once.'

'What are the islanders saying about Itrac?' Kheda asked, diverted.

'Half want to see her waddling around like a broody duck.' Risala was scornful. 'The other half see that she has far too many tasks as it is to add the trials of pregnancy and childbed.'

'Let's hope Olkai's informers pass on that message loud and clear,' said Kheda with feeling. 'And there's no likelihood of Itrac inviting me to give her a baby any time soon – though Dev has his own explanation for that,' he added sardonically. 'Given that no domain would actively seek an alliance with such an insignificant warlord, he says that Saril plainly must have had something else to recommend him to his wives. He reckons Itrac doesn't want to risk taking me to her bed and finding I don't measure up.'

'That sounds like Dev,' said Risala with contempt. 'He should let his hair and beard grow in rather than shaving to look like a man's man or a *zamorin*, even if he is a barbarian. Then some girl might take him to her bed just for the novelty of it and he'd be a lot easier to live with.'

'Or even more intolerable,' countered Kheda.

'Mind you, there's no end of speculation around the cookfires as to where you might find a nicely fertile second wife,' continued Risala, blue eyes bright with mischief. 'Or even a second *and* a third, to sit and nurse their swelling bellies while you and Itrac restore Chazen's fortunes. You fathered enough children for Daish, so there's no doubt as to your virility.'

'That's just what I need.' Exasperated as he was, Kheda couldn't help grinning. 'Some lesser daughter prepared to risk the miasma of magic hereabouts in return for such a rise in her status. Have there been any rumours about who might put themselves forward? Perhaps that explains Rekha's boldness.'

'What are you talking about?' Risala was puzzled.

'Rekha Daish did her best to seduce me earlier.' Kheda shook his head with mingled amusement and disbelief.

'What did you do?' Risala demanded with unexpected sharpness.

'What do you think?' Kheda raised his eyebrows. 'I made my excuses and left as fast as I could, to try to work out what she was cursed well after.'

'Naturally.' Risala cleared her throat.

'Do you think I was tempted?' On an impulse he didn't stop to examine, Kheda reached out and took Risala's hand.

'Were you?' She looked down at him, eyes shadowed beneath her raggedly cut hair.

'A little.' Kheda stood up and brushed the black locks away from her face with gentle fingers. 'That bothers you, doesn't it?'

'Yes.' She didn't blink, sapphire gaze fixed steadily on him.

'I missed you so much while we were on that interminable voyage.' Kheda caressed her pointed chin. 'More than I realised I would. More than anyone else. I missed having someone I can talk to without weighing every word. I missed having someone I could trust not to judge me. I missed having someone who knows the worst of me and is still my friend.'

'I just missed you.' Risala pressed her face against his hand.

'As for Rekha . . .' Kheda shrugged. 'I'm far more tempted right now.'

'Good,' she breathed. 'It's taken you long enough to get around to it.'

He bent and kissed her. Her lips yielded, roughened by wind and sun. He could taste the salt on her. Risala reached a hand up to the back of his neck to kiss him harder, demanding more.

Kheda broke free to catch his breath. 'I'll never hear the last of it from Dev if I get my elegant new clothes all creased.'

'That's something else the islanders like about you.' Risala kissed him again. 'You're not some Redigal Coron, to be ruled by your body slave.' She lifted her other arm up to encircle his neck.

Kheda set his hands on either side of her waist and drew her close, feeling his own passion rising as he kissed her long and urgently. Risala closed her eyes with a sigh of fervent pleasure.

Kheda paused in his kisses, though he still held her tight. 'Itrac doesn't need her life complicated by me taking a concubine.' As he spoke, he slid one hand beneath Risala's loose tunic, feeling her warm skin, her firm ribs.

She lifted his hand to cup one of her modest breasts. 'And I can hardly be your eyes and ears if every eye is on me.'

'Not if people think you're anything more to me than my poet.' Kheda felt her enticing softness harden beneath his palm.

'Because the servants and slaves will soon spread the gossip.' She pressed herself against him, claiming his lips with her own.

'So we really shouldn't be doing this.' He kissed her again. 'Not where anyone might see us.'

'No,' she agreed before kissing the corner of his mouth. 'It's foolishness.'

'I could get used to this kind of folly.' Kheda shivered involuntarily. 'But they would call you an old man's folly.'

'I'm old enough to know my own mind.' Risala's words were muffled by his kisses. 'And you're in your prime, not your dotage.'

'Jevin, is that you? Are we wanted?' Dev's voice, artificially loud, rang out in the night beyond the archway.

Risala released him from her embrace and Kheda reluctantly wrenched himself away. 'And speaking of folly, I have to go and spend a charming evening trying to stop Rekha and Itrac scratching each other's eyes out before we've seen the new-year stars align themselves.' Despite the heavy footfalls on the steps outside, Kheda kissed her one last time, swift and thorough.

'I don't think I have a poem suitable for that.' Risala slid down from the table and tugged her tunic straight. 'So I'll go and get that bath I was talking about.'

Kheda took a deep breath to try to calm his racing blood at the notion of her wet nakedness. 'Are we going to continue this conversation?'

'What conversation?' Dev appeared in the archway.

'When we can find the time, and the privacy.' Risala looked at Kheda, her expression eloquent.

'What's going on?' Dev demanded with scant courtesy. 'Any news I should know about?'

'Not as such.' Kheda walked swiftly past Dev and out into the velvet night where the lamps along the walkways glowed like amber. 'Just an unexpected turn of events.' He smiled into the darkness. 'And a reminder that the unexpected need not always turn out badly.' He took another long, deep breath and strode towards Itrac's distant pavilion, leaving Dev hurrying to match his pace.

Though best not get there too soon or Rekha will certainly see that you welcomed another woman's embraces after you spurned her. This evening's going to be fraught enough without adding that complication.

But what will tomorrow bring, if you and Risala can find somewhere away from the ever-present eyes?

CHAPTER FIVE

'Well, we won't be overheard, but I wouldn't call this private, Kheda.' Risala looked around the deck of the *Amigal* and then up at the *Gossamer Shark* towering above the little ship. Dev looked down on them both, stony-faced, from the rail above. 'What made you change your mind about continuing what we began in the observatory?' she asked bluntly.

'I was hardly in the mood for dalliance after an evening sitting between Rekha and Itrac,' Kheda said ruefully. 'And besides, as I saw all the shipmasters watching our every move, weighing our every word . . .' He sighed. 'I really cannot complicate Itrac's life by being seen to take another woman. And you were right: you can hardly be my chief spy with everyone knowing you're my lover.'

'And if they don't know?' Risala looked steadily at him. 'What then?'

Kheda hesitated.

'What then?' the girl asked again. 'Come on, Kheda, there are no secrets between us. I want to know where I stand. I've been waiting for eight days. You didn't even come to tell me you were launching this expedition the very next morning. I had to hear it from Dev.' Her tone was reasonable but firm.

'There was a sign when we read the stars: silverlight shimmering all around the Ruby and the Spear,' Kheda began slowly, 'which were opposite the arc of foes, which is where the new-year stars aligned.'

'I didn't ask why you decided to launch this expedition so quickly,' Risala began. 'Never mind.' She turned away from Kheda, reaching a hand out towards the little ship's mast.

'And there's this,' Kheda said abruptly. As Risala turned back, he dug into a pouch on his belt and pulled out a string of tiny shark's teeth pierced and threaded on a narrow leather thong. 'When I was taking the omens at the pearl reefs, they caught a shark for me. There was an infant shark inside it. It nearly bit me as I read the entrails.' He tossed the shark's teeth necklace over and Risala caught it reflexively.

'An infant shark alive inside its mother? I've never heard of such a thing.' Risala looked wide-eyed at the talisman for a long, tense moment. 'The last wild wizard, the one that we had to hunt down, he wore a necklace of shark's teeth. Is that what you're thinking of? What do you think such a sign could mean?'

'I don't know what I'm thinking,' Kheda said rather wearily. 'But yes, I remembered that savage wizard.'

The warmth of his blood on my skin when I caught him and cut his throat from ear to ear. The weight of him in my arms and the stench of his death. Dev tells me to souse such memories in liquor. Is that why the barbarians drink so much, to make killing easier? Don't they see how that devalues their deeds?

'After I left Itrac and Rekha, I spent most of that night seeing if Chazen's forefathers recorded any lore on sharks that might explain such a portent.' Kheda shook his head. 'I found nothing to make sense of it. But after what you said about not having fulfilled Shek Kul's commission, it set me thinking how we need to be free of all these invaders and all their mysteries.' He looked at her. 'That applies to you and me as much as to the Chazen domain. We can't look to our future until we're free of the past.'

Risala made a noncommittal noise. 'Then let's get rid of these last savages as soon as we can. What exactly do you want me to do?'

Kheda looked out across the broad blue channel where the fleet of boats was riding a substantial swell. 'We know they are still infesting the Snake Bird Islands.' He gestured towards green tufts of islands barely visible on the horizon. 'And I very much doubt any would manage to escape the *Gossamer Shark*'s patrols, even if they didn't simply drown in these waters. All the same, I want to be certain there is still no sign of any of the vermin lurking in Balaia or Dalao.' He turned to look at a scatter of long, low islands on the far side of a vast reach of shallows where sea grasses grew thick, placid brown and grey turtles grazing on them. 'Can you sail around the villages and make doubly sure for me?'

Because I can't spare any swordsmen for such a duty. Because even if I can't take you to my bed, I'm torn between wanting you close to me but wanting to keep you out of danger.

Risala looked around the small fleet idling on the waters. 'I take it there'll be someone keeping station hereabouts, for me to report to and who will send you a courier?'

Kheda nodded. 'The *Yellow Serpent* has earned that privilege.'

'Then let's be about it.' Risala looked up at Dev's impatient face and smiled sunnily before offering the string of tiny shark's teeth back to Kheda.

He waved it away. 'No, you keep it. The one piece of shark lore everyone agrees on is that their teeth are a talisman against drowning or their attack. I want you kept as safe as possible.' He looked at her and hoped she could see the longing in his eyes.

'You keep yourself safe, too,' she said huskily before lifting her fingers to whistle shrilly to the trireme. 'Now go on and do what you have to do.' She turned her back on him and went to unlash the little ship's tiller, to guide the *Amigal* close to the looming trireme's stern.

Kheda watched the dangling rope ladder carefully and caught it deftly. He climbed, resolutely not looking behind him.

There should be no secrets between us. Every time I say there aren't, I wait for the thunderclap or some other sign in a clear sky to set everyone wondering who the liar is and what falsehood has been spoken.

Though I haven't lied. I just haven't told you all I might. When we have time to ourselves, there's more I will tell you. Will you be able to explain it to me? In all Rekha's endless chatter about the Daish domain, how they are thriving, all the children and Sirket most of all, as she gave me message after message from Janne, she made no mention at all of Sain, beyond assuring us in passing that Daish's erstwhile third wife is prospering in her trades for the domain.

Did Sain truly send no message? Am I dead to her? Or is she so full of hate or sorrow that there was no expressing it? How well did I serve her, in offering her Daish wealth and status in return for alliance with her brother's domain of Toc, with its sheltered sea lanes to the eastern reaches, beyond Ulla Safar's fat and grasping hand?

None of the women who've shared my bed seem to relish the memory or to have profited by it. Itrac Chazen doesn't even want to take the chance. Hadn't I better wait for some more hopeful portent before embarking on any new liaison?

Especially with Risala. I never felt such longing for a woman before, such fear that I might lose such a jewel.

'Are we ready to go, my lord?' Dev reached out a hand and helped Kheda over the *Gossamer Shark*'s stern rail.

'We are.' Kheda nodded to the shipmaster, resolutely ignoring the dull ache of desire for Risala that perversely was slower to fade every time he thought of her. 'Let's make for the Snake Bird Islands, Master Mezai.'

'As you wish, my lord.' The mariner waved a signal to the rowing master on the oar deck below and folded muscular arms across his sleeveless mantle, a short garment of pale blue patterned with waving sea grasses. The rowers bent over their oars and the sail crew hurried to spread the great expanse of billowing canvas hanging from the square-rigged mast to take advantage of the wind at their stern. Even with this bonus, the rowers still toiled long and hard to cross the dark-blue waters where the shallows fell away into mysterious darkness. His record of these reaches tucked in his lizardskin belt, Shipmaster Mezai stood close to his helmsman, lending his strength to the steering oars as the fierce current sought to drag the heavy vessel off course. Kheda watched astern as the little fleet slewed across the waters, fighting the insistent tug of the seas that would so easily sweep them out to battle the dangers of the open ocean.

We have different battles to fight and I have calculated our voyage carefully to arrive on this day of such ill omen for our enemies. The Greater Moon is dark and rides unseen in the arc of the heavens where our foes might look for signs in their favour, while the Lesser Moon has moved to the arc of alliance where the Mirror Bird spreads its wings in defiance of magic, to reflect the future from the heavens to the earth beneath.

He felt the solid weight of one of Chazen Saril's star circles in a pocket of his trousers. It was one of the smallest ones, barely the size of his palm, as well as one of the oldest, the engraving on the brass plates worn faint and the metal dull with use.

A good choice for a talisman as I seek to protect this domain, surely? This isn't a good time for delay, though. A few days and we'll see one of those curious cascades around the compass that realigns the heavens completely.

'Time to get your armour on, my lord.' Dev's impatient voice brought him promptly back to the prospect of a fight.

If I can't enjoy the release I long to share with Risala, I can at least work out some of my frustrations with a sword.

By the time Kheda had donned his padded under-tunic and gleaming hauberk, this time remembering his hated plated leggings, the *Gossamer Shark* was entering the placid turquoise waters between a small reef and an even smaller island. Two fast triremes followed her, with the three additional heavy vessels that made up this armoured flotilla bringing up the rear. A white beach lay like a crescent moon against a thin strip of meagre forest sheltered by the central rise of the island. The long grassy hillock reached from one end to the other, falling away on the far side to a ragged shoreline of broken rocks offering no haven for any vessel.

'There was only the one village here?' Kheda surveyed the wretched remnants, now silent and empty among the nut palms and berry bushes. The little settlement still showed all the devastation the invaders had wrought. All but the largest huts had been torn apart by unnatural winds summoned to some savage mage's service. Unquenchable fire called out of the empty air had burned the saller granary to ash, now washed by the rains into a black stain between the charred stilts that had held the precious store aloft. Paradoxically among all this destruction, the invaders had built a crude stockade from rough-hewn forest wood. One side of this had been broken down where Daish or Redigal swordsmen had rescued those hapless Chazen islanders who had been thrown inside. The half-hearted attempt at a ditch dug across the open beach was already filling with wind-blown sand and the sharpened stakes that had been cut to give it teeth were tossed haphazardly at the bottom.

By the time the rains come again, I don't want to see any

such signs of ruined lives and hopes left standing to blight our future. Let that be a test of my leadership, that I did right in taking on this troubled domain. That I did right in bringing barbarian magic to deprive those savages of the magic they relied on, so that we could finally put them to the sword.

'Do we know for certain there are still savages hiding out here?' Dev demanded, leaning over the side rail to peer intently into the tangle of vegetation.

'We hear them in the night, if we anchor off the reef.' Mezai nodded dourly. 'Shouting their gibberish. There are screams, sometimes.'

'You're sure there are no Chazen islanders left here?' Kheda demanded.

'Sure as we can be.' A frown creased Mezai's broad face as he rubbed a hand over his sweating head. Some ancestor from the far western reaches had bequeathed him sparse, tight curls that dotted his head like peppercorns.

'Let's make quite certain, shall we?' Dev grinned viciously at the *Gossamer Shark*'s fighting force now lining the side rails. A full complement for the heavy trireme, drawn from the Beyau's hopeful warriors, was and eagerly seeking out any sign of their elusive foe. The archers in particular were keen to find a target for their newly forged battle arrows. 'I don't imagine they'll last long against Aldabreshin steel with their fire-hardened pointy sticks,' the mage continued confidently.

Just how do you expect to learn anything from these savages, even supposing we can capture one alive for you to interrogate? Just how does a wizard go about seeking such answers, anyway? Some torment of sorcery? How do you expect to do that undetected?

Kheda glanced at the barbarian before turning to acknowledge the swordsmen's commander as he approached the stern platform. 'Are all your men ready, Arao?'

'They are,' the tall warrior confirmed, his face the colour of old bronze in the bright sun. His armour was mismatched and well worn and he moved in it with the ease of long familiarity. His swords were some of the finest Kheda had ever seen.

'Remind them that these savages might still be rousing themselves with that root pulp they chew,' Kheda said tersely. 'If they are, they'll fight through pain that would ordinarily drop the bravest Archipelagan.'

'I remember.' The warrior cracked the knuckles on his dark-brown hands. 'I told the lads.'

Kheda saw the swordsmen looking his way and favoured them with a confident, approving smile. He looked for Ridu but couldn't pick the youth out of the armoured mass.

'Do we know if there's water here year round?' Arao looked to Mezai. 'If so, we can look for them at the springs.'

'There'll still be water here for at least another turn of the Greater Moon,' Mezai confirmed.

They drew closer to the shore and a shiver of anticipation among the *Gossamer Shark*'s swordsmen sent a rattle of chain mail the length of the boat.

'We're not going to learn anything paddling around out here,' said Dev abruptly. 'Let's get ashore and start turning over rocks to see what crawls out.'

'I'd say they're hiding in those scrubby trees.' Arao peered at the meagre forest running around the margin of the little island.

'Then let's reclaim this land for Chazen.' Kheda looked from Arao to Mezai. 'Signal the *Dancing Snake*, the *Shearsword* and the *Brittle Crab* to land their forces with us. I want the *Green Turtle* and the *Lilla Bat* to circle around to the far side and come in as close as the coral allows. We'll beat our way across the island, dig out any burrows and kill whoever we find. They can fill anyone running out of the trees with arrows, and any of them trying to swim for it on a nut log or some such. They may have made rafts.'

Arao nodded. 'We don't want the vermin on the other islands knowing we're here to put paid to their wickedness any sooner than need be.'

'My lord.' Mezai blew lustily on his curled signal horn. The light *Green Turtle* and the heavy trireme the *Lilla Bat* immediately wheeled about, each ship showing a curl of white foam like bared teeth along its brass-sheathed ram.

There was absolutely no movement among the ruined dwellings as all four remaining triremes deftly turned stern-on to ground on the shelving white sand. Stern ladders were thrown down from the *Dancing Snake* and the *Shearsword* and the warriors slid into the shallow water, swords drawn and fearsome challenge in their shouts. They raced ashore, the twin columns from the two heavy triremes spreading out to line the beach with steel, sunlight bright on their armour. Each boat's swordsmen looked to their captain. The captains shared a nod and all began a slow advance up the white sand. They reached the village unchallenged and then stopped.

As the *Gossamer Shark*'s warriors disembarked to wait in reserve on the water line, Kheda saw a few men prod with their swords at ragged panels of woven palm ripped from huts. Others gathered together in uncertain knots, glancing at their captains for guidance.

Every man as tense as a jungle matia out to kill a cornered snake, confident in its sharp white teeth and thick brindled fur but with no wish to risk a bite all the same. And if you had a matia's striped tail, you'd be lashing it, wizard.

'There's no one to fight,' said Dev with disgust.

'There's something amiss.' Kheda moved to the ladder, his feet feeling sweaty, cramped and clumsy in his armoured leggings. 'I'm going ashore. Tell them to shoot anything that looks like a threat.' Kheda gestured to the archers now clustered along the *Brittle Crab*'s decks and on the fast trireme's stern platform, searching the threadbare cover of the trees and bushes in vain for any target.

'My lord.' Mezai didn't dare openly disapprove of Kheda's decision but his feelings were obvious.

'There doesn't seem to be any immediate danger.' Dev was peering intently at the scene on shore.

As he spoke, one of the *Gossamer Shark*'s sword captains moved up the beach to a heap of debris and levered a fallen palm panel aside. He recoiled sharply and swords rose on either side of him in a snarl of bright steel.

'Let's see what's what, my lord.' Dev's voice was tight with frustration.

Kheda nodded, seeing faces turning towards the poised ships, a few of the swordsmen pushing up the visor plates of their helmets, visibly bemused. 'Whatever it is looks to be more of a puzzle than a threat.'

Dev was already sliding down the heavy trireme's stern ladder with alacrity. Kheda hurried after him, the crystal water of the shallows dragging at his thighs. An unmistakable, loathsome scent tainted the lazy breeze as they reached the shore. Sickly sweetness with an underlying rankness twisted Kheda's stomach and he saw dark smears in the furrowed sand half-concealed by the trampling feet of the swordsmen.

So it's not such a hardship after all to have some leather between your feet and whatever slaughter went on here.

The armoured men parted to let the warlord and his supposed slave pass, seriousness on every face, coloured by confusion.

'What have you found?' Kheda demanded of the battle captains.

'Dead meat,' said the senior man from the *Dancing Snake* helplessly.

Kheda frowned. 'Let me see.'

'And keep a watch while we do,' snapped Dev, shooting sharp glances in all directions.

The other captains shouted orders, sending their men to line the forest edge and bar any attack from the paltry trees. The *Dancing Snake*'s man led Kheda to the pile of rotting palm panels and the scent of decay strengthened.

'There's a body?' Kheda looked from the *Dancing Snake*'s sword captain to the *Gossamer Shark*'s Arao, demanding an explanation. 'Ours or theirs?'

'Hard to say.' Arao hooked the corner of the topmost panel with his sword and hauled it aside.

Blue-backed flies buzzed with displeasure, scattering to circle around the men's heads before returning to their enticing discovery. It wasn't a body – at least, not all of one. There was just a foot, not even with the stump of its ankle attached. Half-buried in the dark, stained sand beside it was most of an arm, raggedly severed half-way between shoulder and elbow.

Kheda sank to his knees to study the remains more closely, trying not to breathe in the putrid smell. In death the skin was a greyish muddy colour, bruised and swollen. In life, it could have been any of the vibrant brown hues that characterised the Chazen people.

Or the dark skin that the invaders hide beneath their paint and mud.

'I've seen shark kills washed up in pieces like that,' Arao said dubiously.

'I've heard tell of fishermen losing feet to beaked turtles. Could it have just washed up here?' The *Dancing Snake*'s man looked at Kheda with more hope than conviction.

'This hasn't been in the water,' Kheda said firmly.

'How long's it been here?' asked Dev.

'A couple of days.' Kheda noted the tiny yellowish maggots clustered along the raw surface of the severed foot, fighting blindly to squirm beneath the skin and gorge on the bounty beneath.

Flies aren't fussy feeders. Pearl oysters, human flesh, it's all the same to them.

Arao swallowed hard and looked down the beach. 'We'd better find out what else is here.'

'Yes,' said Dev absently. He was staring across the beach towards the trees, his eyes distant.

You're fidgeting as if you've got maggots under your toenails. And from the look in your eyes, if I didn't know better, I'd think you'd been pickling your wits with your cursed barbarian liquor.

'Dev, come with me,' Kheda said sharply.

'What?' Dev looked at the warlord, slow to collect himself.

'Arao, I want every piece of wreckage or driftwood turned over. I want every stain on this beach dug up. I want every one of those torn apart and anything inside laid bare!' Kheda was already walking across the sand, pointing this way and that at the derelict huts. Arao reinforced his orders with terse shouts and the warlord turned to Dev as the barbarian caught him up. 'What's the matter with you?'

'Nothing,' snapped the wizard.

Almost immediately, shouts came from several directions. A man prodding a stain in the sand had found something, as had a group scattering a heap of tide-washed detritus with their swords. One held up a second severed foot on the point of his blade.

'Do you think we've got a pair?' Dev chuckled, dark eyes shining oddly.

Kheda caught a look of contempt from Arao as the other swordsman overheard.

I know just what you're thinking: he's still an ignorant, star-crossed barbarian, even if he does wield Aldabreshin steel in the service of your warlord.

'What's over there?' Kheda looked towards two men investigating the space beneath the raised platform of the ruined saller granary. Whatever they had found was enough to drop one to his knees, vomiting noisily.

'Let's see.' Dev hurried towards them. Scowling, Arao took up the body slave's station at the warlord's side.

Kheda had to stop and take a determined swallow to settle his own stomach when he saw that two *Shearsword* men had dragged the head and shoulders of a man out from beneath the splintered wood. The corpse still had both his arms but that was all. Shattered ribs were ground into a gory mess of torn flesh along with the broken remnants of his shoulder blades. All that remained below that was a short tail of vertebrae clotted with blood and sinew.

'At least he's not one of ours, one of Chazen,' the swordsman who'd managed to retain his breakfast said through clenched teeth.

The dead man was unmistakably an invader. His coarse, wiry hair was caked in coloured mud with small bones and black feathers tipped with scarlet woven into it. Handprints in a thick white paint made a pattern of sorts down each arm.

'Their leaders decorate themselves like this.' Kheda used his own sword point to turn one of the broken corpse's hands. The fingers were torn and scored, vicious wooden splinters sticking out of the dead flesh. 'But no wizard, I would say.' He risked a brief questioning glance at Dev.

The barbarian shook his head, bending to peer into the empty gloom beneath the buckled and splintered floorboards of the granary. 'I'm more interested in what killed him. That's cursed drastic damage to do with stone knives and wooden clubs.'

'I can't see anything like a clean cut.' Kheda stood up and considered the torn margins of the severed chest. 'No Archipelagan blade did this.'

'There's one of those stone knives over there, my lord,' the *Shearsword* man with the stronger stomach volunteered.

Kheda looked where the sharp-eyed warrior was pointing and saw dull black obsidian in the white sand. There was no sign of blood or tissue on the invader's blade. 'Why would he throw his weapons away?'

'Surrendering?' Dev was still studying the partial corpse, baffled. 'And then what? There are no swords anywhere. Are we supposing whoever caught the poor bastard held him down and sawed him in half with a sharp bit of broken rock?'

That thought set the hapless *Shearsword* man who'd made the gruesome find spewing hopelessly again.

'Go back to your ship.' Kheda clapped the warrior on one mail-clad shoulder. 'Get some clean air in your lungs and a little fresh water in your belly. Nothing else, mind, not for a while. You, go with him.' He nodded to the other swordsman. 'You've acquitted yourselves well enough for today.'

'Yes, my lord,' the unafflicted warrior said gratefully, bowing low before shepherding his companion down towards the sea.

'Arao, go and see what your men are turning up.' As the warrior walked slowly away, after a last dubious look at Dev, Kheda took a few steps to distance himself from the pungent remnants of the dead savage. He turned to Dev, his voice low and urgent. 'You're sure he wasn't one of their wizards?'

'What?' Dev looked vacantly at Kheda for a moment.

'No.' The barbarian shook off his abstraction and laughed briefly. 'He wouldn't have been hiding under a granary floor if he had been.' The barbarian wizard's face hardened abruptly. 'Though something very odd has gone on here.'

Before Kheda could ask what he meant, one of the *Dancing Snake*'s sword captains hailed them from over by the remnants of the invaders' stockade. Kheda led the way past reluctant swordsmen uncovering more mangled remnants of flesh and bone.

'You were right to say this is a puzzle, but I still don't think we've enough bits to make more than a couple of people,' remarked Dev.

Kheda ignored the barbarian as he looked inside the crude wooden circle, one side of it almost completely broken down, the timbers half-buried in the sand.

'Do you want a head count?' the *Dancing Snake*'s warrior offered reluctantly.

'Add up the feet and divide by two?' Dev suggested with the hint of a grin.

The inside of the stockade was a charnel house. Blood splashed up the inner faces of the crudely split logs, dried black by the hot sun. Black flies clustered on broken limbs and half-crushed heads scattered piecemeal across the torn and sodden earth. Fat, pale maggots writhed where their feasting had been disturbed, squirming in noxious slime pooled in shaded hollows. The stench in the enclosed space was revolting and Kheda retreated hurriedly.

'Shipmaster Mezai heard screams in the night.' He turned his back on the carnage. 'They must have been fighting among themselves.'

'There can't be much food on an island like this.' Dev stared past Kheda at a lifeless head, as if he might read some answer in the clouded, oozing eyes rimmed with greedy flies. 'Do you suppose they ended up eating each other?'

Kheda saw one of the warriors turn away, face anguished.

You lost someone, family or friend, to the invaders. This reminder of their suffering must be excruciating.

He shot the barbarian a quelling look. 'They may have grievously mistreated the captives they took but there was never any sign of such an obscenity.'

'They'd have kept prisoners fed and watered if they were going to end up on a spit, even fattened them up, maybe,' Dev persisted thoughtfully, heedless of Kheda's glare. 'Besides, they used to take the elders, all scrawny and tough—'

'Enough!' Kheda silenced Dev with a hard slap on the side of his helm with his mailed gauntlet. He didn't allow anyone, swordsman or barbarian, time to speak before giving new orders with cold determination. 'Arao, search this isle from end to end and side to side. If there's anything larger than a palm rat in those trees, I want to see it running scared. If we catch a single living savage, we will find some way of getting answers out of him. In the meantime, bring some sail crew ashore to gather up this carrion. Throw it all in this stockade and pile every other bit of wood on top. I want this vileness burned to ashes!'

He had barely finished speaking before Arao's lead had the sword captains summoning their men with curt commands, dividing the warriors into troops. As the swordsmen began disappearing into the scrubby forest, swords raised, tense and alert, sail crews from the triremes disembarked and set about the gruesome task of cleansing the beach.

'Come on, let's see what's what.' Dev headed for the fringe of nut palms, his bald, leathery face uncharacteristically eager.

'Where do you think you're going?' snapped Kheda.

The barbarian turned, dark eyes momentarily confused. 'You want me to scry out these savages here in the open?'

'I don't want you doing anything just at present.' Before Kheda could continue, a shout rang through the trees. Archers aboard the *Brittle Crab* swung their bows up ready, barbed broad-headed arrows nocked.

'*Shearsword! Shearsword!*' Two swordsmen supporting a third emerged from the trees, yelling to identify their trireme.

'Dev, get my physic chest.' Kheda ran across the soft sand, feet slipping and clumsy in his leggings. 'What's happened?'

The two men lowered their companion gently to sit on the ground. The injured man was biting his lip hard enough to draw blood. Kheda saw that something had driven clean through his foot, leather sandal and all, to leave a dark, bloody hole.

'Deadfall, in the trees,' the man gasped. 'Saw that and the trip stick. Didn't see the stake-pit under the leaves, though.'

'Naturally,' Kheda said wryly.

'Just where you'd step to avoid the trip for the deadfall,' spat one of his companions, rearranging the swords shoved askew in his belt by his exertions.

'Lie flat so that the wound's higher than your heart.' Kheda drew his dagger and slit the lattice of laces tying the thick deerhide around the swordsman's foot. 'What's your name?'

'Pai, my lord.' Lying back, he gritted his teeth as Kheda carefully peeled back the bloodstained leather.

'You've won yourself light duties for a good few days with this.' Kheda bent to examine the wound more closely before looking up and raising his voice. 'Dev! Where's my physic chest? One of you light me a fire and get some water boiling.'

One of Pai's companions glanced towards the stockade where a small fire was now taking hold.

'No,' said Kheda sharply. 'Don't get an ember from there, light a fresh fire. Let's not risk ill luck in the wound. We'll soak the foot in an infusion of blueshadow leaves and then pack the wound with chamaz pulp. It has to heal from the inside first or it'll fester.' He felt carefully for the bones of the foot. 'You've not done too much damage, surprisingly enough.'

'Thank you, my lord,' stammered Pai, sweat beading his ashen face.

Saving his foot won't do him much good if he dies from the shock of it all. Best give him a few hemp leaves to chew to take the edge off that.

Kheda looked round for Dev and saw the barbarian hurrying back across the sands as more commotion erupted from the forest further down the beach.

'*Gossamer Shark! Gossamer Shark!*' Five men were carrying another out from the shadow of the trees, one to each limb and the fifth supporting his head.

'Keep this held up.' Kheda handed Pai's foot to one of the men who had carried him out of the forest and hurried to see what had befallen the new casualty.

'Spear trap, my lord,' gasped the swordsman supporting the man's head.

'Four stakes to it,' added one grasping the casualty around a thigh. 'At belly height.'

'Knocked him clean off his feet,' one of the two supporting the wounded man's shoulders explained.

'Lay him down.' Kheda pushed back the man's chain veil to uncover his face and saw that his skin was grey and clammy. The heartbeat in his neck was rapid and feathery under the warlord's fingertips. 'What's his name?'

'Naeir,' said the other one supporting his shoulders. 'It was a sapling, bent back sideways, sharpened stakes on the end. We never saw it, not till it hit Naeir,' he babbled frantically.

'Did he hit his head as he fell?' Kneeling, Kheda felt the unconscious man's abdomen but the chain mail, dirty with fragments of wood and leaves, frustrated his searching hands.

I can't tell how badly he's hurt without getting his armour off. But getting it off could make things worse, if he's bleeding inside. Liver or spleen could be ruptured, even his stomach. Then there'll be no saving him.

Dev appeared and set the warlord's physic chest down beside him. 'How old was the trap?' he asked.

The men looked at him, uncomprehending.

'How old was the trap?' Dev repeated himself with scant patience. 'Was the wood still green, with leaves on the twigs? Did some sly bastard set it this morning to catch you lot if you came looking for him? Or was it dried out from being rigged there half a season ago?'

'That's a good question.' Kheda looked up at Dev.

As the barbarian opened his mouth to say something more, a sudden storm of shouts and screams swept across the beach. Startled, Kheda was rising to his feet when a brutal buffet of sand-laden air and a deafening roar knocked him to his knees again. Before he could recover his footing or clear his stinging eyes, someone grabbed him by the arm and dragged him, stumbling, across the sands into the dubious shelter of the trap-laden forest. They dropped behind a tangle of sard-berry bushes choked with striol vines.

Kheda spat sand and fragments of things he didn't want to think about out of his mouth. 'What—'

'Look!' It had been Dev who had dragged him off the beach. Now the barbarian was crawling and twisting through the bottoms of the bushes, his chain mail scorning the striol thorns.

Kheda wriggled after him on elbows and knees, the metal plates in his leggings digging into the backs of his legs. He swallowed hard. 'What is that?'

Dev looked at him as if he couldn't believe the question. 'It's a dragon, Kheda. You've heard of them, I take it, even down in these godforsaken islands?'

The warlord gaped at the wizard. 'What's it doing here?'

'Whatever it chooses,' Dev answered with strangled sarcasm.

Yes, you asked for that, didn't you?

Kheda lay as flat as he could beneath the inadequate cover of the stunted bushes and gazed at the beach with utter incredulity.

This can't be real. This can't be happening.

No? Then what's that? A mist-dream conjured by some barbarian smoke addling everyone's wits?

Stars above, it's as big as the Gossamer Shark*!*

The dragon, wherever it had come from, had landed on the widest part of the beach, where the sea swells left the sand untouched. It stood, four massive clawed feet firmly planted and its thick, muscular tail curling around as it folded its awesome wings. A crest of thick scales running down its spine and tail glowed like living flame in the bright sun, culminating in a heavy ridged spike at the tip of its tail. The overlapping scales along its back and haunches were dark red as the bloody heart of a recalcitrant fire – and a formidable defence, that much was obvious. As the colour of its hide lightened down its flanks to an orange-tinted gold, the scales gradually grew smaller. As the creature shifted its stance, the flexible folds of skin between limbs and body stretched and bunched, pale as sunrise in the angle of its hind leg and belly.

It turned its enormous head to look at the triremes now fleeing the beach and lashed its tail, the heavy spike gouging a deep furrow in the sand. All four vessels were rowing frantically for open water, oar blades chopping the sea into a frenzy of foam. The lighter *Brittle Crab* was already half a length ahead. The dragon dropped its snout towards the water, fine forked tongue flickering out, never quite touching the rising and retreating surf. Scales framed its head with a lethal ruff of spines that would baffle any opponent trying to seize it by the neck. Heavy crimson scales armoured its broad, blunt-nosed muzzle, softening to lighter colours in the folds beneath its long jaw. That softer skin didn't extend far below its head, however. The underside of the long, flexible neck was armoured with more elongated scarlet scales.

After a few moments, it turned away from the water and surveyed the beach, slowly and deliberately. Its eyes glittered like liquid rubies, lit from within by a single spark of feral intelligence. It glanced over at the ruined stockade now blazing fiercely. The dragon drew its coppery lips back in a snarl that revealed a single row of long, pointed, pure white teeth. It opened its mouth and hissed; a low, menacing noise, as its red tongue flickered in and out.

Abruptly, it sprang, the colossal power in its hind legs sending it across the beach with barely any need to spread its huge wings. It landed on top of the stockade, crushing the pyre beneath its great feet. Lashing head and tail from side to side, it scattered the fire, snapping at the gouts of flame with a growl deep in its throat. The blaze died instantly to leave black ash and cold cinders. The dragon snuffled at them, sending a flurry of sooty dust into the air.

Movement caught Kheda's eye. Everyone had fled the beach in utter panic. Two swordsmen burdened with the unconscious Naeir had only managed to reach a knot of young nut palms standing some distance from the sparse margin of the forest. With the dragon apparently occupied, its back towards them, they seized their chance to try for better concealment, Naeir carried awkwardly between them.

The dragon's head whipped around. It sprang a second time, unfolding the outermost crease of its wings to glide through the air. It landed, sending a tremor through the sand like the aftershock of a distant earthquake. With a bellow like the roaring fury of a forest fire, it swept the nut palms aside with a single sweep of a forelimb. The tree trunks landed half a ship's length across the beach, snapped into splintered pieces.

The swordsmen dropped Naeir and fell to the sandy ground, curling up in a hopeless attempt to save themselves. The dragon crouched, belly to the sand, cocking its head. The fire in its eyes brightened as it reached out one forefoot, a single claw adroitly extended. Ignoring the other two for the moment, it prodded the unconscious Naeir. Getting no response, it bent its massive head closer while running that single vicious claw down the length of the man's hauberk.

The grating noise sent a shiver of icy dread down Kheda's spine. He watched, frozen with horror, as the beast drew back its head to consider the fallen warrior, long neck arcing as it looked at this mystery first from one side and then the other.

It doesn't know what to make of the armour. It's like that young matia you saw when you were out hunting with Sirket. It was doing well enough with the little lizards but it hadn't a clue what to do when its mother brought back that jungle scurrier. Even when she'd bitten between the shiny orange and black segments to break its back, the youngling hadn't wanted to risk its pincers as it writhed in its death throes.

The dragon bent its head to Naeir's feet, mouth agape.

Then it changed its mind, twisting its maw as if to bite his head. At the last moment, it stopped, long tongue flickering out to run delicately along the brow band of the senseless swordsman's helm.

That was too much for one of the other cowering warriors. He scrambled to his feet and ran for the forest, prompting a stifled outcry of encouragement from the swordsmen hidden among the trees and brush. This incautious outburst died on a note of despairing horror as the dragon rose and reached out one massive forefoot. The swordsman disappeared beneath it, crushed into oblivion in the sand. The dragon hauled his body back and bent to sniff at it. The ruff of scales around its head flared and its eyes burned hot scarlet as it opened its mouth to hiss on a rising note.

Abandoning the contemplative approach, it seized the armoured corpse between its teeth, head shaking from side to side. The swordsman's arms and legs flopped loose and rattled against the creature's scaly jaws. It spat him out with a growl of irritation and smashed its great foot down on him once again. After a moment, it repeated the blow and then stamped down a fourth time before bending to lick delicately at the oozing blood now obscuring the steel of the dead warrior's hauberk. Lifting its head, it studied the gory mess for a moment, then carefully extended one claw and drove it through the dead man's neck, pinning the body to the ground. Bending down, it nipped his legs between its vicious teeth with surprising precision, metallic lips drawn back. With a single tug, it ripped the broken torso out of the chain mail, the head left pinned, and devoured it in a single bite. Now that it had the trick of it, dispatching and consuming the other two men was the work of a few moments for the beast.

Bear witness, that's one of your duties as warlord. Find

some way to save the rest of your men, that's another. What are you going to do?

Kheda wracked his brain helplessly as the dragon finished its appetiser and looked towards the island's scrub and meagre trees, interest brightening its eyes. It began slowly pacing the length of the beach, long tongue still tasting the air, teeth and lips gruesomely bloodstained. Warlord and wizard froze, hugging the ground, as the beast drew level with them, barely breathing until it had passed, watching its great claws tearing up the indistinct footprints, long tail dragging a line in the sand behind it.

'I reckon we know what happened to those wild men now.' Dev's voice was improbably distant.

'How do we stop it happening to us?' whispered Kheda savagely.

'Can you feel the power that thing carries with it?' Dev breathed, husky now, almost lustful.

'What?' Kheda propped himself on one elbow and stared at the wizard.

'The magic.' Dev looked at him unseeing, his eyes dark and wandering.

As if he'd been drinking deep of his barbarian liquor and filling his head with their tainted smokes for good measure.

'What are you talking about?' Anger seizing him, Kheda shoved at the mage, sending him rolling sideways, unresisting. 'And keep your voice down.' He twisted to look hastily in all directions, though there was no one to be seen among the glossy yellowy-green of the leaves.

That doesn't mean there's no one else hidden within earshot.

Is this where all your connivances with magic are to be finally unmasked?

Will there be anyone left alive to carry the tale to Itrac or anyone else?

Dev rolled back on to his belly, propping himself up on his elbows and hanging his head, breathing deeply like a man who'd just slaked his passions. 'The magic, Kheda.' His voice was a fervent whisper. 'A dragon is a magical creature; it's in its very nature. No one knows how or why. I've heard tell of their aura, of the wild magic that hangs all around them, but nothing I've ever read describes just how potent it is.' He chuckled, a low, licentious sound.

'What is it doing here?' Kheda demanded.

'There have been mages in Hadrumal who could summon dragons.' Dev's face sharpened unpleasantly. 'Precious few of them and they always kept the mystery mighty close. But even a fool can stumble on a wise man's secret. Maybe these wild men have managed to find themselves a wizard again.'

'A wizard who called this monster here?' Kheda stared at Dev, aghast.

'Maybe,' the barbarian mage said slowly. 'And maybe it got out of hand and ate him along with the rest of his cronies. I don't see it taking much heed of anyone, do you? Or maybe some bright spark on this scrap of an island has finally had his stones drop far enough for him to feel the magic in his blood.' Dev scrambled on to his knees, helmet knocking against the twigs of the sard-berry bush, dislodging fruit to stain the ground around him. 'And when he stuck his head above the parapet, there's some bigger, badder wizard been hiding himself who decided to cut him down to size. Maybe he has the trick of this and sent his new pet out to rid himself of a rival. Or just to fill its belly with anyone who won't get in line behind him.'

As the wizard talked, rapid words stumbling over each other, he was digging a hollow in the dry, sandy earth with the dagger from his belt, scooping out the loose soil with the other hand. Dropping the blade, he sat back on his heels and tugged up the bottom edge of his chain mail and the thick padded tunic beneath it. Holding back cloth and armour with his forearms, he fumbled with the draw-string of his trousers.

'What are you doing?' asked Kheda, revolted, as the wizard exposed himself.

'Got a water bottle on you?' snapped Dev. 'No, I didn't think so. Me neither. Now listen. That beast's a dragon born of fire, plain enough from the colour of it, never mind the way it snuffed out that pyre you made of the stockade. Well, I was born to see the elemental fire within things. If someone's summoned it, I should be able to follow the trail of the spell that summoned it here through a scrying, even if it is in a puddle of my own piss.' The wizard grimaced as he relieved himself.

Kheda concentrated on watching the dragon, which was now well past them, pausing to sniff at the dead embers of the burned stockade before continuing its measured progress along the curve of the beach.

'Then we make a run for it through the woods, flag down the *Green Turtle* and the *Lilla Bat*, taking our chances in the rocks and surf.' Dev didn't sound thrilled at that prospect. His voice strengthened as he continued. 'Then we work out how to sneak up on this clever bastard without him calling his new playmate down on us.'

'And gut him like a fish.' Kheda finished the sentence for the wizard.

But why would any wizard capable of summoning a dragon use it against his own people? Wouldn't he simply set the beast about finishing the destruction these foul invaders began last year?

Dev didn't answer. Kheda looked around to see green magic filling the puddle of urine, darkening as the liquid slowly seeped away into the dry earth. He looked about hastily for any condemning eyes before returning his gaze to the wizard. 'Well?'

A sheet of emerald flame erupted from the damp

hollow, sending Dev recoiling backwards, hands clapped to his face, muffling a guttural cry of pain. Flames crackled in the air around him, translucent green paling to a sickly yellow before strengthening to a vivid gold and then darkening to ferocious orange.

'Dev!' Kheda was on his hands and knees, ready to go to the barbarian's aid, when he realised that the flames had no source, no fuel. The mage's clothes weren't burning beneath his chain mail, nor were the leaves and twigs of the tangled underbrush. It was as if the very air was ablaze, wrapping the wizard in fire.

Is it illusion? Dev told me of such things. No, his hands are blistering. It has to be fire – but magical fire. How can I quench it? What will its touch do to me?

All the same, Kheda scooped a double handful of the loose sand from Dev's digging in his cupped palms, instinct driving him to quell the fire. Then movement on the beach held the warlord motionless. The dragon had whirled around and was running back along the sand in their direction. Before it had looked almost clumsy with its heavy plodding gait. Now it was racing like a hunting hound, long body at full stretch, head outthrust on its sinuous neck, tail straight as an arrow behind it.

It's heading this way! What is it after? The magical fire? It must be!

Kheda threw himself on the wizard, knocking Dev awkwardly on to his back, his legs twisted beneath him. Straddling the barbarian, he tore Dev's hands apart, seeing his face beneath scorched and burned as if the mage had stood too close to a fire when a resin-filled log ignited. The blisters on Dev's hands burst beneath Kheda's grip, the flesh slick and raw. Kheda felt the impossible flames fasten on to his own hands, crawling up his arms, the fine black hairs curling and disappearing, the skin reddening and growing sore.

'Dev!' Kheda yelled. 'Stop it!'

But the barbarian had his eyes screwed tight shut. His whole body was tense beneath Kheda, shuddering like a man in a fever. The flames burned ever brighter, ever hotter, and the roar of the dragon filled Kheda's ears. He let go of Dev's hands. They fell loosely on to the wizard's chest. Kheda braced himself with one hand on the wizard's breastbone and reached for his dagger with the other.

If the beast is seeking Dev's fire, his death will put an end to that.

Better yet, cut his throat. You can tell anyone who saw the fire it was the dragon's work. There'll be no one to gainsay you.

Yes, but who's going to save all of us here, never mind Risala, Itrac and all of Chazen, from this new magic if Dev's dead?

Kheda let the weapon fall and wrapped his bare hands around the wizard's throat. He gripped, hard, the knuckles of his forefingers digging into Dev's lined, sun-toughened neck just behind the angle of his jaw. Dev went limp beneath him and the flames vanished in the blink of an eye. Kheda looked around – tense, poised on his knees – to see where the dragon was and what it was doing.

It had stopped dead, scouring up a rut in the sand with the violence of its halt. Head swinging from side to side, its tongue continued that ceaseless flickering in the air. Its eyes shone with a crimson fire, searching the forest's edge. The blood hammered in Kheda's head, inheld breath a choking fire in his chest, hands and forearms scorched and sore.

The dragon continued to look from side to side, gaze sliding over the bushes that concealed the two men. All at once it sprang upwards, vast wings unfolding and beating against the air with a deafening clap. As it soared overhead, Kheda looked up to see the dark lines of the creature's bones through the leathery wing membrane when its flight momentarily blotted out the sun. Impossibly swift, it rose through the sky and disappeared over the hillock of the island.

Dev stirred beneath him, throwing Kheda off with a convulsive heave of his hips as he coughed. 'Good thinking,' he commented grudgingly as he rubbed at his neck with clumsy fingertips.

Kheda got to his feet, peering up through the sparse trees to search the fragmented clouds for any sign of the dragon. 'Is it coming back? Where's it gone?'

After the ships? Would it attack a trireme? What about a lesser boat? Risala, where are you?

'I'm not inclined to try finding out,' rasped Dev, now sitting up. 'Not with magic, anyway.'

A rustle in the bushes startled Kheda. It was three swordsmen, muddy-faced with terror.

'Go and gather everyone together,' the warlord barked. 'Stay under cover as best you can. As soon as we're all together, we'll head for the far side of the island, to see if we can signal to the *Green Turtle* and the *Lilla Bat*. Don't forget to keep your eyes open for those cursed traps,' he added.

The three of them just stood there, slack-jawed and uncomprehending.

'Go on!' Kheda urged.

His commanding tone reminding them of their duty, they turned and disappeared into the trees. Kheda heard other voices behind him, those who'd fled into the trees making themselves known now that his carrying words had put new heart into them. Twigs and leaves cracked and rustled as people began pushing their way towards him.

Kneeling to retrieve his fallen dagger, Kheda pushed his head close by Dev's. 'Your magic got away from you, mage. That happens again with anyone else at hand to see it and we're both dead – and not just because it looks as if the dragon can sniff out your fires. Give me one good reason why I shouldn't just kill you and have done. You said wizards can summon those beasts. What else do you know about these evils? Quickly, before anyone else might hear!'

'I'm sorry, my lord, but I know precious little about dragons,' said Dev sourly. He paused to blow on the backs of his raw and weeping hands to cool the pain. 'But I do know someone who knows a cursed sight more than most.'

CHAPTER SIX

'Velindre, come in.' The man opening the age-darkened oak door was at least half a head shorter than the tall, blonde woman he welcomed.

'Cloud Master.' She inclined her head, face expressionless as she swept across the threshold. Her firm chin was held high, the long plait of her golden hair falling straight as a rule down her spine.

'Rafrid will do. This is all quite informal.' He was quite possibly twice as broad across the shoulders as his visitor, with a barrel chest for good measure. With his long back, the way he belted his blue woollen tunic under his paunch made his grey-breeched legs seem incongruously short. The hobnails of his sturdy leather half-boots had scarred a path across the polished floorboards from the door to the table laden with books and parchments, and from the table to the tall triple-mullioned window on the far side of the room. The sky beyond the diamond-shaped panes of glass was the same soft grey as the narrow slivers of the stone walls visible between bookshelves burdened with scholarship past and present.

The man's eyes were a harder, flinty grey, age and experience lining his brow and dusting his dark hair with silver. 'Please, have a seat. Can I get you something to take the chill off the day? A little wine or cordial? A tisane?'

His manner was brisk rather than solicitous as he gestured towards the modest hearth where a polished copper kettle hung on an iron spar ready to be swung over the self-effacing flames. An oil lamp glowed golden on the table even though it was barely midday.

'Thank you, no.' Velindre took a ladderback chair from an irregular circle of mismatched seats. She set it between the table and the fireplace on a rug whose pattern had long faded into obscurity. Sitting with her back straight, she folded her hands in the lap of her indigo gown, its full skirt cut short enough to avoid the worst of winter's mire. As she crossed her long legs neatly at the ankles, her black leather boots, finer sewn than Rafrid's, showed that she'd been through a succession of puddles on her way there.

'You know why I wanted to see you.' Rafrid sat in his own round-framed wooden chair, shoving at the cushions behind him as he looked expectantly at Velindre.

She laced nail-bitten fingers together, knuckles whitening. 'Not really.'

An angled crease between Rafrid's grizzled brows deepened. 'If you're as unforthcoming with the apprentices, I'm hardly surprised I'm hearing complaints.'

'From whom?' A faint blush highlighted Velindre's angular cheekbones and she silently cursed her fair complexion. 'Excuse me.' Standing, she moved the chair a few paces from the fire and sat down again. 'I'm a little warm.'

'And you one of the most talented mages born to command the air here in Hadrumal?' Rafrid wondered sardonically. 'I find it difficult to believe that you can't keep yourself cool.'

Velindre folded her arms tightly across her modest bosom. 'If you won't tell me who, you might tell me what's being said about me.'

'You spend very little time with the new apprentices compared to the other mages of your standing.' Rafrid leaned back in his chair, tossing a battered patchwork cushion to the floor. 'And I gather that any of the more experienced apprentices making a formal request to study with you as your pupil can expect refusal without explanation or apology.'

'There are plenty of wizards keen enough to nursemaid the new arrivals.' Velindre shrugged one shoulder, her face impassive. 'I'll take on any apprentice with two or three years' learning to steady their affinity who comes up with a course of study I consider worth pursuing.'

'You're not excused from your responsibilities just because others are more mindful of all they owe to this island and these halls of learning,' Rafrid began sternly. 'We all have our own magical interests to pursue. It's not the business of other wizards to give you the leisure to concentrate exclusively on your own studies.'

'I am fully mindful of all I owe to Hadrumal and my fellow mages,' Velindre said frostily. 'I have lived here all my life.'

'I'm well aware of that.' Rafrid scowled, resting his elbows on the arms of his chair and twisting a heavy ring around the middle finger of his writing hand. A sizeable sapphire, dark and mysterious, was set deep into the silver. 'You're Hadrumal born, as were your parents, both of whom have added significantly to the scholarship of wizardry. Yet your parents have always found time to nurture the lads and lasses arriving on our dockside still reeling from the shock of discovering their magebirth. As for further study, your mother in particular has an unequalled record for guiding pupils on paths that seemed entirely unpromising at first glance.'

Velindre sat in silence, her narrow lips thinned almost to invisibility. Rafrid drummed his thick fingers on the edge of his table, his square jaw hardening.

'You used to spend more time with apprentices,' he

pointed out with a visible effort at reasonableness. 'You've had past pupils who made notable progress and not just in the understanding of the element of air. Why the change of heart over this last winter?'

'Tell me how much time I'm to set aside for apprentices.' Velindre uncrossed her feet and stood. 'And how many pupils I'm required to take on.'

'Kalion did you no favours encouraging you to think that you stood a chance of being elevated to Cloud Mistress,' said Rafrid bluntly.

Velindre lifted her chin defiantly. 'I suggest you take that up with the Hearth Master.'

'I have done,' Rafrid assured her dourly, 'with him and Troanna both. Our esteemed Flood Mistress is under no illusions about what I think of her meddling.'

'I'm surprised you want me spending time with apprentices, since you think so little of my abilities,' said Velindre tartly.

'Don't be a fool,' he retorted, scathing. 'I think very highly of your wizardry. Your admirable focus on our element has led you to some remarkable insights. I can't recall seeing anyone with more feeling for the elemental air in the twenty years I've known you. What you're lacking are the necessary instincts for the demands of an office such as this.'

He waved a curt hand at the parchments littering the table. 'As Master of Hiwan's Hall before my elevation to this office, I got used to keeping all these balls in the air, better than a festival juggler. You've always been able to put your own interests first, and that's all very well, but an element master – or mistress – needs to take a wider view. He can't stay aloof if his feelings have been hurt. He can't turn unapproachable if he doesn't want his studies disturbed for days at a time. He needs to keep an ear to the ground, not have his head in the clouds.'

'And you had Planir's ear when it was time for him to make his nominations to the Council.' Velindre came perilously close to sneering.

Somewhat to her surprise, Rafrid laughed, a full-throated chuckle. 'You flatter me if you think our esteemed Archmage would hand me such an honour just because I fancied wearing this pretty blue ring myself.' He leaned forward, waving the faceted sapphire at Velindre, who flinched as if he'd offered her a blow. Rafrid scowled blackly for an instant before he continued. 'The only opinion of mine that Planir sought was who should replace me as Master of Hiwan's Hall. I don't know who first suggested that I should be elevated to this rank of Cloud Master, but I do know that Planir took a long time to think it through and consulted with wizards far more eminent and experienced than you or me, here in Hadrumal and beyond.'

He paused for a moment and when he went on, his voice was level, even kindly. 'I don't pride myself on defeating you, Velindre. I simply want to justify the faith our fellow mages have shown in me. I'm charged with the better guidance of those born to master our element and with helping those born with an affinity to another to a fuller understanding of the interactions of air with earth, fire and water. I want your help, not your hostility. That's what the apprentices need, and our pupils.'

Velindre said nothing, her sharp face icy calm.

Rafrid sighed with exasperation. 'Make yourself available to any apprentice wanting your instruction from breakfast till noon. Your time's your own after that. I'll let it be known that you'll be considering new pupils over the Equinox festival. There should be two or three keen enough and bold enough to put forward their ideas for your consideration. After Solstice, you can expect your contemporaries studying the other elements to recommend their most promising pupils in the normal fashion.'

'As you wish, Cloud Master.' Velindre turned to depart, her hazel eyes impenetrable.

As she reached for the door latch, the Cloud Master spoke again. 'The next time a bunch of apprentices come to me, I want it to be because they can't sing your praises loudly enough. I told this last lot that you're one of the most skilful wizards on this isle. Don't let me down.'

Velindre showed no response as she opened the door, about to step out on to the stairs.

'Give some thought to what Otrick would have made of your behaviour lately,' Rafrid called after her.

Velindre slammed the door behind her so hard that the reverberations echoed all the way down to the bottom of the stairwell, pursued by the angry clatter of her booted steps on the aged treads.

'What would Otrick have made of all this?' she muttered, furiously scrubbing away the sting of angry tears with the back of one hand as she snatched her thick cloak from a peg. 'What would he have made of your prosy lecturing? Do you think he'd have started apprentices on summoning showers to freshen up a turnip's wilting leaves?'

Her stride lengthening, Velindre crossed the flagstoned courtyard walled on all four sides with ranges of accommodation. She glanced up at the garrets with their little gabled windows jutting through the stone-slated slopes of the roofs, chimney stacks spaced between them. Which of the apprentices crammed into those poky rooms had had the gall to complain about her?

Her gaze slid down to the first- and second-floor rooms, wider windows shut firmly against the bitter weather. Who were those ungrateful pupils who'd begged for her guidance and now felt entitled to whine when she'd cast them off to stand on their own two feet?

They were better off trailing around after the likes of Colna and Pemmel anyway, she thought with contempt. The uninspired deserved the insipid. Let them coddle the apprentices and the pupils; she had better things to do. She would find some insight into magic that would restore her reputation within the higher ranks of Hadrumal. She would find something to make Planir sit up and take notice, something to make the Archmage regret his mistake in passing her over.

She glanced back over her shoulder at the central tower of the wizard hall, at the triple-mullioned window of Rafrid's eyrie at the centre of the four quadrangles. What would Otrick have made of him as Cloud Master? The old scoundrel would have laughed himself breathless and then sent everyone into hysterics with his incisive dissection of Rafrid's inadequacies.

She raised a hand to her eyes as the pain of Otrick's loss stabbed her anew, heading blindly for the dim passage that threaded through one corner of the courtyard.

'Excuse me, miss.' A laundry maid tried to step out of Velindre's path, hampered by her wide wicker basket.

'I beg your pardon.' Velindre flattened herself against the plastered stone wall to let the servant pass. She felt the damp and cold on the back of her neck and pulled up the hood of her midnight-blue cloak, tying it loosely. The first impetus of her anger spent, she walked more slowly out through the gate and into the narrow lane running behind the Leeward Hall. So her mornings were to be taken up with the misapprehensions and misunderstandings new apprentices always spouted.

'No, you've not been sent into some irreversible exile. Ships that have the Archmage's trust come and go from Hadrumal all the time,' she mouthed as she walked along the cobbles. 'Yes, you'll be able to go home to visit your families – once you've learned how not to set chimneys alight when you're angry or freeze the water in the well when you're miserable.'

Velindre felt a measure of sympathy for the mageborn of the mainland, most without any wizard nearby to guard and guide them through the first manifestations of their affinity, never mind the fearful rumours still perpetuated by the ignorance of the mundane populace. Then resentment put such feelings to flight.

'No, the Council of Wizards isn't a cabal of astute and powerful mages secretly directing kings and princes down the paths of wisdom. Don't you think the mainland might be less riven by faction and self-interest if that were the case? No, it's a circle of self-satisfied men and women who struggle to look beyond the sea mists they use to hide Hadrumal, scrying spells notwithstanding.'

She took a still narrower lane cutting across her path and leading between high stone walls towards the long, curved high road that was the backbone of the modest city of Hadrumal. Behind her lay the warren of humbler buildings housing the craftsmen and tradesmen who supported the island's mages in their studies. Reaching the high road, Velindre looked towards the fog-shrouded hills gently rising beyond the city, where the island's yeomen raised their stock and tended their fields, the remote towers of the wizard halls a distant curiosity.

She could go and stay with her father's brother. Let these apprentices who were so keen to study with her prove their worth by traipsing all that way every morning. Let Rafrid make a fool of himself trying to drag her back to the city. And her aunt and cousins wouldn't give a Lescari penny piece for the gossip around the wizard city, any more than they had in those timeless summers she had spent on their farm as a child. There wouldn't be whispering in corners and bright-eyed, hushed speculation as to just why it was that Archmage Planir had found her lacking and why the Council had handed the prize that should have been hers to Rafrid, of all people.

No. That would be running away. Neither her father nor her mother would approve of that, always supposing they looked up from their books and parchments for long enough to notice her absence. As she walked along the flagstones, she glanced at the pale tower of Wellery's Hall, its yellow stone a contrast to the grey sky. Over to the east, the squat stump of Atten Hall's central tower was barely visible over the intervening roofs.

They would be expecting her to still be working towards a seat on the Council in her own right. They'd set that path before her ever since they'd first encouraged her adolescent fascination with her burgeoning affinity. Hadrumal needed to be guided by wizards with a sound understanding of the full potential of magic in the wider world. Then the clear-sighted leaders of this hidden isle could instruct the blinkered rulers of the mainland along better paths than the ones they inevitably chose for themselves.

Velindre's mouth quirked wryly. That remained to be seen. No matter. Her stride lengthened again, setting her cloak flapping, its azure silk lining bright as a summer sky. She passed the dark hollows of several gateways before turning into a courtyard with a fountain at its centre. The basin was dry and the statue at its centre invisible beneath a swaddling of straw and sacking. Was there no one in this hall with the time to spare for a charm to protect the stone from the frosts?

As Velindre passed the fountain, a stairwell door in the far wall opened and a slight woman emerged. She was almost as heavily muffled as the statue, with a mossy green scarf pulled right up to her vibrant chestnut eyes.

'Ely.' Velindre moved to intercept her.

The woman twitched her scarf down with a gloved

hand to reveal a fine-boned face with wisps of black hair just visible around the edge of her knitted cap. 'Whatever you want, keep it short.'

'Rafrid's just lectured me about my responsibilities to the apprentices.' Velindre grimaced extravagantly. 'You must know who Troanna would like to see given a leg up, or Kalion, perhaps?'

'You still think it's worth keeping in with them?' Ely cocked her head to one side, birdlike.

'Naturally,' said Velindre, unperturbed. 'And Rafrid can go jump a rope if he doesn't like it.'

'I'll see what I can find out.' Ely shivered inside her cloak and her turquoise earrings trembled. 'Did Rafrid say anything else?'

Velindre shrugged. 'About what?'

'He's one of the few who get to see our esteemed Archmage in private.' Ely's elegant, finely plucked brows disappeared beneath the ribbed welt of her hat. 'Did he let slip anything about Planir's mood? Any clue as to what might be going on behind that granite façade?'

Velindra shrugged again.

'Oh well.' Ely's carefully painted mouth tightened with irritation. 'Have you seen Galen anywhere?'

'I came here looking for him.' Velindre raised her pale golden brows at Ely. 'You and he *are* keeping company again?'

'He has his uses,' Ely admitted with a sideways smile. 'Especially when it's this cold.'

'More fun in your bed than a warming pan?' Velindre wondered with faint amusement.

'Sometimes,' Ely said a trifle sourly. 'Still, who knows, he might make Stone Master someday.'

'Who knows,' echoed Velindre. 'I won't keep you. Just send any likely apprentices my way.'

Ely pulled her scarf up over her face again. 'Keep your

eyes and ears open for news of Planir, if you're playing the dutiful underling to Rafrid.' She clumped away across the empty courtyard in bulky sheepskin boots and vanished beneath the arch of the gateway.

Velindre looked up at Galen's windows. He had no more chance of becoming Stone Master than he had of becoming Archmage, even if Planir consented to relinquish the lesser of the two offices he held. Ely was deceiving herself if she thought she was going to enjoy any influence as Galen's lover. She had better stick to seeking advancement through the gossip she garnered and supplied to Flood Mistress Troanna and Hearth Master Kalion. She certainly wasn't going to win a Council seat on her own merits. Ely's promise as an apprentice had never really come to much.

Velindre chuckled as she made her way from the courtyard. She hoped for Ely's sake that Galen had learned more of a lover's skills than he'd had when they had all been pupils together, in those days when anything had seemed possible. Her smile faded.

Hadrumal's high road was largely deserted. A few carts trundled along the cobbles to deliver faggots of firewood or anonymous sacks and chests to the closed shop fronts of the tailors and cobblers, the bookbinders and ink-sellers. One wine seller had opened his shutters and profligate candles brightened the interior, soothing chilled apprentices cradling cups of mulled wine fragrant with herbs and spices.

Velindre slowed as she caught the tempting scent of new bread, warm from the oven. Then she picked up her pace. She was hardly in the mood to swap pleasantries with neophyte mages half her age. Stepping across the runnel of muck and rain in the gutter, she crossed to the opposite flagway where mismatched shop fronts yielded to the ancient stonework that bounded the paradoxically named New Hall. Passing beneath the black shadow of a gatehouse with carvings long since weathered to obscurity, Velindre crossed a courtyard where hollows in the flagstones worn by countless generations of feet were dark with moisture. Reaching beneath her cloak, she drew out a keychain and unlocked the iron-studded door at the base of the central tower. Inside, a stair spiralled tightly upwards.

Snapping her fingers, Velindre summoned a pale-blue flame to light her way up the dark stone stairs. She passed the door to the rooms on the first floor without slowing. At the door to her second-floor sanctuary, she paused, keys in hand, looking up the silent stair towards the empty rooms above.

What would Otrick have said to her? It was becoming difficult to recall the exact sound of his voice. There were days when memory of his face was blurred in her mind's eye.

She unlocked the door and walked into her study, flicking the pale flame into the fireplace where kindling laid ready instantly caught fire. Dust from the coal crackled. The brass catches and polished chestnut of the tall cupboards set on either side of the fireplace glowed as the flames grew stronger. The opposite wall was shelved from floor to ceiling on either side of a narrow door, books and parchments neatly ordered. A few curios interrupted the array: a flute made from a bird's hollow bone and a small glass case containing a precisely labelled collection of winged seeds dried to papery fragility. Propped here and there were studies of birds and precisely detailed seascapes, some in oils, others in chalk or ink.

A single high-backed, leather-covered chair stood beside the fireplace while two uninviting, unpadded chairs flanked a wide table where leatherbound books ordered by size awaited her attention, inkstand and quills precisely arranged to hand. Velindre ignored the books in favour of the fresh, floury rolls and a slab of dense yellow cheese left by one of the hall's maidservants. A substantial chunk of sweet bread thick with preserved plums had its own plate, flanked by a small flagon of red wine and a crystal jug of well water.

What would Ely do if Galen offered to marry her? Velindre wondered idly as she tore open one of the rolls. Did she know he'd once had the folly to propose to Velindre? Was he still looking for something between a wife and a mother, who'd darn his socks and sew his buttons and tempt him with dainty meals, and certainly never threaten him with wizardly talents outstripping his own? Well, that hadn't been the first dalliance Velindre had had sour with such rivalry, nor the last.

Otrick never had felt threatened. She poured half a glass of the rich, red wine, and, lifting her eyes to the plaster cornices of the ceiling, silently toasted the old wizard's memory. The most powerful Cloud Master Hadrumal had seen in twenty generations had never known any such insecurity.

Sipping her wine, still standing by the table, Velindre stared out of the window across the roofs of the quadrangle and beyond to the sodden meadows with their dull green tussocky grass, the salt marshes beyond sere and dun. Winter wind tossed the dead reeds this way and that and Velindre watched the eddies and flurries of the air only visible to those who shared her affinity.

Beyond the salt marshes there was the dull rolling grey of the sea that sent the ever-changing clouds and storms to break on the rocky shores of Hadrumal. Rising swells rimmed with white merged seamlessly into the leaden sky. She watched the damp air above the waves rising sluggishly, helpless to resist soaking up the seductive warmth brought up from the sun-kissed southern seas by the mysterious currents that threaded through the pathless ocean. The barely warmed air soared high into the uppermost reaches of the sky. Velindre watched the roiling mass cool and shed its load of moisture to swell the towering clouds. Perversely heavier now, the chilled air slid haphazardly down the sky, driving a rising wind to whip the waves to higher crests and steeper faces, until the swells collapsed in a crash of foam and fury. Above, the clouds darkened and the first flashes of lightning presaged the coming storm.

How often had she stood here to look out at the weather with Larissa? How long would it be before she could no longer recall Larissa's face or voice? Velindre set down the glass of wine and bent to unlace her boots, kicking them away to land with a thud on the floorboards. Ely and Galen and Kalion and all the rest of them had better watch their step with Planir. The man was entitled to grieve, Archmage or not, and his liaison with Larissa had been no casual sport. Velindre knew that from the late-night confidences they had shared. Perhaps it wasn't in her best interests to tie herself too closely to Kalion in particular. There had been precious little sign of Planir's usual good humour when the Archmage had been dining in the common hall with the apprentices a few nights ago.

'Velindre!'

The faint voice was so unexpected that she started, knocking into the table, sending wine spilling around the foot of the glass. She whirled around, long plait flying wide.

A disc of ochre light as big as the palm of her hand burned in the middle of the empty room. It grew, rimmed with searing scarlet brilliance.

'Who's there?' Velindre asked calmly, collecting herself.

'Dev.' The voice was faint but she recognised him at once.

The circle of magic was now the size of a hand-held looking glass. Velindre stood before it. 'Where are you?'

'Where do you think?' Magic flowed down the ochre disc like thick golden oil trickling down a coloured window. 'The Archipelago and a long way south.'

'I can see that.' The blurred radiance cleared and Velindre could see Dev's bald head and that familiar wicked grin. 'What do you want with me? You're Planir's eyes and ears in the Archipelago, aren't you?' she said waspishly.

'Still sulking?' Dev's grin broadened. 'I heard he'd passed you over for Cloud Mistress. You didn't really think you'd be raised so high, did you?'

'Go and impress Planir with your mastery in working a bespeaking over such a distance.' Velindre turned her back on the magic.

'It's you I need.' Dev's irritation set the spell ringing like a plucked wire.

'Why?' Velindre turned back to study the circumscribed vision within the burning circle. 'Where exactly are you?' She sat down on one of the upright chairs and picked up her wine, blotting the spillage with the muslin that had wrapped the cheese. 'What have you got yourself mixed up in now? Is that armour you're wearing?'

The spell flickered a little as it widened. Which was hardly surprising given the countless leagues the magic was reaching over, Velindre thought privately. She saw Dev standing on the deck of a small sailing boat on an open stretch of sparkling cobalt sea. The Aldabreshin sun was so bright in the dimness of her room that she could almost feel its heat on her face.

'You're never going to believe this,' grinned Dev. 'I'm—'

'Wait,' Velindre interrupted sharply, sitting forward to peer through the clouded magic. 'Who in Saedrin's name are those two?'

A dark-skinned man in richly exotic Aldabreshin armour stood some way behind the wizard. The Archipelagan was braced protectively in front of a slightly built girl wearing loose creamy trousers and tunic and a vivid red scarf over her shock of black hair.

Dev moved aside and extended a mocking arm. 'Velindre Ychane, mage of Hadrumal, may I present Chazen Kheda, warlord of the Archipelago's most southerly domain. Oh, and Risala, who's probably spreading her legs for him, though that's the least of her considerable talents.'

'Who presumably don't speak Tormalin,' said Velindre caustically. Both Archipelagans were squinting suspiciously at the circle of the spell, with no sign that they had understood Dev.

'I speak some of your northern tongue.' The girl surprised both wizards with her retort. 'So don't think you can lie to us about what she's saying, Dev.'

The bald mage recovered quickly. 'A girl of considerable talents raised in a northern domain that evidently trades with the mainland.'

'And she's got your measure.' Velindre noted the female talking to the warlord. 'Tell me, how are you expecting to escape an Aldabreshin warlord without being skinned alive now that you've openly worked magic in front of him?'

'It's a long story.' Dev grinned.

'One you don't want to tell Planir?' Velindre guessed shrewdly. 'What makes you think I want to hear it?'

Instead of answering, Dev asked his own question. 'What do you know about dragons?'

'Dragons?' she repeated with a frown.

'Dragons,' confirmed Dev with smug excitement.

'Those dragons that survive live in the far north, beyond the far peaks of the Mountain Men's territory.'

Velindre spread her hands, mystified. 'You won't see them in the Archipelago.'

'We're seeing one now,' said Dev robustly, 'come from somewhere to the south. And there are mageborn living out somewhere beyond the southern horizon, because they turned up here last year and wreaked every kind of havoc. They're nasty bastards, Velle.'

'With dragons to command?' Velindre let him see her scepticism.

'Last year it was just howling savages throwing spears and handfuls of fire.' Dev was suddenly all seriousness. 'Which, as you can appreciate, was remarkably effective against these Archipelagans who pride themselves on staying free of filthy sorcery. Kheda here had the sense to find me to put paid to the wild wizards and plain steel cut their followers down nicely enough after that. We thought we'd come and mop up the stragglers and soon be on our way home for wine and cakes, but a dragon's turned up and it's eating anyone it reckons looks tasty. We must have let one of their mages slip through our net,' he concluded with savage bitterness.

'You think this wizard summoned the dragon? Why now?' Velindre demanded. 'Why not summon it when you attacked him and his allies with your magic? What exactly did you do?'

'Never mind,' said Dev impatiently. 'What I need to know more about is dragons and just how they're summoned. Maybe this mage has simply lucked into the trick of it.'

'I don't think it's something you stumble on by accident,' retorted Velindre. 'Otrick was the only mage in Hadrumal who had the knack of summoning a dragon and he was the finest Cloud Master inside the last ten generations. And I'm sorry, Dev, haven't you heard? He's dead.' The usual dull grief gnawed beneath her breastbone.

'I know that, and I know you were his longest-standing pupil and closest to him in every sense.' Even in his intensity, Dev couldn't restrain a lascivious smile. 'Come on, Velle, didn't he let something slip by way of pillow talk?'

'Otrick didn't need to boast about his magical prowess to convince any girl to slip between the sheets with him,' Velindre said pointedly.

'It was always worth your while bedding me, don't pretend differently.' Dev grinned, unrepentant. 'There must be something – in Otrick's journals, in his records. He was a secretive old bastard but he knew what he owed to wizardry as Cloud Master. There must be some clue.' His voice gained an edge. 'If one of these wild mages is still alive and he's learned how to summon a dragon, there's nothing to stop him between here and Hadrumal. I've seen these bastards let loose and I wouldn't give—'

Dev clapped his hands to his ears as the girl's piercing scream startled him. In the same instant, the Aldabreshin warlord began shouting, a torrent of words that rang with horror. The ship rocked madly from side to side, all three of them staggering. The girl would have lost her footing but for the warlord's strong arm catching her.

'Ah, shit!' The bespeaking dissolved on Dev's raw yell of fear and fury.

'What is it?' Velindre shouted impotently at the empty air. 'Dev!'

The only reply was a faint ringing struck from the crystal water jug.

Velindre sprang to her feet, the chair falling away behind her. She ran to a cupboard beside the fireplace and flung it open. Pulling out a shallow silver dish, she sent pewter plates bowling noisily across the floorboards. Ignoring them, she reached up to a neatly ordered row of stoppered and sealed bottles. Her hand hesitated, then, biting her lip, she snatched at one, leaving the cupboard door swinging as she hurried back to the table by the window.

She emptied the crystal jug of well water into the silver bowl and, hands trembling, tried to unstopper the little bottle. Her fingers slid on the wax, bitten fingernails giving no purchase. Velindre slammed the bottle down on the table before taking a deep, calming breath and then carefully working the stopper free of the neck. She let a few drops of dark-green oil fall into the water, the piercing aroma of volatile herbs stinging her eyes for an instant. Ramming the stopper home, she set the bottle aside and placed her hands on either side of the bowl.

'If you can bespeak me over that kind of distance, Dev, you bilge rat, I can sure as curses scry back to you.' She stared into the water with grim intensity.

The drops of oil spread into an infinitesimal rainbow lustre on the surface of the water. Emerald fire flared in the depths of the bowl, reflections striking back from the curved silver sides. The radiance shimmered against the oily sheen, fluttering, darting back to the bottom of the bowl before striking up again only to meet the same barrier. The light doubled and redoubled, still confined within the bowl. Velindre stood motionless, hazel gaze fixed on her spell. Only when the captive brilliance rivalled the lightning now flickering in the clouds beyond her window did the magewoman release the magic.

In a flash, the surface of the water reflected the distant scene she sought. Velindre flinched, then froze, poised over the bowl, mouth open on an incredulous gasp. All she could see was some portion of a massive scaly back and the flexing of a great leathery wing. The scales were dark crimson, thick and uneven along the creature's spine, the wing a lighter red, more vivid, almost waxy with the sun shining off the ridges of the bones.

A dragon born of fire, mused some dispassionate corner of her mind even as the rest of her wits went begging for some explanation.

She slid one palm around the side of the bowl. The vision shimmered for an instant and then shifted, as if Velindre was now some bird, like one of the great white wanderers that drifted on the winds of the southern oceans. She flew high above the dragon on the wings of her spell to get a better look at it. Now she could see what the beast was about. A chill went through her that had nothing to do with the wintry storm now enveloping Hadrumal.

The dragon was circling the ship she'd seen Dev on. Twisting in the sky with startling agility for such a mighty beast, it bated like some enormous hawk before darting around in the other direction. The downdraught from its wings tossed the vessel this way and that like a child's nutshell boat on a puddle. The little ship's sail hung in rags from its ropes. Velindre held her breath as Dev's boat rolled over on to its beam ends, wallowing for an agonised breath before hauling itself back upright once more.

Where was Dev? Where were the other two? Velindre searched the deck. There was nowhere for them to hide and no one to be seen. Had they gone below?

The dragon obscured her view, diving closer to scour the deck with a sheet of flame from its gaping razor-toothed maw. The wood blistered and charred, remnants of canvas and rigging flaring to blow away as ash on the wind. The dragon drew a tight circle around the ship and lashed at the single mast with its sturdy tail. The pine cracked and splintered, crashing down on to the deck.

Velindre's spell brought her no noise of the distant destruction. The only sound in her dim study was her own breathing, harsh with helpless distress.

The dragon smashed its tail down on the burned decking, making surprisingly little impression. Mouth wide in a soundless snarl, it shot up into the air, wings beating strongly. Tumbling over itself, it dived straight down towards the crippled ship.

'No,' Velindre whispered, disbelieving. Surely a dragon born of fire couldn't risk diving into the sea?

At the last instant, the dragon pulled out of the stoop, swinging its hind legs forward to pound the scorched deck into broken splinters even as it clawed at the sky with its forelegs. Wings beating, it dragged itself away from the murderous embrace of the ocean, climbing back into the sky.

There was no escape for the boat. The weight of the dragon, even for that fleeting moment, had pushed the shattered deck below the surface of the ocean. White seas roiling with the downdraught of the dragon's passing flooded across bow and stern and poured through the cracked and broken planks. The ship floundered helplessly as more and more water cascaded into the hold, relentlessly forcing the hull beneath the waves. In a final convulsion, the vessel's bow came up, stern disappearing into the blue depths. The sharp prow slid down, vanishing in a flurry of foam. The dragon swooped low one last time, circling the hidden grave of the little ship. It flapped its wings and flared a crest of scales around its head in what looked uncomfortably like triumph.

Velindre searched the bland face of the ocean. Had Dev died in the ship's hold, dragged down into the drowning depths? A fire mage, even one of his talents, would be hard pressed to work any magic to save himself, engulfed by the very antithesis of his element. Had he swum for it before the beast made its final attack? What about the other two? All she could see was nameless detritus floating up from the wreck, nothing big enough to be a man's or a woman's body.

The inconvenient beast was filling her view once more. She could see its head clearly for the first time, as if it were coming straight towards her. Ruby eyes glittered above its broad, blunt muzzle, heavy crimson scales fringing its jowls and bristling in a mane of spines around the back of its head. It opened its mouth and she saw its brilliant daggerlike teeth.

Longer than daggers, that same dispassionate voice within her mind commented silently. The dragon's red tongue flickered in and out and she noted a searing red illuminating its eyes from within. The light playing on her face turned from blue-green to greenish gold.

Velindre cursed the beast absently under her breath and drew back from the bowl, waving a hand across the water to lift the spell's vision still higher above the sea, to give her a wider view of the immediate area. Was there an island close enough for Dev to have swum to?

Nothing happened. The dragon still filled the spell. Now its wings were lost beyond the edges of the magic, just its head and body visible. With every beat of its wings, it grew bigger within the silver confines of the bowl. Now all she could see was its head. It opened its mouth and a coil of flame burst out towards her, white hot with unstoppable magic.

Velindre recoiled as the water within the bowl boiled, steaming and spitting, sending splashes leaping over the rim to mar the polished table top. She thrust her hands out before her, repudiating the magic she had worked. The water calmed but the scrying held, vivid emerald light shining up from the bowl with a halo of sunset gold. The magewoman moved slowly forward, irresistibly drawn by intolerable curiosity. The breath catching in her throat, she looked warily down into the water.

The dragon looked back at her. There could be no question of it. Against all she had ever been taught. Contrary to all she had ever read or surmised of this scrying spell. In defiance of everything Hadrumal's wisest men and women had told her about remote magics. The dragon could see back through the spell as clearly as if it were looking through a pane of clear glass. More than that, the beast was looking straight at her, wild curiosity lighting its fiery eyes. The water began boiling again, and with some sense that she could not explain, Velindre could feel the dragon's intent. It wanted to find her. It wanted to destroy her with the same savagery it had loosed to annihilate Dev, his companions and the very boat they had been standing on.

Velindre knocked the bowl off the table with a wild sweep of her arm. It went flying, water splashing to stain the plaster below the window with oily streaks. Irrational fear seized her and the crystal jug followed, shattering into countless fragments. Upturning the table completely, Velindre stumbled backwards, tripped over the chair she'd discarded earlier and fell heavily to the floor.

The room remained gloomy and grey, the sun far distant behind the clouds now wrapped around Hadrumal. The only sound was the distant crack and rumble of the storm. None of the drops and puddles of spilled water glowed with any hint of magic. Velindre lay motionless for a few moments, skirts in disarray around her stockinged legs, waiting for her pounding heart to slow.

Sitting up slowly, she rubbed her bruised elbow thoughtfully. She smoothed down her gown and stood, absently rubbing her hip, still stinging from the impact of her fall. Leaving the calamitous scene of by the window, she went to recover her boots and pulled them on, face pensive. A pang of hunger surprised her and she spared a glance for the bread and cheese and plum bread that had bounced across the floor. Shards of glass and earthenware now rendered it all wholly inedible.

No matter. She had better things to do than eat. Moving briefly to the mantel, she tugged the bell pull to summon some nameless maid to deal with the mess. Leaving the door ajar behind her, she ran lightly up to the floor above, her urgent steps echoing down the stone spiral. Heart racing once again, she laid a pale hand on the latch of the study door and whispered the old mage's name under her breath. The tumblers of the lock clicked obediently and the door swung open.

What would Otrick have said to that? To the notion that a dragon had been looking back through the magic of a scrying spell to see who was working it at the other end? He'd have been intrigued by the idea. He'd have been utterly, resolutely determined to learn how such a thing might be so, to ascertain how he might do just such a thing in turn.

The faceless maids came here, too. The table was polished and gleaming. Even the haphazard parchments on the bookshelves were somehow kept free of dust. The cushions in the corners of the tall winged chairs on either side of the fireplace were plump and neatly placed. The hearth was laid ready with kindling and coal.

A fall of soot prompted by the dampness in the air had spotted the hearthstone and the raw smell caught in the back of her throat. Velindre shivered with distaste. This ordered emptiness wasn't Otrick's. The sideboard had been cleared of the old pirate's prized collection of cordials and wines summoned from merchants trading from one end of the long-lost Tormalin Empire to the other. He had always boasted that he had the finest palate on Hadrumal, even with his breath redolent of the acrid sweetness of chewing leaf.

Velindre turned her back on such bittersweet memories

and studied the bookshelves with a frown. There were gaps. Too many gaps. Some of the general tomes had doubtless been returned to the archives and libraries. The old mage had been an inveterate borrower of books and remarkably negligent when it came to returning them. Where were his journals, and those carefully bound records of his own thoughts and investigations into every aspect of the elemental air he had been born to command? Otrick had been meticulous in recording his conclusions and his musings on how he might make further trial of his affinity, of his powers and how they might rival or complement those of other wizards born to different disciplines.

Of course, other wizards and their pupils had sought and gained Planir's approval to compare their own deliberations with the dead Cloud Master's recorded wisdom. Velindre scowled as she tried to put names to the faces who had trooped up and down past her door. She was paying the price for ignoring them now. No matter; she'd just have to make a list. Sitting at the empty table, she opened a drawer to find parchment inside and one of the steel-tipped reed pens Otrick had favoured, but when she flipped the brass top of the inkwell open, she found that the crystal vial offered only a stain of dried darkness.

Lightning flashed and thunder followed, a crack as if the sky itself had split. Rain lashed the lofty tower, a buffeting wind howling at the tall windows where she had stood with Otrick, listening rapt as he revealed so many mysteries of the magic that they shared. The rascally old wizard's reputation as the finest Cloud Master Hadrumal had seen in an age was no idle boast. Velindre gazed out of the window, lost in memory as the storm raged unheeded.

Though there was the one crucial mystery he had

never shared with her. Otrick had been able to summon dragons. Well, one dragon, at least – a creature of cloud and fury only loosely under his command. That much he had admitted to her in the warm intimacy of one chilly midnight, moonlight lancing through the snow falling slowly outside the narrow window to spill on the coverlet like the fall of her long golden hair on the pillow. She'd never seen it herself, but mages who had no reason to lie swore to it. Besides, Otrick had never lied to her.

Now Dev had seen a dragon. Dev, who would lie black was white and fire was water if it would serve his purposes, which were rarely honourable and always self-interested. But she had seen it for herself, so that was hardly an issue. And this wasn't one of those rare beasts glimpsed above the most distant northern peaks where not even the hardiest Mountain Men could claw out a living. This was a dragon born of fire threatening to set the Aldabreshin Archipelago ablaze.

And Dev had been fighting mysterious wild mages down in the uncharted southern reaches of the Aldabreshin Archipelago. Did Planir know about this? Surely such news should have been brought before the Council of Hadrumal? Untamed magic was a threat to every mage, those in Hadrumal and those living less exalted lives among the mundane populace of the mainland. What would Kalion make of such news? What *use* would he make of such news, and the realisation that Planir had kept such a secret from the Council?

The memory of the dragon's burning eyes drove such thoughts of petty alliance and connivance out of her head. Had the dragon been summoned by some wild wizard, using whatever lore Otrick had kept such a close secret? How else could it have come there?

Dev wanted to know how such a thing could be done.

Why? To confront this mysterious mage with a dragon under his own command? Could he do it, if he had the lore? Was he strong enough in his wizardry to make such a challenge? Dev had certainly been talented, and supremely arrogant besides, when they'd both been apprentices in Hadrumal. What had he learned during his years of snooping around the Archipelago? What could he have discovered in realms where death was the penalty for using magic?

Otrick had been able to summon dragons but he was dead and ashes in a funerary urn. Dev wanted to know how to summon dragons but he might very well be dead and food for the fishes of the southern seas. Who else was thinking about dragons, across the whole of wizardry? No one, not as far as Velindre knew.

What if she rediscovered this lore? What if she learned how to summon a dragon and bend it to her will? More than that, what if she was the one who put paid to this wild magic coming up from the south, saving Hadrumal from a threat more destructive than any whirlwind? Wouldn't that earn her a place on the Council as of right? Wouldn't that make Planir choke on his choice of Rafrid for Cloud Master? Wouldn't that silence the whispers behind hands raised in the libraries and the sniggers behind her back as she passed through the halls?

So where was the lore? Velindre's gaze slid to the door leading to Otrick's spartan sleeping chamber. It wasn't a memory of that winter night that spurred her to her feet but recollection of a distant summer. She had been revelling in the first maturity of her magic and in the flattering attention of Otrick, then in his prime and so different from the callow youths who were her fellow pupils. Walking slowly across the study, she pushed at the bedroom door.

She had been asleep under a thin linen sheet, no coverlet necessary in the still heat that was slow to fade even in the late watches of the night. Something had woken her and she had found herself alone in the bed. Otrick had been sitting in the window seat, relaxed in his nakedness and absorbed in his writing. She had watched him for a few moments before falling asleep again. His hair had still been dark then, not yet faded to the icy grey of his latter years. Not that white hair had made him look any less piratical or diminished any of his appetites.

Cross with herself, Velindre brushed aside such reminiscences and walked quickly to the window seat. She threw aside the long, flat cushion and tried to lift the planking beneath. After a sharp tug, the wood came free and she summoned a tongue of magelight to illuminate the hollow beneath. Small books bound in brown leather were stacked in piles ten deep. She reached for the topmost, then, changing her mind, delved deeper, down to the bottom of the hidey-hole.

She stood up with her prize and crossed over to sit on the bare mattress of the bed, flicking through the pages to see Otrick's familiar irrepressible scrawl, now sorely faded. The magelight blinked out at the snap of her fingers and reappeared to hang by her head, shining a fierce light on the open book. Returning to the beginning of the journal, Velindre began reading with steady concentration. Some considerable number of pages later, a note caught her eye.

Dragons would appear from time to time among the crags of the Cape of Winds that is the last reach of southernmost Tormalin. No one knew where they came from. Few knew the secret of killing them. Those that did could live like kings for a year on the proceeds, if they ever brought the spoils back to a safe harbour. That's what Azazir has been saying, anyway.

Velindre turned the page and read on, oblivious to the storm tearing the clouds to rags and drenching the city beyond the windows with rain.

CHAPTER SEVEN

Is this my death? Burned to oblivion with magical fire? No one foresaw that for me.

What does it mean for Chazen, for Daish, for all those of my blood? Will this portent be robbed of its force if no one knows the manner of my death?

White light blinded him, searing through eyes screwed tight shut. Heat enveloped him, hotter than the murderous noon of the dry season's height, menacing and oppressive. It was pressing in from all sides, through his armour, through the padded tunic beneath, to scald his skin with his own sweat.

This can only be the start of the pain. How bad will it get before I am truly dead?

He felt as light as ash blown on the wind. There was no hard deck beneath his feet, nor cold sea drowning him even as it quenched the all-consuming fire. Then Kheda found one sensation to puzzle him as he waited for the final agony.

Whoever is holding my hand is going to break my fingers if they're not careful.

The light went out like a snuffed candle. Kheda's legs buckled and he fell to his hands and knees, feeling soft leaf mould instead of deck planking. The smell of hot metal prompted confused recollection of a visit to Ulla Safar's famous foundries. Raising a shaking hand to scrub the dizziness from his eyes, he burned his forearm on the breast of his hauberk, the sweat coating him hissing against the hot steel.

'Shit, shit, shit, shit.' Dev's profanity slowly penetrated Kheda's bemusement.

The warlord opened his eyes to see the wizard frantically unbuckling his sword belt. The steel of Dev's hauberk was blued all across the front, like one Kheda recalled a novice warrior leaving incautiously close to a hot fire.

He couldn't help himself. Kheda laughed, but as he sat back on his heels, his own chain mail seared the back of his knees even through his trousers. He scrambled to his feet with a curse of his own as Dev began struggling out of his hauberk, doubled over and shaking himself like a wet hound.

'Let me help.' Risala stretched out trembling hands towards Kheda, the blue of her eyes rimmed with white and her jaw clenched tight.

'No, it's too hot.' Kheda used the tail of his belt to push the leather back through the buckle, dark curves scored on the leather by the hot brass. Bending over, he shed the hauberk in one swift movement. It hit the ground with a rushing rattle and a faint charred smell. Kheda straightened up, panting, and ripped off his steaming under-tunic, the cotton blackened. The touch of the gentle breeze on his bare skin was both welcome and painful.

How did we get here? Magic – it must have been. One more debt you owe Dev. One more taint to foul you.

They were in a small clearing in the middle of a dense tangle of forest.

'No, don't.' He caught Risala's hands as she moved to embrace him. 'I'm burned. Are you?' he asked urgently.

'No,' she said with belated realisation.

'You can thank your lucky stars you weren't wearing any armour.' Dev stood bare-chested like Kheda, holding well-muscled arms away from his sturdy body. 'Curse it, this smarts.'

Keeping hold of the hand that wore Shek Kul's ring,

Kheda kissed Risala's fingers fervently. 'Better burned than dead.'

'You're the healer. Can you see any plant that will take the sting out of this?' The wizard's barbarian skin was distinctly paler where his clothes habitually protected him from the sun. His back and chest were an angry red just short of blistering.

'Leatherspear, that's what we need.' Kheda looked around for pale-green spikes tipped with black among the clustering rustlenut saplings. He swallowed, his throat dry and rough. 'And water.'

'Where is it?' Risala looked up, squinting through the tattered canopy of a spinefruit tree for a glimpse of the dragon. She was shaking faintly, her fingers still entwined with Kheda's. 'And where are we?'

Dev didn't seem to hear them, eyes distant, face twisted with fury. 'The bloody thing sank my boat, my *Amigal*.'

A furred vine coiling up the spinefruit tree burst into crimson flame.

'Dev!' Kheda said sharply.

'I traded the length of the Archipelago in that boat for ten years and more,' the wizard growled, looking up at the obstinately empty sky.

The vine disintegrated in a flare of scarlet fire, leaving a black score wrapped around the tree.

Kheda crossed the glade in a few rapid steps. 'Dev!'

'Cursed bloody worm!' The black furrow in the grey bark began to smoulder, edges glowing golden.

'Dev!' Kheda slapped the wizard hard across the face, his hand ready to add a back-handed blow. 'Get a grip on yourself!'

'Before you set this place alight,' Risala added harshly.

Dev blinked and the unreasoning rage faded from his eyes. 'You obviously don't know how dangerous it is to hit a wizard in a temper.'

'I'm surprised you lasted ten years in these islands if that's what happens when you lose your temper.' Kheda nodded at the charred spinefruit tree.

'A lot you know.' Dev rubbed a hand over his bald head and winced.

'Where are we?' Risala moved to the edge of the clearing.

'On the island where we first saw the dragon,' Dev said heavily. 'A wizard can only use magecraft to go somewhere he's already been. I didn't think there'd be anyone to see us here.' His expression challenged them both.

'You could hardly take us back to the residence, I suppose,' Kheda acknowledged tersely.

Appearing out of thin air in a blaze of magic would take some explaining. Would Itrac believe some obliging eccentricity of the dragon had thrown us home? Or would she just have you killed, for the sake of the domain, since you were so plainly suffused with sorcery, warlord or not, willing or not?

'Someone will send a ship from the fleet to look for us, once we're overdue . . .' Risala broke off, biting her lip. 'But they'll be looking for us in the wrong stretch of the sea.'

'Which at least is a problem we can do something about,' countered Dev, his anger still simmering. 'Or would you rather have been burned to cinders by the dragon?'

Kheda looked to the north, the sea hidden by the scrubby forest. 'The fleet will have seen the dragon, I suppose, even though we were out of sight.'

'Do you think they believed all that goose grease about you needing to take the omens around an empty horizon?' wondered Dev.

'It was the truth,' retorted Kheda. 'And I'll continue to seek all the guidance I can in the earthly and heavenly compasses until you come up with something better with your magics and your barbarian friends.'

Though I saw no omen to give me any clue we were about to be attacked. Was the dragon already bearing down on us, corrupting the patterns of nature?

'Well, I can get us back to the residence now.' Dev rubbed his hands together and grinned. 'If you can think of a likely spot where we can arrive unseen.' He shifted his gaze to Risala. 'And if you can come up with some tale to explain how we got there, mistress poet.'

'This carrying us away with magic, that's what you did before.' The girl looked at the barbarian mage, frowning. 'When that wild mage found you and me spying on him?'

'Yes.' Dev shrugged.

'That was just you and me and not nearly so far as this,' Risala said slowly. 'You couldn't have kindled a candle after that. You were exhausted.'

'But this time your magic's getting away from you, Dev.' Kheda gestured at the scarred spinefruit tree. 'Here and before, when you tried scrying on the beach. What's going on?'

'We may not know much about wizards but we know you.' Risala fixed the barbarian with a piercing stare.

Dev opened his mouth and then shut it, as if he had changed his mind about what to say.

We tell Aldabreshin children that someone who opens their mouth and then forgets what they were going to say was about to tell a lie. Does the same hold true for barbarians?

Kheda pressed Risala's hand against his thigh.

'It's the dragon,' the wizard said finally. 'It's a magical creature. It has a magical aura. I drew on the beast's own magic to get us here. I don't think it even noticed.' He grimaced, rubbing the back of one hand across his forehead. 'I've got a headache, but nothing worse than I'd deserve after a late night drinking white brandy. I've enough magic within me to carry us somewhere closer to the ships. How about that for an idea?'

Kheda looked at Risala. 'When he did this to you before, did you end up parboiled in your own sweat?' She shook her head and he looked back at Dev. 'Then why did it happen this time?'

Dev looked at him for a long moment. Sable finches chattered insouciantly in the trees. 'It's like I said: the dragon has an aura. My magic got away from me with that much raw elemental fire filling the air. That's the element I have an affinity with.' He sounded more resigned than angry, then his voice strengthened with his usual cockiness. 'And now, forewarned is forearmed. Believe me, keeping my hide whole as a wizard in the Archipelago has taught me more fine control of discreet magic than any mage of Hadrumal possesses. It won't happen again.'

'It had better not,' Kheda said stiffly. 'If it does and you're seen, you'll be hunted till some mob has skinned you alive and nailed your hide to a pole. And I won't be able to lift a finger to save you.'

'Can't we get off this island without magic?' Risala walked a few paces away and looked from one side of the clearing to the other. 'And come up with a story to explain where we went? The sooner the better.' She glanced at Kheda. 'Word of this dragon will fly around the islands faster than the beast itself. If rumour that you're dead follows, your whole rule could be fatally undermined.'

Kheda nodded grimly. 'And if some courier dove takes that rumour beyond the domain, who knows who will chance the danger of these waters for the sake of claiming our pearl harvest.'

Could Janne talk Sirket into sending Daish warriors?

He resolutely set aside such worries. 'We have to get back to the fleet. If they've seen the dragon, they'll have fallen back to the rendezvous point on the far side of Dalao.'

'Unless the dragon sank them, too,' Dev interrupted with a scowl.

'We just have to hope the beast didn't.' Kheda sighed heavily.

'That's a wager we've no choice but to take,' agreed Risala.

'We can build a raft, but we've the current to cross.' Kheda looked reluctantly at Dev. 'Could you use your magic to save us from being swept away?'

'Never mind that,' said Dev brutally. 'We need to go hunting whatever wild mage summoned this dragon. You've no notion what a wizard could do with that amount of power to call on. He'll take this domain away from you in a matter of days and there'll be nothing you can do about it.'

'But we killed all the wild mages,' protested Risala with a touch of despair.

'What if we only killed those who were strong enough to make a fight of it?' countered Dev. 'You saw how they fought among themselves, to the death. I reckon there was someone with the sense to keep his head down.'

'Are you about to tell me you told me so?' asked Kheda savagely. 'That we should have killed all who were left and sooner than this?'

Is this my fault, for turning my attention to rebuilding Chazen before we had fully reclaimed it?

'A mageborn with even the slightest power could have hidden himself from all your hunting parties.' Dev waved the irrelevance away. 'He probably hasn't much power of his own, or we'd have seen him lead some fightback before now. But if he's mastered this trick of summoning a dragon, that's all he needs to change that. Drawing on the elements around them, that's the basis of this wild wizardry, that's why it's so crude,' he commented with contempt. 'With a dragon's aura at hand, he's got all the power he could ever use. He can do pretty much anything he fancies.'

'Only as long as he's got some way to stop the dragon eating him,' said Risala with faint hope.

'How does he do that?' Kheda looked warily at the barbarian mage.

'Who knows? I'm making up theories as I go along,' Dev said bitterly. 'I have to bespeak Velindre as soon as we can find some suitable metal.' Petulantly, he kicked a scrap of weathered bark at the flaccid lump of his chain mail. 'I could have used a helmet but they're both at the bottom of the sea.'

Because he can see in any pool of liquid but he needs a magical reflection in metal to speak to this confederate of his. Is it significant, that when I'm willing to countenance his magic, circumstances make it impossible for him to use it?

'Better them than us.' It took Kheda some effort to sound positive. 'Let's build a raft and work our way north through the Snake Bird Islands. If we go well past Dalao before we attempt the crossing, we can ride the current south as we cross it. If we judge it right, we shouldn't get swept too far past our target, not beyond Balaia at the very worst. We'll say I saw some omen that drew us to the far side of the current before the dragon attacked.' The thought of the lie soured his stomach.

No one will challenge my word; I'm the warlord. The people of the domain trust me to seek out and interpret the portents for them, not to lie and feint and deceive. Perhaps that's all part of the curse of magic staining these islands. How much more evil an omen is this dragon's arrival?

'And another thing,' he added vehemently. 'I want no word spoken of any wild mages out there when we get back. We keep that between ourselves. As far as anyone is concerned, the dragon is just a beast like any other.'

'Hardly,' Dev objected. 'Not with magical fire at its command.'

'Then it's a magical beast, but it's still a beast,' Kheda said resolutely. 'Bad as that is, it'll be worse if those who survived the savages and their wizards last year think such catastrophe is coming down on them again.'

'And what will you do when someone stumbles across this wild mage?' asked Dev sarcastically.

'I imagine I'll be as surprised as anyone else,' Kheda said stolidly.

'We need to get down to the sea.' Risala peered through the trees, one hand drifting to the half-moon dagger at her belt. 'Do you suppose the dragon ate all the savages Shipmaster Mezai said were hiding here?'

'If it didn't, I can burn them to charred bones and no one need be any the wiser. We should worry more about those traps the bastards built.' Dev scooped up his fallen swords. 'Watch your step, and leave that,' he said sharply, seeing Kheda bend down to pick up his armour. 'You can't wear that on a raft. If we go over, you'll sink straight to the bottom and be drowned for certain.'

'True.' Kheda grimaced. He caught up his own weapons and followed the others down a narrow path between the battered and drought-stunted spinefruit and rustlenut trees.

Though a warlord losing his armour isn't going to be seen as the best of portents. That'll have to be another wager against the future. If we can get back to the fleet, if I can send someone to reclaim such a potent symbol of my authority, then won't that be proof I'm acting in the best interests of the domain, whatever my compromises with the vice of magic?

And what if you don't get your armour back? Will that mean you were wrong to turn your back on your father's wisdom, on the precepts that guided the forefathers of Chazen and Daish and every other domain? Is it your deeds to this point that have brought the unfettered evil of a dragon upon everyone?

Apprehension thick in his throat, Kheda followed Dev down the steep slope of the far side of the little island, leaving sufficient wary distance so that any trap catching the mage would miss him. Risala came after the warlord, careful to match her steps precisely to his. The spinefruit trees were more sparsely scattered on this side of the island, which meant that rustlenuts had seized the rains' recent largesse and were sprouting in all directions. Vicious tangles of strangling vines fought over the open spaces and the ground was riddled with burrows easily as treacherous as any traps.

At least there are no signs of any but animal footprints.

'Do you suppose the savages ate all the matias?' Kheda wondered as he jumped to save himself from a twisted ankle when a hollow collapsed beneath his foot. Brindled fur and shreds of dry leaves blew away on the breeze.

'They'll be deep underground.' Sweat darkened the spine of Risala's ochre tunic. 'They've too much sense to be out in the heat of the day.'

'Watch your step.' Dev wiped his forehead with the back of one hand. 'It's a sheer drop to those reefs.'

They went on, cautiously, as the trees thinned to reveal crumbling black and grey rock above seas foaming around exposed corals.

'How do we get a raft down there?' Risala asked dubiously.

Kheda looked along the shore in both directions. 'That might be easier.' He pointed to a dip in the cliff. 'I think we can get safely into the sea down there.'

Dev was looking inland. 'I can see a spring.'

Better yet, the damp gully offered a modest sprouting of leatherspear where the twists in the underlying rock forced out the precious water. Kheda drew his belt knife and cut a handful of fleshy spikes. Splitting them lengthways, he slapped them deftly on Dev's back as the wizard bent to cup his hands under the dripping water. 'Hold still.'

Dev reared up. 'Shit, that stings!'

'Only for a moment.' Kheda moved to let Risala get to the spring, squeezing juice from the swollen base of a leaf and anointing his own tender skin.

'Let me help.' Risala shook water from her hands and took a leatherspear leaf, smearing the viscous sap over Kheda's back.

Kheda shivered as she pressed her thumbs into the knotted muscles on either side of his spine.

Just the touch of your hands stops my heart. What have I done to deserve such a woman devoted to me, even when I dare not act on my own desire? Will that be my reward, proof that I am doing right, if I can finally see a way to take you for my own that dishonours no one? If you still want me.

'You sounded very confident about making a raft,' Dev challenged Kheda as he sliced more strips of leatherspear to soothe his reddened chest. 'I'll tell you for nothing that I'm no boat builder.'

'All we need is the right wood and lashing,' Kheda told him firmly before quenching his own thirst from the meagre trickle. 'Risala, you cut vines and we'll look for some likely trees. And we should all look for gourds. We'll need something for carrying water.'

'Let's get busy.' She picked her way carefully along the cliff and began unravelling a skein of strangling vine from an outcrop of rock.

'Dev, we'll use your swords for the tree-felling.' Kheda turned to scan the scrubby forest for tandra saplings. 'I'll keep mine in case we meet some savage who needs cutting down to size.'

'Of course, my lord,' Dev agreed sarcastically as he followed Kheda up to a more level patch on the slope where a few tandra trees were holding their own. 'So how do you know how to build a raft?'

'My father, Daish Reik, took me and my brothers out into the domain on hunting trips.' Kheda pushed a tandra sapling about as thick as his forearm, testing the tenacity of its roots. 'We spent as much time learning the nature of the seas and forests as we did hunting. He said we needed to know how our people fed and clothed themselves.' Despite himself, Kheda smiled with wry humour. 'And he insisted we learn how to feed and clothe ourselves with nothing more than a dagger to hand. He said even the most skilful augur can't always foretell what'll happen. Let's start with this one.' He stepped back to give Dev room.

'He wasn't wrong.' The mage unsheathed his swords, passing his second blade to Kheda.

Daish Reik often said there's vital truth in chance-heard words. Could he have foreseen something in my future to make him suspect that I might need such skills?

Dev began hacking at the tree. Light as it was, the sappy, fibrous wood caught at the steel.

'Careful,' warned Kheda. 'You don't want to break the sword.'

Dev freed the blade, considered his next move and then renewed his assault. 'So he had you making rafts?'

'More than once.' Kheda used Dev's second blade to cut down wrist-thick rustlenut shoots.

'Mind your back.' Dev pushed at the tandra sapling and it toppled over, the last fingers of wood linking the trunk to the ragged stump snapping with a sharp crack.

'Another handful of those and we'll have enough for a raft.' Kheda stuck Dev's sword in the ground and drew his dagger to strip the bark from the rustlenut wand.

'What happened to your brothers?' Dev asked bluntly as he threw down a second sapling to crush more burgeoning tandra shoots.

'I thought you knew enough Aldabreshin etiquette to avoid such questions.' Kheda concentrated on carving a deep notch into both ends of the rustlenut wood.

'It's just you and me here now.' Dev was unrepentant. 'So were you Daish Reik's firstborn or just the eldest left alive because you were chosen to become the acknowledged heir? I know you people beat the odds by marrying off inconvenient elder daughters barely out of their leading strings to change their names, and sons that don't measure up vanish, never to be mentioned again.'

'I was Daish Reik's eldest child.' Kheda slowly peeled a second length of rustlenut with his dagger tip. 'Thus his heir without any need for such subterfuge.'

Dev paused to wipe sweat from his forehead and cocked an inquisitive brow. 'But you said you had brothers. Most warlords make sure they have a few spares, in case one of your noxious Aldabreshin fevers gets the first one. What happened to them?'

'That's none of your concern.' Kheda stripped bark with a rasp of his blade.

Daish Reik taught us all to meet every challenge one step at a time as well. Right from the days when he had us building rafts to see if any of us were fated to drown, relieving him of the decisions that are a warlord's heaviest burden and gravest responsibility.

'And you call us barbarians.' Dev grunted as he chopped at the next tree, ripping out chunks of fibrous wood. 'What are you going to do with any surplus sons Itrac presents you with?'

Kheda finished notching the second rustlenut wand and tossed it aside. 'That's between me and her.'

'What is?' Risala asked, her scratched hands full of coiled vine, her face curious.

Dev chuckled and concentrated on bringing the next tandra sapling down.

'Something that doesn't concern Dev,' Kheda said shortly. He took up the mage's second sword again and began slashing the twigs and leaves from the tandra logs.

Risala studied him for a moment before sitting to twist deft double cords from the wiry vine.

'I wouldn't be doing my duty as your faithful slave if I didn't remind you of *your* duty to get a son or two on Itrac,' Dev said piously as he joined Kheda in crudely shaping the logs. 'I've heard at least one lot of gossip saying you went looking for a *zamorin* slave so as not to be outclassed, since Janne Daish plainly cut off your stones and locked them in her jewel case before sending you into exile in Chazen.'

'And you didn't care to give them the lie by letting them know you're no such thing?' demanded Kheda, stung.

'I couldn't find any gourds that weren't worm-eaten,' Risala announced into the tense silence, winding her vine cord into hanks. 'We'll have to land as we go to find water.'

'So where are we building this raft? Here or closer to the water?' Kheda gathered up the sticks he'd been working on.

'Here's as good as anywhere.' Risala stood up and looked at him expectantly.

Kheda searched her face.

No sign of your true feelings. Is that for my benefit or Dev's?

'Let's get the base lined up.' He bent to drag the tandra logs close together. 'Dev, you take that side.'

Once the tandra logs were pressed close together, Kheda slid a rustlenut wand under one mismatched end of the putative raft and laid a second across the top. He pressed the notched, springy wood together and nodded at Dev. 'Keep those ends together. Risala, lash them as best you can.'

The tandra logs shifted and squeaked as Risala secured the rustlenut struts mercilessly tight with the vine cord.

'I can't hold it much longer,' Dev warned, his bare shoulders bulging with effort as he pressed down on the wood.

Risala didn't waste any time winding cord around the notches Kheda had cut to secure the lashing on the other side of the raft. 'Now for the other end,' she nodded.

'Not bad,' Dev allowed grudgingly a few moments later as they all straightened up. 'How do we steer it? And we'll need paddles.'

'Pass me that cord.' Kheda stretched out a hand to Risala. 'Dev, cut a notch in between the first two logs on either side, at this end.' As the wizard set to with his dagger, Kheda lashed a pair of rustlenut stakes into a sturdy cross. 'We tie this fore and aft to keep it upright and make a sweep to go in the crook,' he explained as he fixed its two feet at the end of the raft. 'And yes, Dev, we need a couple of paddles.'

'I'm getting some water before I do anything else.' Dev stumped off along the cliff edge towards the meagre spring, peeling the remaining shreds of leatherspear from his chest and tossing them aside.

'What were you talking about?' Risala asked quietly, coming to stand close to Kheda.

He caught her around the waist, bending to kiss her swiftly. Her lips were dry, the skin around them paradoxically damp. She smelled of fresh sweat and old leaves. 'He wanted to know what became of my younger brothers when my father died and I declared myself warlord in his place.'

'Do you want to tell me?' Risala asked with studied neutrality.

'I want no secrets between us.' Kheda held her close and looked into her eyes. 'Daish Reik's deathbed decree offered them the choice of a quick, painless death or castration and passing into my hands as *zamorin* slaves. All but two chose the latter and went to serve Daish unnoticed as spies in other warlord's households.'

'A better Fate than living *zamorin*, blinded and imprisoned like Chazen Saril's brothers.' Risala shivered despite the heat. 'Does Itrac know this?'

'No,' said Kheda with belated realisation. 'We've never discussed it. But she must know I agreed with Janne, Rekha and Sain that they could all keep one son, and send any others to be raised far away. I wanted Sirket to have brothers to stand at his back but not close enough in age to sharpen their daggers to stick in it.'

'You should talk to Itrac about it,' Risala said, blue eyes serious.

Dev was coming back and she made to move away, but Kheda held on to her. 'If we come through this to a future where you might give me children, their lives will be wholly in your hands,' he assured her.

She twisted free of his embrace. 'Let's get a drink and make those paddles.'

After Kheda had taken his turn at the trickle of tepid water, they fashioned three crude oars in stolid silence.

Kheda picked up one end of the raft. 'We should be able to get into the sea down there without breaking our necks.'

Dev lifted the other end and Risala followed with an ungainly armful of paddles and swords. They moved carefully to the dip in the cliff where a dark pool of clear water was sheltered by a greenish-brown outcrop of coral battered by surging waves.

Kheda looked at Dev. The wizard nodded and they threw the raft into the water. Kheda jumped after it, kicking out as the water closed over him, shaking his head to clear his eyes as he broached the surface. The raft bobbed placidly and he pulled himself aboard, lying flat so as not to overturn it. Catching his breath, he rose carefully to his knees.

'Here!' Dev tossed the crude paddles down to Kheda.

The startled warlord caught the first two but the third skittered off the knobbly planks into the water. 'Don't throw the swords!' He laid a sweep in the cruck of the cross-frame and forced the ungainly craft closer to the cliffs to retrieve the errant oar.

'I'm a barbarian, not a complete fool,' said Dev scornfully.

Risala made a neat dive into the sea, swimming around the raft to climb on to the opposite side from Kheda.

'Get in as close as you can.' Dev was lying on the cliff, reaching down at full stretch to offer the swords.

Kheda used the stern oar to drive the raft closer to the rocks. Risala reached up and took the swords as an opportune swell lifted them.

Dev jumped into the sea feet first, sending spray in all directions. He bobbed there for a moment, scouring dirt and dust from his reddened chest. 'Shit, this stings.'

'Salt water will do a scalding like that no harm.' Kheda lashed the stern sweep securely into its frame.

'But the sun will leave me dried out like trail meat without a shirt to cover my back.' Dev eased himself warily aboard the raft. 'Let's have a paddle.'

With Risala and Dev kneeling, fending off gently before paddling furiously against the implacable thrust of the waves, Kheda wrestled the clumsy vessel through the tortuous maze of corals using the stern sweep. There was no respite out in the open water. Some stray thread of the southern current seized the little raft, threatening to sweep them into the wider waters beyond the island.

'You steer.' Kheda shook Risala by the shoulder. He kept firm hold of the stern oar as she clung to him, manoeuvring gingerly around the tiny craft. She took the steering oar and passed him her paddle with a resolute nod.

Kheda let go of the steering sweep and knelt to join Dev in driving the raft beyond the merciless current's reach. The knots and lumps of the tandra wood dug painfully into his shins and the searing sun hammered down on his head and back. He was sweating freely, though the breeze snatched away the beads of perspiration on his forehead and chest. It seemed an eternity before he realised that the pull of the water below the raft had slackened. Kheda felt breathless with relief as much as from the exertion They were within bowshot of the next scrap of island.

'Do we want to land for a rest?' Risala was clinging resolutely to the stern oar, feet planted wide on the rough-hewn logs, her bare brown toes gripping the wood. She nodded at a break in the reef that offered access to the beach.

'Let's get around this island and see how we're faring.' Kheda looked at Dev, who was resting his improvised oar across his thighs, bald head thrown back, his eyes closed. The wizard jerked a single nod of consent.

They made better speed now, beyond the grip of the current, but the new danger was drifting too close to the mottled, foam-wreathed reef running parallel with the shore. They crawled along the shoreline. Kheda stopped looking at it. It seemed that every time he glanced up, the same stubborn cluster of nut palms had barely shifted to mark their painful progress.

'Let's land when we're past the next strait,' Risala said tightly.

'And find a spring,' rasped Dev.

'We'll have to wait till it's cooler before we go on.' Kheda found he was nearly mute with cloying spittle and swallowed painfully. 'Or we'll all end up dead of heat prostration.'

We'll just have to take our chances with the fleet still being at the rendezvous point.

They toiled on until the raft slipped sideways into the mouth of a channel running between the little islet and a lump of thickly wooded land that tantalised with a moist green scent.

Dev looked down the channel. 'Shit!'

'Savages!' The raft dipped as Risala's shudder ran down the steering oar.

Kheda dug his paddle deep into the water, fear lending energy that put his weariness to flight. 'They're not looking this way.'

'Not yet.' Dev matched him stroke for stroke.

'It looks like a whole horde of those hollow log boats of theirs.' Risala kept watch as she wrenched their course around towards the far shore.

The rocky ledge ahead was steeply undercut by the ceaseless waves. Kheda looked desperately for some place to land as wild wordless cries echoed down the strait. 'What are they doing?'

'They're not after us,' Risala said with breathless relief. 'They're attacking some of their own.'

'Mezai said the trireme crews heard screams in the night,' Dev puffed.

Kheda pointed urgently with his dripping paddle. 'There, behind that boulder.'

They pushed the raft through an awkward eddy and on to a narrow shelf of sand behind a tumble of broken rocks.

'You'd think they'd be too busy running from Chazen

swords to bother slaughtering each other,' Dev observed as they hauled the raft out of the water.

Kheda peered out over the water but the trees hid the battle from view. 'We'd better hide until they've gone away. We'll never outrun them on open water – those log boats of theirs are cursed fast.'

'We can look for a spring, can't we?' Risala set a hand on the hilt of her dagger.

Dev settled his swords in his belt. 'I don't suggest we stand and fight if we bump into anyone.'

'No, we cut and run,' Kheda agreed. 'Let's try to see what's happening. Best we know what's behind us before we go any further.'

He led the way cautiously through the welcome shade of the forest. Defiant yells crushed inarticulate cries of pain that were pierced in turn by desperate screams. Rage and agony struggled for supremacy in the bitter cacophony.

'This way.' Dev pushed past Kheda towards the water, where reflected light rippled through the thinner trees.

Risala halted. 'I'm going to find a spring or some fruit or something. I'm parched.'

Kheda stopped, torn. 'Shout if you see anything dangerous.'

'More dangerous than Dev?' Risala's half-smile lifted Kheda's spirits just a little.

Kheda pushed cautiously through a dense screen of tassel-berry bushes to find a finger of pocked and pitted rock thrust out into the strait. Dev was already lying flat on the rough sandy ground, chin resting on his interlaced hands, intent on the scene before him. Careful of his swords, Kheda lowered himself to join the wizard. The rock was hard and gritty under his bare stomach.

'It's the usual mayhem,' Dev said thoughtfully. 'The attackers from over yonder are getting the worst of it.'

Some way off, though still too close for comfort, the flotilla Kheda had seen as they rounded the point was attacking an invader's encampment on this larger island. 'Not built in the ruins of a Chazen village, that's something to be thankful for.' He spoke the thought aloud.

The invaders had merely cleared a wide swathe of trees and brush, using the lumber and leafy branches to fashion crude shelters. There were a few blackened scars where cookfires had burned and some heaps of unidentifiable detritus.

Dev's dark eyes were fixed on the fighting. The shallow boats that had come over from the outlying island had almost reached this near shore when savages lying in wait had launched their own hollow log boats from the cover of bushes running down to the water. They hadn't gone straight for their foes but had paddled out to the middle of the channel to cut off their retreat before driving them on to the hostile shore. The wild men fought out on the water, riding their perilous vessels as they stabbed and smashed at each other with wooden spears and stone-studded clubs. The dull thud of bludgeoning and the sharp crack of bone was a counterpoint to aggressive yells and pain-filled screams.

The two mobs of savages were indistinguishable from each other. Their brief leather loincloths were virtually the same colour as their skin and all were impartially plastered with crude designs in pale paint, swirls and spirals and palm prints. All had their hair caked in mud, some decorated with feathers or leaves. None boasted the gaudy cloaks or brightly coloured garlands that the savages' mages usually affected.

Is it just the knowledge that their enemy's wizard can rust the very weapons in their hands that keeps these people from using metal to offer and receive a cleaner death? Or do these wild mages choose to keep them in such barbarism, all the better to rule them?

Sickened, Kheda watched an uneven fight turn into a massacre. The rough and ready weapons were brutally effective. Men disappeared into the sea, some with screams cut short by the smothering water, others stunned and silent, not a hand outstretched to save themselves. Bodies washed up against those who had nearly reached the shore. There was fighting on the waterline now, desperate attackers swinging murderous clubs against new foes racing out of the forest with blood-curdling cries.

'No sign of magic,' Kheda said with hollow relief. 'Precious little sign of tactics, either.'

'Why do you suppose they're gathering up the bodies?' Dev squinted across the bright water.

A noise behind them sent both men reaching for a sword, heads whipping round, ready to spring to their feet.

'I found some setil melons by a little stream.' Risala had halted a prudent distance back. She displayed the warty green globes in the lap of her tunic. 'What's going on?'

'They're killing each other.' Kheda took a melon and, slicing off the top, scooped yellow seeds out of the vivid red flesh with his knife.

'This lot's doing most of the killing.' The wizard also took a melon and cut himself a hunk, spitting the seeds out as he chewed.

'Are they killing them or taking them prisoner?' Risala sat in the cover of the scrubby shoreline trees. 'Is there a stockade for captives?'

'Hard to say.' The melon's aromatic tartness quenched Kheda's thirst astonishingly fast. He waved away tiny black flies that had appeared from nowhere.

'They didn't dig any ditch or plant a palisade.' Dev bared his teeth to scrape the last flesh from the melon skin.

Kheda sucked on another piece of melon as he watched the triumphant savages sweep the debris of the battle back towards their own shore, bodies and log boats alike mere bobbing brown shapes. A few of the defeated wild men staggered to their feet in the shallows, only to be felled with lethal thrusts of wooden spears.

'They don't seem overly concerned with keeping them alive,' Risala observed with distaste.

Dev snapped his fingers at her. 'Give me a melon, a whole one.'

Risala tossed him a knobbly green fruit without comment.

'What are you doing?' Kheda watched the wizard slice off the top and scoop out the seeds, staring intently into the hollow.

'If there's no wizard, then there's no one to tell them they're being scried on.' He shrugged. 'If there is, then that's one question answered at least and we can make a run for it.' He broke off as he saw something in the juice.

'What is it?' Kheda pressed close to the mage to get a look at the spell.

'See for yourself.' Dev swatted at the greedy flies obscuring his view.

Kheda peered into the melon to see the victorious savages piling bodies in a crude heap. Some were plainly dead, heads distorted with wounds, shattered bone and grey ooze pale against their dark, matted hair. Others still struggled feebly, gasping for air that shattered chests could no longer supply, spitting bloody foam as broken ribs tore their innards. Wooden spears jutted from pierced bellies and limbs, welling dark blood against pale timber barely dried.

'Dev!' Risala darted forward to snatch the melon and hurl it out into the water.

'What the—?' Dev gaped at the girl.

Kheda froze, looking to see if any distant savage had heard the sudden splash.

A flap of great leathery wings reverberated along the strait. Kheda grabbed for Risala and pulled her down beside him, sheltering her body with his own. The noise of wings came again, rending the air with a sound like tearing calico. The savages raised an exultant ululation.

'What's going on, Dev?' Kheda demanded in a harsh whisper.

Dev's eyes were wide and wondering. 'Cursed if I know,' he hissed, frustrated. 'And I won't be scrying to find out.'

Frantic drumming of spears and clubs on the hollow log boats echoed along the strait, volume swelling, pace increasing. It stopped, cut off by the thunderous crash of the dragon's landing.

Did it really make the earth shake or is that just my imagination running riot?

Kheda moved as far forward as he dared, to the edge of the rocky promontory where the three of them lay.

The dragon had landed and was crouching in the middle of the area the savages had cleared. Its lashing tail smashed a scatter of crude shelters. The wild men were all prostrate on the ground, not moving even when the beast's mighty tail sent broken timbers thumping down on their unprotected bodies. The dragon threw back its head and roared, an ear-splitting, unearthly sound penetrating flesh and bone. Flocks of panic-stricken birds surged up from the forest all around. Even the pied forest eagles that had few foes to fear burst screeching from the trees and fled.

Kheda reached for Risala and she held his hand tight. The warlord spared Dev a glance. 'Are you all right?'

'It's the magic. I can feel it.' Dev's eyes were wide and bright and the breath was shaking in his chest, as if he had a fever. 'I'll be all right,' the mage said through clenched teeth, 'as long as it doesn't come any nearer.'

Kheda shared a glance with Risala that told him they were in unspoken agreement.

If it does, that's when we start running. And don't you dare follow us, you star-crossed barbarian.

The dragon roared again, not so loudly this time, more intimidation than challenge. Rising to its feet, it stalked towards the tangled heap of dead and dying savages. It snapped at the helpless victims and severed limbs fell from its mighty jaws as it tossed its head back to swallow.

'Stars above.' Kheda watched, aghast, unable to look away.

'So that's how you stop a dragon eating you,' Dev said with a strained attempt at sarcasm. 'Make sure you've taken enough prisoners to fill its belly.'

'Is that why the invaders didn't care that their captives were too old to be useful slaves?' Risala wrinkled her nose. 'They just wanted meat on hand in case a dragon arrived?'

'But none of their wizards summoned a dragon last year.' Kheda looked at Dev. 'Why not?'

Dev glared back. 'I'll weave a quick net of elemental air to grab one of those shoving his face in the dirt, shall I? We'll hope he's managed to learn enough Aldabreshin to explain, shall we?'

'Look.' Kheda extracted his aching fingers from Risala's fierce grip with some difficulty and laid his hand on top of hers. Down on the shoreline, a single figure rose slowly to his feet from among the huddled mass of savages. 'Is that their wizard?'

'The one bastard astute enough to discard anything that would single him out for death at our hands?' Dev narrowed his dark eyes, sweat beading his forehead.

There was nothing to distinguish this wild man from the rest. The beast paused in its grisly feast and regarded him, cocking its massive head quizzically. It opened its mouth, rags of flesh dark on its white teeth, and hissed, low and menacingly.

The man kept his eyes lowered, not meeting the creature's burning gaze. Head bowed, he reached into some recess of his scant loin cloth and threw something in the dust before the dragon. Its head darted down and the scales fringing the back of its neck fanned out. Tongue flickering, the beast rumbled deep in its throat, making the air throb. Losing interest in the meat scattered around it, the dragon crouched, hind legs coiled beneath it, front legs bent, claws digging into the sand. The light at the centre of its lurid red eyes shone fiery gold.

The solitary bold savage walked slowly to one of the remaining shelters. The dragon's brilliant gaze tracked his every step. The great beast froze, motionless, as the man ducked inside. He reappeared almost immediately with a wooden chest. Still with that same measured pace, he approached the dragon and set the brass-bound box down just within striking distance of its long neck. Then his nerve broke and he scrambled backwards, tripping over one of his companions to go sprawling in the dust. He cowered, drawing up his legs like a terrified child, one arm impotently lifted to ward off the dragon's murderous bite.

The creature ignored him, stretching out its head to sniff at the coffer. Dusty earth stirred around its forefeet as it dug its claws deeper into the ground. Its forked tongue flickered out, tasting the dark ironwood and the tarnished bindings. Then, with the same delicacy it had shown when extricating the hapless Chazen warriors from their armour, it extended one forepaw and drove a claw into the top of the chest. One powerful twist broke the coffer into kindling and the dragon sniffed at the contents.

'What is he giving it?' Risala asked, baffled.

'Is that the mage we must kill?' demanded Kheda.

'I don't sense any hint of magic in the man,' Dev said slowly. 'It's hard to be sure, though, with the dragon filling the whole island with its aura. Only . . .' His voice trailed off.

Kheda couldn't recall when he had last seen uncertainty in the barbarian's eyes. 'What?'

'To be a wizard, you must be mageborn and have an innate affinity with one or more of the essential elements of nature,' Dev said slowly.

Born to twist and corrupt nature.

'I know that.' Kheda bit down on his distaste.

'It's like any skill – there are some with more aptitude than others. There are some with so little capacity that all the training in the world won't make them useful.' Dev nodded towards the dragon still intent on nosing at the fragments of the little chest, ignoring the wild men prone all around. 'I think we did kill all the wizards. If that man is mageborn, I don't reckon he's got anything more than negligible ability in the ordinary way of things. But he can draw enough strength to work plenty of mischief if he can keep the dragon close at hand – if he can keep it from eating him.'

'How can we kill him?' demanded Kheda.

'With that thing playing watchdog?' Dev chewed his lip. 'I can't see us doing that. Still, it should take him a few days to work out what to do with his new power. And just having the dragon around might promote a few other new wizards from the spear-carriers. Maybe they'll start fighting each other. Maybe we'll get lucky.'

'What will the dragon do then?' Kheda wondered with a hollow feeling of dread.

'Not a lot, I would hope,' said Dev. 'As long as there are plenty of dead for it to eat.'

'He knows what else to give it to keep it happy,' added

Kheda thoughtfully. 'What do you suppose that is?'

The dragon was lying down now, tail curled around its haunches, forefeet cradling whatever the wild man had given it. Stretching out its long neck, it plucked another lifeless body from the heap of dead and slowly ate it with an audible crunching. Sliding backwards on their bellies and elbows, the surviving savages retreated into the forest.

'It's gems. It has to be,' Risala said suddenly. 'The invaders were never interested in other loot. They'd barely take more food beyond what would fill their bellies after a fight.'

'Why give gems to a dragon?' Kheda looked at Dev.

'I don't know.' Vindictively the wizard crushed a fly crawling on a scrap of melon rind. 'Velindre might, but I'm not bespeaking her within fifty leagues of that thing, even if I had the means to do it.'

'We need to get away from here.' Kheda tried to see where the savages had gone but the all-concealing foliage made that impossible.

'We'll take some melons with us.' Risala crawled backwards to a nut palm and, cutting a few fronds, began plaiting them rapidly. 'And we need hats in this sun.'

'You were quick off the mark back there,' Dev said grudgingly as he glowered at the contented dragon.

'Nothing like the thought of being eaten alive to sharpen the ears.' She shuddered.

Kheda waited impatiently until she had finished the basket. He shovelled melons into the lopsided container and gathered it up. Hot and sticky with juice and sweat, dust and grit coating his arms and chest, the weight of the basket ground painfully against his skin. The discomfort was nothing compared to the torment of this new threat to Chazen.

A dragon. Which looks quite happy to stay as long as these savages keep feeding it their carrion. Whose very presence may be enough to give these wild men new mages. We barely survived their last assaults backed by their murderous sorceries.

'There you go, my lord.' Dev tossed a crudely woven hat to Kheda. 'Sorry if it's not quite suitable for your dignity.'

'I'll let it pass, just this once,' Kheda said dryly as he clapped the hat on his head.

They reached the shallow shelf in the rock where they had left their raft.

'Would these new wizards lose their magic if we could drive the dragon off or lure it away?' Kheda asked suddenly.

'Probably,' Dev said slowly.

'Would the dragon kill them if they lost their magic?' Kheda shot back. 'Would they lose their hold over it?'

'If you managed to feed them some of Shek Kul's cursed herbs?' Dev was quick to see where Kheda's thoughts were leading and scowled beneath his own palm-fringed hat. 'Making them no more than *zamorin* as far as magic goes? Perhaps. I don't know.'

Kheda set his jaw resolutely. 'Then let's think how we might do one or the other.'

'I'd rather see if Velindre's got some lore to help us,' objected Dev disagreeably.

Wouldn't it be better if we could rid ourselves of this new danger without resorting to magic? Using Dev last year was the lesser of two evils but you are still cursed with that evil, if this dragon's appearance is anything to go by.

'We'll have to see.' Kheda glanced over his shoulder. There was neither sign nor sound of the dragon moving from its resting place and he breathed a little easier.

'The trip won't get any shorter for us hanging around.' Risala gathered up the paddles as Dev shoved the raft into the sea.

'We'll each take a turn steering.' Kheda passed the basket of melons to Dev as the wizard balanced gingerly on the raft. 'You first, Risala.' He handed her on to the raft and she took firm hold of the steering oar.

'Then me.' Dev was threading a spare length of cord through the spars holding the logs together, lashing the basket down. 'I'm not paddling you two all the way home and I'm not risking magic that could draw some wild wizard after us.'

'Ready?' asked Risala, shoving her own hat backwards on her head.

'Ready.' At Kheda's nod, the two men began paddling.

No one wasted breath in talking as they worked their way along the coral-crusted shore and into more open water. Kheda spared half an eye for any sign of wild men among the trees as he pondered their predicament.

Could we find some means of killing the dragon or driving it away? Will this woman of Dev's find some lore to help us? Will there be any sign presaging such good fortune when there's a wizard involved? Will there be any sign showing me which is the better choice for Chazen?

First things first: we have to keep this dragon from laying waste to the domain while we wait for some salvation from these northern wizards or for inspiration as to how we might save ourselves.

Let's take a leaf out of that bold savage's book. It wants meat first and foremost. Very well. We send every trireme and warrior Chazen has to call on to round up every last one of these savages. We hold them captive on the islands closest to the beast. If the dragon comes, it can feast on them.

The rocky end of the island sank beneath the turquoise waters, reaching out long fingers of many-coloured coral. In the open waters beyond, an undulating russet reef guided them into a calmer channel between two barren islets rising barely a handspan above the rippling waters.

Though there's no telling where the dragon might go. Best make ready for its arrival anywhere in the domain. Tell the islanders to surrender their ducks and hens. Hunters will have to snare as many deer and forest hogs as they can. Will that sate its appetites? Or has it only got a taste for human flesh?

Crude as they were, their palm-frond hats helped to baffle the punishing sun and the calm waters in the sheltered channel made for easier paddling. Kheda slowed and scooped up water to rinse his sticky hands and face and to wash some of the dust from his chest. 'Dev, take a turn steering.'

What of its other appetites? Risala must be right. It must be gems that savage gave it. Why does it want gems? Does that matter? Stick to the question at hand. How do we stop it devastating the domain? The gift seemed to placate it. Is that what we must do? Pour out what little wealth Chazen has just to keep the beast from causing mayhem?

He paddled on, curbing his longer stroke to match Risala's determined efforts.

It has to be worth a try. Isn't one life worth more than even the finest talisman gem? Then that's another reason to take the battle to the remaining savages, to take back the jewels they have stolen. But can we do it without being eaten by the dragon ourselves?

Dev used the stern sweep to help drive the raft on and Kheda recalled the barbarian's expertise in managing the ill-fated *Amigal* single-handed.

A scatter of irregular reefs demanded all their attention. Wider isles further off baffled the prevailing wind and the sun struck up a dazzling sheen from the water. They left the treacherous uncertainty of the corals and found themselves crossing a shallow stretch of sea rippling crystal clear over white sands. Invisible currents sent the carpets of sea grasses below swaying around the grazing turtles. The raft's shadow crossed the path of a smaller turtle. It shied away, rolling over to show the pale underside of its mottled grey and brown shell as it flailed its scaly flippers.

The invaders scorned turtleshell and pearls when they looted. I suppose that means the dragon has no interest in such things. Is that ill fortune for Chazen or good luck? Do we lament that our own resources cannot save us or rejoice that we don't have to squander the pearl harvest to buy off this monster?

'There's good eating on one of those,' Dev remarked.

'Got anything to catch it with besides magic?' Risala looked at Kheda. 'You've been rowing longer than anyone. You should take a turn at steering.'

'How long have we been at this? How far have we come?' Kheda tried to stand and discovered how cramped and stiff his legs were. His stumble almost overset the raft before he caught the stern oar and managed to recover his balance.

Dev muttered something derogatory under his breath as he settled himself to another stint of paddling. Risala shot the wizard a filthy look.

Kheda scanned the seas and islands ahead and a flash of white caught his eye. 'What's that?'

Dev and Risala both looked up.

'Where?' she queried.

'What?' he demanded.

'Over there, past that easterly island.' Kheda watched the wing of pale canvas disappear behind a clump of nut palms.

'I see it.' Dev let his paddle trail in the water.

The boat reappeared on the other side of the islet.

'Do you think it's one of ours?' Risala looked back at Kheda for reassurance. 'We've never seen the invaders using sails.'

'If it isn't one of ours, it soon will be.' Dev made sure his swords were secure in his belt before setting to with his paddle once again.

'I don't want any bloodshed,' Kheda warned sharply. 'Not unless there's nothing else for it.'

With a dragon in the islands, we don't need the ill omen of Chazen blood spilled in Chazen waters by Chazen steel.

CHAPTER EIGHT

Kheda woke from a dream of sweating bodies entwined in velvet darkness to hear sunbirds singing cheerily outside his shuttered windows. Strong sun striped the wide bed. He threw off the embrace of the light quilt that had rebuffed the night's breezes and pushed himself upright, stifling a rueful groan.

It was barely sunrise when I first woke. I never meant to go back to sleep. Where's Dev?

A soft footfall sounded in the bathing room beyond the door in the opposite wall.

'Dev? Is that you?' Kheda swung his feet to the floor.

'It's me.' Risala appeared in the archway with an armful of towels. She was dressed in a modest cotton dress neither crisply new nor overly worn.

Unobtrusive, all the better for finding out just what the people here are making of the web of lies the three of us have spun for them, her own mouth shut, eyes and ears open.

His blood pulsed at an unbidden memory of her soft skin beneath his hand.

Was it you I was dreaming of? That dress is almost the same colour as your eyes.

'Good morning.' He managed a casual greeting as he eased past her to the bathing room.

'You look rested.' She surveyed his nakedness with the faintest of teasing smiles.

'Why didn't Dev wake me?' Kheda took a moment for the urgency in his loins to fade before he relieved himself, returning, rather more composed, to the bedchamber.

'I don't know.' Risala opened the shutters and Kheda crossed to the window.

He turned the ivory column on the sill so that the vane faced the sun and read the shadow's mark across the swooping lines carved into the cylinder. 'The morning's half gone.' He turned to shout peremptorily at the heavy outer door. 'Dev! Breakfast and plenty of it!'

Risala perched on the edge of the bed as Kheda threw open a clothes chest and looked for trousers. 'Your lady wife is wearing green this morning.'

'We need to show a united front, do we?' Kheda glanced at her before pulling out an emerald pair of trews.

Risala nodded. 'The *Yellow Serpent*'s rowers have been talking.'

'We can hardly blame them for that. Anyway, a creature that size was hardly going to stay a secret for long.' Kheda stepped into the trousers and pulled the drawstring tight. 'They must have left a groove in the sea, they got us back here so fast. That deserves some praise.' He leaned against the wall, arms folded across his bare chest. 'At least we got back here quickly enough to prove that the hasty rumours of my death were exaggerated. What are people making of Itrac's reactions to the *Mist Dove*'s first report?'

'Hardly anyone knew what was going on.' Risala wasn't unsympathetic. 'Just that she'd shut herself in her pavilion, barring her doors against all-comers. Thanks to Beyau and Jevin, her hysterics stayed safely behind those locked doors, and all her servants are loyal, they won't betray her with gossip. As for the rumours . . .' Risala shrugged. 'There's some speculation that she might have lost an early pregnancy.'

Let's hope those loyal servants keep that from her ears.

'There was no word of a dragon around the anchorage?' Kheda persisted.

Risala took a moment to consider her reply. 'There was rumour but it just wrong-footed everyone, especially when there was no word from Itrac. It's incredible, after all. Who'd imagine we'd see a dragon in these reaches? Who's heard of one outside a poet's verses?'

She smiled faintly before continuing, wholly serious. 'You've reappeared, which is good news even if the *Yellow Serpent*'s men have confirmed that the beast is real. That's hardly good news, but at least your presence gives the people some reassurance and for the moment the dragon is still well over the horizon. Everyone's waiting to see what you do, what orders you give. They're all telling each other long and loud that there's no point making any decisions until they know what's afoot. Better to know where the dragon is, rather than head off blindly and run straight into its jaws. I don't think they're too keen to throw themselves on Daish mercy again.'

Kheda rubbed at the back of his neck. 'So it's not as bad as it could be. The domain's not in an uproar.'

'It would have been a cursed sight worse if we hadn't got back when we did,' Risala countered. 'And the people need your leadership. Otherwise dread will spread like mildew.'

'Slow but insidious.' Kheda looked at her, his voice low. 'Do they believe what we said happened to us and the *Amigal*?'

'I think so.' Risala wrinkled her nose with a suggestion of doubt. 'They want to believe that it's possible to escape a dragon, especially those who have friends or family on the triremes you've left out there to continue the hunt for the savages. And they've no reason to think their warlord wouldn't tell them the truth,' she concluded wryly.

'I'd better get to the courier-dove lofts.' Kheda pushed himself away from the wall. 'And see what news there is from the *Mist Dove* and the others. Do you know if there have been any whispers on the wind from any other domains? Is Janne Daish inviting people to wonder why a magic so evil touches this domain, even if it chooses not to touch me?' A knock sounded on the brass-bound door giving on to the hallway. 'Dev? Have you been grinding the saller to make that bread?'

The door opened to reveal Itrac. 'Good morning, Kheda.' Waving Jevin back, she pushed the door closed on his anxious face. She turned to face Kheda, her expression unreadable behind a mask of cosmetics. Risala slid off the bed to vanish swiftly away through the bathing room.

'Itrac, good morning.' Kheda brushed a chaste kiss on her cheek and then waited, uncertain what to do or say for the best.

How can I tell you I don't blame you for panicking at the news that you might have been widowed a second time in strange and ominous circumstances? How can I do that without shaming you by letting you know I heard about your hysterics?

'Jevin is bringing your breakfast.' The first wife of Chazen was wearing a long, wide-sleeved tunic over close-fitted trousers all in leaf-green silk shot with silver lights. Ropes of pearls bound the shimmering cloth at ankle, wrist, waist and neck and a crescent of silver-mounted nacre held back her long black hair, which was plaited into a torrent of narrow braids. 'Dev was as weary as you. I told Beyau to leave him in his cubby hole.' Itrac shrugged her disdain for a body slave who insisted on a permanent sleeping place of his own, rather than at the foot of his master's bed. 'He'll hardly be fit to serve you if he doesn't sleep himself out.'

'We had a tiring voyage back here,' Kheda said carefully.

'And suffered in the sun when you had to make your own way back to the *Yellow Serpent*.' Avoiding Kheda's eyes, Itrac went to a tall coffer and took out a stubby jar with a rag-swathed stopper. 'Let me oil your back before you finish dressing.'

'Thank you.' Kheda took the jar from her and poured a little of the emollient into his own palm before returning it. He rubbed the lotion into his hands.

Back to navigating the intricate complexities of the married life. You're offering an intimacy but one that means you don't have to face me. What does that tell me?

'Now we have a dragon to plague us.' Behind him, Itrac's voice was as firm as her fingers rubbing balm into his muscles. 'After all the trials of invasion last year.'

'There is indeed a dragon.' Kheda concentrated on relaxing his shoulders. 'Though I'm not sure it's here to plague us. For the moment, it seems most interested in devouring those remaining invaders. It's entirely possible that their wickedness has brought this evil down upon them.'

'Truly?' Itrac's hands stopped circling. 'That's how you read this?'

'It's certainly more than possible,' Kheda said steadily. 'I shall need to read the omens with considerable care, to see if things become any clearer.'

In the meantime, that's the word we'll start spreading as far and as fast as courier doves and dispatch galleys can carry it. And I'm sure the portents can be suitably ambiguous, in case the beast makes a liar out of me.

'Hesi, on the *Yellow Serpent*, he said the dragon overflew them.' Itrac resumed her rubbing and Kheda could feel a faint scoring from her silver-varnished nails. 'It drove that boat your slave insists is his on to a reef?'

'Some whirlwind was following in its wake.' Kheda tried to strike an appropriate balance between awe and ease of mind. 'It seems the poets were right: such creatures stir up chaos wherever they go.'

Thank you, Risala, for recalling that nugget from some endless epic or other. I imagine poets on every island will be unrolling those song cycles now. What will that do for morale?

'So we will see the whole domain riven by this chaos?' Itrac's hands and voice both trembled.

'Not if I have any say in it.' Kheda turned to take her hands in his, looking deep into her brown eyes. 'As I said, for now the beast seems content to eat those foul savages and I'm content to let it. I've ordered our triremes and warriors to drive the wild men into its very jaws, if they can do so without risking themselves.'

'But you said we needed all our boats guarding the main sea lanes . . .' Itrac faltered.

'Which is why I decided to clear the western isles of the last invaders,' Kheda reminded her. 'That's what our warriors need to be doing, isn't it, dragon or no dragon? Besides, I'll wager word of this beast clears Chazen waters of every parasite and pirate. They'll be splashing their way north as fast as they can row. There can be a pearl in the least promising oyster, can't there?'

He gripped her fingers tighter to stifle the next question on Itrac's lips. 'And we saw something very strange when we washed up close by the beast, something so strange no poet would dare imagine it. The creature covets gems, Itrac. Don't ask me why, but it does. Dev and I saw a wild man buy his life with a handful of them. That's how we managed to escape its notice, while it was besotted with its prize. We must send jewels to the triremes, so that they can buy their lives by distracting the beast with them, if need be.'

'Jewels?' Itrac's eyes widened with pure astonishment.

Kheda nodded. 'We keep this to ourselves, naturally, but don't you see, this knowledge can buy us more time as and when the beast has eaten its fill of those invaders. I'll stuff its mouth with every jewel Chazen can lay hands on before I let it devour a single one of our people.'

'And when it's eaten every gem we can lay our hands on?' There was desperation in Itrac's eyes.

'All the while we're keeping it sated, with carrion or whatever else it wants, we'll be looking for the means to kill it,' Kheda told her purposefully. 'I will not give over this domain to that creature, Itrac. I refuse to believe we cannot kill this dragon. Those invaders came backed by magic and terror and we killed their wizards. I found the means to defeat their sorcerors in Shek Kul's archive. I've already sent dispatch galleys to every warlord we're allied with who has a library worth having between here and the northernmost reaches. There must be lore about such beasts somewhere.'

'You've seen some portent telling you this is the best thing to do?' Itrac's face shone with frantic hope.

'I have,' Kheda lied doggedly. 'And I shall go on using every divination known to me to see us through this peril.'

That much is no lie. I'll use every means I have of battling such evil. Every means, even if that requires consorting with wizards again.

Tears filled Itrac's eyes. 'Chazen Saril never showed such courage. He wouldn't have gone looking for answers, for ways to fight back, not like you did. He'd have run from a dragon, just like before when the invaders came. He wouldn't have come back for me.'

'Let's look to the future, not to the past.' Kheda led Itrac towards the bathing room. 'And let's not mark that tunic, or your head maid will scold me till the rains have come and gone again.' Taking up a cotton cloth, he dipped one end in a ewer of fresh water and gently scrubbed her hands clean of the oily lotion. He refused to catch his own eye in the mirror above the washstand. 'Now, which tunic do you think I should wear?'

Itrac dabbed the cloth at the corners of her eyes before

following him back into the bedroom, her face a mask of hard-won calm once more. 'The emerald with the golden embroidery.' She opened Kheda's jewel coffer. 'That will go well enough with turtleshell.'

'We can take it as an omen in our favour that this dragon doesn't seek to plunder this domain's riches.' Kheda donned the tunic and accepted the bracelets she offered him.

'We could.' Itrac sounded doubtful. 'Though I doubt that's what Rekha Daish will be saying.'

Kheda settled a chain of carved turtleshell links on his hips. 'When did she sail north?'

'Four days since. I got word of the dragon, that you were lost. I'm sorry, I shouldn't have let her know but I was so shocked by the news.' Hurt and chagrin coloured Itrac's words equally. 'She left straight away and took all her triremes with her.'

'Rushing off like a startled fowl? And four days ago?' Kheda shrugged. 'When I was already safely aboard the *Yellow Serpent* and on my way back here. That galley will take eight days to make the voyage back to the Daish residence. So let's make sure Rekha arrives home to find a courier dove waiting for her, assuring her that I am alive and well and inviting thoughts on what this new puzzle might mean for Chazen and Daish alike. Do you suppose she'll have made herself very foolish telling everyone I'm already dead?'

Do you understand my meaning? That as far as I am concerned, you stayed here level-headed and prudently waiting to learn the truth of the matter? That it was Rekha who took fright and fled?

Do we have Rekha to thank for the rumour that you were secluded because you'd lost a child? Doubtless she'd argue that was all she could think of to plausibly hide the truth.

'I hope not, for her sake.' Despite her words, the

prospect evidently amused Itrac as she handed Kheda a collar of turtleshell plaques. 'Perhaps she won't be so hasty. You've been thought dead and confounded everyone before.'

'She should know that, better than most,' agreed Kheda lightly.

'I don't see why we want to invite Daish opinions on this matter.' Itrac frowned as she studied Kheda's appearance.

'It's only courteous; Daish will need to prepare if there's any chance of Chazen boats fetching up on their shores again.' Kheda grinned maliciously. 'Besides, don't forget how desperate Rekha is for pearls. I said I'd spread every jewel in Chazen in front of this dragon to keep it quiet. And I will, but only after I've drained Daish dry of all the stones it can spare and more besides. If Rekha Daish wants Chazen pearls to hide the disaster of their reefs' harvest, she can trade weight for weight in gems.'

If that doesn't convince everyone that my allegiance is now truly to Chazen, nothing will. What choice do I have? If this dragon isn't dealt with, it'll ravage Chazen and then move north. I have to do all I can to prevent that for Sirket's sake, even if I have to plunder his domain to do it.

'I was looking to trade the pearls for the means to rebuild. Stars above, we need so much.' Itrac fell silent, her painted face contemplative. 'But perhaps that's why the harvest has been so abundant, to give us the means to evade this evil.' She paused, eyes distant. 'We don't want Rekha to know why we need the gems. I don't quite know what she would do with such news, but better to keep her ignorant if we can. She'll do her best to find out what we do with the stones, though. Misdirecting her will take some cunning.'

'Trade and all its intricacies are your prerogative, my lady of Chazen.' Kheda took a pace towards the door. 'And while you're about your duties, I had better be about mine. I've been idle too long this morning.'

'You were tired.' Itrac took a sideways step to surprise him with a quick, hesitant kiss on his lips. 'What will you be doing?'

'Taking the omens first and foremost.' Kheda jerked his head in the direction of the unseen observatory tower. 'Then learning what news has come in from the *Mist Dove* and the rest of the triremes. I want to see the bird master as well, to find out what courier doves we're holding from Ritsem and Redigal. I'd better make sure all our allies know I am alive and well, never mind whatever hysterical news Rekha has spread. And I'll see if there's any useful lore in the Chazen library. We may know how to contain this menace, but the sooner this dragon is dead, the better.'

So I need Dev to bespeak that wizard woman of his as soon as possible. Everything else is just so much treading water.

'But your breakfast . . .' Itrac looked towards the door.

'Send Jevin to wake up Dev and have him bring food and drink to the observatory.' Kheda grinned. 'I must put my duty to the domain before my belly.'

'Naturally, my husband,' replied Itrac with amusement. 'Will you eat with me this evening?' she asked hopefully.

'I will, with pleasure.' Kheda went into the hallway, ignoring the servants who froze as he appeared.

You'll need to make time to bolster her nerve. Besides, Risala will be occupied elsewhere. Though we should discuss what verses she thinks would spread a little calm and stiffen resolve around the islands, and how we might get her discreet allies to prompt poets to recall them.

Other residence slaves were working in the shade of the pavilion's northern face. Maidservants paused in their sewing and polishing, apprehensive faces turning to Kheda. A sturdy youth pulling a handcart stacked with bright brass water jars stopped by the steps, open-mouthed but fearful to ask what might be about to befall them. Kheda nodded acknowledgements, his confident smile resolutely fixed, and strode out into the bright sun. As he took the path towards the observatory, he forced himself to slow his pace.

If I'm seen rushing about, these people will mistake purposeful haste for open alarm and we'll have half of them fleeing before the day is out.

A white-haired islander was sweeping windblown sand and grass from the hard, trampled path.

Too old to be hauling sacks and barrels but too hale to accept an idle seat in the shade. There's mettle in Chazen. A warlord should be proud to lead such people.

'Glad to see you safely home, my lord.' The old man stepped aside, leaning on his broom of palm fronds, the well-muscled arms of his youth wasted to wrinkled slackness. For all his courtesy, his leathery face was anxious as he gripped his broom with gnarled hands.

'I'm glad to be here,' said Kheda breezily.

'My lord . . .' There was pleading in the old servant's voice.

'Yes?' The question died on Kheda's tongue as he saw faces turned towards him all across the anchorage.

Have they all been waiting for sight of me? What are they looking for? Confirmation that there's someone here to lead them to safety this time? Itrac can't be the only one remembering how Chazen Saril fled those invaders to wash up in Daish waters, broken by his fears, unmanned.

Can't they think back to their own terror? Do they realise how much they were asking of him, that he fight magic with bare-handed ignorance?

Do they realise just what they're asking of me? Would they ever truly want to know what answers I'm seeking?

The rowing boats ferrying the residence's food and fuel from the isles edging the lagoon slowed as the islanders trailed their oars in the water, mouths open as they registered Kheda's presence. The purposeful activity aboard the closest light trireme halted as bare-chested oarsmen hurried up from the rowing deck to line the unrailed sides and join the archers on the bow platform. The shipmaster and his steersman bowed low beneath the upswept arc of the stern as they saw Kheda look in their direction. Hails sounded further out across the water as the crews of great galleys anchored in deeper waters acknowledged their warlord.

Kheda turned his attention to the sweeper. 'You wanted to ask me something?'

'I hear tell there's an ill wind blowing in the western isles.' The old man swallowed, unwilling to tempt the future by mentioning the dragon.

Past the old man, Kheda saw Itrac appear on the steps of Kheda's own pavilion, her garments vivid despite the shade, the pearls adorning her all the whiter for it. He saw her look in his direction, hesitant.

'I'm seeking lore from every library I have access to and every ally who might know something of such beasts.' Kheda stretched one hand out towards Itrac. 'I'll be looking to the heavens, to the earthly compass, to every divination tested by time and use to guide me to the means to turn this ill fortune aside. We will be rid of this evil, my friend.'

And it'll all be for nothing if we can't hold these people together. They thought you might be dead. They think that Itrac might have lost the hope of a child for the domain, and that's assuredly an evil omen. They had better see us happy and united. It's not just what you do that builds loyalty, it's what you're seen to do. Daish Reik taught you that.

Kheda strode purposefully back down the path towards Itrac, hands outstretched. She saw him and hurried to meet him. He took her hands and drew her to him, folding her in a close embrace.

Somewhere distant, unseen, a cheer was raised. Other voices took it up, swelling the sound to a defiant roar. Stamping feet and the drumming of spars and ropes on deck planking ran beneath it. The swordsmen and archers of the heavy triremes raised their weapons, scabbarded swords clashing together, daggers making drums of wood and leather quivers to add a hard edge to the rousing sound.

Itrac slid her arms around his chest, pulling Kheda to her. She kissed him hard, her mouth opening beneath his, moulding her body to him. Her breath trembled on Kheda's cheek and he felt a disquieting shiver of lust beneath his cold calculation.

This is lust, not love. It's the thought of Risala that warms me with real passion. Have you seen that, my wife? Which was it that you felt for Saril, if truth were told? Are your kisses as calculated as mine?

As Itrac refused to release him, the ovation from the closest boats took on a distinctly ribald note. Kheda used laughter as an excuse to break away. After a moment's uncertainty, Itrac joined in. They moved apart, still hand-fasted. The applause was finally subsiding into individual shouts that Kheda was quite glad he couldn't make out.

'We have work to do, my lady.' He bowed to Itrac.

'We do, my lord.' Her smile was wide with new confidence, her eyes bright. 'Till this evening.'

He watched for a moment as she walked briskly back towards the heart of the residence. Servants and slaves returned to their tasks again amid a buzz of conversation. The figures aboard the ships in the anchorage set about their chores with renewed energy. One piper sent a swirl of melody up to challenge the raucous wheeling gulls, then a second joined in with a swooping counterpoint. Soon a murmur of disjointed song rumbled along beneath the jaunty flutes. The old sweeper chuckled, brushed some nonexistent debris from Kheda's path and bowed low as the warlord passed.

Let's hope that little display keeps curious eyes away from those things you must never be seen doing, lest the shock and horror of discovery rip this domain apart.

Kheda walked rapidly across the island to the clean-swept expanse in front of the observatory. Risala was waiting in the hall at the bottom of the stairs.

'That was a convincing show of joint resolve.' She sounded amused.

You don't sound jealous. Are you? You've kept your distance these past days, or was that because we couldn't escape Dev? What does it mean if you're not jealous of any woman who thinks she has a claim on me any more? Well, there's nothing I can do about it for the present, so I don't think I want to know either way. But you're wearing that string of shark's teeth around your sleeve. Isn't that token of something?

'We need to find some reason for Itrac's seclusion that nails the lie about her losing a baby,' Kheda said without preamble. 'And where has Dev got to, curse him!' He led the way into the westernmost of the semicircular halls at the base of the observatory. 'Are we alone? Are you certain?'

'There's no one here but me,' Risala assured him. 'I checked.'

'We need mirrors.' Kheda looked around the room with its filigree-fronted bookcases and shelves full of candles, pendants, metal tablets and dried herbs, the paraphernalia for every manner of divination. 'Dev must work the magic to speak to that woman again. We have to find out everything she knows about dragons as soon as possible.'

Risala unhooked a highly polished circle of steel from the wall, its rim chased with bronze sailfish. 'Where are we doing this?'

'Up aloft.' Dev appeared in the doorway carrying a laden tray and scowling blackly. 'And with that door locked behind us. We definitely don't want anyone walking in on us here.' He dumped the brass tray on a polished beralewood table and spooned poached sard-berries into a bowl of steamed golden saller grain. 'Do you have an excuse for shutting everyone out that won't raise more questions than it answers?'

Kheda's stomach rumbled as hunger surprised him. 'We'll say I was reading mirror omens.' He scooped up rustlenuts crushed with oil and herbs with some bread. 'You said you needed a mirror. Choose one,' he ordered indistinctly through a mouthful of sweet green arith.

Wordlessly, Risala set the mirror she was holding on the table and went to fetch a second, this one square and framed with a lattice of tiny lustre tiles in red and gold.

Dev shovelled berries and saller grain into his mouth, purple juice staining his lips. 'Does it matter which one I use?'

'Yes,' Kheda retorted, tearing another round of bread apart. 'Risala, are you hungry?' He gestured towards the food.

'I ate earlier.' She laid a third mirror carefully on the table, an oval of brightly polished copper whose reverse bore a silver mirror bird spreading the shimmering fan of its tail.

'Is any one more valuable than the others?' Dev set down his empty bowl and grinned. 'Any of them a gift from someone you particularly dislike?'

'Just choose one,' Kheda ordered, chewing rapidly.

Dev shrugged and picked up the mirror bordered by lustre tiles. 'This is as good as any.'

Hardly an omen, but that's Ulla-domain workmanship and I can't think of anyone I detest more than Ulla Safar.

'Upstairs then.' Kheda nodded in the direction of the stairs and picked up the other two mirrors.

'I only need one,' said Dev, irritated.

'I'll be telling everyone I was looking for mirror omens.' Kheda picked a weighty key from a brass bowl on a shelf. 'I'm not going to risk making our plight even a little worse by lying about that.'

'Suit yourself,' said Dev with faint derision. 'Risala, make yourself useful and find me a candle.'

'You're his slave, Dev, I'm not yours.' All the same, she found a taper in a metal box beside an oil lamp and held it up for the wizard's approval.

'That'll do.' Dev nodded.

Kheda paused to lock the outer door as Risala followed the mage up to the observation platform. He climbed slowly up the stairs. The sunlight was fierce after the coolness within the building.

Is that why you're sweating? Or is it your guilt at suborning magic yet again? And this time you're doing it in the very heart of this domain that's already suffered so much sorcery.

From the vantage point, Kheda glanced around the skein of islands to see purposeful activity in all directions, residence workers and mariners alike oblivious to their warlord's duplicity. 'Let's get this done. Do you have everything you need?'

'Some shade wouldn't go amiss,' Dev said sourly. He dropped gracelessly to sit cross-legged in the middle of the roof, holding the mirror in one hand and the taper in the other. The virgin wick flared with scarlet sorcerous flame.

Kheda found he couldn't keep looking out over the unsuspecting anchorage and turned to stare at the empty seas to the south. Behind him, Dev spoke in some hurried incomprehensible tongue, his forceful scorn needing no translation.

'She says she hasn't found anything yet.' Risala came to stand by Kheda, her back to the sea, all her attention on the mirror that Dev was holding. 'She's talking about searching in some library.'

'We have libraries,' Kheda muttered.

'She's been looking for some journals,' Risala said slowly. 'She hasn't found them.'

From the tone of the barbarian's brusque interruption, Kheda concluded that Dev wasn't impressed by that news.

'She's asking him about the dragon,' Risala continued in an undertone. 'She wants to know if he's seen it again and what it's been doing. She wants to know all about it.'

'What is he telling her?' Kheda asked, curious. 'Has he said anything about the gems? What has he said about his own magic going awry?'

'No, he's saying nothing about that,' Risala said thoughtfully. 'He just wants to know about her researches.'

Dev's voice was harsh as he demanded answers. The unseen woman sounded to be giving as good as she got. Kheda could just hear her scathing replies, faint and tinny, like someone whispering paradoxically loudly into a copper goblet.

'She's saying he's welcome to try for himself if he thinks he can do better,' Risala commented with amusement.

Kheda slid Risala a sideways grin. 'I'm glad you're here to keep him honest.'

She didn't see his smile, intent on Dev's rapid exchanges with the distant wizard woman. 'They're disputing who might have these journals and who she should ask next.' Risala shook her head slowly, eyes still fixed on the mirror, her voice running low beneath the arguing mages. 'She's insisting she knows what she's looking for. She's sure these journals will hold all the lore we need. It's just finding out who has them. I don't think Dev's convinced.'

Kheda could hear that for himself, along with the rising note of defiant argument in the woman's words.

'Now she's talking about having to go on some journey to find out what we need to know,' Risala continued hurriedly. 'She says that's the best way to be certain, something about going to the source. I think there's a joke there but I don't follow. Dev's not amused. He seems to think there are people who'll know what we need closer to hand. He doesn't see why she can't do whatever it takes to win them over.'

She broke off, frowning as the conversation flowing back and forth through the enchanted mirror threatened to degenerate into a shouting match.

'Dev.' Kheda yielded to his frustration and turned around.

'What?' snapped the wizard before silencing the distant woman with a curt word.

'Is she truly on the scent of some lore that can help us? Do you believe that much?' Kheda demanded. 'Do you trust her?'

'She wants this lore worse than you do.' Dev laughed unpleasantly. 'It's just a question of the quickest way to find it. I'd stick to searching the archives at hand if it was me but she wants to make a trip—'

'Whatever she chooses to do, how soon does she think she might have some lore we can use against the dragon?' Kheda interrupted. 'Honestly? We need to know how long we have to hold the beast off for.'

'And what's the longest it might take her,' added Risala.

'If things don't go as well as she seems to expect,' Kheda agreed.

'Hope for the best but plan for the worst.' Risala quoted one of Kheda's precepts back at him with a grin.

Dev posed the question in his rapid barbarian tongue. Kheda listened with frustration to the uncanny, unintelligible conversation between the mages. The mirror burned with a red-gold radiance vivid even in the bright sunlight. The magewoman was a distant image, featureless as she gesticulated.

Hope for the best but plan for the worst. You cannot wait till you have all possible information before making plans. You will never have all the facts. Make your best plan based on knowledge, experience and instinct, and act upon it. Believe you are right. If it turns out you were wrong, deal with the consequences as and when they arise, and never admit to self-doubt. You did not make an error, because that was the best plan of action at the time. You cannot change the past, only the future, so make a new plan, the best you can in the here and now.

That's what your father told you and that's what you taught Sirket. It sounds so simple to be a warlord.

But won't relying on some accursed wizard's best guess inevitably lead me into error?

What else can I do? Isn't this woman's guess better than nothing? I have to base my actions on something. The people of Chazen must believe I have a plan or we'll lose them to their fears. Lose your people and you've lost your domain. First and last, that's the ultimate reality of being a warlord.

The wizard woman's distant reply had been going on for far too long to be a simple answer. Tension crawled between Kheda's shoulder blades along with sweat prompted by the punishing sun. Dev responded with some lengthy, forceful protest, his tone ugly.

'What is she saying?' Kheda asked with growing concern.

'That she won't just tell Dev what she learns regardless,' Risala answered, her voice tense with anger. 'She's saying she wants to come here, to see the dragon for herself. Then she'll share what she finds out. Unless we agree, she won't tell us a thing.'

'How does she propose to do that?' Kheda saw that Dev was crushing the end of the taper in his hand, knuckles white around the beeswax. His scorn sprayed the mirror with spittle that vanished as soon as it touched the radiant metal.

The distant wizard woman's face filled the magical void burning in the surface of the mirror. The contrast with Dev was startling. This wizard woman was all barbarian with blonde hair drawn back off a curiously ageless face, though she was plainly no longer in the first flush of youth. There was no softness in those angular bones, no yielding in the thin-lipped mouth speaking with clipped precision. Her eyes were a surprise, – brown where Kheda would have expected blue, though paler than any he'd ever seen on an Archipelagan. They were also wholly resolute.

'She isn't going to back down over this,' he said quietly to Risala.

'She certainly looks determined,' the girl agreed.

Kheda spoke up. 'How does she propose to come here?' he asked Dev. 'I thought you said a wizard couldn't go somewhere they'd never been.'

Dev ignored him, still arguing furiously with the woman. Her replies by contrast were icily calm.

'She can't ever have travelled in the Archipelago,' commented Risala. 'She'd have been enslaved before she got further than the northernmost reaches looking like that, never mind getting skinned for being a wizard.'

'She knows she's got the whip hand over us all, though,' Kheda said with reluctant resignation.

'She knows she needs an escort. She just said so.' Risala rubbed a hand through her black hair, frowning. 'She wants a ship sent to Relshaz to fetch her.'

'That's madness.' Kheda stared at her. 'There's the entire length of the Archipelago between us. We haven't that time to waste.'

'She's adamant.' Risala looked at him. 'She's not going to give way on it.'

'How soon?' Kheda took a step forward and shook Dev's shoulder roughly. 'How soon can she get to Relshaz with this dragon lore? If she can bring us what we need to be rid of the beast, I will send a ship. If she can't guarantee to help us, tell her I won't waste any more time on this and I certainly won't send her men or a vessel we need in Chazen.'

The woman abandoned her dispute with Dev, her eyes shifting to look straight at Kheda. He stifled a shudder of revulsion.

Scrying is one thing. The intimacy of this communication is quite another.

Dev asked the questions, challenge in his voice coloured with insulting disbelief. The woman replied with cold precision in her incomprehensible tongue, strange eyes fixed on Kheda all the while. She finished speaking and silence rang loudly across the open observatory. The only movement was the ceaseless whirling of the circle of brilliant magic on the mirror.

Dev let out a slow, contemplative breath. 'She's talking about a long trip but as luck would have it, she can make most of that journey by magic. The last bit will be the trial and then, assuming she can find the man she's looking for . . .' He shook his head reluctantly. 'If she can find him, yes, he should have the lore we need. Whether he'll share it is another question altogether.'

'Promise him gems, pearls, whatever it takes,' Kheda ordered tersely. 'Your barbarian coin, if need be.'

'He won't be interested.' Dev laughed derisively. 'He's long past interest in such trifles. If Velindre can't convince him to share what he knows, no promises of riches will shift him.'

'And if she can?' Kheda asked.

'Then we should certainly have something to make any dragon think twice about plundering Chazen,' said Dev softly.

'Do you think she can achieve this?' Kheda demanded. 'Do you trust her? Is pursuing this worth our while? Tell me honestly, Dev.'

'If anyone can convince the wizard she's talking about to share his lore, she's the woman to do it. And it's not as if we have any other bright ideas, is it?' He looked up at Kheda. 'I'd say the odds are better than even money. I'd take that bet.'

The woman said something, shifting her gaze to Dev who nodded reluctantly.

'If she can persuade him to talk, she'll be at Relshaz barely a day later. What will take the time will be getting her down here, which is plain stupidity – we don't have time to sit here with our thumbs up our arses while she takes a pleasure cruise.' Turning back to the woman he began talking again, objections rapid and angry. She shook her head, mouth stubborn.

'Dev, shut up for a moment.' Kheda closed his eyes, the better to think. 'Can she undertake to be in Relshaz in forty-five days, near enough?'

'You're planning on flogging a trireme crew half to death?' Dev looked up at him, incredulous. 'When did a Chazen trireme last make that voyage so fast?'

'Can we survive this dragon's presence that long?' Risala asked tersely.

'What other choice do we have?' Kheda waved her question away. 'Just ask her,' he snapped at Dev.

Shaking his head in disbelief, the mage obliged. The wizard woman's emphatic nod needed no translation.

'Will she be able to recognise a Chazen trireme in the docks of Relshaz?' Kheda continued.

'Kheda,' Risala warned. She pointed and he saw the

residence steward Beyau heading purposefully for the footbridge leading to the observatory isle.

Waiting impatiently through a rapid exchange between the mages, Kheda handed Risala the key to the door at the bottom of the stairs. 'Get down there and tell Beyau to come back later. Tell him I'm still reading omens.'

Risala nodded and ran lightly down the stairs.

'Dev,' Kheda said, calculating quickly, 'the Greater Moon is waxing. Tell the woman to be in Relshaz at the end of its next complete cycle, the one after this when it'll just about coincide with the Lesser Moon's darkness. Do you understand? I don't know what that would be in your barbarian calendar.'

'Sometime around the thirtieth of Aft-Spring, my lord, depending on which almanac we're using,' Dev said with heavy sarcasm. He said something brief to the woman in the spell, with a note of warning. Then he blew out the taper and the magic vanished to leave the polished metal shining vacant and uninformative in the sun.

'I need a drink before my brain boils.' Dev abandoned the mirror on the observatory's tiles and headed for the stairs.

'Wait. We're taking omens, remember?' Kheda heard Risala talking to Beyau below. He nudged the lustre-trimmed square of the mirror with his foot. 'Does this have to be intact for your magics? The frame, I mean, not the metal.'

'No.' Dev halted at the top of the steps, puzzled.

'Take this and keep it with your own gear.' Kheda drew his dagger and bent to pick up the mirror. He reversed the blade and carefully stabbed at the delicate glass tiles with the brass hilt. The glaze splintered and crackled under his assault. 'You don't use any other mirror for that bespeaking enchantment, do you understand me? Now sit down. I said I was going to read mirror omens for the domain and I intend to.'

Dev didn't reply, simply snorting as he went to sit in what little shade was offered by the waist-high wall encircling the observation platform.

Kheda picked up the undamaged mirrors he had brought up with him and left on the wall's broad rail.

In times of confusion, hidden truths can often be seen more clearly in reflections. Isn't that what you were always taught? Perhaps, but do you honestly think you'll see any omens with the memory of that magic clouding your mind?

He studied the mirror bird on the back of the copper mirror for a moment before flipping it around. Lifting the mirror so that he could see the open horizon and the empty sea behind him, he moved slowly, shifting his feet little by little until he had surveyed the entire circle of the compass as it was reflected in the shining metal. The vista remained entirely, unhelpfully blank.

He heaved a sigh and began again. This time Risala appeared at the top of the stairs. 'I told Beyau you were busy. He asked for you to send word as soon as you're free to see him.'

'There's not a lot to keep me here,' Kheda said heavily.

'Wait till moonrise, that's a more auspicious time for mirror omens,' she suggested softly.

Dev spoke up from the far side of the observatory. 'You were talking about looking in Chazen's library for any useful lore. We could do that and be in the cool. You Archipelagans might know something that would wipe that smirk off Velindre's face. Stronger things have happened. I wouldn't mind seeing that,' he concluded, a trifle vindictively. 'Even through a bespeaking.'

Risala dismissed the wizard with a wave of her hand, her eyes on Kheda. 'Let's get out of the sun.'

The warlord nodded and headed for the stairs. They

were wide enough for Risala to tuck herself beside him and slide her hand into his.

'That's enough of that.' Dev pushed past into the library. 'Where are the keys to the bookcases?'

'Next to the ceromancy bowl.' Kheda laid the mirrors he had carried down on the table.

Risala stood by Dev's shoulder, surveying the books, and pulled out a thin tome bound in stained scarlet leather, age darkening the edges of the pages. 'It would be no bad thing if we could keep the domain safe without magic,' she said in a low voice as she laid the book flat and opened it carefully.

'I think that's rather less likely than this woman of Dev's finding what we need.' Kheda scanned the crabbed, faded writing where some long-dead scribe had dutifully recorded the omens and predictions of some Chazen forelord, along with verdicts on the accuracy or otherwise of his interpretations. 'I only hope we don't end up paying too high a price. She looks the type to drive a hard bargain.'

Risala glanced at Dev, who had moved to examine a second bookcase. 'How are you planning to get her here from Relshaz? You can't leave the domain. You can't abandon Itrac to cope with all this alone.'

'Which is why you're going to be my envoy.' Kheda laid a hand on hers.

'What?' Risala stared at him, open-mouthed.

'You're the obvious person to send. You're my poet, so that's your excuse for searching out lore. You're from the northern reaches and we're telling the other warlords hereabouts we're looking for lore from the north, something like those herbs that helped us to bring down the wild wizards.'

'Since you put it like that,' Risala acknowledged reluctantly.

'You can take a message to Shek Kul while you're about it. We owe him that much and who knows, he might even have some ancient learning about dragons to share with us.' Kheda stroked Risala's hand absently. 'Have you ever been to this place, this Relshaz?'

'Yes, once,' Risala said slowly. 'And Shek galleys trade there regularly. I can find out what I need to know.'

'The *Green Turtle* was our escort back here and that's the fastest trireme in Chazen. The shipmaster can have my authority to claim any man he wants from any other crew in the anchorage.' Kheda looked towards the securely locked door, the seas invisible beyond. 'We'll promise each man all the pearls he can hold in his cupped hands on his return. That will do more than whips to make them row faster. The shipmaster will get a sack of them when he arrives back, as long as you can tell me that no gossip about your destination ended up floating around the trading beaches.'

'But what if something happens while we're away?' Risala laid her own hand over Kheda's.

'Then we will have to cope with it as best we can.' Kheda looked into Risala's eyes. 'And I will at least know you are safe.'

Can you see everything that you mean to me? Do you know all that I would say to you, if we were alone and free of this?

'I don't want to be safe if you're not,' she said, meeting his gaze levelly. 'But all right, yes, I'll do this, so we can be safe together.'

'How are you planning on explaining Velindre away?' Dev asked suddenly, turning from a bookcase further down the room, a heavy volume bound with lacquered wood resting open on his forearms. 'You saw her face; she couldn't be anything but a barbarian. What possible business could she have to be travelling the whole length of the Archipelago? Curious eyes will follow you all the way back, my girl, and Velindre hasn't got my experience of keeping her magecraft hidden,' he concluded with frank concern.

'She'll just have to play the slave.' Kheda smiled despite himself. 'Picture that face of hers through Aldabreshin eyes. What would you think if you'd never seen her before, if you didn't know who or what she was?'

Dev's eyes narrowed. 'I don't follow you.'

'Oh,' said Risala with sudden comprehension. 'I do. Of course. Yes, that should work, with a bit of planning.' She broke off, eyes distant.

Kheda looked at Dev, deadly serious. 'Assuming this magewoman is as good as her word, we still have to hold this dragon at bay, or keep running from it, from now till the Summer Solstice or later, unless we're uncommonly lucky with the winds and the tides. If you've any ideas—'

'I think you'd better see this,' Dev interrupted.

'You've found something?' Kheda took a step and then realised the mage was looking out of the window over the southern ocean. 'What is it?'

'The dragon,' said Dev simply.

'Where?' Kheda ran to the window, Risala at his heels.

The dragon was a dark shape, far away, high in the cloudless sky.

'Is it coming this way?' Kheda tried to swallow the apprehension choking him.

'I'm not sure.' Dev frowned.

Risala watched the distant creature. 'Do you suppose anyone else has spotted it?' she asked with hollow hope.

Shouts of alarm ringing across the lagoon answered her barely a breath later.

'Outside,' Kheda ordered. As he unlocked the door and stepped out, he looked towards Itrac's pavilion. A flurry of maidservants was hurrying her towards him, clustering close as if her presence would somehow protect them from the beast.

'We may not need to disguise the magewoman after all.' Risala shrank back into the shadow of the doorway.

Kheda flinched as a couple of arrows loosed by over-ambitious archers clattered uselessly on the wooden walkways.

'Don't wet yourself just yet, girlie,' Dev said slowly, eyes fixed on the distant dragon, face thoughtful. 'I don't think it's coming this way.'

'Are you sure?' Kheda watched, breath catching in his chest at the beast cut lazy arcs across the sky.

They stood in a tense silence broken only by Itrac's arrival.

'Kheda.' She managed to walk across the bridge to the observatory isle with commendable poise, leaving the gaggle of terrified maids behind. 'What does it mean?' Her voice rose to a perilous pitch.

'It's heading back west,' murmured Dev.

'Are you sure?' Kheda hissed.

Dev nodded, turning the gesture into a florid bow that Itrac didn't even notice, all her attention on Kheda.

'It means we're removing ourselves to the rainy season residence just as soon as our household can make ready to leave,' Kheda said firmly, calmly, as he walked towards her. 'In case it gets curious and comes for a closer look.' He took her hands as Itrac shivered with revulsion. 'See, my lady, it's going away. We're safe enough for the moment. All the same, I want you and all those beholden to us well out of its way. I don't want even the shadow of its wings falling on you.'

And I want Dev as far away from the beast as possible, in case he betrays us all with some slip of magic. I might just save myself by cutting his throat, but I can't afford to do that until this woman of his has brought us some way to defeat the dragon.

'You have killed beasts bigger than this creature.' He raised his voice to address the gathering crowd. 'Chazen boats have fought and conquered whales out on the ocean deep year after year. Chazen is the only domain to go hunting whales, instead of waiting for them to strand themselves on the shore. You have chased and defeated sea serpents that no other domain's men dared to pursue, even when their nets and fish traps were being ripped to pieces. This dragon can summon up fire by some unnatural magic polluting its blood, so we had better not underestimate it, but we faced men with magic and the wit to work malice with it besides last year. We defeated them.

'We'll fight this dragon, once we learn its weaknesses, and we'll fight it on ground of our own choosing,' he continued, putting an arm around Itrac. 'In the meantime, a planned retreat is no rout and no mischief-making by anyone who wishes Chazen ill can make it one. It's no great challenge. You've a practised routine, even if we weren't expecting to make this move for a few more turns of the Greater Moon.'

Confusion stirred among the slaves and servants, surprise at seeing their lord so composed outweighing their incipient fear.

'You'll need to keep a firm hold on everything,' Kheda warned Itrac in a low voice, 'or we'll find ourselves caught up in a panic regardless.'

'Familiar tasks should calm everyone's nerves.' She was still trembling but she set her jaw.

'I still have to check with the courier-dove loft,' Kheda realised suddenly. 'In case there's news from the *Mist Dove*.'

Which would be worse: bad news or no news at all?

'Come and tell me anything you find out.' Itrac stepped

forward, quelling her women's questions with a flurry of rapid instructions. 'Pack your lord's clothes and his jewels. Start stripping the beds and the furniture. Send for Beyau. He needs to see to it that the observatory is cleared. We're sailing for Esabir.'

Kheda watched her go.

Chazen's people have mettle and so does their lady.

'Looks like an ant heap someone's stirred with a stick.' Dev stared out over the lagoon where the galleys and triremes seethed with activity to match that on the land.

'I'd better find the *Green Turtle*.' Risala scanned the bustling scene.

'Dev, go and play the proper slave for once and see that my rooms are packed up properly.' Kheda jerked his head towards his personal pavilion. 'Risala, wait, come with me for a moment.'

'If it's quick enough for him it'll be no good for you, my girl,' Dev said over his shoulder as he strolled away.

'What is it?' Risala followed Kheda into the hallway.

'This.' He opened a tall black cabinet inlaid with nacre and countless coloured woods. It was full of small, closely fitted drawers. Kheda pulled them open, searching, heedless as he pulled too hard and several clattered to the floor. 'This.' He turned to Risala holding a twist of carved ivory pierced and threaded on a leather thong.

I found this, raw and uncarved, on that voyage to the north, that led me to you, as well as to Dev and the means to defeat the wild mages. I saw it as a sign I was on the right path, as I carved it into something I thought only existed in myth. I was certainly blind to that portent.

'The dragon's tail.' There was a strange edge to Risala's unexpected laugh. 'It doesn't look much like the real thing, does it?' She pressed her hands to her face. 'We never saw this in it, did we?'

'I don't suppose the poet whose descriptions I had in

mind when I carved it had ever seen the real thing. There's probably some significance in that but I haven't got time to worry about it.' Kheda hurried forward and hung the talisman around her neck. 'We can't second-guess the past and I'm more concerned with the future. It may just be a way of reading the stars but all the forefathers in every domain say the opposite arc of the sky to a moon is where the dragon's tail lies.' He stumbled over his words. 'And that's where the unseen portents lie, because the dragon never looks behind it. I don't want it looking at you.'

Risala seized his face and drew him to her, kissing him with desperate passion. Then with a suddenness that left him standing there, shocked, she tore herself away and ran out of the building.

CHAPTER NINE

With the brightness of magic snuffed, the room felt smaller, darker, colder. Velindre felt as if the leaden grey of the sky above Hadrumal was seeping through the tall lancets of her window to dull the white plaster of the wall, dimming the parchments on the table before her. She shivered and waved a hand at the coal scuttle beside her hearth, sending a flurry of nuggets on to the glowing embers. She abandoned the table and sat on a footstool set before the fire, hugging her blue-gowned knees as she looked unseeing at the golden tongues of licking flame.

So Dev was still enjoying cloudless blue skies and brilliant sun. He hadn't drowned or burned in that dragon's fires. There had to be plenty he could tell her, not least how he was managing to work magic as an Aldabreshin warlord's trusted servant. Velindre shivered again, this time with revulsion. Tales of Aldabreshin savagery were no idle invention to frighten apprentices into caution. She'd learned that much from days and nights reading ceaselessly in the empty silence of Otrick's study. The old wizard had been intrigued with the Archipelago, not least with the Archipelagan obsession with omens and portents.

Velindre chewed at a thumbnail already bitten to the quick. The firelight struck threads of bright gold in her hair which was drawn back from her angular face in a thick, sleek plait, as usual. Dev reckoned the lore he needed so fast was to be found in the endless shelves of Hadrumal's hushed libraries. No. Velindre had long since tired of reading reams of speculation and half-understood observations in the hope of satisfying any gnawing magical curiosity. Otrick had cured her of that.

But what if she delivered such lore? Could she trust Dev's promise of safe passage through the Archipelago? Could she trust him not to just take whatever she showed him and twist it to his own advantage? Could she afford to delay and debate such questions? If she was going to do all she'd boasted, she had precious little time to spare. And if she couldn't, sure as curses no one else in Hadrumal would be able to. If she could, no one else in Hadrumal would ever doubt her abilities again.

She sprang to her feet and crossed to the door in lithe strides, catching her dark cloak from its hook, swathing the cornflower blue of her high-necked gown as she hurried down the echoing stone stairs. The raw wet wind buffeted her as she emerged from the base of the tower. She waved an irritated hand and the wind swirled away, forbidden to stir even one pale hair escaping from her hood.

'I want a fire for my feet and warm ale for my belly.'

'Let's see what Brab and Derey think about the ocean's currents.'

A pair of apprentices threatened to cross her path. Youth and maiden both had wet hair plastered to their heads, faces tight with cold and their brown cloaks bulked out with books cradled safely in their arms.

'Excuse me.' Velindre swept past them with a shrug of indifference.

Out beyond the ancient stone arch and the weathered oak gate the high road was busy, foul weather notwithstanding. Velindre threaded between men and women of different ranks and ages, master mage and raw apprentice all equal beneath heavy cloaks, hoods and hats worn against the drenching rain. Intent on their own occupations, the commonalty of Hadrumal hurried this way and that, their conversations focused on lives that owed little to wizard halls or affinities.

'I said, I told him, you want to think who'll be mending your stockings in ten years' time before you go playing fast and loose with every girl who catches your eye.'

'May I get past?' Frustration building, Velindre found her progress curbed by a pair of slow-footed matrons with a handful of brats in tow. She reached a narrow side lane with relief and hurried between lofty stone walls stained dark with rain, her boots clacking on the slippery, sloping cobbles either side of a rain-filled gully. She cut across to take a back alley where the sodden, hard-trampled earth muffled her steps.

Reaching the back gate of Atten Hall, she paused to catch her breath and compose her thoughts. The five chimes of midday sounded around her, the echoes of different timepieces tangled among Hadrumal's towers. Good; her father would be rid of his pupils, or if not, her arrival would prompt their departure. He'd have half his mind on what the maid was bringing for his lunch, so he might just let slip what she needed to know.

Pushing open the black iron gate, she walked up the flagstones running through the physic garden. The beds of rich soil were black and empty, neatly dug over and marked out with stones. Here and there, pale scraps of straw bore testament to the stable muck brought to nourish the sleeping herbs and seeds. Hardier shrubs were set back against the walls of the court, dark green and brown against the weathered stone. Withered creepers clutched at skeins of trellis, waiting for spring.

This hall was centred on the broad, squat tower standing alone in the middle of the garden, a style Archmage Atten had brought from his mainland home long ago, along with the coterie of wizards who had chosen to follow his teachings. That tradition had long since outgrown the tower and now its topmost windows could barely see over the ranges of accommodation built inside the walls that enclosed it. Three had serried ranks of casements while the fourth had the long tripartite windows of a large hall where those hopeful mageborn invited by Atten's successors sat at long tables to listen to instruction, to debate lofty concerns or, more prosaically, to eat their meals.

Velindre advanced on the central tower, the door's brass fittings gleaming in defiance of the weather. Inside, harsh matting was finally losing the battle with the mud of the winter. Velindre paused to wipe her boots and heard her own breath echoing in the hush. The stairs were a square spiral on the southern side of the tower. Subdued light filtered through broad mullioned windows on the landings leading to the apartments on every level. Some doors stood hospitably open, faint sounds of movement within. Others were closed on intense discussions just on the edge of hearing. Velindre ignored them all, heading for the topmost floor.

Her father's voice rang through the emptiness as his door opened, encouragement mingled with warning. 'First thing in the morning, the day after tomorrow. I want arguments on both sides from all of you.'

A trio of apprentice mages appeared on the landing, two girls and a rangy youth not yet grown into his height. 'There can't be an alchemist from Selerima to Toremal who still believes in phlogiston,' he protested under his breath, all the arrogance of the Imperial city in his accent. His linen shirt was snowy white, breeches and tunic impeccably tailored in sober grey broadcloth, only a trimming of scarlet buttons marking his affinity.

'The Duke of Triolle, he's been paying out gold for years to all manner of charlatans promising him the secret.' The shorter of the girls shrugged; Lescari intonation as robust as her figure and the vivid red dress that flattered her pale skin and dark hair.

'What would he do with it?' wondered a willowy Caladhrian girl who'd opted for a pale-rose gown. 'If it really existed.'

'I hate to think,' muttered her female companion darkly.

'Madam.' The Tormalin youth caught sight of Velindre on the stairs and swept a creditable bow given the armful of books encumbering him.

'Apprentice.' Velindre inclined her head tautly as the trio hurried past her. Sudden laughter floated back up the stairs to be cut short by the slam of the door below. Velindre took a deep breath and knocked briefly on the open door. 'Father?'

'Come in,' barked the stern voice.

Velindre entered and blinked, frowning. 'Do you have something against daylight, father?'

'I've nothing against it.' The old wizard sat shrouded in darkness by a hearth whose fire was no more than a feeble glow. 'Nor yet any great interest in it, either. I'll leave the skies to you cloud mages.' His tone was uninterested.

Velindre crossed the room with some difficulty, given the plethora of small tables laden with books and the countless volumes stacked on the floors. She reached the windows and tugged at heavy red velvet curtains, an exact match for the distempered walls.

'You'll get precious little light at this time of year,' observed her father. 'All you'll do is let in draughts.'

'You still think any apprentice who can't illuminate his own reading isn't worth teaching.' Velindre managed to shed a thin shaft of light on the leather-backed chairs that ringed her father. For all the clutter, the room showed no speck of dust. No smudge marred the gleaming brass of the fender or the white marble of the fire mantel.

'As rules of thumb go, I've always found it sound.' The white-haired man said. He was sparely built, the height he'd boasted in his prime now bent into a stoop and the flesh fallen away from his aged bones. His face was gaunt, wrinkles carved deep on either side of his beak of a nose, eyes deep set above hollow cheeks. Eyes the same colour as Velindre's burned with the same intensity, undimmed by the burden of his years. Straight and swept back with pomade, his hair was cut precisely at jaw length, his wrinkled chin clean-shaven above a knotted silk scarf. He wore an old-fashioned gown of maroon velvet over layered jerkins, one long-sleeved, one sleeveless, and knee-breeches the colour of old wine. Thick woollen stockings warmed his shrunken calves, his feet in soft leather shoes that gleamed with polish.

Velindre approached and submitted to her father's dry kiss on her forehead.

'What do you want?' prompted the old man briskly. 'Spit it out, girl.'

'Do you remember Dev?' Velindre sat on a chair and looked at the fire rather than her father.

'Of course,' the aged wizard answered with a hint of scorn. 'I remember all my students. A great deal of talent that I rapidly realised would go to waste. Far too ready to take issue with the supposed injustices of life. Always harking back to whatever ne'er-do-well village he stumbled away from. He was never going to make anything of his abilities unless he turned his back on such distractions and applied his intellect to his affinity.' The old wizard's voice was censorious as he folded his age-spotted hands on his chest.

'Did you know he'd gone to be Planir's eyes and ears in the Archipelago?' Velindre glanced at her father.

The old man shook his head, indifferent. 'Planir's another one who should concentrate a little less on the wider world and a little more on the proper business of wizardry.'

'Dev's found a dragon in the Aldabreshin south,' said Velindre carefully. 'One attuned to elemental fire, from what I saw.'

'You scried it?' Curiosity sparked in her father's eyes. 'What's your interest in this?'

'Dev wants to know more about dragons.' Velindre shrugged with unconcern. 'He bespoke me, as Otrick's former pupil, since I'm carrying on his work.'

'Otrick?' The ancient mage's laugh was a dry creak. 'I thought you were finally over that old pirate's foolishness of sailing hither and yon and whistling up winds to see where they lead you.' His disdain was withering. 'Cloud Master or not, Otrick led you astray from your studies. You might have stood a chance of the Council approving you as Cloud Mistress in your own right if you'd stayed here, applied yourself and shown them what you have to offer. You've a good mind. You just need to use it.'

He tapped one bone-white finger to his snowy temple before withdrawing into his high-backed, deep-winged chair. 'Your mother was a fool for encouraging you. She's another one with her head in the clouds. Well, Rafrid's no fool, even if he is one of Planir's cronies. And a mastery isn't what it used to be. I could have been Hearth Master, but nowadays, well, Kalion's welcome to people hanging on his cloak day in and day out, knocking on his door with their whines and complaints. I don't see him adding anything to the sum of wizardry, and that is a waste of a fine mind,' he concluded sourly.

'Dev wants to study the dragon's innate magics.' Velindre returned to studying the fire. 'He needs to get closer to it without ending up burned to a crisp. Otrick knew how to summon a dragon and how to control it but I can't find any record of exactly how he did it.'

'A charlatan's festival trick writ large,' the old wizard scoffed. 'Otrick was always a mountebank at heart. Among his many other vices.' Dislike sharpened his tone. 'Not that such dalliances were any of my business. You were a grown woman.'

Velindre kept her gaze on the flames and held her voice level and emotionless. 'Otrick is dead, so we can't ask him about such lore. The only other mage I can find recorded as having this trick of summoning dragons is Azazir.'

Her father threw up his hands in exasperation. 'If Otrick was a disgrace to wizardry, Azazir was a blight. What that fool cost Hadrumal in lost trust, in sowing fear and ignorance among the mundane of the mainland – there's no measuring it! We're still paying the price to this day,' he growled, fleshless fists clenched. 'With our Archmage bowing and scraping to every petty prince, just to make sure the mageborn can travel unhindered to Hadrumal before their emergent affinity is the death of them.'

'You knew Azazir.' Velindre looked up at her father, challenge in her eyes.

'I did,' he retorted, 'and if I'd been on the Council back then I'd have voted for his death, not just his banishment. Do those dolts who laugh over his exploits tell you how many drowned thanks to his fooling with the rivers or how many starved when his meddling caused famine?'

'I've heard all the tales. What they don't say is when Azazir died,' Velindre persisted. 'Rumour has it he's still alive, somewhere in the wilds.'

'Does it?' the old wizard growled with disgust.

In that instant, Velindre saw in his eyes that that much was true. 'Well?' she managed to ask, keeping all exultation out of her voice.

'He used to talk about embracing one's affinity, about immersing oneself in it.' The aged mage looked past her towards the slim shard of sky visible through the window. 'Which is all very well for a water mage, but I told him, just try that with fire. He didn't care. He was the most irresponsible, most dangerous wizard I ever encountered. He was all for seeking sensation, ever more sensational and never mind making sense of it, never mind understanding the interplay of element and reason and cause and effect. If he thought there was a chance he could do something, work some wonder with his magic, he'd try, never mind stopping to think if he should. He had a higher duty to his affinity, that's what he would say, to find out where its limits might lie. Never mind his duty to wizardry. Never mind wiser mages than him warning that there might be no limits to some sorceries. Never mind when more than one of his apprentices died a foul and lingering death,' the old man concluded with cold anger.

'Do you know where he is?' Velindre asked in measured tones.

Her father's eyes snapped back to her. 'No one will take your scholarship seriously if you associate yourself with a madman.'

Velindre met his gaze. 'There's precious little true scholarship about dragons, Father. It's one of the few areas of study where there's real work to be done. I want to know more and if Azazir is my only source, that's where I'll have to start.'

'Stubborn as your mother,' the old mage muttered. 'You haven't told her about this, have you? No, I'd have heard the two of you arguing from here if you had. And I suppose I've no small reputation for strong will.' A reluctant smile cracked his aged face.

The silence in the room was tense and brittle.

'I'll find him one way or the other,' Velindre said calmly. 'I'm going to do this, Father.'

'Perhaps you should see what it means to go chasing

some madman's idle fancies.' The old mage pointed to a distant table where flat leather folders lay precisely piled. 'Fetch me that third folio of maps.'

Velindre retrieved it and he untied the rubbed-silk cord to open the tooled green leather.

'You've been to Inglis, haven't you, on one of Otrick's foolish voyages? Do you feel inclined to take the road north at the tail end of winter? That journey's not for the faint-hearted.' He pulled out a half-sheet and stabbed at the parchment with a chalky nail.

'So the Council's banishment doesn't just mean quitting Hadrumal.' Velindre's brow wrinkled as she studied the point he'd indicated on the map.

'Azazir was told to lose himself. He was told if he injured anyone, ever again, that would be the death of him. You don't believe the Council would do such a thing?' The old man mocked Velindre's startled disbelief. 'Believe it, and there's more than me who will call for that madman's death if he ever shows his face in the lowliest village. And we'll know if he does. Planir knows what's due to his office of Archmage. He keeps a weather eye on a menace like Azazir,' he said with grim satisfaction.

'So Planir will know if I visit Azazir?' Velindre asked warily.

'Would that stop you?' He thrust the parchment at Velindre. 'You were easily his equal, even if you were apprentice when he was a pupil, and you've twenty years' standing since then. Besides, he's another one full of Otrick's high-flown nonsense about experimentation and observation. You might both learn something from a little closer acquaintance with Azazir, even if it's not what you're expecting.'

The hairs on the back of Velindre's neck prickled at his ominous tone. 'Something valuable, I take it, if you're prepared to help me with this.'

'More valuable than some foolery with dragons.' The old wizard handed her the green leather folio and leaned back in his chair, gathering his mantle around him. 'Put those back where you got them. And don't say I didn't warn you, if you decide to pursue this folly.'

'Thank you for the map.' Velindre rose and left, not looking back.

Outside, the rain had stopped and the clouds had lifted. A breeze was rolling down from the hills to scour the heavy dampness out of the air. Velindre relished the freshness as she walked rapidly through the empty back alleys. There wasn't time to waste, not given the urgency in Dev's voice. Whatever his many and varied faults, he didn't indulge himself in foolish alarm, like some dog barking vacantly at every footfall.

She pictured a very different city in her mind's eye. So Inglis was the closest place worth marking to this mysterious lake where the equally mysterious Azazir was lurking. A city of white stone, well planned and well built, entirely unlike the haphazard accumulation of Hadrumal. A peaceable city, thanks to the powerful Guilds who paid a well-muscled and well-drilled Watch, which incidentally ensured that they had loyal men to hand to deter any challenge to their hegemony. A city built on the endless resources of timber, fur and metal-bearing ores of the empty northern wastes.

Velindre smiled thinly as she arrived back at the New Hall's ancient gate, blurred carvings unlike the sharp elegance of Inglis's cornices. Her father might believe that the city was all respectability and serious trade. Otrick had known better and, thanks to him, so did she. Otrick had known the dockside taverns where those mariners who risked voyages out to the ocean deep could be found. Mariners who should more properly be called pirates, never mind their brandishing of some parchment from the Inglis harbour guild, licensing them to pursue some vessel condemned for not paying the requisite tariffs.

A translocation spell would take her there in short order. Velindre climbed the stairs to her study. Arriving somewhere discreet would be best, to avoid one of the wizards in Inglis reporting her arrival to Planir. Earth mages always found plenty of work and plenty to interest them among the mining concerns around Inglis. Planir had been Stone Master before he'd been Archmage and indeed still was, despite the displeasure of some on the Council. Well, Velindre had no interest in explaining herself to Planir until she had something to show for this boldness, something to give the Council pause for thought over their choice of Cloud Master.

She locked her study door. One of the better inns would suffice, where gold would shut the mouths of any chambermaid or potboy who happened to see her. Tossing her damp cloak over a chair, she went through the inner door to her bedchamber. Throwing open a tall cupboard, she surveyed the gowns lying on wide shelves, linen and stockings in cubbyholes beneath, boots and shoes thrown into the hollow bottom. She'd need heavy clothing as well as some furs and a sturdy saddle-horse when she got to Inglis.

Dev's timing was lousy as always. Velindre grimaced at the thought of the pristine white winter that would still be gripping those mountains. Even half a season later, she might have approached some privateer for passage north, but not now. No sailor would risk his ship among the inlets and coves still choked with floating ice.

Furs and horses would cost money. She found a soft leather bag among her neatly darned stockings and weighed it in her hand for a moment before setting it down again. That should suffice. Planir had been unwontedly generous when she'd asked for coin to hire ships these past summers to continue Otrick's studies of Toremal's ocean winds. More to the point, the Archmage never asked for an accounting and she'd never felt the need to give him one.

She pulled a leather bag with stout handles and brass buckles down from the topmost shelf and threw in a handful of sturdy stockings and smallclothes, woollen chemises and flannel petticoats.

What would her mother do? As soon as word reached her that Velindre had left Hadrumal, her father's eyrie wouldn't save him from interrogation. Would he tell her mother where she had gone or keep it to himself, out of simple malice? Perhaps, perhaps not, if he decided he had erred in helping her. Would her mother set Planir on her heels? Possibly. It would be an excuse to remind the Archmage of Hadrumal's concerns. Her mother was a voluble critic of all the time he lavished on dealings with mainland princes.

Velindre rapidly sorted through her gowns for those of the heaviest wool and moved to her washstand to gather up soap and toothpowder and her silver-backed hair-brushes.

Would she come looking for her daughter herself? One of her father's cruelly apposite jokes prompted a thin smile. It must be her mother's affinity for air that gave her moods that veered as rapidly as the grasshopper weathervane on the tower of Wellery's Hall. Velindre knelt to pull the straps of her bag tight with vicious jerks. More to the point, her mother's rivalry with Otrick hadn't died with the old wizard. She would dearly love to learn the trick of summoning dragons.

Twisting to reach the laces tied at the small of her back, Velindre shed her gown and petticoats for a close-fitted bodice and divided riding skirt. Picking up her purse she thrust it deep in a secure pocket. She drew on a second pair of thick stockings before finding heavy buckled boots in the bottom of the cupboard. With the laden bag dragging at her arm, Velindre returned to her study and shrugged a thick cloak around her shoulders from a hook behind the door. She closed her eyes and finally allowed herself to feel the currents of air stirring in the room.

There was the dry draught coming under the door, heavy with the tang of stone in the dust it carried. Tight-fitted as the windows were, faint breaths of the rain-rich air outside eased through the casements and swirled around the room. The draught from the stairwell curled around the furniture as the air from outside brushed along walls and ceiling. Both currents were inexorably drawn to the fireplace as the heat from the coals sucked at the air in the room. The fire drove away the volatile moisture but had less success banishing the implacable touch of stone. It lost interest, settling for driving the warm air up the chimney, throwing it to the mercies of wind and weather above. Released, the air rushed away, exulting, mocking the fire, revelling in its return to the endless dance that encircled the world.

The air around Velindre crackled with eagerness. She felt its desire to be gone, to join that dance. Pure sapphire light surrounded her, bright even through her closed eyes. Brighter than the crisp chill over Inglis. Pale as icy dawn over snow-capped peaks on that far horizon, where the blue-white of the glaciers melted imperceptibly into the sky. As she drew ever more air to her, pressing it to the service of her spell, Velindre remembered the room where she had stood to see that view. Not the most prized room the Flower of Gold could boast, but luxurious enough for her and Otrick. She pictured the frame of the window, the wide-eaved roofs beyond, every detail of the distant mountains.

Now the elemental air was shaking her to her very

bones, desperate to do her bidding, to carry her wherever she wanted. Velindre gripped the handles of her bag, the ridges of the stitching digging into her palms. Blue light blinded her. Its touch was a shiver on her skin. It rang in her ears on the very edge of hearing. Cold breath filled her lungs, invigorating, cleansing. Eyes snapping open, she gave the magic its freedom and the room vanished in a burst of sapphire fire.

A woman screamed. Velindre raised a hand and scrubbed at her eyes to drive away the disorientation of working the spell over such a long distance. The woman paused to refill her lungs with a shuddering gasp and screamed again.

Still dazzled, Velindre saw that she had arrived in the bedchamber she'd envisaged to find a balding, middle-aged man and a matronly woman staring at her, mouths open. What they were doing abed in the middle of the afternoon was immediately apparent from the clothes strewn haphazardly around the floor. The woman was too astounded to think of covering her pendulous breasts but the man was clutching the brightly embroidered counterpane to his nether regions, a furious blush staining his jowls. He glanced with wrathful frustration at a sword belt hanging from a chair by the merrily crackling fireplace and Velindre realised that the overriding urge for modesty was all that was keeping him from the weapon.

'I apologise for the intrusion. Forgive me. I'll leave you to your . . .' Gritting her teeth against the belated realisation that scrying ahead might have been advisable, she unlocked the door with a snap of magic and slid through it. As she secured it behind her with another instant spell, she heard the frantic jangling of a bell down below.

Curse the aging lecher and his fat, foolish paramour. Didn't they have better things to do with their time? She certainly did. Velindre managed to get half-way down the hall before a wave of exhaustion overwhelmed her. She leaned against the polished wooden panelling of the corridor and fought the dizziness shivering down from her head to her toes.

'Madam?' The blurred figure of a chambermaid appeared. 'Are you all right?'

'I am, thank you.' Velindre forced her leaden feet down the stairs as the maid hurried onwards to answer the insistent bell's summons. Her knees felt weak and treacherous and the bag she carried seemed twice as heavy as it had in Hadrumal. Stiffening her spine with sheer determination, Velindre reached the inn's spacious hallway before shouts up above turned curious faces to the painted ceiling. She slipped out of the main door and hurried away down the sloping street. No one raised any hue and cry before she vanished from sight.

The cold outside was biting. Velindre's fingers ached with it and she realised her gloves were buried deep in her luggage.

'Carry your bag for you, lady?' A hopeful youth hopped over a trampled gap in the thigh-high ridge of grubby snow swept into the gutter between the high road and the flagway. Bright as the sun was, the winter's chill was far too well established for the heaps to melt. Lines of soot marked successive snowfalls. 'Where are you headed?' He wore fur-trimmed hide boots and thick chequered wool breeches beneath a sheepskin jerkin with long sleeves and a high upturned collar that almost reached the knitted cap pulled low over his ears.

'Can you recommend a quiet inn?' Velindre tried to curb her shivering as she surveyed the boy. Blond brows hinted at the Mountain blood that so many shared hereabouts. He had a round, honest face and an engaging smile, which probably meant he was a complete rogue. Honest and dishonest alike made a living serving the traders who were always coming and going in a city like Inglis.

'Don't even think of running away with that.' Proffering her bag, Velindre surprised the boy by winding bonds of clinging air around his feet and knees. 'I'm a mage of Hadrumal and if you rob me, you'll regret it to the end of your unfortunately curtailed days.'

He looked down, wide-eyed. Velindre curled a single tendril around his waist and pulled it tight to cut short his startled gasp. She smiled and let the magic go with a momentary flare of magelight. 'On the other hand, if you help me with intelligence and discretion, I'll reward you handsomely. Do we understand one another?'

'Yes, my lady,' the lad said with a rush of apprehension and excitement.

Seeing honest greed outweighing the guile in his eyes, Velindre let him take the bag. 'Take me to the closest inn that caters to guests of reasonable quality.'

'There's the Rowan Tree, my lady. Will that do?' he offered hesitantly. 'I'm Kerrin, my lady.'

'Are you?' she replied with little interest. 'If that's the closest suitable inn, it will do.'

Abashed, the youth didn't say anything else, simply ushering Velindre towards a wide crossroads where trampled snow gleamed, treacherous as ice, in the interstices of the cobbles. She followed him towards a prosperous-looking building fronted by dark marble steps. It took all her resolution to climb the short flight of stairs, her hand shaking as she gripped the cold iron balustrade.

'A private parlour.' Velindre fixed a supercilious hall lackey with a piercing glare. 'Hot water and herbs. Quick as you like.'

The lackey stood his ground. 'I'm not sure we can accommodate you, my lady.'

Velindre reached inside her cloak and fumbled with the strings of her purse with numb fingers. She tossed a couple of coins on the polished stone floor. 'I think you'll find you can.'

The lackey wasn't proof against Tormalin gold crowns. 'Of course, my lady. Forgive me. Ametine!' He scrabbled for the coins, trying to bow and to indicate the door of a private parlour at the same time.

'Hot water, if you please,' Velindre repeated to the startled maid shooting out of the kitchen. 'And herbs for a tisane. Now, if you please.' She handed the girl her cloak.

The boy Kerrin shoved open the parlour door and Velindre went in. Her eyes fastened on a lavishly cushioned day bed beneath a window opening on to a quiet, snow-covered yard.

'What now, my lady?' The boy dropped her bag on the neat carpet with a dull thud.

'There are things I need you to buy for me.' Velindre sank on to the green velvet cushions and fought to stop her eyes from closing. 'A heavy fur cloak, hat and gloves. Don't think to fob me off with rubbish or to make me pay Toremal prices. Inglis is awash with fine furs at this season, with the trappers coming back from a winter in the mountains. I want a well-mannered saddle-horse hardy enough to take me up into the hills. It'll need grain and I want food for a journey of ten days or so. The minimum, mind you; I don't want the bother of a pack animal. Find me a warm blanket and an oilskin for good measure.'

She broke off as the hall lackey appeared with an obsequious smile and a brass oil lamp with a frosted glass chimney. The golden light warmed the chestnut wainscoting.

'We're nowhere near a thaw, my lady,' objected Kerrin, shifting from foot to foot.

'Did I ask for your opinion?' Velindre raised her brows at him in spurious enquiry. 'No, I thought not. Can you do what I want or does this lackey earn the commission I'm prepared to pay?'

The lackey's eyes brightened.

'I can do it for you,' Kerrin assured her hurriedly.

'Leave me your belt.' She pointed at the tooled leather strap cinching his sheepskin tight to his waist.

'My lady?' He was confused.

'Leave it or just leave,' she said coldly. 'As long as I have something of yours, I can find you with my magic. In that case, I'll trust you with my gold. If not, you can be on your way and this lackey can see to my needs.'

The lackey suddenly looked rather less than eager.

The boy chewed lips chapped from the long winter cold. 'All right.' He slowly unbuckled the belt and laid it on the round table in the middle of the room.

'What's your business here, my lady mage?' asked the lackey fawningly as he stirred the banked fire and added fresh logs from the basket.

'None of your concern,' she told him crisply, fighting the weariness threatening to tighten across her brow into a headache. 'I shall be on my way before nightfall as long as this boy can find me a horse and provisions. Until then I want some peace and privacy. Provide it and you'll be handsomely paid.' She turned her attention to Kerrin and held out a handful of weighty gold coins. 'Waste your time and mine idling with your cronies and you'll regret it.' She glanced at the lackey. 'I shall want a shallow bowl of cold water and some ink for scrying after the boy.'

'Yes, mistress.' The lackey took his opportunity to depart.

'I'll be quick as I can, my lady.' Kerrin ran a finger around the inside of his collar, sweat beading his forehead.

'Your tisane, madam.' The maid Ametine nudged the door open with an elbow, a heavy wooden tray balanced on her other hip. She set it on the table and the tall silver jug breathed a puff of steam. Her eyes widened at the sight of the gold Kerrin was tucking inside his glove. 'Can I blend you a tisane, my lady?' She smiled eagerly, brushing her hands on her skirts. 'We have borage and chamomile, linden, dog rose, valerian—'

'A scant spoonful of dog rose,' Velindre interrupted, 'with just a touch of chamomile and the same of valerian.' She snapped her fingers to regain Kerrin's wandering attention. 'When you've found a suitable horse, bring it here. I'm not paying up till I've seen it for myself.'

The maid spooned dried herbs into a hinged ball of pierced silver, setting it in a tall glass with a silver holder and pouring in hot water. 'Honey, my lady?'

'Thank you.' Velindre nodded before fixing Kerrin with a penetrating stare. 'Well, what are you waiting for?'

Ametine brought the tisane over, ducking a curtsey. 'Will that be all, my lady?'

'A bowl of plain water,' Velindre said again, 'and some ink.'

Kerrin's shoulders flinched as he left the room.

'At once, my lady.' Ametine bobbed her way backwards to the door and disappeared.

Velindre blew the steam from her drink and sipped it carefully. Grimacing at the heat, she cooled it with a breath of enchanted air. That was better. Now she had better get some rest, if she was to be out of the city by nightfall. There might not be many mages who could travel such a distance with a single translocation spell but she was no more immune to the draining effects of working such magic than any other wizard. Careful to keep her boots off the cushions, she drank down the tisane and set the glass cup on the floor. Lying back against the padded headrest of the day bed, she let her eyes drift closed as she waved a hand at the door. The lock snicked and vivid blue light ran around the frame before vanishing into the wall. Velindre was already asleep.

A tentative knock at the door stirred her.

'My lady?' It was the maid Ametine.

Velindre woke at once and was pleased to find that she was well refreshed. She was less well pleased to see that the winter sun had already quit the sky outside, leaving only its golden afterglow on high, pale clouds. 'Come in.' She waved a hand and the door unlocked itself, swinging open.

Watching it with some misgiving, Ametine hovered on the threshold with a tray holding ewer, bowl and snowy towel.

Velindre realised belatedly that no one had brought her water and ink for scrying. Was she going to need it?

'He's back, the boy,' the maid stammered. 'With two horses.'

'Is he? Come in, girl.' Velindre swung her feet to the floor and stood up, shrugging discreetly to ease uncomfortable rucks in the chemise beneath her bodice and skirt. 'I wonder, is there a man born who can do exactly what he's asked, no more and no less?'

'Sure I don't know, my lady.' Ametine offered a hesitant smile, setting the tray down on the table.

Velindre carefully washed the sleep from her eyes and dried her face. 'I wonder what he's brought for my gold. Where is he?'

'Out the back, my lady.' The maid bobbed an uncertain curtsey.

'Let's go and see.' Velindre found her gloves and rebuckled her bag. 'My cloak, if you please.' She left the boy's belt on the table. Let him ask for it back, if he had the nerve.

'This way, my lady.' The maid led the way through

the kitchen passages to the Rowan Tree's extensive stable yard, collecting Velindre's brushed cloak from a peg as they went. The lackey she'd encountered earlier was nowhere to be seen but Kerrin was waiting on the swept cobbles, a horse's reins in each fist. He grinned widely as Velindre appeared in the doorway. 'Here we are, madam mage.'

'Good evening to you.' A dour-faced man was standing nearby, muffled up against the cold.

'These are your beasts?' At the man's nod, Velindre set down her bag and pulled on her cloak, considering the animals in the light of the lamps already lit around the stable yard. Both were unrelieved brown with black manes, their forelocks falling over blunt, undistinguished faces. Heavy-set beasts, they were none too tall in the shoulder but deep in the body and thick in the leg. Their rugged coats ran down to feathery wisps falling over wide, black hooves shod with sturdy steel.

Velindre walked forward and held out a hand for the first to sniff. It shied away from her, a rim of white around its dark, liquid eyes. Velindre turned to the other horse, which sniffed the fur-lined kidskin without reaction, shifting its hooves with a grating noise. Velindre rubbed her hand down the horse's thick neck and felt it quiver beneath her as the animal nosed forward, ears pricking.

'Good lad,' she soothed as she pulled off a glove, bending to run her hand down the front of his foreleg. With wizard senses to augment her touch, she could be certain there was no heat or swelling in the leg. At her prompt, the horse lifted his sturdy hoof for her inspection. After checking all four legs and feet, Velindre stood upright and rubbed the animal's velvety muzzle with a smile for the obliging animal. 'I'll try this one,' she said to the horses' owner.

'As you like,' said Kerrin readily. 'This one's a bit flighty, I'll grant you, but he won't give me bother.'

Velindre looked quizzically at him. 'I don't recall offering to buy you a horse.'

Kerrin chewed his lip. 'You're not going up into the hills alone, my lady, surely?'

'I certainly am,' she assured him, moving to check the girth on the saddle of her chosen horse. She pulled it tight and poked the animal in the ribs just for good measure in case it was inclined to hold its breath. 'Where's the mounting block?'

'You're not setting off now?' Ametine gasped, wringing her hands in confusion. 'It's nigh on dark.'

'What has that to do with anything?' asked Velindre with ominous calm. 'Or with you, for that matter?' She settled herself in the saddle and, walking the horse carefully around the yard, she nodded with satisfaction at the animal's well-schooled responsiveness. 'You'll do, won't you?' She patted his shoulder and turned her attention back to the disgruntled youth now leaning against the wall by the back door of the inn. 'Did you get the provisions I asked for? And everything else?'

The boy rubbed a hand over his head, knocking his knitted cap awry. 'Well, yes, but—'

'Go and get them,' Velindre invited with a hint of irritation. 'Now, Ametine, isn't it? My luggage, if you please?'

Ametine brought the heavy leather bag over and Velindre secured it to the metal rings attached to the front of the saddle.

Kerrin appeared from a tack room by the outer arch of the yard carrying an oilskin bundle bound with leather straps in his hands, bulky furs slung over one shoulder and a small sack hanging from the other arm. 'I did what you bid, but you can't be thinking—'

'The cloak, if you please.' Velindre held out a commanding hand. 'Tie everything else to the back of the saddle.'

'But madam—'

She cut off his protest by pulling the cloak off his shoulder. Standing in her stirrups, she settled the heavy fur around herself. She found a round hat in one deep pocket and gauntlets in another, beaver pelt, wonderfully warm and silky. She pulled them over her kidskin gloves, ignoring Kerrin who was muttering under his breath as he secured the food and grain on the horse's rump. She wouldn't go hungry, Velindre noted. In fact, she'd best discard what she could as soon as she was outside the city, lest the horse prove overburdened.

'You can't set off now. You'll be dead and froze by dawn.' Ametine's breath smoked in the lamplight and she was shivering in her indoor maid's livery. Now that the sun was down, the temperature was falling like a stone.

The bells of the city proclaimed the end of the day with ten brisk chimes as Velindre offered the silent horse-trader a double handful of white-gold crowns. 'That should pay for the horse. What's his name?'

'Oakey.' The horse-trader tipped his hat briefly to her and clicked his tongue to get the unwanted horse walking out of the stable yard. Oakey whickered briefly after his stable mate and Velindre soothed him with a pat beneath his mane before fishing in her purse again. 'Ametine, here's payment for your time and trouble. You can share it with your absent friend or not, as you see fit.'

She tossed a couple more Tormalin crowns to Kerrin, who looked up at her sullenly. 'I appreciate your offer of an escort and I'm sorry if you've made a fool of yourself telling your friends you're heading into the wilds on some adventure.' It was too dark to see if the boy was blushing but his ducked head suggested to Velindre that she'd guessed right. 'Believe me, boy, you don't want to go where I'm heading,' she said sternly. 'And any mage worth the name doesn't need an escort, whatever the weather, so don't think of following me in some misguided hope of riding to my rescue in case of marauding trappers. I shall see any such trouble long before it finds me. I'll also see you if you're fool enough to try coming after me, and I will be seriously displeased.'

Satisfied to see apprehension replace the mulishness in Kerrin's face, she carefully gathered up her reins in her double-gloved hands and drew the horse's head around towards the open archway. The inn's ostlers watched her ride out, shaking their heads in bafflement. Several turned questioning faces to Ametine but she had already disappeared inside the warm inn.

Out on the road, Velindre turned the horse's head up the hill. 'Come on, Oakey.' The reluctant animal was evidently none too pleased to be heading away from a companionable stable yard with a bitterly cold night coming rapidly on. She used her heels to convince him otherwise, urging him to his fastest walk, wary of the cobbles in sheltered corners already slick with frost. Best to be out of the city gates before dusk, when some watchman was bound to take it into his head to ask where she was going, laden for travel at such a time. Not that any watchman could stop her. All the same, any gate-ward mentioning such a meeting to some superior among the Guilds would increase the chances of her visit being reported back to curious ears in Hadrumal.

The inns of Inglis were doing a roaring trade satisfying fur trappers eager for light, warmth and companionship. Velindre soothed Oakey with a firm hand as a riot of song spilled out of one tavern door along with golden candlelight and a man who'd tripped over his own feet. A linkboy with his lantern swaying on a pole stared open-mouthed at her. Velindre ignored him, forcing her recalcitrant steed on.

She soon reached the long bridge that snaked across

the wide expanse of the River Dalas on a succession of tall, solidly built pillars. Ice gathered in the narrow arches shone pale against the black water in the fading light. What would a water mage be doing in the far north in winter? she wondered idly. Was Azazir curious as to the nature of freezing?

The bridge was strewn with sand though there were few enough carts or carriages out to take advantage of the Guilds' forethought. Most people were content to stay by their own firesides, counting the days till the festivities of the Spring Equinox. Did the Aldabreshin celebrate the Equinoxes? Velindre realised she didn't know. No matter. Dev would know all the local customs and playing the guide was the least he could do in return for the lore she'd be bringing him. She only hoped Azazir would be able to explain his secrets without too much of the rambling and digression that so many of the oldest wizards seemed prone to indulge in. She didn't have time to waste and she certainly hadn't come this far to fail.

Oakey slowed as the animal sensed that her thoughts were elsewhere. Velindre prompted him back to a faster walk with hands and heels. With a shake of his head, the horse pressed on through the empty streets of close-shuttered, primly respectable houses. Velindre paid closer attention to their route. She'd only had a few occasions to come this way on previous visits to Inglis and had never had cause to go far inland before.

A gate-ward was warming himself by a brazier beneath the towering gatehouse astride the highroad. 'We lock up at second chime of the night,' he warned as Velindre passed by him. 'You'll have to find another way in if you're late back.'

'I'll remember.' She nodded perfunctorily.

There were plenty of houses beyond the pool of light cast by the torches smouldering above the archway. Inglis had gates for the better collecting of tariffs and dues, their tall towers serving as lookout posts, but there were no walls warranting serious defence. Who was there in these northern wilds to attack the city?

Is that what Azazir is seeking? Velindre wondered. She found herself increasingly curious about meeting this notorious wizard. Solitude and freedom to explore all aspects of his affinity, away from the noise and nosiness of Hadrumal. Otrick had always said he learned more from a day out on the storm-tossed headlands of this ocean coast than he did from half a season in Hadrumal's libraries. She had certainly outstripped every other apprentice of her affinity among her contemporaries once Otrick had accepted her as his pupil and taken her away on those voyages of startling discovery.

Though there had been the few times when she had wondered if their wild trials of wind and wave were going to end in disaster. Best not forget also that Azazir's experiments had resulted in his banishment from Hadrumal. Her father would be content to see the mage dead and it must have taken something considerable to stir him to that degree. She shivered, not cold inside her cocoon of fur and wool but just a little apprehensive. Oakey slowed again with a whicker of protest and she felt his muscles tensing obstinately beneath her legs. As she let the animal come to a complete halt, he laid his ears back irritably.

'We're going to make a good start on this trip tonight, whatever you might think, my friend.' As she spoke, Velindre leaned forward to stroke the horse's coarse, bristly mane. Magelight glimmered between her fingers and spread to wrap horse and rider in a shimmering aura, no brighter than the moonlight now shining from above. Velindre glanced upwards. The sky was clear, pricked with bright stars, and the Greater Moon was rising in a golden half-circle above the dark, featureless mass of the forested hills before her. 'Come on, Oakey,' she encouraged. Insulated from the deepening cold by the subtle magic now enveloping them, the horse gave a grumbling snort and plodded obligingly on.

CHAPTER TEN

Concentrate on the omens. This is your first arrival here as warlord of this domain. Will there be portents to offer some clue as to Chazen's future? As to your future?

Kheda stood on the bow platform of the *Gossamer Shark* and surveyed the bustle in the anchorage sheltered by the great green bulk of the island of Esabir. The vessel stood out from the shore, flanked by the *Dancing Snake* and the *Brittle Crab*, all on guard as the three great galleys that had brought the warlord's household north were unloaded. Small boats ferried coffers, bundles and crates ashore or brought food and water to the grateful crews of the heavy triremes. Low conversations in the belly of the boat behind Kheda were punctuated by the rattle of bowls as freshly steamed saller grain mixed with shreds of meat and green herbs was dished out to the oarsmen.

He resolutely ignored the disturbances, concentrating on the vista before him. The little boats filled the bay so densely that the dark-blue waters were barely visible.

Itrac could almost walk ashore dry-shod over their decks. Could an enemy make an assault so easily?

The steeply shelving beach allowed ships to anchor close in to this shore, a boon to the domain's galleys when the rainy season storms wracked the seas. Under other stars, an enemy might exploit such a vulnerability, so a formidable embankment had been built along the edge of the beach, topped with a thick wall of pale-grey stone. The wall zigged and zagged so that arrows from every bastion could defend its neighbours. Massive catapults squatted on the forward-thrusting platforms to secure a commanding view of any approaching ships.

This residence had never fallen to attack. That was your boast, Chazen Saril. Much good it did you. The wild men's wizards reduced your mighty catapults to burned wood and melted metal. Redigal Coron's warriors found the fortress empty, doors standing wide for anyone to walk through.

Well, you abandoned your people, Saril. They were hardly going to make a stand and die for your sake.

A steady stream of laden servants and slaves trudged through the black wooden gate set into a deep recess flanked by angular towers striped with arrow slits. Warriors patrolled the wall, swordsmen and archers, the sun bright on their mail and helmets as they kept watch not only north out to sea but also to east and west where the encroaching forest was kept ruthlessly in check with shears and scythes.

A fortress to defy any assault, never mind it's a rainy season residence and we all agree that no wise lord makes war when swords rust in their scabbards and armour rusts on a warrior's back, when bows break in an archer's hands, glue and sinew fatally dampened. We all agree, but the histories tell of warlords now and again who have defied such wisdom. Some lost but some won, so we build our towers and ramparts.

What hindrance will they be to a dragon? Have we gained anything by this unseasonal move, trading the cooling breezes of the south to spend the worst of the dry season heat so hemmed in by trees and hills? Will we end up at each other's throats as tempers fray when the temperature rises?

The still air already hung around as hot and heavy as a smothering blanket. He looked about for water and was startled to find Dev at his elbow, proffering a silver cup with a slice of black fig floating in it.

'You're right, my lord,' the barbarian commented, studiedly casual. 'We can keep a far better guard on the sea lanes from here, just in case any greedy eyes are turned to our pearl harvest.'

Nice try, Dev, reminding all the listening ears that we've had good fortune to balance the unprecedented evil of the dragon's arrival. But there's nothing to be gained by running from an unpalatable truth.

'And we can escape the beast in the forests and hills if it dares to come here,' Kheda added.

'If it comes before we have the trick of defeating it, my lord,' Dev countered dutifully.

Kheda looked up beyond the towers of the residence to the steep mountains running east to west and dividing this third largest of the domain's islands. With the morning mist long since burned off by the fierce sun, the ragged uplands were a daunting prospect, sheer heights thrust through the trees shrouded by an all-concealing cloak of vines. Here and there pale rock clawed through to the open air, pitted and stained and sheltering hollows of black mystery. At the water's edge, the high ground broke apart in two distinct ridges falling into sluggish seas sheltered from the southern winds by the bulk of the island. The residence was set in the fan of flat land between them, the beach defences running the full length of the shore between the shattered headlands. There were no paths, no tracks over the heights to give any aid to an enemy trying to attack from the landward side of the island.

The warlord sniffed as the fickle breeze brought a faint reminder of the fetid, humid, swamp-choked islands spreading to the north and east.

That must be where the people hereabouts fled from the wild men's invasion. There must be provision for keeping a hidden boat somewhere, a fast galley for the warlord and his family.

'The people of this island and the residence saved

themselves and much of Chazen's wealth from the trials of last year,' he observed to Dev and for the benefit of the listening oarsmen. 'Make sure you bring me the names of all those who deserve rewarding.'

Do you understand me? Firstly, let's remind these people that they lived through such terrifying trials once. Secondly, let's find out exactly how they did it, in case we need to flee a worse foe.

'Indeed, my lord.' Dev bowed smoothly. 'Are you ready to go ashore?'

Kheda nodded and they walked back towards the stern platform, past the heavy trireme's warriors sitting cross-legged on the side decks. Kheda noted the resolution on their faces as they scoured imperfections from swords and daggers with oil and whetstone or buffed mail to brilliant silver with dampened cloths dipped in harsh sand. He beckoned to Shipmaster Mezai as they reached the helmsman, who was sitting with hands resting lightly on his twin steering oars.

'As soon as you're resupplied, patrol the waters hereabouts. Tell the local villages' fishermen to keep a good watch on the lesser sea lanes as well, just in case someone thinks all our attention will be on the south and west and they can sneak through while our backs are turned.'

'Yes, my lord.' Mezai nodded, then hesitated. 'And what—'

Kheda snapped his fingers and Dev knelt to open a sturdy coffer waiting to go ashore along with the warlord's physic chest. 'The dragon's shown no inclination to attack any sizeable vessels, but if it shows any undue interest in you, see if you can distract it with these.' Dev handed Kheda a soft leather pouch, which he passed straight to Mezai. 'The beast seems to crave gems. I doubt you'd get it to quench its own fires by diving for them, so have your best archers shoot them on to some shore, then make a run for it.' Kheda shrugged. 'Not that I imagine it will show itself this far north. It still seems more interested in pursuing the last of the savages in the west.'

'Evil bringing its own fate down on itself, my lord.' Dev secured the jewel chest and stood up.

'We'll hope that holds true, my lord.' Mezai sounded more hopeful than certain, though.

'There's no disgrace in running from a dragon.' Dev grinned. 'Do you think there's any ship in any domain that wouldn't do the same?'

Kheda gripped Mezai's shoulder, looking him in the eye. 'I'll want you and your ship ready when the *Green Turtle* gets back. Then we'll pursue the beast with whatever lore they might have in the north for driving such predators away.'

'Can't be that difficult, if barbarians can do it.' Mezai made a valiant attempt at a joke but there was suspicion in his eyes as he glanced at Dev.

'Let's be thankful we had a barbarian to hand to remind us they're plagued with dragons in the north, along with their wizards,' said Kheda with casual indifference. 'And since there are still barbarian kings and princes uneaten to trade with the northern Archipelago, they must have some means to stop the beasts laying waste to their lands.'

'There haven't been dragons around the Cape of Winds in three generations, my lord,' Dev assured him obsequiously. 'Not since the last of them was hunted down and killed.'

'And since barbarians can never resist bragging, doubtless there'll be some record of such events in one or other of the domains that touch on the barbarian waters.' Mezai looked around to make sure his crew weren't forgetting that.

'Indeed.' Kheda paused, as if a thought had just occurred to him. 'Of course, we'll keep the beast's lust for gems to ourselves. If it chases any other domain's ships and they don't know how to distract it, that will serve them right for encroaching on our waters, won't it?'

'Yes, my lord.' There was some distaste in Mezai's assent.

Kheda took one last discreet look at the trireme's crew as he turned to climb down the ladder to a waiting rowing boat. There were some unfriendly eyes following Dev as the supposed slave waited near the stern ladder.

Are you all reassured by my apparent confidence or wondering if I am an utter fool to rely on a barbarian slave's word? I certainly don't know what we'll do if the dragon turns up to prey on Chazen's more densely populated islands. How many jewels does it take to buy a life from the beast? Will pandering to it just encourage it to stay where there are such easy pickings?

'We'll go to the courier-dove lofts as soon as we're ashore,' he said briefly to Dev as the barbarian climbed carefully into the boat. 'I want to know exactly what's happening in the west. There should be dispatches from the *Mist Dove* by now.'

'Indeed, my lord.' Dev waited as the jewel coffer and physic chest were lowered from the trireme and stowed them safely beneath the little boat's stern thwart. Kheda shifted his feet and glanced at the two youths side by side on the central thwart.

Are you reassured to see me in silks, apparently confident that I don't need armour here in the heart of my domain? Or have you heard that I lost my hauberk thanks to the dragon?

Kheda carefully drew the fronts of his sleeveless mantle of midnight-blue gossamer across the knees of his emerald silk trousers. The overgarment was sewn with pale-green feathers around the shoulders and hem, matching the panels of embroidery on the front and back of his round-necked tunic, where azure roundels of feathers each framed a hawk's head.

I remember this mantle. So now I've taken Saril's clothes as well as his domain, his residences and his remaining wife. And my erstwhile wife took his life. Are the people here going to look me in the eye or spit in it?

'Let's get your lord ashore,' Dev said breezily to the rowers.

The two youths shared a dubious glance before leaning into their oars, keeping their eyes on their own feet as they rowed.

Kheda felt Dev stir beside him and saw the barbarian open his mouth, a glower cutting a deep line between his angular black brows. Kheda silenced him with an unceremonious elbow to the ribs. One of the rowers looked up only to drop his gaze immediately as he caught the warlord's mildly questioning gaze.

Noise all around pressed in on their tense silence. Crewmen from the great galleys shouted instructions to the islanders down in their little boats. Warning calls rang out as unwieldy loads were manhandled down the steep stairs fixed on either side of the massive ships' sterns. Muffled hammering floated out of the oar ports as the ever-toiling carpenters laboured in the hidden holds. Above decks, rowers were making good wear and tear sustained by rowlocks and oar sleeves.

There were small open galleys with just a single bank of oars and fishing skiffs everywhere. More had followed in their wake from every village the warlord's fleet had passed on the voyage to Esabir.

Are you hoping my presence will somehow protect you from the dragon? I'll do all I can, but are there enough jewels in the domain to turn its attention from so much easy meat?

'Looks like life got back to normal hereabouts pretty swiftly.' Dev was watching the local fishermen vying for space on the beach, eager to sell their loads of crab and lobster to Itrac's household cooks.

'This was one of the last islands taken by the savages,' Kheda said neutrally. 'And one of the first to be relieved by Redigal Coron's ships.'

'We're not going to go hungry, are we?' Dev watched flat-bottomed boats rowed by local women in gaily patterned gowns bringing baskets piled high with all manner of leafy greens or succulent roots brushed carefully free of soil. Other boats carried crates of ducks or village fowl blinking balefully at trussed braces of silver jungle birds, their heads hanging limply from deftly wrung necks. 'Look, my lord,' he said fervently. 'Red meat.' He pointed to the motionless dappled flank of a hill deer still tied to the pole some hunting party had used to carry it out of the forest.

'It was an honour to serve you, my lord.' As the rowing boat grounded on the steep beach, the two boys hastily drew their oars inboard and leapt out to drag the unwieldy vessel ashore as far as they could.

'Thank you.' Kheda walked carefully up the boat to climb over the prow. 'Dev.'

Heads turned on all sides, conversations fading away. Kheda nodded and smiled to islanders and residence servants who stopped in their tracks to bow low. He glanced back to see Dev loftily rewarding the two boys with a few tokens from the pearl harvest before recovering the warlord's jewel and physic chests.

'What now?' Dev hurried to catch up, the twin coffers balanced on his muscular shoulders.

'We accept our welcome with all the pleasure we can muster.' Kheda continued smiling to all sides as they gathered an eager train of islanders and children wide-eyed with excitement. 'We want these people as pleased to see us as we are to see them.'

These people who served Chazen Saril long and loyally, who haven't seen me for more than a day at a time because

I still feel such an interloper here. Am I to try buying their loyalty with pearls just as I try to buy that dragon's forbearance with gems?

They passed beneath the vicious maw of the sea gate where three separate portcullises hung ready to slice down through the arching vault pierced with holes promising a rain of death by spears, boiling water or worse for any enemy caught between them. The compound beyond the beach wall was thronged with activity as newly arrived servants and those who remained here year round scurried to make everything fit for the warlord and his lady. Bows were rapid, even perfunctory, and no one paused to trail after Kheda. Goats tethered here and there to keep the grass cropped short watched all the activity with slant-eyed indifference.

'Is there a back way out of this rat trap?' Dev glanced uneasily at the fortifications ahead and behind.

'There must be. Chazen Saril may have sought peace but his forefathers didn't overmuch.' Kheda looked ahead to the residence. 'That's something you need to find out. And you had better make sure you know your way around by nightfall, for both our sakes. I won't inspire much confidence if I get lost in my own residence.'

'You've been here before, haven't you?' Dev objected.

'Not recently and never for very long,' Kheda admitted ruefully. 'And then I always had Telouet to show me where to go.'

'Yes, he was everyone's friend, was Telouet,' said Dev, a trifle sourly. 'Let's hope they're willing to let me in on their secrets.'

'You're my personal slave, whatever else you may be,' Kheda said crisply. 'Remind them of that, if need be, but keep yourself in check.'

It's bad enough that preparing the ground for Risala's return with tales of banishing dragons from the wizard-

plagued north has reminded everyone that you're a barbarian in their midst. We cannot have anyone suspecting that you're anything more.

Are we far enough away from the fire mountains in the centre of Esabir, in case the dragon does appear and you lose control of your magic again? If it does, and you do, you'll lose your head and hide for it, do you realise that?

'Maybe I should grow a beard,' Dev muttered. 'Show them all I'm properly tamed.'

'It's probably better if they carry on thinking you're *zamorin*,' Kheda said frankly.

'You don't think they'll wonder why you trust your safety to some castrated lapdog?' the barbarian said softly, mocking. 'Maybe there'll be a maidservant here who I can bed to put paid to that worry – with your permission, naturally, my lord. Saedrin knows, I wouldn't mind easing the ache in my stones.'

'Not unless you can swear to me you don't talk in your sleep,' Kheda shot back as they strode across the greensward.

'It's all right for you; you can take that prize piece to bed any time you choose.' Dev slid the chests he was carrying down to the ground with a sigh of relief and bowed low. Kheda ignored the barbarian's insolence as Itrac emerged from the main gate of the residence. Servants scattered in all directions as she hurried towards them, something white clutched in one hand.

'My lady.' Kheda hurried to meet her, a chill running through him despite the heat of the day. 'Is there some news from the west? From the *Mist Dove*?'

'What? Oh, no.' Itrac was dressed in all the elegance befitting a domain's first wife. Her trousers of green silk were patterned with intricate flowers of blue and gold, a tunic of the same cloth fitted close to her body, emphasising her slenderness. The neckline plunged to her breastbone, cloth caught with golden clasps, emphasising the swell of her modest breasts. Strings of sapphires and emeralds swathed her elegant neck, her eyes vivid with sapphire and emerald cosmetics. The sun struck blue and green fire from her rings as she brushed at her intricately braided hair.

For all her finery, she looks no more than a child, and a child caught in some mischief not of her making.

'What is it?' Kheda held out his hands. 'My beloved wife,' he added for the benefit of slaves and servants frozen in their bustle on all sides.

'I find an unlooked-for letter from Daish awaiting us.' Itrac crushed the reed paper with an audible crackle. At her heels, Jevin was scowling openly.

'Concerning our invitation?' Kheda raised his voice a little. 'That Rekha Daish join us at the Equinox, so she might take word of the auguries in this domain back to her lord, that he might compare them with the fortunes written in Daish skies?'

'When I would have the household prepared to welcome her properly.' Itrac's hand trembled and Kheda saw a torrid confusion of emotion in her eyes. 'When I would have refreshed my memory as to Chazen's various trading accounts with Daish. But it seems we are to expect their beloved lady tonight.'

'Are we?' Kheda managed to keep his tone light. 'What an unexpected pleasure.' He didn't mind anyone hearing the cynicism in his voice.

'More unexpected than you know, my lord.' Emboldened by Kheda's reaction, Itrac let slip a hint of irritation. 'We are to entertain that domain's first lady, Janne Daish, not Rekha. We had better make haste to make ready.'

'No, we'll make ready as and when we see fit.' Kheda resolutely avoided looking at the household servants and slaves as Itrac's mouth opened with surprise. 'Our household has worked hard with this unexpected move from the south. I'm not inclined to repay their efforts with yet more demands. He shrugged with unconcern. 'If we're not ready to receive Janne Daish when she arrives, she can stay aboard her galley. It's her choice to arrive earlier than invited.'

A deliberate choice, I've no doubt, to throw Itrac off balance, on to the back foot with mortified apologies for shortcomings in her hospitality.

'You're right, my husband.' Itrac lifted her chin, face serene. 'Our people serve us well and deserve our consideration. Chazen concerns outweigh those of Daish.' Behind her, Jevin was now grinning widely.

'Naturally.' Kheda hid his qualms as Itrac's bold statement prompted whispers all across the open ground. 'It's a hot day, my wife. Let's take some refreshment before we continue about our own duties. It's time everyone had a break.'

As he gave a lordly wave of his hand, maids and menservants alike promptly set down their loads and abandoned their errands. Some dropped to the grass; others headed for a stone spring house where water barrels were being filled. Those carrying provisions up from the shore shared out fruit and cloud bread.

Kheda drew Itrac to him, tucking her hand through his arm as they walked towards the main gate of the residence. The outer wall constructed of Esabir's pale, gritty rock towered over them. It was set with angular towers banded with different stone, dark as shadow. Here and there, dark smudges were mute testament to the magical fires of the invaders. Kheda acknowledged the salutes of the warriors standing on the wall-walk.

'Each contingent has its own tower, my lord,' Jevin explained from the rear, 'where they eat and sleep and keep their armoury.'

'Most impressive,' Kheda said approvingly.

Do they keep as alert a watch on what goes on inside the walls? Where will their loyalties lie if Dev and I need to get in and out without arousing suspicion when Risala returns?

Kheda led the way into the inner compound through a gatehouse easily the equal of the one in the beach defences. Here springs bubbled up from fissures in the riven grey rocks and had been channelled into a lattice of rivulets enclosing delightful arbours, songbirds busy among the bright blossoms. Miniature waterfalls tumbled into pools with splashes of glee. As they passed, white and silver dart fish hid among swollen green spears soon to bear scarlet flagflowers or the sprawling, rumpled leaves of azure lilies now fading from their first magnificence.

'I wouldn't fancy trying to mount an attack along these dainty little paths,' Dev observed to Jevin.

'Try running through the water and you'll find pits and beds of spikes.' The younger slave pointed to shadows beneath the ruffled surface of a pool.

'Not that anything stopped the wild men, by all accounts,' Itrac said tightly.

I'm not the only one who hasn't wanted to come here. You've made restoring the southern dry season residence your excuse for avoiding all the memories lying in wait for you here, haven't you?

'Not here, perhaps, but we stopped them eventually,' Kheda reminded her. 'Chazen and our allies.'

Will leading that rescue be enough to see me accepted here?

He looked up at the heart of the complex. A solid fortification of banded stone barred their way, outer wall pierced only by small windows at the very top. The single access was through a substantial forebuilding boasting octagonal towers at each corner. Colonnades ringed the walls at ground level, providing shade and benches for those who had come to call on their lord. The benches were full of men and women scrambling to their feet, faces hopeful as they bowed low. Warriors looked down from the heights of the battlements above.

'My lord!' Beyau, the steward, hurried out of the shadows of the colonnade. 'Please forgive the disorder.'

'We've barely unloaded the galleys,' Kheda said mildly. 'I'll give you till sunset before I have you flogged for an incompetent.'

After an instant of wide-eyed startlement, Beyau guffawed. Kheda grinned and squeezed Itrac's arm. 'We'll look at the gardens. Come and find us when there's some lunch ready.'

Beyau fell into step beside Dev and Jevin as Kheda led the way through the bowing throng to an archway leading into a garden. The forebuilding was a hollow square, its inner face similarly ringed with colonnades. As yet no suppliants had been admitted and the benches stood empty on the intricate lattices of blue and brown tile underfoot, still gleaming here and there with the fast-fading dampness of a mop. One stretch was bright with new tile.

Kheda nodded towards it. 'What happened there?'

'The savages made a fire with the roses.' Beyau scowled.

'They're recovering, I see.' Kheda glanced at Itrac with a smile.

The rosebushes no longer filled the garden at the centre of the courtyard but those that had survived were making a valiant effort, just coming into bud, their flourishing leaves glossy and green.

'Let's take that as an omen,' she said with brittle brightness. 'Did you see any other portents as you landed, my lord?'

'No,' Kheda realised belatedly. A flash of sunlight caught his eye and he looked up to see that the topmost level of the rear tower to the east of the forebuilding was enclosed with glass panes whose angles did not match those of the octagonal walls.

Twelve facets. Chazen Saril's observatory. My observatory now that this is my domain. What will I see from there?

Gates opened from this outer courtyard into the main residence, paired guards ready at each one. Itrac unobtrusively steered Kheda towards the eastern entrance, through the anteroom beyond and out into another, considerably larger, secluded garden.

'If you'll excuse me, my lord.' Beyau slid past as Kheda halted beneath the shade of another colonnade. 'I'll see to your refreshments.' He hurried away towards the doors on the eastern edge of the garden. The inner face of the fortification's boundary wall was lined with sleeping quarters and workrooms for servants and slaves, resident or visiting. The warlord's accommodations were a complex of courtyards framed by single-storey buildings of the local grey stone, topped with ochre-tiled roofs with skylights here and there catching the sun.

'Is that upper servants' accommodation?' Kheda hazarded, glancing at Itrac. 'Or the kitchens?'

Itrac didn't hear him. Her eyes glistened with tears as she looked at the garden in the heart of this first courtyard. 'Chazen Saril's . . .' She corrected herself hurriedly. 'The Chazen warlord's physic garden.'

'And his audience halls beyond,' Kheda said thoughtfully.

Where I will be expected to sit in judgement as lawgiver for the domain when I'm not out here doing my duty as healer and teacher of healers. Which I must do, if I'm to reassure these people. They have to believe all is well, or at least as well as can be expected. But how can all be well if I can't find a way to slip out of here unnoticed to save them all with whatever abhorrent magic Risala brings back from the north?

How can all be well if I'm only making a sham of being this domain's warlord?

A faint sound turned Kheda's head. He saw Dev idly tracing the intricate tiles with a dusty toe, his expression bored. Jevin was watching him, indignation and something colder shading his face. The younger slave realised that Kheda was looking at him and his face darkened with a blush of embarrassment as he dropped his gaze.

'The audience halls are through there, Dev.' Kheda pointed abruptly to the wide arch at the southern end of the garden leading into a formidably large building. 'Three of them in succession. Just keep going till you hit the great reception room and turn west. The warlord's apartments run all along the back wall of this fortress. Go and make sure everything is as it should be.'

Dev shifted the coffers he was carrying on his shoulders and sauntered away. 'As you wish, my lord.'

Kheda released Itrac's silk-draped arm from the crook of his own and took her hand. 'I remember when this was Chazen Saril's garden,' he said softly. Gentle yet insistent, he left the colonnade for the white sand paths threaded through the carefully chosen arrangements of herbs. Jevin hesitated before staying leaning on a pillar, following Itrac with his gaze.

Purple poppy to dull pain mingled with red lance to cleanse the blood, bringing the bees to both. Firefew to ease the chest planted with mossy pepper, so effective against parasites of all kinds and incidentally keeping yellow mites away from the firefew. All shaded by carefully trained wax-flower trees offering up their leaves for wound washes and their trunks to support white vines, so insignificant in themselves yet valuable with such potent roots. Potent yet perilous, so barberry bushes keep anyone from incautiously digging those up.

'I'm glad to see the household here still honouring Chazen Saril with their care of this place.' Kheda surveyed the herb beds. No impertinent weeds marred the rich, black soil raked smooth between the myriad plants. The only sign that unfriendly hands had ever been at work here were scorch marks on the papery bark of the wax-flower trees.

'He loved this place.' A single tear trickled slowly down Itrac's cheek, leaving a faint trail of golden face paint. 'That's where we met, in my father's physic garden. We all liked flowers, me and Olkai and Sekni . . .' Distress choked her and she looked away, stricken.

'I know.' Kheda squeezed her hand with sympathy. 'For every book of herb lore I studied out of duty, Saril must have read ten or more, for sheer love of plants and their properties.'

He wasn't brave or overly astute, but he was content in his modest domain, with his wives drawn from lesser daughters, all charmed by his amiable adoration for them. Will I ever be so content here, without bonds of blood or affection to tie me to Chazen?

Other warlords may have mocked Chazen Saril as one who was ruled with a silken whip, but there were plenty who envied him his quiet life. How I miss the sound of the gates shutting on the Daish residences, knowing Janne would unbend from her wifely dignity within those walls and Rekha might even set aside her intricate tally of trades.

But my marriages as Daish Kheda are as dead as Chazen Saril. And how much more Itrac has lost, barely older than my own eldest daughter. At least my children know I am still alive, even if I am lost to them in all other ways.

'It's so strange to be here without them.' The desolation in Itrac's voice cut Kheda more deeply than her tears.

'Saril and your sisters in marriage still share in this domain, as long as the gardens you planted still flourish.' Kheda put his arm around Itrac's shoulders and drew her close. 'Sekni's benevolence will lend virtue to the tinctures made with these herbs. Olkai's goodness will sweeten the perfumes made from her flowers.'

I had better take care that these gardens do flourish. Their failure to thrive would be an omen everyone in Esabir could read.

'You're right.' Itrac wriggled free of his embrace and wiped a tear from her eye with a careful fingertip. 'What's done cannot be undone. The chances that led us both here have been stranger and harder than we could ever have imagined but we must believe they are for the best. What's happened just proves that you were right to claim this domain,' she pressed on resolutely. 'There's the omen of the pearl harvest, and what hope would we have of driving out this dragon without your slave's recollections of such beasts in the north being defeated? Chazen Saril was a good man in times of peace but he could not meet such trials.' Her voice wobbled despite her determination.

'We none of us know what we can bear till we're tested,' Kheda said distantly.

If Chazen Saril failed the trials of magic and invasion, that still didn't entitle Janne Daish to put him to a trial of his life, not on her judgement alone. I lived with her half my life, shared my bed and my blood with her in our children, and I never knew she could be so ruthless. Now she comes here, doubtless with the same unshakeable confidence in her own interpretation of what must be done.

'Where are you going to accommodate Janne Daish?' he asked briskly.

'The guest apartments are between the other gardens.' Itrac turned towards an arched passageway ending in a gate leading towards another green oasis. She looked uncertainly at Kheda. 'Olkai Chazen always invited the wives of the domain's allies to share her own apartments but I don't think I want to do that.'

'I think that's probably wise,' he agreed with a twinge

of shame that Daish was no longer trusted. He followed Itrac, Jevin falling in step behind them. This next garden was flanked to the north by accommodation for lesser guests. To the south, doors opened on to a labyrinth of playrooms and nurseries that had been the riotous province of the domain's children.

'This was Sekni's garden.' Itrac pointed at dark-green glossy fans of leaves sprouting from low woody trunks. 'See, she planted pitral to catch the rains. She loved the sound.'

Kheda glanced at her.

You're hearing the lost voices of Sekni and Olkai's children, just as I hear the echo of the sons and daughters Janne and Rekha have taken from me.

'Olkai's garden was through here.' Itrac led the way through another shady passage separating more luxurious guest suites. 'Where we grew the perfume flowers and kept the aviaries.'

White augury doves looked out of their intricate cages, cooing softly amid the irresistibly soothing fragrances of the brightly coloured garden. Dun quail bathed in the dust or preened themselves, oblivious to the presence of warlord or lady.

'So those are now your quarters as first wife of the domain and you're entitled to your privacy.' Kheda looked to the south where wide doors opened on to an audience room, the faintest of breezes stirring the light drapes within. 'I'm sure Janne and her entourage will be entirely comfortable in any of these other apartments.'

Sounds of activity within prompted Jevin towards the first wife's suite. 'With your permission, my lady?'

Itrac nodded and crushed Janne's letter, still in her hand, still further. 'Tell the maids to make the ash-flower suite ready for my lady of Daish.'

'Only once they've seen to my lady of Chazen's

comforts,' Kheda said pointedly. 'You should take your time to bathe and eat and satisfy yourself as to the standing of our trade with Daish. It's been a long voyage and a busy day and it's barely half-over.'

Itrac glanced around to be sure they weren't being observed. 'And when Janne Daish arrives?' She looked at him, beseeching.

'*If–*' Kheda emphasised the word '–you're ready to receive her, do so. If not?' He shrugged. 'Don't. I think it entirely possible that I will be occupied until at least the early evening,' he mused. 'So Jevin can take word to Birut that we're both occupied with affairs of our domain and that Janne Daish can take her time to recover from the rigours of her journey. She's not so young as she was, after all.'

'I don't think Jevin had better take *that* message to Birut,' Itrac said with a faint smile.

'We don't want to make an enemy of her,' Kheda agreed frankly, 'but it won't hurt to remind her that you're first wife of Chazen, with all the status that entails and the respect it requires.'

Itrac's smile widened. 'All the same, we won't keep her waiting too long.'

'No, but just long enough.' Kheda looked around the garden. 'If you'll excuse me, I'll go and see if Dev's got himself lost or found his way to my apartments.'

Itrac laid a hand on his arm after another furtive glance around. 'When we've put all this upheaval behind us,' she said hesitantly, 'might you look for a personal slave with blood ties to the Archipelago? Let him go back to his northern barbarian lands?'

'That's something I shall be happy to do,' Kheda promised fervently. He hesitated. 'I can get to the central corridor through your audience hall, can't I?'

'Yes, my lord.' Itrac very nearly laughed.

Jevin appeared at the doorway to her personal apartments. 'My lady, are you ready to eat?'

'I should check the omens from the observatory first.' Kheda kissed Itrac lightly on the forehead. 'You go ahead.'

The audience hall opening off the garden was cool with lengths of muslin shading the arched windows. Blue and golden flowers painted into posies on the white-tiled floor surrounded a fountain whispering in a central marble basin. Carpets at either end of the room drew the eye with their vivid pattern of white and blue vine flowers worked on a golden ground. The patterns were echoed in the painted walls where climbing roses coiled elegantly around fretwork trellises. Banks of yellow cushions were piled ready for those invited to sit with the domain's lady; silver trays on side tables were set ready with ewers and goblets.

The household slaves certainly managed to hide a good deal from the wild men. I wonder how. I wonder if they managed to save Chazen Saril's store of talisman gems as well as the fabrics and furniture.

Kheda went through a central arch to a smaller square reception room with doors on either side leading to the private apartments that Chazen Saril's other wives had shared. An arch opposite opened on to the broad corridor that he recognised as separating the women's quarters from the warlord's preserve. He strode down the long passage past paired ironwood doors opening on to identical suites ready to welcome visiting warlords invited to some council or other.

Not that the other warlords of these southern domains ever came to sit at Saril's feet and receive his wisdom. Am I the one to raise Chazen to such status? If I get rid of this dragon, they'll sit up and take notice, that much is certain. Even Ulla Safar. Janne Daish can chew on that till it chokes her.

He passed through a reception room luxurious with furnishings of brocaded silks, soft carpet beneath his feet and the wall hangings painted with hunting scenes suitable for a warlord's dignity.

'There you are,' said Dev with relief, appearing through a door leading to some indeterminate hallway. 'Are you eating your lunch with Itrac or should I try to find a maid to send to the kitchens?'

'I want to visit the observatory,' Kheda said briefly. He paused. 'I think it's this way.'

He opened another door to find a lesser reception room furnished with carpets whose bold scarlet pattern of interlocking canthira leaves on a rich brown ground was relieved with a white lattice of sashflowers. Low tables of rich russet fora wood bore broad brass bowls of scented petals. There wasn't a speck of dust to be seen anywhere; two maids clutching polishing rags bowed as they disappeared through a far door.

Kheda waited until the door was closed. 'You're going to have to play a much more convincing slave here than you did in the southern residence,' he warned Dev in a low tone. 'A lot more of these people lived here before. They had time and warning to flee the invaders, not to get caught and killed.'

'I'll bow and scrape like a good lackey,' promised Dev with an unpleasant curl to his lip.

'There's a lot more to it than that,' Kheda told him as they passed swiftly through another hall. 'I need you to find out as many of these servants' names as you can. I need to know slaves from free islanders. If they're slaves, I need to know where they came from and how they came to be bonded. I need to know who can be trusted, who can be bribed, who will do their duty and no more and who would take a knife in the chest for their lord. Not that I suppose there are many that loyal to me. I also need to know who's particularly loyal to Itrac.'

I need Telouet, not you, you blunt-witted barbarian.

'If I can win them over, especially the older retainers, that'll colour the attitude of the whole household,' Kheda continued. 'It wouldn't hurt to know exactly how they saved themselves from the invaders, either, where they fled to and how many were lost. And you'll sleep on a slave's pallet at my door,' he added. 'No arguments, Dev, otherwise the whole household will be wondering about you.'

'We barbarians always say that you Aldabreshi treat your slaves like dogs,' Dev muttered with contempt. 'Are you going to put a collar and leash on me?'

'Don't tempt me,' Kheda said tartly. 'There are warlords who would, and have you eat from a plate on the floor till you learned some proper humility.'

The warlord halted as he found himself on the threshold of Chazen's great audience chamber. Its simplicity came as a stark contrast to the rest of the residence's luxuries. Here the floor was plain white tile, the walls unadorned plaster. The centre of the roof had been raised with a clerestory whose windows were a marvel of the glazier's art. Glass in jewel colours wove intricate designs that captured the sunlight to spill it to the floor below in dazzling patterns.

Patterns that change with every cloud crossing the sky, different with the sun's rising and setting every day. Did Chazen Saril see omens in those colours? I know nothing of such lore.

There were no carpets, no cushions: those coming before their lord would stand and be grateful for the privilege. A beam carved and sheathed in bronze like the prow of a trireme projected from the far wall, drapes of white silk making a canopy. A backless, cross-framed chair of gilded wood stood there.

'So you get to sit in judgement but you don't get to slouch.' Dev grinned.

Kheda made a sudden decision. 'There'll be time enough to sit in judgement over this domain when I've secured it. I need guidance from the omens and I need news from the outlying isles if I'm not going to lose it to this ravaging dragon. I'll be getting dispatches from the *Mist Dove*, but you need to make friends with the mariners down in the anchorage, especially those from the dispatch galleys who'll be taking the courier doves here and there. You'll be surprised what they pick up.'

'I'm supposed to do this while keeping my head down and not reminding anyone that I'm some god-cursed barbarian from the magic-plagued north?' Dev asked quizzically. 'And hoping they won't ask awkward questions about just how you and I managed to kill off the invaders' wizards with just Risala along to give us an uplifting poem or two?'

'You keep telling me how clever you are.' Turning his back on the canopied chair, Kheda left the audience chamber and walked through three successive reception rooms with luxurious furnishings and vigorous wall paintings in bold colours until he reached the physic garden.

Dev grinned. 'I've already found out something useful. Beyau showed me the back way out of this warren, on account of me being your trusted slave, even if I am a strange barbarian. A tunnel runs right along the foundations of the back wall and there are several ways in from your apartments and from one of the lesser reception rooms. It goes all the way out past the eastern headland and into some caves. There's caves all under that high ground, apparently. That's where the household stashed all the loot before taking to the boats and running away from the wild men.' Dev's grin turned into a chuckle. 'Beyau's looking forward to showing Janne that the residence is quite restored to its former glory, thank you very much. He took exception to a few things Rekha had to say, apparently.'

'Keep well clear of Birut, Janne's body slave,' Kheda warned sharply. 'He'll suspect you on principle and he's shrewd enough to notice things Jevin doesn't. And tenacious, if he gets a scent of something awry. Walk carefully round him; I don't want Janne contriving anything she might use against us.'

'I don't imagine she'll surpass her last exploit,' Dev said, more thoughtful than mocking. 'So where is this observatory? And the courier-dove loft?'

'The courier doves are housed in the forebuilding.' Kheda gestured towards its towers rising high in defence of the residence where swordsmen and archers maintained their unceasing watch.

'All the warriors in the domain will be cursed small use if that dragon turns up,' Dev said with faint malice.

Since there was nothing to say to that, Kheda led the way across the physic garden to a flight of stairs leading up to the fourth, glass-crowned tower of the forebuilding. 'The observatory's up here.'

Opening the door, he was startled to find a grey-haired servant looking back at him, equally surprised.

'My lord.' The man bowed, clutching a sizeable tome bound in brown leather to his dun tunic.

'Who might you be?' Kheda asked, once his heart had slowed a little.

'Tasu, my lord.' The man stayed bent low. 'The keeper of the books here.'

'Then show us what you've kept safe for Chazen,' Kheda invited briskly.

The two of them followed the old man up more stairs to a room taking up the whole width of the tower below the glass-walled observatory. It was shelved from floor to ceiling with books packed tight on all sides. A broad table of black wood polished by years of use stood in the middle of the room, reading slopes scattered haphazardly across it, stools pushed tidily beneath.

Kheda surveyed the shelves with pleasure. 'I'm delighted to see so much of the Chazen library intact. I was afraid the invaders would have burned the books to warm their naked arses.'

'They did, my lord, those that they found.' Tasu hid a smile with a wrinkled hand, ostensibly smoothing his grizzled beard. 'Which were copies or books of little value. When the beacons told us we were invaded, we had sufficient time to get the important books to the caves along with the bulk of the residence's treasures. We left some furnishings, mostly worn or discarded. We hoped they'd think they had taken a domain of little substance. We left enough food to see them on their way, not sufficient to encourage them to stay.' His smile faded. 'Then we sealed the caves with the bravest of the swordsmen inside, in case they should need to fight in last defence of Chazen's learning and wealth. We lost ourselves in the depths of the forest, those of us who were able to flee. The warriors and the slaves drew lots to see who should stay to hold the forebuilding to give us time to escape, so that whoever was attacking wouldn't just come hunting the rest of us.' He looked at Kheda, dark-brown eyes beseeching. 'We didn't know we were facing magic, not then. They died, my lord, at wizards' hands.'

'No one knew, not then,' Kheda told him firmly. 'And if you stayed, you risked a foul death or a worse captivity.'

'We thought we were safe when Redigal ships arrived with word that Daish Kheda was not dead as we'd heard but alive, and bringing the means to foil the wild magics. We were most relieved to hear you were claiming the domain since it was Chazen Saril who had died.' His voice faltered. 'Now a dragon has come. I'll tell you honestly, my lord, and you can have me flogged if you wish, but there are some asking if all our efforts have been worth the pains.'

'I'd never flog an honest man for asking a fair question,' Kheda assured him.

'How do we foil a dragon?' Tasu looked helplessly around at the bookshelves rather than risk Kheda's gaze.

'It seems the barbarians of the far north know how,' Kheda said carefully. 'I've sent Chazen's fastest trireme to see if any northerly Aldabreshin domain holds some clue as to how we might kill the foul beast or at very least drive it out. While we wait, since it seems happy to devour the remaining invaders, I'm inclined to let it. If it moves against Chazen people, we'll do all we can to contain it while we wait for the means to defeat it more permanently.' He looked up at the plaster ceiling, which was studded with facsimiles of the shells of curious sea creatures for no readily apparent reason. 'While we wait, I'll study the earthly and the heavenly compasses and all the lore you can offer me, so we'll be able to pick the best of all possible times to attack it. I don't know if all that effort will be worth my pains or yours, but if I'm warlord of this domain, I must do all I can to save it or die in the attempt.'

Which will show me, one way or the other, whether I've been right to associate myself with magic to fight magic.

Kheda changed the subject briskly. 'Are you known to the courier-dove keepers?'

'Yes, my lord.' Tasu was too bemused to bow.

'I shall want all messages from the fleet keeping watch on the western isles brought up to the observatory.' Kheda crossed the room to a far stair leading up to the topmost level. 'Could you do that for me?'

'Yes, my lord.' The old man nodded obediently.

'Could you go and see if any news has arrived since this morning?' Kheda asked courteously.

'Of course, my lord.' Tasu made his way to the stairs and began a cautious descent.

Dev followed Kheda up to the glass-walled observatory. 'You're not needing those messages before sunset, then?'

'He won't take that long.' Kheda blinked in the sunlight pouring painfully bright through the twelve panes of glass. Each was engraved with a reminder of the nature of portents to be found in that reach of the earth and sky. The black wooden pillars separating each window bore carvings of the augury stars that progressed around the compass, inlaid with white ivory and bright gold. Vivid enamel depicted the heavenly jewels here and there; Sapphire, Emerald, Topaz, Ruby, Amethyst, Diamond, Pearl and Opal. With the sun beating down on the black wooden roof above, it was stiflingly hot.

Dev went to look at the enamelled jewels. 'These positions must mark when this observatory was built. We could work out when that was with a bit of thought and one of Saril's star circles.'

'I thought you said all Aldabreshin stargazing was just so much nonsense.' Kheda tried to shake off the oppressive sensation of the still, stuffy air. 'Open a window.'

Dev studied the catches for a moment, then threw open the little casements at the top of each window. 'All your guessing and gazing after portents is nonsense,' he corrected. 'Your measuring of the passing years is second to none for accuracy. So, are we hiding up here to avoid Janne Daish and, if so, for how long, because we still haven't had anything to eat and it's past noon.'

'You can eat after you've found something to use for your speaking spell and discovered how your friend's search for lore we can use against the dragon is going,' Kheda ordered. 'And quickly, before Tasu gets back.'

'What will you be doing when he gets back?' Dev

started opening drawers in the twelve-sided table engraved to match the rest of the room.

'As I told Tasu, finding the best days for attacking the beast.' Kheda pulled up a stool and reached for one of the star circles in the centre. 'Casting the heavens for all the possible days when Risala could arrive. Calculating how long it'll take to reach the westernmost islands after that. Factoring in possible delay in finding the beast, and on account of the weather. The rains will be all but on us, if they haven't actually started.'

'A fat lot of use that will all be,' commented Dev as he took a brass base plate from a dismantled star circle out of a drawer and set a reed pen alight with a casual brush of a finger.

'Only if you can't come up with the means to defeat the dragon,' challenged Kheda as he concentrated on aligning the star circle. 'Where's this woman of yours now?'

'She'll blister your ears if you call her that when she gets here,' Dev said absently. 'And I don't just mean she's got a sharp tongue on her. Ah, there she is, asleep, isn't that sweet?' He chuckled.

'Wake her.' Kheda looked up, hearing the door at the bottom of the stairs opening. 'As quick as you can.'

Crossing the intricate floor carvings, he hurried down the stairs to find Tasu standing with one hand pressed to his bony chest, catching his breath. Kheda forced approval rather than irritation into his voice. 'That was quick.'

'Yes, my lord.' Tasu took a deep breath and held out a handful of small silver cylinders. 'One of the lads ran up to the lofts for me, my lord.'

'Make sure he makes himself known to me.' Kheda unscrewed the tops of the message cylinders with deft fingers and pulled out the frail slips of paper. 'Let's read these in here.' He ushered the old man inexorably into the book-lined lower room.

'May I ask what news, my lord?' Tasu looked drawn and anxious.

'Good news,' Kheda said slowly, holding up the fine paper to read the tiny writing, 'from the *Mist Dove*, at least. They've only seen the dragon once in the last ten days and it was killing the invaders. Since then our warriors have been clearing the westernmost isles of the vermin without its interference.'

'Good news indeed, my lord,' the old man echoed.

Kheda looked around the book-lined walls. 'I want to be ready to deal with this beast if it shows its face around here, and when we can make a plan to kill it. Can you find me all the most recent records of portents that proved particularly significant for the domain? And anything from longer ago that you think might have some relevance to the days ahead. And there was a curious omen when we were out at the pearl reefs, an infant shark found alive inside its mother. Do you have any lore on sharks here?'

'I can look, my lord.' Tasu's eyes brightened.

'And could you do me one more service?' Kheda smiled. 'Could you go and find someone to take a message to Beyau, and to my lady Itrac. I've decided I'll take my lunch up here.'

'Very good, my lord,' said Tasu dutifully, turning to go back down the stairs.

Kheda reached out and took a book from a shelf, apparently absorbed in it as the old man departed. As soon as he heard the door at the bottom of the stairs close, he ran up to the observatory, taking two steps at a time.

I should just have time to find out what news Dev's got from this woman of his.

CHAPTER ELEVEN

'Are you sure you won't stay the night?' The woman stood in the doorway, wringing work-hardened hands.

'No.' Velindre made sure her rope-tied bundle of blanket and food was comfortable on her shoulder. 'Thank you all the same,' she added as a stiff afterthought.

'There's scant daylight left and what with the promise of rain yonder, this is no time to be setting out,' the woman persisted. 'You could wait till tomorrow, go out with a full day ahead of you. I'm sure some of the men would go with you.' She waved vaguely down the hill.

'Thank you, but I don't need your solicitude or their help.' Velindre curbed her irritation. 'Didn't you understand what I meant when I said I was a mage of Hadrumal?'

The woman stood reluctantly aside and Velindre stepped out on to the muddy track that cut through a scatter of skulking huts. The village had been built from the mismatched plunder of rockfalls judging by the irregularity of the walls beneath the snow-caked wooden-shingled roofs. Most were single- or double-roomed dwellings, few boasting even an attempt at a garden or yard. The only sizeable building was down where the track widened to a trampled expanse that even the most optimistic would hesitate to call a village square. It was twice the width of any other building and steam rose from a wing extending behind it to shelter a brew house.

Velindre realised too late that looking at the rough-hewn tavern had been a mistake. The handful of dour-faced men lounging against the wall had been covertly watching the women emerge from the hut. Two pushed themselves upright with alacrity and began walking up the lane, the rest trailing behind, faces alight with curiosity.

'Thank you for your hospitality.' Velindre nodded to the woman. She turned to go, gathering her heavy fur cloak around her. 'I think the horse is more than adequate recompense.'

'Are you sure you don't need him?' The woman struggled with her unwillingness to reject such a gift. 'This is hard country for travelling on foot and with you a lady from the south—'

'A *mage* from the south,' Velindre corrected her. 'No, take the horse and welcome. I'd be casting him loose otherwise. All I ask is that you look after him; he's been a good beast to me.'

The woman detained her with an insistent hand. 'Shouldn't I keep him till you come back this way? I'll give you a bed again and welcome.'

'I shan't be coming back this way,' Velindre assured her brusquely. 'Good day to you.'

'I wouldn't want you to come back and not find us,' the woman continued, as if Velindre hadn't spoken. 'See, with a horse, me and the children, we'll make for the lowlands when the thaw comes, go back to my own family.' The children in question, three of them and none taller than their mother's apron strings, peered around the doorframe, blue eyes wide.

'The animal is yours. Make whatever use of him you want.' Pulling her arm away, Velindre began walking up the track, cursing under her breath as she stumbled on frozen ruts. Solid boots thudded on the ice-hardened earth behind her and she tensed, clasping her double-gloved hands together beneath the all-concealing fur cloak.

'Taking a walk, mistress mage?' One of the village men hurried to draw level with her. He had the short, stocky build and fair complexion of the mountains, with a heavy leather coat further padding his bulk.

Velindre ignored him, increasing her pace.

'What was your business with the Widow Pinder?' A second man came up on her other side. He was taller than the first, with the dark, curly hair and olive skin of southern Tormalin blood incongruous with the snow and ice all around.

Velindre kept walking, face expressionless. She fixed her eyes on the fir forest ahead, dark above the leafless skeletons of the lower slopes.

'Widow Pinder's eldest, she was telling my Sonille that you're some wizard woman,' a voice from behind taunted.

Sniggers told Velindre that the remaining three idlers from the tavern were trailing a handful of paces behind her unwanted escort.

'Go on, then, show us some magic,' mocked the man with the Tormalin blood.

'Magic's not welcome round here.' The stocky man scowled at her. 'Is that where you're headed?' He pointed up past the ridge of hills sheltering the little village, towards a forbidding range of high peaks. Clouds were gathered just beyond, dark grey and ominous in an otherwise clear blue sky. Higher up, white clouds were spread by the winds into feathery streaks. The grey clouds weren't moving.

'He asked you a question, lady!' The Tormalin man darted forward to plant himself solidly in Velindre's path, hands on his hips.

Velindre made to step round him. A second stocky man with muddy brown hair appeared from behind to block her way. With the fair-haired man on her other side and the two remaining loafers behind her, she was effectively surrounded.

'Haven't you got anything better to do with your time?' she asked with faint derision. 'Let me pass. My business is none of yours.'

'You tell us what it is and we'll decide that,' the fair-haired man said boldly.

'We don't want no more wizards setting up home hereabouts,' growled one of the pair behind her.

'You've seen a wizard hereabouts?' Velindre turned around, surprising a flare of panic in the thin-faced speaker's eyes.

'That's a wizard's work, isn't it?' He waved a shaky hand at the distant leaden cloudscape before hastily snatching it back. 'There's valleys up there no one's got near in years.'

'Everyone knows it's magic keeping us out.' The Tormalin man scowled. 'Even if the wizard hides himself away up there.'

'Find themselves caught up in tangles of plants knotting themselves, people do,' the brown-haired man insisted, 'or get turned around so often they find themselves back where they started.'

'Life's hard up here.' The thin man's companion added his voice to the debate. The scars on his face attested to his words. 'We work hard for our furs and our tin and it's share and share alike. We don't close off the land with magic and hoard it all for ourselves.'

With the slope of the track added to her already greater height, Velindre looked down on him with undisguised disdain. 'I assure you, I have no interest in furs or tin.'

'What's in those valleys?' The fair-haired man stepped closer, his shoulder nudging her arm, belligerence curdling his face. 'Come to share the spoils with that wizard, have you?'

'Is it gold?' the brown-haired man asked hopefully.

'Magic or not, you must need some help. We could lend a hand.'

'As long as we're fairly paid,' warned the fair-haired man.

'Let's say whoever's up in those hills wants your help.' The Tormalin man laid a heavy hand on Velindre's shoulder. 'Then he can pay us for your passage through our territory, can't he?'

'You've never actually seen a wizard, have you?' Velindre looked the Tormalin man in the eye before glancing at his hand, amused. 'Not this mysterious mage you say lives beneath those clouds nor any real wizard.'

'What's that to you?' The brown-haired man looked uncertainly at the man with the scars, who glanced uneasily at his hatchet-faced friend.

'Seen plenty of fools up from the south who think it's easy pickings up here.' The fair-haired man tried to seize her other arm through the thick fur of her cloak.

Velindre flung her hands wide. A burst of blue light blew the five men away with a brutal gust of magical wind. The fair-haired man fell backwards, landing hard to sprawl gasping, arms waving feebly as the breath was knocked clean out of him. The Tormalin man tumbled sideways, ending up in a crouch like a whipped cur, clutching at a tuft of frosted grass, his jaw slack with inarticulate astonishment. Taken entirely by surprise and with the downward slope treacherous behind him, the brown-haired man fell in a tangled heap with the one with the scars. Only the hatchet-faced man kept his feet. He stumbled backwards down the track, hands raised in feeble denial, his head turned aside and eyes screwed tight shut, too scared to want to see what might be coming next.

'I told you my business was none of yours.' Entirely composed, Velindre stood, her hands held wide, dark fur cloak and golden hair streaming behind her as if she stood in the teeth of a winter gale. Not a twig stirred on the winter-stricken trees on either side of the track. 'I take it you'll believe me now when I tell you plainly that you have no hope of detaining me.'

She thrust a hand forward and a ribbon of sapphire light hobbled the hatchet-faced man. 'Whereas I can make your lives very unpleasant if you have any notion of following me.' With a snap of her fingers, she called down a bolt of lightning from the clear blue sky. It struck the rowan she pointed to with one long, pale finger and the tree burst into crackling white flames.

Movement down the hill caught her eye and Velindre realised that almost the entire meagre population of the village was watching from doorways or around the corners of their ragged-edged huts. 'I will know if you try following me,' she continued with precise menace, 'just as I will know if anyone decides to offer the Widow Pinder any trouble for giving me a bed for the night. I recommend you bold heroes make that plain to your neighbours.'

With a wave of her hand, she snuffed the flames consuming the rowan. The only sound was the faint patter of the tree's few remaining leaves and berries falling to the ground. Velindre gestured discreetly towards the tree and a charred branch broke away with a tearing crash. As the shaken men all jumped, startled, and looked at it, Velindre wrapped herself in a swathe of dazzling cerulean light and vanished.

The cowering men rubbed their eyes, blinking painfully as they stared gaping at the place where she'd been. Smiling unseen, the magewoman retreated slowly up the hill. It had been some while since she had worked invisibility around herself, she realised with faint amusement. Who would have thought an apprentice's trick like blinding someone with magelight would prove so useful? Drawing the air close in around her, she deftly bound water and fire into the spell to cloak herself entirely from view.

But enough of this foolishness, she decided. She had no time to waste. The trip had already taken longer than she had expected. Not that Dev had had any cause to complain that she was idling, she thought with irritation. And she wouldn't be dealing with this nonsense if he hadn't startled the widow and her children by bespeaking her like that. It was hardly surprising that the eldest girl hadn't been able to keep something like that to herself.

Velindre walked away up the track, first looking ahead at her path and then back down the hill, to be sure those bold heroes were returning to their startled village.

The fallen men were picking themselves up. The scarred man took a cautious pace towards the charred skeleton of the rowan tree, his fair-haired companion following, careful all the while to keep the first man between himself and the uncanny spectacle. The Tormalin man and the one with brown hair were edging towards their hatchet-faced friend, who was still rooted to the spot with terror even though the skeins of azure light around his legs were fading. The Tormalin man gave him a sudden shove. The sharp-faced man cried out before taking a step to save himself as he found he was no longer bound by the spell. He took to his heels, slipping and sliding as he fled for the solace of the tavern. The hatchet-faced dun-haired man and the one with the scars followed him, barely slowly enough to preserve their dignity in front of the wide-eyed villagers.

The Tormalin man and his Mountain-bred friend stayed where they were, looking suspiciously up the track. Velindre hurried for the shelter of a starveling hazel thicket. These fools weren't deaf, she reminded herself, or blind to any other trace she could leave. They might be miners in the summer; in the winter seasons they trailed game far smaller than an adult mage. She looked at the ground, shaking her head at the momentary disorientation of not being able to see her own feet. She could see the ridges of the hard ground unyielding beneath her clumsy boot soles; no tracks there. But her weight had crushed blades of sere grass poking up through the sodden black leaves where the vagaries of the wind had left the ground clear of snow.

It had been a while since she had had to work two, no, three such spells in harness. Velindre summoned a second layer of dense air to cocoon her invisibility spell, baffling and muffling any crunch of her footfalls on the icy ground, any swish or snap as she brushed past the clawing hazel twigs. She lifted one foot and stepped up on to a soft cushion of magic. Pausing to be sure of her balance, she stepped forward, summoning a second squashy pillow of air to raise her a hand's width above the ground.

Not that this was quite the sophisticated working with elemental air that Hadrumal would expect from a Cloud Mistress, she thought with distant amusement. And Planir's rebukes for apprentices who felt entitled to cow mundane fools with gaudy trickery were legendary. Which was all well and good, but life was certainly different out here where the Archmage's writ didn't run.

She stumbled as the chancy air drifted beneath her feet and abandoned such idle thoughts in favour of concentration. Walking further into the trees at a painfully slow pace, she looked over her shoulder for any sign of pursuit after every few steps. If those fools from the village couldn't hear her, she wouldn't hear them approaching either, thanks to that same magical spell.

By the time she crested the ridge behind the village, her neck was stiff, her legs ached as if she had been walking all day through soft sand and a faint queasiness threatened to turn into a nauseous headache. Setting her jaw, she forced her way through a copse of shivering aspens and cast away the magic surrounding her. Her booted feet hit the ground with a jolt and she drew a welcome breath of fresh, cold air. Hastily she gathered up the magic dissipating around her and cast out a web of unseen magical threads, drawn taut to tremble with the noises of the forest and bring every sound magnified for her ears alone.

Meltwater dripped from trees welcoming the optimistic sun that was strengthening with each new day. In the dark hollows of the forest, though, the chill of night was already returning, prompting protesting creaks from the icy streams frozen solid in their stony beds. Untrammelled breezes ran ahead of the shadows, trailing casual fingers through tangles of ivy clinging to the mossy larches. A faint scuttle of tiny paws whispered through the frost-bitten undergrowth. Velindre breathed more easily. There was no sound of footsteps or the harsh breathing of men intent on a hunt.

Velindre looked across the wide expanse of snow pierced with scattered trees that separated her from the next rise in the rumpled land. Then she settled the rope of her bundle more securely on her shoulder beneath her cloak and began walking. The track from the village soon petered out, disappearing beneath the drifts of snow and the black swathes of leaf litter.

Would any of those oafs tell their tale the next time they made the wearisome journey to Inglis? And show themselves for the fools they had been? That was hardly likely, she concluded. What about the widow woman? Would she tattle to all and sundry about how she had given unknowing shelter to a mage unafraid to use her magic to teach ignorant buffoons a much-needed lesson? Velindre shrugged. What of it? If the woman did tell her tale, who could carry it to Hadrumal? She was well beyond Rafrid's reach already and it was hardly likely that Planir would rebuke her if she returned with untried lore from both Azazir and this dragon loose in the Archipelago.

She studied the distant coil of grey clouds with growing interest. Even with long leagues still to go, she could feel a faint resonance of magic as the storm defied the natural currents coursing through the air. She found herself intrigued. Never mind Dev's distractions with this dragon; just what would this Azazir have to teach her about the elemental air? If she was going to find out, she had to get to the valley beneath that unmoving, unbreaking storm. She considered the wide expanse ahead of her, deep snow reaching half-way up the dark stands of firs.

This looked like a good time to try another prentice mage's trick: the impudent connivance that allowed the bold and reckless to dart between the highest points of Hadrumal's roofs and towers when festival cheer overcame caution. Rafrid would doubtless be spending his Equinox issuing the usual reprimands and curtailing offenders' privileges. Velindre smiled with vindictive amusement as she fixed her gaze on a patch of open ground beneath a stained outcrop of rock away on the far side of the woods. A rush of air carried her across the intervening half-league with a single stride. Another step took her to the top of the ridge and a third made light of a sprawling glassy expanse of frozen marsh.

From the bottom of the next ridge, she searched for a suitable foothold among the trees lining the heights above her. Seeing bare earth and stones where a storm had felled some mighty fir, she threw a coil of magic towards the open space. The ensorcelled air writhed, spiralling away up to be lost in the uncaring blue sky. Velindre was taken aback. It was several moments before she recovered her authority over the fickle winds. She cast her spell again. Once more, the magic recoiled from the patch of empty ground where she wanted to go. This time the spell curled back around her, threatening to carry her backwards and dump her unceremoniously among the sodden tussocks of the valley. She barely disentangled herself from the magic before she lost her footing, startled into cursing under her breath.

Face wary in the dark fur framing it, she made a third attempt, this time abandoning the spell as soon as she felt the first tremor of failure. She smiled thinly with slow realisation. The magic frustrating her own was being worked through the water suffusing the air. Only a very powerful mage could manifest his intent through the infinitesimal amounts of vapour in this cold, dry emptiness. Azazir evidently knew how to use his own element to dominate the air. Would she learn how to rule water with air so effectively? All the inconveniences of crossing these last interminable leagues on foot would be well worth it if she could, never mind what Dev and this warlord of his might owe her for any lore about dragons.

She had better learn something worth the tedious toil ahead, since further magical travel was plainly out of the question. Velindre sighed and searched for any semblance of a track leading up through the trees.

Intellectual curiosity about what Azazir might or might not know had faded in the face of grim determination by the time Velindre was half-way up the steep slope. The hem of her fur cloak was caked with snow and her boots dragged leaden at her feet. Legs aching fiercely, she pressed on, the icy ground slick and unforgiving. She caught at saplings with her gloved hands to pull herself up awkward stretches and silently cursed the bleak rocks breaking through the soil and forcing her sideways to find a clear way forward once more.

As she worked her way down the north face of that ridge and across the valley beyond, Azazir's dampening magic weighed more and more heavily on the blasts of air she was summoning to clear snow out of her path. She was reduced to fighting her way through waist-deep drifts with no more than the unaugmented strength in her arms and legs. By the time she was at long, long last approaching the foot of the first true scion of the mountain range, the sun was sinking, turning the rocks breaking through the threadbare ground to a cold, steely grey.

Velindre clenched her fists inside her gloves to quell the trembling of fatigue. At least she wasn't cold. Azazir might have the reach to stifle magic beyond her arms' length but he couldn't overcome her innate abilities, whatever his unlooked-for talents. She sighed and pressed on up the punishing slope, the heavy fur cloak dragging at her shoulders.

Half-way up, she lost her footing and fell to her knees. As she did so, her hand landed on a fold of the beaver fur. It squelched beneath her weight. Velindre frowned and stood up carefully. She stripped off her doubled gloves, her suspicions growing hand in hand with hot anger. Taking a double handful of the cloak, she squeezed the fur tight. Water oozed over her fingers. There was a curious glitter to it, almost like quicksilver. She looked for a moment at the bright drops, then shook them off. Rather than falling to the ground, the moisture flew back to the fur, vanishing in an instant – all but one bulbous drop which sat on the surface of the dark fur until a blackness winked across it, like the blink of an eye.

Velindre tore at the clinging ties of the heavy cloak and dropped its sodden weight to the ground. It was saturated with water, she realised with sudden fury, but not through any normal turn of events. She rubbed a hand over the shoulders of the woollen cloak she was wearing underneath. The cloth was dry and faintly warm with the heat of her body. None of the wet from the fur had penetrated it, nor the thick flannel shirt and sturdy woollen gown beneath. Sitting on a bare patch of cold, dry earth, she fought to pull off the clumsy gaiters she was wearing to keep the mud and damp from her boots and stockings. The leather was grotesquely swollen with moisture, but the boots beneath were still dry, their polish unmarred. She reached for her thick outer gloves and found that they, too, were weighed down with more water than the fur could ever hope to hold without magical deceit. She wrung one out and the water gathered itself on the moss in oval drops, again with an uncanny semblance of watching eyes.

'That's a subtle working, Master Azazir,' she remarked, partly to the motionless drops of water and partly to the empty air. 'Do you discourage all your visitors like this?' She stood up, shaking out her thick skirts and drawing her woollen cloak close. 'Or is this a test for mages, to see if they can do without the conveniences of winter clothing? Believe me, I am more than equal to keeping myself warm without furs.' As she spoke, the drops of water abruptly ran away to be lost in the frosty ground.

Never mind Dev and his distant difficulties. Velindre gritted her teeth. This contest was becoming one she wasn't prepared to yield, however good this unseen Azazir might think he was. Drawing on her kidskin gloves with hard-faced resolve, the magewoman enveloped herself in still air warmed with a hint of fire. Abandoning fur cloak, gloves and gaiters, she began climbing again. Determination drove her on and her spirits rose as she realised she was actually making better progress without the hampering bulk of those outer garments. Then the fire in her spell was abruptly snuffed and the gathering chill of the frozen forest dusk bit through the air surrounding her. Gritting her teeth, she pressed on until a small saddle between two jagged spurs of rock offered a place to catch her breath.

She couldn't snare any spark of fire. The element was fleeing in all directions from the cold damp now suffusing the air. Frost was already glazing the rocks, visibly thickening even as she looked at it. Dev would have been no use here, she thought inconsequentially. He wouldn't even have got close enough to learn anything of dragons. In the gathering dusk and chill, that notion wasn't as comforting as it might have been.

'My compliments, Azazir. I see you have a considerable mastery of fire, which is all the more impressive given that it's the element antithetical to your own.' She stood, listening, but heard nothing. Closing her eyes the better to concentrate for a moment, she wove a denser cloak of air around herself. If she couldn't warm herself from without, at least she wouldn't lose any more of the precious heat from within her body. The ground was less steep now and she could walk without using her hands. That was fortunate as she found her cocoon of air under insidious assault, the threads of air weighed down with more and more moisture until they snapped, tearing shreds of the protective magic away. Velindre found herself reaching further and further afield for untainted air to draw into her magic, the effort exhausting her more effectively than the weight of the sodden fur cloak.

'I only want to talk to you,' she snapped with weary irritation. 'I don't see why you should freeze me out like this. Don't the customary courtesies between mages apply in this forsaken place?'

A sound suspiciously like laughter brushed past her ear. She snatched at a breath of fleeting fire to cast light into the shadows of the trees. She just had time to see that there was no one there before the fire slid out of her grasp with ominous finality. The noise had come from a chuckling brook splashing over a rock-strewn stream bed.

She tried to find the fire again but her search was

fruitless. Unease gathered chill beneath her breastbone. Without at least a modicum of fire, the other three elements were cursed to lie inert and useless. That was one of the first things any prentice wizard learned and a circumstance that frequently gave those with an affinity for fire an unwarranted sense of superiority – especially given that fire could be snuffed, which surely made it the most vulnerable of the elements when all was said and done. Velindre gathered her wits, realising that cold and fatigue were making her foolish. She had to concentrate on the here and now, where Azazir certainly gave the lie to any claim of fire's pre-eminence, in this remote fastness where he'd honed his magic.

Magic that was unlike anything she'd encountered in Hadrumal. That's what she was seeking. Velindre took two more determined strides onward before she turned back to look at the stream. With winter still ruling these northern lands, it was the first open, running water she had seen there. How much higher was she than those uppermost villages where the miners and trappers were still smashing the ice in their wells of a morning and the brooks were frozen solid?

Then she saw the direction this implausible unfettered water was taking. The stream was flowing uphill to vanish over the lip of the valley ahead. Her mouth fell open, astonished as any ignorant villager. Recollecting herself and narrowing her eyes, she dropped to one knee, stripping off a glove. She pressed her palm to the spongy, mossy turf and concentrated with every mageborn sense within her.

The ground should have been frozen, moisture locked within the soil, earth and water alike waiting lifeless for the sun's warmth to drive out winter's cold. Never mind Dev; let Hearth Master Kalion come here, Velindre thought with mingled awe and apprehension. Let him make his pompous arguments for fire's precedence in the face of Azazir's dominance. This ground wasn't frozen, but neither was it warmed by any discernible heat. It was simply saturated with water quite untroubled by the plunging temperatures. And the water was moving oddly, flowing uphill unhampered through the solid rock and cloying clay. The earth lay passive, submissive, its elemental resonance entirely subdued. Velindre looked up. The grey clouds were directly overhead, in coils of air held captive by the all-commanding water, meekly doing its bidding. Green radiance crackled in the clouds like uncanny lightning.

She walked on slowly, increasingly reluctant yet irresistibly intrigued. Her wizard senses were soon shaking under the assault of the water's ascendancy, just as her ears were ringing with the sound of a thousand streams rushing towards the valley ahead. She left the larches and spruces behind and soon the brambles gave up the unequal struggle to maintain a foothold in this unnatural land. The mosses persisted furthest of all, a mottled green carpet reaching almost to the crest before her. Almost but not quite. The valley was rimmed with bare earth. Not mud, she noted with faint apprehension.

The ground was dry and easy enough to walk on. She paused, sensing the water surging just below the surface. Without the magic holding it back, it would turn the solid ground into a morass of clinging clay. She took another step. No, it would become bog, a sucking mire to drown her, filling her ears and eyes and mouth with deafening, blinding, stifling muck. She could feel the lethal potential just waiting beneath her feet.

Squaring her shoulders and lifting her chin, Velindre walked up the slope, which ended in a knife edge against the empty sky. She looked down into the valley. 'My compliments, Azazir . . .' The words died on her lips as she saw the vista before her.

There was nothing growing in the valley. Trees, shrubs, grass and mosses, all had been washed to oblivion by the countless streams cascading down the steep sides. Here and there a stretch of soil remained, some curious patch of gravel bright with minerals untouched by the water gliding across it. Mostly the ground had been stripped back to rock, the bones of the earth laid mercilessly bare. The soil hadn't been permitted any revenge on the streams, however. The lake filling the bottom of the valley was unclouded, no dirt sullying the crystal expanse. Pure power alone suffused the waters, filling the lake and the air above it with an emerald radiance.

The rocks around the shore glistened in the low light. Some of the outcrops were sharp, angles unblunted by the scouring floods. Others had been polished smooth, veins of ores and crystals exposed. Some protrusions had been carved into fanciful shapes. There was a horse with flippers instead of hooves, a fish with a mouth of distorted snaggle teeth, a lizard-tailed goat. Exaggerated faces peered up at her or out over the lake, some laughing insanely, others fixed in grimaces of terror or pain. One image caught her eye time and again: a coil mimicking the cloud held in that endless, unmoving turmoil above. Velindre looked more closely at the nearest such spiral carved into the rock just below the valley's rim. From this angle it looked like a serpent consuming its own tail.

Velindre began a cautious descent of the treacherous slope. The ground abruptly gave way beneath her. Her flailing feet could find no purchase, nothing to stand on. She sank waist deep into water rushing to fill the newly opened gully, her hands caught in the floating folds of her skirts. Icy currents soaked her to the skin, the chill prying between her legs, sliding beneath her clothes to crush her chest in a freezing embrace. The weight of her woollen cloak choked her, pulling her backwards till her yellow plait of hair floated on the surface of the water. She gasped and struggled as the waters closed over her head in an emerald flash. The torrent carried her over the rocks, sweeping her into the lake in a cascade of jade foam.

Eyes and mouth closed tight shut, she fought with the brooch securing her cloak. A prick of pain as she ripped it free was instantly numbed by the cold. The heavy cloth sank away and she fought with the buckles on her boots with nerveless fingers. Kicking them off, she tried to swim to the surface, the breath burning in her chest. Her legs were hampered by her skirts, dragging her down. She fumbled with the buttons at her waist, tearing herself loose. She struggled free of her sodden, constricting bodice, fighting the panic rising in her throat.

Free at last, she kicked for the surface, opening her eyes only to find an impenetrable barrier of emerald light denying her. The lake had her in its grasp. She couldn't reach the air above or the earth below the deeps. There was only water. It surrounded her, it suffused her, the cold magic willing the very blood in her veins to stop, to become one with the still peace of the pure, unclouded lake.

Velindre forced herself to go limp, arms and legs floating wide. She closed her eyes and concentrated on the air within her lungs. Meagre it might be, but it was air and it was hers. It was some tiny fraction of the emptiness beyond the water's barrier. It had circled the seas in the great storm systems where water did the air's bidding. It had crossed the lands where fire made a plaything of moisture in the heat of summer. The air alone knew the infinitesimal voids in the earth where water could not pass.

The green radiance wavered above her, stained with an aquamarine smear. Sapphire light splintered the waters, thrusting Velindre upwards to lie gasping, shivering on the surface of the lake. She pushed a hand into the water and a sheet of ice formed beneath her, edged with vivid blue light. Emerald fire crackled angrily around it, but the sapphire boundary stayed unbroken. She dragged herself up to half-sit, half-kneel, leaning heavily on her hands. Her skin was as white as her clinging shift and stockings and she shivered uncontrollably. Laughter echoed around the lake, sly amusement striking back at her from every rock face.

Velindre waited until she had some semblance of control over her voice. 'My compliments again, Master Azazir. I have never seen such mastery over an element.' She forced her head up, throwing aside her sodden plait and wiping freezing trickles from her forehead.

Green light swirled around the fragment of ice she rode on. She watched warily, stealthily seeking whatever air she could find. The eddy spun faster, mossy radiance darkening as a vortex formed, reaching down into the depths of the lake. Spiralling walls of water rose up all around the magewoman. Now the surface of the lake was level with her elbows, now her shoulders, now her head. Velindre thrust out a hand, turquoise light spreading from her outstretched palm. Her magic held back the lake as it fought to close over her head once again. She knelt upright and brought her hands up, the light strengthening to bathe her in a piercing azure. Her magic spread, forcing the emerald-laced waters back. The vortex swirled beneath her and for the barest moment, a ripple opened a gap between the ice she rode and the hollow beneath. Velindre thrust one hand down, blue fire plunging through the gap to rip the green spiral apart, scattering it to the depths of the lake. The waters rocked violently and she let her magic go to cling to the ice, fingers burning with the cold. That same laughter echoed around, now coloured with a buoyant excitement.

'I would much prefer to talk to you face to face,' Velindre called out with all the dignity she could muster.

She scanned the water and the valley in the fast-fading dusk. How far was it to the edge of the lake? Could she rely on the air to carry her over such an expanse of magically malevolent water? There was no point in even thinking of working a water magic through her own sympathy with that element. She could never hope to wrest any control from Azazir.

'How would you recognise my face?' Cruel laughter rippled through the words.

'I wouldn't, obviously.' Velindre looked around in vain to see where the voice was coming from. 'The Council of Hadrumal hasn't seen fit to hang your portrait in any of the halls,' she added tartly.

'The Council of Hadrumal doubtless thinks I'm dead, if they think of me at all.' There was an undercurrent of menace in the breathless words. 'And I don't imagine you're here with their blessing. What's to stop me killing you?'

'I'll do my level best, for a start.' Velindre seized her chance and wrapped herself in a web of bright-blue magic. It wasn't warmth but it was better than nothing. She had to ward off the cold somehow or that would be the death of her, never mind this mysterious wizard. 'Besides, kill me and you'll never know what brought me here.'

'What makes you think I would care?' the voice queried.

'Otrick's diaries,' she shot back. 'His writings say you were a mage who never let a question go unanswered.'

'Why are you reading Otrick's diaries? Did he send you here?' The voice was right behind her.

Velindre skidded around on her knees and gasped. A man was standing on the surface of the lake. Or at least, the translucent form of a thin, wiry man had risen out of the water, entirely naked, with a semblance of a long beard and straggly hair flowing back into the effigy. Currents of green magic fleeted within the shape, momentarily mimicking blood and bone before disappearing. The apparition opened its mouth.

'Did Otrick send you?' Azazir repeated, with an emerald flash in his colourless eyes.

'Otrick is dead.' The admission was startled out of Velindre. She bit her cold, wet lip and found her face was too numb for her to feel it.

'Is he?' Azazir didn't sound overly concerned. 'He taught you, didn't he? I can see his quirks in your magic.'

'Yes, he taught me.' Velindre nodded jerkily. 'But not everything he knew. Not everything the two of you knew. There's more I want to learn.'

'You have a powerful affinity,' Azazir remarked, coming close to the sapphire magic that surrounded her. Green radiance pulsed and faded within his watery body. 'Like Otrick. But do you understand, like he did?'

'Understand what?' asked Velindre warily, struggling to stop her teeth from chattering. 'And I won't understand anything if I freeze to death. I have to get ashore and dry off.'

Azazir ignored her, stretching out a colourless hand. 'Do you understand the limits of magic? Do you understand that the only limits are those we impose on ourselves?' He touched the azure magic and the ensorcelled air sank into the waters of the lake. Velindre gasped as the fierce cold bit deeper than ever into her drenched, inadequate clothing.

'Hush,' whispered Azazir, eyes glowing phosphorescent.

The air that Velindre had bound with her sapphire magic rose up from the lake once more. It brought a mist of fine droplets with it, suffused with emerald magelight. The blended magic shimmered turquoise.

'Did Otrick see it in you?' Azazir continued, drifting around behind Velindre to reappear on her other side.

'See what?' she snapped, doing her best to keep him in sight. It wasn't easy. Azazir began circling her, his insubstantial feet drifting through the surface of the lake, leaving a trail of emerald radiance sinking away into the depths.

'Is that why he sent you to me?' the water wizard mused. 'To do what he couldn't? Is that what he sees in you? The courage he never had, to yield, to become one with his element? Is that what you want to learn?'

Velindre felt herself growing dizzy as the aquamarine magic blurred her vision.

'Because there are marvellous magics to be made when you truly blend the elements, you know,' he whispered seductively.

'I want to learn what you know of dragons,' she said resolutely, trying not to look at him, fumbling for some control over her own element.

'Of course you do.' Azazir nodded with a happy smile. 'Which is why you'll do what I want. Whatever I want.'

Inside a heartbeat, three things happened. Velindre realised that Azazir was quite insane. She realised that his magic had entirely suffused her own and that she had no idea how to disentangle herself. Then he stepped through the turquoise radiance and seized her, his translucent hands digging into her arms. She gasped with pain and opened her mouth to protest but it was too late. Azazir pressed himself against her and the shape he had adopted was already losing its form as his very substance flowed inexorably into her own.

CHAPTER TWELVE

'It's no good.' Dev's voice thickened with frustration. 'I can't find her.' He hunched over the water as he fought with the scrying spell. 'I can't even get the spell to hold still.'

Finding his teeth aching, Kheda forced himself to unclench his jaw. He drummed his fingers on the far side of the vast grey marble bath raised in the middle of the floor. The swirls of the polished stone were copied in the smoky tiles of the floor. 'Try the mirror again.' He gestured towards the square of steel with its cracked lustre border, half-hidden behind a row of unguent jars painted with the same patterns of reef and sea that decorated the bath chamber's walls.

'There's no hope of fire magic finding her inside Azazir's influence,' muttered Dev bitterly, his attention still fixed on the obstinately magic-free water. 'And if we beat our heads against that truth much longer, we'll be late for that banquet of yours. Do you want to be discovered at this because some lackey comes to find us?'

'Would fresh water help?' Kheda searched his wits for some constructive suggestion.

If we've lost this magewoman, where do we look for any help against this dragon?

'Fresh water?' Dev looked up with an ill-tempered scowl. 'It's not the water and it's not me. I found Risala for you, didn't I? You saw her enjoying her pleasure cruise. I told you, it's Azazir's—'

'Hush.' Kheda was certain he'd heard a footfall. 'Someone's coming.'

'Announce yourself to your lord!' Dev's hand went to the scabbarded sword thrust through the sash of his black tunic and he slipped past Kheda to open the door with a jerk.

'Do we need to be so formal, Kheda?' A woman stood there looking at Dev, faint curiosity raising her brows.

'Janne Daish.' Kheda drew a short, sharp breath before waving her backwards and stalking through the door to the warlord's private sitting room.

Janne retreated, stopped and wiggled her toes. 'I do like these floors of wooden blocks,' she remarked. 'So much warmer and easier on the feet than tiles.' She moved towards a thick silk carpet of palest blue piled high with soft sea-green cushions embroidered with clams and sea stars bordered by swaying sea grasses.

'Through here, if you please, Janne Daish.' Kheda waited in the arch between this inner chamber and the warlord's anteroom where chests of ebony and ironwood stood in the corners between low tables set with alabaster vases bright with fresh flowers. There was a vivid white and gold carpet but no cushions for waiting visitors. He inclined his head, stopping well short of a bow. 'To what do I owe this unexpected visit?'

Unexpected and unwelcome. What do you want?

She smiled with amiable tolerance for the edge in his voice as she strolled into the anteroom. 'After everything Rekha said about how splendidly Itrac has restored these residences, I had to come and see for myself.'

'Forgive me.' Kheda smiled thinly. 'I didn't mean your visit to the domain. I meant your appearing here, in my apartments. You and Rekha seem to have become very casual about etiquette of late.'

Janne looked sharply at Dev, who was waiting in the

archway to the inner chamber, head bowed, every measure the attentive slave. 'You may leave us.'

'My lord?' Dev looked at Kheda, his Aldabreshin accent note perfect.

'Wait outside.' Kheda nodded. 'You're looking well,' he continued neutrally as Dev obediently closed the outer door behind him. 'And wholly first lady of Daish by virtue of being the warlord's mother rather than his wife. You look ten years older than you did as my consort.'

'It's such a relief, for me and Birut.' Janne smiled, untroubled. 'You never did appreciate how much work it took to make you the envy of every other warlord, and me the despair of their wives.'

The grey in Janne Daish's hair was no longer concealed by the crimson and indigo dyes she had been wont to use. Her long tresses were coiled into a crystal-studded net of plaited white silk held back behind her ears by a silver crescent headdress. The effect was subtly unflattering, revealing the years blurring her jawline and the wrinkled skin of her neck. No effort had been made to hide her years with cosmetics; she wore the minimum of frosted silver around her eyes, lips merely glossed with a purple the same shade as her gown. The high-necked dress of red-shot silk was cut to conceal, not to enhance, the charms of her voluptuous bosom. The wide white sash embroidered with red and purple flowers emphasised that her waist was thickened with child-bearing, while the full skirts hid her elegant legs.

All the same, I would still embrace you, draw your head upon my shoulder. You were all the wife I ever wanted. And you know it.

'I see you're weary.' Kheda regarded her with a hint of pity. 'The voyage must have been tiring for a woman of your years.'

If you want to play the matriarch, let's see how you like

being treated as if you were twenty years my senior instead of merely nine.

'I'm curious about your new body slave.' Janne looked after Dev. 'A barbarian, isn't he? Were none of our neighbours willing to trade you a better trained slave after all you'd done for Chazen?'

What are you expecting me to tell you? That I dared not approach Redigal or Ritsem, Aedis or Sarem, for fear of them refusing to send a slave to a domain stained with magic? If only it were that simple.

'He's of barbarian stock.' Kheda shrugged at the irrelevance. 'I found him when I was searching for lore in the north.'

'Is he *zamorin* or beardless by choice?' Janne's long sleeve fell back as she adjusted her headdress with fingers heavy with silver rings set with amethyst. 'A lover of men?' she elaborated unnecessarily. More violet stones circled her wrist.

'That's a remarkably impertinent question, even for one who was once my wife.' There was no warmth in Kheda's voice. 'And I owe you no answers, since you decided I was no longer wanted as your husband. I've questions of my own, mind you. What brings you here instead of Rekha? What are you looking for, besides pearls to conceal how scant the Daish harvest has been?'

You wear amethysts to calm anger and promote humility, so you're serious about whatever negotiations brought you here. The heavenly Amethyst rides in the arc of honour and status, along with the Hoe that is the symbol of a man's hard work in service of the domain, whatever his rank. Do you expect me to keep calm, to put my duty as Chazen warlord above my own feelings?

Now it was Janne who shrugged. 'You can't blame me for being curious about that voyage, not when it brought such changes to all of our lives.'

Kheda ignored the barb. 'He belonged to a trader in the central domains. I needed someone to help me sail a boat south. Dev was willing to trade his service for a place in my household.'

'When he didn't even know you had a household to return to, much less a domain,' Janne observed, sceptical. 'What did this trader want in return?'

'That's between me and him.' Kheda realised that Janne's own faithful shadow was nowhere to be seen. 'Where's Birut?'

You don't want him privy to this conversation. Why might that be?

'He's spending some time with Itrac's Jevin,' Janne replied easily. 'I don't want to see her embarrassed when more demanding guests visit – the Aedis wives, for instance. The boy's willing but Rekha said he lacks the experience to be serving a first wife. Birut will show him a few things.'

'You chose Jevin for Itrac,' Kheda recalled, 'when we already knew she was the only Chazen wife still living.'

'We suspected,' Janne corrected him. 'We didn't know for certain that Sekni was dead.' She held his gaze, eyes dark and impenetrable, her face expressionless even without the concealment of cosmetics. 'One acts differently when one only suspects, rather than knowing something beyond all doubt. The most important thing was having her guarded, so that no one like Ulla Safar could force her into marriage and claim this domain along with her body.' She paused. 'So much has happened since then, and so much that was unforeseen.'

'Foretelling is a warlord's prerogative,' said Kheda sharply. 'You'd better not be interfering with Sirket's interpretations of the omens.'

'I do not interfere,' retorted Janne, piqued. 'I offer support. I strive for the domain's good above all else, in the light of whatever Sirket reads in the earthly or heavenly compasses.'

'As I strive to see the best path for Chazen, since Daish is closed to me now.' Kheda pictured the charts of the shifting constellations and heavenly jewels that he'd been drawing all afternoon.

The Spear's in the arc of marriage now, token of male potency and call to arms, along with the Ruby, talisman for courage. Is that a warning for me, when the heavenly Pearl that is a symbol of Daish rides with the Winged Snake that is symbol of male and female intertwined? They are in the arc where the Emerald talisman of peace and growth presides over omens of good health and a peaceful future. What am I to make of that?

'I had so hoped to see Chazen prosper.' Janne sounded deeply regretful, tracing the silver-edged flowers embroidered on her sleeve with one long-nailed finger. 'But ill luck seems to stalk this domain.'

'I take it you're referring to this dragon?' challenged Kheda.

Janne took a sudden pace closer, lifting her face towards him, eyes hard, her voice low. 'Such a portent of evil and coming less than a year after those wild men wrought havoc with their savage sorcery. See what you started, when you brought whatever magic it was you found in the north to defeat the invaders. Did your father teach you nothing? Did you think your actions, alone of all men, wouldn't have consequences to echo through the days and years to come? You were never so foolish as ruler of Daish, not until you were touched by the corruption of magic. I wish you'd never sailed to Chazen's aid when the beacons first told of his misfortunes. I hate to think what calamity will befall you next, or these hapless people, all on your account.'

'At least you made sure none of this misfortune can

fall on Daish,' interrupted Kheda sarcastically, 'refusing to let Sirket relinquish rule to me, driving me out as you did. You were never a fool, Janne, so why are you talking like one now? What would have become of Daish if I hadn't found such lore and sailed south with it? Do you think Chazen Saril would have halted the wild men? Don't you see they'd have swept north to plunder Daish as well?'

He shook his head vehemently. 'No, Janne, I don't regret anything I have done. Can you say the same? You saw that Chazen Saril was destroyed by grief and fear but you didn't help him. You decided to put his life to trial instead. Do you wonder if it was his death in Daish waters that's blighted your pearl harvest?'

'I have no doubts that I was right to put Chazen Saril to the ultimate trial,' Janne said resolutely, folding her arms. 'I wagered my own life as well as his and yours.'

'And we're still standing, so you must have been right?' Kheda waved an airy hand. 'I wouldn't be so confident in your interpretations, Janne. This dragon is an evil, granted, but for the present it's eating as many of those savages still hiding out in the western isles as it can find. That's doing Chazen no harm. Would you like to see the dispatches from our triremes confirming that? As for Chazen's better fortunes, I think it's all to their good that I've mastered my unreasoning fear of magic and sent an envoy to the north to find out all about this new foe. That barbarian slave of mine recalls tales of such beasts being defeated in the far north. That's another stroke of luck, isn't it? You can take some comfort in the fact that my rule will protect Chazen better than Saril's would have done in the present circumstances.'

'What have you learned about this dragon?' Janne demanded.

'That's Chazen business and none of Daish's concern.' Kheda smiled.

'You don't think we're entitled to worry that the beast will come north?' queried Janne with mock surprise. 'When you tell me these wild men would have done just that without your boldness in suborning whatever magic brought them down? Don't lecture me about shameful deeds, Kheda.' She turned away to walk slowly around the anteroom, ostensibly studying the ebony and ironwood corner chests.

You could always tell when I was shading the truth, but that was when I seldom lied to you and trusted you with my life. Let's see how much that has changed along with everything else.

Kheda deliberately smiled more broadly when Janne's path brought her around to face him once more. 'I'll tell you this much: we already know how to contain it, once it has rid us of the savages. We're seeking a way to kill it. I imagine that'll be expiation enough to satisfy all our neighbours that the wild men's magic has been cleansed from Chazen. Blood has always been the ultimate purification for such evil. Who's to say this dragon isn't to lead to better things for Chazen in the long run?'

'You think you can kill it?' Janne asked, honestly incredulous.

You certainly didn't expect to hear this, did you? What were *you expecting?*

'As I said, unforeseen good still follows on from my voyage to the northern domains.' Kheda leaned back against the wall, hands folded behind him. 'That slave, Dev, tells of barbarians killing dragons in the unbroken lands. You must have heard that a poet came south with me last year? She's seeking out such lore.' He gestured towards the unseen north. 'We expect her back around the breaking of the rains. The storms can wash the beast's blood into the seas and Chazen will be set fair for a new beginning.'

'Yes, I'd heard some poet girl was deep in your confidences. What does Itrac make of that?' Janne asked with sweet spitefulness. She took a moment, pretending to consider the silver cranes engraved on an alabaster vase. 'I imagine your poet will find that word of this dragon has gone before her, though. Ill news flies faster than the fleetest courier dove.'

'And so?' Kheda prompted coolly.

Janne raised her finely shaped eyebrows, disingenuous. 'Whoever has that lore will look to trade it to best advantage. We both know that.'

'Then you will be pleased to hear that Chazen is celebrating an abundant pearl harvest,' Kheda responded blithely. 'Which is more than merely fortunate – it's a significant omen; a positive token that we will restore this domain to its former peace and happiness.'

'And you're seeking to trade pearls for gems.' Janne nodded approval. 'A wise precaution, when you don't know who you'll be trading with for this lore. There are always some who prefer jewels. Pearls have their vulnerabilities, not least their finite life.'

I know that serene smile of old, Janne. You think you've got the upper hand here.

'We're looking to trade for many things.' Kheda fashioned a puzzled look. 'Metals, finished wares of all kinds—'

'But you need gems most of all, for some overriding necessity.' Janne laced her hands together, studying her scarlet nail polish. 'I paid my compliments to Itrac Chazen before I came looking for you, naturally. The girl seemed very anxious to set out her negotiating position.'

Leaving you confident that you'll get everything you want from such an inexperienced girl. A confidence that's hardly misplaced, let's be honest.

'It's hardly polite for us to discuss your trades with

Chazen in Itrac's absence. In fact,' Kheda continued, harsher, 'it's hardly appropriate for you to be visiting me in my private chambers before my lady wife and I have welcomed you to our domain with fitting ceremony. You make us look ill-mannered, Janne Daish.'

'Shall we stop these games?' Janne folded her arms again, amethyst bracelets rattling. 'Itrac isn't up to playing against me – or Rekha, come to that – and well you know it. This isn't about pots and pans and cloth to cover your people's nakedness. You need gems, presumably to pay off whatever barbarian has this lore you seek to kill this dragon. I don't suppose those northerners have the wit to appreciate the true value of pearls.'

She looked at him, face unforgiving. 'You're playing the same dangerous game as before, aren't you? You've done it once and you seem to have got away with it. All the same, you don't want anyone enquiring too closely into just where you might be getting this lore, or whatever it might be that you're contemplating using against the beast. You certainly don't want anyone suspecting that you might suborn sorcery against it, not when there are still questions whispered about your unexpected victory against those invaders last year. Not everyone's convinced by your tale of secret herbs and spices stupefying the savages' wizards so that you, your slave and your poet could bring them down with poisoned arrows. Don't worry,' she assured him pleasantly, 'I keep my own counsel on all that happened, on all that you admitted to me.'

'Because all that I did, I did as Daish and you'd be condemned along with me if the truth were known,' Kheda interrupted. 'You'll continue to keep silent, will you? Just as long as we hand over an abundance of pearls in exchange for some meagre gleanings from the Daish treasury? If you don't want to play games, Janne, don't try threatening me.'

'You misunderstand me, Kheda.' She looked hurt. 'Don't blame me if your guilt pricks you.'

'What guilt?' he retorted. 'I showed Ritsem Caid and Aedis Harl the concoction that we used against the savage mages. I still keep the remains of it in my physic chest. I explained how I learned the secret from Shek Kul in the north, under his seal of secrecy. No one can deny that the northernmost domains have been plagued by wizards from the unbroken lands in the past. It's not so difficult to believe that they would have found some way to defend themselves. The wild wizards' bodies were found pierced with arrows and they were most assuredly poisoned.'

'What set them all fighting among themselves so conveniently?' countered Janne angrily. 'So that you and these unattested northerners could pick them off?'

'No one knows,' Kheda shot back at her. 'And who's to tell, since they're all dead? You could spread your suspicions that I somehow inveigled a barbarian mage into their midst, Janne, but you've no hope of prooving it since his body was burned to ash with the rest of them. The only way you can condemn me is by admitting your own foreknowledge, with all the grief that would bring down on Daish. No, Janne, your threats are empty and you know it.'

Just as long as you don't get suspicious about Dev. I really must keep him away from you and Birut.

'What about this poet of yours?' Janne challenged. 'What does she know?'

'Nothing, and if she comes to any harm at Daish hands, you'll regret it for as long as you live.' Kheda took a pace towards Janne and she saw something in his face that made her shrink back, coming up hard against an ironwood chest. 'You're right. Let's stop these games. What brings you here, so anxious to trade for our pearls, so anxious you're not even prepared to leave it to Rekha?'

'I thought I'd do Itrac the honour of dealing with her, first wife to first wife,' Janne shot back. 'I thought I'd do this domain the favour of showing all the others that we Daish women consider that the danger of magic has faded. That has to be worth a good deal to you.'

'That stinks worse than ten-day-old fish.' Kheda laughed with open disbelief. 'Rekha must be busy placating Moni Redigal. That's it, isn't it? Moni must be agitating for her share in your pearl harvest by now.' He took another step and leaned over Janne. 'Every day you delay, the greater the risk that the truth will come out, that everyone will find out that the Daish reefs are barren this year.'

'Have you told Itrac about the deal with Moni?' Janne thrust at his chest with a forceful hand. 'You've no qualms about betraying Daish trade secrets to your new wife?'

'I must do my best for Chazen.' Kheda allowed himself to be pushed back. 'You laid that duty upon me.'

'You seem to forget you've a dragon stalking your isles,' retorted Janne. 'What will you do for Chazen if I refuse to take your pearls for these gems you're so anxious to have? You need gems for barbarian lore, or for some barbarian mage you're relying on to rid you of the beast. Don't deny it,' she concluded with malicious satisfaction.

'I think the dragon's presence strengthens my hand.' Kheda smiled cruelly. 'I told you we can contain it. I'll share one Chazen secret with you, Janne, for old times' sake. We can do more than contain it. We know how to lure it from place to place. Why else do you think I'm so confident that we can kill it when we choose?' He stepped forward to look down on Janne again, this time resisting her attempt to push him away. 'We could lure it to Daish waters if we felt so inclined.'

'You wouldn't!' Janne stared up at him, aghast.

'If we don't have the gems to trade for the lore we need

to kill it?' Kheda leaned forward, his weight resting on his hands, which were set flat on the chest on either side of Janne. 'What would we have to lose? If I'm to see Chazen lost, after all the pains I've suffered for this domain, I'll take Daish down with me.'

Can I convince you of that? Can I convince you that I hate you so much now that I'd forget my love for my children and my duty to all the innocent people of Daish?

'Then I want a better price than a few sacks of pearls,' Janne hissed, 'if you're so convinced you can cleanse yourself of all suspicion and free this domain from all taint of magic with the shedding of this dragon's blood.' Her breath came fast and shallow.

'Offer me terms,' Kheda invited with cold precision.

'Itrac was very eager to convince me that she is happy in this marriage, that your future will soon be secured in a child.' Janne stood up, forcing Kheda away. The vase with the silver cranes toppled over to fall and crack into pieces on the floor, the sound startlingly loud within the enclosed space. They both ignored it.

Janne took a pace forward, coming so close that her gown brushed Kheda's tunic. 'Too eager. You still haven't touched her, have you, Kheda? Don't try lying to me. I know you too well. I know the look in a woman's eyes when she's remembering a night in your arms. I don't see it in Itrac's face. And I know your taste in women and your scruples. She's barely older than our eldest daughter and you were never some monster like Ulla Safar to violate hairless girls. I'm sorry. I shouldn't have said that.' She paused for a moment, eyes closed.

'So, Kheda, that's my price. Don't touch Itrac. Don't take any acknowledged concubines either. I don't know if this gossip about you and that poet girl is true – she's barely older than Itrac after all. I don't care. Leave her well alone or use your physic chest to make sure she never quickens with a child. Don't leave the responsibility to her because folly or ambition will win her over some day. If you want Daish gems to save Chazen, then you make sure there's no child born to this domain. I want only Daish blood to have any claim on Chazen when you die.'

'Should I beware of any food from your hands, in case you decide to see if that day's to come sooner rather than later?' Kheda compelled himself to hold his ground, even though he could feel the taut warmth of Janne's breasts through the thin layers of silk separating them. 'Why do you want Daish to claim Chazen, when you've condemned us all as tainted with magic?'

'Don't you want to see a better future for Chazen?' Janne's eyes didn't move from his face. 'Sirket's posterity will be untouched by magic. You're not, of your own deliberate choice, and neither is Itrac, innocent victim though she's been in all this. You could secure an untainted future ruler for this domain and free all the domains hereabouts from the fear that echoes of your actions may yet cause disaster in years to come. I want to see Daish free of that burden.'

'And I would be leaving my son an inheritance to make him the equal of the most powerful lords in these reaches. You know exactly how to tempt me, Janne.' Kheda still refused to retreat. 'I might be more convinced if you hadn't baulked at any action that would have tied Daish to lands so tainted with magic last year. You wouldn't see Itrac protected by a tactical marriage to Sirket.'

He looked at her with cold contempt. 'I see your principles aren't so strong when your pearl harvest fails. You really are desperate to get your hands on the Chazen reefs, aren't you? You tried to tempt me with Rekha and the children and when that failed, you've come to play a harder game. Can I expect to find you slipping into my apartments tonight, to offer ease for my hardness? What's happened to the Daish reefs? A plague of black prickle-stars eating corals and oysters alike?'

'You're telling me that this dragon's blood will purify this domain.' Janne stood still, rigid, face upturned to him. 'If I'm wagering that's true and that you'll do what you're boasting and kill the beast, if I'm staking Daish gems on your word, and Daish's safety from the creature, I want a worthwhile return.'

'You still think you're in a position to dictate terms?' Kheda prodded Janne's chest with a hard finger. 'I'll tell you what you'll get and, more importantly, what you won't get. You'll get sufficient pearls to conceal the bareness of the Daish reefs for this year and this year alone. You won't get me scorning Itrac for you or Rekha and having you stake a claim on Chazen through Sirket or any other of my children. On the other hand, you won't get every boat spreading whispered speculation around every domain within reach about just what the dire omen of the pearl-harvest failure could mean for Daish Sirket's rule.'

Because I wouldn't do that to my son. But this is something I'm not going to forgive in a hurry, Janne; you're fomenting such antagonism between our domains that I cannot offer him the least advice.

Kheda took a breath to cool his anger. 'In return, I will get sufficient choice gems from the Daish treasury to suit my purposes – and don't forget, I know exactly what's in those treasuries, so I'll tell you exactly which jewels I want. Then you won't see the dragon plundering those Daish islands that lie nearest to Chazen, so that all our neighbours' galleys start shunning your waters as well as ours, since they're stained with magic. As for the future, we'll let the consequences of all our actions play themselves out. We'll see just who's vindicated by omens and events.'

'Yes, we will. Who knows what the stars to come will

reveal.' Janne whirled around and walked towards the door, the silk of her gown swishing angrily.

'Are we agreed?' Kheda demanded harshly. 'Pearls for gems?'

Janne halted, not looking back at him. 'And this conversation never happened.'

'I'll send Dev to Birut with a list of the gems I require,' Kheda called as she wrenched the door open and stormed through it. Janne made no response.

'She didn't look any too pleased.' Dev came in from the corridor wearing a crooked smile.

'Quiet!' As Kheda walked back into the warlord's private sitting room, a blur of green and scarlet beyond the high windows caught his eye.

A flurry of fig-thieves erupted from a spread of rustlenut trees on the distant heights that loomed beyond the forbidding outer wall of the fortress. Kheda shaded his eyes with a hand to see a yellow-banded eagle slice through the hysterical flock. Then a second eagle appeared, sending the little birds darting this way and that in terror. The first predator swooped low, wheeling and disappearing into the topmost branches of the copper-leafed trees. Then the second reappeared seemingly out of nowhere to scatter the fig-thieves again. Each eagle flapped its mighty wings and rose high into the air with a plump corpse in its talons.

Kheda caught his breath as a third eagle darted out of a stand of ironwood trees barely visible against the shadows of the high ground. It looked as if it would fly straight into the lower of the original pair, only veering away at the very last second. The startled eagle tumbled ungainly through the air, letting go of its prize. The attacker was ready, stooping to catch the lifeless fig-thief before vanishing into the dark-green gloom. The bereft eagle flapped disconsolately after its mate, venting its rage in a harsh scream. A thread of that mournful, angry cry floated through the air to brush Kheda's ear.

'What is it?' demanded Dev.

'An omen,' Kheda said slowly, 'in the arc of the sky where one looks for portents for the self. What are the stars in that reach of the sky?' he mused, speaking more to himself than to Dev. 'It's the Bowl, still hidden below the horizon, though. Token of shared food and drink, so of mutual support and faithfulness.'

'Which means what?' Dev persisted. 'For you or for Chazen?'

'The eagle is a warlord's symbol,' Kheda said slowly.

'So are you the one robbed or the opportunist snatching advantage?' asked Dev, idly amused.

'My lord?' An apologetic knock at the outer door startled warlord and barbarian alike.

'Tasu?' Kheda whirled around. 'There were three eagles, a pair and one other. Three always signifies a potent omen, that much we can be sure of – usually notice of something entirely unexpected, according to my father. What do you have to add?'

The old man advanced through the anteroom. 'Could you see which birds were cock and which were hen, my lord?'

'No,' said Kheda slowly, 'which could have been significant. Was that some wiser female robbing an inexperienced younger sister? Can we expect Janne's rapaciousness to defeat Itrac?'

'What were the little birds?' wondered Dev mischievously. 'Aren't they all part of this?'

'My father always said there's unlooked-for wisdom in chance words.' Kheda stared at him. 'You may be right, for all you're an ignorant barbarian.'

'That's me.' Dev grinned.

Tasu coughed uncertainly at this exchange. 'Fig-thieves

are no innocents, my lord. They're pests with their incessant sneaking into storehouses and granaries and they foul whatever they don't plunder. Little short of fire scares them off,' he concluded thoughtfully.

'Do you suppose they signify the invaders?' Kheda wondered. 'Am I the yellow-banded eagle throwing them all into confusion?'

'Or is that the dragon?' asked Dev slyly. 'Or if you're the first bird, is it your present wife or your former who's flying off with a plump dinner?'

'You're not really helping.' Kheda warned Dev off with a scowl.

Or is that more unlooked-for wisdom in an ignorant mouth?

'This might be some kind of warning.' Tasu frowned. 'Such noisy birds carry their alarm to the whole forest. None of those eagles will hunt successfully in these woods today.'

'Perhaps the eagle *is* the dragon,' Kheda said slowly. 'It's certainly spreading alarm among the wild men, according to the *Mist Dove*'s dispatches.'

'Is there anything in the night skies to make sense of such an omen, my lord?' Tasu asked humbly.

'The Diamond, the warlord's talisman, is sharing the sky with the Sea Serpent, token of unseen forces at work. There's a warning there but it counsels self-sufficiency as well,' Kheda mused. 'And both are in the heavenly arc where one looks for omens for siblings and anyone close through friendship rather than blood.'

Itrac may not be a true wife to me but she must count as close as a sister in this so-called marriage of ours.

'Is there anything significant in direct opposition?' prompted Tasu.

'The Opal,' Kheda said briefly, 'which unlocks emotion and rides in the arc of travel and ambition, along with the Sailfish whose self-assured boldness can so easily slip into exaggeration. Maybe that's why Janne Daish has journeyed here so confident that she'll secure all she wants,' he said sourly.

'What exactly has any of that to do with eagles?' Dev wondered with spurious innocence. 'And forgive me, my lord, but we're supposed to be going to dine with my lady Itrac and our guest from Daish.'

'Indeed,' said Kheda heavily. 'And what a delightful prospect that is.' He turned to Tasu. 'What brought you here? Have any more courier doves arrived?'

'No, my lord,' the old man said apologetically. 'Though I did check right before I came to see you. It's just I found something about sharks. You said you were curious about their lore, what with the omen—'

'Yes,' said Kheda, diverted. 'What have you found?'

'There's this.' Tasu took a heavy book bound with red-tooled black leather from under his arm and opened it. 'In an otherwise positive context, a shark can be an encouragement to perseverance.' He tapped smoothly flowing writing below a detailed portrayal of all manner of sharks. 'You see, there are sharks, many of them, that must keep swimming otherwise they drown.' He frowned. 'Which is a curious fate for a fish. I'm sorry, my lord, it's not much but it's all I found. A shark can be a sign that you must just keep on going, keep doing all you can.'

'Otherwise we're all sunk,' said Dev quietly. 'There might just be something in that.'

Kheda looked at him. 'We're doing all we can, aren't we? I certainly trust Risala to keep going north at best speed.'

'I'm sure we're all doing everything we can,' said Dev meaningfully, 'whether or not we can see each other doing it.'

'I'll bid you good evening, my lord.' Tasu shut his book with a brisk clap. 'I wouldn't want to intrude further.'

'You're not and thank you.' Kheda grinned. 'I'll see you tomorrow.'

'Good night, my lord.' Tasu withdrew with a low bow.

'What now?' asked Dev tersely.

Kheda jerked his head towards the bath chamber. 'Try again.'

The wizard groaned and turned but another knock on the outer door halted him. He went to open it instead.

'My lord.' Beyau was twisting his warrior's hands together with some considerable emotion.

'I take it we're ready to offer Janne a dinner to equal any Daish could present?' Kheda shot Dev a wry look. 'We'll keep the conversation strictly limited to the food and the seasonings. Itrac will follow my lead there.'

'It'll be a splendid meal, my lord, but it'll just be you and my lady Itrac who will enjoy it.' Beyau couldn't keep the indignation out of his voice. 'My lady Janne Daish has just sent word that she wishes to dine alone in her suite tonight.'

'Daish courtesy is certainly lessened of late,' said Kheda with sudden irritation. Then he smiled with patently false sympathy. 'The exertions of the voyage must have caught up with her. She's neither as young as she was nor as tireless as she thinks she still is. Make sure our household offers every comfort that a woman of her years might welcome.'

'I can think of a few suitable things, my lord.' Beyau chuckled before schooling his face into proper immobility. 'So where will you dine, my lord?'

'I certainly don't want to miss out on such a feast even if Janne Daish is so weary.' Kheda glanced in the direction of the various wives' apartments. 'And everyone's had a long and busy day, so I see no need to have the whole household dancing attendance on me and Itrac. We'll eat in my private audience chamber, with just our own slaves to wait on us. Let the kitchens know; I'll tell Itrac. Dev, you tidy up in here and then help set things out for the meal.'

'Yes, my lord,' the barbarian replied stolidly.

'Of course, my lord.' Beyau bowed low before turning to go.

Then all the servants and the slaves who aren't waiting on us can eat their food hot from the kitchens, instead of waiting for we exalted three to tire of the plenty and allow them the cooling leavings. That should win me some goodwill, and that never goes amiss.

Kheda walked through the corridors and courtyards, nodding to acknowledge the servants and slaves busy with the constant care of the residence. Garden servants in workaday cotton were removing faded blooms from the splendid arrays of flowers or sweeping the spotless tiles with rustling palm-frond brooms. Inner-household slaves protected their silk sleeves with long, soft cotton gloves as they polished finger marks from gleaming brassware and adjusted painted hangings showing vistas of all the differing isles of the domain.

He knocked on the door to Itrac's private sitting room. Jevin opened it. 'My lord.' He bowed and looked past Kheda for Dev. 'You're alone?'

'Dev's arranging my private audience chamber for our meal.' Kheda entered the room. 'It seems Janne Daish finds herself too weary to dine with us. I see no point in the two of us rattling around the banqueting hall.'

'As you wish, my lord.' Itrac stood in the middle of the room, wearing a shimmering gold gown cut close to flatter her slenderness. Kheda noted both anger and apprehension in her eyes, and with her paler skin, he could see the hint of a blush underlaying the rose powder on her cheekbones. Her gold-painted lips were pressed tightly together. 'Or we can dine in the banqueting hall if you'd rather,' he offered.

'What?' Itrac looked at him, momentarily confused. 'No, I'd rather it was just the two of us. As you say, it's been a long day. And I've had about all I can stomach of Janne,' she added in a sudden rush of anger. 'She's been walking in and out of my rooms ever since she arrived, as if she were mistress here. She won't take a hint, from me or the servants, and that slave of hers is deaf to anything Jevin says to him. She kept reminiscing about how informal we'd all been when Olkai and Sekni were here.'

'You should have sent word to me.' Kheda saw Itrac flinch at his harsh tone. 'No, I'm not cross with you, just with her discourtesy. But why didn't you send word? I thought we agreed we'd meet her together.'

'I didn't know how to get rid of her without being insulting. It seemed silly to make a fuss, when she was being all sweetness and sympathy and offering compliments on how well I'm managing the domain.' Itrac bit her lip, twisting her long, gold-tipped fingers among the graduated strings of yellow lustre pearls that reached to her waist. 'Then I realised she was treating me like a little girl who's been out in the sun too long. And she kept reminding me that Olkai and Sekni are dead and gone, even though she was saying how proud they would be of me.'

Indignation rose above the tremor in her voice as she went on. 'And now, after we've disrupted the entire household to try to provide a fitting banquet, when she was the one setting us all awry by arriving early, she says she's too tired to join us!'

I used to admire her manoeuvrings, when they were to further Daish interests. It's not so amusing to be on the receiving end of such manipulations.

'So now she's got you wound to such a pitch that you'll be awake half the night fretting or fuming and she'll have the advantage of you in the morning when it comes to negotiating your trades,' Kheda pointed out. 'Let's not fall into that trap. Let's just commiserate with her weariness and do all we can to make her comfortable. She'll thank us profusely, at the same time letting slip some hint that we're falling short of perfect hospitality – which, of course, she forgives, after all we've been through. Which we will, of course, ignore.'

'And what if she spreads tales of our inadequate welcome to the other domains?' Itrac twisted one of the thick gold rings she wore on every finger.

Kheda paused for a moment's thought. 'I think you might share your concerns that she's become sadly exacting in her old age. We're sorry for her, seeing how her insecurity must be gnawing at her. As soon as Sirket marries, after all, she will lose all her status and need to find another home.'

He realised he was pacing back and forth across the room and stopped abruptly.

'I don't think anyone will believe that Janne's going senile,' Itrac said, subdued. 'She already knows we want to trade pearls for gems. I wasn't intending to talk trade at all, not till tomorrow, but she kept coming in chatting about this and that. She was telling me what we needed and how she would help and if I hadn't said no and told Jevin to escort her back to her rooms, she'd have probably set sail tonight to put everything in hand as if I'd agreed to it all.' She looked at Kheda, beseeching. 'That must be why she's feeling so insulted.'

'That's why she's withdrawn, now she realises she's underestimated you,' Kheda corrected. 'I think you'll find she's more inclined to treat you as an equal tomorrow. Anyway, it's me who insulted her.'

'How?' Itrac asked, wide-eyed.

'Firstly for her discourtesy in coming to my private apartments before we'd publicly received her.' Kheda hesitated. 'And she thinks she can get all the pearls she wants from us because we're so desperate to pay some barbarian for tales of how to kill the beast. I've put her right on that, never fear. Hold out for a fair trade and she'll back down, trust me.' He took one of Itrac's gold-ringed hands and gave it an encouraging squeeze. 'Because if she starts making trouble for us, we can start making trouble for her. Remember, she really doesn't want anyone knowing just how poor the Daish pearl harvest has been, not officially.'

'I don't know how to say things like that, not without making an open threat.' Itrac looked at him anxiously. 'Olkai always used to deal with that kind of thing.'

'Just do your best, Kheda encouraged. 'It's not as if there will be wives from other domains whispering behind their hands as they gauge your skills.'

'I suppose not,' Itrac allowed, with an inelegant grimace. 'Jevin, leave us,' she said abruptly. 'Go and see if Dev needs any help.'

What do we do if the boy comes upon him working magic?

Kheda realised there was nothing he was going to be able to do about it. Itrac plainly had something pressing to say to him, holding tightly to his hand when he would have withdrawn it.

'Janne seemed most concerned that I shouldn't ask too much of myself as Chazen's only wife.' Itrac swallowed, looking down at her feet. 'She was sure you'd have more sense than to look to father a child in such troubled times. She said everyone knew that I'd chosen Saril for love and that this marriage is only a safeguard for me. She said your taste had never really run to virgins, that you'd left Sain to come to you in her own time, since that was also purely a marriage of alliance. She said Olkai would have told me the same, if she'd lived.'

'While she tried to persuade me that I should scorn

you and allow one of my children by Daish to claim Chazen,' Kheda interrupted. 'Janne's very good at dripping honeyed poison into unwilling ears. I wonder she didn't hint at some inadequacy in the marriage bed on my part, that you'd not be missing much.'

He realised Itrac was pulling away, rebuffed by his churlishness. He took both her hands in his and leaned forward to kiss her scented cheek. 'I told her to mind Daish business while we minded Chazen's, the two of us, as we see fit, in our own time, without her interference or anyone else's.'

Itrac turned her head to meet his kiss with her soft lips, her eyes closing on the diamond glint of a tear beneath her lashes. 'I think I'm ready to be a proper wife to you, Kheda,' she breathed. 'And Janne can go—'

A loud knock at the door startled the two of them apart. 'My lord?' It was Dev. 'Your dinner's ready, my lord.' He bowed to Itrac. 'My lady.'

'I'll be along in a moment.' Itrac slipped away into her dressing room. 'Don't wait.'

Kheda looked at Dev, who was grinning broadly in the doorway. 'What's amusing you?' he asked finally as they reached the corridor leading to his personal apartments.

'Jevin tells me I'll be sleeping out in the corridor tonight.' The wizard smirked lasciviously at Kheda's side. 'Finally decided to exercise your rights there, have you?'

'I haven't decided.' Kheda scowled. 'Though it seems Itrac has. I'm wondering how Janne will read it—'

'What was Tasu saying about shark omens?' Dev silenced him with a backhanded slap to the chest. 'You should stop looking over your shoulder and up at the skies and all around the compass and just do what's in front of you. Or who's in front of you,' he amended with a lewd chuckle. 'You've every right to take Itrac in any way you want. You've had that right for half a year now and, Saedrin save us, your stones must ache like you've caught them in a vice. What more is there to think about? Itrac's a choice piece. Or isn't she quite what you fancy? So close your eyes and imagine she's Risala.'

Kheda halted and shoved Dev hard against the wall, knotting a hand in his tunic. 'Shut your foul, ignorant barbarian mouth—'

'You could do with something to ease your tension, sure as curses,' Dev continued, entirely at his ease. 'And as it happens, I think this household and the whole domain would be usefully reassured to see their warlord throwing a rope to their lady at long last. Come to that, I think she might benefit from a little firm reassurance herself. She'll certainly be fit for nothing in the morning if you turn her down tonight, now she's got her nerve up. That bitch Janne will see it in an instant and take all the advantage she can, you know that.'

'You know—' Kheda broke off, unable to deny the unpalatable truths in Dev's words.

'I'm a faithful slave who is supposed to give you honest advice,' the barbarian said viciously. 'So listen when I give it. You've been saying how we need keep everything sailing along on a nice even keel till Risala and the *Green Turtle* get back, and that's not going to be any time soon. This is no time for you to rock the boat. Now get your hands off me before I break your face,' he concluded in an undertone.

'My lord?' Beyau appeared further up the corridor, his voice uncertain.

Kheda let go of Dev and stepped back. 'We're just coming.'

'Our lord and lady only require their personal slaves.' Dev looked past him to Beyau.

'That's right.' Kheda forced a smile. 'The rest of you can take some time for yourselves.' He walked slowly back towards the open door where the tempting scents of a sumptuous dinner sought to draw him on.

So I'm cornered, with no option but enjoying an intimate dinner with every delicacy and beautiful, willing Itrac as the final dish. When I'd rather be sharing dried meats and stale water on some crowded trading beach with Risala, with no more than the chance of just talking with her.

So much for a warlord's absolute power.

CHAPTER THIRTEEN

He had taken her out of herself with a rush of ecstasy that swept all her resistance away. She became dimly aware that he had cast her off. No matter. She didn't need him. She was free to revel in the delight suffusing her.

Now she was the rushing breeze, making cats' paws on the surface of the sea, tugging at ruffles of foam until the waves did her bidding, rolling and breaking. Other breaths of wind hurried to join her game, following in her train, adding their meagre strength to her growing might. Now she was the sterner draught driving in off the ocean to scour the land, relentless as she brushed obstacles aside, commanding all lesser breezes. She ignored the weakling eddies of air seeking shelter in the lee of trees and hills, sweeping past to rise into the skies beyond, carried on an exultant surge of pleasure.

Here she was rarefied, dancing in the emptiness. The sky was her plaything, the clouds her delight. The highest wisps of vapour trailed behind her like wind-tossed hair. She drew them out into glittering threads, finer than the sheerest gossamer, and threw a milky veil over the distant sun. She was an artist, weaving beauty out of sheer inspiration. Which was entertaining in its way, but what was the point of possessing such power if she didn't do more? What could she do with it? What couldn't she do?

She drew the zephyrs to her, commanding them to suck the heat from the earth below, rising high on their appropriated might. Snaring the flurries, she drove them out over the water, wrapping them into squalls fat with captured moisture. Storm clouds filled the void, coalescing under the pressure of her ominous unseen presence. The water was too weak, falling as frantic rain in a vain attempt to escape the air's crushing sense of purpose. She sent a gale to drive the downpour into the shore, cowing the submissive earth, lashing it with hail. Crackles of lightning illuminated the darkening clouds as the rising currents of air inexorably reclaimed the fallen rain at her command.

At a whim, she set the thunderclouds spinning. The storm swirled at her bidding, drawing gusts from further and further away into the frenzied dance. The rush of the winds, wheeling ever faster, was music to her ears. The power was dizzying, enthralling. She trembled with it, revelled in it, euphoric. Ripples of ecstasy shook her. She was air, pure and simple and omnipotent.

No, she wasn't. She was Velindre. She was a mage of Hadrumal and if she couldn't master herself better than this, she had no claim on the rank of Cloud Mistress. She fought her way free of the encircling clouds, seeking the centre of stillness, the better to regain some control over herself and the element and the seductive sensations that suffused her.

With that refuge gained and some fragile hold over her wizardly senses secured, Velindre considered the catastrophic storm. How to put a stop to this self-indulgence before it ran utterly beyond her control? The wheeling tempest loomed all around her, threatening to rush headlong into maddened violence. The clouds in the heights were spreading out to claim more and more of the sky. She concentrated on maintaining that hard-won calm, within and without, and finally saw what she must do.

Fire was caught up in the storm's coils, capturing the sea spume and drawing the moisture high up into the skies where the wind flogged the white billows till they bled great gouts of rain. Fire was the element that set all others in motion, she remembered dimly. But fire could be snuffed. Velindre reached for the warmth drifting through the seas far below and drove it away. She seized a fugitive breeze and wove a carefully selective barrier between the ocean and the whirling storm clouds above. Rain fell, slipping gratefully through her spell to escape into the cooling deeps. Try as it might, the storm could draw up no moisture to replace the downpour. The clouds cooled, the rain lessened. Velindre tore a rent in the tempest's formidable wall, sending the thunderclouds stumbling and falling away from one another. The deadly intent of the storm dissolved into confusion.

The magewoman opened her eyes. She was standing on the shores of Azazir's lake, cold and wet in her sodden chemise and stockings. Mud oozed between her toes. Her tangled hair hung loose around her shoulders, wet and clinging. She blinked painful tears from her eyes as the sun rose over the rim of the barren valley with piercing brightness. Low beams struck pale gleams from the glistening rocks around her and tinged the ominous clouds still circling relentlessly above in a strange yellowish haze.

'Hadrumal.' Azazir's contempt was chilling.

Velindre slipped and almost fell as she turned to see him beside her. She opened her mouth but she found she had half-forgotten how to speak.

'You can't rise above their small-mindedness any more than Otrick could.' Azazir stood there, a man made out of elemental water that sparkled in the early sun, motes of green magelight rising and falling within him. 'Arrogant, self-willed, all of you. Incapable of letting yourselves go. Incapable of finding your true potential.'

'Self-control is not self-will,' Velindre retorted with effort. 'And losing one's mind is hardly a route to wisdom.'

'Self-control,' sneered Azazir. 'Self-doubt and denial.'

'Self-restraint,' spat Velindre, wiping sodden hair out of her eyes. 'Something you've never bothered with. Not pausing to wonder if you should do something, just because you've established you could – you don't call that arrogant?'

'I serve a higher calling.' Azazir's unearthly eyes glowed green. 'I serve my element. I will not be confined by Hadrumal's petty rules and fears.'

'I wish to master my element,' Velindre retorted, 'not to have it master me. Loss of myself is too high a price to pay for whatever power I might gain in following you. Where is the man you once were, Azazir?'

'Gone where you haven't the courage to follow, that much is plain.' The translucent mage smiled with open derision. 'Go back to Hadrumal and try to live with yourself, within those confines, now that you've tasted true freedom in your magic. Try to content yourself with your plodding progress, groping for knowledge in your fearful obscurity. Don't tell me you haven't learned more in these past days than you could in a lifetime on that rock!' Laughing, he walked towards the water, growing paler and more transparent with every step.

'Wait!' Velindre found she was trembling and not merely from cold, fatigue and slowly building outrage at his assault on her. 'What did you mean, "in these past days"? How long was I . . .' She struggled and gave up. There were no words to describe where she had journeyed.

'Who knows?' Azazir halted almost on the water's edge. Ripples ran towards him, eager to narrow the gap. 'Who cares? I abandoned almanacs and hourglasses along with all of Hadrumal's other constraints.'

'I said stop!' Velindre raised a shaking hand and summoned a wall of air to block the mad wizard's path. The questing lake waters flowed away on either side, baffled. 'Yes, you're right. I've learned a great deal from this experience.' She stifled a shudder at the recollection of such insidious delight. 'But I haven't learned what I came for. I came to ask you about dragons.'

'Dragons?' Azazir turned with a smile of delight that was the most terrifying thing Velindre had seen yet. 'What business could a frigid inadequate like you have with dragons?'

'Not so inadequate,' Velindre retorted coldly. She looked up and wrenched the winds free from the strangling grip of Azazir's ceaseless storm. With a battering blast of air, she drove the rain aside and seized the warmth of the sun riding high above. In an instant her clothes, such as they were, were dry, and she had driven the deathly chill from her bones.

'Not so inadequate?' echoed Azazir, mocking. He raised a hand and his magic crashed through the barrier she had erected between him and the lake, brutal as a breaker from a winter storm at sea. Her spell disintegrated under the assault. He looked up at the clouds and they swirled inwards, crushing the shaft of sunlight she had pulled down. 'Want to try that again?' He grinned at her, open challenge in his eerie eyes. 'Now that I'm ready for you?'

'I came here to learn, not to fight.' Velindre shook her head. 'The lowest apprentices know better than that.' She drew a breath to keep her voice calm. 'You're right,' she repeated. 'I've learned an astonishing amount. Or rather, I've seen that I can work instinctive magic with a power I've never known, if I allow myself. Instinct isn't knowledge, though. If it was, every migrating bird is a secret sage.'

'I see they still teach how to chop reason into shards of logic in Hadrumal.' Azazir laughed, his mood as fickle as the glitter of sunlight on the lake. 'Shards so fine that there's nothing left. Knowledge is overrated, my girl.'

'But you hold knowledge Hadrumal has lost,' Velindre persisted, bolder now that she was dry and warm. Her golden hair obscured her face, coiling and frivolous in the teasing breeze. She brushed it back with irritation. 'That's what I'm seeking: the knowledge you shared with Otrick. What do you know about dragons?'

'You're persistent, I'll give you that.' Azazir turned his back on the uneven surface of the lake and the waters sank back to a glassy smoothness. 'Or rather, I'd say Otrick gave you that. Among other things.' His smile took on a lascivious curve that sat bizarrely on his liquid face.

'Don't think you're in any condition to follow him there.' Velindre was surprised into an incautious response. 'And I've long since given up on lesser liaisons.'

'My condition is whatever I choose it to be.' Azazir walked away from the water and with every pace he took on a greater solidity. His skin turned a pearly white, pale as a fish's belly, shining with a faint suggestion of scales. His hair and beard bristled, long and unkempt and washed to a colourlessness somewhere between grey and white. Only his eyes stayed the same, lit from within with that same green madness. 'So you want to know about dragons, my cold and constrained lady mage? What do you already know?'

'I know they laired in the Cape of Winds from time to time, where the mountains of Tormalin run into the sea.' Velindre kept her eyes resolutely on the mad wizard's face. 'Where they were hunted for their hides and teeth and claws. One voyage could set a man up for life, if he came back. Plenty didn't, from all I've read. And I've also read, in Otrick's notes, that there always had to be a wizard on the ship otherwise the dragon hunters wouldn't sail.'

'But you don't know why,' Azazir taunted her. 'No, you wouldn't. Hadrumal has been happy to see that knowledge erased from its dusty libraries and learned tomes.'

'Why?' demanded Velindre.

Azazir stepped close to whisper in her ear. 'On account

of all a dragon can do for a mage. Because of what a mage can do with a dragon.'

Velindre spread her hands. 'I don't understand what you mean.'

Azazir's grin had all the reassuring warmth of a death's-head. 'No, you wouldn't.'

'Then teach me,' Velindre challenged, hands on her hips. 'If you don't want to see that knowledge lost up here in the wilds.'

'Why should I care?' Azazir studied her intently.

'Because you want to see wizards exploring their full potential,' Velindre shot back. 'How can they do that without a fuller understanding of all they might achieve?'

'You think you're up to it?' His smile turned cruel.

'I think I can take what I learn back to Hadrumal and share it with others,' she said steadily. 'Whereas you'll be condemned out of hand if you go back.'

'All right. I'll show you what I know of dragons. Then maybe you'll see why I live up here in the wilds.' The emerald madness in Azazir's eyes faded as cunning lit his face. 'Whether you can learn from it, whether you can set aside your fears, with your mind hobbled by Hadrumal's teachings, that's another question.'

'Let's see, shall we?' Velindre raised her eyebrows expectantly. She fought not to shiver, not with cold but with apprehension.

'Yes, let's,' murmured Azazir as he squatted in the mud and thrust his bony white fingers into the cloying ooze. The ground trembled and the lake glowed suddenly green in its crystal depths.

The spiralling clouds above fell apart to blow away. The sun flooded the valley with brilliant light and frail spring warmth. Velindre looked around to see the mud all along the shore drying out, the glistening rocks turning dull.

Dust wafted from the ridges of the valley's edge, confused and helpless.

She turned her attention to the lake. That was where all the water was going, concentrating all the elemental power the mad wizard had gathered here. She frowned. Why were the ripples receding from the shore? Shouldn't the water be swelling the lake? She took a step forward, the parched ridges of mud now hard enough to bruise her unshod foot.

'Careful,' warned Azazir, intent on the depths. 'You don't want to catch its eye. It'll be hungry.'

The waters seethed, boiling into white foam shot through with cold green phosphorescence. A dragon erupted from the lake. The long, sinuous body seemed to flow endlessly upwards, water streaming from its glowing scales. Its underside was pale as the lightest jade, its sides dark as deepest agate. A crest of emerald spines snapped erect along its backbone, running up its snakelike neck to crown its long head with a diadem of lethal spikes. It spread vast wings, greater than any ship's sails, leathery membranes translucent in the sunlight. It rose higher, long tail finally leaving the lake, water streaming from the viciously barbed tip. The dragon soared up and circled the lake, coiling around itself in defiance of the empty air and the pull of the ground below. It opened its long, predatory jaw and screamed out a challenge, its glittering white teeth as long and as sharp as swords. With the last echoes of the ear-splitting shriek still reverberating around the hills, it folded its wings with a clap like thunder and dived back into the water. A cascade of spray exploded from the lake, falling to vanish into the thirsty ground.

Velindre couldn't help but tremble, standing with her hands clasped to her face.

'Did you feel the power? You should have done. Air and water are so often partners in magic. That's why you were so open to me before.' Azazir was at her shoulder, pressing his cold body against hers. 'Did you feel the power? That's why Hadrumal doesn't want its wizards knowing how to summon dragons: because that dragon's aura has a more powerful resonance for the likes of me than the highest, mightiest waterfall in the world. You could do more with the merest touch of a cloud dragon's aura than with all the storms of a winter brought together. A fire mage wouldn't know such power if he stood on the lip of a flaming mountain's crater. There's no place in the darkest depths of the earth that would hold such power even for the likes of Planir. That's why Hadrumal doesn't want us knowing about dragons.'

'I felt power, yes . . .' Velindre stared at the water. 'Pure power. I could have worked water magics far beyond my own affinity—'

'It's barely a hint of the power surrounding real dragons.' Azazir squatted to sweep a hand across the undulating edge of the lake. Out in the deeps, emerald radiance rose lazily to the surface. The dragon broached with barely a ripple, lolling in the crystal waters, wings folded close to its long, lithe body.

'That looks like a real dragon to me,' Velindre observed, motionless.

'Look at it,' commanded Azazir.

'I am looking,' Velindre retorted.

'Look at it like a wizard,' he ordered with some irritation. 'Not like a gawping peasant.'

Velindre narrowed her eyes and studied the dragon idling in the water. She could see the beast in all its savage glory, coiling this way and that to send countless little swells hurrying to the shore. More pertinently, she could half-see, half-sense the magic that pervaded it. She realised that elemental power was as much a part of the creature as the scales and sinew, bone and blood that a peasant would see, in that instant before he soiled his breeches and fled. What was there for a wizard to see? She focused on that roiling nimbus of elemental power, tracing the pulses, the ebb and flow.

'There's a void.' She frowned. 'Where its heart should be.'

'Well done,' approved Azazir. 'It's a simulacrum, not a true dragon. For which you should be very grateful; a true dragon would know you for a mage and see you as a rival to be slain. It would bite your head off before you could think of escape.'

Velindre strove for understanding. 'You mean this is an illusion?'

'Does it look like an illusion to you?' Azazir snapped. 'Would I give up so much of myself, the power that I have amassed over a lifetime, to make an illusion?'

Belatedly, Velindre noticed how the mage's appearance had changed. He was still naked, but the shimmering patina of fishlike scales had faded, leaving his ancient skin wrinkled and scarred, mottled with age, his ribs visible. His hair and beard were a sodden mess, stray strands clinging to his hollow cheeks. His eyes, deep set and shadowed, no longer glowed with that unearthly light, for all they were still as green as emeralds.

Discomfited at seeing the old man thus revealed, she turned back to the frolicking dragon now blithely lashing the lake with its tail and snapping at the resulting spray. 'So this is something between an illusion and a true dragon?'

'And it's an innocent. It knows nothing of a true dragon's magic or cunning.' Azazir cackled suddenly, startling Velindre horribly. 'It's a mighty beast all the same and real enough to bite the head off anyone coming up here to bother me. Do the hunters and trappers still whisper about me, wondering what riches the mad wizard is hoarding?' He laughed again, sounding quite insane enough to deserve the title. 'They don't get past the dragon even if they force their way through my other spells. It's tied to me, you see, because I'm the one who made it.'

'It'll do your bidding?' asked Velindre, incredulous.

'Does that look like a lapdog?' mocked the ancient wizard. 'No, but if I look on something and know it for an enemy, the dragon feels it, too. Dragons kill their enemies. They're creatures of unfettered power and untamed instinct, even such fleeting ones as this.'

'You told me not to move, in case it ate me.' Velindre tried to pick out the crucial questions from the clamouring maelstrom inside her head. 'But I'm no enemy to you,' she insisted, emphatic, in case the old wizard let slip any doubts to the distant dragon.

'No, but you could be food.' Azazir gazed happily on his creation. 'I told you, I don't control it. It'll go off to hunt soon enough and there's no man or beast in this forest that will escape it.'

Velindre turned her thoughts resolutely from what Hadrumal's Council would say or do if they knew Azazir was wont to set a dragon eating fur hunters. 'You called it fleeting. What did you mean by that?'

'You don't think I would reduce myself to this for long?' Azazir studied his withered hands. 'You saw the void at its centre. It has no heart, nothing to hold its power together or to hold the other elements at bay. It will fade, in time.'

'How much time?' Velindre asked immediately.

'That depends,' said Azazir with a sly smile, 'on how much power went into its making.'

'How do you make something like that?' Velindre wondered aloud.

'Simple.' Azazir waved an airy hand. 'And quite the

most difficult thing you'll ever attempt. The first step is like creating an illusion; I assume Otrick taught you that much? Summon all the elemental power you can, bring it together and use that to fabricate the creature. You'll probably still fail,' he predicted gleefully.

'You said it wasn't an illusion.' Velindre swept her hair back off her face again, irritated.

'It isn't,' said Azazir with biting precision, suddenly angry. 'Once you have the shape of it in the midst of your magic, you summon still more power, if you're capable, which I doubt. Force enough elemental power in on itself, letting none escape – none at all – and it will reach an intensity where the magic grows out of its own substance, doubling and redoubling. Once you've achieved that, the creature will live, for as long as the magic remains. While the magic remains, its aura is a source of purer power than you can possibly imagine . . .' His voice trailed off, his expression avid. 'Of course, the more you draw on it, the sooner the magic is gone. When the element exhausts itself, the dragon fades.' The passion in his eyes dwindled to be replaced by something akin to weariness.

'Simple, as you say,' Velindre murmured sceptically. 'How do you guard against being consumed by the magic you're summoning?'

'Like some mageborn taken unawares by their manifesting affinity?' Azazir looked at her, sardonic. 'That, my dear, is your problem. As is finding sufficient power. My element is all around me here. You couldn't give yourself over to the air, even for a little while. What makes you think you can attempt such a spell?'

'Otrick could do it,' retorted Velindre, 'without letting himself run howling mad on the wings of a storm.'

'You think you're the equal of Otrick?' Azazir guffawed as if he had heard a ripe tavern jest.

'I would be,' Velindre murmured, more to herself than

to the mad old wizard, 'if I could do this.' She gestured out to the water where the green dragon was now floating, wings outstretched, basking in the sun. 'What will that one do, if I can summon up another dragon?'

'A rival coming into its territory?' Cruel expectation lit Azazir's face. 'It'll fight. They may be born of the elements but they're beasts when all's said and done. True dragons claim a territory for themselves where they hunt, where the elements are at their rawest, to give them power for working their own magics. They fight among themselves for the choicest territory, to the death or until the loser yields and flies away. That's why dragons would come to the Cape of Winds, following the heights and the storms when they'd been driven out of the far mountains.' As he spoke, his eyes drifted towards the north.

'So they were never the strongest,' he continued, 'for all the hunters would boast of their bravery in taking on such a mighty quarry. Even a dragon isn't so mighty if it's already wounded, with its magic exhausted. Dragon and mage alike – spending too much of our substance on our spells can be the death of us,' he warned Velindre with a sharp expression.

'So the hunters just found them exhausted and butchered them?' she asked with distaste.

'You think they needed a wizard along to help them do that?' Azazir's screech of laughter made her jump. 'You think they'd pay a wizard half of everything they made just to whistle up a wind or calm the seas on the voyage? No, you stupid chit. Even a wounded, weary dragon could kill a boatload of hunters without blunting a claw.'

He fell silent, one wrinkled hand absently stroking his straggling, knotted beard, dark-green eyes hooded and contemplative. He looked old beyond imagining. 'No, the wizard was there to summon up a simulacrum like that one, to fight the wounded dragon to utter exhaustion and sap what remained of its elemental magic so that it couldn't breathe death or lethal illusion on the hunters. If a wizard could manage that, he'd more than earned his share, wouldn't you say? Then dissolving the simulacrum was his problem while the hunters tracked the exhausted dragon to wherever it was laired and hacked it to pieces as it lay helpless. If they were lucky, it wouldn't take their heads off in its death throes. That happened more than once,' he added with ambiguous neutrality.

He rubbed his hands briskly together. 'Let's see if you can do it. Let's see if you're even half the mage Otrick was.'

'I don't want to summon up a dragon just to set it fighting that one for your amusement,' Velindre said with distaste.

'That's Hadrumal talk, all ethics and imbecile niceties. Besides, you're assuming you'll succeed. I'm inclined to think my beast is perfectly safe.' Azazir clicked his tongue disdainfully. 'You came up here to learn. I've told you what you need to know. Where else are you going to try it? Down in the lowlands where the beast can gorge on some villageful of idiots? Or here where I can fetch you back if you summon so much elemental air you're overwhelmed by it?'

'You'd do that?' Velindre looked searchingly at the old mage. And how could she let such an opportunity pass? she asked herself.

'Otrick was a friend, the best of my friends.' Unexpectedly, Azazir sounded almost sane. 'I didn't have many. I'll help you for his sake and yes, there's part of me that doesn't want to see such knowledge lost at Hadrumal's decree,' he acknowledged vindictively.

She had come so far and she could hardly hope to experiment with such beguiling, perilous knowledge back in Hadrumal. Velindre gazed out at the basking dragon.

'You say it will fade in a day or so, regardless of what I do?'

'Or when I get tired of lending it my strength.' Azazir looked at the oblivious creature with faint resentment, his moment of humanity ebbing away.

Velindre bit down on her qualms. Otrick had done this, after all, without disasters bringing down the wrath of the Council.

'Will you watch my working?' she demanded. 'Tell me where I go wrong, if I should fail?'

'*When* you fail.' Azazir nodded. 'For the first few times. Until I get bored.'

'Then let's see how hard this can be.' Velindre reached up into the brilliant blue sky in search of breezes. Faint winds were just starting to rise from the bare slopes of Azazir's valley, now that the unhindered sun warmed the bare earth and rock. She noted them but did not bring them under her control just yet, looking further afield. As colder winds blew in from the surrounding heights to claim the space those first breezes had just vacated, she caught them and wove them together. More gusts followed and she captured them, but these shallow wafts offered nothing like enough elemental power to try the process Azazir had described. She looked higher into the sky where the winds were stronger, following their own imperatives high above the distant snowfields and mountainsides, shearing away from the bizarre disruption of the elements around Azazir's lake. Velindre drew on the alluring recollections of the wild ride the old wizard had thrown her upon. She reached out and summoned the elemental force with unexpected ease.

She reminded herself to feel the earth beneath her feet and the sun's warmth teasing her hair, soothing her skin beneath her crumpled chemise. There was no birdsong in the barren valley but she could hear the splashing of the green dragon and the slapping of ripples on the muddy shore. This was never going to work if she didn't keep firm hold of herself, denying the illicit temptations Azazir had shown her.

'Get on with it.' Velindre saw the old wizard wave a dismissive hand at the lake and the air shuddered with a rushing crash of water as the dragon dived for the depths. 'He won't stay gone for long and if he sees you working magic, he'll most likely attack.'

She stared unblinking up into the sky. Even as she drew down the power of the uppermost winds, she searched beyond them. There was one secret Otrick had taught her that few, if any, other wizards in Hadrumal knew. Maybe Rafrid knew it, maybe not. No matter. If she could master this spell, no one would dispute her pre-eminence over him. And Azazir could eat his mocking words.

There, she had it. In the very highest reaches of the sky, just before the air became too thin to sustain them, the fleetest winds she'd ever encountered were racing unhindered by the rumpled earth below, indescribable power at their core. No wonder the early mages who had followed Trydek to find refuge from dangerous ignorance on the mainland had approved his choice of Hadrumal, when they'd found such strength in the upper air above it. And Otrick had made it his life's work to find other such winds.

She summoned the intoxicating strength and blue light crackled all around her as a ribbon of elemental energy fell from the cerulean blue. Velindre gathered all the lesser currents of air to it, braiding them around that sapphire heart of unfettered power. Blue magelight flickered and vanished, snapping and fluttering. Flurries of dust along the lakeshore died as the breezes hurried to do Velindre's bidding. The air cooled as the heat of the sun fled in disarray. Spray danced up, impatient to join its sympathetic element. Velindre spared just enough concentration to banish it. The droplets ran away to hide in the lake, duly chastised.

The sapphire light glowed bright, a swelling column reaching up from her upturned palms into the vast emptiness of the sky. It held steady, pulses of brilliant light running up and down its length. Velindre drew her hands just a little distance apart and focused all her mageborn instincts on the space between them. The azure beams within the column of light flickered and then began coiling in on themselves. The light grew brighter, paler, lightning-white with pulses of sapphire shooting down from the uppermost sky to vanish into the incandescence building between Velindre's outstretched hands.

Now she had to create the illusion of a dragon. She drew out a thread of blue-white magic to mark the long line of the creature's back above the shoreline before her. Chilling the air, she studded its back with spines like icicles, rising from a ridge of thick scales grey as frost. Spreading her hands, she ended the tail in a heavy blunt spike and turned her attention to the arrow-shaped head, long, lean jaw white as the purest cloud, opening to reveal a mouth of blue shadow and an array of ice-white teeth cruel as a mountain winter.

'Don't stand there admiring it,' scolded Azazir. 'Give it some substance. Don't stop gathering the magic.'

Velindre struggled to maintain her grip on the pulsating mass of elemental energy. The column of azure light was rippling alarmingly, sapphire pulses shooting skyward. The dragon began to fade, barely sketched as it was. She bit her lip, tasting blood in her mouth as she fought for control over the fickle element.

Slowly, painstakingly, Velindre wove the magic together and strengthened her creation. She gave it long elegant limbs where sapphire light made bones and sinew and cloud clothed them in muscle and scale. She hammered out white armoured plates for its flanks before moulding smaller belly scales, opalescent as sunrise clouds. Mist coalesced into vast translucent wings shimmering with faint rainbow haze.

'Very pretty,' murmured Azazir with scant admiration. 'But can you make it fly?'

Sparing just enough attention to ensure that her carefully drawn creation did not fade, Velindre concentrated on gathering every scrap of elemental power that she could find between the uppermost skies and the valley she stood in. She felt herself suffused by possibilities, her hair spreading in a halo, her skin crawling with the touch of untamed energy. Focusing on the brilliant heart of the column of light, she forced the elemental might into the maelstrom of magic, confining the roiling power in an ever tighter circle.

Some remote, dispassionate part of her mind wondered how many times she had told arrogant pupils never to summon more magic than would be released in their spell. How foolhardy was this? All the same, she concentrated every fibre of her being on winding the circle of power ever tighter, ever smaller. A pinpoint of sapphire light flared in its burning white heart.

'That's it!' Azazir crowed. 'Now cut it loose, throw it to the dragon or we'll both be dead!'

With a thrill of horror, Velindre realised that the sapphire spark was doubling in size with every beat of her heart. It was sucking the power out of the sky of its own volition. There was no way she could contain it. Distantly she recalled Otrick musing on just how the wizards of fearful mainland fable might have wrought their legendary destructions. Now she knew. If she didn't confine that raw, burgeoning power within the simulacrum of the dragon, mages and non-mageborn alike all the way to Hadrumal would see just such a disaster unfold.

She hacked at the column of braided air with pure blue energy. In the instant before the sapphire spark could burst free to scour the valley even more bare than Azazir had made it, she thrust the elemental power into the motionless form of the dragon. The cerulean light vanished, recoiling in all directions, whipping back up to the highest reaches of the sky.

The dragon shivered and blurred, distorted as a distant mirage. Then azure fire kindled in its eyes and it yawned, long slatey-blue tongue tasting the air. It sprang upwards, spreading its great wings and flexing them, tail lashing wildly. Velindre caught her breath as it slipped down the sky, awkward and ungainly. Then she saw the creature catch the whisper of a breeze and seize it, curling the air to support itself with pure instinctive magic. The dragon soared high, graceful and beautiful. It looked from side to side, gathering the winds to itself until a nimbus of blue magelight surrounded it.

Velindre reached out to the aura and shivered. It was that pure, invigorating power that had seduced her in the heart of the storm, yet now it was something more, laced with the dragon's uncomplicated delight in its union with the element that had borne it. She couldn't help herself; she drew the magic to her, opening herself to it. The dragon's head whipped around and it dived to land on the shoreline with a faint thud, talons gouging the dry mud. Cocking its head to one side, it glared at Velindre, hissing faintly.

'Let it know you're more powerful than it is,' Azazir warned.

'How?' Velindre asked in a strangled whisper. Her knees felt like water. She licked her dry lips and her tongue found a raw edge on a chipped tooth; she'd clenched her jaw that hard. Close to, the beast was more terrifying than fascinating.

'Think of it as an unruly apprentice.' Azazir was callously amused.

Velindre locked gazes with the dragon. It took a stealthy pace towards her, mouth opening wider. Those teeth were incredible, like shards of indestructible ice. She flung an abrupt bolt of lightning just in front of the dragon, smudging its white purity with a shower of dust and stones. The creature retreated, head sinking low between its forefeet, icy spines flattened to its long neck. The light in its eyes faded a little and its long tail curled around its hind legs. Its long blue tongue flickered out to taste the ground where the lightning had landed and it extended a curious forefoot to the blasted hole.

'Good,' Azazir approved. 'Now—'

Whatever he might have said was lost in the water dragon's emerald fury as it stormed up out of the lake. It ran across the surface of the water, shrieking a challenge that echoed around the barren valley. Unfurling its pale-green wings, it sprang into the air before it reached the shore and plunged down, vicious talons extended on all four feet.

The cloud dragon writhed out of the way barely in time. The water dragon lashed out with its spiked tail and caught the newcomer full in the side, ripping at its white scales. Purple blood oozed from the wound. The white dragon whipped its head around and fastened its teeth on the green dragon's hindquarter, worrying at its leg. The water dragon screeched and extended its wings, flapping wildly and whipping up a cloud of dust as it fought to pull away. The cloud dragon held on until it was standing at full stretch on its hind legs, wings outspread to keep its own balance, still tearing at its rival's flesh. Green-brown blood from the water dragon's vicious wound stained the pristine whiteness of the cloud dragon's face and neck.

The green dragon opened its mouth to breathe a torrent of burning spittle at its tormentor. The white dragon recoiled and released it, sinking back on to its hind legs, still ready to spring, its head weaving from side to side as it licked its bloodied teeth with its slatey-blue tongue. The water dragon wheeled in the air, holding its wounded leg tight to its long body, remaining clawed limbs still extended in warning. The white dragon darted up and this time the green dragon's lurid breath caught its wing, searing the white membrane like acid. The cloud dragon shrieked in uncomprehending agony, tumbling through the air as it tried to escape the pain. The green dragon pursued it, wings pumping to rise above the shining white creature. Once it was above it, it tore at its white head and neck with its glaucous foreclaws, agate-spiked tail lashing at the wounded white wing. Now the cloud dragon's head was soiled with its own purple blood, one eye torn to a blind, ruined socket.

It rolled in the air, falling away, trying to escape. The green dragon shrieked its triumph and groped down with its unwounded hind leg, desperate to rip into the white dragon's unprotected belly. Its exultation was cut short as the cloud dragon breathed a lacerating hail of icy blades straight in its face. The green dragon threw its head back and the cloud dragon shot upwards, jaws fastening on the water dragon's throat. Wings beating frantically, it forced the creature back, rising above it for the first time. Now the water dragon was on its back, the soft hide between belly and hindquarters exposed, only one clawed hind foot raking the air to defend its vitals. It tore frantically at the cloud dragon's armoured neck and shoulders with its forefeet, claws skidding off the thick ridged scales.

Forelegs flailing to defend its head from the water dragon's tearing claws, the cloud dragon ripped with its hind legs, opening great gouges in the jade-green scales of its foe's belly. The water dragon lashed back with its tail. Throwing a muscular coil around the white dragon's own tail, it hollowed its back, wrenching those vicious hind claws away from its wounded underside. Writhing upwards, it bound itself so close that the white dragon had no room to claw at it again. With a single powerful beat of its wings, the green dragon forced the two of them out over the surface of the lake. Then it folded its mighty wings closed with a snap that whipped smoky spray from the water.

The white dragon flapped hysterically, but with holes gaping in its wing, it couldn't escape the dead weight of the water dragon pulling it down. It released its killing bite, head straining upwards. The green dragon thrust down with its head, brownish blood muddy on its emerald scales, dark tongue questing for the waters below. With the cloud dragon still caught in the coils of its tail, it fell into the lake. Both creatures vanished into the depths, trails of purple and muddy green blood blurring the crystal purity of the water.

'Not so strong, your little effort.' Azazir drew a deep, satisfied breath. The shining pallor of fish scales gleamed beneath his skin and green light shone in his eyes.

The battling dragons erupted on to the surface of the lake in a blaze of sapphire and emerald light. They reared up, batting their wings for balance, each ripping away scales from the other with foreclaws and teeth. The cloud dragon was hissing, the water dragon's cry a resonant moan that sent a shiver down Velindre's spine.

She watched, tears filling her eyes, as the two creatures' struggles grew weaker, blows landing without strength, evasions becoming clumsy and useless. Finally the cloud dragon collapsed backwards, head drifting on the subsiding ripples. Its motionless wings spread outstretched on the water and its tail dangled away into the depths. The water dragon fell forward on to its enemy's body, claws scraping ineffectually. It gaped, stretching its sinuous head forward to rip at the cloud dragon's throat, but this last effort was beyond it. It collapsed, tongue lolling over its teeth.

Velindre watched, tears falling unheeded down her cheeks, as the creature she had woven with her magic dissolved. The wings blurred to mist, sapphire bones momentarily revealed like a spread of fingers before they vanished. The long, lithe body turned to grey fog tainted with the dusky purple of a storm cloud. The head was the last to fade, the remaining azure eye now dull and lifeless, turned to Velindre in mute reproach. She shivered as it disappeared.

'Draw the magic to you, don't let it blow away on the wind,' Azazir rasped.

Velindre watched the green dragon fading, its wounds widening, cutting the creature into butchered remnants that drifted apart on the water, mercifully growing fainter, with scales, claws and teeth the last to disappear. She saw Azazir transmuted to a hollow semblance of man once again, filled with green-hued water, emerald madness in his eyes.

'Now do you understand?' He turned to her, eerie intensity lighting his face. 'Now will you stay?'

'Yes, I understand,' she said tersely. 'I understand why Otrick so rarely summoned a dragon. I understand why he kept such magic to himself. He would never create such a creature so lightly, to see it fade and die so soon, still less to watch it killed like that.' Revulsion choked her.

'So you understand nothing,' Azazir said with contempt. 'You had better leave.'

'Gladly,' snapped Velindre, 'but not in my underclothes, thank you all the same.' Cutting violently through the confusion of magic that now permeated the lake, she searched the barren rock of the bottom. She brought all her scattered belongings to land at her feet in a flash of sapphire light.

'Better hurry,' warned Azazir as he rubbed his hands together. His fingers were flowing through each other as the dry mud beneath his feet turned liquid once more. The dry rocks began to shine in the sunlight as they were coated with cold moisture.

Velindre looked up to see that the sky was still unclouded and snapped her fingers to summon a flame of pure fire. It burned elemental red, hanging in the air, and she set her clothes drifting around it, steam rising from the sodden cloth. She pulled on her damp boots, stamping as her stockings rumpled uncomfortably beneath her heels. Finding a silver-backed brush in her sodden bundle, she dragged the bristles angrily through her protesting hair.

'What are the differences between a true dragon and simulacrum?' she demanded. 'What else do I need to know?'

'What else?' Azazir's voice rippled with the myriad streams now cascading down the sides of the valley. 'Why should there be anything else?'

'Because there always is,' Velindre said grimly, subduing her imperfectly brushed locks in a tight plait. 'Especially with wizards. You said there was a void at the heart of a simulacrum. What is there within a true dragon?'

'I wondered if you'd remember to ask about that.' Azazir's laughter was like a winter brook tripping over stones. 'Maybe you might be Otrick's equal, one day.'

'Well?' demanded Velindre.

'A true water dragon has a heart of emerald.' Azazir looked out at the lake and excited ripples raced towards him. 'Ruby for a fire dragon, sapphire for one living among the clouds. Amber for a dragon born of the earth, for some reason. That's the other thing the hunters were ready to risk their lives for, to cut out a dragon's heart. There are no purer gemstones.'

'They killed them for jewels?' Velindre was astounded.

'So, will you be trying this again?' Azazir looked at her, his head on one side, expression – as far as it could be seen – contemplative. 'Or will you just run back to Hadrumal, tail between your legs, too frightened to admit where you've been?'

'Otrick would summon a dragon in times of direst need,' Velindre said carefully, noting that she was now standing in mud up to her ankles. 'I imagine I would do the same, if I could see no other way of saving myself or some vital situation.'

'Be careful where you work such magic,' warned Azazir softly. 'The dragon will go hunting out of blind hunger, not realising what scant time it has to live its borrowed life. It won't only hunt meat. It senses the void at its heart, even if it doesn't understand it. It'll seek gems to fill that emptiness and it will rip apart a building if it gets so much as a sniff of a diamond ring.'

'What happens if it finds them?' Velindre wrenched her ill-fitting skirt over her head before fighting her way into her bodice, now shrunken in oddly inconvenient places.

'I imagine it'll win a true life for itself,' mused Azazir as he gazed out over his lake, which was starting to glow green once more. 'Then you would have a lot of explaining to do in Hadrumal.'

Velindre gathered up everything else she cared to salvage inside her blanket and tied it into an awkward load. 'I'll bear that in mind.' She took a deep breath. 'I don't suppose anyone will come here again, not from Hadrumal, but if they do, there's no need to say I was here . . .'

Azazir ignored her, walking away. Angered, Velindre reached out to hold him back but her fingers simply rippled through his arm. He gave no sign he had even noticed, first striding, then running towards the lake. He dived into the crystal waters and vanished in a flash of emerald radiance.

Velindre looked up to see the roiling grey clouds that had capped the valley before returning in full force. She closed her eyes and sighed. Where should she go: to Hadrumal or Relshaz? She had this secret now and there was no unlearning it. Was it a secret she wanted to share?

What would Dev, of all unreliable, untrustworthy people, do with such knowledge? But these wild wizards had the lore, if one of them could forge a dragon to plunder the Aldabreshin islands. Could she bring herself to hand such dangerous power to Dev, so that he could raise a dragon of his own to rip the interloper to pieces?

How long could it be before the Archmage got wind of this dragon loose in the Archipelago? Wouldn't it be better to be in Hadrumal when that happened and be on hand to present the assembled worthies of the Council with a solution? Necessity would force Planir to overlook her visit to Azazir. Let them deny her the rank of Cloud Mistress then.

But could she live with herself if hoarding this hard-won lore meant that Dev died and innocent people besides, even if they were savage Archipelagans who would murder a mage as soon as look at her?

She was cold, dishevelled and exhausted. Her body ached for the reassurance of a warm bath, clean clothes, food and wine. She needed peace and solitude to make sense of this whole unnerving experience, but she couldn't face the lofty isolation of her silent room in Hadrumal. She needed people around her after the desolation of Azazir's madness. People who wouldn't be asking any questions until she had some answers.

Velindre opened her eyes and seized the last wisps of

air still struggling to escape imprisonment inside Azazir's unnatural storm. Picturing one of the more discreet inns among the bustling cacophony of Relshaz, she fled the silent lakeshore in a flare of sapphire light.

CHAPTER FOURTEEN

'You've got a funny idea of pleasure, my lord,' Dev mused as he climbed up on to the *Mist Dove*'s bow platform. 'We barbarians would generally prefer living in luxury with a beautiful woman open to our every suggestion to spending a full turn of the moon up to our arses in blood and slaughter.'

And we civilised men know that taking a girl to your bed because you feel sorry for her and angry with some other woman is seldom a good idea. At least, I used to know that. I certainly owe Itrac better than that, when we get back. Though I don't know what that will mean for me and Risala, whenever she returns. Will she have thought better of tying herself to my fate, when she can still turn aside to make a new life for herself?

'Do you have any news for me?' Kheda looked meaningfully at the supposed slave. 'Did you have an enjoyable shave?'

The wizard grinned, running a hand over his bald pate before he put his helmet on. Then he slid a covert glance at the side deck to be sure the trireme's archers weren't close enough to overhear him. 'She left Jagai waters yesterday.'

'She's a couple of days out from Relshaz, then.' Kheda fixed Dev with an unblinking stare. 'Is there anyone there for her to meet?'

'I don't know,' Dev replied with repressed savagery. 'The stupid bitch is brushing aside my questions. I don't know where she learned that trick.'

Has this magewoman learned the tricks we need, that we were promised? Or is there something Dev isn't telling me?

He bit down on the questions crowding on the tip of his tongue, conscious of the storage space under the planking beneath their feet.

Do you know who's in there? Some of the sail crew? The ship's carpenter, about some innocent business? No, so watch your words.

The *Mist Dove* was rowing steadily past a shallow white slope of sand where a coral islet barely broke the waves. The *Gossamer Shark* and the *Brittle Crab* flanked the heavy trireme. Kheda looked out past the upswept prow, frustration burning like acid in the back of his throat. 'Risala has courier doves. She'll send word when she reaches Relshaz. Itrac knows to send out a dispatch galley with news from the north at once. Until then, all we can do is go on.'

How long can I rely on that sole omen of the infant shark? When will I see something more to guide me? And what an irony this is: I'm risking my life consorting with wizards and I'm still reduced to relying on birds carrying messages because Dev and this magewoman have somehow lost touch.

'Go on slaughtering savages?' Dev raised an eyebrow. 'I suppose it's a living.'

'You imagine we're enjoying this?' Kheda rounded on the wizard. 'You don't think we're all sick to our stomachs of the stink of blood and bowels?' He gestured at the armoured swordsmen sitting along the rails of the trireme or lying down on the side decks. All showed signs of fatigue, some sitting with heads hanging or eyes closed, faces drawn. Hauberks and helms betrayed signs of rough cleaning but foulness still stained metal and leather. Only swords were bright and unspotted. Plenty of warriors were busy with whetstone, rag and oil while the archers sat to check that the fletching on their arrows was secure and that no damp threatened the soundness of their bows or mildew compromised their strings.

At least I got my armour back and no one was killed fetching it. Is that any kind of omen?

'It has to be done,' Kheda said with weary determination as he wiped away a trickle of sweat from underneath his helm's brow band. 'And it will be done. We will clear every last island of these savages and then Chazen can look to the future.'

And pursuing them gets me away from the residence where everyone pursues me looking for answers and judgements. Where Itrac increasingly wants something more than affection, something I find I just cannot give her.

'This little campaign of yours is certainly doing wonders for my swordplay,' Dev commented idly. 'I can really play the part nowadays. And it's keeping everyone's mind off the dragon,' he added in a lower, thoughtful tone.

Kheda rubbed a hand over his beard. 'Is it possible we've already killed whoever was summoning it?' he asked quietly. 'There's been no sign of it, no word, since the full of the Lesser Moon.'

'I wouldn't bet your residence on it,' Dev said frankly. 'Let's see what's happened at this village we're heading for first. That sounds like the work of some wild wizard with a rush of blood to the head.'

'It's done no good for morale, has it?' Kheda leaned back against the prow post, surveying the trireme's tired contingent. 'We thought we had the last of then penned in on the rocks beyond Corui with nowhere to go but the empty ocean and then we get news of a village razed to the ground two days' hard pull behind us.'

'Which is what makes me suspect some prentice wizard has felt his stones drop.' Dev cracked his knuckles. 'Who wants a quick and lethal lesson in his art.'

'You're to keep watch for the dragon,' Kheda told him

forcefully. 'We want to kill them all before it arrives. Try to think of anything we might do to drive it off, if we can't get away in time, even if we've no idea how to kill it as yet.'

'Without getting myself killed?' queried Dev sceptically. 'By the beast or by my own side,' he added in a low tone.

Kheda looked up at the empty skies. 'We can tell every archer to watch for it. Perhaps a storm of arrows will send it looking for an easier meal.'

'As I said, my lord, I wouldn't bet your residence on that,' Dev scoffed.

'Then we'll have to try throwing gems at it.' Kheda shrugged. 'You know where the chests are.'

A warlord's ransom in jewels extorted from Daish and stacked in the stern cabin of this trireme. It's a good thing any pirates have long since fled these waters for fear of the dragon.

He frowned as he saw activity on the shore on the far side of the strait the *Mist Dove* had turned into. Skiffs with deft triangular sails were drawn up on the sand and bare-chested fishermen were landing a fresh catch and haggling with islanders in creased and sweat-stained cotton who sat on sacks of saller grain, baskets of vegetables by their feet. Youths waiting out on the water saw the triremes and began shouting and waving.

Ready to give us all the precious saller from storehouses that barely hold enough to see them to the end of the dry season. They'll strip their village plots of reckal roots and send children into the forest to forage for hira beets instead, if that's what it takes to support their warlord and his warriors, so we can put an end to these savages, so they can return to a life with only the usual chances and hardships to fear.

'They're a bit cursed close to this village that was attacked, aren't they?' Dev frowned. 'They don't seem overly worried.'

'It's possible no one got away to raise the alarm.' Kheda looked towards a slew of larger islands rising in low palm-fringed green hummocks. Pale reefs in the channels between them made a turquoise and lapis mosaic of the waters. 'Maybe the savages killed everyone there.'

'Hadn't we better warn that lot dallying on the beach?' asked Dev.

'I don't want to start a panic,' said Kheda slowly. 'Let's see how bad it is before we do anything rash.'

I'd rather kill every last savage and take those islanders the news that the danger they didn't even know about is gone without threatening their fragile peace.

'Shouldn't be long now,' Dev murmured.

'Get me some water, will you, please?' Kheda licked lips dry with thirst and apprehension. He watched Dev make his way back along the ship through the warriors on the side decks.

Each day's warmer than the one before. We've this last cycle of the Greater Moon to fight through before the rains break and the heat will rise like a stoked furnace between now and then. We must finish this butchery before we have to abandon this campaign because the men in armour are boiling in their own sweat.

As Kheda watched, Shipmaster Shaiam got out of his seat and, after a brief discussion with the helmsman Yere, said something to the young warrior Ridu who was sitting on the top of the ladder leading down to the rowing deck. The word was passed along and the swordsmen on both side decks drew themselves up, alert. Archers had their bows at the ready and every eye was turned outwards. Across the water Kheda heard the purposeful rattle of the troops aboard the *Gossamer Shark* and the *Brittle Crab* making ready. He walked back to the stern, meeting the grim determination on the faces of the Chazen warriors with nods of equal resolve.

'Keep a lookout for those log boats of theirs, Shaiam.'

'We'll crush them under the ram and the scum can drown, my lord.' The shipmaster ran long, dark fingers through the plaits of his beard, crow's feet around his eyes deepening as he watched the fleeter, narrower *Brittle Crab* pull ahead of the other two ships. 'That's if they run, my lord. I think they're more likely to be hiding in the cane brakes again.'

'Then we'll hem them in and hunt them out again.' Kheda turned to follow the line of Shaiam's gaze.

'Hunting such wily prey in this thick cover has cost us good men already on this campaign, my lord,' the shipmaster said tentatively. 'Setting a few fires might send the savages running for the open.'

'And fire would purify the land their foul feet have trodden.' Kheda nodded. 'Unfortunately that cursed dragon seems to relish fire. I'm disinclined to draw its attention this way.' He managed a wry smile. 'Not till I've learned how we're to kill it.'

'Do you truly believe your slave, that there are barbarians who know how to kill these creatures?' asked Shaiam quietly. He glanced down to the oar deck where Dev was carefully filling a brass ewer from a water cask. 'Can we trust a barbarian's word? Magic runs through their lives like rot through wood.'

'Dev's been an Archipelagan longer than he was a barbarian.' Kheda shrugged with well-feigned unconcern. 'And we've seen Aldabreshin wisdom find ways to foil magic in the northern reaches. That saved us last year.'

'True, my lord,' Shaiam allowed. Distaste still creased his face.

'Let's deal with one problem at a time,' suggested Kheda. 'Let's see what's become of this village.'

'My lord.' Dev climbed up the steep stair to the stern

platform, carrying the ewer and a broad-based brass goblet.

'Thank you.' Kheda drank gratefully before refilling the goblet and offering it to Shaiam.

'My lord.' The shipmaster bowed before quenching his own thirst.

The brassy scream of a horn from the *Brittle Crab* silenced the chatter from the oarsmen and all activity on the side decks halted. Everyone watched the fast trireme round a headland choked with tangled dark-green vines and edged with jagged grey rocks.

Shaiam shouted orders down to the rowing master, the trireme's piper translating his commands into shrill whistles. The shipmaster stood by the helmsman's chair, one hand gripping Yere's shoulder. The youth's cheerful face was deadly serious as he glanced from side to side, judging the courses of the other two ships, hands gripping the twin steering oars.

The oarsmen on their triple-tiered seats below leaned over their sweeps and the oars crashed into the water. On the side decks, the swordsmen lined the rails, dulled armour still catching the sun here and there. The archers stood alert on the prow platform, ready to loose a rain of arrows in an instant. The *Gossamer Shark* was running level with the *Mist Dove*, white spume foaming up around the mighty ship's brass-sheathed ram. The two ships swung around, giving a wide berth to the broken waters where the eager current gnawed at a long finger of land.

As Yere pulled on his steering oars and the rowing master shouted his orders to each rank of rowers, the *Mist Dove* wheeled around. Kheda, Dev and Shaiam turned as one man to get a clear view of the long beach protected by the curve of the headland. It was empty – both of defiant, painted savages and of any sign that there had ever been a settlement there.

'Shaiam?' As Kheda voiced his surprise, a querulous horn sounded from the *Brittle Crab*, seeking instructions.

'This is where we were told the village had been seen.' The shipmaster was splitting his attention between watching Yere's steering and riffling through the pages of his route records.

'A new village,' Kheda reminded him. 'A fresh start for some of those who escaped last year. Perhaps we've been misdirected.'

'Perhaps.' Shaiam looked at the vacant shore, baffled. 'We certainly haven't gone astray,' he insisted.

A second horn sounded from the *Gossamer Shark* as the heavy trireme took up position guarding the *Mist Dove*'s seaward flank.

Kheda saw that the warriors on the side decks were similarly bemused, more and more faces turning to the stern expectantly, their hands still resting on their sword hilts. The murmur of speculation among the rowers below grew louder.

'Shaiam, this can't be the right beach.' He tried not to sound too severe.

'I can't see how we made a mistake.' Yere twisted to pull his own book out of a deep pocket in his over-mantle. 'It was the *Lilla Bat* that saw it. I know their helmsman—'

'They said it was just like before,' Shaiam insisted. 'A village burning, a stockade for prisoners, wild men clubbing women and children to death!'

Kheda looked at Dev and jerked his head towards the stern post. The two of them retreated as far from Shaiam and Yere as possible.

'Is there magic at work here?' Kheda demanded in a low tone, under cover of a vehement argument erupting around the helmsman's chair as the rowing master and Ridu arrived to demand an explanation.

'Hiding the wild men?' Dev looked past the curve of the stern. 'I don't think so.'

'Don't think, be certain!' snapped Kheda.

Dev scowled before narrowing his eyes. He rubbed his palms lightly together, lips moving soundlessly. 'It's—'

He got no further. The trireme shuddered from end to end and the stern reared up out of the water. Soaked by a wave of spray, and with the deck tilting abruptly beneath them, Kheda and Dev both lost their footing. They slid down the planking, Kheda bracing himself behind the shipmaster's chair. Dev barely managed to grab hold, fingers slipping on the smooth wood. Kheda grabbed at the neck of the barbarian's hauberk, hauling him up to share the inadequate perch.

Yere clung to his useless steering oars, feet slipping on the deck. Shaiam was hanging on to the helmsman's seat with one hand, the other maintaining a precarious grip on Yere's tunic. Ridu and the rowing master were nowhere to be seen. Down in the body of the ship, the rowers were clinging to their oars as the swordsmen fell in amongst them. Other warriors had fallen over the rails to land among the oar blades with yells of shock and pain.

Kheda looked to see what incomprehensible disaster had overtaken the ship's bow. The dragon looked back at him, cavernous mouth agape, its long crimson tongue flickering over those glittering white teeth. It had landed full on the front of the ship, hind legs breaking down the upswept prow posts before seizing a foothold on the brass-sheathed ram, claws tearing through the thickness of the metal. Its massive front feet, with vicious curved claws the colour of old bone, splintered the planking of the bow platform and the downdraught from its outspread wings sent showers of debris to land in the water.

Those swordsmen who hadn't fallen to death or injury were flinging themselves from the rails into the sea. Some died under a hail of arrows hissing in from the *Gossamer Shark* and the *Brittle Crab*, both vessels coming as close at they dared. Shouts of terrified consternation mingled with the screams of the *Mist Dove*'s stricken crew.

Ignoring the arrows skidding harmlessly off its crimson scales, the dragon ducked its head towards blood oozing through the shattered wood at its forefeet. It paused to lick at a man's torn leg protruding from the wreckage before scorning it with a rumble deep in its colossal chest. It took a pace forward, drawing in its enormous leathery wings. More of its weight bore down on the hapless trireme. The upper decks buckled and broke, crushing the oarsmen trapped beneath. The ship sank deeper, the rising waters cutting short the screams from the rowing deck.

The dragon looked up at the stern and advanced, step by ponderous step. The *Mist Dove* levelled out as it sank still further, seas rising to the middle oar ports. The dragon looked down, careful not to let its feet slip into the chaos of bloodied foam, shattered oars and broken bodies. Its heavy, blunt head swept from side to side, forked tongue still flickering over those murderous teeth. Pinpoints of golden fire burned in its ruby eyes as it nosed among the injured and dying men tangled up with the shattered planks. Then it looked up at the four men still clinging to the sloping stern platform. Crimson scales fringing its head and jaw bristled and its great red flanks swelled as it opened its maw. The fire in its eyes burned white hot and it breathed a great gout of scarlet flame.

What hope is there for Chazen now?

When his next breath wasn't one of searing fire, Kheda forced himself to open his eyes. He wished he hadn't when he saw Yere and Shaiam being consumed by the flames. The shipmaster threw himself blindly away from the ship, searching for the sea. There was no escape. The malicious red fire that enveloped him kept on burning even after he had sunk beneath the waves. The helmsman burned to a blackened skeleton still clinging vainly to the charred steering oars.

Why aren't we dead?

Kheda saw the scarlet flames abandon Yere's contorted corpse to split apart the deck that had been risen above the worst of seas. The wood crackled and disintegrated into feathery ash blown away by the punishing downdraught of the dragon's wings. But the planking where the warlord knelt was somehow proof against the enchanted flames.

Dev crouched beside Kheda with one palm outstretched, denying the dragon's fire. Frustrated, the crimson flames crawled around their refuge to reunite behind them, racing up the trireme's stern posts to devour the seasoned timber like the driest kindling. The sorcerous red fire was burning whatever remained above the waterline. Scarlet flames sprang across the cowering seas to devour wood, cloth, flesh and bone floating helpless in the turmoil.

The dragon roared, deafening Kheda. The blaze all around leapt up as high as the beast's scaly spine, wreathing the creature in fire. Its scales glowed like molten metal as it breathed another furnace blast straight at the two of them. Dev kept his arm outstretched to deny it as he swept his other hand around to gather a handful of enchanted fire from the burning stern. He flung it at the dragon, a blazing missile shooting straight at the creature's eye. It sprang up, great wings fanning the flames to even greater fury. The *Mist Dove* rocked violently, relieved of the massive weight, and water poured over the burning decks. The seas were still helpless to quench the murderous magical fires.

'Come on!' Dev dragged Kheda towards the side of the sinking ship. The water was lapping around the hem of his hauberk and rising fast, a cold grip around his thighs.

'We'll drown,' protested Kheda numbly, looking at the impossible distance to the dubious refuge of the shore.

'No, we won't,' yelled Dev. 'Do you want to burn to death?'

The deck beneath their feet fell away, leaving Kheda frantically trying to swim, to keep his head above the water. Lumps of wood battered him in the roiling foam. Bodies jostled among the wreckage, arms and legs limp. Kheda couldn't tell if they were alive or dead as they appeared and vanished in the chaos. The water was cold but cuts and scratches he didn't know he had stung like fire.

The weight of their armour dragged both men below the surface. Kheda managed to draw a last, despairing breath before the sea closed over his head. Dev still had hold of his hand, their fingers intertwined. Kheda opened his eyes, trying to prise Dev's fingers loose with his free hand. Dev held on still tighter. He shook their linked fists, face twisted with anger. Kheda stopped fighting to free himself and they sank together.

The water became calmer beneath the uppermost surge of the waves. Sooty black trails from burning shards of wood followed them down towards the pale ripples of the sea floor. Bodies floated around the still smouldering hulk of the ship, slowly sinking as the curious sea riffled their lifeless hair and clothing. Some were intact, others cruelly maimed and burned. More were caught twisted among the remains of the stricken trireme.

The pain in Kheda's ears was indescribable. Water was forcing its way up his nose. His eyes felt raw. He looked up, his chest burning. The surface of the sea was opaque confusion, shining like nacre. He blinked and rubbed at his eyes. Everything under the water was blurred and weirdly distorted. Noise filled his ears but he couldn't make sense of it. He couldn't tell where any sound in the deafening turmoil was coming from.

Dev tugged at his hand, still kicking to drive them at least some way towards the shore before they landed on the sea bed. They came to rest with a soft thud on the undulating sand. It was hard and unyielding beneath Kheda's feet. Kheda tugged, panicked, at the neck of his hauberk then realised that he could barely feel the weight of the armour. Before he could make sense of that, an invisible swell nearly knocked him off his feet.

Still holding tightly to Kheda's hand, Dev let himself drift down to lie almost prone on the sea bed. The warlord saw that the wizard was pinching his nostrils tightly closed with his spare hand. Kheda blew the water out of his own nose and did the same. Somehow that eased the vicious pain in his ears. He squinted at the mage, seeing Dev still blurred and looking oddly bleached.

Stern face demanding obedience, Dev released Kheda's hand. The warlord half-lay, half-crouched on the sea bed, not knowing what to do. Dev turned and began half-crawling, half-swimming towards the distant beach.

Kheda tried to stand up again and once more a swell knocked him down. He sat on an unyielding ridge of sand for a moment. His chest was a hollow cavern of agony and the strain in his throat was becoming intolerable. Terror paralysed him like a stone fish's sting.

I can't swim for the surface and I won't make it to the shore. I can't help it: I'm going to take a breath. Then I will drown. Will it make any difference to Chazen if I die a natural death instead of being burned to ash by the dragon's fire?

Dev appeared beside him, face twisted with a fury apparent even through the blurring still plaguing Kheda's vision. Kheda opened his mouth in a mute, hopeless plea. Dev reached out to force Kheda's jaw shut, his fingers digging in painfully. The wizard raised a warning finger in front of his eyes and pointed towards the shore. Somehow in the midst of his panic, Kheda realised that foul as the feeling of being half-suffocated was, it wasn't actually getting any worse.

Will it make any difference to Chazen if I'm saved from a natural death by wizardry?

Dev turned and began his laboured crawl back towards the shore again. This time Kheda followed, pushing with his feet and knees, doing his best to drag himself with his spare hand. The fingers pinching his nostrils threatened to cramp as he grew colder. He found himself fighting against the water and the drag of his chain mail, even though he couldn't feel its weight. Jaw clenched so tight his teeth ached, he ducked his head and continued fighting his way towards the pale promise of the open air.

The sea bed sloped more steeply upwards and the ridges in the sand grew closer together, telling Kheda that they were getting closer to the shore.

I suppose it makes sense to move more like a crab than a man down here.

He looked up and in a heart-stopping moment of relief thought they were within reach of the open air. He tried to stand and raised a frantic hand only to realise that the surface was still more than an arm's length away. A roll of surging white foam knocked him sideways, shoving him this way and that. Kheda fell back to the sea bed, using hands and feet in a desperate scramble until his head broached the surface. He gulped down clean, salt-scented relief before choking on a mouthful of water as a wave broke over his head. When he could breathe again, he retched and coughed.

'Come on.' Dev's hand grabbed the scruff of his neck and hauled him forwards. 'Before it sees me.'

'Where's the dragon?' Kheda wiped water from his eyes

and tried to run in the knee-deep surf. He lost his footing and fell, only saved from another ducking by Dev's strong arm.

The wizard hauled him upright and gave him a feeble slap across his nerveless face. 'Move, curse you!'

Kheda's armour felt five times the burden it had ever been as the waters fell away behind them. Where his hands and feet had been numb before, now he realised that the water and rasping sand had left his skin sodden and tender. He staggered after Dev as the wizard reeled across the sand like a man drunk on barbarian liquor. The mage barely reached the shade of a cluster of nut palms before he collapsed, chest heaving, breath rattling in his throat.

Kheda rubbed at his stinging eyes. His hair and beard were sticky with salt. Looking out to sea, he saw the *Brittle Crab* and the *Gossamer Shark* racing desperately away from the island. The dragon wheeled above them. 'They can't outrun the beast,' he said despairingly.

'They won't have to.' Dev forced himself up on to his hands and knees. 'It'll be back.'

'Look!' Kheda pointed to men crawling ashore among the wreckage of the *Mist Dove*. 'We must get everyone together, before the savages attack.'

'There are no savages.' Dev's words were muffled as he scrubbed his face with his hands. 'There never were any savages. The dragon wrought an illusion. It wanted us to come and see what had happened.'

'It can do that?' Kheda gaped.

'I don't know what it can do.' Dev broke off, shuddering. 'I know what it wants to do. It wants to kill me. It's realised I come in a ship. It's realised Chazen ships are hunting the wild men. So it showed a Chazen ship a Chazen village under attack by the wild men. Ah!' He gasped with pain and began frantically tearing at the lacings of his hauberk.

'What are you doing?' Kheda asked in alarm.

'The dragon,' said Dev, jaw clenched as he fought his way free of his armour. 'It's back.'

A black shape blotted out the sun and Kheda saw the creature's evil shadow sweep across the sand.

'Run!' Dev threw his chain mail away as hard as he could. The ungainly sprawl of metal burst into flames, the plates writhing and buckling, the rings melting into drops of liquid steel.

With the deafening sound of the dragon's wings directly above, Kheda took to his heels. The stand of nut palms exploded into flames as the dragon wheeled overhead, blasting the sand with its fiery breath, scorching whatever was left of Dev's armour into oblivion. It crowed with exultation before landing with a thud that shook the whole beach. Thrusting its massive head into the flames, it began ripping at the burning trees with its murderous foreclaws.

Warlord and wizard crouched in a tandra thicket. Kheda saw that some of the men washed up on the shore who had fallen terrified to the sands were cautiously lifting their heads. One made a dash for the dubious safety of the trees. The dragon ignored him, still intent on reducing the nut-palm thicket to smouldering fragments. More of the men ran for their lives.

They'll never believe I swam ashore in this armour.

Kheda threw his helm aside and began wrestling his way free of his own hauberk.

'I've got to get away from it,' Dev said fervently, shaking like a man wracked with fever.

'We've got to get away from all this tinder.' Alarmed, Kheda saw the dry husks of tandra pods start smoking. A tuft of the white fibres within flared up. He flailed at it with his armour before the oily black seeds ignited.

'It knows its magic speaks to mine,' Dev said with difficulty. 'That's how it's going to find me.'

'This beast's too cursed clever by half.' Kheda looked at the dragon standing in the midst of the blackened nut-palm stumps. The creature had lifted its head and was surveying the trees and brush that fringed the beach. 'But you said it was doing a wizard's will. Where is he?'

'I've no idea,' said Dev tightly. 'All I know is that thing wants me dead.'

The dragon took a few paces along the shore and blasted a striol-choked spinefruit tree into fiery oblivion.

Could I escape, along with whoever else has washed ashore, while it hunted him down?

But Dev saved my life, so I'm bound by every code of honour to try to save his barbarian, magic-cursed hide. Besides, this magewoman won't be too inclined to offer her help if she learns that I left him to be eaten by the beast.

'What do you suppose it wants more?' Kheda said slowly. 'Do you think we could escape it if it was sated with gems?'

'They're all at the bottom of the strait along with the *Mist Dove*.' Dev watched with sick apprehension as the dragon studied the spreading blaze it had created, tongue tasting the air.

'No, they're not,' Kheda said with growing determination. 'Look.'

Several of the survivors were seizing chests or coffers from the broken wreckage scattered on the shore before scurrying towards the forest.

'That fire's coming our way.' Dev began backing out of the tandra thicket.

Kheda stood his ground despite the scarlet flames crawling towards them, crackling and spitting. 'Can you distract it somehow, while I try to find some gems? We can at least buy some time to run. How far do we have to go before it loses your scent?'

'I've no idea,' spat Dev. 'There's no hiding from it—'

Kheda slapped the mage hard across the face. 'You're a lot of despicable things but you've never been a coward. Don't start now!' He caught Dev's arm, barely saving himself from the wizard's fist in his face. 'How can you distract it?

Dev rubbed his flushed cheek. 'We could see what it makes of your armour if I set it melting,' he muttered without conviction. 'Leave it there.'

'Just keep one step ahead of it.' Kheda gripped Dev's arm, trying to encourage the mage. 'I'll be back.'

Dev pulled away and disappeared into the trees. His bare feet left scorched, smouldering prints in the dry leaf litter.

Kheda caught up his swords and ran along the edge of the shore. He scanned the trees urgently for any signs of the *Mist Dove*'s crew.

'My lord!' An ashen-faced oarsman peered out from behind a spinefruit tree. He flinched and ducked back again as a ball of fire erupted in the trees behind Kheda.

The warlord flung himself into the shelter of the spinefruit's shadow. 'Do you have any gems?' he demanded. 'Did you pick any up?'

'No, my lord,' the hapless rower quavered.

Kheda looked back to see a pillar of flame snaking up into the sky. The dragon sprang into the air and circled it, lashing at the writhing scarlet fire with its tail. It was all far too close for comfort; Kheda could feel the heat on his forehead.

'Come on.' He drew a sword and began hacking a path through the tangled underbrush. 'Chazen!' he yelled. 'To me! We need gems to fill the creature's mouth or we'll all get eaten!'

A couple of terrified archers appeared on either side of a tandra thicket. Neither had bow nor arrows but one clutched a small coffer in his shaking hands. Kheda hurried forwards and seized it. His heart sank. It was his physic chest.

'That's something,' he said tightly. 'Look after it. But we need gems.'

'My lord.' Another rower appeared, this time holding one of the coffers of jewels so grudgingly sent from the Daish treasury.

'Good man,' Kheda breathed with heartfelt relief. 'Are there any more?'

There were stirrings further along the shore. Unseen, some man called out to another, passing the word of Kheda's appearance and of his search for gems.

'Come on.' The warlord led his stunned, disparate band further away from the dragon.

The creature was now roaring horribly at the pillar of flames. Every time it blasted the taunting inferno into oblivion with its fiery breath, the stubborn blaze sprang back up again.

That hauberk was definitely bad luck. Whatever Dev's doing, how much longer can it last?

'My lord.' A handful of shocked oarsmen appeared from behind a sandy outcrop.

'Gems.' One thrust another small coffer at Kheda.

The warlord took it and looked around the stricken handful of survivors. A strange calm came over him as he put the only plan he could think of into halting words. 'I'll see if I can distract the beast, then I'll make a run for it. Get yourselves over to the far side of this island. Find the most northerly point. Wait until dusk and try to flag down a fisherman. Don't light a fire, that'll only attract the beast. I'll try to join you.'

'My lord—' the man still clutching the physic chest protested inarticulately.

'Give me that.' Kheda took the ebony and silver coffer and knelt to open it. He found a small wax-sealed box and tucked it inside the front of his sweaty, sandy tunic. 'Go on. You have to take word of what's happened back if I don't return.' He looked at the men now staring at him, aghast. 'I can't and won't ask any of you to do this. This is my duty to you as your lord.'

And how better to find out if I am truly doing the right thing by Chazen, or if I'm truly cursed to die by the magic that I've brought to this domain.

'Go!' he barked, with all the authority he could summon.

Slowly, the survivors of the disaster backed away. As they turned to see where they were going, they began to move more quickly. Soon they were running away through the forest, heedless of the noise they were making.

Kheda picked up the two jewel coffers by their rope handles. They weren't overlarge but were still heavy enough to drag painfully at his arms as he walked slowly out from the shelter of the trees.

The dragon had finally managed to quell the impudent flame Dev had raised against it and was stamping violently on the ground where Kheda had left his armour. Its vehement throbbing growl made Kheda's head ache.

The warlord walked slowly down to the waterline and scanned the debris, glancing up at the dragon with every second step. He saw another battered chest and splashed into the shallows to retrieve it. Movement caught the corner of his eye and he halted, knee-deep in the water. The dragon was looking at him, heavy blunt head cocked to one side. Faint trails of smoke rose from its nostrils. It snorted and the smoke stopped.

Kheda straightened his back and stared the dragon straight in the eye. It looked back at him, unmistakable intelligence in that white fire lighting its ruby eyes. Kheda swung one of the coffers at arm's length, backwards and forwards, the arc lengthening with every swing. Putting all his strength behind it, he flung the little chest down the beach. The dragon's eyes followed it as it flew through the air and landed with a solid thud further down the waterline.

Kheda stood still. The dragon stared back at him before turning to look over its shoulder into the unrevealing trees. Kheda threw a second chest, the effort forcing out an unintended groan. The chest landed and broke open. The dragon's head whipped around and the light in its eyes glowed brighter. It took a pace forward before looking at Kheda again.

He threw the third chest as far as he could. It fell not far from the first, Daish workmanship holding firm.

Just what I don't need. What do I do now? There's no way I'm going any closer to open the cursed things!

The dragon took another few paces forward, its attention switching between the two unopened coffers and the one spilling bright jewels over the white sands. Kheda began walking slowly backwards, feeling his way as best he could to avoid tripping over broken wood and bodies. The dragon ignored him as it crouched low to run its tongue over the scattered jewels.

Kheda risked a glance over his shoulder as he shifted his path towards the tree line. A few more men were dragging themselves out of the water and scrambling across the sand. He looked back to see that the dragon wasn't interested in them, and was advancing on the two unopened chests.

Now Kheda was half-way between the waterline and the trees. He abandoned caution as the dragon broke open the second coffer with a splintering claw. He ran for the forest, but rather than join the fleeing rowers, he doubled back towards the blasted ruin of the tandra thicket where he'd left Dev. His heart pounded in his chest as he tried to recall the path the wizard had taken. Caught unawares, he skidded to a halt as he saw the black footprints charred into the dry leaves. Curbing the urge to shout out the barbarian's name, he forced his way through the entangling brush. Behind him on the beach, the dragon's growl had softened to an unnerving croon.

Dev hadn't got far. Kheda fell over him behind a green-stained outcrop. The mage was lying in the shade of the rock, eyes tightly closed, arms wrapped around himself and shaking violently.

Kheda dropped to his knees. 'Dev,' he whispered urgently, shaking him. He snatched back his hand as the coarse hairs on the wizard's forearm slid away to dust beneath his seared fingers. The heat within the mage was singeing him hairless.

Back on the beach, the dragon roared with sudden fury. Kheda heard the deafening clap of its wings. He looked at Dev. Before he had time to think, he caught up a rock the size of his fist. He winced as he smacked it into the side of Dev's head. The wizard moaned and went limp. Kheda ducked as the dragon made a pass overhead, the wind from its wings setting the leaves rattling. As the shadow passed, he tried to drag Dev further into the shallow hollow beneath the overhang and tested the wound he had inflicted with careful fingers.

You don't seem to have cracked his skull. That's one good thing. Or is it? No one would have batted an eyelid if you'd returned without your awkward slave, who could then be safely praised as a hero for spending his life in your service.

No, we've been here before. I didn't kill him then and I won't kill him now, not unless it's the only way to save ourselves from the dragon. I owe him more than that.

And he owes this domain a more valuable death, if it comes to it. There's still much his blood could do to wash away the stain he's brought to these islands.

Kheda glowered at the unconscious Dev as he reached

inside his tunic and brought out the wax-sealed box. Cracking the tightly fitted lid open, he found that the speckled powder inside was still largely dry. Forcing the unconscious wizard's jaw open, he tipped a hefty dose on to his tongue. After a moment's thought, he ripped the sleeve from his tunic and bound the wizard's mouth closed. Then he ducked down as the dragon swept overhead again.

Going back to the shore. Then we're going the other way.

Forcing himself upright, Khcda dragged Dev's senseless body on to his shoulders and began breaking a path though the undergrowth, heading away from the nightmare on the beach.

CHAPTER FIFTEEN

Sitting in a high-backed chair upholstered with painstaking needlepoint, Velindre allowed herself a moment to enjoy the warm sunshine pouring through the unshuttered window. Then she opened the crisp new almanac lying in the lap of her lavender gown and ticked off the twenty-ninth day of Aft-Spring. Carefully setting her pen down on the octagonal table at her elbow, she blew the ink dry and then closed the book. Her thin lips narrowed to invisibility. Thirty days here and still no closer to a decision.

She gazed out at the paved square beyond her window, its enclosed garden watered by a glittering central fountain. The sweeper was about his leisurely business brushing the flagstones free of dust, at the same time showing broad shoulders to keep the square free of Relshaz's hopeful indigents. A nursemaid in yellow livery shooed a gaggle of excited children out of one of the genteel houses with whitewashed walls and ruddy earthen-tiled roofs. As they rushed towards the circumscribed freedom of the central garden, some nameless youth pushing a handcart paused to talk to the nursemaid. After a glance up at the blind windows, the girl slipped something into his hand before hurrying after her charges. One of the two little girls was denouncing her bolder brother as he swung on the green-painted rails, hands on her diminutive hips.

Velindre lost interest in the pedestrian byplay, looking up at the scudding clouds dotting the clear blue sky. There was little enough power to tempt her. Relshaz was too far south to find the lofty ribbon of air she had pulled down over Azazir's lake, and too far north to find its counterpart that raced high across Hadrumal. All was as yet untroubled by the thunderstorms sweeping in off the gulf to break over Lescar and Caladhria, as the wide inland plains threw off the summer's heat. Far beyond the horizon, she could sense the long reach of Toremal cradling the broad gulf, its mountains denying passage to the turbulent winds of the open ocean.

There was little enough power but there was still sufficient to tempt her. Sweat prickled beneath her shoulder blades and under her breasts despite the moderate temperature of the room. With her newfound skills she might be able to summon the dragon once more, even with such dissipated breezes in these placid skies.

Another dragon, she corrected herself savagely. The first one was dead at the hands of Azazir's simulacrum. And it was no true dragon, merely a creature of magical contrivance and convenience.

But it had been a creature all the same that had delighted in the soaring element that so thrilled her. A creature condemned to fade and die before it had barely begun to comprehend where it was or what it was. Unless she threw it into a brutal fight to the death against some other wizard's equally enslaved magic.

Sweat beaded her forehead as she felt suddenly nauseous. Getting carefully to her feet, she crossed to a sideboard and poured herself a glass of wine. She was standing, motionless, holding the wine undrunk when a knock at the door startled her into spilling it all over the prettily embroidered linen draping the polished wood.

'You have a visitor, my dear.' The amiable widow who was renting her these two comfortable rooms beamed as she opened the door. 'You said you had no acquaintance in Relshaz,' she chided.

'I don't,' Velindre said curtly as she moved to hide the spilled wine from view.

'Well, dear, she says she's a friend of yours.' The widow's smile faltered and she brushed at the frivolous lace hanging from turtleshell combs supporting her complicated *coiffure*. 'She says she's Madam Esterlin. Shall I show her up?'

'No need,' laughed a genial voice from the hallway. 'Velindre, my dear, no wonder you stay so slender, climbing all these stairs day in and day out.' A generously proportioned woman in an elegant gown of jade silk appeared in the doorway, fanning herself with a silver-mounted spread of vivid green feathers.

The widow bridled as the visitor sailed past her into the room. 'I'll leave you to your conversation.'

'Thank you.' Velindre managed a brief nod for her landlady. The widow shut the door with a force that spoke of her indignation.

The newcomer grimaced as she deposited a light wool wrap and her fan on an old-fashioned satinwood side table. 'I don't think she'll be bringing us wine and honey wafers.'

'Probably not.' Velindre folded her arms. 'This is an unexpected pleasure, Mellitha.'

'Unexpected, that much I'll grant you.' The newcomer's laugh had a harder edge now that the door was shut behind her. Her shrewd grey eyes took in every detail of the room, lingering on the table by the lustre-tiled fireplace where twenty or more leather-bound books were organised in precise piles. A thick sheaf of notes on expensive reed paper was set squarely between them. 'I was surprised to learn you'd been in the city for nearly half a season without calling on me.' She looked at Velindre, her plump face expectant.

'You're curious to know what I'm reading?' Velindre crossed the room in long strides to pick up the topmost book. 'Lawsenna on the history of Southern Toremal and–' she lifted the volume beneath '–Den Jaromire on the beasts and birds of the Cape of Winds.'

'You've sailed the Tormalin ocean coasts extensively.' Mellitha nodded with apparent understanding. 'Though I'm curious as to why my book merchant mentioned you've been buying everything and anything he can find on the nature and lore of dragons.'

Velindre replaced the books carefully. 'I'm hardly your pupil to explain myself to you. Still,' she continued, to forestall the words on the other woman's lips, 'I was Otrick's pupil, as you well know. It's not so remarkable that I'd be retracing his steps in my reading.'

'No, but I know full well you did that ten years ago and more. He told me as much himself.' Mellitha crossed the room in a rustle of lace-trimmed petticoats and sat in the chair matching the one Velindre had vacated. 'Since we're being so frank with each other,' she went on with distinct sarcasm, 'it's not so much what you're reading that piques my interest as where you're reading it. I'm surprised to find you away from Hadrumal.'

'One can learn many things beyond Hadrumal's shores,' Velindre responded smoothly. 'Otrick taught me that.'

'I would have thought Otrick taught you how to pour a fine wine without spilling it.' Mellitha leaned back in her chair to look at the stained cloth behind Velindre. The sunlight picked out the silver thick in her chestnut hair. 'Did he teach you how to rise above disappointed hopes?'

Velindre smiled coldly. 'You can reassure Flood Mistress Troanna or Archmage Planir, or whoever it is you're reporting to, that I'm not sitting here weeping over my shattered dreams.'

'I imagined Rafrid's elevation would still be a sensitive

subject.' Mellitha waved an airy hand bejewelled with rings. 'You misunderstand me. I'm not here on anyone's behalf. Oh, when Planir's curious about something in this ant hill, I'll kick over a few stones if it suits me to find out more, but that's seldom called for. I have plenty of things to occupy my time, far more interesting things than reading inferior copies of books I found tedious the first time around in Hadrumal. Which is why I'm curious to see you reading them.'

Velindre found her nausea retreating. 'These things that occupy you, they're matters of magic?' she queried.

'Relshaz has little or no interest in magic.' Mellitha chuckled. 'And the games around the magistracies here make the scrambling for the high seats on Hadrumal's Council look very tame.'

'I've no doubt,' Velindre said distantly.

'I came to see if Otrick or anyone else had ever let you consider opportunities beyond Hadrumal for a woman of your intelligence and affinity.' Mellitha looked out of the window at the serene square. 'I've lived more than half my life here. I've made a handsome fortune, satisfied my own desires as I've seen fit and raised four happy, healthy children, all grown and gone now, leading their own lives as they see fit, mageborn or not.'

'I don't think I'm cut out to wheedle contracts to gather taxes out of a council of venal magistrates.' Velindre smoothed her skirts as she returned to her seat.

'No, I don't think you are.' Mellitha rested her chin in her hand, studying Velindre. 'I think you intended to head back to Hadrumal with some startling discovery spun from Otrick's wilder speculations, to make Planir and all the rest regret not raising you to Cloud Mistress. I think you've stumbled on something you didn't expect. You're certainly hiding from someone. Or should that be everyone? Why do you think I've gone to all this trouble of visiting you in person? Because I couldn't raise you through any kind of spell, and even if I don't play Hadrumal's games, you can rest assured there's no one there who's my equal in scrying.'

Velindre couldn't help her glance towards the closed door of her bedchamber, where the mirror was shrouded with a heavy shawl and both ewer and basin stood dry and empty.

'You're not looking well, Velindre,' Mellitha continued after a few moments' tense silence. 'You were always thin, but now you look positively gaunt and that's not flattering for a woman past the first flush of youth.'

Velindre still said nothing.

Mellitha stood up and fished in the mesh purse hanging from the plaited silk girdling her well-cut gown. 'Come and see me if you feel like confiding in me. I'll tell my servants I'll always be at home to you.' She laid a folded and sealed piece of deckle-edged paper on the wine table beside her chair. 'Or just come to dinner, if you don't want to talk.' She gathered up her wrap and fan as she sailed blithely to the door. 'I'll give you one piece of advice to be going on with. I used to tell my four children, if you skin your knee, don't pick at the grazes. It'll take all the longer to heal. The same is true of wounded pride.'

'If I talk to you . . .' Velindre forced the words out. 'Will you keep my confidences?'

'Yes.' Mellitha stood motionless, one hand on the door handle. 'I told you, I don't play Hadrumal's games.'

'I have to talk to someone.' Now that she had started, Velindre regretted it. At the same time, she wondered if she would be able to stop. 'To someone mageborn, someone who might just possibly understand. Or I'll go mad.'

'We wouldn't want that, my dear.' Mellitha walked swiftly back to her chair.

'Did you ever know Azazir?' Velindre stared out of the window at the alluring blue sky.

'Only by reputation,' said Mellitha cautiously. 'They say he's mad.'

'That doesn't equal the half of it.' Velindre shivered even though she was sweating again. 'He's gone beyond madness. He's lost himself utterly in his element.'

'It happens.' Mellitha's voice was cold. 'I take it you've seen him?'

Velindre nodded jerkily.

'Do you think you might be going down the same path?' Mellitha asked softly.

Startled, Velindre looked at her. 'No.'

'Good.' Mellitha's grey eyes were steely. 'Because that's not something I could keep from Hadrumal. Anything less than that . . .' She shrugged. 'That's no business of anyone else's.'

Not entirely reassured, Velindre looked back out of the window. 'Azazir knew how to summon dragons, did you know that?'

'Him and Otrick both.' Mellitha nodded. 'Is that what you're planning on astounding the Council with?'

'I had some such notion,' Velindre admitted, running a shaking hand over her mercilessly braided hair. 'Have you any idea how they do it?'

Mellitha shook her head. 'I was never that curious to raise some creature that might bite my head off.'

'I know how,' Velindre said simply. 'And now I wish I didn't. Only I went to find out to help someone else. If I don't tell him, he'll most likely die as a result. But he could well end up dead if I do.' The words rasped in her dry throat.

Mellitha rose and fetched them both a glass of wine. 'Who are we talking about?'

'Dev.' Velindre sipped at the wine and felt it strengthen her. 'Did you ever meet him?'

'More than once.' Mellitha chuckled. 'He's another one who was never born for Hadrumal, never mind his wizardry.'

'He's down in the far south of the Archipelago.' Velindre swallowed another mouthful of wine. 'He's been helping a warlord fight some wild wizards who appeared out of the southern ocean last year. He thought they were all dead but this year a dragon's appeared, so presumably there's at least one left.'

'Or one's recently arrived from wherever the first contingent came from?' Mellitha raised her perfectly shaped eyebrows.

'Either way, Dev wanted to know how to summon a dragon of his own.' Velindre fell silent again.

'To attack the interloper?' Mellitha prompted. 'Like those old tales of the dragon hunters around the Cape of Winds?'

'He has no idea what he's asking for.' Velindre drained her glass.

'Fire to fight fire, presumably.' Mellitha looked intently at her.

'Literally, as it happens.' Velindre found she couldn't smile at the jest. 'Which would give him two things,' she continued with brisk dispassion. 'Firstly, access to far more power than he could ever imagine, and I don't know how well you know Dev, but I certainly wouldn't trust him with that. He could easily find himself slipping down the same road to Azazir's obsession. Because a dragon's aura is fascinating beyond belief, Mellitha. You can see all the things that have always been just beyond the reach of your wizardry and you think you could finally grasp them if you just reached out a little further. And when you find you can't, you tell yourself it doesn't matter because you'll manage to do it next time and anyway, the power you're feeling now is the purest and sweetest you've ever known.'

Her words slowed. 'Have you ever had a lover who brought you such bliss that all you wanted was to feel his hands on you, that every moment you were apart felt wasted, even when you were well past the first flush of passion?'

'Just the once,' Mellitha said dryly.

Velindre looked at her. 'And you realised eventually that however good the loving, there is more to life than ecstasy in bed?'

'Eventually.' Mellitha dimpled, her youth momentarily returning in her eyes. 'Then I decided the best trick was having the ecstasy and the rest to go with it.'

'Absolutely.' Velindre laughed despite herself. 'And once you've had that, you're not inclined to settle for anything less thereafter.'

'Quite.' Mellitha looked at her quizzically. 'But what has your life with Otrick or mine with whoever else got to do with dragons?'

Velindre's smile faded. 'It's hard to think of anything more desirable than the elemental thrill of a dragon's aura. You spend your days thinking of all the reasons why you should summon one up – for the good of wizardry, for the better education of the mundane populace. To drive untamed wizardry out of the southern Archipelago.'

'And Dev did always have a taste for white brandy and dream smokes,' said Mellitha thoughtfully. 'You said there was a second thing he'd gain, besides a dangerous new obsession.'

'He'd get a dragon.' Velindre pressed her hands to her face as she struggled for words. 'I don't mean the magical aura, I mean the beast itself. It's pure element, Mellitha, shaped and bound with magecraft, and it's an innocent. Yes, it's dangerous beyond reason, and I certainly don't trust Dev with something like that to do his bidding – always assuming he could bend it to his will – but there's no malice in it. It's a creature of instinct and all its instincts are mageborn. It revolts me, the thought of creating such a creature to fight like a pit dog, suffering pain and death, never even knowing why it's there. It's a perversion of all that's good and honourable in magecraft,' she concluded bitterly. 'And I'm talking like some dewy-eyed fool of an apprentice, I know, and I should know better.'

'But you say there is already a dragon in the southern Archipelago, doing the bidding of some unknown wizard?' Mellitha returned to the crux of the problem tormenting Velindre.

'Who will quite probably kill Dev if I don't show him how to fight back on equal terms,' the blonde magewoman agreed. 'And will certainly cause even more mayhem across the Archipelago, killing innocent Aldabreshi and giving them yet more cause to hate and fear and murder any mageborn they happen to come across.'

'And given that no wizard in his right mind travels in the Archipelago, there's no telling how far north this unnamed, untamed magic will come.' Mellitha pursued Velindre's predicament inexorably. 'How much blood do you want on your conscience? How exactly are you going to explain keeping such a secret from Hadrumal? I take it Dev hasn't told anyone of his little adventures?'

'I don't imagine so.' Velindre sighed. 'So that's what I've been doing – trying to learn more about dragons, to find some alternative. I haven't found one yet.'

'Some other means of killing one or driving it off?' Mellitha frowned.

Velindre nodded. 'Or some way of finding the wizard who summoned it and killing him. Saedrin save me if the Council ever finds out about that.'

'You say a dragon summoned through Otrick and Azazir's spell is a creature of pure element? No–' Mellitha raised a hand and her emerald rings sparkled in the sun '–I don't want to know how. I don't need to know. Perhaps there's another alternative. Give me a moment to think.'

Velindre sat looking out of the window. The children in the square below played their blithe games, shouting and laughing, and the clouds tracked across the sky. The five chimes of noon sounded across the city and their echoes died away.

'You said the dragon is pure element shaped and bound with magecraft?' Mellitha said after some considerable while. Velindre nodded.

'Do you suppose it might be possible to undo that binding?' the older magewoman suggested slowly. 'Or to introduce some other element into it, to somehow contaminate the wizardry within it?'

'I don't know.' Velindre looked at her, mouth half-open. She rubbed her forehead with the back of one hand. 'It might be possible.'

Mellitha smiled. 'It's all very well shutting yourself away to beat your brains out against a problem but it's often said that a problem shared is a problem halved, even if you share it with an old wife like me.'

'It would be nigh on impossible to undo your own creation once the simulacrum is made,' Velindre said thoughtfully. 'I don't know if I could do that to another mage's dragon.'

'Do you suppose it would improve matters if that dragon had been made by a wizard attuned to the same element as yourself?' Mellitha asked. 'Or as Dev – you said he was looking to fight fire with fire.'

'That's certainly something to consider,' mused Velindre, 'but how would he introduce another element? Would it have to be antithetical? Or perhaps we could do it between us – air and fire are sympathetic elements.'

'This looks like one of those possible answers that brings a handful of new and harder questions along with it,' said Mellitha ruefully. 'Loath as I am to say it, you're more likely to find the answers in Hadrumal than Relshaz. Hearth Master Kalion is a pompous fat fool in many ways, but he'd certainly be someone who could advise you. Or your father, though I imagine he'd be too busy telling you he told you not to visit Azazir in the first instance.' She smiled as Velindre looked sharply at her. 'I've been a daughter as well as a mother, my dear.'

Velindre stared out of the window again. 'I've been wondering if the wisest course might just be to lock what I've learned in the darkest recesses of my memory. The collective wisdom of the Council seems to be that such dangerous knowledge should be lost. It would have been washed from the annals of wizardry whenever Azazir finally achieves the ultimate dissolution he seems intent upon.'

'Lost knowledge has an inconvenient way of reappearing,' Mellitha said briefly. 'And keeping your own counsel on this won't help Dev, will it?'

'No.' Velindre sighed.

'I'm sorry, my dear, but I have other appointments.' Mellitha stood up, gathering her wrap and fan. 'Come and see me if there's anything more I can do. Come and see me anyway. I meant what I said about the wider world offering far more than the narrow halls of Hadrumal.' She favoured Velindre with a sunny smile before bustling out of the room and away down the stairs.

Velindre stood up with sudden decisiveness and crossed to the door of her bedchamber in a few quick strides. Taking the shawl off the mirror, she set a beeswax candle in a single silver stick before it and lit the wick with a snap of her fingers. Deftly, she wove the bright circle of bespeaking and then frowned. The mirror stayed obstinately empty. She snuffed the candle and tried again. She had no better success.

The crease between her blonde brows deepening, she

crossed to the marble-topped washstand and, lifting out the floral ceramic ewer, passed her hand over the broad, shallow bowl. Moisture slowly coalesced out of the air until a small puddle had gathered in the bottom. She passed her hand over the bowl again and the water glowed green. But there was still no image riding on the iridescent surface.

Where was Dev? Too far away, in a place so entirely unknown to her? It wasn't as if she had any possession of his to focus her spell. Or was he hiding, as she had been, in case she betray him with such magic? Velindre hurriedly banished the spell. She had no wish to condemn Dev to the agonising death the Aldabreshi reserved for wizards. And the more she thought about it, the more foolish her own plan of travelling south began to seem, risking such a fate herself. But she had better let him know that she was almost certainly returning to Hadrumal.

She walked slowly back into the sitting room and picked up the almanac, her lips moving unconsciously as she calculated the days since she had last spoken to Dev. Would that ship he had promised her be waiting in the docks, ready to carry her away? The Aldabreshi had their own ways of sending messages among themselves, with their ciphers and puzzles to hide their meanings. If the ship was there, this warlord's envoy would surely have some means of getting word to Dev.

Velindre left the room and the door locked itself with a soft click as her purposeful steps faded away down the stairs. She didn't pause as the door to the widow's sitting room opened. 'I'm going out. I may be some while.'

She pushed the outer door open and walked rapidly down the house's steps. Her pace didn't slow until she left the guarded privacy of the square for the bustling thoroughfares beyond. There were more people clogging up the streets and alleys in Relshaz every time she visited,

Velindre thought with irritation. But this busy commercial street was by far her quickest route to the docks.

Women were slowly perusing the displays laid out on drapers' counters and ribbon sellers' doorposts. Those hurrying with more purpose jostled the magewoman on their way to appointments with the dressmakers and milliners whose workshop windows opened above the shop fronts. Some of the women walked in two and threes, heads close together, arms linked as they sought to carry on a conversation. Others barked orders to the maids or menservants at their heels laden with packages or bolts of cloth. Merchants' inducements, hawkers' blandishments and the rising notes of intense haggling added to the hubbub.

'Something for that lovely fair skin of yours, my lady?' An importunate pedlar darted in front of her, thrusting forward a wooden tray, leather strap looped around his neck. 'Well into spring now, madam. You don't want that delicate complexion spoiling in the sun. I've calomel powder here—'

Velindre would have stepped around him but the flagway was too crowded. 'Get out of my way,' she said coldly.

The pedlar's cheeky grin widened now that she had been forced to acknowledge him. 'Such gorgeous golden hair you have, my lady. Northern blood makes for such beauties—'

'My forebears may have had northern blood, I neither know nor care.' Velindre fixed him with a forbidding glare. 'I am from Hadrumal and if you don't let me pass, I'll curdle every jar of unguent and snake oil that you possess.'

Mouth slack with shock, the pedlar pressed himself back against a sweetmeat seller's handcart. Velindre pushed past to leave the two men arguing as the throng closed behind her. Seeing several women with entourages of maids and children pausing for mutual consultation and effectively blocking the flagway ahead, Velindre glanced at an urchin clutching a broom and ready to sweep a crossing in exchange for some copper. She reconsidered as a heavy dray rumbled past, barrels clunking together as the horses checked, their path obstructed by a carriage slowing to find an indistinct side alley. It would be quicker to force a path between the indignant women than to wait for a gap in the traffic.

She pressed on until she had left the thriving mercantile heart of Relshaz. Now she had reached a quieter quarter where windowless warehouses rose high on each side of the narrow lanes. Waggoners bringing their creaking carts to be emptied or lashing their reluctant horses to pull a new load slowed to look at the unaccompanied magewoman with open curiosity.

'What are you looking for, blondie?'

'Are you lost? I'll trade you a ride for a ride, sweetheart.'

'What's a handsome piece like you doing in these parts?'

Velindre ignored honest concern and ribald jocularity alike. Taking a cross street and then cutting through a short entry, she emerged on to a broad dockside solidly built of pale stone. There were precious few Relshazri to be seen here. The storehouses were guarded by dark-skinned men in gleaming mail, expressionless behind their all-concealing beards. Each one carried more swords and daggers at his brass-studded belt than he had hands to use. Shutters above stood wide open, women in flowing gowns of brilliant silks sitting on the shallow windowsills. They sipped from sparkling glass goblets as they looked down at dutiful slaves carrying bales of linen cloth and nameless barrels. Their laughter rang out across the unintelligible harshness of orders and rebukes shouted hither and thither.

Velindre looked at the great swollen-bellied galleys bobbing gently, safe within the embrace of the massive breakwaters that reached far out into the open waters of the gulf. She had always known that all the goods of these civilised countries were brought down to Relshaz by the rivers and roads that threaded through the vast hinterland. It was another thing entirely to see the countless quantities of cargo waiting to be taken aboard the ships. She had never seen any need to visit the docks when she'd been in Relshaz before. She had never caught more than a glimpse of the Aldabreshi who set aside their lethal quarrels and fragmented alliances alike for the opportunity of trading the goods of the Archipelago for the mainland's bounty. It was a trifle unnerving to see armoured slaves carrying iron-bound chests behind Aldabreshin men on their way to repay some Relshazri merchant's generosity. Masters and slaves alike wore vivid jewels set in gold and silver around their necks and wrists in ostentatious token of the rewards of such trade.

One such Aldabreshin merchant paused to stare openly at Velindre, with her golden hair and pale, unpainted face. Her plain-cut lavender gown was certainly unlike the calculatedly seductive dresses of the decorated Archipelagan women. The magewoman ignored him, walking along the dock for a better view of the lean, predatory triremes tied up further around the sweep of the seawall. Dev had said it would be a fast trireme from the Chazen domain. Perhaps Mellitha could help her identify it discreetly.

A hand caught her arm just above the elbow. 'You would be Velindre,' a soft female voice said in fluent if strongly accented Tormalin.

Velindre found a thin-faced Aldabreshin girl half her age at her side, her head barely reaching the wizard's shoulder. She wore a plain straight dress of cotton as blue as her piercing eyes. Her straight black hair barely brushed her shoulders, unlike the flowing tresses of the other women on the quayside.

'I saw you, with Dev's warlord.' Velindre tried to free her arm but the girl was stronger than she looked. Her bony fingers held firm, unyielding.

'My name is Risala.' She retreated, pulling Velindre with her. 'Over there.' Now the girl was pushing her forward, towards a dark doorway.

'I don't think so.' Velindre stood firm, catching up a passing breeze to bolster her resistance. She saw that a crescent dagger had appeared in the girl's hand. 'You're threatening me? Have you any idea what I could do to you?'

'I'm protecting you,' the girl retorted. 'Or at least I'll try to, till both of us are cut to pieces. Work any magic on this wharf and there will be bloodshed. Do you know nothing about the Archipelago?'

'We're not in the Archipelago.' Velindre wrenched her arm free. 'This is Relshaz.'

'Do you think the Relshazri will deny themselves Aldabreshin gems and hardwoods and all the infinite craftsmanship of a myriad domains because some swordsman couldn't restrain his revulsion at seeing a wizard threatening our ships with sorcery?' asked Risala sarcastically. She looked warily around. 'Come. We need to talk before you join the ship.'

Velindre narrowed her eyes. 'We need to talk about whether or not I'm joining your ship.'

Risala opened her mouth on a question before changing her mind and urging Velindre towards the dark doorway once more.

The wizard yielded and curbed a rebellious impulse to flood the shadowy room with magelight as she entered. 'What is this place?' she asked instead.

Risala replaced her dagger in the sheath hanging beside a small purse on her plaited lizardskin belt. She fumbled for a spark-maker in the leather bag and lit the wick of a shallow cup-shaped lamp. The soft golden light revealed a cloth-covered table set with a fine Aldabreshin ewer and goblets in beaten bronze. 'Please, sit down.' She gestured towards a low stool before crossing the darkness to lock the door behind them. 'This is a warehouse belonging to an ally of my master. He knew it would be empty, so he is allowing us to use it.'

'Your master?' Velindre sat down warily. 'You're Chazen Kheda's slave?'

Risala's laugh surprised her. 'Slave? No, I'm a free islander and not even Chazen born.'

'But he's your master nevertheless?' Velindre looked around the blackness of the windowless, cavernous room. 'Calling yourself "free" sounds like making a distinction without a difference.'

Risala poured pale golden liquid from the ewer. 'I thought it was all agreed that you would join us.'

'I need to speak with Dev before I go aboard your ship.' Velindre sipped from her goblet to cover her hesitation. 'Things have turned out to be a little more complicated than I expected.' She wiped a drop of the sweet wine from the corner of her mouth.

'You do know how to defeat the dragon?' Risala demanded.

'Yes,' said Velindre slowly, 'but I need to know more before I agree to try, or even agree to share that knowledge. These are things I must discuss with Dev.'

'What things?' Risala held the ewer tightly between her hands.

'Mage concerns,' responded Velindre composedly. 'I have been trying to reach Dev but he seems unwilling or unable to respond to my spells.' She ignored an uneasy spasm in her belly at the latter notion. 'I don't suppose you want me to work the necessary magic here, so I shall return to my lodging and try again. You can wait here, I take it, for a day or so? I'll let you know where we go from here, both of us, as soon as I have an answer from Dev.' She drained her goblet to avoid looking at the Aldabreshin girl.

Risala topped up the magewoman's drink before she could refuse. 'You're going back on your word?'

'It is more complicated than you imagine.' Velindre found that her throat was dry in the dead, dusty air of the storehouse. That was peculiar – everyone knew Aldabreshin wine was too weak to intoxicate but she would have imagined it would quench a thirst.

'You do know how to defeat the dragon?' Risala repeated her question.

'I've discovered a great many things about dragons, which Dev almost certainly does not know.' Velindre stopped short before continuing, 'I need to discuss these matters with Dev before we can decide our best course of action.'

'I thought we were agreed on the only course of action that matters.' The girl set her own goblet down beside a twist of oiled silk and turned a silver and emerald ring around her finger. 'We must rid Chazen of the dragon.'

'That may be easier said than done—' Velindre broke off as a wave of dizziness swept over her. 'You don't understand . . .' Further words clogged in her throat, her tongue thick and awkward. Darkness rushed in from every side, closing around the little lamp's flame. Velindre stared at the golden point of light, her jaw slack. She didn't even feel the spittle sliding down her nerveless face as she fell sideways off the stool and the blackness claimed her. The last thing she heard was the treacherous Risala shouting something in incomprehensible Aldabreshin.

CHAPTER SIXTEEN

'It's coming.' Kheda watched the fire shrink in on itself in defiance of every natural pattern.

It narrowed and then doubled in height. The solid wall of flame advanced. Trees were silhouetted against it, lilla, tandra and ironwood. Their leaves and branches flared to ash, their blistered trunks vanishing in the scarlet blaze.

Dev glanced over his shoulder to see where they were retreating before returning his sickened gaze to the pursuing fire. 'It wants me dead,' he muttered. 'It looked me in the eye.'

Kheda flicked his gaze up to see the dragon sweeping this way and that across the sky, studying the forest ahead of its fiery barrier. 'While it's trying to kill you, it's not killing anyone else.' He sucked at a hand scratched by a stray tendril of thorny striol. 'All we need is to keep one step ahead of it until we know how to kill it.'

We cannot return to any residence, or risk any ship, if your very presence is going to bring down disaster on us. It may not be following your magic, barbarian, but it's still got your scent somehow. Seventeen days, we've managed to evade it so far. How much longer will we be able to, now it's started burning the forest that covers us?

'My lord!' A swordsman appeared at the edge of a gully cut deep into the forest floor. 'This way!'

The dragon's menacing bellow of challenge sounded overhead again. The wall of flame picked up speed, turning the forest to charcoal before their startled eyes. It roared towards them.

'Run!' Kheda shifted his swords in his sash and raced for the shelter of the gully. Dev followed hard on his heels.

The swordsman was scrambling over rocks of all sizes littered between earthen walls parched and crumbling under the long assault of the dry season. The river that had washed the broken stones down from the island's heights was barely a chain of mossy puddles lurking beneath feathery ferns, biding its time until the rains should swell it to foaming ferocity once again.

'This way, my lord.' The swordsman glanced over his shoulder. 'There's a cave and less tinder for the cursed beast to burn around us.'

Mindful of the shattered ground underfoot, Kheda couldn't resist looking up to see the wall of fire accelerating along the edge of the cleft so fast that it left the sturdier trees barely scorched. He shrank into the shadow of a mossy overhang as the dragon wheeled overhead, peering down. The wall of fire curled around a stand of ironwood trees. The circle contracted, flames rising higher and burning white hot. The ironwood trees burst into blinding flame.

Kheda turned his attention back to getting through the gully without breaking an ankle. Stumbling on a patch of loose shale, he grabbed Dev's shoulder to save himself. The wizard's tunic was dry and hot to the touch, while the warlord laboured under the chafing weight of a coarse cotton tunic sodden with sweat.

'Do you need another dose?' he hissed urgently, shaking the mage.

'No.' Dev plunged on, crushing pungent ferns underfoot.

'Here, my lord.' The swordsman disappeared into a dank cavern.

Kheda followed, forcing a rueful smile. 'That was a little too close for comfort.'

'Yes, my lord,' the swordsman replied obediently.

None of the other men pressed against the irregular walls of the cave said anything, mere shadows in the darkness, only their eyes shining as they looked at Kheda.

'Who's here?' The warlord paused for breath, chest heaving, as the men gave their names in muted tones. 'Where's Ridu?'

'Not back yet,' said a surly voice from the blacker recesses of the cave.

Is it better to challenge that or let it pass? Which would just make things worse?

He looked out of the cave entrance. 'We'll be safe here—'

Kheda's next words were lost as the scrubby bushes lining the opposite edge of the gully burst into flames, swaying with the violence of the dragon's passing. Kheda saw the flash of its pale golden underbelly as its roar of fury shook loose earth from the sides of the crumbling cleft. Dev stood motionless, eyes tight shut, face like carved stone.

The dragon's roar came again, more distant this time. No one moved or spoke. They waited in the musty darkness and listened to a third roar and a fourth.

Like listening for the thunderclap after the lightning flash in the rainy season, to find out how close the danger might be.

'Is everyone here but Ridu?' Kheda asked. He nodded at the ragged murmur of assent. 'Do we have anything to eat tonight? Have all the villages hereabouts been warned?'

'We've plenty of food,' one relieved voice assured him.

The next man sounded more dubious. 'We've told the islanders to hide themselves as best they can.'

'It hasn't flattened any more villages now that we've

given each spokesman a bag of jewels to cache somewhere obvious,' Kheda pointed out.

'A lot of the villagers are going down to the coast regardless.' The surly voice spoke again. 'And taking boats to other islands.'

Kheda's eyes were becoming accustomed to the gloom and he picked out a tall, lean man blowing on his hands as if to cool them. 'Zicre, isn't it?'

The man froze. 'Yes, my lord?' he said warily.

'If you're hurt, come into the light where I can take a look,' Kheda ordered. 'And where's my physic chest?'

The men in the cave shuffled themselves awkwardly to let Zicre through and Kheda's physic chest was passed to the fore.

'Do we have fresh water?' Kheda nodded as someone confirmed this. 'Then let's all have a drink. We may as well stay here till Ridu gets back. Take a rest while you can. Zicre, let's see those hands.'

Kheda moved closer to the edge of the cavern as the rest of the men made themselves as comfortable as possible with the ragged assortment of wraps and quilts they had dumped to one side. Zicre joined him and gingerly extended his fingers.

'What happened here?' Kheda saw that both hands were red and swollen and a raw burn ran along the outer edge of his sword hand, black grime crusted around the weeping edges.

'Change in the wind,' the man grunted. 'Too close to the fire.'

'Greenfoot oil will clean it and roseate starflower should help with the healing and keep it from festering.' Kheda knelt to open his physic coffer, silver bindings tarnished against the ebony.

'If you say so, my lord.' Zicre looked past him out into the gully, face expressionless. Like all the men he wore rough cotton clothes smudged with soot and sweat.

At least we all agreed that we didn't need the burden or noise of armour that wasn't going to save us in any case, if the dragon caught up with us.

Kheda stood up, tipping glutinous lotion from a small blue bottle on to a scrap of cotton waste. 'This is going to hurt,' he warned as he took the man's hand, holding it tight as he swabbed firmly. 'But the quicker I do it, the sooner it will be over.'

Zicre hissed and caught his breath. 'Thank you, my lord,' he said through gritted teeth.

Kheda turned Zicre's hand over as he continued with his ruthless cleansing. 'No real oar calluses. You hadn't been aboard the *Mist Dove* long. What did you do before that?'

'Huntsman, my lord,' said Zicre tightly, 'from the western slopes.'

'Here on Boal?' Kheda looked up at him as he returned the blue bottle to the chest. 'On the far side of these mountains?'

Zicre nodded, bracing himself for the touch of the ointment Kheda was uncorking.

'When all this is over, you must show me your forests.' Kheda coated the burn thickly with grey salve flecked with pinkish fragments. 'We'll hunt together.'

'If we haven't been hunted down first,' Zicre said incautiously. He ducked his head and studied the burn, clenching and unclenching his fist.

The low murmur of conversation deeper in the cave halted abruptly.

'We've kept ahead of it so far,' Kheda said calmly as he replaced the ointment in the physic chest. 'It's a more dangerous beast than anything else in these forests, I'll grant you. Personally, I'd rather be tracked by some rogue jungle cat with a taste for villagers or pursued by a water ox crazed with foaming madness, but it's still just a beast and we are men. We have our wits and this is the second largest island in the domain, so we have league upon league of forest to hide in. It may be hunting us, but we're not hook-toothed hogs to blunder off a cliff in terror or spotted deer to just lie down and die of heat prostration.'

'But why is it hunting us?' Zicre burst out.

Kheda checked to be sure the lacquered wooden box with the cracked and smudged wax seal was safe before he closed the physic chest. 'We were all on the *Mist Dove*,' he said carefully.

'Why did it attack the *Mist Dove*?' demanded someone hidden in the cave. Emboldened, a murmur of assent rose to be lost in the hollow space.

You're the warlord. They look to you for answers. You can't give them the truth, so are you going to dishonour them by giving them lies?

'That was the ship that led the fleet.' Kheda shoved his physic chest backwards and used it as a low stool. He looked into the darkness, meeting the unseen challenge squarely. 'The beast may even have realised that I was aboard. Zicre, you have loals in these forests, don't you?'

'Yes.' The erstwhile hunter was taken unawares by the question. 'Black-cloaked ones.'

'Have you ever seen what happens when one gang decides to take over another gang's stretch of forest?' Kheda asked.

'Not seen it so much as heard it,' Zicre said slowly, 'and found the big males from the gang under attack beaten to bloody pulp and half-eaten.'

'Loals know to concentrate on killing the strongest leaders among their rivals.' Kheda shrugged. 'I think that cursed beast is at least as clever as a loal.'

'Loals can't curse us with magic,' muttered a sullen voice in the darkness.

'You all survived attack by men with magic last year,' Kheda shot back. 'You wouldn't be here if you hadn't. I don't call that cursed, to live when so many died. I don't see any curse on Chazen, not with the best pearl harvest in living memory coming out of the sea. We've all survived worse than this dragon.'

'But what are we going to do, my lord?' asked someone desperately. 'Just let it chase us till it's burned every tree on the island?'

'If that's what we must do, to keep it from flying off to burn and devour our homes and families,' Kheda said harshly. The undercurrent of response in the cave took on a surprised note. 'And while it's chasing its tail pursuing us, our other ships and warriors are hunting down the last of the invaders,' he reminded the mutinous darkness.

And when will they kill whoever has summoned this beast to plague us, tell me that?

'I read you the last dispatches from the *Gossamer Shark*. The remaining invaders are scattered on the barren islets beyond Corui now. We'll soon rid Chazen of those vermin. Then, as soon as we find out the barbarians' trick of killing dragons, we'll be rid of that bane as well, won't we? The *Green Turtle* should bc back sometime around the breaking of the rains. We just have to keep one step ahead of the beast till then.' He grinned. 'And it won't find these forests so easy to burn when the real storms start, will it?'

The assent from the darkness was more dutiful than convinced.

'Water, my lord?' A swordsman stepped out of the shadows offering Kheda a battered wooden cup. He shot a look of covert contempt at Dev. The wizard was lying on the bare earth just inside the cavern entrance, eyes closed, apparently asleep.

'Thank you.' Kheda took the cup and drank gratefully.

'Zicre, can you find somewhere to keep watch for Ridu? I don't imagine you'll be able to sleep with that burn. If the rest of us get our heads down we can move on tonight.' The warlord closed his eyes and leaned back against the water-sculpted wall of the cave. He wasn't that tired but it seemed wisest to put an end to this dangerous conversation.

You can take your dissenting notions out of here with you, Zicre, and keep them to yourself. To think I wanted Chazen people to learn to speak their minds to me. As my father said, Be careful what you wish for, lest you get it.

Weariness of mind and body surprised Kheda as the urgency that had kept him on his feet since dawn and through all the long days evading the dragon's pursuit retreated.

Where is Ridu? Is he going to have any news from Itrac? Has she had any news from Risala? What will this mage-woman of Dev's do whenever she gets here, when she finds out what I've done to him? Will she just vanish in a puff of smoke and take whatever knowledge she might have along with her?

A hand shaking his shoulder startled Kheda awake. 'What is it?' he demanded.

I never meant to sleep. Oh well, no harm done.

'It's Ridu, my lord.' It was Zicre, speaking quietly.

'I'll see him outside.' Kheda rubbed a hand over his beard and glanced at the men dozing further back in the cave. 'No need to disturb everyone.'

He stepped over Dev, who didn't appear to have moved since he'd lain down. Ridu was waiting out in the gully, enjoying the shallow breeze funnelled by the earthen walls. Kheda realised that the worst of the day's heat had passed, not that there would be much evening cool this close to the coming of the rains.

'My lord.' The youthful swordsman looked younger than ever stripped of his armour. He held out a small wooden box. 'The *Yellow Serpent* was at the rendezvous. It brought dispatches.'

'Excellent news.' Kheda breathed a sigh of relief and took the box, sinking down on to a convenient boulder. 'Sit. Zicre, get him some water, please.' He cracked the seal on the box and opened it to find several pages of individually folded and sealed reed paper inside. 'My lady Itrac's taking every precaution, I see.' He looked over at Ridu. 'Are there any stray ships creeping around Chazen waters?'

Ridu shook his head as he drank thirstily, spilling water down his grimy tunic. 'No, my lord,' he gasped. 'Everyone's terrified of the dragon.'

Kheda looked at the youth thoughtfully for a moment before cracking the seal on Itrac's note and scanning the contents. 'All seems well enough on Esabir,' he mused.

Apart from the fact that we've nearly emptied the treasury of gems to save the palm huts and saller granaries of Boal's threadbare hill villages. And we won't be replacing such wealth any time soon, with not so much as a single trading galley venturing into Chazen waters since Janne Daish went home. Is that her doing? Would she need to do anything, with a dragon overflying our sea lanes? At least there's no other cause for alarm in Itrac's news.

Kheda refolded the paper and took out a second missive. His heartbeat accelerated as he recognised Risala's writing on the outside. He tugged at the cord around his neck and pulled the emerald and silver ring that was the key to Shek Kul's cipher out from beneath his tunic. It was the work of a moment to make sense of the few brief lines of flowing script. He looked up at Ridu with a smile before calling across the gully. 'Zicre, there's something of an end in view. Risala, the poet I sent as my envoy to the north, she's on her way back. She left at the crossing of the moons.'

Is that any kind of sign? Where were the stars and heavenly jewels when the last fading arc of the Greater Moon was matching the first renascent arc of the Lesser?

He looked up at the blue sky bleaching towards early evening, soiled with the dust of the dry season hanging heavy in the air. It took a distinct effort to picture the arcs of the unseen night sky.

Both moons are talisman against dragons, presumably because, as we now know, the beasts scorn both pearls and opals. I wonder if this magewoman of Dev's will know why. So it must be a good sign that the Greater Moon was in the arc of life, along with the Mirror Bird that turns aside magic. The Lesser Moon rode in the arc of duty alongside the Horned Fish, another sign of renewal.

Was there anything significant opposite either moon, where the ancient sages said the dragon's tail trailed? Opposite the Lesser, we had the Amethyst that warns against arrogance and the Canthira Tree that's reborn through fire in the arc of foes. As it happens, that's beside the arc of life. So with the Diamond beside the Pearl in the arc of children, along with the Net that offers support for us now and in the future opposite the Greater Moon, we have positive omens in twin opposition across the compass.

And the Ruby that's talisman against fire was shining among the stars of the Spear in the arc of death.

'The compass of the heavens when she set out must surely presage the dragon's fate coming from the north.' He looked from Zicre to Ridu and back again with a broad smile, though he found it strangely difficult to summon up excitement over such signs. The thought of seeing Risala again was enough to drive everything else out of his mind.

That's what's really putting the smile on your face.

He looked down at the paper again, reluctant to put away even this insubstantial contact with her.

There must be some way we can escape everyone else's eyes and find a little peace in each other's arms. I'm doing my duty by Itrac, aren't I?

'My lord.' Ridu cleared his throat. 'May I speak freely?'

'About what?' Kheda looked up sharply. 'I mean, yes, but we'll have some privacy, Zicre.' He shot a stern glance at the erstwhile hunter.

'I'll keep watch over there.' The lean man shrugged and took himself off down the gully.

Kheda looked at Ridu. 'What is it?'

'I stopped in the villages for food, as you instructed.' The young warrior gripped his sword hilts so hard his knuckles whitened. He stared down at the ground. 'I heard talk.'

'Go on.' Kheda forced himself to speak calmly. 'Talk about what?'

'About the dragon.' Ridu looked up, face muddy with apprehension. 'About why it's hunting us in the hills like this. Every village spokesman is asking his seer and any travelling augur if there are any signs to explain it.'

'And what do these fortune-tellers say?' Kheda kept his face pleasantly interested.

Ridu swallowed and glanced towards the cave entrance. 'They are wondering – just wondering, my lord,' he qualified hastily, 'if the beast is hunting your barbarian.'

Kheda froze with shock. 'Why would it be doing that?' Blood pulsed in his throat.

Ridu looked at Dev with naked suspicion. 'It started out hunting down the wild men. They weren't wizards but they came with them, tainted by their magic. Barbarians live surrounded by magic. They think nothing of it.'

Kheda tried to work out if Zicre was close enough to hear this. 'Dev's lived in the Archipelago for more than half his life,' he lied steadily. 'He's not been hunted by a dragon before.' He regretted those words as soon as they left his mouth.

'There hasn't been a dragon to hunt him before,' Ridu retorted.

Undeniably true.

Kheda pursed his lips. 'I would need some more definite sign before I wanted to believe such a thing.'

'The dragon never comes after any of us who go to find food or to carry dispatches,' Ridu pointed out with growing boldness. 'Would it be a sign if we sent Dev off alone and waited to see if the beast followed him?'

'I'll bear it in mind.' Kheda realised he had crushed Risala's letter in his hand. 'But I won't do any such thing until we've found out what lore the *Green Turtle*'s brought back from the north.'

'A lot of the soothsayers are seeing no very hopeful signs that barbarian lore can help us.' Ridu looked at him, honest doubt in his eyes.

'We'll have to wait and see.' A noise in the scorched trees above the gully made Kheda look up. 'Zicre, what's that?'

'Loals.' The former huntsman came back down the gully. 'I suppose that could be a sign of sorts, my lord.'

Kheda decided to ignore the insolence and watched the black-furred creatures picking their way along the edge of the gully, chittering with what sounded like displeasure at the ash stirred up by their steps. At this distance, when they stood upright to see their path more clearly, the animals looked oddly human, only betrayed by their strange rocking gait. The group paused some distance downwind above one of the larger pools left by the subdued river.

The biggest loal looked suspiciously at the three motionless men and barked a challenge, lips curling back to better display its impressively pointed eyeteeth. Its dark eyes were whiteless, shining points of light above its long, black-furred muzzle. It sprang down into the gully, poised on all fours, long tail lashing as it sniffed the air and barked again.

'Are they always this bold?' Kheda asked quietly.

'One that size is entitled to be bold, my lord,' Zicre replied with a grin, tension momentarily leaving his lean face. 'He could rip your arm off and club you senseless with it.'

'Let's allow him and his family their evening drink, then,' said Kheda dryly. 'You go and get something to eat. I'll be a moment or so.'

The biggest loal watched warily as the two men picked their way carefully over to the cave. Sniffing the air again, it sneezed, scrubbing at its muzzle with its strangely human hands. Evidently deciding that Kheda was no immediate threat, it turned to chitter up to the rest of the group who climbed cautiously down into the gully. The half-grown infants released their grip on their mothers' fur to drop down and lap at the puddles. Kheda watched with amusement as the first ones to quench their thirst began flicking mud at each other while the adults turned to foraging under stones for grubs and worms.

They all froze with barks of alarm and Kheda jumped. Then he realised that all the loals were looking at Dev who had got up from his uncomfortable bed across the cave entrance. He glanced incuriously at the creatures and walked over to join Kheda on his boulder.

'So you're going to throw me to the dragon if Velindre doesn't come up with the goods?' he asked with something of his old combativeness.

'What else was I supposed to say?' Kheda hissed. 'I won't let it come to that. I owe you better and you know it.'

'I'm not sure I'd mind if it did catch up with me.' Dev

hung his head, hands dangling loose between his knees. 'I sure as curses don't want to live like this much longer.'

'You put it behind you before,' Kheda began cautiously.

'Last time you gave me half a pinch of that cursed powder in a bottle of wine and that stifled my wizardry for a day or so,' spat Dev furiously. 'It feels as if you've poisoned every mageborn instinct in me this time. You might as well have cut off my stones and made a real *zamorin* of me.'

'It's keeping you alive,' countered Kheda resolutely.

'I'm starting to think I'd rather be dead,' Dev muttered with passion. 'You've no idea what this is like.'

I had no idea it would make you this vulnerable and wretched.

'No,' Kheda agreed with reluctant pity. 'I'm still sorry for it, though I'd do it again—'

'So the dragon couldn't eat your handy decoy.' Dev's face twisted with bitterness.

'I wanted to save your life. I didn't know it would still be able to follow you. At least it has no more than a vague idea where you are now.' Kheda went to unfold Risala's letter. 'You just have to keep taking the drug until Velindre gets here. It shouldn't be too much longer—'

'What happens then?' Dev sat upright, horror on his drawn, dirty face. 'What happens when the dragon gets a sniff of Velindre's power?'

'I don't know.' Kheda looked to make sure there were no curious faces at the cave mouth.

But she'll surely be a far more tempting morsel than Dev in this sorry state.

'I won't be able to do a thing to save her.' Dev stared at him, distraught.

'Risala says she has the secrets we need.' Kheda raised the crumpled paper slowly. 'Won't she be able to save herself?'

Won't she be able to save both of them, and the boat they're on and all its crew? What will the domain make of the dragon destroying the vessel I've been telling everyone all our hopes are riding in?

'My lord.' Ridu appeared at the mouth of the cave, cold baked fish wrapped in lilla leaves in his hands. 'You must eat, both of you.'

Kheda nodded and got to his feet. 'You have to try, Dev,' he insisted in an undertone.

'I don't see much point,' muttered the mage miserably. 'I probably won't keep it down.'

'There must be crush-root growing somewhere.' Kheda looked at Dev with growing concern. 'That could help.'

He caught Dev's arm as the wizard stumbled over a rock. The sharp sound startled the loals. The whole group fled in moments, leaving nothing behind but damp overturned rocks and the echo of their shrill cries.

What kind of a sign might that be? I don't know and I'm starting to think I don't really care.

He took more of the wizard's weight on his arm and they made their way to the darkness of the cave.

CHAPTER SEVENTEEN

The harsh Aldabreshin tongue was the first thing Velindre heard as her senses returned. Slowly she realised that the darkness was no longer complete. There was light beyond her eyelids. She was lying somewhere, on her side. There was something soft beneath her but no coverlet.

Velindre tried to open her eyes but found her lashes sticky and crusted. She tried to raise a hand to rub at then but her movements were clumsy and awkward. She rolled on to her back but any further movement was beyond her. The air was stale and stifling, unexpected heat oppressive.

Someone caught her hand and placed it carefully on her midriff. 'All right, don't fret.' She felt a hand on her neck, checking her heartbeat.

She recognised that voice. It was the girl who had drugged her. Velindre tried to twist away but her body wouldn't obey her.

'Lie still,' soothed the girl.

Risala, that was her name, Velindre remembered. Further recollection fled at the shock of a cool, damp cloth on her forehead. The magewoman could do nothing but submit as her eyes were gently cleansed. She lay rigid with growing anger as memory returned. She had been here for some unfathomable length of time. She recalled struggling to wake, time and again, tormented by thirst. The water she had been given to drink had thrust her back into the abyss of unconsciousness.

'There you are,' concluded Risala with satisfaction.

Velindre blinked and squinted, her blurred vision clearing to reveal that she was lying in a cramped, windowless room. Bright sunlight edging through a narrow door fell on the wooden walls and floor. She did her best to scowl at Risala, who was kneeling beside her.

'What did you do to me?' Her accusation was a harsh whisper. Her mouth was dry and foul.

'I'm sorry.' Risala's apology was perfunctory. 'We couldn't afford any more delay – still less risk you refusing to come at all. Not when we knew you had the lore we need.' She slipped an arm behind Velindre's shoulders to raise her up, bringing a wooden cup to her lips.

Velindre found some strength returning to her nerveless arms but not enough to resist. Not enough to slap this bitch's face. She resolved to bide her time and sipped at the liquid in the cup. Citrus juice cut through the staleness in her mouth and she licked at her rough, dry lips. 'So you enslaved me?' She would have said more but a fit of coughing seized her, leaving a burning ache in her chest.

'Not exactly.' That seemed to amuse the girl, to Velindre's impotent fury. Risala tugged at a cushion to prop the magewoman's head up and sat back on her heels. 'Don't worry. The soporific will soon wear off.'

Velindre looked down towards her feet, wondering when she would be able to move. Then she would be gone from here as soon as she could find some breath of air to work with. She looked at her legs, distracted by the realisation that she was now dressed like her captor. Both of them wore loose trousers of undyed cotton reaching to mid-shin and sleeveless tunics in faded red. Velindre's skin was startlingly pale compared to the Aldabreshin girl's rich brown complexion.

Her thoughts wandered. She'd never worn anything red, not since she'd been a child. Her parents had dressed her in neutral colours until their acute observation might determine the nature of any inborn affinity she might possess.

She dismissed the irrelevance angrily. She must still be half-stupefied. No matter. She'd be gone from this inadequate prison just as soon as she could gather her wits and her strength. Her stomach gurgled noisily. 'I'm hungry,' she said with as much dignity as she could muster. 'Am I to be starved as well as enslaved?'

Risala smiled with that infuriating amusement again. 'I'll get you some food.' She disappeared through the open door.

Velindre looked after her, trying to make sense of the noises beyond. With a jolt that was half-surprise and half-fear, she identified the slap of water against a ship's hull and the creak of oars and ropes. A pipe was sounding out a regular rhythm somewhere in the pattern of light and shade beyond the door and she could half-hear, half-feel the rush of the sea running beneath the wooden floor of her prison. Idle conversation floated over the boards above her head.

With a further shiver she realised that she had no way of knowing what was being said. She might be fluent in every tongue spoken from the polite debates of Toremal's enlightenment to the haphazard archives of Solura's robust feudalism, but that would do her little good here. She'd never had cause to learn anything of Aldabreshin languages or dialects. These uncouth barbarians had never produced any scholarship worth noting. Nor would they, as long as they persisted in their superstitious fear of magic. That superstitious fear would be the death of her, if she didn't get away.

Velindre realised that more than disquiet was coursing through her. With an unpleasant crawling sensation, warmth was replacing the numbness in her legs. Bracing her hands against the flower-embroidered quilt beneath her, she managed to sit upright against the planking. She froze at the abrupt realisation of another violation, far worse than the loss of her clothes: her hair had been cropped so short it barely covered the nape of her neck. She ran a shaking hand over her head, unbidden tears starting to her eyes.

Risala reappeared in the doorway, a covered bowl in her hands. 'Weep if you want to,' she invited with sympathy. 'It's the soporific. It distresses some people.'

'I'm not distressed, I'm angry,' Velindre said with shaky accusation. 'You cut my hair.'

'I did,' the Aldabreshin girl admitted with more genuine remorse than she'd shown thus far. 'I've kept it for you. I'm sorry, but it had to be done.'

'Why?' snapped Velindre, scrubbing the tears clumsily from her cheeks.

'Eat this, slowly.' Risala knelt to place the bowl between Velindre's hands. Once she was satisfied that the wizard woman had secure hold of it, she lifted the lid. 'I'll explain what I can.'

The bowl was warm between Velindre's hands and against her cotton-clad thighs. A savoury scent rose and her stomach growled again. Swollen golden grain was sinking slowly in a clear broth along with chunks of pale fish. Resentful, she picked up the long, shallow spoon of unadorned silver and began to eat. The sooner she regained her strength, the sooner she would be gone.

'I'm sorry we had to take you like this.' Satisfied with the magewoman's apparent compliance, Risala sat on a folded quilt by the door. 'But the lives of hundreds depend on the lore that you promised, and much more besides. We must be rid of this dragon.'

The concoction in the bowl was delicious. Velindre forced herself to pause in her eating. 'What has any of that to do with cutting my hair?' she asked coldly.

Risala considered her for a moment, blue eyes opaque. 'You do know what happens to those who use magic in the Archipelago?'

'Yes,' said Velindre curtly, shoving the spoon viciously into the delicately poached fish and aromatic grain.

'Then you appreciate the necessity for some disguise.' Sarcasm coloured Risala's tone. 'We've a long way to travel and there are plenty of domains who've suffered at barbarian hands. More than one warlord prefers killing any unexplained traveller with pale skin or yellow hair over risking further theft or insult. Travelling openly as a northern barbarian would draw every curious eye towards you, never mind risking inevitable suspicion that you might be a mage.'

'And you have the gall to call us barbarians,' Velindre muttered, returning to her food. 'So what's my part in this masquerade? Slave?'

'Yes, for the moment. To be safe under Chazen Kheda's protection, you'll have to play the part of a slave. Forgive us, but it's the only way someone so obviously barbarian–' Risala corrected herself '–someone born in the unbroken lands would ever come to the far southern reaches of the Archipelago.'

'You want my help but you dress me in rags and crop my head like a criminal?' Velindre scraped crossly at the last few spoonfuls of broth.

'There's more to it than that.' Risala sounded sufficiently awkward to make Velindre look up.

'Slave or free, you'll still be turning every head,' Risala said frankly. 'The best way to quell that curiosity is to make it known that you're a eunuch—'

'What?' Velindre was dumbfounded.

'Hear me out.' Risala leaned forward to retrieve the bowl that was threatening to roll from Velindre's lap. 'It must be an omen in our favour that you've the build and colouring to make it believable—'

'That I'm some mutilated man?' Velindre was still too astonished to be angry.

'That you're *zamorin* who was made so in early youth.' Risala set the cover back on the bowl and leaned against the wall. 'If a little boy, and I mean one barely walking, is taken to be made *zamorin*, he's bathed in hot water and the seeds of his manhood are squeezed each day until they disappear—'

'I don't want to know this,' Velindre protested, appalled.

'You need to know, if you're to be believed.' Risala overrode her. 'A eunuch, *zamorin* in our tongue, who has been made in that way keeps a smooth skin, grows tall for the most part and, if he has barbarian blood to begin with, will often stay fair-haired and fair-skinned. You'll be entirely believable as such a *zamorin*, as long as you dress in loose tunics,' she added apologetically.

Velindre couldn't help but glance down at her modest bosom, barely showing through the folds of cotton as it was. She had lost still more weight in her drugged sleep on this voyage. 'You'll make me out to be one kind of freak, to stop people thinking I'm some other more dangerous oddity. That makes some kind of sense.' She scowled. 'Was this Dev's idea?'

'Dev knows nothing of this,' Risala interrupted. 'It doesn't concern him. My concern is to get you to Chazen waters undetected and this is the best way to achieve that. You'll have far more privacy if people think you're *zamorin* than you could in any other guise. *Zamorin* made as little children are actually quite uncommon; it's hardly something to do lightly, to cut such a young boy off from his chance of fathering children.'

'An unfortunate turn of phrase,' commented Velindre coldly.

Risala studied her for a moment before going on. 'Most *zamorin* are made as grown men, at best, after thorough consideration and with good reason. At worst, yes, there are domains more interested in the profit to be gained from trading in such slaves than in the violence they do to their captives and their futures. Depending on how it is done, yes, some *zamorin* are cruelly mutilated. So all *zamorin* are given a good deal of privacy for bathing and suchlike. You'll have to do something remarkably stupid to be discovered. Do you think you can manage to avoid that?' Her tone was unexpectedly cutting.

'What do I have to do, to play a slave?' Velindre's eyes narrowed. 'Fetch and carry and keep my mouth shut? I think I can manage that. And you can hardly have me stripped and whipped without revealing our secret,' she concluded with bitter satisfaction.

'Dev has been telling us you're very clever. Perhaps, but you're as ignorant as any other barbarian.' Risala drew up her knees and laced her hands around them. 'Let me guess: you're convinced that all Aldabreshi live lives of indulgent ease, their cruel feet stamping on the necks of downtrodden captives who are worked to death burdened with chains?'

'I've seen the slave market in Relshaz,' Velindre countered frostily. 'Every unfortunate who ends up there can expect shackles and manacles, not to mention the lash if they so much as look sideways at the wrong person.'

Risala shrugged. 'It's no business of ours what you mainlanders do with people whose fortunes in life bring them to such a pass.'

'You prey on such unfortunates readily enough,' retorted Velindre.

'What do you mainlanders do with those destitute or desperate enough to give themselves over to theft or violence to keep themselves alive?' Risala countered. 'You flog them or hang them or leave them to die like dogs in the gutters. No one need fear such a fate in the

Archipelago, slave or free. Besides, what has a slave to complain of, when his own choices have led to his ruin, if a warlord or his lady is prepared to take up the burden of guiding his life toward a better future?'

'What is there to complain of?' Velindre stared at the girl. 'In slavery?'

'You've never seen life beyond your own waters.' Risala cut her off with a sharp gesture. You need to hide your ignorance if you're to play your part well enough for us both to stay safe.' She rose to her feet. 'Keep your mainlander opinions to yourself or we'll both be at risk.'

Velindre looked up, uncomprehending, as the ship lurched and voices rose on the deck above. Feet ran, slapping unshod on the planks. There was a splash and the vessel was brought up with a jerk as an anchor bit into the sea bed. Cheerful approval rang through a sudden tumult of voices in the main body of the ship.

'You also need to learn some skill in our language. We can't use Tormalin much further south than these waters.' Risala stood, one hand on the half-open door. 'We'll keep you away from other people as far as possible but we don't want you giving yourself away every time you open your mouth.'

'I'll do my best,' said Velindre sarcastically.

'Let's go ashore and see what you make of our brutal licentiousness.' Risala smiled with that irritating amusement.

'Ashore?' Velindre was taken aback, but only for a moment. 'Very well.' She got gingerly to her feet.

'How do you feel?' Risala held out a supporting hand.

Velindre brushed it aside. 'Light-headed,' she admitted cautiously. 'Fresh air should help.'

The only question in her mind was where she should flee to. Back to Relshaz or to Hadrumal? Either way she would be provided with the means to bespeak Dev before the day was out. He could go whistling for any lore on dragons until he apologised on bended knee for dragging her into this insanity.

The magewoman followed Risala through the narrow door to find herself on an equally narrow gangway running between tiered ranks of rowers. They all looked back at her with frank curiosity, sitting in the shade of the trireme's side decks. Velindre looked up at the strip of brilliant blue splitting the uppermost level.

'Up you go.' Risala urged her towards a broad-runged ladder.

Her desire for the touch of the breeze was more than hunger, more than thirst. Velindre climbed as fast as she could, her knees still weak, her hands clumsy as she pulled herself upwards.

Risala followed close behind her. 'This is the Kaasik domain. We're just over half a cycle of the Greater Moon south of Relshaz.'

Velindre ignored the barbarian girl. She ignored the bearded Archipelagans on the cramped stern platform of the trireme. Best to return to Relshaz, she decided, and seek advice as well as some decent clothing from Mellitha. She reached for the breeze toying with an ochre pennant flying from the arching stern post.

There was nothing there. She could see the wafting silk and hear its faint rustle and snap, but she couldn't sense the air that stirred it. Velindre looked at her hands in disbelief. The breeze drifted across her open palms. She felt it but couldn't take hold of it. Gooseflesh prickled on her bare arms despite the heat of the sun. She seized Risala by the shoulders, shaking her viciously. 'What have you done to me?'

Wincing as Velindre's fingers dug into her, Risala looked past the furious magewoman to one of the mariners, her few words quelling. Then she looked Velindre in the eye, blue gaze emotionless. 'We did what had to be done. We cannot risk any inadvertent display of your skills. And I didn't imagine you'd stay long if you were able to leave.'

'What have you done?' Velindre's voice cracked with fear and fury.

Risala looked over the wizard's shoulder again, insisting on something in brisk Aldabreshin before returning her gaze to Velindre. 'It is a different kind of soporific.'

Velindre gripped the skinny girl so hard her own hands ached. 'As soon as I can work the slightest magic, I'll be gone. You can all be cursed to whatever fate awaits you, along with your dragon.'

'You'll be in Chazen waters before that happens.' Risala spoke through gritted teeth, her eyes creased with pain. 'You can talk to Dev. If he can't convince you to stay, we won't stand in your way.'

'I'll be long gone before that.' Velindre declared, but the girl's self-assurance was making her uneasy.

'The mage soporific is in all the water aboard this ship,' Risala said bluntly. 'Refuse to drink and you'll be insensible before you recover your spells. Then I'll just pour the draught down your throat like I've been doing so far.'

One of the mariners behind Velindre said something loud and threatening. She glanced over her shoulder to see the man brandishing a naked dagger back and forth. His dark face was stern and unfriendly. The other two men had their hands on their own dagger hilts.

Reluctantly, she let Risala go. 'You seem to have covered all the angles on this game board.'

Risala's laugh surprised Velindre and the three Aldabreshin mariners. 'I didn't think you played the stones game on the mainland.'

Velindre shook her head. 'I was thinking of a game called White Raven.'

Risala looked at her, uncomprehending, before shrugging. 'No matter. We'll have plenty of time to discuss such things. Let's go ashore. The sooner you learn even a little about our ways, the safer we'll all be.' As she spoke, she unbuckled the lizardskin belt from around her waist and Velindre realised that the girl had been wearing two daggers all along. She slid one off, sheath and all, and offered it to Velindre.

'So your eunuchs aren't entirely emasculated.' The wizard woman frowned as she took it. 'What's to stop me sticking this between your ribs the first time your back's turned?'

'Anyone who finds me dead will kill you in the next breath.' Risala said something to the three men, who all laughed. The foremost waved his dagger at Velindre one last time before sheathing it solidly.

Feeling chilled once more, Velindre followed Risala to the stern of the ship, unbuckling her own belt to thread the plain black leather through the dagger's sheath. She saw a long ladder hanging down to the water. A piercing whistle beside her made her jump. The bearded Aldabreshin chuckled and pointed to a youth sculling a small flat boat towards them with a single oar over the stern.

'He'll take us ashore,' Risala explained.

Velindre's hand went instinctively to her belt. 'Where's my purse?'

'Safe.' Risala was unperturbed. 'It's no use to you here.'

The youth caught hold of the lower end of the ladder and Risala swung her legs over the slope of the stern timbers, climbing rapidly down.

Velindre followed more carefully. The dagger at her belt was hard and inflexible, digging into her thigh. The sensations of wearing trousers were unfamiliar and unwelcome. Worse than anything else was the motionless emptiness all around her. She was cut off from the most basic, instinctive sense of the elements that had been with her for so long she had come to take it for granted. It was worse than being blind or deafened. Nausea rose in her throat.

She landed in the boat with trembling legs and sat down hurriedly. 'So what—'

Risala cut her off with a merciless smile. 'When we're ashore.'

Velindre realised the lad at the single stern oar was watching her, dark eyes bright and curious. She caught his gaze and held it, summoning all the disdain she felt for this place and its deceits. Her bruised spirits rose fractionally when he looked away, unease replacing his cockiness.

The shallows were crowded with a bewildering array of small boats, scurrying to and from the larger ships at anchor out in the deeper water. Velindre searched for any more familiar-looking vessel among the sleek triremes and the fat-bellied galleys with their square-rigged sails furled in hanging swags. There was none that she could see. She concentrated on keeping her growing wretchedness at bay until they reached the shelving golden beach and stepped into the ankle-deep surf.

Risala exchanged a few words with the youth.

'What does he get out of ferrying us?' Velindre desperately sought distraction from the realisation that the earth was inert beneath her feet as the two of them walked up the sand.

'The satisfaction of having done a good turn to a Chazen fast trireme. The shipmaster won't forget his face, if the lad comes looking to take an oar out of these waters sometime in the future.' Risala ticked off points on her fingers. 'And he's proving to whomever Kaasik Rai has presiding over this trading beach that he's reliable and trustworthy. If he keeps his wits about him, he should be able to make a few trades of his own.'

'Trading what?' Velindre demanded. 'You want me to learn. Teach me,' she snapped.

'His services.' Risala paused to survey the scrubby fever trees that separated the beach from the dry and dusty clearing beyond. 'And whatever his fortunes bring him by way of gifts from people like us.'

Velindre made a derisory noise. 'What gifts could you offer him?'

'You'd be surprised.' Risala reached inside her faded, saggy tunic and produced a small, soft leather bag. Untying the drawstring, she tipped it to let a few glistening pearls roll to the lip of the leather. Each was as large as a woman's smallest fingernail.

Velindre blinked. 'What are these worth hereabouts?'

'Whatever someone is willing to trade for them.' Risala secured the pearls inside the bag once again. 'We don't reduce everything to some nonsensical number of stamped bits of adulterated metal. Make sure you remember that,' she warned. 'Life in the Archipelago is a balance of co-operation and obligation. Every man in a village plays his part in building his neighbour's new hut so that he'll have help when he needs it. One woman will watch another's children so that woman can weave cloth for both of them. Fishermen trade crabs for a share in a villager's vegetable plot.'

'And the ties of obligation bind everyone more securely to their place and station of birth than chains around their ankles,' Velindre murmured under her breath.

The earth was no more than dry dirt beneath her feet. The sea was barely ten strides away but it might as well have been ten leagues. She could feel the sun's heat on her skin, the brush of the breeze, but that wasn't the elemental consciousness that united her with the whole of the natural realm. She was hemmed in by mere physical sensation. She felt sick again, weak and abject.

Fighting a rising urge to fall to her knees and weep, determined not to give this chit of a girl such satisfaction, Velindre looked along the line of twisted trees. Solitary traders she would call no more than pedlars sat in the shade of the fringed, red-tipped leaves. 'What are we looking for?' she asked tightly.

'This and that.' Risala led the way along the shore, surveying base-metal plates and spoons on offer beside bracelets and necklaces of polished shell, next to small boxes of intricately carved wood. Beyond the pedlars, more prosperous groups of merchants were distinguished by family resemblance or some common motif on tunic or sleeveless overmantle. Silver and brassware were displayed on carpets spread on the ground. There were bowls and ewers and jugs, plain or chased with florid designs of plants and animals. Some were ornamented with fine enamels or coloured stones. One family had claimed a long stretch of beach, erecting several awnings to protect bolts of fine cloth from the bleaching sun. Some of the soft pastel muslins were plain, some printed with bold designs. Others had smaller, more convoluted patterns in vivid dyes.

'Ikadi traders,' murmured Risala.

'How do you know?' Velindre wondered.

'Their daggers.' Risala tapped the hilt of her own weapon. 'Every domain has its own design. We're wearing those of Chazen.' She smiled with discreet amusement. 'Archipelagans don't feign like barbarians. Everyone can see everyone else's origin, their rank and status.'

The cloth traders' grey-haired, grey-bearded patriarch sat on a brilliantly coloured carpet surrounded by rolls of vivid silk. He was intent on a conversation with an elderly woman in a loose red gown with frolicking green birds embroidered around the hem. Nodding with satisfaction, the grey-haired woman bustled off towards a cookfire set beneath the spreading shade of a tall, warty-barked tree. As she gestured, several little girls began ladling rich meaty stew into bowls. A woman plainly mother to the children and daughter to the grey-haired cook was deftly slapping unleavened breads on to a searing griddle. The merchant and several of his sons came over and sat in a circle as the little girls handed out the bowls. Tearing scraps from the flatbread to scoop up his stew, the grey-beard nodded and chewed as the younger woman spread her arms to indicate the lengths of cloth she required. The little girls eyed the brighter muslins eagerly.

'You must use coin when merchants from Relshaz or Caladhria come south to trade.' Velindre tried to keep her desperation out of her voice. There would surely be someone she could pay for passage back to safer waters, if she could find out where this thief had stashed her purse. No, she need only get far enough away for whatever poison the traitorous bitch had given her to fade from her blood. She summoned up all the anger she could to overwhelm the sick fear lurking at the edge of thought.

Still searching the assorted traders, Risala shook her head absently. 'Only warlords who trade directly with Relshaz hoard their worthless metals. They can get rid of them buying slaves.' She shot a sideways grin at the stony-faced wizard. 'Kaasik Rai won't have any dealings with barbarians.'

'Why not?' Velindre couldn't help asking, pointlessly affronted.

'Some mainlander merchants came down here a year or so back.' Risala indicated the long curve of the bay with a sweep of her hand. 'Six big galleys that decided they didn't want to trade through Kaasik Rai as would be customary courtesy for such visitors. They came straight to the trading beach and offered barbarian coin for whatever they fancied. They had no notion of honest bargaining, offering the same insulting sums for pieces of vastly different value. They grew more and more angry when the traders wouldn't take their tokens. They saw every refusal as a ploy to drive up the price.'

They were passing by a merchant sitting between two wide, shallow chests holding beautiful glassware nestling in soft cotton cloths. Risala gestured towards what looked like long-necked bottles, each capped with a pierced silver dome. One was as clear as crystal, adorned with precisely engraved flowers. The other was blue-green glass with threads of white spiralling upwards. 'Which rose-water sprinkler would you say is more valuable?'

'I don't know,' said Velindre caustically. 'I'm no merchant.' She took a deep breath as her stomach roiled at the smoke from a cookfire.

Risala smiled briefly at the hopeful-looking merchant before shaking her head and moving on. 'If you were from the eastern reaches, you'd favour the coloured one. If you were thinking of trading down to the far west, you would want the crystal piece. Knowing that would affect what the merchant would take in trade, as well as any history between you, any obligation owed or sought. How can you reduce such complexities to some arbitrary weight of impure metal?'

Raised voices interrupted her. Every head on the beach turned to see one of the youths who'd been fetching and carrying for the cloth merchant standing toe to toe with some other bare-chested lad. The cloth merchant's boy shoved the challenger, modest beard bristling. The bare-chested youth responded in kind, sending the cloth merchant's boy stumbling backwards. He followed up his advantage, shouting insults. The cloth merchant's boy recovered his footing and yelled back.

Two tall men in gleaming chain mail appeared out of the trees. One had his sword drawn, striking vivid glints from the sunlight. The murmur of more normal conversation resumed as everyone else on the beach turned tactfully away to leave the youths explaining themselves.

'Kaasik Rai's men keep the peace.' Risala glanced at Velindre. 'Those barbarian traders soon discovered that. They left after suffering a beating sufficient to match the offence they had offered. And Kaasik Rai decided that branding them was appropriate, not least so that everyone would see them for what they were if they ever returned.'

'The Relshazri didn't object?' Velindre was almost shocked enough to forget her weakened, sickened state.

Risala shook her head. 'Archipelagan trade is too precious to be risked because some ignorant individuals bring down suffering on themselves.'

Cold fear halted Velindre. 'So some imprudent mage meeting a hideous death in the Archipelago would be of no concern.'

'No wizard would be so foolish as to travel these waters.' Risala steered her inland with a merciless hand at her elbow. 'As a scholar, you will know that.'

'A scholar?' Velindre shook her arm free. 'First I'm a eunuch and now I'm a scholar?'

'The two often go together.' Risala nodded. 'If you've no stake in the future through your body, you want to leave your mark for posterity with your wits. Many of our greatest philosophers, mathematicians and physicians have been eunuchs.'

'Oh.' Velindre couldn't think what else to say. 'So what manner of scholar am I?'

'You had better be an historian.' Risala smiled. 'Reading our histories as we sail will do wonders for your understanding of our language. I've the pearls to trade for books to get you started and that's the man I've been looking for.' She pointed to a white-bearded ancient sitting on a battered chest bound with tarnished brass, idly kicking his feet as he listened to a younger man sat cross-legged on the ground reading steadily from a sheaf of white reed pages. The old man had a stoutly bound book open on his knees and was following the text with one gnarled finger.

'He's taken a copy of the scholar's book.' Risala nodded at the younger man. 'When the scholar's heard him read it back, to be sure he hasn't made any errors, he'll certify it as accurate and it can be bound properly.'

'And how does he pay for it, if you don't use money?' Velindre demanded.

'He offers what he thinks it is worth.' Risala spoke as if that were obvious. 'As well as something of equal value to whatever other teaching he's had. Noted scholars, highly appreciated poets, particularly astute seers – they'll often find a warlord to house and feed them. So you need to be able at least to bluff you way through this, so no one thinks it too odd that Chazen Kheda is willing to be known as your patron.'

The sensation of crushing emptiness all around was threatening to wholly overwhelm Velindre. She focused desperately on the strange incomprehensibility of the Aldabreshin language instead. 'What's he saying? What does the book say?'

The white-bearded scholar spared the pair of them a faintly irritated look. Risala drew Velindre some way back. 'It's philosophy.' She listened for a moment before continuing in a low voice. 'Consider the round lute. Only one string is plucked but the others around it resound in sympathy. The experience of any individual affects all those around. Consider the fig tree. If its fruit falls in its shadow, the seedlings cannot thrive. If a loal carries the fruit away, whatever is lost on the way can grow into a new tree that feeds many more animals than just the loals. If a village's hunters kill all the loals, eventually they will have no fig trees. Other animals will go hungry. All our actions have consequences, even if we cannot see them at first hand.'

'That seems a little simplistic.' Velindre sniffed. 'Like your rationalisation of slavery.'

Risala looked at her. 'Perhaps we had better buy you some books of philosophy as well as some history.'

'Why not?' Velindre agreed. 'I shall need something to focus my mind on or I will go mad, thanks to your cursed poisons!'

The white-bearded scholar looked up again, scowling.

'Keep quiet.' Risala drew the magewoman further back. 'We've a long voyage ahead of us and you don't want to draw attention to yourself.'

'How long?' Velindre demanded with low urgency.

'It's thirty days or so till the rains should break. After that, perhaps another ten days, if the storms don't delay us too badly.' Risala looked away to the south, face tightening with apprehension. 'I only hope we're not too late.'

Velindre could not have spoken even if she'd had anything to say, the choking sensation in her throat was so vile. She pressed her hands to her face, shaking, fighting to control her horror at the prospect of such a long voyage deprived of her magic.

CHAPTER EIGHTEEN

'You could find something to read.' Kheda looked up from the much-amended star chart he was annotating further. He studied Dev across the books and charts piled on the table in the middle of the observatory. The mage was staring into the lamp in the centre of the table without blinking, without moving, even when the wind rattled the windows with slews of rain. Kheda paused to listen for any sound down in the rooms below.

If anyone comes up here wondering what we're doing, we'll have to say we're just about to retire for the night. Or say that something woke me, if it gets much later.

'What?' The mage dragged his eyes away from the flame.

'Find something to read,' Kheda repeated. 'To take your mind off . . . everything.'

'Everything?' mocked Dev, his gaze sliding back to the lamp. 'Piss on that. All I want to read is the word that Velle and your would-be concubine are finally in Chazen waters.' He tore himself away from the flame reluctantly to look accusingly at Kheda. 'Didn't the courier doves bring any word from Risala? You got plenty of messages today. What did they all say?'

'There was nothing new, which is at least good news of sorts.' Kheda moved a book whose open pages detailed potentially significant conjunctions of the lesser constellations. Slips of paper fine as onion skin curled beneath his fingers. 'There's been no sign of any wild men since the first of the rains.'

'So are they finally all dead or just hiding from the wet?' asked Dev sarcastically. 'Has the dragon eaten them all? Has it shown itself anywhere? Or has it flown off before its fires are damped by some storm?' The mage reached for a ceramic cup and drank deeply. 'Or maybe one of your swordsmen finally skewered the bastard wizard summoning it.'

'No one's seen it.' Kheda rubbed one of the slippery messages between finger and thumb. 'But Shipmaster Mezai sent word that the last two caches of gems he left have been plundered.'

'By savages or the dragon?' Dev didn't sound that interested, staring at the golden flame imprisoned in the glass of the lamp again.

'Hard to say.' Kheda flicked the scrap of paper away. 'Does it matter as long as the gems are keeping the beast sated?'

'How long before Mezai has to come back for more gems?' Dev demanded. 'Have you got any to give him? Have you got something to throw at it here, when it comes to smash these towers into rubble?'

'Yes,' Kheda retorted. 'And there's no reason to expect it will come here. We wouldn't have returned if I thought there was a chance of that. We waited till we'd passed a full ten days without seeing it, didn't we?'

'I suppose it could be something to do with the rains breaking, with the antipathy between fire and water.' Dev thrust himself away from the table, sending insecure books and papers sliding perilously close to the edge. 'But it's just waiting for another sniff of my magic, sure as curses.' He stared out into the dark, clouded night, arms folded tight, shoulders hunched. 'Unless it's got Velle's scent and sent her and the *Green Turtle* to the bottom of the sea.'

'Don't even say such things,' said Kheda sharply. 'And we'd have heard if anything like that had happened to the ship. Besides, you said yourself it might be that the beast only pursued you because of your affinity with fire.' He stumbled reluctantly over the words. 'It may well be that your magewoman is safe, if her ties are to the air.'

'So how long before Velle brings me some magic to make the bastard creature sorry it ever flew into these waters?' Dev murmured viciously, leaning on the windowsill, staring out into the night.

'Soon, I hope,' Kheda said curtly. He found his hand straying to his thigh beneath the table, to the pocket in his black trousers.

It's your imagination. You cannot feel such an insubstantial piece of paper. What are you going to do with it? Burn it? Keep it for a talisman, some token of hope to cling to, until its promise is fulfilled?

Risala wrote that she should arrive today. Today is nearly past. What could have held her up, besides the weather? What if she doesn't arrive today or tomorrow or the next day? How many days before Dev refuses to drink the decoction to stifle his magic? How long before someone discovers him drunk and raises an uproar? What do I do then, when the least punishment he should expect is a flogging and the loss of his sword hand, so no one is ever tempted to trust him with their life again?

Kheda watched without comment as Dev refilled his cup from a small blue glass bottle. Dev drank greedily, desperately, spilling a few colourless drops on to the plain brown tunic he wore, little different from Kheda's own.

The barbarian looked at him belligerently. 'Do you want to try some?

'No.' Kheda shoved aside the chart he had been altering and reached for a wide brass star circle instead. A few turns of the star net over the base plate of the heavens told him what he already knew: the positions of the heavenly jewels and constellations in the compass changed nothing.

Both moons are together in the arc of foes. Opal and Pearl are both talisman against dragons. Why? Is Dev right to suspect that the beasts prefer the four stones he tells me that barbarians associate with the perversions of magic? Does that mean I should be wary of any conjunction involving Ruby or Sapphire or Emerald? But there's no amber in the sky and he says that's one of their elemental jewels. How could barbarian beliefs affect our reading of the heavens anyway?

We still haven't seen the dragon, so that's some reassurance that I was right to see protection in these two days in the entire year that the moons meet in this reach of the sky. None of the men would have followed me back here if I hadn't been able to point to that. And the Sailfish is there in the same arc, and that's a good omen when it rides with either moon. And the shoals of squid have come with the rains, to spawn in the moonlight and feed islanders, beasts and birds alike. That's surely a good omen that the natural order is unshaken by the dragon's magic.

But where is any portent to encourage me to believe that we can defeat this creature? Both moons are waning. If we could see beyond the clouds, the Greater would be little more than a shaving of gold and the Lesser has passed its full. Will our success or failure depend on Velindre arriving before the conjunction of these talismans loses its potency?

Kheda stared at the star circle and did his best to ignore the repeated clink of the bottle against the rim of Dev's cup.

What of the rest of the heavenly compass? The Ruby is at the quarter turn from both moons in the arc of travel, talisman against fire set among the stars of the Winged Snake. Does this mean that the beast has already left us? Are we finally free of its unnatural fires? No one's seen it for days on end now. Well, we'll find out when Velindre arrives. We'll let Dev recover his magic and see if the beast comes down on us again. As long as she's some hope of killing it when it does.

He forced himself to concentrate on the jewels dotted around the star circle's net.

The Amethyst lies directly across from the Ruby, where the Mirror Bird spreads its wings protectively over those as close as kin. Can I believe that the Mirror Bird's fabled ability to turn aside magic will protect Risala? And Itrac? The Mirror Bird promises clear sight of the future, but the Amethyst warns against arrogance. And it's a jewel to promote true visions through dreams. Should I have agreed when Itrac offered to sleep beneath the tower of silence, to see if the wisdom of the past might show her some insight into the future?

Kheda's head jerked up and he stared out into the black night, towards the unseen tower where the most worthy dead of Chazen were laid so that their substance might be carried across the whole domain, rather than confined to the isle where they were buried.

'How long are you going to be shuffling paper?' Dev scowled at him from the other side of the observatory. 'Aren't you tired?'

'Are you?' Kheda traced the pierced brass of the star net with a thoughtful finger.

'I might be,' grunted Dev, 'if I drink enough of this.' He reached for the blue bottle again.

Do you think I'm staying wakeful out of sympathy, because you're tormented by your surrender to the potion that dulls your magic? Or because I find I still don't wholly trust you, even if you're a wizard in name only at the moment. I wish I knew which it was.

'I'll bet Itrac's lying awake down below warming her quilts for you. Don't you think you'd find more fun between her thighs?' Dev sneered unpleasantly. 'Or if you want to keep staring up at the stars, I'm sure she could get on her knees—'

'Shut up.' Kheda turned his attention resolutely back to the star circle. 'The liquor's making a fool of you again.'

Dev slumped back on his stool. He leaned forward and rested his chin on his folded forearms, staring silently at the lamp once more.

Kheda rubbed at the crease between his brows as he studied the patterns in the pierced and engraved brass.

If this was going to be a truly significant conjunction, the Diamond would make the fourth point of a square. It doesn't. If it were just one step back around the compass, the warlord's gem, in the arc of duty, would be showing me that the way forward is to attack. But that conjunction's impossible. None of the other jewels could be in their present arcs with the Diamond in that reach of the sky.

It's caught in the meshes of the Net, in the arc of marriage. And I am husband in flesh as well as in name to Itrac now. We are bound together. Does the Net, symbol of unity, join with the Diamond's aspect as talisman of fidelity to tell me our union is essential to support the domain? What does that mean for me and Risala, when I desire her like no other woman I've ever known?

He surveyed the piles of books, some still crisp-paged, their leather stiff, embossed gilt gleaming in the lamplight. Many were much older, reduced to limp decrepitude. Some were so worn that even daylight couldn't reveal whether they'd originally been bound in black or blue. Kheda sighed and reached for one whose pages were edged with grime, the leather flap that should fold over to secure the precious wisdom with engraved brass clasps entirely missing.

'Let's see if Chazen Saril's great-great-grandsire saw anything in the earthly compass at this same moment in the heavens' dance. Then we'll go to bed.'

'What?' Dev looked up as a rattle of wind-tossed drops against the window panes covered Kheda's last words. The mage managed a wry half-intoxicated smile. 'At least your rains came in good time. Isn't that a positive omen?'

'It is,' Kheda agreed slowly. 'And there were none of the usual quarrels towards the end of the dry season.'

'You don't think folk had more on their minds than bickering over vegetable plots or wood-cutting shares?' Dev's mood hovered precariously between amusement and contempt.

The shocking slam of a heavy door in the silence of the sleeping halls below cut off his next words. Footsteps and voices sounded on the stairs.

'That's Tasu,' Dev said, gathering up his cup and bottle to hide them below the table.

'It's Risala.' Kheda stood up, kicking his stool away. His hand went to his thigh, to the message slip hidden in his pocket.

Dev's eyes narrowed. 'You were expecting her.'

Kheda didn't answer, moving to open the door. 'It's all right, Tasu.' He smiled at the sleep-fuddled servant clad only in a hastily clutched wrap. 'Go back to bed.'

Risala appeared behind the old man. 'We didn't mean to wake you,' she apologised softly, 'but we saw the light in the observatory and we have news for our lord that cannot wait.'

'News and books, so I see,' Tasu said thickly. 'Let me dress—'

'The books can wait till the morning, Tasu,' Kheda interrupted.

'If you're sure, my lord.' The old man did his best to cover a yawn with one hand, the other clutching the length of cotton around his wrinkled, sagging belly.

'I am,' said Kheda firmly. 'Good night.'

'Good night, my lord.' The old man turned reluctantly

to ease past Risala and, further down the stairs, someone Kheda did not recognise at first.

He looked at Dev and, at the wizard's nod of confirmation, studied the newcomer more closely. She looked much the same age as him and Dev. Her face had lost the smoothness of youth and lines of age and experience traced faintly around her eyes and mouth. They would deepen with laughter or anger, he realised, not yet fixed and immutable as they would be ten or fifteen years hence.

The magewoman he had glimpsed in Dev's indistinct spells had certainly changed. Voyaging the length of the Archipelago through the dry season's fiercest heat had tanned her pale skin to a golden brown and bleached her hair to the whitest blonde. Tall for a barbarian woman, she was easily the height of most Aldabreshin men, and with her angular features, cropped head and masculine garb in dark-grey cotton, her appearance was far from feminine. She still looked exotic but her brown eyes should reassure most people that she had some Archipelagan blood.

'You were right.' Kheda smiled at Risala. 'A good few among the household will take her for *zamorin* without being told. They'll spread the word among servants who've never encountered such an unusual slave.'

'Such slaves that are coveted by many warlords.' The woman startled him by speaking in slow, careful Aldabreshin as she set down the armful of books she carried. 'What do you intend to do if you get an impressive offer for me?'

Kheda found himself retreating back behind his table as the magewoman studied him with equally frank appraisal. 'I will decline, with thanks,' he said with calm precision.

'You're looking very well.' Dev strolled slowly around behind Velindre. 'And very fine, in those trousers,' he added, running his tongue along his upper lip as he brushed a hand across her rump.

She rebuffed him with a blow from the leather bag she had slung over one shoulder and set a hand on the dagger hilt at her belt. 'Lay another finger on me, Dev, and I'll cut it off.' She sounded more bored than angry as she switched to their barbarian tongue.

Kheda noted that the barbarian woman's voice was naturally pitched quite low.

Further strengthening the illusion of this disguise. Is that an omen in our favour, that she can play this part so convincingly?

Dev stepped back, hands raised in mock apology. 'You can't blame a man for being tempted.'

'He says she's looking well.' Risala translated tactfully as she crossed the room to stand close to Kheda. She deposited her burden of books and let her own bag fall to the floor.

'I know.' Kheda saw that she had found time on her travels to have the infant shark's teeth mounted in silver and made into a necklace. She was wearing the ivory dragon's tail as well and he felt his heart miss a beat. 'Dev's been teaching me their barbarian tongue while we've been waiting. Though she looks tired to me, and so do you.'

Risala's dark skin didn't show the same weariness bruising Velindre's eyes but her face looked as washed out as her old blue tunic and trousers.

'You should see the *Green Turtle*'s oarsmen.' She tried to make a joke of it. 'We wanted to get back as soon as possible.'

'Your Aldabreshin's coming along, Velle.' The bald mage closed the door and leaned against it.

'And I've been learning a good deal about Archipelagan customs and beliefs.' She leaned towards Dev and sniffed. 'Including the many good reasons why they despise indulgence in alcohol. I didn't expect to find you three parts drunk.'

'You just be grateful I haven't soused myself insensible,' the bald mage retorted. 'All the while you've been dallying your way down here, I've had to take their poison to dull my magic.' He flung an accusing hand at Kheda.

'As have I,' snapped Velindre. 'But I found more constructive uses for my time—'

'We can use this barbarian tongue among ourselves,' Kheda interrupted, 'but elsewhere you should speak Aldabreshin as best you can. Your accent is unusual but so is your presence here, as a northern-born *zamorin*.'

'I told the shipmaster she was a little hard of hearing,' Risala broke in, 'to explain her hesitancy in speaking and to cover some misunderstandings.'

Kheda nodded. 'Dev can tell Jevin the same.'

'What's one more slight after so many?' commented Velindre acerbically.

'You're the one who wanted to come here,' Dev taunted her.

'When I didn't know what it would entail.' The magewoman turned on him with a forced smile of vicious satisfaction. 'At least you've been neutered, too.'

The two wizards stood, motionless, studying each other. Both were drawn, the skin tight on their bones, flesh beneath melted away. Their eyes betrayed the fearful, incomprehensible hunger gnawing at them from within.

Kheda looked on with a shiver of unease and felt Risala slip her hand into his. He held it tight.

'What do you think?' Dev challenged Velindre. 'Shouldn't we take this curious nostrum back to Hadrumal? Shall we offer its relief to all those snotty newcomers who weep and wail and wish they'd never been cursed with magebirth? The first thing they do is beg someone to take their affinity away.'

Velindre slapped Dev's face, taking them all unawares. 'Don't you dare make light of this.' The magewoman's voice was husky with emotion. She turned on Kheda, face accusing. 'Why have you poisoned him? If you think you can force us to do your bidding like this—'

'He didn't force me,' Dev interrupted sourly. 'Do you honestly think he could? It's been the only way to stop the dragon searching me out and biting off my head.' He laughed without humour and crossed to the table, bending to recover his cup and bottle. 'I got a better deal out of it than you. It's not quite white brandy, but a glass of oblivion from his lordship's medicinal still dulls the pain better than some tedious history treatise. Though your father would approve of your choice – no problem can't be solved by the application of intellect, isn't that it?'

'He wouldn't be surprised at your solution.' Velindre's attempt at contempt didn't quite come off.

Kheda broke into the ensuing uncomfortable silence, choosing his words carefully in the awkward barbarian tongue. 'As soon as we're rid of the dragon, we'll send you back with every recompense it's in my power to give. Have you brought us the lore we need?'

'Let's sit down.' Risala bent to fish under the table for a stool and Kheda let her hand go with reluctance.

'I found Azazir.' Velindre addressed herself to Dev as they both sat on the far side of the table. 'He had a lot to tell me about dragons and I've learned how to summon one, like Otrick used to do.' Her Tormalin speech soon became too rapid and strange for Kheda to follow.

'Sounds fascinating,' Dev interrupted, 'but how do we find the wild mage behind this? We've seen no sign of the bastard!'

'I imagine he'll show himself soon enough if I summon a dragon to fight his creation,' said Velindre with distaste. 'It'll take both of us to put an end to this,' she went on reluctantly. 'Summoning the dragon will have drained this savage of most of his magic. That's doubtless why he's been hiding. But that's only the case for as long as the dragon lives. Of course, I'll be as drained as him if I create a dragon to fight his. You'll have to subdue the wild wizard, Dev, while he's vulnerable, before either dragon is dead. Once the creature dies, the element that makes it is freed. The mage's full strength will be restored.'

'Subdue him?' queried Kheda sharply. 'We want this savage wizard dead.'

Velindre slid a sideways glance to Dev. 'If we did capture him, we might learn a lot from him.'

'All I want is this evil gone from my domain.' Kheda felt Risala take his hand once again under the cover of the table and held it tight. 'And I'm not interested in replacing one evil with another. How will it benefit Chazen to simply summon one dragon to kill the first? How will you stop this new beast from terrorising my people?'

'Just how much control would you have over the creature?' asked Dev thoughtfully.

'You like the idea of a dragon at your beck and call, do you?' Velindre was unwillingly amused. 'I'm sorry to disappoint you. These dragons aren't real.'

'It was real enough to sink a heavy trireme and kill most of the men aboard,' objected Kheda, exasperated.

'And to sink my *Amigal*,' agreed Dev in a rare moment of accord.

Velindre paused before continuing. 'The creature has physical substance woven from the element that supports it but it cannot live for more than a few days.'

'No, that's not right.' Kheda shook his head. 'This beast has been prowling these islands for five full cycles of the Greater Moon by now.' Sick disappointment threatened to rise and choke him.

After all this, after all this risk and the danger of exposure for us all, I've got a wizard who doesn't know what she's talking about.

'It may look like the same dragon, but it isn't.' Velindre addressed herself to Dev again. 'This mage will just be summoning one when he needs it.'

'Not least because it would be so much more powerful than him, if he's the novice we think he is.' Dev shrugged, looking over to Kheda. 'Which might explain why it hasn't been seen lately. Perhaps he's overreached himself and is laying up somewhere to recover.'

Kheda glanced at Risala. 'Does this make any sense to you?'

'I know nothing of magic.' She tilted her head, noncommittal. 'I don't want to know. Up till now, I'd have trusted her confidence, though, and Dev's arrogance.'

'When have I ever let you down?' The bald wizard grinned.

'There's always a first time,' Kheda retorted.

'Trust me to help you with this or set me on a ship heading north again.' Velindre began leafing through the papers in front of her. 'Where was the dragon last seen? That might give some clue as to what the wizard summoning it wants.'

Kheda reached over and gathered up star charts and a miscellany of courier-dove messages from all across the domain. 'You won't find anything relevant there.'

'Would you have such a thing as a map?' She looked up at him. 'I know you don't trust your mariners with them but surely a warlord must know the extent of his domain?'

'I don't think you've learned as much of our ways as you think you have,' said Kheda politely. 'A map can only ever be a frozen representation of a single moment. A warlord would be a fool to rely on such a thing. We learn to recognise every reach of our waters with our own eyes, so we can see any changes and consider their meaning at once.'

'Charts aren't a lot of use around here anyway.' Dev pulled a blank sheet of paper towards him and reached for a pen. 'Not given the way the sandbanks and mud channels shift once the big storms of the rainy season hit. Now, this is roughly where the dragon's been seen the last few times.' He sketched with brisk accuracy. 'And these are islands where caches of gems have been left to keep it quiet—'

'What?' Velindre stared at him, mouth open.

'The dragon – well, presumably this wizard you say is controlling it – he certainly wants gems,' explained Kheda. 'That much we do know.'

'Whose idea was this idiocy?' Velindre looked from Dev to Kheda, her eyes wide, struggling for words. 'Have you any idea what you've done?'

'No,' retorted Dev, waspishly. 'Why don't you tell us, if you're so wise?'

'A summoned dragon seeks gems to extend its life, so it doesn't fade in the way I said it would.' Velindre paused, rubbing a hand over her mouth. 'I can't imagine that any mage would be foolish enough to allow that to happen.'

'Don't expect any reason from these wild men,' Kheda said bitterly. 'We've seen none. They simply plunder and destroy.'

'Are you saying we'll never be rid of it?' demanded Risala, alarmed. 'What happens if this dragon has already got enough gems?'

'It's certainly amassed a fair hoard by now,' Kheda said slowly. 'Let's not give it time to add whatever final jewel makes all the difference. How soon can you summon this dragon of your own?'

'Not before I recover my own magic,' snapped Velindre.

Kheda looked at Velindre. 'When did you last dose her? With how much?'

'The day before yesterday,' Risala replied promptly. 'With just a couple of pinches.'

Kheda nodded. 'Your strength should return by dawn, both of you.'

'You *were* expecting them to arrive today.' Dev repeated his earlier accusation.

'You said that foul herb or whatever it was poisoned every cup of water I drank.' Velindre glared at Risala with equal outrage. 'You said it would take days for my affinity to recover!'

'I lied.' Risala sounded unconcerned but her hand tensed in Kheda's. 'I told you I'd do whatever it took to bring you here to rid Chazen of this evil.'

'You fell for that?' Dev taunted Velindre.

'I've taken as much insult and deceit as I'm prepared to tolerate from you barbarians.' The magewoman rose to her feet, directing the full force of her fulminatory anger across the table at Kheda. 'As soon as my magic returns, you won't see me for dust. You can deal with this dragon as best as you are able.'

'That's a steaming heap of horseshit, Velle, and you know it.' Dev caught her sleeve and dragged her down to her stool. 'You wouldn't have come all this way, doped or not, if you didn't intend to see it through. How else are you going to make fools of every mage who doubted your fitness to be Cloud Mistress?' He thrust the map in front of her. 'We won't have time to waste once my magic returns because that bastard will send his creature out to find me again. The one thing those savages can do is tell when anyone's using magic. So drop this masquerade. Where do we go and what do we do?'

'We should go somewhere as isolated as possible.' Velindre was icy calm but her skin wasn't so sun-bronzed that Kheda didn't see a furious blush rising from the round collar of her tunic. 'So we don't all get skinned and nailed to a gate for our trouble. Then Dev can indulge himself playing with his fires until the dragon turns up.'

'You've no idea how good that sounds.' The bald mage grinned at the prospect. 'So while I'm playing teaser mare in the stud yard, what will you be doing to make sure that other mage gets properly served?'

'Watching the skies.' Velindre looked thoughtfully at the black night beyond the window. 'It's no bad thing we've arrived in the rainy season. I should be able to use the elemental forces of any developing storm. That and the currents of the upper air.' She surprised Kheda with a sardonic smile. 'These latitudes are peculiarly well suited to this kind of working. Perhaps that's an omen in our favour.'

'Hardly,' he said, stung by such mockery.

'Not if that's what brought these wild mages here in the first place,' Dev began thoughtfully. 'Did Azazir say—'

'Tomorrow, Dev. I've had a long day.' Velindre rose to her feet, face stony. 'Can I expect a bed or shall I find some corner to curl up in like a dog?'

'This would all go more smoothly if we avoided the insults,' retorted Risala.

Her interjection gave Kheda time to bite back the wrathful rebuke rising to his own lips. 'I can offer you a hammock with soft, fresh quilts,' he said politely. 'Will that suffice?'

'What do you mean?' Velindre looked at him and then at Dev.

'We've a boat ready and waiting, my girl.' Dev stood up, adjusting his sword belt. 'And as soon as we've dealt with this mage and his beast, I'll be sailing north. You're welcome to a ride, if you can think of something to trade for your passage.' He winked lewdly at her.

'I think you'll find I can make shift to get myself back to Hadrumal,' Velindre assured the bald mage, wiping the smile off his face.

'Let's just hope the dragon doesn't smash this boat to kindling like the *Amigal*,' Risala said soberly.

Kheda squeezed her hand. 'Let's not tempt the future with such notions.'

'It's the middle of the night.' Velindre looked at him, perplexed. 'Won't we attract unwelcome attention? What are we going to say if people ask questions?'

'They won't. I am the warlord, after all,' Kheda said simply. 'People may wonder but they won't ask questions. We'd face far more curiosity if we wait till morning,' he added wryly, 'also because I'm the warlord. You've no idea how difficult it can be to do anything unobserved around here.'

'We'll get clear of this place and anchor up somewhere quiet tonight,' Dev agreed, 'otherwise we'll have twenty boats sniffing along our wake, wondering where we're going.'

'Whereas if they wake up to find us gone –' Risala nodded '– they'll have no choice but to accept that their warlord knows what he's doing.'

'As long as he comes back with news that the dragon is dead,' Kheda said incautiously. 'And proof,' he added, looking at Velindre.

'That may not be as simple as you might think.' She frowned.

'We can discuss that on the way.' Dev urged them all towards the door. 'Come on, Velle. Don't you want to command some magic again?'

'We had better go out armoured, Dev, otherwise half the guard will insist on coming along to defend me. Go and get our hauberks.' Kheda pulled a sheet of paper towards him and flipped open an inkwell.

The wizard groaned. 'When we get back to Hadrumal, Velle, I'm never going to wear so much as a gold chain around my neck.' He disappeared down the stairs.

'If I'm not to get any rest before we go on, I take it I can at least use the privy?' Velindre enquired icily.

'At the bottom of the tower,' Kheda said shortly.

'Do you suppose she'll forgive me?' asked Risala a little shakily as she watched the magewoman depart. 'Or will we be repaid for all this with some revenge once her power returns?'

That's an unwelcome thought. Though wouldn't we deserve such a fate, for bringing magic into the domain? Will it truly make any difference that our motives have always been pure? Or am I to see Chazen saved from this beast only to have my own duplicity revealed for all to see? Is that how the ledger will be balanced?

'Dev's been assuring me she'll see this through, so she can go back and settle some scores among their kind.' Kheda hesitated over his writing before setting his pen down and folding the letter in three. 'Let's hope that's more important than balancing her ledger with you. Besides, she'll know that all you did was at my behest. If she wishes to take any revenge, let her take it on me.' He took up a stick of wax and, removing the glass of the lamp, melted the end, catching the drop on the folded letter.

'No, we're in this together.' Risala's voice was muffled as she bent to pick up her bag and Velindre's. 'We always have been. You wouldn't have found Dev without me.'

'No, I wouldn't have.' Kheda pressed the seal of his ring into the pliant wax. 'But you would never have been caught up in magic without me.' He looked at her. 'Can you forgive me?'

'I'd rather risk magic to be with you than be without you.' Risala smiled slowly in the golden lamplight.

'If we can rid Chazen of this dragon and all this

magic—' The sound of voices rising from the bottom of the stairs interrupted Kheda.

He hurried down the spiral, Risala at his heels. To his relief, Tasu's door was firmly closed. The two of them picked their way quietly down the few further steps to the silent vestibule where a small lamp burned dimly in a tiled alcove. Velindre was waiting there, arms folded, face unreadable.

'Kheda?' A soft voice spoke in the dark shadows of the colonnade.

'Itrac?' Kheda went through the arch out into the black and silent garden. The rain that had persisted for most of the afternoon and evening had finally stopped. He took a deep breath of the cool, reviving air, redolent with the richness of the damp earth.

Velindre and Risala retreated into the vestibule of the observatory tower as unobtrusively as they could.

'Jevin was waiting to see when you came to bed.' Itrac stepped forward, her gaze fixed on Kheda's face. 'He said Dev was collecting your armour and swords. You're going somewhere, now, tonight?'

Unseen herbs rustled in a stray breath of wind and a few drops of water pattered on the invisible leaves of the wax-flower trees. All was quiet. There were no lights stirring in the steward's quarters on the far side of the garden.

'Risala has brought lore from the north, as I hoped.' Kheda looked at Itrac. Her wide, dark eyes were free of cosmetics, her neck and wrists bare of gold or silver. All she wore was a white silk chamber robe, loosely tied. The fabric was so fine that he could see her warm brown nakedness beneath. He crushed the letter he had just written for her in his hand. 'We may be able to rid Chazen of this dragon and the last of the wild men. We must go now, tonight. The moons—'

'I don't want to know,' Itrac interrupted sharply. 'I

don't need to know, my husband,' she amended, less shrill. 'Is there anything you need from me before you go? More jewels arrived from Daish today—'

Kheda saw that Itrac also had a letter held tight in one ringless hand.

Is that Janne's writing? What questions has she been asking, as she tries to find out what I am up to? What subtle poison flows along with her ink for you to breathe in without realising? Will any of that matter, once this is resolved one way or the other?

He turned to Velindre. 'Do we need gems?'

'No.' Velindre shut her mouth resolutely on further explanation.

Kheda turned back to Itrac. 'We're done with pacifying the dragon. We will be rid of it, my wife, if it's the last thing I do for Chazen.'

'Don't risk such a wager with the future.' She stepped forward, reaching out to him. 'Just make an end of this nightmare and come back safe to me.'

'I'll do my very best,' he assured her fervently as he took her hands. 'There is something you can do for me. This is a time for stealth, not force of arms. I must leave as discreetly as possible.'

'What ship are you taking?' Her eyes searched his face, confused. 'What do I tell the household?'

'Don't say anything until you have to. Let everyone think I'm still here for as long as you can. Then pretend appropriate surprise that anyone needs to ask and say I've taken that new skiff I had built on a search for important plants that the wild men destroyed.' Kheda nodded towards the unseen physic garden. 'The rains will bring the usual ailments, after all. And say I'll be searching out some unusual things at the behest of that *zamorin* scholar who's presently under my protection.' He jerked his head backwards towards Velindre and Risala. 'The *zamorin* is from the north. You remember it was northern lore helped us against the savage wizards last year? Trust me, Itrac.'

'Always, my lord and husband.' Itrac sounded apprehensive all the same. 'When will you be back?'

'I don't know,' Kheda said honestly. 'As soon as possible, I'll promise you that.'

Itrac's mouth trembled and she stepped forward to press herself against him, sliding her hands around his waist and burying her face in his neck. Kheda held her, helpless, feeling her warm tears on his skin.

'We should go.' Risala spoke softly behind him.

'Before someone hears voices and comes to see what's amiss,' Dev's voice agreed in the darkness beyond Itrac.

'Good night.' Itrac pulled away abruptly. She skirted past Dev and vanished without another word. Jevin followed, a black shadow passing across the fading white of her robe.

Kheda stood looking after her.

Can you do this, left all alone? Can you keep the household together and the domain beyond, proof against all the rumours and fear? You are bound to Chazen in a way I will never be. Let's hope those bonds are strong enough.

'We need to go, my lord,' said Dev forcefully.

Kheda nodded. 'Then let's.'

'What's it called?' Risala's face was unreadable in the strange shadows cast by the subdued light of the lamp she took from the vestibule to guide their way through the darkened residence. 'The boat, I mean.'

'I haven't decided yet.' Kheda led the way through the colonnade to the doorway into the wide anteroom between the warlord's inner garden and the outer tower. A lamp glowed golden on the far side of the room. The sentries guarding the double doors out to the courtyard stiffened, their hands resting lightly on their sword hilts.

'Open to your lord Chazen Kheda.' Dev stepped

forward to stand at his right hand, voice authoritative.

Both youths bowed low, doing their best to conceal lively curiosity. One pulled at the heavy bar sealing the door against assault and his companion pushed it open with another bow.

'Thank you.' Kheda walked through without slowing his pace or turning his head. Risala followed, two paces behind Dev, Velindre lagging a little further behind. Kheda walked briskly through the outer colonnade. Unseen in the darkness, the roses filled the night with their perfume. He paused to breathe in their heady fragrance.

They have flourished and bloomed after suffering such wanton damage, renewed, restored. Let that be an omen.

'My lord.' Dev's voice broke into his thoughts with scant courtesy. 'Put your armour on before we leave the residence.' He was wearing his own chain mail and carrying Kheda's, as well as being encumbered by a bulky bag slung over one shoulder. All their swords were thrust through his belt where they clashed awkwardly.

'Of course.' Kheda donned his armour quickly, aware of watching eyes high on the tall towers. The topmost turrets were dark, with no lamps to ruin the sentries' night vision, but he could hear the rustle of feet and the faint clink of armour. Only the observatory tower was silent.

Kheda pulled the studded belt tight to draw the weight of the hauberk on to his hips as it dragged at his shoulders. 'Let's go.' He took his scabbarded swords from Dev and secured them in the tight grip of his double-looped sword belt as he strode towards the northern outer gate.

'Open to your lord Chazen Kheda.' Dev's voice was calm and emotionless as he stepped past the warlord to confront the sentry.

The man looked from the impassive body slave to Kheda, who kept his face equally expressionless. The sentry bowed low and withdrew the door's heavy bar.

Pulling open one half of the door, he stepped through it. 'Bow to your lord Chazen Kheda,' he commanded the guards springing to their feet in the arcade beyond.

Kheda nodded briefly to the detachment of warriors as he walked down the steps and into the outer enclosure. The ground was cool and damp beneath his bare feet. Above, the sky was clearing. The light from the distant, just barely lopsided orb of the Lesser Moon turned the countless streams and pools to cold quicksilver. The outer wall was a black barrier before them.

'Watch your step,' Dev warned Velindre and Risala before stepping forward to repeat his challenge to the waiting sentries.

Kheda gave them a curt nod as he went out towards the shore with his ill-assorted entourage.

You don't know what to make of this, do you, faithful warriors of Chazen? Will you spend the rest of the night debating whether I'm disappearing again? Will you wait for all to be made clear when the dawn comes? Will you accept Itrac's reassurances even if I've not won your trust as yet?

Kheda kept his face as blank as marble as they passed through the final gate and walked out across the cold and wet grassy expanse between the residence and the shoreline defences. They were barely out of earshot of the warriors guarding the residence when he heard Velindre whisper to Dev in their barbarian tongue. He struggled to follow her words.

'This place is going to be buzzing with speculation before we're out of sight,' the magewoman hissed. 'Wasn't there some less obvious exit?'

'What would you suggest?' Dev countered. 'Shall we wait till morning and carry ourselves over the walls with magic? We could blend fire and air together and vanish in front of their astonished eyes. How much panic would that provoke around here?'

'I'm hardly suggesting open wizardry,' retorted Velindre scathingly. 'Just a little more discretion.'

'The warlord has to be seen to leave the residence.' Risala spoke up in firm Aldabreshin. 'If everyone wakes up tomorrow and finds he's not there, it won't be good enough to say he just slipped out of a side door while everyone was asleep. There'll be servants who'd set rumours running that he was dead or incapacitated, out of sheer mischief or because their true allegiance is to Daish or Aedis or some other domain.'

'Yes, they'll all be whispering behind their hands and wondering what we're up to but they won't gainsay Itrac's explanation,' Kheda said neutrally. 'Not without good reason, not for a good while. The best way to avoid that will be sending good news back here as soon as possible, if you two can possibly contrive some.'

They approached the arch piercing the mighty wall drawn across the beach. There was no gate here, merely the outermost portcullis prudently lowered. Kheda heard the growl of the winches and the rattle of chains pulling the lattice of wood and steel upwards almost before Dev had completed his challenge to the warrior commanding the wall guard.

'This way.' Once outside, Kheda felt uncomfortably exposed on the open shore.

'There must be curious eyes all along that rampart,' Velindre muttered behind him in the tongue of the Archipelago this time.

'Let's get the boat in the water and sail away before anyone else wakes up, shall we?' invited Dev.

'At least the rains mean there aren't too many people sleeping on the beach,' Risala observed.

Out in the open water, the *Green Turtle* rode in silent sleep after dutifully delivering Risala and Velindre. The galleys and smaller boats at anchor were dark shapes on the silver sea, their crews below half-decks or lying beneath awnings of oiled hide drawn tight over open hulls. There were a few tents on the sand, solidly planted above the high-water mark with their ropes storm lashed. There were no lights or sounds bar one sleeper's shockingly raucous snore.

Risala stifled a giggle as they passed the snorer's tent and Kheda shot her a grin in the faint moonlight.

'Come on.' Dev was intent on the modest boat floating on an extended tether at the furthest end of the beach. Velindre followed him, her pale head colourless in the moonlight.

Kheda reached for Risala's hand and she took it as they hurried after the wizards.

'It's smaller than the *Amigal*,' Risala remarked as she joined Kheda and Dev to haul on the rope as they pulled the boat closer into shore.

'Not by much.' Kheda leaned back, using all his weight. 'And it handles better.'

'The *Amigal* handled better than any boat you people will ever build.' Dev scowled.

The new boat grounded on the unseen seabed with a grating thump and rocked gently, water lapping at her sides.

'How do we get aboard?' Velindre looked on askance from the dry sand.

'We wade.' Kheda pointed to a rope ladder hanging over the boat's square stern. 'And we climb.'

Dev was already waist deep. Velindre followed, her leather bag held high as she waded through the water.

'Come on.' Kheda looked at Risala.

'It has no name.' She looked at him, frowning. 'And I don't imagine you've got an augury dove tucked in some pocket or other. This is hardly the best way to start this voyage.'

'There are enough omens of ill luck that you can't control without going out of your way to invite more,' observed Velindre, pausing in the lapping waves.

Kheda looked at her. She met his gaze calmly. 'As I said, I've been doing a lot of reading on my way down here. How else do you think I learned your language?'

Dev was already aboard and busy with the sail's ropes. 'We'll be ready to move in a few moments,' he warned testily.

Kheda heard a brief flurry of liquid sound floating high in the air. He looked around with surprise. 'A reteul and singing from the east. Is that enough of an omen for you?'

A bird of good omen, as they share their song with past and future, the birds of the present singing the same melody as those that laid their parents in the egg, the same song that those as yet unhatched will know. An omen to remind me to trust in the past and hope in the future?

Risala smiled with relief. 'I would say so.'

Kheda looked at her, the desire he'd kept in check through her absence seizing him anew. Then another realisation twisted painfully beneath his breastbone.

The reteul's a sign of constancy, each pair mating for life and all the birds of any one island sharing their song with each other alone. No other island's birds will have the same song. What does that presage for your future with Risala?

'What are you two waiting for?' Dev leaned over the boat's stern to help Velindre aboard.

'A good omen,' Risala retorted as she splashed through the water to the ladder.

'And a name for this boat.' Kheda followed and hauled himself up, clambering awkwardly over the rail encumbered by his armour. 'We'll call her the *Reteul*.'

'It's my boat and I'll thank you to remember that. I'll think about a good name.' Dev had already shed his hauberk and was lifting a long oar over the rail. 'This'll be a cursed sight easier once I have my magic back,' he muttered darkly in Tormalin.

Velindre was lifting a trap door set midway between the stern and the mast. 'What's down here?'

'A single hold.' Kheda ducked to shuck his own chain mail. 'With everything we need for a voyage of some distance,' he added, straightening up.

'We've been ready for days. What kept you?' Dev grunted as he shoved at the shore. 'Come on, lend a hand.'

Kheda picked up a second long sweep and went to help him.

'What kept us?' Risala moved to the mast and began efficiently adjusting ropes and sailcloth. 'Apart from the rainy season winds coming up from the south at full force?'

'I shall need to spend a little time seeing just how the winds and weather work in these latitudes.' Velindre sat on the deck, feet tucked up, perfectly composed.

'I've had enough of living as half the man I should be.' The *Reteul* was afloat now and Dev dug his oar viciously into the shallow water, barbarian words harsh. 'As soon as we're clear of this anchorage, you two can manage the boat between you. I'm going to sleep until I can wake up a wizard again.'

Kheda matched the mage stroke for stroke as they rowed the *Reteul* out into open water. Risala raised the triangular sail and deftly caught the slight night wind. The boat moved through the darkness as stealthily as its namesake as the two wizards disappeared into the hold.

'How rapidly the rain has cleared,' Risala remarked, looking up at the star-strewn sky. 'How long do you suppose that can last, at this season?'

'I don't know.' Kheda surveyed the dim and dangerous waters ahead. 'If any cloud hides that moon, we'll be blind.'

Is this how it will end? All my deceits and these wizards

along with them drowned in the all-concealing sea?

'I'll keep watch from the prow.' Risala walked briskly forward to be hidden by the mast and sail.

Kheda set a course for the open western horizon. As the obedient boat skimmed lightly over the sea, he realised that Velindre and Dev were talking down in their hammocks, their voices just audible through the open hatch to the hold. He strained to understand the Tormalin tongue they were using.

'So what do you make of life as a eunuch?' the bald wizard enquired with amusement.

'It's not without interest,' replied Velindre dryly. 'There's a strange freedom to having everyone assume you're one thing while you're really something quite different.'

'Why else do you think I spend so much time in these islands?' chuckled Dev.

'No, that's not what I mean.' Velindre fell silent for a moment. 'I'm thinking more about being freed from expectations. Everyone's always expecting something in Hadrumal, something more, even if they don't know what it is. You're always searching for it. Hereabouts? Everything's set out for you, depending on where you were born. Everyone knows what's expected of them. Few people seem to see any need to move out of their allotted sphere.'

'You call that freedom?' scoffed Dev. 'That potion of theirs has dulled your wits as well as your affinity. And there are plenty of people in these islands out to escape their lot with smuggled liquor, dream smokes or a willing girl. I've made a good living selling all three. Fancy coming into business with me when we're done here?'

'Go pleasure yourself with your sword hilt,' Velindre replied without heat. 'You might know more about these islands if you didn't spend all your time in the bilges. I've read a handful of their philosophers debating the precise nature of freedom on my way here. Archipelagans don't think like us but they certainly think. This is a far more curious place than I ever imagined.'

'You're not here to be curious; you're here to help me kill this dragon and whatever cocky bastard of a wild wizard's raising it.' There was a cruel hunger in Dev's voice. 'Can you do this? Can we? Truly?'

'I believe so.' Velindre sounded definite.

'Better show me the trick of it,' Dev observed casually. 'Just in case.'

'Hardly,' the magewoman retorted. 'I don't trust you with that kind of magic.'

'What if you need me to save your skin?' challenged Dev.

'I'll just have to make sure I don't,' Velindre countered.

There was another silence, this time so long Kheda thought both barbarians had fallen asleep.

'I'll show you the trick of it when I take the knowledge back to Hadrumal, along with word of all that's happened down here,' said Velindre at last. 'I'll want to call a witness before the Council. You're hardly ideal but you'll do.'

'Flattery will get you everywhere,' muttered Dev.

Velindre's reply was inaudible and after that there was nothing more to be heard.

Once they were past the coastal reefs of Esabir, Risala moved to satisfy herself that the sail was rigged to best advantage. Then she came aft to sit on the stern thwart with Kheda, the tiller between them. They sat in silence as they sailed through the moonlight.

'What's Dev been like, stripped of his magic?' she asked some little while later.

'Oddly diminished,' Kheda said after a moment's thought. 'As unpleasant as ever, when he puts his mind to it. He's just not been putting his mind to it as much. What about the woman, Velindre?'

'More desperate than diminished.' Risala shivered and not merely from the cool breeze. 'I wouldn't have wanted to be sailing with her without a crew of loyal Chazen to cow her. Still, she threw herself into her studies, by way of distraction. She can certainly pass for a scholar now.'

'The only thing that distracted Dev was alcohol,' Kheda admitted, shamefaced.

'I saw,' said Risala with some alarm. 'That could hardly reflect well on you.'

'No one else knows.' Kheda shook his head. 'No one saw him drunk. What else could I do?'

Risala had no answer to that. They sat in silence as Kheda steered the little boat well clear of a dark islet rimmed with pale, noisy surf.

'The mood in Chazen is strange,' Risala commented. 'On a knife edge.'

'There have been positive omens.' Kheda looked at her. 'Not many, I'll grant you, but such as have been seen, all have counselled patience and trust in a beneficial outcome.'

'Word seems to be circulating.' She nodded thoughtfully. 'The people are telling each other to trust in them.'

'In the omens?' Kheda asked quizzically. 'Not in me?'

'I haven't heard open doubts expressed.' Risala shrugged, a shadow in the dim moonlight. 'It's been a perilous season.'

Kheda concentrated on steering a straight course. 'What are people making of the way this dragon seems to have taken to some lair rather than burning or plundering any more islands?'

Risala shrugged again. 'No one seems to know what to make of anything to do with the dragon.'

'Do you trust me?' Kheda stared straight ahead, hand

light on the tiller. 'Do you believe I'm doing what I honestly think best for Chazen?'

'Yes,' Risala replied without hesitation.

Kheda waited, sensing there was more to come.

'People believe you're doing your best by Chazen and by Itrac.' Risala's voice was studiedly neutral. 'There are wagers circulating around most anchorages as to when she'll quicken with child.'

'I wish I thought I was doing the right thing by her,' Kheda admitted without reserve. 'I can't help thinking of Sain Daish when I look at Itrac. They're much of an age. I keep wondering what Sain thinks of me now. That was a marriage of convenient alliance like this one and I thought keeping her in luxury and pleasuring her in bed was all that was required of me.' He trusted that the veil of night was hiding his expression. 'That was certainly all Rekha ever expected. But Sain was shy and nervous and I barely had a chance to get to know her before all this confusion threw us apart. Her life could have been very different if her brother hadn't married her off to me.' He caught his breath and concentrated on steering the boat as an unseen current tugged at the tiller.

'The word around the Daish anchorages is that Sain Daish devotes herself to her son and the other children.' Risala folded her hands in her lap, looking at them. 'You gave her that much, at least.'

'I miss them so much,' Kheda said with raw emotion. 'The children. Every day. I never understood what it meant when I read the sages saying children are hostages to the future. I don't know if I can bear to give Itrac a child when I can't be sure of my future in Chazen. Even if I could find it in myself to love her. I loved Janne and look where that got me. I never knew her, not truly. Itrac doesn't know me. She doesn't know what I've done. She's just clinging to me because she has no other hope.'

'I know you,' Risala said swiftly. 'I know what you've done. I'll love you no matter what.'

'I'm still waiting for the day when I can believe I'm worthy of that,' said Kheda tightly.

Risala bit her lip. 'Then I can live in hope of that.'

The night sea rushed away on either side of the hull, whispering secretively to the islands unseen on either side.

'Do you think this magewoman can do all she claims?' Kheda finally asked after a long, long silence.

'She certainly believes she can,' Risala replied cautiously. 'I'll trust in that. These mages don't lack confidence. And after everything Dev did last year, such self-belief seems justified, don't you think?'

'Do you suppose all mages are like them? I think they're very strange people,' Kheda said frankly.

'Strange even for barbarians,' agreed Risala. 'I thought she might be less strange without her magic but . . .' She let the words end in a shrug.

'I found the same with Dev.' Kheda nodded. 'Let's hope his self-belief returns with his magic.'

'That seems to be all these wizards believe in,' mused Risala. 'Themselves and their magic. Each of them alone, I mean. They scarcely credit another's wizardry unless they've seen it with their own eyes.'

'They seem so jealous of any power they suspect might be greater than their own,' Kheda observed. 'Not so unlike the invaders' mages when you think about it.'

'Just like the dragon, from what Velindre told me on the voyage here.' Risala stared ahead. 'Let's hope we can put an end to all this.'

'I want to rid this domain of every magic once and for all,' agreed Kheda.

'And then?' Risala continued looking unblinking towards the prow.

'I hope a great many things will be clearer once we are

rid of this dragon and these wizards,' Kheda said fervently.

Risala rose and walked to the hatch. 'I'll fetch a quilt and try to get some sleep up here on deck, so you can wake me at dawn.'

Kheda watched in silence as she settled herself accordingly. Then he concentrated on sailing the boat, resolutely turning his mind away from any other thoughts.

CHAPTER NINETEEN

Kheda saw Risala stir with the dawn. The *Reteul* was slowing as the wind lost its strength with the passing of the night and the sea was a calm grey, barely a shade different from the sky above. The rain-bearing winds from the south that had driven the little boat through the night had drawn a coverlet of high cloud across the sky and the rising sun's light was a mere pearly glow.

Is that any kind of omen? More importantly, will that make any difference?

Risala resolutely threw aside her quilt. 'Do you think that cloud will thicken enough to bring rain or blow away to the north?'

'This early in the wet season, either could happen.' Kheda smiled as she rubbed her face with her hands, yawning widely. 'Good morning.'

'Just.' She peered around at the featureless horizon. 'Where are we?'

'Dev said he wanted somewhere empty of people and I'm not about to argue with that—' Kheda broke off, unable to stifle his own yawn. 'We're about half a morning's sail from the middle of the Serpents' Teeth. There are some barren islands where we can anchor. Then our friends from the north can try tempting this beast to its death.'

Risala looked at him critically. 'You need some rest before we do that. Just give me a few moments.' Getting up with a groan, she walked to the head of the boat to relieve herself. On her return, she stopped at the cask of fresh water lashed to the base of the mast. She splashed water over her face before cupping a drink with her hand. 'Take the quilt and get some rest. It's going to be a busy day.'

'Don't let me sleep through the excitement,' he said wryly as he surrendered the tiller.

The quilt was still warm as he wrapped it around himself, pulling a fold up to shade his eyes. He was so weary that the faint scent of Risala's perfume stirred no more than uncomplicated longing before sleep claimed him.

Dev's voice waking him some incalculable time later was far less welcome.

'You know why women rub their eyes when they wake up?' the wizard was saying, mischief in his voice. 'Because they haven't got stones to scratch, that's why. The question is what do *zamorin* do? Have you got the answer to that one, Velle?'

'Shut up, Dev.' The magewoman sounded bored.

Kheda rolled over and blinked in the bright sunlight as he pushed the enveloping quilt aside. He could feel the *Reteul* rushing through the water with renewed energy and a brisk wind raised gooseflesh on his drowsy skin as he sat up. 'Where are we?'

'A good question.' Dev scowled. He was leaning against the rail on the far side of the deck.

'Just within sight of the Serpents' Teeth.' Risala smiled briefly from her seat in the stern before turning all her attention to the seas ahead. 'You'd better take the tiller, if you know these waters. The winds and currents seem to be fighting among themselves.'

'You'd better not wreck my new boat, girl,' Dev warned.

'That won't happen while I'm aboard.' Velindre was standing just forward of the mast, gazing upwards, her arms outstretched. 'Not now.'

'It feels good, doesn't it?' Dev cracked his knuckles, looking as dangerous as Kheda had ever seen him.

'Oh yes.' Velindre glanced over her shoulder and Kheda saw new energy in her face. Her pale golden hair seemed brighter than before and her tanned skin looked smooth and sleek. The gaunt hunger and shadows that had disfigured her eyes were gone.

More than a good night's sleep has restored you. And you, Dev. I had let myself get too used to having you around, doing my bidding, even before you agreed to have your magic stifled. Foolish of me. As foolish as one of those warlords who raises some jungle cat from a kitten or keeps whip lizards in a garden to awe his visitors. Sooner or later such beasts turn on their captors without conscience or understanding.

'It's just like my bitch of a mother always said,' Dev declared with vicious amusement. 'You don't truly value something till it's taken away from you. I don't know about you, Velle, but I'll be dead before I surrender my affinity again!' He paced around the deck, light on his feet, weight balanced like a wrestler, hands straying between his dagger hilt and his swords. In his sleeveless tunic, his arms looked more muscular than ever, veins and tendons taut.

Just looking for someone to fight.

Dropping the quilt down the hatch into the hold and securing the wooden trap door, Kheda tried to stifle his disquiet at being on a ship with two mages in full command of their wizardry. He walked to the stern and sat beside Risala, resting his hand next to hers on the tiller.

'If you use magic to bring us to a safe harbour, won't that draw the dragon to us before we are ready for it?' He looked past Velindre to gauge the ferocity of the breaking seas and gusty winds around the distant black rocks of the Serpents' Teeth.

If we're sunk here, we're dead, no question of it.

'Only if the mage raising the creature is scrying in this direction.' She sounded entirely unconcerned, smiling as she tilted her head back, revelling in the wind's caress on her face. 'We'll do something a little more dramatic to draw his eye this way, when we're ready.'

'When will that be?' demanded Dev at once.

'Soon enough.' Velindre stared up into the clouds.

Kheda did the same. The sky was a broken mosaic of blue and white, shuffled by the winds that were driving the rains up from the open ocean. The warlord looked back over his shoulder to see a darker line of denser cloud gathering on the southern horizon, turning the azure of the sea to a deep slatey blue. 'There'll be a bad storm before the day's out.'

'Then let's get this done before it arrives,' said Velindre breezily.

Kheda couldn't contain his scepticism. 'It's as simple as that?'

Neither wizard answered, both intent on the skies.

'Breakfast?' Risala offered in a low voice.

'Please.' Kheda smiled.

'Take the tiller.' She unwrapped a fold of white muslin on the seat beside her to reveal torn lengths of unleavened saller bread wrapped around pale curd cheese. 'How long have you kept this boat stocked and ready to sail at a moment's notice?' she wondered, amused.

'Since at least ten days before you could possibly have returned,' Kheda admitted. He took a blushing avori pear plump with all the sweetness of the first rains.

Dev turned around with a cocky smile. 'I told him he needed to do something more than sit around with his thumb up his arse till the dragon arrived to bite my head off.'

Kheda frowned and tested the tiller. The *Reteul* didn't respond, cutting an uninterrupted line through the waters.

He looked over the stern and caught a fleeting glimpse of palest blue radiance curling through the boat's arrow-straight wake.

'You have grown bold, Velle,' jeered Dev. 'You never used to be so confident that you could emulate Otrick.'

'Look up there, Dev,' Velindre challenged. 'Up as high as you can. Use your element's sympathy with the air. See that?'

Kheda and Risala stared up into the sky along with the bald mage before sharing a shrug of incomprehension.

'There's nothing there,' she whispered. 'Is there?'

'Not for us.' Kheda chewed on the leathery bread. The sharp tang of the cheese sat uneasily with the misgivings roiling in his stomach.

'I see . . .' Dev's voice trailed off, bemused. 'Something, yes. It's so swift.' He stood motionless, astounded.

'It's the very highest and fastest of winds. It flows in narrow bands drifting across only a few latitudes,' observed Velindre. 'You may take that as an omen in your favour, Chazen Kheda, that the power I need to summon your dragon happens to be available in this domain. If you're so inclined.' Her voice was wholly neutral.

'Can we trust any portent offered by a mage?' Risala wondered under her breath.

'At least she doesn't mock such things outright like Dev.' Kheda shrugged. 'Perhaps that's a sign in itself. I don't know.'

'What I can't tell is where this savage mage is finding a comparable source of elemental fire,' the magewoman continued pensively. 'Have you felt anything when you've seen the dragon?'

'The creature's aura has always overwhelmed me.' Dev looked around the horizon before fixing on the rapidly approaching rocks of the Serpents' Teeth. 'Let's get this wild wizard here and I'll find out what's fuelling his magic,' he promised with feral intent. 'And I'll turn it against him.'

'Do you get the feeling we're riding in the hollow of a tempest?' Risala murmured beside Kheda.

'Just as long as it blows this dragon back out to the southern ocean,' responded Kheda grimly, 'along with whatever invaders are still clinging to its tail.' What little appetite he had deserted him and he tossed the half-eaten bread over the stern with an apologetic grimace at Risala.

'Let's see if you can make good on your bragging, Dev.' Velindre was walking back to stand between the stern and the mast. 'There's nothing to be gained by delay.'

She raised her hands, one stretched forward and one aft. Blue light flickered all around her and the *Reteul*'s sail bellied outwards at the thrust of a wind laced with azure sparkles. Kheda recoiled from the crackles of vivid sapphire light crawling over the tiller.

'Just leave it,' Velindre said calmly. As she gestured with one down-turned palm, the tiller adjusted their course just a fraction. With her other hand upraised, she curled her fingers slightly upwards. The ropes of the rigging shifted themselves, sliding obediently to trim the sail. Satisfied, Velindre halted them with a sideways cut.

'Sit down and enjoy the ride,' advised Dev with a wide grin. 'She knows what she's doing.'

'You should try rounding the Cape of Winds with me,' Velindre challenged with a hard smile of her own.

The *Reteul* surged forward at speeds far in excess of anything Kheda had imagined possible. The prow rose high in the water, bouncing as it scorned the rolling swells. Risala slid from the stern seat to sit on the deck, holding on tightly to the rail. Kheda joined her, reaching round her shoulders to take a firm hold himself. Risala shuffled backwards into the crook of his arm and he pressed himself closer. Velindre stood unconcerned in the middle of the deck, as easily balanced as if she were on solid ground.

'Do you suppose this little display will catch our friend's eye?' Dev couldn't quite match her insouciance, forced to shift his feet every now and then.

'You said they seem limited to their own element for the most part.' Velindre ushered the magical wind a little around to the east. 'I think it's up to you to do something spectacular with fire. Besides, I'll need to gather my strength.'

'Already?' Dev scoffed. 'I could take on half the Council and scorch their arses black.' He laughed gleefully.

'Let's concentrate on whipping this one mage into submission,' suggested Velindre. At the snap of her fingers, the sapphire light laced around the tiller glowed more brightly. 'And this is a wizard who can summon a dragon, don't forget. None of Hadrumal's Council can do that.'

Risala gasped as a massive wall of spray came crashing over the bow and surged down the deck towards them.

Dev brushed it aside with a scarlet flash of magic that instantly reduced the water to lingering steam. 'There'll be two who can, once we get back,' he promised exultantly. 'Then we can raise a dragon to chew on anyone who gainsays us.'

Kheda flinched as a ragged dark rock passed terrifyingly close to the *Reteul*'s rail. Wind-tossed spume spattered his face.

By all means, please do. Rid us of this beast and go wherever you wish as long as it's beyond Archipelagan waters. Do whatever you want with whatever arcane secrets you've uncovered, just as long as you do it as far away from here as possible. Go away to make as much trouble as you like among your fellow mages. Perhaps that will stop anyone else as dangerous and devious as you insinuating their evil into our lives.

He felt Risala trembling beside him. He was shaking,

too, from the chill of wind and sea as well as cold apprehension. They both tensed as the boat slowed to an abrupt halt.

'I can't concoct serious fire magic out here on the water.' Dev looked around, brow furrowed. 'Not something that will catch our wild friend's eye.'

'That looks like a good place to mount our challenge.' Velindre pointed and the *Reteul* made a stomach-churning wheel.

Kheda rose gingerly to his knees to see where the magewoman was taking them.

They were nearly at the far western edge of the chain of reefs and dark rocks that had separated Chazen waters from Daish since time before record. Here the outcrops were larger than those in the east, more akin to the humped coils of a monstrous sea serpent breaking through the turbid foam. The rocks rose sheer from the water, ridged and steely grey, resolute as they defied the crashing waves. Here and there stunted tangles of nameless shrubs clung to the topmost crags, among countless nests of white moonfishers and pied coral-divers built safely above the water.

The sea was not to be scorned. The grey stone was disfigured from waterline to the highest ragged knife edge. Every face was dappled with pockmarks gouged by the incessant spray. Plants that had thought to colonise the lower ledges raised only bleached, dead fingers in mute warning to any that might follow. Here and there the ripping tides had forced their way through some weakness to carve a new path, joining forces with the waters beyond to wear the stone down into submission. Pillars that had once been sturdy bastions stood alone, undercut by the ceaseless sea, frozen in the endless instant before they fell to be lost for ever beneath the waves.

'You can see some safe anchorage?' Kheda couldn't restrain his disbelief.

'Beyond that one.' Velindre pointed unperturbed through the impenetrable barrier of a sheer grey outcrop. At her bidding, the sail billowed with blue light and swung around. Blithely ignoring the vicious turmoil of the currents, the *Reteul* danced around the end of the rocky islet. Buoyed on a raft of sapphire light, the little boat eased backwards to nestle snugly in the embrace of a cup-shaped hollow. The cliff edge aloft was a man's height or perhaps a little less above the top of the mast.

'How are you going to be able to hold my boat secure in here if you're throwing all your magic into summoning this cloud dragon?' demanded Dev.

'How can we hide it?' Kheda was already dragging anchors from the lockers beneath the stern thwart. 'I don't fancy trying our luck swimming home, and the beast has decided that sinking boats is a sound tactic before.'

'Where can *we* hide?' Risala looked up at the unforgiving barren face of the cliff above, a rope held indecisively in her hand. 'We've no part to play in this.'

'Give me that.' Dev took an anchor from Kheda and swung it in one hand. The iron flukes glowed red and when Dev threw it, the anchor sank into the stone, melting the splintered rocks like wax.

'We could work a spell together to hide the boat,' said Velindre thoughtfully. 'Then your magic would secure it.'

'Nexus magic?' Dev paused before throwing a second anchor to bite deep into the rocks with a triumphant hiss. 'Who've you been sharing yourself with back in Hadrumal?'

'Just give me your hand.' Velindre ordered, exasperated.

As Dev raised his arm, the magewoman laced her fingers with his. Ruby light oozed from between their tight-closed palms, trickling down Dev's forearm. Velindre frowned and a dusky purple suffused the wizardry, turning the magic to a dull amethyst. Pressed close together, their arms were coated with the opaque radiance. Their gazes locked, the magewoman's hazel eyes staring deep into the bald wizard's; Dev's eyes were so dark brown as to look black. The glow of overt magic faded and as it did so, the deck beneath Kheda's feet faded with it. The wood shimmered and reappeared before vanishing once more.

Like some mirage of a distant vessel carried up over the horizon to offer an always ambiguous portent.

Even with the reassuring solidity of the planks under his feet, Kheda took a step backwards as the deck continued to come and go beneath him. 'Does this sorcery hide us as well?'

The question turned Velindre's head. Dev assaulted her cheek with a rough kiss, pressing his body close to hers with blatant suggestion. 'We always were good together, weren't we?'

'Probably.' Velindre pulled herself free of Dev with a look of contempt. 'I won't be working any conjoined magic with you in Hadrumal, nor doing anything else with you, not unless you learn some finesse. No wonder they call you a barbarian hereabouts.'

'"Probably" doesn't fill me with confidence.' Kheda looked at Risala.

'There are hollows in the rock where you can hide if you want to,' Velindre said impatiently. 'The dragon will have better things to think about than you two.'

'I'll show you finesse if that's what you want. How do you think I kept my hide whole in these islands?' Dev cracked his knuckles absently, surveying the looming cliff above. 'But I thought you wanted fiery uproar to summon this wizard and his dragon. I need solid ground beneath my feet if I'm going to do that.' As he spoke, he vanished.

'Where . . . ?' Kheda looked up to see Dev standing on the edge of the crumbling precipice.

Risala stood, head tipped back, expression dubious. 'How . . . ?'

'Allow me.' Velindre's spiral of azure light carried the three of them up to the heights before Kheda or Risala could say anything more.

'This is better.' Dev was looking along the broken line of the Serpents' Teeth, the rocks disappearing into the distance. 'There's fire beneath the seabed here. Deep, but not too deep.'

'Don't do anything just yet,' warned Velindre. 'It'll take me a little while to summon a cloud dragon.'

'We'll leave you to work uninterrupted.' Kheda's sarcastic courtesy went unnoticed by either wizard. 'Over there.' He tugged at Risala's hand and led her towards a storm-carved hollow where a trio of resolute nut palms had laid claim to what little soil and moisture the winds and rains let fall on the undulating top surface of the rock. Kheda saw they had persisted there for some years, for all they were barely taller than his head. Each successive season had seen the new fronds yellow and wither to fall down around the ridged trunks in tattered curtains.

'It's some cover, I suppose,' he muttered, unconvinced.

'I can't see anything better,' agreed Risala glumly. 'But we're no threat to the beast. There's no magic in us.'

'Nor in half the people it's eaten so far,' Kheda said incautiously.

Wasn't there? Many learned warlords have judged those encountering wizards, however innocently, to be soiled. Most agree there's an irrevocable stain left with those who have suborned magic for their own purposes. Will the dragon smell that on you, sniffing you out wherever you hide? What of it? You're committed now. You brought this magic to this domain. Can you complain if it becomes the death of you, if that's the cost of freeing Chazen from the dragon? Would you have it any other way?

The mages were still standing in the centre of the island, talking about something, gesturing. Risala sat cross-legged between the nut palms, tugging at the wholly inadequate barrier of damp and musty fronds. Kheda eased in beside her, the rock cold and unyielding beneath the thin layer of soil. He welcomed her warmth pressed against him as he watched the wizards' animated discussion.

'Is this how wizards treat the barbarians in the unbroken lands, disrupting their lives at any whim or fancy?' He leaned forward, elbows on his knees, cupping his chin in his hands. 'Don't the men of the north resent that? Not that they could do much about it, I suppose.'

'Velindre says they have little enough to do with the mainlanders.' Risala's comment surprised him. 'None of the wizards seem that interested in them, nor in anything much beyond the whys and wherefores of their own power, as far as I can tell.'

Before Kheda could think what to make of that, the eerie glow of magelight erupted on the far side of the rock.

Velindre stood stock still, hands cupped before her, her eyes downcast and intent on the empty air she cradled. A gossamer filament of faintest blue radiance drifted downwards to fall in lazy coils in her palms. The thread thickened and brightened, shining azure drawn taut between the gathering magic in the magewoman's hands and the unimaginable realms of the skies above. The coil of enchantment wound into a ball, the brilliance darkening to a vivid sapphire. The sphere swelled, summoning ever more magic. The thread of light became a solid shaft of piercing blue. Wind whirled around Velindre, whipping up a spiral of dust crackling with miniature lightning, darkening with every spin.

Unmoved, she stood in the centre of the vortex, the

hem of her tunic not so much as stirring, trousers hanging loosely from her narrow hips. She was concentrating on the magic building between her hands. A new light began to glow in the innermost heart of the sapphire. It might have been blue to begin with but within moments it was too bright to look on. Too bright for anyone but Velindre, who stared at the burning mote unblinking, her face a mask of cold fire.

Dev's magic was a ruby inferno by contrast. Wherever he had summoned the power from, he was using it to send gouts of scarlet fire jumping around the entire rock. Balls of flame bounced hither and thither, trailing blazing veils of crimson light. Wherever they landed, the rock melted into incandescence, white heat dying as soon as the magic sprang away. Bright gold faded through blood red to leave black and splintered craters in the grey rock. Dev laughed like a madman, sending blistering spheres ricocheting around the barren islet, gesturing wildly. Ruby light crackled between his outspread fingers.

Abruptly he swept his hands together and the burning globes raced to join in a towering pillar of flame. The wizard thrust his hands forward and the column split into two, into four, soon divided into a dizzying infinity of spears wrought of scarlet fire. As Dev swept his hands out and around, the flaming shafts obediently surged forward to surround him with a stockade of burning magic. The flames danced and shifted, now hiding the wizard, now revealing him exulting in his power.

'It's not so difficult to catch the bastard's eye!' The bald mage wheeled around and made as if to throw something. One of the incandescent shafts of fire soared high into the sky.

Kheda watched the flaming lance shoot straight as an arrow towards a shadow falling out of the brilliant sun. Dev's magic exploded into a shower of glittering fragments as the dragon met the missile with a blast of blazing breath. It swooped across the scarred island, the clap of its wings like thunder.

Kheda crouched impotently within the wilted circle of nut palms as the leaves rattled and shivered beneath the massive beast's passing. The breath was frozen in his chest, blood pulsing in his temples. Risala scrabbled for his hand and he gripped her fingers tight.

'Any time you're ready, Velle,' bellowed Dev hoarsely. He sent another spear of flame hurtling up after the dragon, and another, and another. The great beast lashed at the first with its tail, shattering it into crimson shards. Wheeling around in midair, it smashed at the next with a forefoot, striking sparks with its claws as it cut the threat to pieces. Another blast of fiery breath melted the last into nothingness. With a deafening flap of its mighty wings it soared high into the sky, roaring with exultation.

Velindre stood remote and isolated in the midst of the whirling column of dust. The shaft of sapphire light encased her now, magic flowing unceasing into the painful, seductive blue-whiteness hovering between her hands. In the instant before the entrancing brightness overwhelmed Kheda's sight, he saw the individual bones of her hands dark against the radiance. Then he had to look away or be blinded. As he rubbed his watering eyes, a shadow momentarily darkened the shaft of light from sapphire to slatey blue as the great fire dragon circled around it. It made as if to strike at the magic with its mighty tail but recoiled before the blow landed, tumbling through the sky, wings ungainly and uncoordinated.

Seeing its pale underbelly exposed, Dev sent spear after spear of blazing light at the creature. For an instant, Kheda caught his breath in sudden hope. Scarlet was spreading in the angle between the dragon's foreleg and breast. It faded and Kheda realised with a chill that it was Dev's magic fading away. The sorcerous shafts had merely shattered on the dragon's impervious scales.

The fire dragon landed at the far end of the islet with a thud that made the whole rock shudder. It crouched, then rose up to stand tall on its massive legs. Long neck extended, it moved its head from side to side, making an untroubled survey of this new challenge. Ignoring Velindre, still frozen within her wizardry, the great beast stalked towards Dev. The barbarian mage's defences continued to weave their dance around him. Now he was also ringed by a channel of molten rock, but the gaps between the blazing shafts were becoming wider. Each cast of a blazing lance had thinned his fiery stockade. With a sweep of his hand, the bald mage brought all the shimmering flames together to form a wall of fire between himself and the great creature. The dragon advanced until its blunt snout was almost touching the blazing barrier. Then it paused, its claws grating on the grey rock.

Has it seen us? Surely not. The wizards are between us and it. They're its enemy. So what do we do when it has killed both of them? What will it do to us?

With a furious bellow, the dragon reared up on its hindquarters and began tearing at the fiery wall with its foreclaws. It ripped away great gouts of flame, tossing scarlet fragments into the air. Dev stepped backwards, gesturing as he sought to recapture his magic. His mouth was open, but his words were lost beneath the deafening roar of the incensed dragon. Some of the blazing wreckage spun backwards at his command, thrusting itself into the widening gaps. More escaped his frantic efforts, plummeting into the sea to be lost in a flare of vapour or soaring high to evaporate in the turbulent sky. However hard the wizard worked, the dragon was ripping away the barrier faster than he could repair it.

Where is this dragon that the magewoman promised us? Isn't Dev her friend? Surely she won't let him die?

But Velindre was still standing motionless within the sapphire core of the spiral of whirling dust. Kheda looked up to see clouds gathering high, high above, where the uppermost winds were pierced by the needle of Velindre's magic. Risala screamed as the great dragon tore apart the last scraps of Dev's defences and pounced.

Kheda felt a yell torn from his own throat as a massive flash of lightning struck the rock. A great concussion knocked him and Risala both back against the blasted nut palms. He scrambled up to crouch among the smoking remnants of the palms' stubby trunks and scrubbed at his eyes to clear his dazzled vision.

Both wizards had vanished.

Now there were two dragons facing each other across the empty rock.

The newcomer's scales were white, the pure white of towering clouds beneath a brilliant sun. Pale blue-grey shadowed the angles between its lithe legs and rangy body, the colour of high, fine cloud against an early morning sky. The spines raked along its back and down the length of its whipping tail were translucent as ice, shimmering with untamed magic. The creature extended its wings slowly, the fine membranes touched with gold like the glow the sun might cast against a fine haze of twilight cloud. Wings bating, the cloud dragon stood tall on its hind legs and hissed a challenge, clawed forefeet extended. Its knifelike talons were bright with the iridescence of a cloud passing before a full moon. Its teeth shone moon-white in its long, lean mouth, flickering tongue the palest blue. Narrow and cunning, its eyes blazed with sapphire fire.

The fire dragon waited, motionless, weight balanced on all four feet, wings half-furled against its sides. Its red-gold flanks were dusted with grime thrown up from the scarred grey rock, coppery claws dull with soot. It sank down until its pale gold belly flattened against the ground, mouth half-open, running its scarlet tongue around its white teeth. All the while it kept its liquid ruby eyes fixed on the newcomer and the crimson scales fanning around its head bristled. Only its tail moved, a ripple slowly passing down the great muscular length of it, twitching the ridged spike at the tip to and fro.

So this must be it. What can I learn here, to pass on to the future, in the unlikely event that I get out of here alive?

Kheda studied both dragons with the dispassionate curiosity born of a calm beyond terror. He began to notice some differences. The cloud dragon was pristine, untouched by age or strife. The fire dragon showed evidence of a life lived hard. Several of the thick scales that armoured its backbone were ragged with broken edges. The ridges of the spike of its tail showed nicks and gouges. Further up its tail, the regular pattern of its red-gold hide was interrupted by darker, smaller scales. A similar scar marred the hindquarter closest to Kheda. One of the claws on that foot was snapped off short and the rest were chipped.

As the fire dragon opened its mouth a little wider, Kheda noted that its teeth were as white as he remembered but lacking the unsullied brilliance of the cloud dragon's maw. The fire dragon's fangs were more ivory in hue and, towards the back of the creature's mouth, slightly stained. One was missing, leaving a bloody hole in the dragon's jaw where a new tooth was just beginning to appear. Its coppery lip was torn there and the creature's scarlet tongue kept returning to run lightly over the sore spot.

Where the cloud dragon was light and lithe, full of energy, the fire dragon's movements were slower and more calculated. It was bigger and heavier. Older, Kheda realised, and somehow wiser. Its eyes were different from the cloud dragon's. The white beast's sapphire gaze shone with ferocity, pure and simple. The fire dragon's eyes burned with cunning as well as aggression. It bided its time, weighing up its opponent, waiting for this challenger to make the first move.

The cloud dragon sprang aloft and in the same lithe movement ducked its alabaster head to send a cloud of white vapour at the fire dragon. The red dragon was gone before the freezing breath struck, not into the air but springing forward to the spot the cloud dragon had just vacated. Behind it, the rock cracked and split, blackened craters rimed with frost defying the tropical heat.

Long neck outstretched, the fire dragon breathed a torrent of scarlet flame up at the cloud dragon's belly. The white dragon shot upwards but the blaze just reached it, catching its trailing tail. The icy spike clouded and dark blue oozed between the white scales. The creature screamed in outrage and turned to dive before abruptly thinking better of that tactic. It shot away sideways barely in time to avoid meeting a second furnace blast full in the face. Recovering with startling speed, it reversed direction to send another cloud of its own freezing breath to envelop its foe.

This time the fire dragon did spread its wings and take to the sky, leaving the icy mist to roll harmlessly across the sloping rock and tumble to the sea below. The cloud dragon shot straight for the red dragon, wings beating, neck outstretched, mouth agape in a lethal snarl. It vanished in a ball of fire, not exhaled by the fire dragon but simply bursting out of the empty air to envelop the white beast. The blazing sphere contracted like the pulse of a beating heart. It shattered outwards, riven by countless bolts of lightning. The cloud dragon was revealed, white scales scorched blue-black around the edges and wing membranes blistered, raw patches oozing cobalt blood. The creature seemed oblivious of its injuries, still intent on attacking the fire dragon hanging impossibly in the air before it.

It was impossible: the real dragon wasn't there to be attacked. The freezing blast of the cloud dragon's breath merely enveloped a shimmering apparition wrought of the fire dragon's own magic. Appearing out of the air behind the white dragon, it sank the coppery claws of one forefoot into the meaty flesh of the cloud dragon's haunch, just above its tail. Flames burst from the wound and crawled across the cloud dragon's hindquarter. The creature writhed and twisted, snapping at the fire dragon in agony. The fire dragon ripped its claws free and slashed at the cloud dragon's eyes. The white beast recoiled just in time but still suffered a deep gash across its muzzle. Lashing out with its tail, it caught the fire dragon in the belly, more by luck than intent. The fire dragon was knocked off balance just long enough for the cloud dragon to flee, the frantic beat of its wings shattering the air.

Bruise-coloured purple blood oozed from the wide gash in its back to trickle down its tail as it shot straight up into the sky. The fire dragon chased it with a startling turn of speed and found itself enveloped in a smothering fog whipped up from the warm sea below. The vapour glowed briefly from within and evaporated to reveal the fire dragon turning its head in all directions, searing the sky with its fiery breath as it searched for its enemy.

The cloud dragon was high above and seized its chance, folding its wings close to fall through the air, all four feet extended below, talons shining in the sunlight. It landed full on the fire dragon's back and dug in its claws, twisting its head down and around, intent on sinking its teeth into the back of the other creature's head. It failed and tried again but found it could make little impression on the shield of rugged, solid scales.

As the cloud dragon worried at its neck and clawed the scales from its flanks, the fire dragon fought to stay aloft with mighty strokes of its vast wings. Despite its endeavours it sank through the sky, borne down by the weight of the cloud dragon towards the deadly embrace of the waters below. Bright scarlet blood glistened on its torn sides, drops spitting as they fell to pit the surface of the sea. The fire dragon lashed at its white tormenter with its heavy spiked tail, striking unerringly at the gaping wound in the cloud dragon's hindquarter time and time again.

The white dragon couldn't stand it. Releasing the fire dragon, it shot away, screaming its rage and anguish. The red dragon pursued it, glowing with reignited ferocity. The red-gold of its sides shone like flame, brilliant under the full force of the sun. The beats of its great scarlet wings were slower than the frantic flapping of the cloud dragon, but every stroke took it closer, inexorably closing the gap between them. With every beat of its wings, it glowed hotter, its ruby eyes burning with determination. Within moments it was close enough to snap at the cloud dragon's dulled and soiled tail.

The fire dragon bit and held and ripped its head sideways, pulling the cloud dragon bodily back through the sky. With a flap of its mighty wings, it embraced the white beast. With its muscular legs, the red dragon forced the cloud dragon's gold-tinted wings close to its sides and, stretching out, entwined its neck and tail with the trapped creature's. The glow suffusing the fire dragon grew ever more intense and the white dragon began to burn. Its pale flesh charred, blackness spreading from the lethal brightness of the fire dragon's touch. Blue blood clotted dark and dried before it had a chance to flow. The membrane of the cloud dragon's wings split and curled away to leave the fine azure bones exposed before they, too, cracked and broke.

The cloud dragon screamed in uncomprehending fear and pain, its long, lean head writhing against the brutal bluntness of the fire dragon's muzzle. The red dragon held on tight, falling with its dying rival, tongue flickering across the cloud dragon's muzzle. Its eyes were unblinking ruby malevolence lit with points of fire as the cloud dragon's eyes dulled, their sapphire light extinguished. The two beasts fell, still entangled, on to the next rocky outcrop in the chain of islets. The impact sent knives of shattered stone in all directions and the rock where the dragons had landed vanished in a cloud of vapour laced with fire and lightning.

Is it gone? Have the wizards finally made good on their promise? Is this an end to it all?

Kheda sprang to his feet, he couldn't help it. Risala was at his shoulder, so close he could feel her trembling. He threw an arm around her shoulders and held her close, trying to see what had become of the dragons.

The fog of magic, dust and mist faded. The cloud dragon was gone. The fire dragon remained. It lay sprawled on the damp rock, its vibrant colours muted. The scales of its back were the colour of clotted blood, its underbelly a dirty orange where wounds oozed dull crimson. Only its eyes were still bright, brilliant ruby lit by points of white-hot fire.

'It's not dead,' breathed Kheda, horrified.

'Where are the wizards?' Risala pulled herself free of his arm and looked around, eyes white-rimmed in her ashen face.

'Let's get out of here before it recovers enough to fly.' Kheda ran to the cliff edge and looked down at the *Reteul*. 'The mages, they're on the boat,' he shouted back over his shoulder. He looked again and saw that the *Reteul* was rocking dangerously in its niche, no longer buttressed with magic. He winced as a slopping wave drove the vessel against the rocks with a grating noise. 'Get us down there!' he yelled urgently to Velindre.

She looked up at him, pale beneath her tan, tears smeared across her cheeks. 'No, no magic. We can't risk it. I'll throw you a rope.'

Kheda stood, fuming, as she searched for one. 'Dev! Show her the locker!'

The bald wizard was sitting on the deck, head hanging, hands pressed to his temples.

Risala came up beside Kheda. 'Dev!'

The bald mage didn't respond.

'Here!' Velindre had found a rope and slung a length awkwardly aloft. It barely reached half the distance between them before it fell back short.

'Throw the coil, not the end,' yelled Kheda, frustrated.

Velindre's second attempt was better aimed and Risala grabbed the rope out of the air.

Kheda seized the Aldabreshin girl's arm as she stepped perilously close to the broken edge of the cliff. 'Let me have that. You go first.' He took the rope out of her hands and slung it around his waist, setting his feet firmly on the dusty rock. 'Slap some sense into Dev. We have to kill that beast before it recovers. I'll cut its throat with my own sword if that's what it takes.'

'If you can.' Risala didn't look at him, concentrating on tying the rope securely around her thighs. Kheda braced himself as she began climbing down the ragged cliff. Several heavy jerks and one startled curse told him when hand- or foothold in the rotten rock betrayed her. Then the slackness in the rope announced her arrival on the *Reteul*'s deck. He moved to the edge of the cliff and looked down, just to make sure.

'Is there anything you can tie the rope to?' Risala looked up at him, face concerned.

Kheda judged the distance to the stubby remnants of the nut-palm trees and shook his head as he tossed the rope down to her. 'I'll just have to risk it.' He knelt to study the split and pitted stone, absently scooping up dust to dry his palms.

Put everything else out of your mind. Concentrate on the task in hand. Distraction can kill you. Forget dragons and wizards and magical trials. Your world is this cliff and your only business is finding solid hand- and footholds in the rock.

He moved slowly, testing every ledge and crack with toes and fingers. He could see where he was putting his hands but his feet were blind: the angle of the cliff made looking down too hazardous. The crash of the seas reverberated around the hollow, drowning out encouragement and advice from the deck below. Kheda closed his ears to all the voices, focusing his attention on testing each new step, each new handhold. Never lifting more than a single hand or foot from the rock at one time, he forced his body mercilessly against sharp edges chiselled by wind and wave.

A shout of warning sounded beneath him an instant after a slippery ledge crumbled beneath one foot. Kheda clung to the rock with sweating hands and did his best to drive the toes of his other foot into some inadequate crevice they had found. The beat of his heart in his ears sounded as if it were echoing back from the stone he had his face pressed against. Once he was sure he was secure, he tested the cliff with his free foot. A minuscule ledge resisted some pressure then broke away. He stretched and found a larger foothold but that also fell away to crash on to the *Reteul*'s deck, startling cries from below.

Kheda carefully withdrew his unsupported leg and turned his head as far as he could, his chest against an uncomfortably prominent point of rock. The *Reteul*'s mast danced before him, ropes taut against the varnished wood. Warily, he tried to look down to judge the distance but found himself committed as he lost his grip. Half-jumping, half-falling, he dropped to his hands and knees on the *Reteul*'s deck with a bruising thud, falling forward and sideways.

'Are you all right?' Risala was at his side in an instant.

He stood up. 'I'll survive.' His feet and the arm he had fallen on ached abominably. 'We need to get this boat out of here.' He looked expectantly at Velindre. 'And where are my swords? Dev, can we finish the beast with steel?'

The magewoman was weeping silently, tears flowing down her frozen face. 'We can't sail out of here with my magic.' Her voice was soft and low but steady enough. 'The dragon would be on us in an instant.'

'You won't rid your domain of such magic by sticking a sword in that dragon.' Dev looked up, voice loud and harsh. 'I know what it's been doing with those gems. I could feel it. It's made itself real. It's escaped the mage who made it—'

'No mage made that creature,' Velindre interrupted furiously. 'That's a true dragon. It was never a simulacrum.'

'Your spell could never have beaten it? Then it's won.' Kheda spoke the dire realisation aloud. 'It's here to hunt and fly wherever it wants and all you can do is draw it down on us.'

'Is there no way you can put an end to it?' Risala demanded frantically.

'I don't know,' shouted Dev furiously. He dragged himself to his feet and Kheda saw that the wizard's hands and face were seared with shallow burns glistening in the sun. He gestured wildly in the direction of the unseen dragon. 'Yes, it's a true dragon and that's one reason it brought down your pitiful beast, Velle. That dragon is used to fighting and using its magic for its own spells. You'll have to come up with something a cursed sight more clever for it to stand a chance of coming off best.' He turned his withering scorn on Kheda. 'And it'll be up and flying and burning us to a crisp before you could stick your sword in it, you fool!'

He winced and licked at a split in his lower lip. 'All right, Velle, what do you make of this? It's used the rubies from those caches of gems we fed it to focus elemental fire somewhere off to the south. I can feel that much, now that the beast's wounded, now that it's drawing its aura back into itself. That's how it's healing itself,' he warned bitterly. 'So what do we do now, Velle?' He raised his blistered hands in helpless fury. 'Because that's a true dragon which will soon be back at the height of its powers with enough gems cached to draw on all the elemental fire between here and the central domains. You were saying they were territorial? I'd say this is that creature's territory now, my lord Chazen Kheda—'

The fire dragon's chilling bellow drowned out the rest of his words. Its mighty wings ripped through the air and it soared above them, heedless of the insignificant boat in the hidden hollow. It looked magnificent once more, underbelly bright as polished metal, vast against the darkening sky.

'Can you raise a stronger dragon?' Kheda seized Velindre's shoulder and shook her violently. 'Something mighty enough to defeat that creature?'

'I don't know.' She wiped fresh tears from her eyes, still looking after the rapidly vanishing fire dragon. 'Perhaps.'

'How?' demanded Dev, scathing.

'From an ocean tempest,' she retorted.

'If we had one to hand,' mocked Dev. 'And if we didn't all drown while we were about it.'

'Dev.' Kheda snapped his fingers to get the bald mage's attention. 'What is this focusing of magic you're talking about? Has the beast made something that it relies on, something we can destroy?'

'You said killing the dragon would deprive this mage we believed had summoned it of his magic.' Risala was following Kheda's reasoning intently. 'Can we deprive the dragon of its magic if we scatter its hoard of gems?'

'If that weakened it, could you summon a dragon that might truly kill it?' Kheda demanded of Velindre once more.

'If it was weakened and, more importantly, distracted,' she said slowly. 'If I had a truly enormous storm to draw on. But those don't appear to order, and like Dev said, by the time one came down on us, we'd be too busy trying to stay alive to be working magic.'

'I can tell you when a tempest is coming.' Kheda brushed aside her objections. 'Would working your magic lessen such a storm's ferocity, if you were warned in good time?'

'Yes.' Growing interest rose above Velindre's wretchedness.

'You hope,' scoffed Dev.

Kheda silenced him with an upraised hand. 'You said you felt this focusing of elemental fire, Dev. Can you still feel it? Could you find where the beast has hoarded its gems?'

Dev stared at him, silent for a moment. 'Yes,' he said finally.

'Would scattering the hoard bring the dragon down on us, without us having to betray ourselves with your magic?' Kheda looked from the bald wizard to the magewoman and back again. 'You could use your magics together to attack it? If I could forecast a storm coming?'

'Possibly.' Some spark of his usual boldness lit Dev's red-rimmed eyes as he looked at Velindre. 'Focusing magic through a single gem, for a single, limited purpose, that's done seldom enough in Hadrumal. This creature's using a whole hoard to draw on the elemental fire all around, channelling power ceaselessly to itself.'

'There's no record of anyone from Trydek down having any notion of how to create such an all-pervasive spell,' Velindre said with wonder. 'Do you think any of the element masters would have any idea how it's doing it? Maybe Azazir—' She broke off with a shudder.

'Don't think you're leaving now to go and debate with your fellow mages,' interrupted Kheda harshly.

'I've had enough of taking your orders.' Dev's hand went to his dagger hilt. 'And I'm not playing your slave any more!'

'Oh, stop it,' snapped Velindre. 'What do you want to do, Dev? Paddle the whole length of the Archipelago without using a flicker of magic, just to return to Hadrumal and tell the Council you found a true dragon, that it is somehow focusing unimaginable power through a hoard of gems but you've no notion how? That you were too scared to try to find out?'

'You're calling me scared?' Dev drew his knife in one swift motion to threaten Velindre.

Taking him by surprise from his blind side, Risala knocked it out of his hand. 'Don't be a fool, Dev!'

'Enough,' shouted Kheda. 'Dev, that creature's too close. It's making you mad!'

The four of them staggered as the *Reteul* rocked violently.

'The first thing we need to do is get safely away from here.' Risala looked uneasily at the rocky walls enclosing them.

'Easier said than done without Velindre's magic,' sneered Dev.

'I don't claim to be any kind of sailor without it.' The female wizard looked grim-faced at Kheda. 'But I can pull on a rope if you show me the right one.'

'Risala, the two of you see to the sail,' Kheda ordered. 'Dev, get the stern oars out and let's move out into the channel. We'll take it as slowly as we can and you fend off while I steer.'

Still scowling blackly, Dev looked for a moment as if he was going to protest or refuse. Then he turned to free the long sweeps from their lashing below the rail.

Kheda moved to see what damage had been done to the rudder by the unyielding rocks.

Splintered edges but sound enough. Sufficient to get us out of here, at least. And then where to? Not back to any residence, that's for certain.

There's no going back for any of us till we've rid Chazen of this dragon or died in the attempt.

CHAPTER TWENTY

'Do you suppose it'll still be here when we get back?' Risala looked up from the anchor she was resolutely digging into the ground.

Satisfied that the rope he was tying around a sturdy knot tree was secure, Kheda shrugged. 'That depends on how much of the violence Velindre can draw out of this storm with her magic.' The winds were whipping up spray from the sea to mingle with the rain dampening Kheda's sturdy brown tunic.

Is it an omen that the storm we need has arisen in a mere matter of days? Or just to be expected, given the season and the latitude?

'Did you hear that?' Dev was up on the *Reteul*'s deck. The boat was bobbing madly in the narrow tree-choked inlet he had finally grudgingly accepted as an anchorage. He froze in the act of nailing a batten across the hatch to the hold.

'The dragon?' Kheda looked up at the cloud-covered sky, mouth half-open.

'What?' The bald wizard spared him a brief glance. 'No, Velle, I was talking to you. I'm relying on you to draw this storm's teeth. You keep it from wrecking my boat.'

The magewoman was standing a little distance away, face turned into the accelerating wind driving white-crested waves to crash all along the muddy shore. The larger billows were forcing their way up the inlet to wedge the *Reteul* still further into the clinging thicket of knot trees. 'I'll do my best,' she said absently.

'Do we have any more ropes?' Kheda surveyed the ungainly lattice tying the boat to the shore. He shook his head. 'This is madness, Dev. The boat's still right in the path of the fiercest storm of the season so far.'

Dev stood up on the deck. 'The shorter ropes will save it from being smashed against the shore by the first winds and when they snap, the longer ones will hold it as it rides the surging seas.'

'What if they don't?' Risala demanded. 'Where will the *Reteul* be when the storm passes?'

'What will it be?' Kheda muttered under his breath. 'Kindling?

Where will any of us be? Isn't this whole voyage madness? You've failed in your suborning of magic to defeat this dragon so far. All these wizards' theories have been proved wrong. Why are you trusting them now? Do you honestly believe they know what they're doing this time?

He wiped sweat from his forehead with the back of one hand.

What else can I do? I will not return to face the people of Chazen with the news that there is no way to kill this dragon. If I do, we might as well all take to our boats and flee to cast ourselves on the dubious mercy of the neighbouring domains.

I cannot go back. We can only go forward. I can only follow this path.

'We need to get inland before the storm comes any closer,' he shouted above the rising skirl of the wind. 'Bring your swords, Dev. There may be hogs or water ox in the forest. They'll be even more inclined to fight than usual if they're fleeing the storm.' He looked at Risala. 'Keep your eyes open, and stay close to me.'

'Always.' She smiled faintly. 'At least the storm's blown away that foul humidity, and the sweat flies.'

Dev jumped ashore and grinned at Kheda as he handed over the warlord's twin scabbarded blades. 'If you manage to lose this boat for me, I'll take the price of a new one out of the dragon's hoard.'

'Those are Chazen gems,' Risala retorted.

'Stolen by wild men?' Dev queried, dark eyes wide in pretended surprise. 'Hoarded by a dragon? Surely Chazen has no use for jewels so tainted with ill luck and enchantment?'

'Enough.' Kheda thrust his swords securely through his doubled belt and pointed towards a narrow game trail. 'Get into the trees. Velindre!'

The blonde magewoman hurried across the shore as fat drops of rain thudded on the ground. 'The heart of the storm's nearly here.'

'I know,' said Kheda curtly.

'How?' Velindre slowed as the tangled knot trees blunted the knife edge of the wind. 'How did you know today, of all days, was going to bring such a tempest? The skies have been clear for the last few days, the seas calm.'

'As they so often are before a run of wild weather. How did I know it would come today?' Kheda checked to be sure Dev wasn't getting too far ahead before explaining. 'The pattern of the tide told me that this morning. As for knowing it's nearly here, well, just listen.'

They stood motionless as the knot trees rocked around them, muting the sound of the surf crashing against the shore. Contorted grey branches rasped across one another, the slap and rattle of their stubby fleshy leaves quite unlike the rushing turmoil of the ironwoods and tandra trees growing inland where the salt water never encroached, no matter how high the seas rose. Gouts of rain came and went, the abrupt showers mere playthings of the winds.

Velindre shook her head. 'What am I listening for?'

'What you're not hearing.' Kheda walked along the

path, Risala at his heels. 'The loals weren't singing at dawn but the meari lizards have been fighting among themselves all morning.' He quickened his pace to catch up with Dev. 'Now they've gone quiet as well. And no birds sing.'

'Every fisherman and islander knows how to read these signs,' Risala added. 'They'll all be ashore and sheltering in steep, deep valleys or hidden caves.'

'Let's hope that's fortuitous,' Kheda agreed. 'No one will see the dragon killed with magic, if we finally manage to slay this cursed beast.'

'Let's hope so,' murmured Risala.

Do you mean you hope we slay the beast or that you hope we do it undiscovered in the act of suborning magic? Or both? It's much the same, isn't it?

With the tall trees all around, the path was sheltered from the worst of the rain now pouring down steadily, heavily. Kheda could smell the moisture running down the grooved trunks of the ironwoods, channelled along the kinked fronds of the tandra-tree leaves. For the moment, the rain was sinking into the damp leaf litter and the thirsty seeds. It wouldn't be long before the torrents falling from the sky would overwhelm the sodden earth and seek their own course across the cluttered forest floor. Then this hollowed path would become a stream, the bare earth underfoot slick and treacherous. Kheda increased his pace.

Velindre was pressing close behind the two of them. 'All these signs and portents to do with the weather, are they all recorded?'

'Of course.' The wizard woman's ignorance astounded Kheda. 'How else can we reach for the future with one hand if we don't hold fast to the past with the other?'

'How far back do these records go?' The blonde woman in her creased *zamorin* clothes strode along with him. 'And these changes in the tides and the ways the birds and animals behave, they would be portents of what you call the earthly compass? It's just the heavenly compass that's stargazing?'

'Ignorant superstition, you mean?' Kheda stopped so suddenly that Risala bumped into him and Velindre had to pull herself up short. 'Dev explained all your northern attitudes to our lore. Have *you* realised yet just why we hold *your* magic in such contempt? Did your reading on your voyage explain that?' His anger rose with a recklessness to equal the storm winds shaking the trees all around. 'You know nothing of the world that surrounds you and you care still less. How can you northerners hope to choose the best path for your future when you are so wilfully ignorant of the signs laid out all around you? You wizards are still worse, heedless of the violence your magic does to the natural order of things. You twist the very fabric of the seas and the skies and the land to suit your own whims, never mind that you are corrupting and destroying everything that the past has written into the present to guide you.'

'What are you arguing about now?' Dev had stopped where a scatter of boulders had rolled down from some hidden crag and held back the ironwoods and lilla trees to leave an irregular clearing.

'Nothing,' retorted Velindre, indignation darkening the tan on her cheekbones.

Risala looked past Kheda to the barbarian mage. 'How close are we to the dragon's lair?'

Dev jerked his head along the trail. 'Not far.'

'Good. We don't have time to waste.' Velindre squinted up at the sky where racing squalls of darker hue were banding the pewter grey that had hung over them since morning. 'Not if I'm to raise a cloud dragon from the height of this storm.'

She pushed past Kheda and strode along the path, her

cotton-clad legs long and lithe. Dev hastened to stay ahead of her. Risala walked close to Kheda. He kept a wary eye on the forest all around. Lilla trees creaked ominously, torn leaves whipped away before they could fall to the ground. Whole sprays heavy enough to defy the winds came tumbling along the path to whip around their ankles before being snatched by a gust and tossed into the undergrowth. The wind chilled Kheda and the rain soaked them both to the skin, even in the shelter of the trees. The sky overhead rapidly darkened to the colour of twilight. Kheda kept one hand on a sword hilt, straining his ears to try to pick out any hint of a maddened animal above the sounds of the storm-tossed forest.

Are you reading the signs aright? The signs of the tempest, certainly. Those are unmistakable. What of the higher portents? What of the heavenly compass and the stars that have been hidden by cloud every night since that first failure to rid the domain of this beast? But the stars are still there, even if we cannot see them. The heavenly jewels continue their dance around the heavenly compass.

The Sea Serpent has just moved to the arc of marriage where the Diamond that is the warlord's talisman rides. I have no idea what to make of that. But the Pearl is directly across the compass, where the Sailfish swims in the arc of life. That should be a good omen, as the Sailfish rise to greet the moon and fishermen catch the weightiest females just as it wanes.

The Greater Moon is in the next reach of the sky, where we look for portents of wealth and material success, and there's the Hoe, promising rewards to those who strive for land and family. In the furthest reaches of the sky, the Sapphire rides there as well, unmoving for year after year. Does that promise daylight and clarity in such a conjunction? According to these wizards, the Sapphire is the gem of the cloud dragon. Could it be possible that the heavens are showing me that this abomination will lead us to success?

What of the Ruby, if that's the gem of this fire dragon, this true creature of wild elemental magic? That still rides in the arc of travel, hardly a surprise given that the creature had to come from somewhere. What has the Horned Fish to do with the beast? That's a strange creature, warm-blooded and suckling its young in the midst of the cold ocean. Does that show me the dragon has travelled out of its allotted place in its journey here? Hardly something I need telling. The ivory I found on my own journey, that I carved into a dragon's tail, that came from a horned fish. What does that mean?

He paused in his speculation to negotiate a fallen tree and kept a wary eye on a stand of towering ironwoods creaking and swaying wildly as they fought with the storm assailing them from all sides.

There must be something more to the Ruby since the Amethyst lies straight across the compass, where the Canthira Tree spreads its branches and where portents for those close as blood, be they friends or not, can be found. Amethyst for calm and new ideas, new beginnings, with the Canthira Tree that is the first to recover after fire has devastated a forest, whose seeds do not sprout unless they have been through fire. Is that hope for the future to set against this dragon's destruction?

The Pearl and the Opal are the talisman gems against dragons. If the moons mark the dragon's head, what lies at its tail? For the Pearl, it's the Diamond, along with the Sea Serpent. Is that what I have become? A hidden darkness to bring peril and death?

Death itself lies opposite the Opal, in that reach of the sky where the Net embraces such omens, along with portents of inheritance. But there are no significant stars or jewels in that arc of the sky.

What will any of this mean if one of us has our brains dashed out by a falling branch? That will be a plain enough portent: one of utter disaster.

Kheda abandoned such fruitless speculation as the

sound of falling water ahead echoed above the rising clamour of the storm. The two wizards stood where the path ended abruptly at the lip of a deeply carved gorge. The rocks were dark and mossy with the return of the rains and the vivid white foam of the cataract splashed noisily below. Spray drifted up to coat the thick ferns of the gorge's side in a fine mist.

'It's in one of those caves, isn't it?' Risala wiped rain from her eyes as she stared at a riven cliff face rising out of the tangle of forest on the far side.

Unbothered by her soaking clothes, Velindre studied the pewter-coloured rock pierced with an array of black caverns. 'This is a curious place for a fire dragon to choose to lair.'

'Want to lay a wager on which cave?' Dev suggested with a hint of malice glistening on his wet face. 'If you're feeling confident enough to encroach on my element.'

'The merest mageborn tied to water and overwhelmed by that waterfall would feel the fire being drawn to this place,' Velindre commented with interest, 'antipathy in their affinity notwithstanding.' She looked up at the wind-tossed trees craning over the edge of the gorge, the crease between her brows deepening as she considered this new puzzle.

'Is the dragon in the cave?' Risala asked apprehensively beside Kheda. The warlord put his hand on his sword hilt.

And just what use is a blade going to be?

'No, but it can get here in the blink of an eye if it wants to.' Dev grinned. 'And it'll want to, once I get my hands on its hoard. Grabbing anything's stones gets its attention.' He laughed uproariously at his own joke.

Kheda took the opportunity to quench his thirst from a water skin he had slung over one shoulder and then offered it to Risala. 'You're feeling the dragon's magic, are you, Dev? Like you did before?'

'What?' The bald mage looked a little bemused. 'No, not as such, now that you mention it.'

'We can't wait.' As Velindre spoke, a crack of thunder split the dark clouds overhead. 'Go on then, Dev. Go and start kicking its stones.'

'How do we cross the gorge?' Risala peered into the broken chasm. Mere moments in the open rain had plastered her black hair flat to her head.

Kheda looked downstream. 'There's a bridge.'

'What?' Velindre broke off from studying the clouds to look. 'Why?'

'Who cares?' Dev was already moving cautiously towards it. 'It's what we need.'

Kheda hesitated before following him, ignoring the stinging, chilling rain. 'These caves would be places for meditation and seeking portents. Velindre, where are you going to work your magic? Can you do it under cover?'

'No,' the magewoman replied shortly. 'I'll stay here.' She stared up at the sky and her blonde, short-cropped hair bristled with faint blue light.

'Will you stay with her?' Kheda looked at Risala. 'I don't want you with us, if me and Dev bring down this dragon's wrath on our heads by looting its hoard.'

Risala nodded jerkily. 'I suppose it's as safe as anywhere with her.'

Kheda stepped close and took her hand, kissing her softly on one cheek. 'If the dragon turns on her, knock her out,' he whispered into her ear. A tendril of her sodden hair was cold against his face. 'If it has no magic to follow, it may not find her. Then leave her to whatever her own fate may be and save yourself. Someone has to take word back to Itrac if we are lost.'

'You'll tell her of your victory yourself.' Risala twisted to kiss him full on the lips with brief, sweet longing. 'How you saved Chazen.'

'Come on!' yelled Dev, now down at the flimsy bridge. 'We've a lot to do before you two can start celebrating!'

'Try to find some shelter.' Kheda tore himself away and went after Dev as fast as he could across the wet and treacherous rocks.

The mage was already testing the narrow bridge, a swaying structure of ropes woven from hairy vines and floored with crudely sliced lengths of hakali bark.

'Wait,' Kheda shouted.

'If I fall, I'll fly.' Dev shrugged. 'We want to bring the dragon here anyway, don't we?'

'There are footprints.' Kheda knelt where smudges in a patch of bare earth had caught his eyes. 'I'm beginning to wonder who built this bridge. It doesn't look like Daish work.'

'So it's Chazen work,' Dev called, irritated. 'How would you know it? You've never been hunting in these forests, have you?'

The bald mage made his way cautiously across the vertiginous bridge to the narrow ledge of open ground between the gorge and the cliff face with its dark, blank caves.

'Come on!' He beckoned to Kheda, yelling above the fury of the storm. 'If it holds me, it'll hold you. Are we going to do this or not?'

Kheda hurried across the bridge, feeling it flex and swing beneath his feet. His speed carried him over before his balance deserted him and he staggered to a halt beside Dev. 'Which cave is it?'

'Here.' But Dev was looking back over the chasm rather than at the rock face.

Kheda looked, too, to see Velindre bathed in a nimbus of dark-blue light, a point of blazing sapphire between her two hands. The clouds above swirled into a spiral storm, black and riven with lightning. The whirlwind extended its murderous claw down towards the magewoman but her magic reached up and seized it, drawing all the might of the turbulent gale into a column of blue brilliance edged with rainbows.

'She's really getting the knack of that,' Dev breathed, his tone a curious mixture of envy and admiration. 'She better had show me the trick of it when we're done here.'

'Then let's get done here,' snapped Kheda. 'Which cave?'

'This one.' Dev disappeared into a sloping angular entrance.

Kheda followed, and within fewer steps than he had anticipated, the sound and fury of the storm outside were a muted memory. The cave floor was dusty and hard underfoot, smudged with wet footprints. The walls of the tapering cleft disappeared over his head into a black crack that didn't even offer the reassurance of solidity. He ducked instinctively. He could smell dry stone and damp cotton as his wet clothes seemed to press in on him like the enfolding walls.

Turning a corner into darkness, Dev raised a hand full of bright magelight and Kheda followed to see a cavern opening outwards on either hand. The walls were ancient ripples of water-carved rock, with rounded corners opening on to further passages that sank away into unseen depths. On one side a tunnel entrance raised up higher than Kheda's head had broken through to throw down a shattered scree. The roof was a black mystery high above, strung with pale curtains of living rock painted with muted blues and browns. Spines rose up to meet them, trailing curious patterns across the undulating floor and casting impenetrable, sharp-edged shadows.

It wasn't just Dev's magelight showing them this scene. In the middle of the cavern, a fiery glow burned on a bed of sparkling jewels, drifts of sapphire, emerald, diamond and even amber, so rarely found in the Archipelago. Red-gold and radiant, a single rounded ruby of unimaginable size shone in the centre, lit from within with fiery magic and filling the cave with uncanny, brassy light. The air was warm, Kheda realised, and it would be warmer still close to the dragon's creation.

How did the beast meld all those gems together into that? Why did it do that?

'That's . . .' Kheda stumbled over the unfamiliar notion. 'Is that what the dragon is using to focus its magic?'

'Yes,' Dev said softly. He stood, his hand upraised. The mageborn flame in his palm was lengthening, thinning, drawn through the air towards the great jewel until it narrowed to invisibility. 'And guess what else?' He laughed. 'It's an egg. Well I never. I wonder if Velindre knows this, or Azazir.'

'What?' Even as Kheda sought to deny the notion, he looked again and saw that Dev was right. The ruby sphere was unmistakably flattened and tapered as if some bird or lizard had laid it. The glow at its heart was the same living flame that burned in the fire dragon's eyes. He even thought he could see a miniature dragon outlined within it. Then he blinked and the image was gone, only a memory smudged across his vision.

'Then we have to smash it before it hatches.' His mind still reeling at the impossibility of all this, Kheda looked around the vast cave. There was no sign of daylight penetrating the surrounding darkness to indicate any other entrance. An odd thought occurred to him. 'How did a dragon that size get in here?' As he glanced back at the narrow passage to be quite sure it was too small for the beast, movement caught his eye. 'Dev!'

The warlord barely had time to draw his swords before the wild man was on him. As it was, Kheda's backward step betrayed him as he tripped on some stony ridge. The wild man swung a stone-studded club at his head and Kheda barely drove the blow aside before he fell heavily.

'Here, you bastard, eat this!' Dev threw a blazing handful of fire at the savage. The flame flared scarlet and scorched through the air like an arrow. It didn't reach the painted wild man, however, veering wildly awry to arc back across the cave and disappear into the shimmering light surrounding the ruby egg instead.

'Piss on that!'

As Dev cursed behind him, Kheda tried to scramble to his feet, but the savage swung his club again, knocking the warlord's leading sword out of his hand and numbing his fingers. The blade went skittering away to be lost in shadow.

'What are you, some wizard? Then come and fight a real mage!' Dev's belligerent shouts didn't distract the savage, intent on aiming another crushing swing at Kheda's head. The mage's hurled dagger had more success, slicing through the air to strike the wild man a glancing blow on one painted shoulder. The invader glared at the wizard, bellowing some incomprehensible challenge that echoed around the uneven walls.

Kheda seized the opportunity to regain his footing, drawing his dagger from his belt as he did so, wincing as his hand ached viciously.

Not as good as two swords but better than one empty hand. I'd rather have the sword in my leading hand, with the dagger as backup. Armour would be better yet but at least I have blades and this invader is still naked. Let's see how he bleeds.

He feinted at the wild man, who dodged backwards with another swing of his stone-studded club in an attempt to knock Kheda's weapon aside. He was dressed like every other savage the warlord had seen, in a worn leather loin-cloth. His bare legs and body were painted with red-ochre flames, the designs clear against his dark skin in the bright golden light filling the cave. More russet mud caked his bristly black hair

Kheda moved carefully from side to side and watched the wild man's black eyes track his every move with feral intelligence. 'Dev, is this some savage wizard?' he asked conversationally. 'Can you tell if he has anyone backing him up?'

'Not that I can see,' answered the wizard with vicious satisfaction. 'And he's no mage. He must just be in thrall to the dragon or serving it somehow.'

'We'll have to kill him to get to that egg.' Kheda surprised the savage with a rapid thrust. The wild man recoiled before recovering an instant later to threaten Kheda with a crunching blow to his leading leg. Kheda evaded the strike with a sideways step, his shadow sprawling across a ridged wall of flowing stone. The wild man would have sidestepped with him but the barrier foiled him. Kheda dodged the other way and as he passed in front of the wild man, his shadow darkened his enemy's face for an instant.

A roar from outside made the whole cave tremble, stones tumbling down the scree in panic. The very air seemed to pulse with the sound. Crimson fire erupted behind Kheda and the brilliance filling the cave flared once more. Wild man and warlord alike flinched away from each other as their eyes closed irresistibly under the blinding assault.

'I can't reach him with any spells,' spat Dev furiously. 'The ruby devours all the magic.'

'Don't try,' Kheda snapped as he blinked through tears of pain. 'Get between him and the light instead.'

'What?'

The wild man attacked before Kheda could explain, swinging his brutal club in a frenzy. Kheda ducked and dodged and slashed with his sword, leaving the savage's arms bleeding from an array of deep cuts. The wounds didn't seem to slow the wild man. He kept on coming, pressing Kheda ever harder as every new bellow of fury from outside seemed to goad him on.

'Dev! Smash that gem!' The warlord hacked at his foe with a flurry of strokes born more of fearful rage than swordsmanship. His dagger hovered ready, waiting for any chance to launch a fatal thrust. The savage landed a crushing blow on Kheda's shoulder, the warlord barely managing to turn to lessen the impact. His whole arm went numb for a moment and the sword almost slipped from his nerveless fingers. The savage stepped forward, raising his club above his shoulder to bring it smashing down on Kheda's unprotected head.

'Hey! You with the shit in your hair!' One of Dev's swords came spinning through the air to slap against the wild man's chest. The flat of the blade didn't even break the skin and the blow barely gave him pause before the sword clattered to the floor. The savage switched his gaze from Kheda to Dev for an instant, lip curled in a sneer.

As he did so, the mage dodged to one side, letting the full glare of the ruby egg's magical fire fall on the wild man's face. He flinched and blinked and Kheda thrust his dagger deep into his naked midriff. The wild man fell against him, dropping his club to fasten his strong hands around Kheda's neck. They fell backwards, locked in a deadly embrace. Kheda landed hard on the ridged floor, back and ribs agonisingly bruised. He fought with the dagger still embedded in the wild man's entrails, struggling to rip the blade sideways for a killing stroke. The savage's fingers tightened around his throat and Kheda forced his jaw down into his chest, hunching his shoulders, fighting to save himself from strangulation. As it was, he was being rapidly throttled, the breath crushed in his windpipe.

With a last effort as his vision blurred, Kheda threw the savage away with a twist of his hips. An insignificant gap opened between them and he managed to tear the dagger blade across the wild man's belly. Blood and entrails flowed out of the gash to smother his hands. The savage collapsed across him with an incoherent gasp, rank breath foul in his face.

Kheda struggled uselessly for a moment, throwing his head from side to side to get free of the dead man's clinging fingers. 'Dev!' he yelled hoarsely.

The wizard neither answered nor came to his aid. Kheda drew a deep breath and heaved the wild man's corpse off himself. Wincing at his bruises, he staggered to his feet, breathless, looking as if he had been the one disembowelled with the blood and foulness on his midriff. The cavern reverberated at another deafening roar from outside.

'Best keep clear,' Dev called over his shoulder as the final echoes of fury ran away to be lost in the labyrinth of stone.

The mage scuffed his bare feet through the drifts of gemstones, brushing them aside as he approached the brilliant ruby egg. He would have been hard pressed to encircle it with his arms. The golden flame burned in its scarlet heart, white hot at its incandescent centre.

Kheda hesitated and stayed where he was.

This is wizard's work, so leave him to it. What could you possibly do to help anyway?

Dev rubbed a hand thoughtfully over his bald head, beads of sweat glistening like the diamonds scorned beneath his feet. Slowly he drew his remaining sword and extended his arm back and sideways. With sudden violence, he brought the blade up and around in a flashing arc to smash down into the top of the egg. The steel exploded into a shower of burning splinters that ripped through the air to bury themselves in the stone walls all around.

Kheda had ducked away as soon as Dev launched the strike. Hiding his face in his forearms, he winced at the sting of a handful of vicious slivers biting deep into his back and shoulder. He looked up cautiously. 'Dev?'

The wizard was staring over towards the black hole that had been their way into the cave. His tunic was bloody, torn in countless places. Sparks of steel shone in the wounds to his hands and face. He didn't seem to notice.

'This really could all go horribly wrong,' he remarked conversationally. Looking back at the egg, slowly, painfully, he knelt beside it and rested his cheek gently against its shining shell. His dark eyes glowed with reflected red fire and his mouth curved in a slow smile of ecstasy. He laid one hand palm down against the curved surface of the egg and, turning the other over, he cupped his palm and summoned a frail scarlet flame.

'Dev.' Kheda's voice was puzzled, pleading, even though he had no notion what to say or ask of the wizard. He shivered as a sudden chill shook him, gooseflesh raised on his bloody arms. His bruises and lacerations ached viciously and his damp and foul clothes clung coldly to his shrinking flesh.

The flame in Dev's hand burned taller and brighter and the light filling the cavern turned to an ominous scarlet. The golden flame within the egg glowed more fiercely, writhing and twisting. Dev's flame spilled over the edges of his hand and flowed across the egg, dimming that inner radiance. The scarlet fire ran around the mage's face, still pressed to the surface of the ruby, and down the sides of the egg to pool around the wizard's knees. His dagger was melting in its scabbard, drops of metal burning their way through the wood and leather. Stray diamonds and sapphires cracked and shattered where the burning magic touched them. Dev didn't react. His eyes were open but fixed, as if he stared into some unimaginable distance. Scarlet fire burned in his pupils and the rapturous smile on his face widened.

Kheda shivered. All around the chill was deepening, biting deep into his bones. Ahead, the egg burned with a ferocity that he could feel drying his lips and eyes, scorching his exposed skin. He tried to take a step backwards but could not do it.

I cannot leave him. I must see this through.

The golden flame was filling the egg now, expanding from its white heart. Dev's scarlet fire was still pouring from his hand, coating the ruby, stifling the incandescence within.

'Dev!' Kheda took a pace forward and the scarlet fire flared, heat striking him like a physical blow. He winced and stepped back, rubbing at tears provoked by the piercing light. He squinted painfully and saw a horror that froze the breath beneath his breastbone.

Dev's hand was burning: not merely holding the blood-red magic, but being consumed by it. The skin of his palm was gone, revealing the white bones beneath. As Kheda watched, his hand became a skeletal lattice wrapped in scarlet flame. The skin of his wrist began to peel back, tendons shrivelling to nothing, fibrous muscle laid bare, glistening, before the creeping tide of magic devoured it to leave blood-smeared ivory. The twin bones of his forearm were revealed, finger-width by finger-width.

It's like some nightmare of ulcerating rot in a wound. Can I save him, if I can get to him? If I cut off the arm before it devours the rest of him? At the elbow? At the shoulder?

Kheda stepped forward again but the heat was a physical barrier now. Bathed in ruby light, his hands and face ached ferociously. Try as he might, he couldn't bring himself to force his way any closer through the excruciating pain. In the shadows behind him, his back was colder than he had ever known, knotted with fierce pain to counterbalance the searing agony before him.

Is this all I can do? Just watch?

Dev still smiled with that beatific stillness. Where his face was laid against the surface of the egg, the skin had burned away and the flesh beneath with it, his jaw and teeth exposed in a deathly rictus. The fiery glow spread, consuming his weather-beaten cheek and his thin lips, peeling back his eyelids to expose the socket beneath. In the hollow of bone, his eye was a ball of sweating flame. His other eye, as yet untouched, glowed ever brighter with scarlet fire.

The fiery gold within the egg pulsed, its brilliance fading with every labouring beat. The flame still flowing from the calcined bones of Dev's hand darkened to a clotted crimson even as it burned ever more fiercely. The air in the cavern was throbbing and somewhere on the very edge of hearing, a piercing note was building.

Dev drew a long, shuddering breath. The fire had devoured his nose, leaving a ragged pit in the middle of his face, and his mouth was entirely gone. What little remained of his expression was still euphoric but that might just have been the curve of his naked, charring jawbone.

There's no saving him now.

The wizard spoke, startling Kheda horribly. His voice was no different, no trace of the barbarian in his mocking tone as he spoke, his eloquent Aldabreshin speech unaffected by the grotesque ruin of his face.

'I really think you'd better get out of here, my lord.' His words were slow and languorous and the breath rasped in his throat. As Dev blinked his remaining eye, the burning of the other socket was momentarily quenched. He shuddered like a man trying to hold himself back from the cataclysmic throes of passion. 'This really doesn't concern you.'

Never underestimate the wisdom of a dying man's words.

With that long-held truth forcing him back, Kheda retreated in what he hoped was the direction of the tunnel out of this inferno. He tripped and stumbled but could not look away from the sight before him. The crimson flame was spreading outwards now, wrapping Dev entirely in its lethal beauty. The mage twisted this way and that as it consumed him with its incomprehensible delights, greedy crackles stifling his groans of ecstasy. Slowly, resolutely, the blackened bones that were all that was left of the hand where this deadly fire had first kindled began to close into a fist.

Kheda saw the fiery gold within the egg crushed to a dull thread writhing at its heart. With every breath, it shortened, halved and halved again. He looked for the way out. There was no way he could reach it before that tarnished light died.

And that's going to do something horrendous.

He flung himself behind a ridged conglomeration of stone flowed from the cave's roof and grown from its floor. He buried his face in his hands and drew up his legs like a cowering child.

With a soft sigh, the crimson fire exploded outwards, setting the very air of the cavern ablaze. The whole crag shuddered with the anguished howl ripped from the tormented dragon outside. Stone tapers crashed from the ceiling to smash the ripples of the floor into ruin.

The darkness was total. When Kheda opened his eyes, he could see no difference. He could not see his trembling hand in front of his face. All he could feel was his shaking breath on his scored and bloody palm. His ears were still ringing from the deafening noise. If anything else was going on outside, he couldn't hear it.

If you can't see and you can't hear, you can still feel. You haven't come this far, at such a cost, to give up now. Move!

He got to his hands and knees and felt shards of stone viciously painful under his tender skin. Slowly, he knelt upright and waited, eyes instinctively closed the better to concentrate, rejecting the darkness all around.

Just a breath of movement in the air, that's all I ask for. There it is. And a green smell with it, of life and hope, among all this hideous reek of scorched death. And swords to fight with, if there's still an enemy out there.

Sheathing his dagger, he fumbled around in the darkness where his sword had fallen, as best as he could tell. He found a blade and won a cut across his thumb for his pains. Clutching the naked sword, he crawled towards that wisp of air promising escape. Carefully, he swept his empty lacerated hand across the mute stone, shuffling to protect his knees. After every few paces, he halted, waiting until his heart was calmer, trying to ignore the dreadful echoes still reverberating in his ears. His head throbbed, the pain somehow worsened by the strengthening scent of normality waiting for him beyond the confines of the cavern.

Finding the wall by grazing his knuckles against it, he clambered awkwardly to his feet. He flattened his free palm against the water-smoothed stone and eased himself along, stubbing his toes here and there against the invisible malice of the floor. Finally, his hand slipped into a void and the fresh scent of the forest outside steadied him as he stumbled. He rounded a corner and light forced its way down the tunnel to draw him on. Kheda blinked and squinted as the light strengthened, stabbing at his eyes.

He reeled out of the cave mouth and collapsed against the cliff face, mind and senses in turmoil. The light had seemed so bright but there was no clear sun above him, only the cold grey of the storm clouds he had left behind earlier. The punishing pain in his ears wasn't merely the echo of the fighting dragons. They were still roaring high in the sky above, tearing at each other in frenzy. Kheda looked up, appalled, despairing

After all this, after Dev's death, and such a death, and it still isn't ended?

The fire dragon was struggling to free itself from its new foe. The cloud dragon Velindre had summoned from the storm was a very different creature from the white innocent she had sent against it before. This was a bigger beast, longer and stronger, vigour in every line of it. Its spines were the dark blue-grey of a rainy season tempest, paling just a little to armour its head in twilight blue. Cloudy white gleamed beneath its jaw and down the front of its neck but back and flanks were armoured with scales the hue of a leaden overcast. Its underbelly was the colour of the dirty foam lashed from the sea by a whirlwind. Its storm-blue legs were thick and muscular, tipped with talons brilliant as lightning as its hind feet ripped at the dull crimson of the fire dragon's hide. The ruddy beast was held by the cloud dragon's dark, brutal tail entwined with its own.

Both creatures were grievously wounded, each bleeding from great gashes ripped by teeth, claws and magic along their flanks. They had torn the scales from each other's breasts, the flesh beneath lacerated bone deep. Bite marks showed plainly in the cloud dragon's mist-tinted wings, the holes shimmering with rainbow light. The fire dragon had suffered appalling injuries to one of its wings in turn. The membranes between the long, splayed bones had been cut to bloody scarlet ribbons by claws and teeth.

It flapped frantically with its remaining sound wing to save itself from falling, all the while fighting to defend itself. Pulling the stricken creature mercilessly down with its weight, the cloud dragon brushed away its flailing copper foreclaws with contemptuous ease. Every blow of its own that landed sent a burst of blue magic crackling through the fire dragon's hide, warping and splintering its scales, racking the creature rigid with agony. The cloud dragon's broad head weaved from side to side on its long, corded neck. It gaped, teeth like crystal knives vicious in its dark blue mouth. Only its eyes were the same as those of the creature that Velindre had first sent against the fire dragon. They shone, living sapphire beneath its bristling brow ridges, as it darted its head forward to tear at the fire dragon's throat. Ruby blood poured down the red beast's neck and hissed to steam on the cloud dragon's dark scales.

The fire dragon's struggles subsided to no more than token defiance and its feebly flicking tail brushed the tops of the tallest ironwoods. The cloud dragon untwined itself with a convulsive twist and soared upwards with a thunderous sweep of its wings. The fire dragon fell, too exhausted to recover itself. At the cloud dragon's cry, a spear of lightning shot from the turbulent clouds above to stab deep into the fire dragon's side. The beast's back arched in such agony that its lashing tail almost struck its own screaming head.

The red dragon fell to the ground, smashing the forest beneath it as it rolled down the slope, helpless. Trees held it for a moment before breaking under the strain and letting it roll free once more. Its flailing tail swept aside the bushes and clinging vines trailed from the chipped and broken spike. The beast scrabbled at the ground with ungainly claws in a vain effort to slow its rolling tumble. It could not find purchase in the loose soil, merely gouging great furrows in the dark, pungent earth. All along the trail of destruction, the crushed, sodden foliage was ablaze. Birds sprang frantic from their roosts, screeching their terror. Some escaped but the slowest died in plummeting bursts of flame, devoured by elemental fire.

Where's the wizard woman? Where's Risala?

As Kheda stood, transfixed by fear, the cloud dragon carved a lazy circle in the sky, crowing its triumph. It stooped like a falcon as the red dragon moved, struggling to rise to its feet amid the flames that rushed to succour it. With a shattering hiss the cloud dragon breathed out a cloud of vapour that snuffed the fires, leaving the charred stumps of the broken trees coated with ice. It circled again and this time a wind rose to follow its bidding, ringing the fire dragon around with splintered branches and ripped-up tree roots, showering the hapless creature with earth and leaf mould. The wind whirled faster and faster, narrowing into a spiral, pulling in broken wood and soil and even rocks from an ever-widening circle. The cloud dragon circled ceaselessly above. Every time it raised its gaping head to the clouds above and roared, a shaft of lightning shot down to pierce the whirlwind.

The cloud dragon finally dived towards the dark spiral and lashed at it with its massive tail. The whirlwind disappeared to reveal the fire dragon struggling feebly, battered into submission by windborne missiles. Its hide was dulled with dirt and blood and bruises and it barely had the strength to raise itself into a crouch. All it could do was peer upwards, ruby eyes failing in the gloom as it hissed pathetic defiance at its killer.

The cloud dragon bated its wings and hissed back. Ice fell from the clouds around it – not the rare storm-born hailstones that occasionally offered these islands a puzzling portent, but jagged shards with razor edges raining down. They fell only on the fire dragon, pummelling it to stillness. The rest of the forest was untouched.

Kheda watched. He couldn't have moved if the murderous ice had been turned on him.

Someone has to bear witness. Even if I can never tell anyone what I have seen.

Satisfied, the cloud dragon turned to fly high into the sky, rising higher with every stroke of its wings. As it rose, the clouds parted before it, revealing a clear blue sky. As the creature shrank to a mere outline high above, the storm dissolved into rags of cloud that paled and disappeared faster than any natural change in the weather. The sun shone down, bright and warm. The cataract sparkled merrily, rushing noisily down the gorge.

The fire dragon lay still, the fire in its eyes quenched at last. Steam rose all around it as the ice melted in the wounds torn in its flanks and belly. Dark-red blood, no longer bright with ruby radiance, flowed sluggishly to the ground and stained the forest floor an indelible black.

Kheda watched and waited.

Is it truly dead? How do I make sure? Hunters die every year when some jungle cat or whip lizard turns out not to be quite as dead as it looked. I don't want to prod that and find it still has life enough to crush me in its death throes.

He moved warily towards the frail vine and hakali-bark bridge, looking all around and holding his remaining sword ready.

Was this bridge that wild man's work? His and some more of the savages? What will they do now their dragon is slain?

He froze as he saw stealthy movement on the far bank, beyond the ruin wrought by the dragon's fall. Then indescribable relief flooded through him.

'Risala!' His shout sent lira finches fluttering up from the rock face behind him.

She moved out of the shadow of a stubborn ironwood and waved. 'Where's Dev?' she yelled.

Kheda shook his head, unable to speak.

Risala looked at him for a moment, then beckoned him on. 'Over here.'

Kheda took the bridge more slowly this time, stomach quaking at the thought of the yawning chasm below him. He kept his eyes fixed on Risala who looked back, unwavering, her hands held out to him. As soon as he was on solid ground, he ran, slipping on the broken leaves. As he folded her in his fierce embrace, she buried her face in his chest, wrapping her arms around his waist.

Kheda gasped. 'Ah, careful. I may have cracked a rib.'

'Is that all?' Risala looked up, her face smudged with dirt and her black hair tangled with leaves. 'None of this is your blood?' She pulled back and grimaced at the gore coating him.

'No.' Kheda drew her close again. 'There was a savage in the cave, guarding the . . .' He stumbled over the words. 'The gems that the dragon had gathered. It had made some kind of egg, that was central to its magic somehow.'

'Is it gone?' Risala looked up, eyes wide and fearful.

Kheda nodded. 'Dev . . .' He swallowed hard. 'Dev destroyed it and it destroyed him.'

'Oh.' Risala rested her head against Kheda's shoulder.

He stood still, taking comfort from the warm solidity of her body against his. The careless song of the cascade was joined by a few hesitant chirps of birds seeking and offering reassurance, crookbeaks and chequered fowl and the extravagantly tailed glory-cocks. The *zip* and *churr* of the forest's countless insects resonated softly through the underbrush once again.

This is life, this is reality. This is what I have been fighting for through all this nightmare of the unnatural and the impossible. This is what I want, for me and for Chazen.

The aches in his back and side reminded him of the price he had paid.

Let's see the final balance settled.

'Where's Velindre?' he asked at last.

'Over there.' Nestled in his arms, Risala didn't stir.

Kheda waited, eyes closed, for a long moment. He sighed. 'Come on.'

Risala reluctantly pulled herself free and, taking his hand, led him across the blackened scar sliced through the forest. Velindre lay curled like an infant in the shelter of an ironwood's tall buttress roots. Like Risala, she was filthy from the detritus flung from the periphery of the whirlwind. Rips here and there in her tunic and trousers showed bruises darkening on the pale skin beneath. Her face was buried in her arms, hands clasped around her head, and she shook with silent sobs.

Kheda looked wonderingly at Risala, who could only shrug helplessly in reply. He knelt and laid a careful hand on the magewoman's shoulder. 'It's all right, it's gone, it's dead. Where are you hurt? Are you bleeding?'

Velindre shook off his hand with a jerk of her shoulder and snarled something unintelligible into her arms.

'Where are you hurt?' Kheda repeated more forcefully.

'I said I'm not hurt.' Velindre startled him, pushing herself up from the ground to sit, loose-limbed in her soiled clothes. She scrubbed tears from her cheeks with the backs of her hands, leaving dirty smears across her face. 'Yes, it's gone but it's not dead. Don't ask any magic of me till it is.' Her voice broke into fresh weeping.

Satisfied at least that she had no obviously life-threatening injuries, Kheda sat back on his heels. 'The fire dragon, that's dead, surely?' he asked carefully.

Velindre nodded, striving for some composure with visible effort.

'The cloud dragon, that still lives?' Kheda tried to hide his apprehension. 'But it cannot last? You said so. It will fade? In a few days?'

'That's right.' Velindre just about had her tears under control now. 'I brought it here and made it a murderer of its own kind and now it will just sicken and die.' Her voice was thick with self-loathing.

With no notion of any possible consolation to offer, Kheda got to his feet. 'Then Chazen will finally be free of the creatures.'

'Then we had better let Chazen know.' Risala was looking down the shattered slope of the forest. 'They need to know the beast is truly dead.'

'And the sooner the better,' Kheda agreed, joining her to stare at the ruined carcass of the fire dragon. 'Well, they can come and see it with their own eyes, if they feel the need.'

'Let's just hope no one sees that cloud dragon in the meantime,' Risala said tensely

'We don't need that complication, not after all the trials we've been through to get this far,' Kheda agreed heavily.

Velindre pushed past them both, tears still slowly running down her dirty face, intent on the massive corpse.

They picked their way carefully down the slope after her. Sudden doubt assailed Kheda as they grew closer. 'It is dead, isn't it? Truly dead?' He gripped the sword he held tighter still and realised with a shock that it was Dev's blade he had picked up from the cavern floor, not his own.

'Yes,' said Velindre tersely.

Kheda studied the dead dragon through the clouds of steam still wreathing it. It was immense, awesome even in death. Its injuries were appalling, seen close to. Splinters of ruby bone poked through the torn flesh of its ruined wings. Other lumps spoke of more broken bones, dark swelling spreading to force scales apart. Savage bites cut through skin and fat, muscle and sinew. Loops of crimson viscera bulged between the lips of a great rent in its golden belly.

'It smells familiar somehow,' Risala said with wonder. 'How can that be?'

Kheda thought for a moment. 'That bite of quenched fire, it's like a swordsmith's forge, isn't it?'

'What are you planning to do with it now?' Velindre challenged.

'Fire is the ultimate purification,' Kheda began doubtfully. 'I don't like the idea of leaving it here to rot.'

'You don't think you can set fire to this, do you?' The magewoman laughed without humour. 'It won't burn, you fool!'

Kheda didn't answer, seeing the iridescent carapaces of carrion beetles already hurrying through the leaf litter towards the monstrous corpse. He watched as one reached a black smear of the fallen dragon's blood. The beetle waved its antennae briskly and accelerated along the glutinous trail.

You thought it would turn up its little legs and die, didn't you? So the unthinking creatures of the forest will reduce this mighty terror and spread its substance across this island, across this domain, if you don't do something about it. Declaring this valley, this whole island, a place of ill omen isn't going to suffice.

But death changes everything, haven't you always been told that? Is every mention of dragons fraught with ill luck?

He cast his mind back to the endless tomes he had studied during the interminable wait for Risala and Velindre. 'Dragon teeth and claws are mighty talismans in some poems, aren't they?' He looked at Risala.

She nodded slowly. 'And scales and anything made of its hide.'

'Talismans?' Velindre looked up from studying the rugged spike at the end of the dragon's tail. 'To protect you? That might just work, you know,' she commented with sour interest. 'It would certainly give any other true dragon flying this way pause for thought, when it got a sniff of such a powerful rival sliced to ribbons.'

She looked up at the sky, grimacing as she blinked away more tears. 'No dragon is going to want to meet whatever could do that. They're not going to know it was all a sham.'

Kheda looked at the green-hued flies buzzing through the air to cluster around the edges of the dead dragon's wounds.

So the insects are wiser than you. Spreading this creature's substance through the domain could protect it. Death changes everything. What was once destruction is now a weapon in your hand, a defence.

'Then let's flay it and send some token to guard every village.' Kheda looked dubiously at the mountain of reeking flesh rising before him.

'That'll be a long and filthy job,' said Velindre savagely. 'If you can find anyone brave enough to risk touching the creature, even now it's dead.'

'Then I'll do it alone,' Kheda shot back. 'The blood and sweat and labour might even purify me. The stars above know I owe some mighty penance for bringing down magic on these islands in the first place.'

Even as he quailed at the prospect of such an undertaking, optimism rose in Kheda's breast.

'Do you suppose they'll believe us, without coming to see this for themselves?' Risala grinned unexpectedly. 'No one's seen real dragonhide in time of memory. I think we'll find people willing to come and lend a hand to win themselves a dragon scale of their very own.'

'You'll be keeping its heart for yourself, I take it?' asked Velindre, an odd note in her voice. 'I imagine such a ruby would be beyond price.'

'What's its nature now that the dragon and Dev are gone?' Kheda asked her. He looked at Risala. 'Is it talisman beyond measure or curse beyond bearing?'

Both women shrugged helplessly.

Kheda frowned. 'That wizard who led the invaders last year, he was wearing a dragonhide cloak, don't you remember?'

'The one Dev killed,' Risala interrupted him. 'I remember.'

'So those savages, without blades or even clothes, do you suppose they know how to kill a dragon?' Kheda wondered.

'Where is Dev?' Velindre rounded on Kheda.

A chill ran through him despite the hot sun beating down. 'He was burned, in the cave,' he began incoherently.

'And you left him?' Velindre shot the warlord a furious glare before hurrying towards the frail bridge.

'No,' Kheda shouted after her. 'He's dead. He must be.'

His words echoed back from the cliff face. Velindre halted, looked at him and then continued on her path.

'Come on.' Risala looked at Kheda. 'We owe him that much.'

Finding himself at a loss for words, Kheda followed her.

They caught up with Velindre at the entrance to the tunnel into the crag. She looked at them angrily. 'I can't even summon some magelight, not with all my power tied up in that dragon.'

'Wait.' Kheda looked around and spotted a tandra tree clinging to a rocky cleft a little way upstream. He drew his dagger and climbed up the rounded stones to cut a stubby branch and a plump seedpod. It was the work of a few moments to drive a slit into the soft wood and wedge in the black oily seeds along with the silky white fibres that had cocooned them.

'Spark-maker?' Risala proffered one and Kheda snapped the steel wheel with his thumb. The tandra fluff flared and the seeds sizzled, burning with an aromatic greenish flame.

He realised that the two women were looking at him. 'Let's go.' Holding the torch carefully before him, he led the way into the blackness.

They halted in unspoken apprehension where the tunnel opened on to the vast cavern. The light of the torch reached out into the darkness and struck a myriad sparks from the dull stone walls.

'Jewels.' Risala picked at a diamond glint. 'Buried in the rock.'

If I hadn't managed to hide, they'd have cut me to pieces.

'Resources to help rebuild Chazen,' commented Velindre dourly. 'They're yours if you want them.'

'Leave them,' said Kheda abruptly. 'Remember what Dev said about jewels tainted with ill luck and enchantment.'

Never underestimate the wisdom of a dying man's words.

'You can't leave them here.' Risala retreated from the glittering wall. 'Some fool will come and dig them out.'

'Is this Dev?' Velindre had advanced across the cave floor and was looking down at a hairless blackened body, flesh shrunk to a semblance of charred leather. The wizened head gaped in a silent scream, clenched fists drawn up as if the corpse still sought to fight the hideous death visited upon it.

'No.' Kheda approached, glad of the tandra seeds' aromatic smoke wafting around to mask the stench of death. 'This was the wild man who was here.' He raised the torch and looked across the cave. 'He was tending that, I suppose. Dev said it was an egg.'

'An egg?' Risala echoed, disbelieving.

The great ruby was still there on its bed of jewels. It was dull and blackened, its surface opaque with a dull haze of cracks. The sapphires and emeralds around it had been reduced to no more than glistening dust. Glistening dust mingled with pale-grey ash.

That must be all that's left of him.

'Dev brought down some fire of his own on it.' Kheda struggled to explain. 'He killed the magic within it but the fire burned him, too.'

'Fire is the ultimate purification,' Risala murmured as she bent to retrieve Kheda's fallen sword from the floor.

Does that mean the taint of Dev's presence is lifted from Chazen, all that he did, all that he was?

Velindre walked slowly over to the lifeless dragon's egg. She crouched down and laid a hand on it. Kheda shivered at the recollection of Dev doing almost exactly the same thing.

'I want this,' the magewoman said softly. 'You promised me payment for my services to you. I want this.'

'No!' Kheda's rejection echoed harshly round the cavern.

'You can give it to me or I will take it.' Velindre stood up in one fluid movement. 'My magic will return and I won't be accepting any food or drink from your hands till it does,' she added with a harsh smile. 'I want this and I have earned it. We've earned it, Dev and me. What stain would that leave on your future, Chazen Kheda, to dishonour our bargain like that? When he has died in your service, wizard or not?'

Remember it's not only dying words that hold wisdom but chance truths spoken from the most unlikely sources.

'Why?' Kheda cleared his throat. 'Why do you want it?'

'That really doesn't concern you,' Velindre said softly, looking down at the lifeless egg. She glanced back at Kheda and the torchlight reflected in her dark eyes. 'Here's something for you to think about. You want to show all the people of your domain that the dragon is truly dead. That's all well and good as long as they don't ask too many awkward questions about how it died. How will you answer those? Can you offer any other explanation besides the cloud dragon killing it? What then? Everyone will be as terrified as before, or more so. And your rule will have been cursed by two dragons, not just one. Believe me – I can make sure that everyone sees this new calamity flying above your islands.'

She smiled eerily in the flickering light. 'Or you can tell everyone honestly that this new dragon slew the old beast. Then you can bring everyone to see you kill that foul and dangerous creature yourself. You would never have killed that true dragon with your feeble steel but I can give you more than a fighting chance against the dying simulacrum. Wouldn't that be purification enough for you? What wouldn't such a mighty deed do for your rule over this domain, Chazen Kheda? Give me this egg and I will give you that dragon.'

CHAPTER TWENTY-ONE

'Word spread like wildfire, didn't it?' Kheda looked across the clouded waters of the bay, stirred by the passage of countless ships.

'Despite the rains.' Risala stood with him on the stern deck of the *Gossamer Shark*, fingering her necklaces.

The trireme was drawn up on a beach almost entirely hidden by shelters hastily improvised from palm fronds and tents deftly rigged from sailcloth and spare oars. Fire pits smoked damply in the humid air. Most had already been quenched to black scars on the mottled sand. The multitude who'd slept and eaten ashore were gathered in earnest conversation or stood in silent groups considering the undulating green hills indistinct in the dense mist rising from the sodden trees. The sky above was an unrelieved pale grey.

'It doesn't seem to worry them that it wasn't this dragon that sank the *Mist Dove*,' Kheda said softly. 'Most of the islanders never even saw the fire dragon. Some of them never even saw hide or hair of the savages. They all want to share in this, though.'

'They all want to play their part in ridding Chazen of this evil.' Risala studied the crowded shore. 'This is their chance to fight at long last instead of running and hiding. It's something for their children, for their future.'

'Something to expiate whatever wrong choices or steps in the past led Chazen to this plight.' Kheda nodded. 'Something to still the dubious whispers and snide speculations behind Redigal hands or Aedis sails,' he added more prosaically. 'Let's hope so, anyway.'

Away from the shore, fast and heavy triremes alike were anchored in disciplined lines while fishing skiffs clustered in haphazard companionship around the fat-bellied merchant galleys. Flat-bottomed boats toiled through the gaps, outstripped by lithe dispatch boats stirring up spray with dashing oars. Voices shouted questions and instructions, answers and agreement ringing with common purpose.

'It helps that the dragon chose to lair as near to the centre of the domain as makes no difference,' Risala commented.

'Do you think that's significant?' Kheda looked down the length of the ship to the prow where Velindre stood, tall and slender in her guise of a *zamorin* scholar.

Can we trust her, when she grieves so openly for this base creature she created? She seems to mourn it more than Dev. But she's shown us where it is, when she could have concealed it and let it die unseen. She really wants that ruby egg.

'I don't know.' Risala shrugged. 'It certainly can't hurt to have so many hands raised against the beast. I doubt it'll be that easy to kill, even wounded.' She twisted the silver chain of tiny shark's teeth around one finger. 'But we can only go onwards.'

Is that more wisdom in chance-heard words? Or simply a statement of the blindingly obvious? Does it matter? We're committed now.

The *Gossamer Shark*'s helmsman and shipmaster were both down on the rowing deck. Kheda lowered his voice nonetheless. 'Has she let slip any hint that the creature could have found gems to strengthen itself?'

'No.' Risala shook her head with complete conviction. 'She says it's weakening fast.'

'There's been no word of it making any attacks,' Kheda

mused quietly amid the hubbub of the anchorage. 'Not where it could have found sapphires for its sorcery.'

'Plenty of people have seen it on the wing, though.' Risala glanced at him. 'She was right – you couldn't have kept it quiet.'

'Let's hope this course of action all turns out for the best, then.' Kheda shoved the wide belt drawing his hauberk close firmly down on to his hips. The dagged edge of his bronze-ornamented chain mail chinked softly against the gold-embossed metal plates of his leather leggings.

A time to look every measure the warlord, I think.

'Your swords, my lord?' Risala proffered two scabbarded blades and the double belt to secure them. The swords were not a matched pair: one was Kheda's, the other had been Dev's.

Kheda took the weapons, face impassive. 'You'd make a fair body slave.'

'Sorry, my lord, I'm not going up against that creature.' Risala shuddered, and then her face betrayed a new concern. 'Who is going to be at your shoulder?'

'Mezai for one.' Kheda nodded down into the depths of the trireme. 'Along with Ridu, Eshai and probably the whole sail crew.'

Down on the rowing deck, every man was abandoning his oar to don some scavenged chain mail or a thick leather jerkin. The *Gossamer Shark*'s contingent of trained swordsmen moved slowly among the rowers, handing out a miscellany of swords. Eshai, the helmsman, earned himself a sharp rebuke from one of the armoured warriors for trying an amateurish parry in the confined space.

'I couldn't ask you to stand at my shoulder again.' Kheda smiled, his words soft. 'You've already gone into more danger on my account than anyone should have had to face.'

'I've been wondering where the stars stood at my birth,' Risala remarked wryly, 'and what the soothsayer missed, or chose not to tell my mother, for fear she'd faint dead away.'

'I've more need of you here anyway.' Kheda's tone hardened as he gazed at Velindre. 'Keep a close eye on her. She'll regain her full strength once the creature is dead.'

'What do you suppose she'll do?' asked Risala apprehensively.

'I hope she'll disappear in a lightning flash and leave us loudly thankful that we're rid of such an unexpected and dangerous deceiver.' Kheda sighed. 'I don't suppose she will. She's set on having that ruby egg.'

Is it truly dead? There's been no new spark of life within it. Could the death of this cloud dragon give it some new power?

'What can she want with it?' Risala was as mystified as Kheda.

'I don't know and I don't want to know,' he said firmly. 'And I don't really want her revealed as anything more than a *zamorin* scholar.' Kheda looked at Risala, his face grim. 'Can you kill her if she betrays any sign of magic when the beast dies?'

Risala nodded slowly. 'Yes, my lord.'

Seeing the pain in her eyes, Kheda had to fight a powerful impulse to fold her in his arms. At that moment, Shipmaster Mezai came swiftly up the ladder from the rowing deck. Kheda busied himself donning his double-looped sword belt and securing the twin scabbards on his hips.

'Are we ready, my lord?' The mariner was wearing a hauberk showing signs of rust only recently scoured away and with some fierce dents in the solid metal plates inset to protect his vitals. He gripped a heavy blade more suited to forcing a path through virgin forest than to swordplay.

'We are,' Kheda said resolutely.

Mezai summoned the whole ship's crew with a rousing shout.

'Come on, lads, let's have the beast! For the *Mist Dove* and everyone who died on her!'

Kheda bade Risala farewell with silent eyes as he waited his turn to climb down the stern ladders as virtually the *Gossamer Shark*'s entire complement spilled along the side decks. As he slid down the last few rungs to the damp sand, he turned to see countless eyes fixed on him. Hunters from the hills of Boal and Esabir brandished their square-ended hacking blades. Lads with them carried bundles of the sturdy lances that could bring down a hook-toothed hog. Most sweated uncomplaining beneath the thick hide tunics they more usually wore to save themselves from a goring by some water ox, with high collars to foil the tearing neck-bite of a jungle cat springing from a tree.

Fishermen rested on their long, barbed spears, some bare-chested, more with some attempt at armour fashioned from latticed knot-tree bark more commonly used for crab traps. Youths without either weapons or armour stood burdened with swathes of heavy net and coils of thick pitch-blackened rope.

Men more used to sailing the domain in search of trade were ready to join the hunters and fishermen. Like the *Gossamer Shark*'s crew, they clutched a motley selection of weapons and a curious array of armour, new and old, in styles drawn from every local domain of the Archipelago and some from far beyond.

Is that some sign, that merchants and mariners can arm and armour themselves so readily when only a warlord's designated warriors are supposed to carry swords in his service? Dev used to trade in forbidden weapons, didn't he?

Thrusting away that painful thought, Kheda picked out

the bowmen lending their strength to this enterprise. A few carried their bows in hopes of seeing some weakness where a shaft might pierce the dragon. Most of those he recognised as archers from the Chazen residences carried the polearms that usually gathered dust, stored against some disaster when the untrained household would be the last line of defence.

Slaves and servants are all the defence the residence has at the moment. I hope no opportunistic pirate thinks to attack Itrac while every eye and blade is turned against this dragon. At least that bastard Ulla Safar's too far away to try taking such advantage, even if he did hear some rumour of what was going on.

The Chazen swordsmen were drawn up in precise troops amid the milling crowds, steel hauberks bright, polished helmets gleaming even in the dull overcast. Kheda looked for Ridu but couldn't see him. He set the thought aside resolutely and took off his own helmet so that his face could be seen more clearly and an immediate hush fell around him. Ripples of silence raced outwards until the only sound was the idle play of the sea. Every face turned to Kheda: openly anxious, taut with apprehension, all utterly determined.

'You are here to do Chazen a great service today.' The words sounded thin and insincere in Kheda's ears. He cleared his throat. 'We have a difficult and dangerous task ahead of us. We are looking to kill a creature bigger than any I have ever hunted – and if any of you have ever tried harpooning a sea serpent or a whale anywhere near as big, I'm amazed you're here to tell the tale.'

Nervous laughter shivered through a few people. His next words killed it.

'This creature has magic to call upon as well as its size and strength. I don't know what it may try, to confuse us or kill us, but we must expect it to wield its unnatural powers. We must not let this undermine our resolve. We must fight our way through such attacks to kill the creature itself and that will put paid to such malevolence. We will end this evil blighting Chazen.'

He scanned the intent faces all around. Here and there he noted the uncut hair and beard of a soothsayer. The sages were nodding with approval as they clutched their baskets of prophetic stones or held augury doves dozing in little cages.

Kheda's voice strengthened. 'Do not fear the stain of magic touching you. Wiser men than us, through many revolutions of the heavens, are all agreed that the innocent victims of magic are not condemned by its touch. Every portent for Chazen has been positive of late, from the blessing of the prodigious pearl harvest onwards. The domain's future is full of hope. We are here to claim that hope for ourselves and for those we love. The rains will wash this dragon's blood from Chazen soil to be lost in the boundless depths of the ocean.'

A few men raised a belligerent cheer.

Kheda spoke again, his voice louder, harsher. 'We know these beasts can be killed. This dragon we are here to hunt fought and killed the fire-born beast that first arrived to plague us. That evil is dead and gone and scales from its hide are token of that death and talisman to protect the lives risked here today.'

He pointed to men wearing scales on thongs of leather or plaited grass, dull as gouts of blood in the muted light.

'This second dragon paid heavily for its victory. I saw its terrible wounds with my own eyes. The creature is already grievously weakened.' Kheda thrust his helmet back on to his head and drew a sword. 'Let's kill it for Chazen and look to the future!'

This time a full-throated roar burst from the crowd.

'Mezai! Where are the scouts who volunteered to track

it down last night?' Kheda had to raise his voice to be heard in the din.

'My lord!' Before the shipmaster could answer, Kheda saw another familiar face forcing a path through the throng.

'Beyau, what brings you here?' Cold flowed through Kheda's heart. 'Is my lady Itrac all right?'

'She is, my lord,' Beyau assured him at once. 'She gave me leave to join in this hunt. She sent this for you.' He handed Kheda a double-folded and tightly sealed letter.

Kheda took it, aware that all eyes were suddenly fastened on him. He cracked the seals, sweat from his fingers darkening the pale reed paper. He scanned the letter and purposely smoothed an incautious frown from his forehead, replacing it with a wide smile of delight.

'We have another omen of blessing for Chazen.' Kheda brandished the paper high above his head to include everyone in his shouted announcement. 'My lady Itrac Chazen is with child! Let's make sure she brings the new heir into a domain free from the shadow of any dragon's wings!'

His words were drowned out by exultant cheers raised by those standing closest to him. Kheda stood looking at the letter.

Will you leave another fatherless child to be raised by a mother secretly relieved you are gone from her life? Will you leave Chazen with the disaster of an infant ruler prey to Daish ambition, never mind any other domain that might look to take advantage? This is all still far from over.

'This won't be such good news if we make so much noise that we frighten the dragon into flight, wounded or not.' Kheda turned his back on the jubilation spreading across the clutter of boats in the bay, lest he inadvertently catch sight of Risala. 'Mezai, where are those scouts?'

'Here, my lord.' Struggling for some belated restraint, the crowds parted to allow three disparate groups of men through to the warlord.

'My lord.' The leader of the first group bowed low before exchanging a glance with the man pushed forward by the second band. Each contingent showed a stamp of common blood and a harmony in their dress and weapons suggesting they were village hunting parties. The third gang was a loose collection of men whose stained gear and worn faces indicating the harder life of the solitary forest dweller. They had the darker complexions and wiry hair of hill blood rather than the coppery faces and sleeker heads of the coastal dwellers.

'Where is the dragon?' Kheda looked from the first man to the leader of the second group.

'That pass leads to a narrow valley, my lord.' The first man turned to point to a notch in the vine-choked trees cloaking the high ground rising from the shoreline. 'The valley leads up to a broad terrace on the far side of that peak. That's where the beast is lying up.'

Kheda looked but couldn't even see a peak on the distant mountain shrouded by curtains of low cloud.

'It's huddled in between two ridges running down from the height,' the leader of those from the second village added dourly. 'Trying to hide itself under a stand of iron-woods.'

'Is there space to get sufficient men up to fight it on this terrace?' Kheda looked for answers among all the men.

'Space enough.' One of the forest dwellers took a pace forward, rubbing a hand over his close-cropped beard. 'But there's only the one path to get up there.'

'Good day to you, Zicre.' Kheda nodded a brief greeting.

'There's nothing but bare rock and scree at its back,

my lord,' the dour hunter continued. 'We can only come at it from the front.'

'I don't think the beast is expecting attack,' an older man from the first village said judiciously. 'It's not lying up where it could keep watch for anyone starting up the slope.'

'It's certainly sorely wounded, my lord,' volunteered one of the second contingent. 'A blind man could find it in the dark from the stink alone.'

'And get his head bitten off for his trouble,' Zicre commented, grim-faced. 'If it's not lying in wait, it certainly doesn't want to be found.' He fixed Kheda with a questioning eye.

Kheda looked calmly back at him.

What would you ask me, if you dared? How did I know the dragon was here in the first place? Whether it would regain its strength if we left it alone? Could even so great a creature recover from the wounds you've seen? Why are we risking ourselves instead of just waiting to see if the dragon dies?

Because I think Velindre was right, mage or not, when she said this would be a form of purification for the domain. Because I have to know if I am condemned for bringing magic to this domain. What better wager than my life against this creature's?

He looked away from Zicre to the first group of scouts. 'How wide is the path to this terrace? How many men can we send up it abreast?'

'Four or five.' The man got nods of agreement from his companions.

'Is there room for them to spread out, to let more of us come up behind?' persisted Kheda. 'If there's only the one way to reach this beast, we must overwhelm it as fast as we can.'

'Yes, my lord,' several men concurred, their faces serious.

At the rear, Zicre looked grimmer than ever. 'There's space, my lord.'

'Then let's be on our way.' Kheda walked past him and headed for the track between the tandra trees.

Seeing their warlord disappearing into the green darkness stifled the last cheers still ringing around the outskirts of the impromptu horde. The men of Chazen followed their warlord; trained swordsmen, practised hunters, fishermen relying on skills learned performing very different tasks and villagers with unwavering determination to reinforce their shaky arms. The abrupt silence was broken only by the crack of brush and vegetation mercilessly subdued by their passing and the chink and rattle of armour. Even with the cool of the night lingering here and there among the shadowy trees, the air was close and oppressive.

Kheda led the way up towards the notch in the higher ground that gave on to the valley leading up to the dragon's lair. The taciturn Zicre slid through the swordsmen to follow close behind him, swiping unnecessarily at opportunist tangles of striol vine choking berry bushes and lilla saplings striving to claim their share of the rainy season's bounty. Behind, the sound of hacking blades grew louder as men spilled off the narrowing trail into the thicker growth, oaths and obscenities meeting thorns or whipping twigs fighting back.

The sound of hurrying feet on the bare earth and muffled protests stiffened Kheda's spine. He glanced back over his shoulder and acknowledged Mezai and Beyau with a stern face that instantly quelled their stealthy attempts to edge past Zicre, who was still following close behind Kheda.

The forest was still and silent all around. Distant birdsong and the calls of loals were muffled by the mists, with the distorted shrieks of some unidentifiable creature reverberating off an unseen cliff face. A flash of movement caught Kheda's eye and he saw a golden-crowned matia clinging to the wrinkled grey trunk of an ironwood. He blinked sweat out of his eyes and when he looked again, it was gone. He and his men could have been the only living creatures in the forest.

Apart from the blood-sucking flies.

Feeling the burning bite of black sweat flies, Kheda scrubbed fiercely at one cheek with the back of a gloved hand. Beside him, Zicre paused and looked to the rear. Kheda did the same and was surprised to see how far up the incline they had already come. Glimpses of the dull turquoise sea were just visible through the crowded branches of the spinefruit trees overhanging the trail. Down among the trees, the men of Chazen were forcing their way forward, all sweating profusely. The forest around them was thick with mist, drifting upwards to join the unbroken cloud cover. Kheda looked up to see the thin cloud silvering as the hidden sun strengthened. The heat of the day was beginning to build. Somewhere in the pungent depths of the forest a stream chuckled and he saw thirsty men break off from the main thrust to search for the relief of its waters.

Wordlessly, Zicre unslung a battered gourd from his shoulder and drank deeply before offering it to Kheda. The warlord took it with a grateful nod. His tongue felt like damp cotton, thick in his mouth, and the oppressive heat seemed to weigh more heavily with every breath. That and the burden of Zicre's eyes fixed on him.

What are you thinking? Why the unspoken questions in your eyes and the shadow of doubt? I was the one who brought lore from the north to join battle with the invaders and their savage sorcery coming unbidden to these waters. And I lost Daish for my pains, so that's hardly the best endorsement of my wisdom. Is all I've done for Chazen enough to redress the balance? Is that what you're wondering?

Kheda handed Zicre back his gourd. 'You've some herbs in there I can't quite identify.'

Zicre smiled briefly and restoppered the gourd. 'Yes, my lord.'

'What can I trade for the secret?' Kheda wondered aloud.

'We'll see.' Zicre shrugged. 'Later, if we get the chance.'

His dark gaze locked with Kheda's.

You've seen the dragon, haven't you, Zicre? You know what we're up against, wounded or not.

'My lord?' As the scouting parties paused to suck greedily at their waterskins, Beyau and Mezai forced their way through to draw close to Kheda, their faces concerned.

'Is everything all right?' Kheda asked. The shipmaster was drenched with sweat.

Beyau granted the scouts a cursory glance. 'Let me lead the first assault, my lord,' he begged unexpectedly. 'I was trained to be a warrior for Chazen.'

'And you want to test your fate here against the guilt you still feel for surviving when so many of those warriors died?' Kheda asked with quiet sympathy. 'Don't try to second-guess your destiny, Beyau, just accept it and go on with your life. As for leading this assault, no, that is my duty and I will neither shirk it nor let any other man claim it from me.'

He turned his back on the startled faces of Beyau, Mezai and the scattered scouts. As impassive as ever, Zicre walked silently beside him as they covered the last stretch of the track leading to the rocky cleft in the ridge of high ground.

'Not far now, my lord,' the hunter observed quietly. 'We need to stick to the sides of the valley. It's all marsh in the bottom.'

Now Kheda could see the stream he had been hearing

all the way up the slope, flowing down from a peak still hidden in mist. The water of endless successive rainy seasons had carved a channel down the rock only to find its path to the sea barred by this stubborn ridge. It pooled in indecision before turning to seek another route and the reek of ancient decay fuelled afresh by recent downpours rose from the spreading bog.

Zicre smiled humourlessly at Kheda's unguarded grimace. 'If you think that's bad, wait till you smell the dragon.'

Kheda didn't answer, heading down towards the narrow path that Zicre indicated. He moved slowly, to be sure of his footing and to allow the rest of this diverse multitude of dragon slayers to keep pace with him. Not everyone was so careful on the awkward slope and the slippery, crushed vegetation was treacherous underfoot. Kheda couldn't help but grin as startled yells were hastily stifled by splashes from the bog.

Then he caught a gust of a smell so putrid it made him retch. Recollections of revolting encounters flashed through his memory.

That spotted deer dead of an arrow to the throat and unseen in a thicket until an incautious woodcutter filled the campsite with the foetid gas from its bloated belly. The hunt when we came across a hook-toothed hog drowned in a wallow, skull picked clean by carrion birds and beetles, the rest of it disintegrated into a slough of foulness roiling with maggots. That time we found a courier dove fallen into a water cistern and realised we'd bathed in water tainted with that matted mess of slimy decay.

Clapping a mail-backed glove to his mouth, Kheda fought to control his heaving stomach. 'The dragon?' he asked Zicre with a gasp, trying to ignore the sound of vomiting behind him.

The hunter nodded silently as he tied a rag around his

mouth and nose. He handed a second strip of cloth to Kheda. The warlord caught the pungent scent of chaelor oil and pressed it gratefully to his nose.

'How exactly do we set about attacking it, my lord?' The other men who'd scouted out the valley drew up around Zicre as the hunter spoke, all their faces expectant. 'Once we're up on the terrace.'

The men of Chazen were spreading out among the trees; some were still doubled up emptying their guts but most were standing upright, faces muddy with apprehension and nausea.

Kheda took a slow, careful breath to avoid any spasm of queasiness and did his best to pitch his words to carry to the farthest man he could see without speaking overly loudly.

'First and foremost, we cannot risk letting the dragon fly away, so we must foul its wings with nets and ropes.' He glanced at the contingents from the fishing boats. 'Those of you without much armour, tear into its wings, ripping the membranes. For the rest of us–' he included everyone with an impromptu blade in his gaze '–if its hide is proof against another dragon's teeth, it'll be proof against the best swords. So we attack its wounds. We set it bleeding again. It's already weak. We want it weaker still.'

'Weak is one thing, dead's another,' interrupted Zicre, ignoring looks of outrage at his temerity. 'How are we to kill it?'

'The quickest way to any creature's brain is through its mouth or its eyes.' Kheda fixed the hunter with an unwavering gaze. 'That's my task. What I need the rest of you to do is keep it distracted by so many attacks that it doesn't realise what I aim to do, until it's too late.'

Confused protests rose from Beyau and Mezai and others besides, while the armoured warriors of Chazen tried to force their way closer to their warlord, with fervent assurances that they would be at his side, their swords with his.

Kheda ignored them all as he looked at the rugged shoulder of the peak, a dark shadow against the mist lightened under the strengthening sun. 'The path leads up round that spur?' He looked to Zicre and got a silent nod of confirmation. 'The terrace is beyond that?'

He drew a deep breath, grateful for the pungent chaelor oil masking the stench of decay. Setting a punishing pace up the hill, he was soon feeling the strain in the backs of his thighs and calves. As the path widened to claim a broad, undulating ledge at the base of the peak, men drew level with him on either side. Beyau was surrounded by warriors of the Chazen household, their armour brilliant with beads of moisture, the muffled light of the sun turning their naked blades to dull silver. Mezai was in among the fishermen burdened with their nets and ropes, other men from the *Gossamer Shark* gripping clubs and long knives.

A broken knife edge of rock rose sheer on one side, the broad ledge falling away into a confusion of forest on the other. As the slope grew less cruel, Kheda pushed on faster, Zicre still at his side. Beyau and the swordsmen ran with them, faces grim beneath the brow bands of their polished helms. The tramp of the countless feet behind Mezai and the mariners reverberated across the steep valley.

Kheda rounded the shoulder of the peak and the hollow of level ground between the two ridges running down from the peak opened up before them. Some of the biggest ironwoods he had ever seen had claimed this sheltered, fertile spot for their own. Hidden from foresters who would have cut them down long since and thought them a mighty prize, they had soared upwards.

The great grey trees with their lofty crowns of dense green leaves looked no more than saplings behind the massive bulk sprawled in front of them. The reek of decay hung stifling in the air. The dragon lay awkwardly, hindquarters slumped to one side, stormy-blue hind legs drawn up to its pale grey belly, its massive tail, dark as thunder cloud, curling around. The wounds torn in its hide by the dead fire dragon gaped wide, dark bruised flesh barely visible beneath clusters of flies and beetles, intent on feeding and not caring if their prey was alive or dead. Every now and again the dragon's skin twitched in a feeble attempt to shake off the tormenters. A few flies were dislodged, only to return with buzzing eagerness. Where beetles fell away, their place was instantly taken by newcomers from the glittering horde scrambling over and around each other. The ground below the creature was a crushed mass of bushes and saplings foul with blackened blood.

There was more life in the front end of the dragon. It rested on its chest, forelegs braced, white crystal claws digging into the shattered twigs and leaf litter. Its massive blue-grey head swayed from side to side, hoary spines bristling with malice the length of its long, muscular neck. Eyes blue as sapphire glowed with malevolence beneath frosty brow ridges and it opened its mouth to hiss menacingly, long cobalt tongue flickering over teeth like steel sword blades. With a rattling clap, it spread its wings.

It couldn't spread them very far. The rents torn by the fire dragon had ulcerated horribly. Purple slime soiled the cloudy membrane, oozing from the spreading wounds. The creature's defiant hiss turned to one of agony as it let its wings fall back in painful disorder.

The men of Chazen crowded behind their warlord, each man lending courage to those gathered close around him, inadvertently pressing Kheda forward. He raised his sword slowly, then cut it down with an audible swish. He was already running, Zicre on one side, Beyau on the other, mariners, warriors and huntsmen hard on their heels.

The dragon disappeared. A veil of mist opaque as silk came down before their astonished eyes. Kheda barely hesitated, plunging on through the fog. After a moment's indecision, the men with him followed. The whiteness wrapped around them, denser than ever. Kheda looked from side to side and found he could barely make out Zicre or Beyau even though he was close enough to touch them. He slowed just a little.

'Where is it?' Beyau asked through clenched teeth.

'It can't have flown away.' Shivers wracked Kheda and he looked down to see frost forming on his chain mail. 'Not on those wings. And we'd have heard it.'

'What magic is this, my lord?' Zicre's sweat-sodden clothing crackled as he fought against its sudden icy embrace.

'We must kill it before we all freeze to death.' Kheda gasped. The all-enveloping mist deadened his words and he realised he could barely hear anything beyond arm's length either.

'My lord?' It was Mezai, teeth chattering uncontrollably, breath frozen white in his beard.

'Come on,' Kheda said with difficulty, his jaw stiff with cold.

'My lord!' Barely coherent, Beyau threw himself at Kheda and knocked the warlord off his feet. The dragon's head appeared out of the deathly mist, snapping at the void where Kheda had just been standing. Mezai and Zicre stumbled forward, brandishing their weapons. Their yells of wordless defiance were instantly swallowed by the fog swirling ever denser around them.

'I got it!' The ice in Mezai's beard cracked as he grinned, proffering his crude hacking blade.

Kheda pulled himself painfully to his feet, chilled thighs and forearms aching bone deep from the impact on the brutally frozen ground. 'Well done.' An icy smear of dark-blue blood glittered on the burnished steel of Mezai's weapon.

'Here, my lord.' Zicre bent to recover a scatter of small blue-white scales with fingers withered by the cold.

Tossing aside the chaelor-soaked rag, Kheda held out a gloved hand and examined the scales the hunter laid on his palm. They were edged with putrid flesh where they had been ripped from the underside of the dragon's jaw. He closed his hand around them and felt them crumble. When he uncurled his fingers, all he held was glittering powder.

Velindre said it would fade away to nothing.

'Perhaps its hide won't be so tough after all,' said Zicre cautiously.

'Come on.' Kheda threw the dust away, brushing his hand against his thigh.

They advanced slowly, Kheda at the forefront, the other three behind him to make a rough arrowhead, every man's eyes looking in all directions. Shadows in the fog fleeted on the edge of vision. Noises came and went so fast they might just have been imagined. Kheda ripped off his helmet and threw it away.

'My lord,' Beyau protested.

'Seeing and hearing have more value than armour in this.' Kheda strained eyes and ears. 'Are we the only ones going forward? Can you hear anyone else?'

A scream ripped through the mist and the clouded air swirled violently around them. More yells tumbled over each other, punctured by a rattling sweep. Then the mist gathered ever closer, deadening the noise.

'Its tail?' hazarded Zicre through clenched teeth. He brushed frost from the front of his tunic but the oiled leather vanished beneath a fresh layer of white.

'Where's its head?' Kheda gripped his sword tight with aching fingers and peered into the fog. He could feel cold moisture seeping through his hair to trickle down his scalp and temples.

A stealthy current in the air alerted him an instant before he saw the sapphire glint of the dragon's eye cutting through the white mist. Its blue head darted forward, jaw agape, cobalt tongue lashing, blue-black blood dripping from its chin. Kheda didn't flinch, sweeping his sword around and up to slash at the slack hide beneath the dragon's jaw. He ripped the blade away and ducked sideways to lose himself in the mist. The creature's roar of pain made the fog all around throb.

Kheda tensed at a swirl of the vapour then relaxed as the other three emerged and crouched beside him. 'We have to catch its head somehow,' he told them forcefully, 'so we can force it down and have at its eyes. We have to blind it!'

'We'll find a net.' Mezai was shivering so violently he looked like a man in the grip of fever. Jerking his head at Beyau, he stumbled backwards to vanish in the white mist. The swordsman hesitated.

'Go,' Kheda ordered.

Zicre moved to stand with his back to Kheda's. 'Do you think it can see us through this?'

'I don't know.' Kheda shivered as the other man's weight pressed the frozen padding beneath his mail against his chilled flesh.

His words were lost as sobbing forced its way through the dense mist, cut off short in a horrifying gurgle. The dragon's hiss rasped through the blinding fog, seeming to come from all directions. Kheda drew his second sword and shifted his weight from foot to foot.

'Ware!' Zicre shouted and flung himself sideways as the dragon's forelimb raked through the mist, glittering claws ripping across at chest height.

Kheda wheeled around, dodging awkwardly. He flailed blindly with his swords and made contact more by luck than judgement. His blade ripped a claw from its socket, the crystal talon nearly skewering Zicre before it disappeared into the enveloping fog. The dragon bellowed and its head loomed above him, teeth bared, dodging bloody blue saliva. Kheda stood his ground and hacked at the beast's neck and jaw with all his strength. One blade clashed against its teeth. The dragon recoiled, only to snap at the blade, shattering the tempered steel to lethal needles. Kheda flinched from the blinding shower, fleeing blindly. The dragon's foreclaws struck him a glancing blow on his mailed back, sending him tumbling over frozen vegetation that crackled beneath him. He rolled over on to his back, raising his remaining sword. A shadow darkened the fog, pierced by a glint of sapphire flame.

'Hey!' Zicre found a fallen spear underfoot and flung it at the mist-shrouded dragon.

Kheda heard the polearm strike with a solid clunk. The dragon's head whipped across to snap at Zicre, trailing tendrils of haze and slaver. Diamond drops spattered Kheda's armour. The steel rings and inset plates of his hauberk cracked and split where the drool landed.

'My lord.' A hand grabbed his shoulder. It was Mezai.

'Are you hurt?' As Beyau hauled him up, Kheda realised there was a rent in the back of his chain mail.

'No.' He gripped his remaining sword and scanned the white opacity for the dragon and Zicre alike. 'Have you got a net?'

'And grapnels,' Mezai confirmed with bitter satisfaction.

'What's happening?' Kheda strained his ears for any sound that would offer an answer. 'Where are the others?'

Before anyone could speak, the dragon attacked, murderous maw agape and intent on Kheda. The warlord waited until the last instant before darting aside, hacking at the side of the creature's long, scaly face. Mezai threw a grapnel at the dragon's head and the curved tines tangled in the crest of spines at the nape of its neck. It roared and reared up, trying to shake off the biting metal teeth. Zicre appeared and flung himself on the rope to add his weight to Mezai's, pulling the barbs ever deeper into the creature's flesh.

'Chazen! Here! Chazen!' Kheda shouted into the empty mist as loudly as he could, moving between the dragon and the two men, lest it try biting at them.

The dragon was more concerned with the immediate cause of its pain. It ducked its head in a futile attempt to escape the tormenting grapnel. Beyau seized his chance and flung a broad net over the beast's head, the wide mesh weighted with pierced and polished stones. The dragon shook its head with a furious hiss, snapping at the weights dangling just out of reach. It licked at the net and the rope crumbled to dust at the touch of its freezing saliva.

'Chazen!' A second net came spinning out of the mist, the web black against the encircling pallor. It landed squarely on the dragon's head and men followed it. Kheda knew some of them from the *Gossamer Shark*, and others who had volunteered as scouts. The rest he didn't recognise. A double handful ran to lend their strength to Mezai's rope, slipping over the icy ground. Their combined weight began inexorably dragging the dragon's head downwards.

More ropes and nets appeared from all directions, everyone intent on snaring the dragon's head. The creature roared with fury, fighting the binding cords and cables. It clawed frantically, first with one forelimb, then the other.

'Let me get at its eyes!' Kheda stood, watching and waiting, sword at the ready.

The dragon bellowed and reared upwards, dragging those closest off their feet as they clung to their ropes in frozen terror. It slashed at them with murderous talons and two men fell backwards, eviscerated in a single stroke. One rolled over to land at Kheda's feet, the bloody void of his abdomen frozen solid before he came to rest.

'Chazen!' The men of the domain raised their vengeful cry. More rushed forward to haul on the ropes and grapnels tangled in the dragon's spines. Nets smothered its muzzle, caught in its teeth. It tore at the mesh with a forefoot but only succeeded in ripping the lethal fangs from its own jaw.

'Bring it down!' Kheda yelled.

Mezai raised a breathless chant that the warlord recognised from the *Gossamer Shark*'s rowing deck. Hoarse with exhaustion, other mariners joined in. Fishermen picked up the rhythm in the next breath and the hunters and merchants weren't slow to follow. With every man's might brought to bear together in the rhythm of the gasping, tuneless song, the dragon's head dipped. They drew it further down with every beat. The wheezing chorus took on a menacing, exultant note. Kheda watched the creature's burning sapphire eye brought lower and lower. He gripped his sword and waited for the moment to strike.

As the dragon's scaly jaw dipped to touch the ground, hailstones fell so thickly that Kheda couldn't see through them. Big as the most precious pearls, they bruised his head and face brutally. Gasping and squinting through the pain, Kheda stumbled forwards. He could barely keep his footing on the icy spheres and his feet were so numb he couldn't feel them. All that mattered was that he could still see the dragon's eye glowing blue through the mist.

Cries of distress rang through the fog and the coordinated assault dissolved in pain and panic. Kheda pushed past some nameless islander still clinging to a rope despite the jagged ice lacerating his bare hands. Drops of the man's red blood were falling frozen to join the drifts of hailstones now ankle deep.

Kheda was close enough to see the dragon lashing with its blue tongue at the nets draped over its long face. The ropes tangled around its neck and forequarters were breaking and crumbling away as it clawed its way free. It had a dead body pinned beneath the other forepaw, its talons embedded in the man's back, the corpse already half-buried beneath the hail.

Kheda grabbed at a twisted cord tangled in the spines above the dragon's brow and hung on it with all his weight, levelling his sword. The dragon's head darted down towards him, blue tongue seeking him like a serpent. Bracing himself as best he could, with all the strength he could muster, Kheda thrust the blade deep into the creature's glowing eye. The sapphire orb shattered like crystal. Burning white fluid oozed along the sword, etching the steel like acid. Kheda held tight to the hilt and thrust again, leaning in with all his might, twisting the blade ever deeper. The burning whiteness ate away the sword's guard and hissed against the fine chain mail of Kheda's gauntlets. He held his ground as long as he dared then sprang away, tearing off his gloves and tossing them to the ground where they steamed with an acrid metallic stink.

The dragon's head slumped to the ground, long neck limp. The beast writhed in agony, convulsions rippling through its body to prompt shouts of alarm far away in the mist. Its long blue tongue curled around its muzzle, tentatively licking at its ruined eye. A tormented moan escaped it, wretched and pitiful.

'My lord?' It was Beyau, offering Kheda a sword in a hand bloodied by rope burns and blackened by cold.

Kheda looked at the dragon. The creature was now motionless.

'Wait.' He gave head and foreclaws a wide berth as he skirted warily around it, to get a clear sight of its unwounded eye.

The glow of white fire in the sapphire depths was growing fainter. Kheda watched it fade to little more than a candle flame. The hailstones began to melt. The incandescence shrank to a mere pinprick. The fog dissolved to no more than a frail memory, misty around the treetops.

The men around him were exclaiming in relief or giving way to grief as they saw their fallen comrades. Kheda kept his attention fixed on the dragon's eye. The light finally died and a warm breeze rolled up the valley.

'Is it dead?' Zicre looked at Kheda for confirmation, hugging an arm wrenched bodily out of its shoulder socket. Fearful faces all around begged for the same reassurance.

Kheda walked forward and laid a hand on the creature's muzzle. The twilight-blue scales were cold but not with the burning chill of magic. No breath issued from the wide nostrils and the lolling blue tongue didn't so much as twitch when he pushed it with a tentative foot. He looked again at the creature's unwounded eye, now dull and clouded beneath a drooping eyelid. 'Yes.'

Someone raised a shaky cheer of celebration and others soon joined in. Men pressed close all around Kheda, shoving at the dead dragon as if they needed to touch it to convince themselves it was truly defeated.

'My lord?' Mezai looked to Kheda for permission, his knife poised over one of the spines behind the dragon's neck. Kheda nodded and watched the shipmaster dig out the needle-sharp scale. 'How's this for a talisman, my lord?' Mezai grinned, exultant. 'The *Gossamer Shark* won't go down like the *Mist Dove*!'

A group of huntsmen began disentangling the corpse of their friend from the dragon's dead foreclaws, ripping out the talons for their own prize as they did so. Out of the corner of his eye, Kheda saw a troop of Chazen warriors set about hacking off the spiked tip of the dragon's tail, brushing aside the dead flies and carrion beetles that the sudden cold had killed. Emboldened, others used the ropes to scramble up the creature's sides, intent on digging their knives into the wounds already splitting its hide. The mountain hollow grew loud with congratulation, speculation and the heady joking of men who'd half-expected to die instead of see victory. The youth Ridu's hysterical laughter rang out at some inane jest.

Kheda smiled wordlessly and walked away. Men who had fled the fearful fog in the first place or broken beneath the murderous hailstorm emerged from the trees, shamefaced. Some looked hopefully to Kheda for permission to claim their share of the fallen creature's teeth and scales. Others fell to their knees, faces in the dirt, begging for his forgiveness. He ignored them all.

'My lord?' Beyau caught up with the warlord, face anxious.

'Don't you want to claim a trophy?' Kheda gestured back towards the plundered corpse. 'Before the day warms up enough to start it stinking?'

'There's fewer dead than I feared, my lord,' Beyau said stoutly.

'Still too many for comfort.' Kheda slowed reluctantly, seeing that Beyau was limping painfully.

This creature would have died without their blood being shed. Didn't I just bring these men to a meaningless death?

'They made the choices that brought them to such a fate, my lord.' Beyau's face twisted with emotion. 'And this is a victory for Chazen over magic and malice, at last.'

'And a victory must be bought at a price if it is to have any lasting value.' Kheda tried to keep the desolation out of his voice. He stared down at the ground for a moment, before lifting his eyes to the trees and the sky now clearing above them. 'I want a tower of silence built on the beach,' he said slowly. 'Two, if needs be. The men who died here died for the whole domain. Let's hope that gives some value to their families' losses. And those who lived through this slaughter must remember those who didn't, when they're praised as heroes the length and breadth of these islands. See to it, Beyau.'

Still wracked with a chill that the hot sun couldn't warm away, Kheda turned his back on the butchery of the dead dragon and began walking towards the coast. His sword scabbards hung empty in his belt. He realised he didn't know if it had been his blade or Dev's that had finally killed the beast. He decided it really didn't matter.

CHAPTER TWENTY-TWO

The beach on Boal was a long bank of pale sand crowned with low tangles of midar. Violet flowers glowed among the long glossy leaves outspread to welcome the rains. Ragged furrows in the sand showed where the horn-backed turtles had crawled up the beach under cover of night to dig their nests and lay their eggs.

Kheda walked carefully down to the water's edge to stroll along the firm, wet sand. Every now and then an adventurous ripple nudged at his toes. He looked down to see his feet still bruised where someone had trampled them in the chaos of the cloud dragon's death. His face was still scabbed from the hail's assault.

But everything is healing. Everyone is healing. And the families of those that died are honoured for the sake of those who fell fighting for Chazen's future.

He looked along the gentle curve of the shore to the far headland where a solitary pinnacle of shaped white stone rose from a grove of nut palms.

I suppose it makes sense for Itrac to visit this particular tower of silence. Boal is where they were first attacked by the wild men and their magic, her and Chazen Saril and Olkai Chazen. I wonder what she will see in her dreams. Will echoes from those peaceful days offer her hope for an untroubled future? Or will any guidance from the past be lost in the chaos of recent events?

There's not much I can do about that. But I can rid this domain of the last distortion of magic.

He walked towards Velindre, who was sitting some distance down the beach. Still dressed in her guise of *zamorin* scholar, she was leaning back on her hands with her long legs outstretched as she stared up into the sky, intent on the clouds scudding up from the south. A breeze tousled her fine blonde hair, now grown to a softness that nevertheless did little to threaten her imposture. The lines in her face were carved deeper than before, skin burned by sun and wind taut over her angular features.

'There'll be rain this afternoon.' Kheda walked up the beach to the dry sand beyond the high-water mark. Mindful of the carved ironwood box he was carrying, he sat beside the magewoman.

'Indeed.' Velindre's thoughts were on something else entirely.

'You'll be returning to your home soon, so I brought you this.' Kheda placed the wooden box carefully on her lap.

'What?' Velindre dragged herself away from contemplating the skies and frowned. 'What's this? I want that dragon's egg—'

'And you'll get it,' said Kheda curtly. 'This is something else.'

Velindre opened the lid of the box to reveal a plain casket of rock crystal. Iridescent dust inside sparkled in the sunlight. She went to lift the lid.

'No.' Kheda held her hand back. 'Don't open it.'

'Why not?' she asked suspiciously. 'What is it?'

'It's all that remains of Dev.' Kheda stared out over the turquoise sea, far away across the deeper blue of the open ocean to the far horizon where the sea couldn't be distinguished from the line of turbulent clouds presaging the next wave of rainstorms. 'And I don't want it blowing all over this beach. Come to that, the winds from the south could carry some part of him over the entire Archipelago.'

'Which would not be a good thing.' Velindre looked down at the casket. 'All things considered.'

'You burn your dead on the mainland, so Risala tells me,' Kheda continued with distant courtesy. 'We don't do that here, we don't know your rites – but I gathered what ashes I could, in case you wanted to inter them somewhere.'

'Fire may be the ultimate purification but you still don't want whatever remains of Dev making any claim on Chazen's future.' Velindre sounded bitter.

'Whatever good he did for the domain is honoured in the tales of his death in my service that are being told around the evening fires,' Kheda said slowly. 'That will suffice for his legacy.'

Velindre carefully lifted the crystal casket up and studied the contents as best she could. 'The gems that were crushed to powder, they're all mixed in with the ash.'

'I couldn't see any way of separating them.' Kheda shrugged. 'Or any point, come to that. Magic was woven into his very being in life.'

Velindre smiled reluctantly. 'What about those gems that were driven into the walls of the cave? Have you recovered those?'

'We have.' Kheda allowed himself a brief, ruthless smile. 'With them most likely wholly ill omened, as Dev said, we're keeping them separate and they are only to be traded with domains like that of Ulla Safar. He's long wished me ill, so I see no harm in sending him all the bad luck I can, in return for things we need to rebuild Chazen.'

'Which is being rebuilt apace now that galleys have come from Redigal and Aedis and even Ritsem and Jahal,' Velindre observed.

'Now that word of our victory over the dragon is spreading,' Kheda agreed. 'And now we have pearls to trade and a fine harvest of turtleshell.'

'And most prized of all, dragonhide,' said Velindre pointedly. 'And all the other talismans you won.'

'Quite.' Kheda continued staring out to the southern sea.

Doesn't this prove I was following the right course, that Chazen's trade is so quickly restored, with so many keen to share in our good fortune?

'Has anyone remarked on the fact that the second dragon had no gem at its heart?' Velindre's voice was neutral as she nodded at the faceted ruby hanging from the golden chain in the open neck of Kheda's russet silk tunic.

'No,' Kheda said slowly. 'I don't suppose anyone noticed, in all the confusion. If anyone does think of it, they'll doubtless assume I hold it for the sake of the domain.' He glanced at her. 'I'm curious about the scales and teeth taken from the cloud dragon. When it was dying, it was all but disintegrating, but no one's come to me saying their trophies have turned to dust. The lengths of hide sent to Itrac are as sturdy as any other lizardskin.'

'I'm just as curious,' Velindre admitted frankly, still holding up the crystal casket and studying the contents. 'I imagined it would all crumble away to nothing. Perhaps I've stumbled across something Azazir didn't know. Or he knows something he didn't care to share with me.' She sighed. 'There's so much we don't know about dragons.'

Kheda did his best to hide his distaste. 'Surely what you've learned and seen means you've valuable lore to take back to your island of Hadrumal, along with Dev's ashes.'

'And the dragon's egg.' Velindre looked quizzically at the warlord. 'Are you trying to get rid of me?'

'Yes,' Kheda replied bluntly. 'The sooner all magic and all trace of it are gone from Chazen, the better for all of us and our future.'

'You certainly want Itrac's child born under the most

favourable auspices possible.' Velindre nodded with understanding.

Kheda was surprised. 'I am glad you appreciate that.'

'I understand a good deal more about Aldabreshin ways than you realise, my lord Chazen.' Velindre set the casket with Dev's ashes carefully back in the ironwood box. 'I had plenty of time to read on the voyage south and every domain has a tradition of fine scholarship, even if we in the north are ignorant of it.'

'I'll be happy to supply you with all the books you want for your journey home.' Kheda smiled tightly. 'As well as our fastest trireme.'

'I don't need any boat. I can return to Hadrumal in the blink of an eye.' Velindre closed the intricately carved lid of the box gently. 'And I'll take this token of Dev's life and death back with me. He had no family that he ever acknowledged and few enough friends in Hadrumal, but there are those who should know of his fate and some who could learn from it.'

'I'm glad to hear it,' said Kheda honestly. 'You must know we believe a man's life isn't done when he dies. Much that he was lives on, as long as those who knew him live on after him.'

'I don't imagine many mages will think of Dev in those terms,' Velindre said sardonically.

Kheda got to his feet. 'Let me know when you're planning to leave and I'll make sure the egg is delivered to you.' He hesitated. 'You will be discreet. Perhaps you should set sail with Risala for some outlying island. If anyone asks we can say you took a merchant galley north.'

'If she can spare the time from spreading your carefully rehearsed version of events around Chazen.' Velindre looked up at him, hazel eyes like golden onyx in the sun. 'Or carrying it to trusted traders and her friends in other domains. As I said, Chazen Kheda, I know more than you think. And just what do you propose to do for Risala?'

Kheda was thrown by the abrupt change of subject. 'What do you mean?'

'The girl's in love with you.' Velindre lifted a hand to shade her narrowed eyes. 'Can you give her anything better than some precisely calculated share in your favours? Are you capable of returning her love, with Itrac carrying a child that will link you to Chazen for all your futures?'

'That's none of your concern,' Kheda retorted roughly.

'She's still young enough to see everything in absolutes of dark and light.' Velindre let her hand fall and returned to staring out to sea. 'You could hurt her very badly.'

'I value her certainties.' Kheda looked away inland but the bank of the beach hid the seldom-used residence from him. 'Risala can see that all I have done has been for Chazen's good and Daish's before that. She knows all that I have done and does not condemn me.'

And I never thought to burn with such desire for a woman. No, more than simple desire. Is this truly love—

'Then be certain that what you do for her is for her own good.' Velindre's sharp tone interrupted his thoughts. 'I'll return to Hadrumal soon enough but I shall want your safe conduct to travel in the Archipelago again.'

'What?' Kheda shook his head in instinctive denial. 'No.'

'You owe me a considerable debt, Chazen Kheda.' Velindre stood up, brushing sand from her white cotton trousers. 'And Dev said you were an honest man, someone to be trusted. Being such a scoundrel himself, he should know. I choose not to be repaid in pearls or gems or anything else. I have that right, you must agree?'

'Archipelagan customs are for Aldabreshi—' Kheda began.

Velindre overrode him. 'It's been custom for years beyond count that anyone choosing to live in the

Archipelago should be counted as Aldabreshin, whether they were born slave or free, islander or mainlander, man, woman or *zamorin*.'

'Everyone living in the Archipelago is bound to a domain,' Kheda retorted. 'You're not.'

'Nor was Dev.' Velindre shrugged. 'But doesn't rendering some signal service to a domain entitle a traveller to ask for a right of residence?'

'Dev was an object of suspicion to several warlords,' Kheda shot back, choosing to ignore that question. 'Ask Risala. Shek Kul, her lord that was – he told me to find Dev in the first place. If he'd had proof, Dev would have died the death of all who use magic in these islands long since.'

'But he didn't have proof,' retorted Velindre. 'If Dev can live in the Archipelago without being discovered, I'll bet I can. Isn't that how you test your fate in these waters, with such a wager?'

'Only when something of the utmost value is at stake,' countered Kheda swiftly.

'I wouldn't risk myself for anything less,' Velindre assured him. 'I will be searching for something of tremendous value, to mages and Archipelagans alike.'

'We hold no values in common.' Kheda shook his head vehemently.

'I'm not talking philosophy or morality,' said Velindre caustically. 'What about more practical values of safety and security?'

'What do you mean?' Kheda looked askance at her.

'You recall I told you about the currents in the air, those in the highest heavens, that I can draw on for my magic?' Velindre gestured up towards the sky. 'I've been studying them since we came here and I've a few notions that might interest you. I don't think these winds normally reach these latitudes. I think they blow over the open ocean for the most part. Something has driven the torrent of air north.'

'Why should that interest me?' snapped Kheda.

'Because I believe that fire dragon rode those winds to come here,' Velindre replied calmly. 'And if one dragon can do that, so could another and another, who knows? Don't you want some warning if that's likely to happen?' She waved her hand across the flat expanse of the shore. 'Those savages who landed here to bring magic and slaughter, where do you suppose they came from?'

'You've no more notion than I have,' scoffed Kheda angrily.

'No,' Velindre agreed, 'but I think they were following that current of wind in the high heavens, either by reading the clouds or seeing the element alive within it. I think they knew that dragon would be coming here and they wanted to be ready, with whatever gems and food they could gather, before it came.'

She looked inland to the wind-tossed trees, thoughtful. 'I don't believe they came here to take your land. I think those mages were fighting among themselves to establish who was powerful enough to use that dragon's aura. Perhaps only the strongest would be able to hold the beast off with his own magic. I don't think they've any notion of creating a simulacrum of a dragon with elemental power. Why should they, if they have true dragons? If a wizard could win a dragon's trust so that it wouldn't simply kill him as some rival, its aura would give him elemental power beyond imagining to draw on.'

Kheda heard fear and desire in equal measure in her voice.

And you're the only wizard who knows any of this, now Dev is dead. Shouldn't I kill you here and now, to stop you carrying such dangerous knowledge away with you?

Velindre rounded on him. 'So what will you do if some

wild wizard comes here with a true dragon ready to do his will? What will you do if another untamed dragon rides that highest wind to land on your shores? Or perhaps I should say "when".'

Once you start dealing with magic, you can never be free of it, can you?

Gooseflesh rose on Kheda's arms. 'What will you do for us?' he demanded. 'To help us in such circumstances? If I let you travel the Archipelago under Chazen protection?'

'I'll go back to Hadrumal first, to consult our libraries and those few mages I can think of who may be trusted with this theory and not seduced by its possibilities.' Acerbic, Velindre ticked off her points on long, nail-bitten fingers. 'Secondly, I'll look for any other sources of dragon lore on the mainland. Then I'll come back to the Archipelago and search Aldabreshin scholarship for any useful knowledge. That would be much easier with a Chazen dagger at my belt and some token of yours to back me.'

'We know nothing of dragons,' Kheda interrupted. 'That's why I had to turn to you barbarians!'

Velindre shook her head. 'I don't mean dragon lore. I'm thinking of mariners' tales of galleys driven out into the ocean by some misfortune. I want to hear of any strange ships washed up in these southern waters or unknown birds blown ashore by some freak storm. All those things would be taken for portents and recorded somewhere, wouldn't they?'

'What good would such lore do you?' demanded Kheda.

Velindre's face was hard and cold. 'These dragons and these wild men, they must live somewhere. I'll be looking for any clues as to where we might sail to find them. Don't you want to know where such an enemy is to be found? Don't you want to find out what manner of threat they pose to this domain and all the rest of the Archipelago? Don't you want to have some chance of putting an end to their evil?'

'You talk of evil, when you're a mage.' Kheda threw up his hands, to stop himself drawing a knife on the wizard woman. 'Haven't I done enough harm by bringing wizardry into these reaches? Why should I help you find out secrets you can use to your own twisted advantage?'

'I'm not seeking advantage, magical or otherwise.' Velindre shook her head slowly. 'You say I'm ignorant of the Archipelago and Aldabreshin ways but believe me, Chazen Kheda, you're just as ignorant of wizardry as it's practised in the north. Which is hardly surprising, if Dev was your only guide,' she allowed, looking down at the carved wooden casket on the sand between them.

She chose her words carefully. 'Every mage of Hadrumal, from the Archmage down, would see these wild wizards as just as much of a threat as you do. We spend our lives stepping around fear and prejudice, careful not to reawaken resentments or old tales of magical abuse. Rumour of unbounded magic in the hands of southern savages would soon run rife through the ports of the mainland coast. We wizards might not be flayed alive but we could well find ourselves shunned or stoned or worse.'

'I fail to see how that's my concern,' Kheda said resolutely.

'You call us ignorant barbarians, in the north, and up to a point that's true. We know very little of the Archipelago and the barriers you set against our ships have stopped us learning more. You have some responsibility for our ignorance,' Velindre challenged him. 'If rumour of wild magic in the south runs loose, I can see you paying a price for that obduracy. Do you suppose ignorant northerners are going to make any distinction between dark-skinned, dark-eyed Aldabreshi who have no magic and the dark-skinned, dark-eyed sorcerous invaders driving them north? Because you'll have no choice but fleeing north if a wizard with a true dragon doing his will comes here. The shockwaves will run the entire length of the Archipelago to wash Aldabreshin up on barbarian beaches.'

'You're just trying to frighten me.' Kheda shook his head to deny her words.

'Is it working?' Velindre shot back.

He looked at her. The soft rush of surf and the scent of the midar flowers drifted through the tense silence between them.

'You're painting as black a picture as you can imagine,' Kheda said at last. 'I think the chances of such calamity are small. But I wouldn't wager against some new danger coming out of the southern ocean.'

'Then let me help you make ready for it,' Velindre pleaded. 'Yes, I have my own reasons for wanting to fathom this mystery and I don't expect you to understand them. Does that matter when we both have much to gain as well as much to lose?'

'The enemy of my enemy is my friend?' Kheda quoted the old precept with a wry twist to his mouth. 'In a pinch, perhaps, but such friends often prove faithless.'

'What other choices do you have here?' Velindre was unmoved. 'Aren't I the lesser of two evils?'

'That's what I thought about Dev,' Kheda pointed out. 'Our alliance may have benefited me but it hardly did him much good, did it?'

'Aren't we all responsible for the choices that lead us to our individual fates?' Velindre countered.

'You'll be safe enough among the travelling scholars if you answer every question with another one.' Kheda sighed and rubbed a hand over his beard, careful of the grazes on his face. 'I'll give you a token of safe conduct, so you can say you're travelling in the islands under Chazen protection. Though I warn you, there'll be plenty of domains where that'll be of little worth. In return, I expect you to bring me any clue you discover as to where these savages live. You said something about using the clouds to trace this current of air that the dragons rode. I want to know if there's any way I can read it in the skies myself, to know when we are in danger and when we are not.'

'Fair enough.' Velindre nodded.

Kheda forestalled her next words with a curt hand. 'If you're discovered to be a wizard, I shall not lift a hand to save you. I cannot imperil Chazen like that. I will forswear myself and give my oath you stole my token as well as deceiving me as to your sex and your unnatural powers.'

Velindre pursed her thin lips for a moment then nodded. 'I can live with that.'

'You wouldn't say that if you were truly Aldabreshin,' Kheda said swiftly, 'lest there was an omen in such words.'

'Should I hope so, or hope not?' Velindre wondered dryly.

'Go back to the residence.' Kheda dismissed her with a curt jerk of his head. 'We'll sort out the details later.'

Velindre studied him for a moment, then bent to pick up the box containing the casket with Dev's ashes. 'Till later.'

Kheda heard her slip in the loose sand as she climbed the long bank, muttering some incomprehensible oath as the stubborn midar plants scratched at her feet. Out across the water, he watched the rain clouds approaching.

The stars turn and bring rainy and dry seasons one after another. Every year the new-year stars return to realign themselves with the heavenly compass. Even the furthest jewels of the heavens eventually return to the same points, even if it takes an old man's lifespan to see it. Everything is the same and yet everything is different. Everything is affected by what has gone before. Some sages say everything happens in the same instant, outside of time as we know it.

How could I have expected this to be an end of it all? There are no ends, any more than there are beginnings. Everything depends on everything else. These calamities depend on far more than I can see or hope to understand. What do I know of dragons or magic or these hidden wizards of Velindre's? What do I want to know of such things?

So what are you going to do? Are you going to sit on your hands and lament your misfortune like some beggar or slave refusing to acknowledge the part he has played in his own fate? Or are you going to lose yourself in mystic contemplation of the infinite like some soothsayer starving himself to death for fear of making a wrong choice?

No man can halt the wheeling skies any more than he can stop the passing of the days and his life with them. All he can do is watch for the omens to guide him to better choices. Let's see what lore Velindre brings back to show us some path to keep ourselves safe from these wild mages and their dragons. If she manages to make good on such a promise, won't that be an omen, in itself?

He turned away from the uncommunicative sea and looked at the distant tower of silence.

In the meantime, I have offered up another innocent hostage to the future by getting a child on Itrac. I owe her the best future I can contrive, as my wife, as recompense for all she has suffered in the past, even if that was none of my doing. If I can do this, if I can see Chazen's people set fair, perhaps that will balance the account against my involvement with magic.

If I can put an end to this magical danger once and for all, even if it means working with Velindre, perhaps that will outweigh the compromises I have made. Perhaps I can earn myself a better future. Perhaps I can earn the right to make choices for myself alone. Perhaps Risala will be able to wait for me.

THE THIEF'S GAMBLE

Juliet E. McKenna

In Einarinn, the secret of magic is known only by an elite few. They live in deliberate isolation, under the watchful eye of the Archmage. But nothing lasts for ever.

Livak is a part-time thief and a full-time gambler, long accustomed to living by her wits and narrowly avoiding serious trouble. When she attempts to sell a stolen antique to a passing merchant, she finds herself pulled into a new and dangerous world of political intrigue in which the stakes are higher than anyone involved can imagine.

For the antique she has acquired dates from a particular period in the history of Einarinn about which little is known, but much has been speculated. And when the truth begins to emerge, Livak decides to take the greatest gamble of her life.

SHADOWMARCH

Tad Williams

Far to the north, past ancient family seats of crumbling stone, lies the shadowline and the grey places beyond. At its border stands the fortress of Southmarch, a place of mortal men. And beyond, not far into those bleak forbidding lands, lies another castle, the ancient shell of Qul-na-Qar, whose stones were laid in another age.

It is here, within its ancient walls, that the Twilight People gather to hear Ynnir, the Blind King, pronounce the dark fate of humankind.

So begins the saga of Shadowmarch, the magnificent new epic of high fantasy from acclaimed and internationally renowned storyteller Tad Williams.